*The Tontine*

The

# Tontine

## A NOVEL BY THOMAS B. COSTAIN

*Illustrated by Herbert Ryman*

VOLUME II

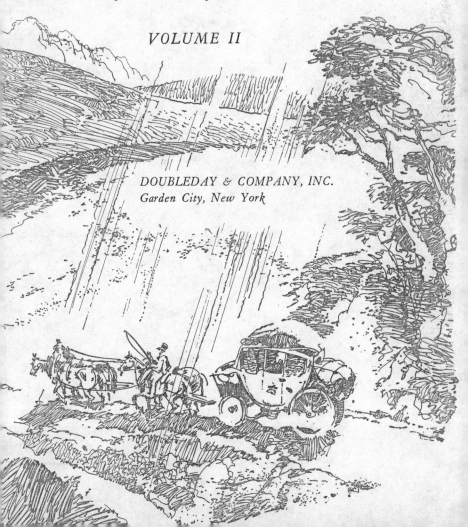

DOUBLEDAY & COMPANY, INC.
Garden City, New York

With the exception of actual historical personages, the characters are
entirely the product of the author's imagination and have no relation
to any person in real life.

# CONTENTS

# BOOK III

## *The Colossus*

CONTINUED

## CHAPTER NINE

1

The guard who escorted the prisoners to their cells was very conscious of the fact that several of them were prominent citizens. He turned the key with reluctance and did not instruct them at once to enter.

"Cells ain't clean," he said. "Had no time to take a mop and pail in to-day."

"Ain't been a mop and pail in here in a matter o' ten years," said a drunken voice from one of the dark cells. "I knows becus I been here most o' the time."

There was a sickening odor of unwashed flesh and bodily wastage, and the ladies drew back in horror. Most of the cells were occupied by human wrecks who got up from their wooden benches and came to the bars to stare at the new arrivals. Some of them were drunk and all of them were unshaved and ragged.

One of the ladies, a Mrs. Edwin Winslear whose husband was a man of wealth and could be expected to create a great commotion when he learned what had happened to his wife, whispered in Nell's ear, "I think I'll die if I have to stay in here another minute."

"This is the worst part of it," replied Nell. "The terrible conditions of the jails. They say the big prisons in London are unspeakably bad."

Mrs. Winslear placed a handkerchief to her nose and continued to hold it there. "Nothing could be worse than this," she said in an agonized voice.

There were only three cells vacant, so the four men were put in one of them and the three ladies in another across the passage. The latter stood together in a shocked group and looked with dismay at the slimy floor and the condition of the wooden benches on which, presumably, they would have to spend the night.

The cell locks had barely been snapped when Sadie Coaster was led in to occupy the third vacant cell. Her husband followed after her, his arms filled with supplies. He had a pillow, a pair of sheets, a pair of blankets, a bellows and a bottle of smelling salts.

Jonathan, standing at the door of his cell, called attention to the comforts which that difficult lady would enjoy. "That's what experience does for you," he said to Nell, who was standing opposite him. "Sadie has been in prison so often that she knows what she needs. I realize I should have been more foresighted and provided some of these luxuries for you."

The female crusader was not pleased with what she found. "*You!*" she said to the turnkey. "Do you know who I am?"

"Yes'm," answered the officer. "Ye're Sidie Coaster. I stepped out and listened to some o' yer talk. E'jeez, ye was pitching it into 'em."

"According to my usual practice, I left nothing unsaid," declared the agitator. She looked about her with rapidly rising ire. "I've been in many jails and this is the worst I've ever encountered. What do you mean, letting things get into such a condition? You, you foul creature, should be in a cell yourself for such neglect of your duties. What kind of a lazy, cheating, drunken man are you?"

"You takes things here as ye finds 'em," declared the turnkey. "And never you mind about what kind of man I am. I suits myself. Our motter here is, No favors to no one. Not even to Sidie Coaster."

"Mr. Dengate," said the lady, turning to her husband, who had deposited the supplies in the cell and had then backed out into the corridor, "can you leave me in such a pigpen as this for a whole night? What will your conscience do to you if you fail to arouse the mayor and the council and the church and the press of this town and let them know the indignities and hardships I am being compelled to suffer? Will you ever be able to raise your head again if you don't have me out of here under the hour?"

"I'll do my best, my dear," said Mr. Dengate.

"There ain't anythin' he can do," said the turnkey sourly. "The mayor's in bed and nothin' will get *him* out. And as for you, sir, ye're not a prisoner, so out ye goes. Visitors not allowed in these 'ere playshul surro'ndin's."

Mr. Dengate looked ruefully at his wife and then departed, followed by the officer, who banged the barred door behind him with a vigor which suggested a ruffled temper. Sadie Coaster began immediately to make arrangements for such time as she might be compelled to remain in her cell. She took the bellows and vigorously blew all the dirt and vermin off the bench, following this with an energetic cleansing of the bars and walls by the same means. Having thus rid her couch, temporarily at least, of the lice which had infested it, she proceeded to spread the sheets and the blankets. She had completed these arrangements and had removed her shoes when footsteps in the outside corridor announced the approach of fresh visitors.

It was the Rev. Peveril Cullen, who was admitted, reluctantly, by the disgruntled turnkey. He entered smiling and proceeded at once to the cell door where Jonathan Bade was standing.

"The whole town is in an uproar," said the minister. "The sympathy is all on our side. The streets are filled with people demanding your release. When I came through the front offices here I could see that Boisterous Billy was in with the chief and they were talking at a furious rate and their faces were red and angry. It won't surprise me at all if he withdraws the charges in the face of the public indignation."

"I doubt it," said Jonathan. "He's a tough citizen and a fighter, your Mr. Isbester."

"He'll be fighting the whole town, and perhaps the whole country, if he doesn't give in."

"What about the children?" asked Jonathan in an anxious voice.

"Safe. No effort seems to have been made yet to find them. They had a fine supper and hot baths and now they're all snoring soundly in comfortable beds. I hear it took a dozen volunteers a full hour to get those poor little bodies clean." The minister bobbed his head and smiled. "There are plenty of families in town now who want to adopt them. I believe we'll find good homes for all."

2

The Rev. Peveril Cullen was the first visitor next morning. A new officer held the keys and waited for him to deliver his message, a younger man, and more friendly.

Cullen was the bearer of good tidings. "It's clear now that the whole town is with us," he said. "A special breakfast is being sent in for you in a few minutes with the compliments of the mayor's wife. The court this morning will be filled with sympathizers. The children have been taken into the best homes in Rixby and the people who have them are defying Isbester to take them away. The written reports went off by special coach last night. When the story gets into the newspapers, all England will feel the same as the people of Rixby do."

"How is our good friend Isbester acting in the face of all this?" asked Jonathan.

"Like a bear who's been gored by a bull. He's not giving an inch." The preacher nodded to Mrs. Winslear. "Your husband, ma'am, is to be allowed in to see you before you go into court."

"I hope," said the lady, shivering with disgust of her surroundings, "that he brings fresh clothes for me."

"There is talk," went on Cullen, "of the men of the town organizing to break this place open and get you out."

"Put a stop to that if you can," said Jonathan urgently. "We must win by orderly means. Violence will hurt our case."

The hearing in court took up most of the morning. The lawyers wrangled and the spectators had to be warned repeatedly to repress their feelings. Boisterous Billy Isbester had to content himself with indulging in scowls and dark looks. The magistrate seemed to reflect a definitely hostile feeling toward the prisoners and the upshot was that they were committed to stand trial at the next assizes.

"I will meet the crown attorney and Mr. Alfred Pund, acting for the defendants, in my chambers at three o'clock this afternoon," announced the magistrate, pounding his gavel loudly for order in court. "We will settle the matter of bail then."

One victory had been won for the defense, however. While the lawyers had fought in court and the witnesses had given their evidence, the turnkey and a corps of helpers had been at work in the cells with mops and pails and bottles of chemical. There was a new atmosphere in the cell block when the defendants were brought back, an aseptic smell which brought them a sense of relief.

Mrs. Winslear settled herself on one of the benches and said, "Now I can face captivity with new courage." She smiled at her fellow prisoners. "My husband is suffering much more over this than I am. Did you notice how pale the poor lamb was in court?"

Sadie Coaster, who had been remanded for a hearing the next day, spoke up from her cell across the corridor. "The one who is really going to suffer," she declared, "is Mr. Dengate. He has failed me in my hour of need."

The official attitude, subjected, it may be assumed, to heavy pressure from the manufacturers of the town, hardened during the afternoon. There was a long and acrimonious session in the magistrate's rooms and then a decision was handed down which caused a wave of anger to sweep across Rixby. Bail was refused.

"I knew that fellow Isbester would fight with fang and claw," said Jonathan when the word was brought to the defendants. "I really believe he would like to see us hanged."

That night there was an indignation meeting of townspeople on the Market Square and the sound of voices raised in righteous expostulation reached the prisoners faintly. The meeting failed of the desired effect, however, for the barred door remained closed to them, not only that night but for several nights thereafter.

Sadie Coaster was released on the third day. On the fifth morning of their incarceration the turnkey threw open the door and announced, "A vis'ter fer Miss Groody," and in came a boy of fifteen in an Eton coat and striped trousers, holding his silk hat in his hand.

Nell cried out in delight: "Sammy, Sammy! Here I am!" The heir to the Carboy fortune saw her and ran across to the cell which she now occupied by herself. He pressed close against the bars.

"Aunt Helen!" he said. "I had to come. As soon as I heard about it, I went to the Head and told him I had to be with you. He agreed and gave me my leave of absence. I didn't have enough to pay my coach fare up, so I went around and borrowed from all the fellows. And oh, Aunt Helen, there was a meeting of the boys at school and they passed a resolution in your favor. And I hear there was a riot about it in Oxford."

"That is wonderful news," said Nell, succeeding in kissing him on the end of his nose through the bars. "But it's much more wonderful to see you and know that you cared enough to come such a long way to see me. You must be very tired after your long trip."

The boy nodded in assent. "I was outside so I didn't sleep any last night. I was afraid I might fall off." He added after a moment's silence: "They were talking about the case, Aunt Helen. The other passengers and the driver, I mean. They'd all read about it in the London newspapers. I got into a real argument with one of them because he was blaming my grandfather. I said my grandfather didn't have a thing to do with it. That's right, isn't it?"

"Of course, my dear," said Nell. "You must always stand up for your grandfather."

Across the narrow space which divided the cells, Jonathan had been watching the grandson of his former employer. "Do you know who I am?" he asked.

"Yes, Mr. Bade," said the boy. "You are my grandfather's lawyer." He then demonstrated that he had been keeping advised of things. "I mean, you *were* his lawyer."

"Exactly. Your grandfather and I have parted company. I don't expect we'll ever be on friendly terms again. But I want to add something to the advice you've just received. Your grandfather is a great man. No matter how much you may hear him criticized—great men always come in for abuse, you know—you must never lose any of your pride in him. You must always be ready to fight for his good name."

Young Samuel nodded his head gravely. "Oh yes, sir. Oh yes, indeed."

Nell reached through the bars and touched the boy's cheek. "How grown up you are! You are going to be very tall."

"I'm going to be six foot," said the boy proudly. "Aunt Helen, what do you think I ought to do about a place to sleep? There seem to be a lot of inns here and they all look alike."

The other male member of the committee, who was headmaster of a school, spoke up from the opposite cell. "I have a boys' school. How would you like to go there?"

Sammy turned about to see the speaker. "Why, sir, I think that would be very nice."

"My boys would be proud to have an Etonian in their midst. You could have my room. The meals are wholesome but not fancy."

"They're not fancy at Eton, sir."

The boy remained for another half hour, telling them everything he had heard about the case on his travels to Rixby. Then, as he began to show symptoms of drowsiness, the headmaster gave him a note and directions to follow in reaching the school. He departed with considerable readiness.

Nell watched him depart with a deep feeling of pride. "My little son!" she thought. "He'll always be that to me, although I must hide it far back in my mind. He's changed a great deal. He looks like my dear Allie still but he's beginning to take after his grandfather too. I don't think he'll ever be as tall and handsome as his father but perhaps he'll have other qualities to make up for that." Her eyes became misty. "To think he came all this way to be near me!"

3

Samuel Carboy arrived in Rixby on the sixth day. At first he thought the town was enjoying a holiday. No one seemed to be working and the streets were filled. There was something unreal about the situation, something strange and paradoxical. Only one tavern was open and it was doing no business. The people loitering about in groups had little to say and, when they did speak, it was in low tones. The shops were open but no one was buying. Clearly they were waiting for something.

Carboy leaned from his carriage and asked a police officer what the town was celebrating.

"This is the Day, sir," answered the officer.

"The day? What day? I don't understand this, Officer."

"The Day, sir, when the Lord comes to Rixby—if the Rev. Peveril Cullen is right about it. The Day of the Second Coming, sir."

It came back to Samuel Carboy now that a crackpot preacher, to quote his thoughts, had been predicting the end of the world here in Rixby. He grunted.

"Is nobody working?"

"Not a soul, sir. They want to be outside where they can see what happens. Do you notice how they're keeping an eye on the sky all the time. And will you believe it, sir, that the skies are clear for the first time this year? That must mean something. Nature is ready to receive the Lord when He comes, sir."

"You'll all be back at work tomorrow, Officer."

The policeman frowned as though he considered this statement nothing short of sacrilege. "I'm a believer myself, sir. All day I've been watching the sky for a sign. We'll have it soon, sir."

Carboy grunted again. "It'll be better if you watch what's going on around you. A pickpocket would have an easy time of it in this crowd of waiting oxen."

"Sir!" exclaimed the policeman. "Would anyone be so wicked as to commit a crime on the very day that the Lord is coming to judge us? No, no, sir. We'll have nothing but peace and praise-giving this day. Can't you see that everyone is waiting and watching?"

A church bell began to peal the hour. The sound seemed muted as though the faithful bell, which had been summoning people for more than a century to prepare for this event, was aware that its usefulness would soon be over. It seemed rather sad about it.

The Colossus said, "Bah!" and ordered his coachman to drive him to the Whale and Anchor. Finding with some difficulty a man who was ready to serve him, he sent a note around to Mr. William Isbester to the effect that he had arrived and desired a full attendance of the directors of Slasher and Welldon at a meeting with him in his rooms in half an hour. Then he rang the bell vigorously three or four times in the hope of getting some lunch but received no response. It was evident that the members of the staff had joined the watchers in the streets. He was in quite a temper, therefore, when the directors arrived, promptly but apprehensively.

Samuel Carboy looked the group over with an indignant eye.

"Well!" he said. "I hope you are proud of yourselves."

"And why shouldn't we be proud of ourselves?" asked the president, bristling.

"Boisterous Billy Isbester," said Carboy, speaking the name slowly and accenting each syllable. "You don't seem to realize what a lot of dunderheads you are! What do you mean getting into a mess like this? Didn't you see, in God's name, that you were playing right into their hands?"

Isbester's face turned almost purple with anger. "I have done my duty as I see it," he said. "I've acted to protect the business and the shareholders."

"You've made a blasted fool of yourself!" exclaimed Carboy. "Don't you know that the whole country is seething with indignation? Don't you realize that your ill-considered stand has put us in the wrong completely in the eyes of the world? You've hurt all business, making manufacturers seem like monsters and bloodsuckers. Before I left London there was a meeting of bankers and businessmen and they begged me to clean up the mess before it was too late." He looked about him with a belligerent eye. "There's only one thing left to do. You must withdraw the charges against the prisoners——"

"Never!" cried Isbester. "We must fight them to a finish. We must refuse to be stampeded. We must stand firmly on our rights."

"If that's the way you feel about it, I'll turn this into a board meeting and boot you out of the presidency in two minutes."

An uneasy silence settled over the group. They looked furtively at each other out of the corners of their eyes. No one dared to speak.

"We can't make martyrs of these people. They're trying to drive us into some such position as that, knowing how outraged the whole country would be. We must get them out of prison as soon as you can arrange a clearance with the magistrate. Give it out that there's new evidence. That the woman at the mill wasn't laid hands on and that the gates were open. Anything to make it convincing that you've decided to step out of this of your own free will. And now there's another point, the children. I'm told they're in homes throughout the town and that you're threatening to lay charges against every family involved. If any of these children are taken back to work you'll start a crusade. People will come from all over the countryside to take them away from you by force. Don't you realize that no one in the whole of England is taking your side in this infernal trouble?"

"I don't believe anything of the kind," said Isbester stubbornly. "All I'm asking is justice. I'm standing up for the rights of the Slasher and Welldon Mills under the agreement entered into with the parochial board of Rixby."

"And you intend to take action against the families harboring the children?"

"I most certainly do."

Carboy looked about him. "Is the secretary of the company here?"

"Yes," answered the president. "He's here. John Courage, sitting over there."

The secretary, who was a small man with shoulders little wider than a soup tureen and of somewhat the same shape as the lid, nodded to the formidable visitor and flushed nervously.

"Courage, eh! You've been showing too much courage around here, the whole lot of you. You've couraged yourselves into getting a good licking. Well, Mr. President Isbester, get the meeting started. I don't intend to delay a moment in taking steps to clean this mess up. We must now proceed to prove that we have courage enough to quit."

4

It was late in the evening. The heavens had not opened, the hills had not trembled, a Voice like the rushing wind had not spoken from the sky. The streets were still filled with silent people, staring upward, when Samuel Carboy arrived at the police station.

"Good gad!" he said to himself. "Haven't these simpletons been convinced yet that the Lord isn't coming to Rixby?"

The chief of the department bustled out from his office to greet the great man. "Mr. Carboy, sir," he said. "What can I do for you?"

"Are they all settled in the magistrate's office?"

"Yes, Mr. Carboy. The necessary papers are being drawn up."

"Good. And now may I see the prisoners? I want a word with them."

He had papers under both arms and it was clear that he had spent a busy day. Stepping inside the door leading to the cell block, he came to a sudden stop and the red of complete surprise spread over his face. His eyes had lighted on his grandson sitting on a stool in the corridor and eating a pork pie.

"Sam!" he exclaimed. "What in thunderation are you doing here?"

The boy got hurriedly to his feet. "Why, sir," he said, "I came when I found that my aunt Helen was in trouble. I—I wanted to be here with her."

"Did you now," said Carboy. His eyes came to rest on Nell Groody, who was sitting back of a barred door in close proximity to the boy. His head inclined forward in a reluctant nod. "Ma'am, I won't ask if you've enjoyed your little stay in Rixby jail. I won't say I'm glad to see you, because I'm not. You've caused me a lot of trouble, young woman, you and your precious friends. But it's all over now. The charges have been withdrawn against the lot of you and you'll be out as soon as the magistrate upstairs can sign the papers."

"This is very interesting, Samuel," said Jonathan Bade from the cell behind the visitor. "But suppose we refuse to leave our cells? Suppose we demand an airing in court? Has it occurred to you that, if you withdraw your charges against us, we may make some against you?"

Carboy turned about to face him. "Don't talk nonsense," he said impatiently. "You've won, haven't you? What more do you want?"

"We'll want nothing more if this proves to be a country-wide victory and not a local one. Our desire, our purpose, is to have child labor abolished."

The Colossus grunted with even more impatience. "Perhaps it's going to be a nationwide victory for you. At any rate, we're introducing new regulations into all the manufacturing concerns which are under my control. The age limit is being raised. No boy under ten years will be put to work and no girl under eleven. Does that satisfy you?"

"I'm not sure that it does."

Carboy's face began to take on the reddish tinge which indicated anger. "Don't lose all balance, Jonathan, because you've gone over to the long-haired brotherhood and the ranks of reform. You know as well as I do that this country is full of families which can't afford to support children beyond a certain age. When they get old enough, they must earn their keep—and perhaps help the old people. If you try to get more than we're giving of our own free will——"

"Well, hardly that, Samuel."

The industrialist repeated himself. "*Of our own free will.* If you try to get more, the chief opposition will come from the parents and not from employers. What do you think of that?"

"I appreciate," said Jonathan, "that no measure of reform can be accomplished at one step. It comes about by degrees. We'll be content with what you propose as a first step. Provided you intend to pay them something reasonable."

"They'll get more. I'm planning to discuss money with the heads of all my mills. It'll take some time. But we're going to be fair, Mr. Bade, you may depend on that." He took out his watch, snapped back the lid and studied the face. It was apparent that his sight was not as good as it had been. "I have a full evening's work ahead of me—repairing some of the damage the high-minded, do-gooding occupants of Rixby jail have done to my interests in this town."

At this moment a step sounded in the outside corridor and the gloved hand of the police chief came through the bars, holding out a flimsy yellow envelope.

"It's for you, Mr. Carboy," he said. "Came by messenger from Coltown Junction."

After slitting the envelope open with an index finger, Carboy read the message inside. He then held the envelope up with a gesture which suggested pride.

"May a mere man of business, intent only on making money and grinding the faces of the poor, point out that we are quietly changing the whole face of life? You, my idealistic friends, may have heard of telegraphy but I'm not at all sure of that. You, back there." He squinted in through the bars and picked out Mrs. Winslear, who got to her feet and came to the bars. "You, young woman, do you know what the telegraph is?"

"Telegraph?" said the chatelaine of Winslear Hall in a puzzled tone. "I guess it's some kind of wild animal."

"This is a message to me which was sent over wires from London to Coltown. It took only a fraction of a second to send it. *That* is the telegraph. In a year or two we'll have the wires here to Rixby and you'll be able to send messages to your friends in all parts of the country. This Wheatstone paper

I've just been handed summons me back to London. Do you, young lady, see the importance of this invention that the businessmen of the country are putting to work for *your* benefit, and the benefit of everyone in England?"

"I think I do," answered Mrs. Winslear, "but I don't suppose it would have meant anything to those poor children you were starving at your mill. It wouldn't take the place of decent food and kind treatment, would it?"

"Someday there will be a dozen inventions as great as this in daily use." The Colossus crumpled the message into a pocket. "I'm sure it won't change your opinion of me if I tell you I built the one hundred and fifty miles of wire which brought this message to me tonight." He turned to his grandson. "Young Sam," he said, "I'll be leaving around midnight. Do you want to come with me?"

"Yes," said the boy eagerly. "I've never had a long trip in your carriage, Grandfather. Besides, my leave of absence is nearly up."

"I'm relieved to hear you have one. It seemed to me likely that you had just up and come without attending to any such formalities."

"Could we take Aunt Helen with us?"

"Hardly, my boy. I would be happy to extend the hospitality of my carriage to Miss Groody but unfortunately it only holds two."

Nell smiled at the boy. "I'm still a prisoner," she said, "and probably won't be out until tomorrow. It was kind of you to want me." She spoke directly to Carboy. "I know quite a lot about the telegraph. You see, I invested some money in your company, Mr. Carboy, and I had to understand what it was, didn't I?"

"This doesn't surprise me at all, Miss Groody. I happen to know what a very thorough investor you are. You'll make a lot of money out of this one, mark my words."

"Mr. Bade," said Nell, "I want to take one of the children back with me when I go. I think it should be that poor boy who says his name is Huruld. I'm afraid he's too old for adoption but I can look after him and keep him busy in my shop."

"I'm delighted to hear you're willing to take Huruld," said Jonathan. "I've been worried about him. We'll have no difficulty with the rest but no one seemed to want him."

"Come along, my boy," said Carboy. "It's getting late for visitors in this charming apartment. You can have your supper while I finish up some cold, cruel business matters. There's a roast chicken and a fine knuckle of ham. *And* a gooseberry tart. Does that appeal to you?"

"Yes, Grandfather. I guess I'm pretty hungry."

"The time may come, Sammy, when your grandfather will have to serve roast capon and steamed pudding to the young help he employs in his mills. Miss Groody had better watch her investments pretty sharp when we come to that."

The boy got to his feet. "I'm going to ask you all about how that message came to you. I didn't think they could send sheets of paper along a wire."

"It's rather more complicated than that, my boy. Well, ladies and gentlemen," bowing to the company at the bars, "I bid you good night. Also I salute the victors. You've won the first round."

"I'm really more interested at the moment," said Mrs. Winslear, "in the prospect of a hot bath."

## CHAPTER TEN

### 1

All the shades had been drawn at the house in Carlton Gardens and so the fact was hidden from the outside world that preparations for departure went on throughout the night. They had been going on, in a less intensified form, for several weeks. Muskets had been arriving from Birmingham in quite innocent-looking boxes and uniforms had been received from Paris. The uniforms were of the fortieth French Regiment which, most conveniently, was stationed at Calais, and several domestics had been kept busy covering the buttons with new cloth on which the regimental number was prominently displayed. Down in the cellars Dr. Conneau, one of the most devoted of the Bonapartist lieutenants, was printing proclamations on a small hand press.

By three in the morning the preparations had been completed. The tall mirrors had been swathed in sheets and the furniture had been covered. The house had taken on a ghostly appearance and the domestics walked softly and spoke in whispers. All personal belongings had been packed in boxes and were now piled up in the entrance hall.

Prince Louis Napoleon sat at his desk, which was covered with campaign notes and maps of northern France. He struck a bell and said, "The Comte de Persigny," to the footman who answered the summons. His chief lieutenant, looking dusty and gray with fatigue, carried more plans in his arm when he obeyed the summons.

The prince asked in a husky whisper, "My dear Comte, have we overlooked anything?"

Persigny shook his head. "Nothing, Prince."

"Is it your opinion then that we are ready?"

The lieutenant did not say "to the last gaiter button," the answer Napoleon the Small was to receive on a much more momentous occasion thirty years later (and an erroneous answer it proved to be), but he responded in kind. "We have thought of everything, Prince." He gestured wearily. "Every conceivable turn of fortune, favorable or otherwise, has been considered, and provided for."

Louis Napoleon smiled for the first time that night. "Then success lies before us," he said. "The French people are ready. They want us to return. They wait for us to revive the Napoleonic glory."

"I think it would be wise, Prince, if you were to go on board at Margate, the last stop."

Louis Napoleon gave the suggestion some thought. Finally he nodded. "You are right, Persigny. If it can be arranged that everyone else is aboard prior to that, I can slip in without being observed. Where do you propose to start?"

"At London Bridge. I'll be aboard before dawn. The Comte de Lussac will also."

"Has he left already? I haven't heard his voice for some time."

"He has gone to say farewell to his wife. The comte is a most devoted husband."

The prince's lips drew upward in a sly smile. "I had a most difficult time convincing the fair Isabelle that she could not accompany us. Under her beauty she has a will of iron. But she found that my will was even firmer than hers."

The Comte de Lussac arrived at the house on Mecklenburgh Square, where Isabelle insisted on living, before the light of dawn showed above the rooftops. The hand with which he inserted the key in the door trembled a little; for the devoted Bonapartist was no longer young and the twenty-four hours past had been packed with excitement and action. A footman sprang up from the hall chair in which he had been sprawling and tried to restore order in his tousled hair by a hasty roaching with his fingers.

"I leave in half an hour," said the comte. "Let me know as soon as the carriage comes around. I don't want it standing in the streets any longer than is necessary. Do you understand what I am saying?"

"Yes, m'lord."

"Then find Gossing and see if Madame la Comtesse can be wakened."

The footman returned in a very few minutes. "M'lady will see you at once, m'lord."

The comte took the stairs two steps at a time, no mean feat for a man of his years. He was breathing hard nevertheless when he reached the door of his wife's dressing room. Gossing, the maid, wore a most curious smile as she ushered him to the bedroom door. "You are to go right in, m'lord."

"M'sieur le Comte du Lussac," said Isabelle, who was standing in front of a pier looking glass, "this is your dutiful and affectionate wife. I think I make a rather trim valet, don't you?"

"My dear child!" gasped the comte in surprise and dismay.

Isabelle was dressed in shiny black cloth with a most snugly waisted coat and trousers which fitted as closely as the "smalls" of an earlier generation. She was wearing also a masculine hat which fitted her head to the very tips of her ears.

"I went to a tailor who provides clothes for footmen and valets," explained Isabelle. "The hat is a little vulgar, I think, but the man swore it was quite the proper thing."

"Why this masquerade, my dear child?" The comte was still in a condition generally described as "bowled over." "I thought you had decided to stay with your father while I am away."

"I changed my mind," said Isabelle, tilting her head first on one side and then on the other to see if any way could be found to reduce the undoubtedly vulgar effect of the hat. "You see, Hippy, I'm not going to stay. I'm going with you. I am going as your valet."

"No, no! It was all settled, my sweet one. The prince was very firm. You were not to be allowed to go with us under any circumstances." Then his eyes, which had been fixed on the tightly fitted trousers with something approaching panic, saw another reason for still additional dismay. "My child! My beautiful one! What have you done with your hair?"

"I had it clipped off," explained Isabelle casually. "I couldn't go as your valet with ringlets down my back, now could I? And, do you know, I think it looks tiptop this way." She took off the offending hat and revealed the fact that her head was covered with close brown curls which made her look very young and gay. "I may never let it grow again, Hippy. I'll start a new fashion. I'll bring back the Titus cut. Perhaps the queen will take it up. No, no, that's expecting too much. A Titus cut would *not* suit her at all."

"Isabelle, Isabelle!" said her husband, shaking his head in despair. "What am I to do with you? How can I leave you here? You would be up to all kinds of tricks. I am not sure you wouldn't take yourself in these abominable clothes to parties for footmen and balls for housekeepers and butlers! You would make yourself the talk of the town."

"There's only one thing for you to do," declared Isabelle. "Take me with you. I'll wear a false beard if you think I *must* be disguised. But I will *not* be left behind. Now that Nippy"—a name she had coined for Louis Napoleon—"has decided to become the Man of Destiny, I am not going to be cheated out of having a finger in things. There is no use discussing it further. My mind is made up. I've had some breakfast." She had indeed, as the bones of two chops and a cluster of eggshells attested. "I'm ready to go at once."

Her husband looked as though he would like to take her by the shoulders and give her a good shaking. After a moment, however, he smiled and patted her cheek instead.

"I was shocked when I first saw you in these outrageous clothes. But I am compelled to say, my little pigeon, that you look most wonderfully well in them. You are as slender as a girl of sixteen."

Isabelle smiled proudly. "I haven't gained a pound in twenty years. Do you think I would appear in trousers if I had?"

"And now," said the comte, "we must be serious about this. I must tell you——"

"I *am* serious. I am serious enough to brush any obstacles out of my way."

"Including husbands?"

"Including husbands and fathers and the leaders of dangerous missions. Listen to me, if you please, Hippy! I *need* to go." She paused and looked rebelliously at him. "I want gaiety, excitement, a real part to play in life. It happens that I'm a favorite with the prince; at least he likes me well enough to talk to me about his ideas and plans. I'm in his confidence. And now that his plans are coming to a head, I am not going to be left out just because I'm a woman. When Nippy said he wouldn't take me in his party, I made up my mind at once that I would go as your valet. It was the only way left. And here I am."

There was a sound of carriage wheels on the street. "The time has come!" cried Isabelle. "My bag is already packed and in the carriage. Come, come! There isn't a moment to lose!"

## 2

The excursion steamer *Edinburgh Castle*, which had been chartered for the raid on the French coast, dawdled down the river for two days in reaching Margate. No suspicions had been aroused. The fifty-odd young men, obviously all foreigners, who constituted the passengers, had laughed and capered on deck, and dined and depleted the wine supplies, with all the abandon of true excursionists. The group who had come on at Wapping had been in charge of a brisk Frenchman named Parquin who, it had developed, had an eye for the dramatic. By some means he had acquired a young eagle and had brought it aboard the vessel. It was not a large and healthy eagle to begin with and it was showing a tendency to molt. However, it looked well on the mast where it had perched itself and it squawked bitterly at the people on shore who paused to watch the steamer on its slow peregrination down the river.

The prince came aboard at Margate as planned. He looked about him with an eye which kindled excitedly. "My dear Persigny," he said, "it seems that everything has gone smoothly. I'm certain no one recognized me." He caught sight of the not too imposing bird up in the rigging. "A splendid idea! We will loose him on French soil, as a symbol of the freedom we offer the people of France! It will be quite as dramatic as Napoleon delivering his address before the Pyramids."

"Yes, sire," said Persigny, using that term for the first time as an indication of his faith in the success of the mission. "All northern France will be in our grip before they know in Paris that we have landed."

"Our party is complete?"

"Yes, sire. In fact it is rather more than complete. It seems that we have a volunteer."

When they reached the cabin which had been reserved for the leader, Louis Napoleon stretched himself out on the bed with an air of great weariness. "I couldn't sleep last night. All the dangers we may encounter and a fear of the mistakes we may make hung over me like a deep mental cloud. It was almost a nightmare." He roused himself and sat up abruptly. "Did you say we have a new volunteer? Send him away. We can't add to our numbers now. He might be a spy."

"No," declared Persigny. "Not a spy. I can vouch for that."

The prince fumbled impatiently with a badly rumpled tie. "Why all the mystery? Who is it, in God's good name?"

"I think you should find that out for yourself, Prince. And may I add that your breakfast will be served here? It will be brought up almost immediately. A red fish and a platter of eggs."

Louis Napoleon recognized Isabelle as soon as she entered the room after a hesitant tap on the door. In spite of the conflicting emotions aroused in him by her unexpected appearance, he burst into laughter.

"Minx! Hussy!" he exclaimed. "It is clear I underestimated your share of obstinacy."

"I heard my father say once," declared Isabelle, "that the depths of his obstinacy had never been plumbed. I suppose I take after him."

"There is method in this mention of your father," grumbled the prince. "You know he is one of my most valued friends, that I am very much in his debt. It's unlikely we would be making this venture if his contribution had not been so handsome. But you! You are a great nuisance, my dear Isabelle. Will you tell me what you are doing here and why you are dressed in those absurd clothes? Not that I don't approve most heartily of the way you look in them. What a remarkable maker of trousers your tailor is!"

"I am going with my husband," said Isabelle in a gentle voice. "You would not have objected if he had brought his regular man. I'm sure all of you have brought valets. Why, then, shouldn't the comte? Well, I am my husband's valet for the next few days or weeks or months, as the case may be."

"Days, if we are to succeed." The prince studied her for a moment in frowning absorption. Then he shook his head. "What am I to do with you? I must not offend the comte, who is one of my most loyal supporters. Your feelings, my beautiful Isabelle, are much less important, and yet I have some small consideration for them. You are determined to see things with your own eyes, it seems." He continued to frown at her and then he indulged in a flickering and rather bleak smile. "Come here, Madame Impudence!"

Isabelle obeyed the order by crossing the room and standing in front of him, looking up almost demurely from under her long eyelashes. He placed a hand on each of her ears and turned her face upward. "You tempting creature," he said; and then kissed her lingeringly on the mouth.

"I think I'm entitled to that much," he added, letting her go. "It's a great deal less than Napoleon demanded of La Bellilote when she followed him to Egypt in an officer's uniform. And, as it happens, I am going to give in to you. But," his voice becoming firm again, "you must make me a solemn promise. You will keep yourself out of sight. You will go quietly back to your cabin from here. When we land, you will wait long enough before following us to make sure that things are quiet. You will not flaunt yourself, my sweet young gentleman, before the other members of the party. Do you promise all these things?"

"I promise, O King live forever. I will do everything you say."

"This is a trying prank you have played on me," said the pretender. "I am very angry with you. I have given in to you most reluctantly. And so now I advise that you withdraw quietly and give me no reason to regret that you are with us."

## CHAPTER ELEVEN

### 1

Isabelle watched from the porthole of her tiny cabin while the invading party went ashore. They were resplendent in their new uniforms of the

French line and filled with confidence as well as a liberal issue of rum. The *Edinburgh Castle* veered with the wind and she could see down the beach which ran from Wimereux to Boulogne. Even in the faint light of early dawn the firm sand of the beach was spectacularly white.

Isabelle was furious. The prince had repeated his order that she was to remain aboard and had refused to see her when she went to his door and pounded on it until her knuckles hurt. Her husband had refused his help. "This is war," that ardent Bonapartist had said. "We must obey orders." She thought now of going to the captain, who was not too old to be susceptible (there was a gleam in his eye whenever she came on deck), and using all her wiles on him. Perhaps he could be induced to put her ashore.

The wind swung the ship again on its taut cable and she found herself looking north over the waters of the Channel. A British warship loomed large on the horizon. It seemed to be bearing in toward the French coast.

At this point she heard a voice which had a somewhat familiar ring to it hailing them from the Wimereux side. Voices boomed back and forth. She was convinced it was the customs men back again, to ask more questions.

But it was not the customs back again. She heard a rap on her door and the somewhat familiar voice, now entirely familiar, saying: "Let me in, please. I must see you. It's urgent."

It was Jonathan Bade. She had never expected to see him again after his open and furious breach with her father and his espousal of the cause of factory reform. What was he doing here? She pondered this point for several moments. "He can't mean any harm because he's still in love with me," was her final conclusion.

She opened the door of the cabin and said in a mocking tone, "Some legal papers for me to sign, no doubt."

"I've talked the captain into letting me take you ashore," he said, frowning impatiently. "He understands it's every man for himself now."

She became completely grave at this. "What do you mean, Jonathan? Have things gone wrong?"

"I'll explain when I get you off this great rolling tub." He frowned with still more disapproval as he took in the details of her costume. "Have you any proper clothes with you?"

"I have dresses. But why are you here? Why this interference?"

"Get into a dress then. And do it without delay, if you value your safety. A simple dress, if you possess such a thing."

"Close the door, if you please."

In a very short time she called, "You may come in now, Jonathan." He found her in a plain brown dress which would have identified anyone else as a governess but in which she looked like a lady of rather considerable importance in disguise, a princess, a lady in waiting or something of the kind.

"What have you done with—with the things you were wearing?"

"I hung them up. I will have you know that I am tidy."

"You had better throw them out of the porthole. No evidence of this kind must be left behind. In fact, everything you have here had better be thrown out too. I'll do it for you."

Isabelle watched with dismay as he confided her carefully selected wardrobe to the waters of the Channel. He was very thorough about it, leaving not so much as a handkerchief.

"And now that you are through destroying my clothes, will you tell me why you are doing this?"

"You must trust me," he said in urgent tones. "We must get away from here without a minute's delay. This vessel is about to be seized."

While they were being rowed ashore by four broad-backed natives, Isabelle began to ply him with questions. Jonathan did not take his eyes off the shoreline. Far down the white sands they could see the small black figures of the invading party still striding confidently in the direction of Boulogne Harbor.

"Has the prince been betrayed?"

"The prince's plans are well known to practically everyone. That crass and proud man, that puny specimen hobbling in the shoes of genius, might as well have announced his intentions with printed proclamations. Did he suppose the shipping of guns from Birmingham would go unnoticed? Did the importation of uniforms from Paris seem to him a safe way of equipping his men? Didn't he know that the French government has spies in England to report everything he does and says and even what he thinks? If your prince has been betrayed, it has been by himself."

Isabelle had turned in sudden alarm to watch the diminishing figures on the white sands. "Do the French know about this?"

"Of course. The prince expects the troops in Boulogne to receive him with open arms. They will receive him instead with drawn bayonets."

Isabelle began to realize the full seriousness of the situation. She laid a hand on his arm. "I'm sure you know my husband is with them. Will they all be killed? Can't we get warning to them in time?"

"It's too late. They are close to Boulogne now."

"Jonathan, we must try! We can't let them walk to their deaths like this!"

"I don't think there will be any fighting, although a musket or two may be fired off. There aren't enough of your friends to stand up to a full regiment. The worst we need expect is that they'll all be clapped into prison." He paused to watch the receding figures of the confident Bonapartists. "The man must be insane to land with a party of fifty men! He must think the people will rise up to welcome him as they did Napoleon when he returned from Elba. Fortunately, he's only Louis Napoleon."

Isabelle regarded him now with a suspicious puckering of her brows. "And how do you happen to know all this?"

They were drawing in close to the shore and Jonathan was giving the helmsman all his attention. "Don't run her up on the beach. I'll carry the lady ashore. I want you to be well away from here as soon as possible, so that the nature of your errand can't be detected." He sprang into the water, which came well above his knees, and took Isabelle into his arms. "I won't get you wet," he said. "How can anyone so intelligent and beautiful be cold and ambitious and also weak enough to get into a silly mess like this?"

They had reached the sands and she kicked at his knee. "Put me down," she demanded.

He lowered her to the ground reluctantly but with such care that not more than the tips of her shoes were revealed.

"I don't know why I'm letting you carry me off like this," she said. "Will you at least tell me where we are going?"

"We are getting off the beach and out of sight as quickly as we can. The French would like to have proof that you were with the party. They could use it to good advantage and much to your discredit. There are horses for us back of those trees up there on the crest. I'm taking you to Boulogne as fast as we can ride. To keep an important appointment I've made for you."

The narrow path they were taking led into the trees at a sharp upward incline. At the top they found a black-bearded farmer with two horses saddled for use. Jonathan led Isabelle to one and helped her to mount. She looked down at him with a rather strained smile.

"It's only because I have such confidence in you, Jonathan, that I've let you take me away like this. I've accepted everything you've said although you haven't produced any proofs."

"Look!" The lawyer motioned back over his shoulder. "If you want proof, there it is. The French customs ships are overhauling the *Edinburgh Castle*."

He sprang into the saddle and led the way down a road leading to Boulogne. The farmer bawled after them some instructions for the care of the horses when they arrived at the seaport.

"And now," said Jonathan, "I will explain how I happened to know about the plans of the fat little pretender. I have a friend on the staff of the London *Packet*, a Scot of the name of Hector Augustus MacMore who seldom utters a word but who bursts into inspired eloquence as soon as he has a pen in his hand. On Saturday evening he came to my rooms and announced that he was in a difficulty. He had received a letter from his editor who, of course, was away somewhere for the weekend. It explained what Louis Napoleon was up to—the information having come straight from the British Foreign Office—and instructed my friend to proceed to the Continent and get the story for the *Packet*. It happened that poor MacMore had only a few shillings in his pocket. He went to the *Packet* building and found it dark and empty. He began on a desperate search for someone who could loan him the money for his expenses, and finally he arrived at my door. A wonderful institution, the weekend.

"Luckily," he went on, "I had some money and I agreed to give him what he needed on two conditions. First, I was to be allowed to go along. Second, there was to be no mention of the mysterious lady by name—his editor had said there was a lady with the party and that it was believed to be you—unless he saw you with his own eyes. We arrived in Boulogne late yesterday and got verification of the likelihood of a landing today. My friend

Hector remained in Boulogne while I came here. He has no idea where I am or what I am attempting to do."

Isabelle's doubts had been resolved. "How lucky it was," she said, "that your friend found you in London!"

Jonathan kept his eyes fixed ahead of him on the narrow, stone-fenced road. "It may have been lucky. But I am not sure; I hope it was something more than that."

She did not attempt to probe the meaning of this remark. Instead she asked where he was taking her.

"Do you know the Marquis of Invermark?" he asked.

"Slightly. We were together in a party to shoot grouse a few years ago. I don't remember much about him. I think he had a long, solemn face and a juggy nose. I'm sure he didn't say a word to me—and very few to anyone else."

"He's here, in Boulogne. Did you know his wife died nearly a year ago and left him with two small children?"

Isabelle's interest in the juggy-nosed Scottish peer must have been slight, for she said no more than "Yes."

"He's on his way back from Italy with the children, a girl and a boy. The Italian governess decided at the last moment not to accompany them to Scotland, having heard unfavorable reports of the weather. The marquis found a suitable woman in Paris to take her place, named Elise Brizzard. Whether or not she also heard reports of the weather, she backed out at the last minute. So here we have the marquis with no governess and a passport which seems of no use. Do you speak French?"

"W-well enough, I guess." Isabelle turned her eyes from the road to smile at him. "And did he agree to your suggestion that I go back to England with him on the passport of the Frenchwoman?"

"He didn't hesitate a moment. He said it would be breaking the law but he had always been ready to fly to the assistance of beauty in distress."

"It's very noble of him to take such a risk. And I didn't think he gave me a second glance on that one occasion when we met." She hesitated. "Do you think I can pass for a governess, Jonathan? I am much too old and, I suspect, too frivolous-looking. I don't believe there's anything spinsterish about me at all."

"No," he answered. "Nothing at all. You'll have to play a part. I think you'll do well enough."

Nothing more was said for several moments. It was clear that doubts of a more serious nature had taken possession of her mind. She propounded a question finally. "Will it seem rotten of me to run away and leave my husband and the rest of them to face the music?"

"There's no way we can help them. They have probably walked into the trap by this time."

"But shouldn't I stay anyway? I browbeat them into letting me come in the first place. How can I run away at the first hint of danger?"

"I don't believe you would enjoy life in a French prison," said Jonathan dryly. "Isabelle, get it into your head that you can do nothing to help them. You would only increase their difficulties by remaining. The only thing left for you to do is come with me to the inn where the dour Scot is staying. You must take advantage of this opportunity to cross the Channel with his household. It's large enough, by the way, to give you ample chaperonage."

They had ridden clear of a turn in the road and the ancient town of Boulogne lay spread out ahead of them. Jonathan gave a glance at the towers of the Haute Ville showing above the masonry of the old ramparts and then looked with anxious eyes at the modern town which stretched down to the harbor.

"The streets are still quiet," he said with a sense of relief. "Perhaps you can get away before the trouble starts."


2


They turned in under an ancient stone archway leading into the courtyard of an inn which had stood there through the Hundred Years' War. There were three carriages in the yard, one piled high with luggage. Jonathan stopped and inspected them.

"Invermark travels in considerable state," he said. "He's the richest peer in Scotland. Acquired recently, I believe. South America or South Africa."

The marquis received them in a room on the first floor which was large enough to have a gallery on three sides and a huge window on the other. He was not dour-looking as Jonathan had said and, if his nose was really juggy (whatever that word might mean), then jugginess was something rather admirable; at any rate, it was a large and determined nose, with a hint of both kindliness and pride about it. He was dressed soberly in black and with a wide band of crepe on his arm.

Isabelle's plain brown dress seemed to surprise him. "Well suited for the purpose," he said in a voice which owed as much to Oxford as to the glens and braes of Forfar. "I am happy to see you again, Countess. Though I must add that I regret finding you concerned in this farcical affair."

Isabelle could not contain her resentment at this. "It is not a farcical affair, my lord Marquis. The planning was done with the utmost care. To me it seemed a daring and heroic idea. And it was based on reports from the very best French sources." Her cheeks had become flushed. "Why are you so sure the prince will fail?"

"Madame Countess," said the Scot, "France wants peace. The people will brush your prince off like a bothersome gnat. Listen! The town is quiet. The arrival of the plotters has caused no excitement. It may be that his party has already been dispersed or captured."

Isabelle turned to Jonathan with the intention of demanding that they leave. He gave his head a hasty shake to prevent her from any such ill-advised course. He could not prevent her from saying, "Perhaps, my lord, the lack of noise is due to the success with which the plans are being carried out."

The marquis, who had been watching her closely, was secretly delighted with the spirit she was displaying. "How her eyes flash!" he thought. The first glimmer of a smile showed in his deep-set eyes. "Permit me to say that you are a better shot than a judge of conspiratorial plans, Countess. I've never forgotten how you outdid the other guns that day when I had the privilege of meeting you. I don't believe you ever missed." He turned then to Jonathan. "There is no time to lose. I think Ma'amselle should meet her charges at once."

He motioned to one of the servants and two children were conducted immediately into the room, a brown-cheeked girl of perhaps eight and a boy of six, both in kilts.

"Margot," began the marquis, touching his daughter's dark curls with an affectionate hand. He seemed to be hesitating over the need to utter a lie before his children and finally compromised with the truth by saying, "This is a lady from France who will travel with us to England."

"She's our new governess, Papa," said the girl, studying Isabelle with a shrewd pair of eyes. "I think I like her."

The hat which Jonathan had selected for Isabelle from the many she had taken on board had not been to her taste. It had been intended for use on a full head of hair and looked a little absurd on the short tangle of curls left. She had taken it off and was carrying it in her hand.

"Alick," said the peer, turning to his small son, "bow to the lady."

The boy bowed as directed and then burst into laughter. "She's funny," he said. "She's got hair like a man."

"Alick!" said the father. "Your manners will have to be attended to, young man."

The daughter of the house protested even more vigorously. "The lady is lovely, Papa. I'm always going to wear mine that way. You'll let me, won't you, ma'amselle?"

"Yes, my dear," said Isabelle.

The marquis patted his daughter on the head a second time. "As usual, the daughter of the family takes the sound view of things," he remarked.

The children were then led away for a final inspection and grooming. Margot called, "Good-by, ma'amselle," and the boy Alick was heard to say, "That man's funny-looking too, isn't he?"

The streets about the inn suddenly seemed to explode with sound. They heard cheers and jeers and much talk and expostulation in excited voices, mixed with the grinding of horses' hoofs on the cobbled roads and the creak of carriage wheels. Voices cried above the din, "*Vive l'empereur!*"

Isabelle was carried away with excitement. "He's come!" she cried. "You were wrong, both of you. How completely wrong you were. Ah, listen to that cheering! The people are for him. He's going to win." She threw her arms above her head and cried, "*Vive l'empereur!*"

"Have a care!" exclaimed Jonathan. "You must control yourself. And you must not jump so quickly to conclusions."

Isabelle laughed happily. "And you must not be so stubborn," she retorted. Her eyes were beaming with delight. She seemed on the point of dancing. "Jonathan, I must go out. Give me your arm, my old wiseacre. I came over with them, you know. I'm in it. I want to be there to greet the prince."

The nature of the sounds reaching them from the streets had changed. The jeers seemed to predominate over the cheers.

"It won't be safe for you to venture out," said Jonathan. "And—don't let your hopes get too high. I'll go and see what is happening."

When Jonathan had left, the marquis said to her with a smile, "I'm truly sorry that I must be classed also with the—the old wiseacres. Nothing has happened yet to make me believe Louis Napoleon will be successful." He studied her closely. "You feel very strongly about this. Is it because your husband is one of the leaders?"

"No, no, my lord. I was devoted to Prince Louis Napoleon before I met my husband. To me there is something glamorous about the Bonapartist ideals."

"I've never thought they had ideals," commented Invermark. He was quite puzzled by her attitude. "I seem to remember that your father was always openly anti-Bonaparte."

"He was, my lord. But things have changed. He now believes in Prince Louis Napoleon and would like to see him the master of France."

"That is strange, Countess. I find it hard to understand. I can't see how the situation has changed. We got rid of one troublemaker after years of war and dreadful cost. Do we want to set up another?"

"Do you know my father?"

"No, my lady. I've never had the honor of his acquaintance."

"He would soon convince you that it's in England's best interests now to have the Bonapartists in power again."

"Then he approved of you coming with them?"

Isabelle indulged in a laugh. "Oh no, no! My husband couldn't stop me but if my father had known what I was doing he would have tied me up with his own hands."

"It's unfortunate that he didn't know," said the Scot with sudden gravity. "It's most important to get you back to England, my lady, and I'm not certain it is going to be easy. Don't misunderstand me, please. I have no disinclination for the task. The greater the obstacles, the more I am inclined to it."

Jonathan returned soon thereafter, wearing a disturbed frown. "All this noise is being made by tavern scum and the riffraff of the town," he reported. "They don't seem to know how things are going. Some told me the prince was winning and some said he was already a prisoner. It seems clear that things favored him at the start. Some officers of the regiment went over to him as the party marched into town, carrying the bronze eagles of Napoleon."

"*Vive l'empereur!*" said Isabelle in an undertone.

"There was plenty of viving at the start. The streets were filled with people and they began to cheer the prince. Crowds, my dear Isabelle, will cheer for anything. There was a sudden switch. The other officers rallied the troops and came out in force. Louis Napoleon wanted to give battle—the little rooster has courage, even if he lacks judgment—but the others realized they hadn't a chance."

"Where are they now?" asked the marquis.

"They marched out into the country. The regiment is now in full pursuit."

There was a shade of sympathy in the look the marquis bent on Isabelle. "Then it seems," he said, "that they have lost."

Jonathan nodded. "It will soon be over. The little party seems to be trapped somewhere in the fields. The coast guards have seized the steamer so their retreat is cut off. Louis Napoleon will have to surrender."

There were tears in Isabelle's eyes. "He may refuse to surrender."

"Whatever stand he takes, we must leave at once," declared the marquis. "Are you going with us, Mr. Attorney?"

"No, my lord. A page of history is being written today and I shall be an interested observer. In any case I have an appointment to meet a friend here in Boulogne. Hector Augustus MacMore."

"The scribbling chap?" The marquis smiled. "I went through college with him. Well, my good sir, keep your wits about you. There will still be plenty of trouble."

Isabelle, silent and downcast, allowed herself to be ensconced in the second of the three carriages where she had for company the valet, the porter, and a bevy of maids. She tried to smile at Jonathan as the vehicle was driven out under the stone arch but it was not a very successful attempt. He followed slowly on foot.

"Was it luck?" he was asking himself. "Or may I allow myself to believe that whenever my lovely but very foolish lady gets herself into trouble I will be made aware of it in some way? I don't believe it was luck that brought the *Packet* man to my door. He was sent."

3

Hector Augustus MacMore was a huge man. His waist was as round as a pipe of canary and his trousers fitted him so snugly that bystanders were always in a state of alarm for fear he would pop out of them. His great round head was covered by an unruly black thatch of hair.

Jonathan met him at the quay. All the excitement was over and the journalist was waiting impatiently for the English packet.

"I see your pockets are full of notes," said Jonathan.

"We have witnessed today a memorable farce," declared MacMore. "It was like a small boy walking into a lion's cage and saying, 'Lie down, doggies.' But of course it's an important piece of news when a nephew of Napoleon invades the shores of France and announces that he is taking over the government. I have every excuse to extend myself in the reporting of it."

"I hear they've all been taken prisoners. Was there any bloodshed?"

MacMore gestured indifferently. "Many heated words were exchanged and a musket or two was fired off. Three or four of the gallant invaders were killed. One was drowned when a number of them swam out to take possession of a boat."

"Not Louis Napoleon!"

"No. It was the Comte de Lussac. The husband of the impudent English lady who was supposed to be with the party but of whom nothing has been seen."

Jonathan gasped with surprise and consternation. "How extraordinary! It's hard to believe. He wasn't a fighting man, you know, and not likely to be in the forefront." He remained silent for a moment, wondering how this misfortune would affect Isabelle. "Poor child! Losing two husbands by violence in such a short space of time. I'm afraid she'll take this very hard."

The journalist was watching him out of the corner of an eye. "It's odd that she got away," he said.

"Very odd."

"Do you suppose some friend helped her to escape?"

"Quite possible. If it's true that she came with the party. Have you proof of that?"

"None," conceded the Scot. "I questioned some of the prisoners but not one had seen hide or hair of her. They lied like gentlemen; because I am certain she came over on that ratchety steamer with them."

Jonathan had never known the Comte de Lussac and so he felt no sense of grief for him. He was thinking: "Is it possible that Isabelle has had her fill of titles by this time, and the elderly husbands who go with them? Will she be content with a common man next time?" Then he took himself severely to task. "It wouldn't be you in any case, you soft simpleton."

The packet was ready to leave. The two men moved together toward the gangplank.

"Under the terms of my agreement with you, Jonathan, I won't be able to refer to the rumors about the mysterious beauty," said the journalist, watching his companion closely. "Or do you see any reason why the ban might be removed?"

"I see none," declared Jonathan firmly.

"It's most unfortunate." MacMore heaved a deep sigh of regret. "It would add so much to the story, a highly romantic touch. I've never seen the lady but I've heard it said that she's Circe in long plumes and six petticoats. Well, I'm not doing badly. Louis Napoleon was captured, of course, and I've been informed that they're going to pen him in the strongest military prison in France. So, we've seen today the last act in the saga of the ambitious Corsicans. There will be deep sighs of relief in every chancellery in Europe."

CHAPTER TWELVE

1

On a mean and very much run-down street not far from Shadwell there was a building which had once been something a little better than a warehouse although at no stage of its history could it have aspired quite to the dignity of bookkeepers' stools and offices enclosed in glass. It was not large but for certain purposes it would be extremely well located.

"I think this is what I want," said Jonathan Bade, standing on the other side of the narrow road and studying the timbering of the building and the reliability of its roof. "I can have it put into shape in quick order. The large room downstairs will serve for our meetings and the one on the left of the hall will do for serving meals. I'm afraid the kitchen will have to be enlarged."

A pedestrian came to a halt in front of him and said: "Jonathan! What brings you here? And what is there about that old ruin which chains your interest in this remarkable way?"

It was his newspaper friend, Hector Augustus MacMore, looking more mountainous than ever with an array of chins painfully enclosed in a starched collar.

"Will you laugh at me," asked Jonathan in response, "if I say that I'm going to open a mission for the derelicts of the city and that I'm considering the suitability of this place as my headquarters?"

"No, I wouldn't even smile. Not after that demonstration you arranged at Rixby. What are you aiming to be, Jonathan? Another John Wesley?"

"Nothing of the kind. Although I'm going to open this mission and devote all my spare time to it, I have no thought of giving up the law. This little place will never satisfy my desire to raise my voice in oratorical endeavor. I like to speak in public now. Besides, a man must live, you know. Now that I've broken with Carboy, I'll open an office again. I'll try, of course, to devote such legal talents as I have to the interests of the underdogs."

The scribe shook his head doubtfully. "I see we now have another reformer in our midst. A second Howard or Wilberforce." He did not seem inclined to take the new venture seriously. He began to draw bank notes from an inner pocket and to count them with the utmost care. "I was going to look you up this afternoon and pay you the money you advanced me before we left on our Bonapartist adventure. That difficulty will never arise again."

"Why not? Louis Napoleon may break out of his prison or some other event may happen to disturb another sacred weekend."

"When I told the editor what had happened, he went into the business department and raised a merry uproar about it. 'Is the ability of this paper to cover the events of the world to depend on the charity of friends?' he demanded. Well, they had it hot and heavy but my man won his point. An arrangement has been made with one of the banks to send a clerk over to our offices every Saturday morning. He'll carry a leather bag with him, and in the bag there will be one hundred guineas in gold. He'll stay there until Monday morning, sleeping on a couch and eating the sandwiches he brings with him. And if a situation like this ever arises again, he'll dip into the bag and bring out the dibs." He indulged in a grin. "I feel proud to have been the cause of such an innovation."

Jonathan counted the notes and stowed them away in a pocket. "A very good arrangement, it seems to me," he said.

"I've something else to tell you." The scribe indulged in a wink. "Your beautiful countess got out of France quickly and easily. And what's more, the episode has not been mentioned in the press; for which you should be properly grateful to me. Did you know that she traveled to Dover disguised as a governess in the household of the Marquis of Invermark?"

"Who do you suppose arranged that?"

"Need I say? You, of course. I never had a doubt on that score.

"I saw the marquis this morning," went on the newspaperman. "We went to college together and he deigns to remember me; in fact he is practically friendly at times. This morning as I crossed Hanover Square there he was, superintending the removal of the hatchment from the front of his house. He had discarded his weeds and was dressed in a suit of bottle green. His hands were stuffed into his trousers pockets and, moreover, he was whistling. Something must have happened to him to yank him out of mourning in such a thorough way. Can you imagine what it might have been?"

"I have no idea," answered Jonathan. But his heart sank. He said to himself: "Why was I so blind! Even a dour Scot would find her irresistible. First a baronet, than a French comte, and now, perhaps, a marquis! It sounds both probable and logical. A steady upward climb."

"Have you any idea," persisted the scribe, "why he should stop me and ask if I know anyone with a knowledge of French Law?"

"My dear Hector, he is your fellow countryman. You are better able to understand the workings of his mind than I am. I have met him once only. Perhaps he has business interests in France."

"Somehow I don't believe that is it. Could it be that he wants to be of help to someone who has claims on French property? That seems more likely to me."

"What have I done?" thought Jonathan. "He couldn't spend so much time in Isabelle's company without falling in love with her. Why did I throw them together? Why didn't I think of some way of getting her out of France myself?"

"When you have your mission running, friend Jonathan," said the scribe, "I shall do a few paragraphs about it for the paper. And if our mutual friend actually marries your Isabelle, I shall feel free to draw on my store of knowledge about the beginning of the romance. That seems to me quite fair and just."

2

Isabelle had been playing a new game called field tennis which a bishop, or at any rate a churchman of high rank, had invented. It was tennis taken out of the solid walls which closed it in, and played on open ground with a net and a few ground lines. Her opponent had been the Rev. Jack Blissing, who had been a fair athlete in his day but who on this occasion had not succeeded in getting enough of Isabelle's brisk drives back over the net. He had left without waiting for the traditional glass of sherry and so it may be assumed that his pride had suffered.

Her father not being at home, Isabelle gave the butler orders for her lunch as he let her in. "Cold roast beef, Fleck, a heaping salad, an omelet, and a good sweet of some kind. Just bring it to me on a tray. In the strawberry parlor."

"The strawberry parlor is occupied, m'lady," said Fleck. "His ludship is waiting for you."

Isabelle ran to the nearest mirror, a very handsome one of considerable age and distinguished lineage, and inspected herself in the glass. Her cheeks were flushed a little from the play; and all the better for that. Her hair, which she was allowing to grow in, was at a somewhat undisciplined stage, and after a tug or two with impatient fingers she brought the errant locks into a degree of presentability and hurried to the strawberry parlor.

But it was not the Marquis of Invermark who was waiting for her. Young Chip was standing in a window embrasure and looking out into the garden. His huge shoulders were encased in a coat of loud tweed, his legs showed muscular contours through yellow trousers, and his riding boots, with red-painted tops, verged on vulgarity.

"Why, Chip!" said Isabelle, feeling rather let down. "Fleck didn't say it was you." She observed his proportions with a dismayed eye. "Chip, you're getting heavier all the time!"

"Waiting for you does it. I do nothing but sit about and mope. But I didn't come here to discuss my weight. I came to tell you that I'm hearing things. Things I don't like at all, Isabelle. You made me a promise, you know. And you don't seem to be trying to keep it."

Isabelle seated herself in a couch which her father had bought for an extravagant figure, and leaned her brown curls against the elaborately carved crest rail. "Chip, I'll appreciate it if you'll sit down. You're so damned broad"—she indulged occasionally in profanity when at home—"that you're shutting off the light. Take a strong chair, please. Not one of Father's frail antiques."

"Don't want to sit down," declared the future Duke of Outland. He left the window and stationed himself in front of Isabelle. "Why are you seeing so much of the Sawney?"

"The Sawney?"

"Yes. The Scotchman. I hear he's gone clear over the rail about you. Now looka here, Isabelle, I won't have you marrying him. If you keep that sort of thing up, we'll never get married, you and I. And you promised me. Don't deny it; you gave me a solemn promise."

"Did I?" She opened her eyes wide to simulate surprise. "But, Chip, you're a married man. How can it concern you if I marry again?"

"Isabelle, do you remember that time when you got me in to play whist?"

"Yes." She indulged in a shudder. "I don't think I'll ever forget that evening."

"There were two tables and it was agreed we'd divide up differently when the first rubber ended." His round black eyes, as large almost as the bases of beer mugs, were fixed on her sternly. "I had insisted on it."

"I remember. You were at the other table and you wanted to play with me. I agreed to the arrangement because it seemed unfair to make the others at your table carry the whole burden."

"When we finished our rubber," he went on, shaking an accusatory finger at her, "your table was only halfway through. So we went on playing. We never did change sides because we never finished rubbers at the same time. Isabelle! You and I are going to be in the same fix if we don't look out. Whenever one of us is free, the other will be tied up. We must agree now that we can't go on getting married this way. One of us must stop and wait for the other."

"Did you wait when your first wife died?"

"I couldn't," he answered in an unhappy voice. "As I told you at the time, Isabelle, I had gone through my first wife's money—I always had the most damnable luck at the races—and I couldn't get along on the absurd pittance my father offered me. I *had* to marry again."

"And I suppose now you're going through Amy's money as fast as you can."

"It is flying a little."

"And so you want me to wait until it's all flown away and Amy divorces you. You want me to send poor Dugald Malcolm about his business."

"So!" cried Chip. "He does want to marry you then!"

"Oh yes." Isabelle nodded her head. "He does. And I—I'm a little fond of him."

"Why doesn't he marry one of those broad-beamed Scotch lassies we hear so much about? Why does he come looking around down here?"

"He isn't looking around. Such a vulgar idea!"

"I tell you, Isabelle, I'll call him out!"

Isabelle became completely serious at this point. "Chip, if you come blundering into my affairs, or if you as much as repeat one word of what we've said today, I'll never speak to you again. I mean it."

The future duke began to stride about the room, kicking at rugs and giving other proofs of an aroused temper.

"This seems to me a good time, Chip, to tell you that you wouldn't like being married to me," said Isabelle. "You would find me a hard taskmaster."

He came back to his former station at the double quick, his eyes lighting up. "Just give me a try, Isabelle. That's all I ask."

"In the first place I would put you on a diet. I can't imagine what that Amy of yours is thinking of, letting you get so—well, the only word for it is beefy. I would have twenty pounds off you in no time at all."

Chip grinned. "It'd do me good, Issy. I wouldn't mind having you bothering over me like that."

"Then I would take every bit of clothing you possess and make a bonfire. Your taste is nothing short of bucolic."

"I would wear whatever you picked out for me, dear girl."

"Just look at that hat! Is it—is it an Australian hat? Or a Canadian, perhaps?"

"Don't know." He was still grinning in perfect good humor. "I liked it when I bought it. Seemed to have a little dash and daring about it. But since you've taken a scunner to it, I'll never wear it again."

Isabelle began to smile also. "Well, so much for that. You'll stay for lunch with me, Chip?"

"Thanks, no. I can't, worse luck. I'm on my way to the Colling-Holmeses' and I should be there in five minutes. If I'd been able to stay, would you have started on me with the dieting? Cutting down on the beef and putting a custard in front of me?" He leaned over and extended a hand. "Farewell, and remember what I said. No more matrimony for you, my girl. I have a lien on a very beautiful piece of property and I'll have no Sawneys poaching on my preserves."

Isabelle did not accept the proffered hand. She knew from experience that he would immediately pull her to her feet and kiss her soundly before going on his way.

"Good-by, Chip. I'll remember what you've said."

He became completely grave. "I've meant every word I've said. I seem to love you more all the time, my beautiful Isabelle."

She said to herself when he was gone, "How angry poor Chip would be if he knew I've already promised my handsome, dour Scot, and that the day has been set!"

## CHAPTER THIRTEEN

### 1

The Carboy grandson waved in the direction of the stables at the Old Rectory and a figure which looked boyish in spite of a mature roundness of body waved back.

"That's Huruld," said Young Sammy. "He's got a last name now. He's been named Gladstone after a young member of Parliament. At first Aunt Helen thought of naming him Martin because she admired a character of that name in a book by Mr. Dickens. But she found she admired Mr. Gladstone still more and so that's what Huruld got."

"Just the kind of fellow a woman would pick to admire," said Samuel Carboy. He paused on the point of raising the knocker. "Do you still feel the same way? You know what I mean. You said something to me once, you know. In fact you started it."

When his grandson succeeded only in looking completely blank in response to this question, the Colossus knocked at the door.

"A new maid," he grumbled when a neatly dressed girl opened the door. "What's *your* name?"

"I'm Pitcher, sir," answered the girl. "Daphne Pitcher from the village, sir."

"Oh. Is your mistress in?"

"Yes, sir. Will you come this way?"

"Good evening, ma'am," said Carboy when Nell rose from her chair by the fire in the room which had always been called the library because the various rectors who had inhabited it maintained a small bookcase there. It deserved the name now. Nell had become a great reader and the walls were covered with books except for the space over the fireplace, which contained a portrait of the late Daniel Groody, executed by an artist from London; a good likeness, moreover, and costing a pretty penny.

"Good evening, Mr. Carboy. And Sammy!" Nell did not kiss the boy. In fact she had ceased doing so some years before when he began to grow long in the legs like his father and very strong about the shoulders like his grandfather. "You haven't been to see me much lately, Sammy."

"Young Sammy," said the grandfather, "has been too busy to see anyone. He's been too busy making plans. We're here this evening, Miss Groody, because he has a plan he wants to discuss with the two of us."

"How very interesting," said Nell. "Let's all sit down and hear about it comfortably. Would you care for a cup of tea?"

"Tea?" said Carboy doubtfully. "Well, no. But if you had any whisky——"

"I have. And I'm certain Sammy would prefer a cup of chocolate."

"Yes, Aunt Helen, I would. And I hope you've got some of that Spanish bun we used to have. I'd like some."

"Daphne," said Nell when the maid appeared in answer to her ring of the bell, "bring the whisky for Mr. Carboy and make some chocolate for Mr. Samuel. I'll have a cup too, I think. I seldom indulge myself to that extent but this is an occasion, isn't it?

"And now for the plan," she said when their wants had been accommodated.

"Go ahead, youngster," said the Colossus, leaning back comfortably and thinking what an extremely pleasant room it was. "Unfold this mysterious plan for us. I'm anxious to know what it's all about."

"Well, it's this way, Aunt Helen. I told my grandfather that I didn't want to go to college. It's not because I object to college but it seemed to me—because I have such lots of plans in my head that I want to get started on right away—that to go to Oxford would be—well, rather a waste of time."

"Now that makes sense," said Samuel Carboy.

"So, Grandfather thinks I ought to go into the business. I want to go into the business, of course. It's what I hope to do later. But before that happens there's one thing I must do. I want to go to another country for a few years and see what I can do about getting some kind of a career started for myself. If I have any success, then I can come back with something to offer of my own. Perhaps a little capital. Or, at any rate, a bit of experience. I don't want to be handed everything like a rich man's son—or grandson."

"You want to win your spurs!" cried Nell. "What a really and truly splendid idea."

"Wait a minute now before you get running away with enthusiasm." The grandfather was clearly very much disturbed. "I'm afraid of trips abroad. Your father, my boy, went on one and he never came back. I don't want to lose you the same way. It would be safer if you stayed right here so I could keep an eye on you."

"And help me too. Grandfather, that's what I don't want."

"Oh, you could have your own little business and run it to you own liking. What's this country where you want to go?"

"South Africa!" said the boy triumphantly, as though the mere mention of the name should arouse in them the same degree of enthusiasm he had for it. "Oh, it's a wonderful place! I've been reading about it and talking about it whenever I get the chance, and studying maps. It's so warm and it has such strange and wonderful flowers. It's the place to meet with adventures. And, Grandfather, they say there's gold to be found there. That's what I want to do first. Get together a gang of natives and go after gold."

"How long do you plan to stay in this dangerous country?"

The boy answered coolly: "Oh, a few years. Seven or eight. Ten perhaps."

"Oh, Sammy!" cried Nell reproachfully. "What a dreadful idea, to stay away ten years!"

"I certainly put my foot down right now on that," declared Carboy. "I'm not getting any younger, you know. I can struggle along without you for a while. But not for ten years."

"Of course, I would come home any time you really did need me. But, sir, it's just as Aunt Helen said. I want to win my spurs."

They discussed the plan at considerable length while the boy consumed two mugs of chocolate and an incalculable amount of the spiced cake called Spanish bun, and Samuel Carboy paid attention to the whisky bottle. In the end it was decided that the boy should be given his head but that a close rein would have to be kept on him so that he could be brought back home at short notice. The grandfather gave in rather grumblingly, having a very real fear that the past might repeat itself.

"I make one stipulation," he said finally. "You're not to go out into the wild country after gold and get caught by these natives with great long spears."

"Zulus?" suggested the boy. "It's the assagai they carry. A very dangerous weapon. And they're quite wonderful fellows. I've been reading about what great fighters they are."

"Well, no Zulus for you, my boy. You can go only on condition that none of these Zulus ever get a chance at you unless they climb through strong brick walls. And now, young fellow, go out and see your friend Huruld. I've a word to say to Miss Groody."

2

When the boy had left, willingly enough having gained his point, Samuel Carboy got to his feet and stationed himself in front of the fire. He seemed unsure of himself, even a little embarrassed.

"Ma'am," he said, "I believe in getting right to the point. I have something to say and I'm not going to beat about any bushes. Will you marry me?"

"Mr. Carboy!" cried Nell, so completely taken by surprise that she could not think of anything else to say.

"I mean it, ma'am. Is it such a strange idea that you can't believe it? Hundreds of men ask women to marry them every day of the year. I'm a widower. I'd like to marry again but only if you're to be the one. I—I admire you most excessively."

Nell had managed to collect her wits by this time, sufficiently to realize that he really meant what he was saying. His face was a little red but he seemed also to have recovered his usual composure. He was jingling coins in a pocket and waiting for some indication of her reaction.

"I'm sure, Mr. Carboy," she said, "that it's a very great compliment you've paid me."

"Not at all, ma'am, not at all. I can't conceive of any man, free and in a position to marry, not wanting to marry you. You are a most beautiful young woman. And clever too. I sometimes think you're the second best business-man in England. We would make a great team, ma'am."

"The first and the second in double harness," thought Nell, concealing with difficulty a tendency to smile.

"I hope you haven't been prejudiced against me," he went on, "by all the things that have been said. Mostly by that former and not too deeply re-gretted partner of mine. Perhaps you remember what he said—'wallowing in women.' It was a lie! A complete and damnable lie! I've been a widower for quite a few years but I haven't been wallowing in women. Whatever I've had to do with them has been on a basis of decency. They've always been decent women, widows mostly, and everything has been understood: that I sup-ported them for a short time only at an agreed figure and so much more when the time to part arrived. There have never been any hurt feelings—— What are you laughing at, ma'am?"

"I really believe, Mr. Carboy," said Nell, "that this is the most unusual proposal any woman ever received."

It's an honest one, at any rate," he declared. "It's more honest and decent than the usual thing: a young buck on his knees and protesting his devotion and not saying a word about *his* experiences—the housemaids he's seduced and the well-bustled ladies of the town he's tagged after."

"Oh, I see how very honest you are, Mr. Carboy. I think I should take it as a very great compliment."

"Well, you know what I have to offer. Not a title—although I might attend to that later—but everything else. Including, as I said before, my most exces-sive admiration."

Nell looked up at him, standing with his shoulders, those strong shoulders on which so large a share of the business burdens of the kingdom rested, pressed against the marble of the mantel. She realized that she was begin-ning to like him a little, although she had never believed such a thing pos-sible. She was equally certain, however, that she would never like him well enough for what he was proposing.

"Young Sammy put the idea in my head," he threw in, as a final argument perhaps. "He said it would be nice if we could have his aunt Helen with us all the time."

"That was sweet of Sammy. And I *do* thank you, Mr. Carboy, for asking me. But—well, I can't."

"I'm very much disappointed," said Carboy. Perhaps he was thinking how fine it would be if she were like a factory in the Midlands or a mine in Wales so he could send his financial minions to buy her in, whether she wanted to be bought in or not. He looked at Nell, whose cheeks had turned quite pink and who was looking doubly desirable, and it was difficult for him not to indulge in a tirade aimed at breaking down her resistance. All he allowed himself to say, however, was: "I'm going to come in to see you while the boy's away, ma'am. Quite often. We'll both be lonesome without him. And then, if you should change your mind, I'll be handy."

Nell looked at him long and steadily. "I've come very close to liking you," she said frankly. "But I'm not sure it's going to last. It will depend, I think, on the answer you give me to a certain question."

"Well, what's the question?"

"Perhaps it will seem like more than one. Also, it has something to do with the—the answer I've just given you." She paused for a moment, wondering if there was any purpose to be served in going on. "There was another reason for saying no to you besides the one I gave. Have you forgiven me for the part I played in that affair at Rixby?"

"Well," he said, smiling down at her with some degree of reserve, "I thought you were brave and that your intentions were good. But I was sure you'd got yourself into something you didn't understand. You were foolish to get into a scrape with that crew of sentimental twaddlers. It might have turned out very badly. Still, I've never seriously held it against *you*."

"It turned out well. Don't you agree?"

"No," declared Carboy. "I was beaten. By Jonathan Bade, of all people. I don't like being beaten; and so the affair, as you call it, didn't seem to me to turn out well at all."

Nell was watching him with increased earnestness. "You don't think it good that those children were released from slavery? You aren't pleased that the incident has led already to an improvement in conditions in all parts of the country? Aren't you happy at all that it may prove in time to have been a factor in doing away with child labor entirely?"

"It will never do that," he declared. "Certainly it won't until all other conditions of life have been improved to the same extent. And that, my dear lady, is too much to hope for as long as men are men and not little tuppenny-ha'penny saints or angels with silver wings. And in the meantime, because of what happened at Rixby, I must wear myself out, planning and contriving to reduce costs in other directions so that we'll be able to produce as cheaply as our competitors, who continue to employ children to some extent."

"Now that you've taken this one great step in the direction of—of a better world, shall we say?—don't you feel disposed to take more? There's no man in England who has as much power as you, Samuel Carboy, to do good for mankind."

"It's not my function," he responded emphatically. "I don't see why we had to get into this argument but I'll say this much and no more. When the parsons really teach people to live better lives and to be more generous and decent; when the schools put more sense as well as practical education into young heads; when the House of Parliament makes better laws: then the man of business can start in to do his part. And not before."

"Oh, I know there's a lot of truth in what you say. No one man, or one class, can do the whole thing. But, Samuel, Samuel, don't you ever feel disposed to try?"

The look he bent on her from under his shaggy brows, now sprinkled with salt, indicated that he was puzzled over her insistence. "Frankly, my dear, no. I'm doing more work as it is than any half dozen men you could name. I can't be a Wilberforce or a Howard as well."

Nell shook her head. "I'm sorry. I'm very sorry. Because now I must say that you'll be wasting your time—your precious time, Samuel Carboy—if you come to see me. Because I'm not going to change my mind."

## CHAPTER FOURTEEN

### 1

The lights of Grosvenor Square (for that stronghold of wealth and conservatism had at last succumbed to the use of gas) served to relieve the gloom in the narrow streets surrounding it; and so people of fashion were now willing to establish themselves in the outer reaches, building for their use fine tall houses with iron gates and tiny gardens in the rear; thus driving out the more humble homes which had formerly existed there. It was to one of the finest and tallest of these that Julian Grace directed his steps one April morning when, for a change, the rain clouds had decided to go elsewhere.

The house before which he had come to a stop boasted on its iron gate a design made up of an easel, a brush and a chisel, which quite obviously was intended to represent the arts. "This must be the place," he said to himself. If he needed any further confirmation, his shortsighted survey made out a brass plate on one side of the door, bearing the name Thompson Castle, Esq. His ring brought a footman to the door, attired in a tasteful uniform of black and gold and blue.

"I desire to see Mr. Timothy Grace," said the caller. "You may tell him it's his father."

"Come in, sir," said the footman in a tone which did not rise to respect but did not sink quite to the level of condescension. "Mr. Grace is busy in the studio with Mr. Castle. I will tell him you are here."

Julian was left standing in the hall, a dark and rather forbidding place because of the efforts which the owner had made to have it reflect the artistic trends of the day. The walls were covered with heavily framed paintings of all sizes, Japanese fans and oriental gods on brackets. There was a suit of armor on the stair landing which had once been fitted to the frame of a brave knight although it must be said that it seemed better suited to a third-form Etonian. The stairway was massive and ornate and the newal post was a marvelously intricate reproduction of a cathedral with spires and lantern and lady chapel. A door opening off to the right gave a view of the dining room with golden walls and a baroque structure at one end which could only have been a sideboard, made with mirrors and pillars and pediments in dark oak.

Julian paid little attention to all this splendor. His eye had been captured by a room opening off to the left, a parlor without a doubt, and the receptacle for everything that contributed to the pretentiousness of the Victorian era. It had one distinction, a series of four portraits, all of the same subject, a lady; and a most beautiful lady she was, with red hair piled up above an oval face, and large blue eyes, and a rather sensuous mouth.

"Must be the artist's wife," thought Julian. "The famous Kit Killigrew. No, that was her stage name. Kit Castle, that's it. She really *is* a beauty."

The footman returned and said, "Follow me, sir."

The studio was at the back of the house, a high apartment with a quite huge window in the north which brought light into the room without dispelling the suggestion of a calculated cloisteral gloom. A grated door closed off the anteroom to which Julian had been escorted but through it he could see that a very plump lady with an imperious eye and with expensive furs draped on her bare shoulders was sitting next to a man with eyeglasses and a reddish beard, who quite clearly was the great Thompson Castle. Behind a tall screen he saw his son busily engaged at another easel. Timothy, looking very handsome in a paint-smeared frock, was so placed that the sitter could not see him although he could see her. At intervals he would walk to the screen and make use of a convenient hole to stare at her.

On being informed that his father now awaited his pleasure, young Mr. Grace laid down his palette and brush, wiped his hands on a sponge soaked with turpentine and vanished through a door back of the screen. In a few moments he reached the anteroom and shook hands with affectionate fervor.

"I'm most happy to see you, governor," he said. At close range it could be seen that he had developed a strong resemblance to his father although he lacked an inch or two of the older man's impressive height, making up for it perhaps by a debonair and dashing air. "Are you taking a day off from running the navy and ruling all of the seven seas?"

"I'm taking a fortnight off, Tim, as it happens."

Timothy indulged in a low-pitched whistle. "A fortnight? Gad, sir, won't all the ships be getting into the wrong ports and won't little wars be breaking out because of indiscretions, with you away?"

"Not quite, son," smiling, "but I'm going on a—a new journey myself."

Timothy looked up quickly. "Indeed, sir?"

"Tim, I leave tomorrow. I'll have a new suit of fine broadcloth, a new hat, a pair of new shoes and a new portmanteau of considerable magnificence. I go to Thwaites Hall near Leeds. The day after I arrive, I am being married to the daughter of the house, a Miss Esther Thwaites. Her father, Sir Bullstrode Thwaites, is by way of being a satellite of Samuel Carboy's but he's a very wealthy man in his own right."

An almost comical look of amazement had descended on the face of his son. "Governor," said Timothy, "you've nearly taken my breath away. I never expected anything of this kind to happen. Is there any reason, besides the affection you undoubtedly feel for the lady?"

Julian looked at his son with a gravity which contained a certain degree of wistfulness. "Yes, Timothy, there is a reason. I am fond of my intended wife, of course. You must never think I'm going into this for gain or reasons of convenience entirely. You'll like her also when you know her. But, Timothy, I've come to the end of my rope at Three Gables. I've piled up debts trying to maintain it and the place is running down all the time. You haven't honored us with a visit for quite a time but when you do you will notice a sad change. I still have to keep my mother in the Fox wing and that is a heavy expense. She hasn't forgiven me yet and seldom speaks to me. Sometimes I have to carry her tray in to her and she never thanks me."

"My most revered grandmother is a rather difficult person."

"No, Timothy, that's not true. She—she has had a hard time of it, you know. We must take all that into consideration. And, you see, she thinks I should be able to revenge the death of my father by fixing the guilt on Samuel Carboy."

"She wants you to be another Hamlet, eh?"

"Well, something of the kind. I've been to the police about it half a dozen times, more or less, but they keep telling me the case is closed because they couldn't lay their hands on any evidence. They didn't even find the man who threw the stone. As you probably know, Common Jack was shot in the back by one of his own men. So where should I start? I've tried, Tim. That time I spent my vacation so mysteriously I was investigating the case in the town where my poor father was killed. The people seemed to think I was crazy. They had only the barest recollection of the case. After wasting all my time among them, I reached the conclusion that I was neither a detective nor a Hamlet. I gave it up."

"Perhaps we made a mistake that day when Mother died," said Timothy, becoming very serious of mien. "Do you remember how we sat out on the grass with old Noel and decided we would keep up the place, no matter what happened?"

"Perhaps it was a mistake. But it's been a wonderful home, Tim. Sometimes, when the bills were particularly difficult, I've thought of selling the place and moving into a flat in London. If I did that, I would keep Noel only. But that seems like running away and so, finally, I've decided on this other course. My fiancée, Timothy, has considerable means of her own."

"It's hard to get accustomed to the idea," declared Timothy. "But, after all, it's the sensible thing to do, I expect. The Great Man did a portrait of Sir Bullstrode a few years ago."

"You mean Thompson Castle?"

"None other. Apparently it was a success because your prospective father-in-law paid a whopping fee. It has been held up as a model transaction in all discussions over terms since."

"Are you enjoying your work here?"

Timothy raised his eyebrows to indicate that it was a closely balanced matter. "I'm learning a great deal from him. He's ahead of Phillips and right on a par with Pickersgill. His use of color is remarkable and I want to tell you he's a slapdash genius at painting materials. He has no equal at flesh tones. But I'll whisper a secret in your ear. He has to struggle to get a likeness.

He lacks the gift of seeing just which quirk of line is the one that brings a person alive on canvas."

"Isn't that a great weakness in a portrait painter?"

"Well—not necessarily. Many sitters don't want their portraits to be too literal. They want even a likeness glorified to some extent. In this matter of catching the likeness, I'm—well, permit me to be candid and say that I have a rather remarkable gift for it. So we're playing a little trick between us. While he's facing the lady and slathering on the paint, I'm behind a screen, doing the same thing but confining myself to the face. The next step is for him to copy my sketch on the official canvas. The old boy would be furious if he knew I had told anyone. He has a razor-edged pride and practically no scruples whatever. This little matter is being kept a dank, dark secret; and I got a rather handsome addition to my salary because of it. You must never whisper it to a soul."

"Of course not, Timothy." Julian was frowning. "But it seems to me rather shabby."

"Not at all," said his son airily. "We give them exactly what they want, and they don't care about the mechanics of it. Of course, none of them has an inkling of what goes on. Thompson, dear fellow, sees to that." With a quick glance through the grating, he continued: "It's a little uncomfortable, and perhaps dangerous, to talk here. I'll send you up to my sitting room and join you later, after I've put in another half hour on the dear lady's nose. It's causing me no end of trouble."

The sitting room was of a good size although undeniably dark. Seating himself in a corner, Julian crossed one threadbare knee over its disreputable fellow and looked ruefully at a patch on one of his shoes. "In another year," he thought, "I'd have been another Vincent Pardon, with no one to worry about the patches on the seat of my trousers."

Because the room was dark he was not at once visible to a lady who came in on tiptoe, wearing a pleased smile on her rather full lips. He recognized her at once as the model for the portraits below. "They didn't do her justice," he thought; and in this he was right, for Mrs. Thompson Castle, wearing a loose dressing gown of green silk and her red hair in wavy disorder, was worth walking all the way from the City to see.

She walked lightly to a bookcase on the opposite wall, carrying an envelope in one hand. She drew out a volume from the case and was on the point of placing the envelope between the leaves when the sound of the visitor getting to his feet interrupted her. She turned her head, and a startled and dismayed look took possession of her face.

"Oh!" she exclaimed. "I didn't know there was anyone here."

"I'm very sorry if I've startled you," said Julian. "I'm Julian Grace, Timothy's father."

"Of course," she said, recovering herself easily. The envelope had disappeared into a pocket of the green dressing gown. "There is a close resemblance between you. I am very glad indeed, Mr. Grace, to make your acquaintance."

They shook hands and there was a look in her lovely eyes which told him she had meant what she said, that she was indeed glad to meet Timothy's father, even though he had observed an activity on her part at the time when observation was the last thing she had desired.

"Tim is busy in the studio," she said by way of explanation, "and so I decided not to disturb him. I was going to leave a note for him about something I want him to do for us but, as you are here, I'll give you the message instead. Please tell him we'll need him for dinner after all, if he hasn't made other arrangements. A guest has sent last-minute regrets. Please tell Tim to talk to me about it before he leaves for his walk."

"I'll be very happy to convey your message to him, Mrs. Castle."

"Thank you, Mr. Grace. Oh, Tim is so like you. You're a little taller, I think, but you both have the same forehead and eyes and nose. Anyone could tell you are father and son. Is there anything I can get you? A glass of wine?"

"Thank you, no, Mrs. Castle. I'm leaving almost as soon as Timothy comes up."

The large blue eyes of the recent graduate from the London stage gave him the full benefit of a disarming smile. "I am really so happy to have met you at last, Mr. Grace. You see, we are quite fond of Tim, both Mr. Castle and I. You must come for dinner some night soon."

"Thank you. It would be a pleasure."

Timothy came up the stairs almost as soon as the lady of the house had left. He stopped in the doorway and sniffed suspiciously.

"Perfume," he said. "I'm sure Kit has been here. I hope you met her, Father. Isn't she lovely?"

"Quite, son. I consider her one of the most beautiful women I've ever seen." He paused briefly. "By the way, are you reading *Peregrine Pickle?*"

Timothy looked startled and then his face flushed. "Why, no. I read it as a boy, of course. I think I have a copy of it here. Why do you ask?"

Julian was studying him with an affectionate anxiety. "Timothy," he said, "if I hadn't happened to be here, I believe you would have found a note addressed to you concealed between the pages of *Peregrine Pickle.* See here, my boy, are you in love with your employer's wife?"

"What a farfetched idea!" Then a deeper flush turned his face to the red of guilt. "Yes, Father, I am. I'm madly in love with her."

"And is she in love with you?"

The young artist nodded. Then he burst out into a rhapsody of praise. "She's not only the loveliest woman in the world but the sweetest as well. I'm so much in love with her, Father, that I don't know what I'm going to do about it."

"I know what you're going to do about it," said his father in an emphatic tone. "You're going to resign your position at once. And you're going to move as soon as you can pack your things. If you stay here another day, or if you see Mrs. Castle again, you'll become involved in a very dangerous situation. On second thoughts, you had better resign and come away with me. We can send for your things later."

Timothy gave the problem some troubled thought and then shook his head. "I can't. I must finish Lady Brazey's nose. Castle will never get it right if I don't."

"Never mind Lady Brazey's nose!"

"Father," said Timothy after a long silence, during which he had been thinking deeply, "I can't go away without a word with Kit first. No, no, that would be cowardly. We'll have to talk about it. There's no use fuming at me. This is my affair and I must handle it in my own way."

"Will you promise me that you'll tell her this must stop? And stick to it?"

The young artist smiled rather grimly. "I'll try. I know that it's all wrong. So does Kit. But so far we haven't been able to make up our minds about anything."

"But you will now?"

"I'll do my best. That's all I can say. I love her so much!"

"Does the husband know anything of it?"

Timothy shook his head. "No. I'm sure he doesn't. We've been—most discreet."

Julian said sharply: "Continue to be discreet until you've left the house. Do you promise me that? I won't be able to proceed with my plans until you do."

The son indulged in a second wry smile. "Very well, then, I promise. Nothing must be allowed to interfere with your matrimonial plans, Father."

2

"There's really a great deal to be done to this place," said the second Mrs. Julian Grace as the carriage stopped in front of the house. The afternoon sun was pouring across the garden, which Julian had always kept up with almost fanatical care, but his new wife was seeing instead the lack of paint on the house and the sand on the steps of the stone porch.

Her coachman, who wore a long white overcoat and a tall green hat with yellow feathers at the sides, helped her down. When she entered the hall she looked about her and said, "Oh dear, dear, dear, dear, dear, dear, dear!"

"I've had little help and less time," said Julian apologetically. "And I'm not a housekeeper, you know."

"I shall have a frantic time of it, I can see that."

Without waiting to make sure that her personal maid, who had been concealed somewhere in the carriage, probably among the mountains of luggage, unpacked the clothes properly, the new chatelaine of Three Gables began on a tour of inspection of the house. Three times she came to the library, where Julian was sitting, with specimens of the dreadful discoveries she was making, including an old washcloth behind a tub, a torn curtain from an upstairs window and a can of some foodstuff which had decayed rather thoroughly. Julian paid little attention. He was absorbed in a letter.

On reaching the house he had, as was his usual custom, gone to the library first, for it was here that he had spent with Winifred the last moments of her life. He had glanced about him with a subdued air and a hint of mistiness in his eyes which could have been interpreted as apologetic; as though, in fact, he were begging forgiveness. He had remained there because a letter was propped up above the fireplace in the flowing and quite distinctive handwriting of his son Timothy. It was dated from Antwerp.

*Dear Father* [it began]:

You will not see me for a very long time. Kit and I talked it over, as I promised you we would, and we reached a conclusion: that nothing else would do but to run away together. You see, the Great Man is a devout Catholic and he would never consent to a divorce. That left us, as I am sure you will agree after you have given thought to it, with no alternative but to toss our caps over the whatyemacallem and leave for parts unknown.

I visited Three Gables in your absence, to see it (perhaps for the last time) and to gather together a few articles of clothing and some keepsakes. While there it occurred to me that as Noel is so closely affiliated with the old regime it might be better if he were absent when you return with your lady. So I took the good old fellow with me. If you want him back, you can send me word at this address, and the faithful retainer will be shipped to you at once.

My most beautiful and much-beloved lady has connections in Vienna, so I think we shall go there ultimately. I am planning to paint portraits, having (as I so modestly stated before) a decided flair for it. In fact, I have every confidence that we shall do very well and that my beautiful lady (ah, the wonder of her!) will never have reason to regret the fleshpots of Grosvenor Square and its environs.

Under all these circumstances, it may be that I will never venture on a visit to England—not, certainly, until the G.M. changes his mind. It is even possible that this will be a final farewell.

The letter, which had then gone into particulars as to the disposal of such of his belongings as he had left behind, was a very long one. When Julian finished reading it he walked to the front window of the library and stood there without moving for many minutes. His eyes rested most particularly on the summerhouse where his young wife had spent so much of her leisure time but he glanced in turn at all the reminders of her beloved presence, even to the weir because she had always enjoyed watching the water tumbling through on its way to the sea.

"Dearest Freddie," he whispered, "your son has run away with a married woman and your husband has taken another wife. Can you forgive us?"

## 3

The second Mrs. Grace was rather short and rather square, with sandy-colored hair and gray eyes set in her face at an angle seen most often in cats. She was not unattractive but there was a brusqueness in her manner which was decidedly so; and which could be traced, perhaps, to the independent means she had always enjoyed. Esther, in fact, was quite wealthy and would become more so when the time came for the half dozen children of Sir Bullstrode to divide his very extensive holdings.

Her arrival at Three Gables had one immediate result which seemed at first to belong on the happy side of the ledger. She conceived a certain kinship, if not an actual liking, for the aging invalid in the Fox wing. Perhaps it was because they had one thing in common; they were women without beauty or charm who had reason to believe that their husbands had been actuated in picking them for reasons apart from any romantic feeling, the elder Mrs. Grace having been the niece of a duke and the younger being an heiress in her own right. At any rate Julian found them together when he finished his long visit in the library. The senior Mrs. Grace had done an unprecedented thing, she had left her own suite of rooms and had come out to join her daughter-in-law at tea in the strawberry parlor, which was a pleasant spot as it caught the rays of the declining afternoon sun. She was attacking her crumpets and tea with open enjoyment.

She even spoke to her son. "You have chosen well this time," she said.

This open avowal that she had not approved entirely of her son's first wife sealed the compact between the two women for all time. Esther Grace leaned over to touch her mother-in-law's hand as she remarked to her husband, "Your mother and I are going to get along splendidly, Julian."

"Yes, my dear. I am very happy about it."

It became the custom thereafter for the two women to greet him together on his weekend visits, their arms linked, his wife just a little cool to him (because, he was sure, of the confidences his mother had been pouring into her ears) and the elder Mrs. Grace ostentatiously wearing the pieces of jewelry her new daughter had given her. Each return brought him discoveries in the way of changes about the place. The library and the parlor exchanged identities, new drapes were hung everywhere and old pieces of friendly furniture vanished to give place to shiny new Victorian atrocities, heavy over-all carpets replaced the mellow oriental rugs, the garden was completely transformed by an expert and expensive gardener. He was never consulted in advance and he soon came to understand his wife's purpose. She was determined to banish all traces of Winifred, to leave nothing which could sustain his memories of his first wife.

"I know," she said to him once in an almost passionate surrender to her inner thoughts, "that you loved her more than you do me."

"My dear, my dear," said Julian, feeling very sorry for her, "you are being unfair. To yourself as well as me. Such comparisons can't be drawn. The man who married Winifred was not the man who has married you. You mustn't get the two of them mixed up."

The escapade of the absent Timothy was a two-edged weapon in Esther's hands. The young artist who had run away with the once rather famous but now notorious Kit Castle was the son of her rival and what he had done reflected on the memory of the woman who had been his mother. It gave the new wife the right—or so she thought) to think ill of the deceased first wife. She never put this into words but there was an air about her which was both smug and triumphant whenever the matter was brought up. It seemed to Julian that his mother delighted in mentioning Timothy and in speculating on how things were going with the absconding couple.

"One thing is certain," said Esther on an occasion when her mother-in-law had introduced the topic. "I'll never receive that woman."

"Nonsense, my dear," said Julian. "One of these days Castle will come to his senses and get his divorce. Then the young people will get married and —well, things will be different. People will never forget, of course. I'm not sure that I will ever be able to give them a complete pardon. But when that does happen, we must get behind them. It will be our duty to help them face the world and make a place for themselves. That goes without saying."

"That creature," declared Esther, "will never set foot in my house."

They were sitting in the garden when this conversation took place. Julian gave his wife a hurt look and motioned about him. "Are you referring to this?"

"Yes," said his wife positively.

"It's true that you've changed the place completely," said Julian after a moment. "Not for the better always, I'm compelled to say. At considerable expense, I expect, although I'm not in your confidence in such matters. I must acknowledge also, rather to my shame, that you pay for a very large part of the upkeep. But it's also true, and this is a good time to make the point clear, that this house is mine. Moreover, if the possibility we've been discussing ever becomes a reality, the decision as to what stand we take will be mine, my dear."

There was a long silence. "At any rate," said the wife in a smaller voice, "I'll never have that colored man about the place."

"Noel has been my faithful body servant for many years. If he ever returns, he will be taken back without any question."

CHAPTER FIFTEEN

1

A sign in the window read: *The Waterloo Tontine*, and there were two dark rooms inside, filled with paper presses and cabinets for the filing of newspapers and correspondence and half a dozen chairs with stuffing bulging out in all directions. All of the staff who handled the Tontine were present on a dull and drizzly Friday afternoon, in the year 1845; the manager, three inspectors, a copyist and Old Scratchy, the bookkeeper. The latter had taken a stool in the office two days after Hark Chaffery blew his brains out and had remained there ever since. The others were convinced that he never got down from his high perch for meals or sleep, for he was always there when they arrived in the morning and when they left at night. He had become so thick about the middle that he sagged all around the top of the stool and his hair had receded with the years to a pepper-and-salt fringe which made his bald head look like that of a suckling pig on a New Year's Day board.

Everyone liked Old Scratchy but on this particular day his popularity was in danger of suffering a decline.

"A nice time, I must say, to be taking a day off," grumbled Burke, one of the three inspectors. "Here we've got to get all these checks out to the survivors before tomorrow night. What's the matter with you, Scratchy, that you think you've got to be away tomorrow? You've never been away for a single day to the best of my knowledge."

"Can't be helped," said the bookkeeper in a high squeaky voice. "I've promised my brother-in-law Jimmy."

"Jimmy Feast?"

"Yes, Jimmy Feast. Can't break my promise."

"What promise?"

"Well, you see Jimmy's a banker. His boss has decided he's got to take over a weekend job on top of everything else. He's to go to the offices of the *Packet* every Saturday and stay there until Monday. He takes two bags, one with his clothes and another that the bank hands him."

"What's he do while he's there?"

The bookkeeper shook his head in a puzzled way. "Jimmy don't rightly know. He wasn't told. He's to stay in one office and never put his head outside the door. But do you know what he thinks? He thinks it's got something to do with that bag they hand him."

"That sounds reasonable. What's in it?"

Old Scratchy lowered his voice. "He hasn't been told. But Jimmy thinks —and mind, no one of you must repeat a word I've said because it's all very secret—that there's gold in the bag."

Five pairs of eyes came sharply about to study the pudgy face of the occupant of the high stool. "Gold!" said the manager, whose name was Boyston Baird. His voice contained a distinct note of awe. "Gold, did you say, Scratchy?"

"Gold, sir. He says the bag is heavy, so it would be a lot of gold, wouldn't it?"

"Sweet crow!" said Burke. "What would they be sending gold for to a newspaper office while it's all closed up and nobody's there?"

"I just know what Jimmy tells me, and that ain't much." The bookkeeper went back to his work and his pen began to squeak over the page of a ledger. "Jimmy's kind of afraid to go all alone the first time for fear he might get knocked on the head. Common Jack's dead but there's a lot of crooks would have a go at the bag if they knew what it contained. If it *is* gold, that is." His head was now deep in his work. "So I'm going with him and if the lot of you don't like it you can lump it."

Old Scratchy went with his brother-in-law the next day and so even the manager had to take a hand in getting out the first checks. It was, they all realized, a most important matter. The tontine period of thirty years was now over and there was a handsome reserve for the payments which would continue to be divided evenly among the survivors as long as there was a single one left. In recent years there had been a great deal of impatience for the payments to begin and the offices had been flooded with appeals. Many of the men and women who held shares had been finding themselves in financial straits and had clamored loudly for the disbursements to start. It was partly owing to this widespread impatience that any delay in sending the money was regarded as undesirable.

"Seven hundred and two left out of more than eleven thousand starters in this class," said the manager, taking off his starched cuffs and placing them on the edge of the desk. "There's never been such a heavy casualty percentage before. The survivors begin with a larger income than anyone expected."

By midday the five men were realizing that they were glad the number of survivors was no greater. Seven hundred and two letters to write, the same number of checks to be made out, the envelopes to be addressed for each; that was a heavy day's work, even for five men. They began to miss the bookkeeper early and to complain about the errand which had taken him away.

"That greasy stew of suet!" growled Burke. "He'll spend the whole day playing cribbage with his chickenhearted brother-in-law and munching beef sandwiches."

"My hands are numb already," complained the copyist, who had been doing more than all the others put together.

"I was curious to find out why so many had died and lost their shares," said the one called Spunky, deciding to change the subject. "I checked over the old lists the other day. Do any of you realize that eighty-seven met violent deaths of one kind or another? Three, even, were murdered. Eighteen vanished and haven't been heard of since. That fellow in Newcastle who killed himself by wadding his mouth full of blotting paper owned a share. You'd think he would have waited a little longer. As for consumption, it's been popping them off like flies. You'd almost think when they got their shares it was natural to start pining away."

"They'll knock off a little slower now," said the manager, who had such a long black mustache that the ends were threatening to get into the ink. "Only the healthy ones and the tough ones are left. Still, we'll have a wastage of about thirty a year, I expect, and that will mean a tidy increase for those who hang on. This forty-two pounds eleven shillings we're sending each of them today will grow fast. In another ten years, of course, the blokes will begin to pop off by the hundreds every year."

"The survivors will be the luckiest dogs in the world," said Burke. "I've already made my pick for the final winner. Do you remember, Mr. Baird, when I had to go up to Lincoln to see a butcher fellow named 'Barrel' Corgan? He'd put in a complaint. He was sure one of the other members had died and that someone was taking his place and would claim the share. It turned out he was wrong but I had a good look at the butcher and he's good to live to a hundred."

"He won't have a chance against my pick," said Smith. "I called on a little wart of a fellow named Arthur Anselm Race, a violin player, mind you. He was about five foot tall and he weighed all of ninety pounds. He'd never been sick a day in his life and he could eat like a horse without gaining a pound. I'll bet that skinny weasel will outlive your Barrel Corgan, Burke."

"You're both forgetting that women nearly always win the tontines," contributed the manager. He held up a letter he had just addressed. "Here's your winner. The Marchioness of Invermark, old Carboy's daughter. She'll be a handsome widow when all of the rest of them are dead and laid away in their eternity boxes. The marquis, you know, stays most of the time at his castle of Kilmorlie but the butcheous Isabelle doesn't want anything to do with the Highlands. She likes it right here in London. I saw her out riding the other day with six men, all of them young and handsome." He gave his head a glum nod, being both of an envious disposition and dyspeptic. "I'll lay a bet with any one of you that this husband killer will live to be ninety and that when she dies her father, old Castiron Sam, will still be sitting on top of his moneybags. Did any of you see him when he was in the other day with some instructions about the distribution? He looked hardy enough to chew tacks with his breakfast eggs."

"How about Miss Helen Groody?" asked one of the others.

"She hasn't a chance," asserted Burke. "I saw her not long ago. I thought she was looking frail."

"My money's on the Carboy gal," said the manager emphatically. "She'll be the one to collect the thirty thousand pounds a year. And she'll need it less than most people need a penny for a cup of tea."

# BOOK IV

## *A Singular Coincidence*

1

THE ARM of coincidence, often described as long but in most instances decidedly short, is a much-criticized device when employed by a teller of stories. It is acknowledged, nevertheless, that in real life coincidences are continually in evidence, being largely responsible for the saying that truth is stranger than fiction. All people figure in them on innumerable occasions. As this story covers the lives of a rather large group, it follows that coincidence is bound to be met with and that there must be, like it or not, a recording of it.

Four children who will play prominent parts in the balance of the story were born, not on the same day (for that would be stretching the long arm further than even life attempts), but within a matter of two weeks of each other. The blessed events occurred in four different parts of the world and it was to take considerable time for the quartet to get together; though get together they did in due course, sometimes to their mutual advantage, sometimes not. This, then, seems sufficient excuse for the heading which appears on the preceding page: A SINGULAR COINCIDENCE.

The first of the four infants to put in an appearance was a boy. He was born in a rambling white house which stood on a hilltop not far from Cape Town, within full view of Table Mountain and even in sight of the castle at the head of the bay. It was a beautiful place, under skies of speckless blue and air of intoxicating lightness. A grove of silver trees had been cut through to make room for it and farther back on the southern slope there was an orchard where tropical fruits as well as the native pear and the Kei apple flourished. There were colored servants in great numbers hurrying on slippered feet about the house and barefooted field hands at the back door waiting patiently for the word that the beloved mevrou had safely brought her son into the world; for it was never doubted that the first child to arrive would be a boy.

The father was a young Englishman who had been nearly ten years in Cape Colony and had already cut quite a swath in various directions. He owned a gold mine far up in the Great Trek country and his hand was in many concerns in and about the city. The mother was a Boer girl with black hair and gray eyes and a milk-white skin who belonged to one of the very oldest families. One of her ancestors, Dirk van Heerden, had been an official of the Dutch East India Company and had accumulated such a large fortune that Clara van Heerden had been a very wealthy heiress indeed.

The child *was* a boy, a healthy young specimen who was named after his paternal grandfather and so became the second Alfred Carboy to figure in this narrative.

The second of the four was also a boy but his prospects did not seem nearly as bright as those of the fortunate infant far off to the south whose black nurse crooned mournful native lullabies into his ears. This one was born in Vienna and his parents were among the most talked-about people in that great and glamorous city. The father was a portrait painter who had become the rage and who charged large prices for his work. The mother was an ex-actress who had run away with the portrait painter without waiting for a divorce; which meant that the squalling child in his lacy cradle had come into the world without a legal name. He proceeded to live with his parents, quite happily unaware of this lack, in a most expensive apartment in the First District. If he had been old enough he would have realized that his parents had no concern whatever for the future and were living recklessly in the very lap of luxury. When his beautiful, titian-haired mother was recovered sufficiently, she rode in an open carriage with a colored man named Noel on the box. The horses were magnificent and Noel wore a coat with six large silver buttons down the front. They dined off plate which had belonged to the French embassy and the lovely Kit's jewels were fabulous.

He had been named Julian Grace.

The third arrived at Three Gables. It had seemed for a long time that the second Mrs. Grace had failed in her cherished ambition to bring into the world children to claim her husband's first allegiance. But after they had been married nine years she unexpectedly found herself able to fulfill the desire. The boy, for it was a boy again, was a weak little creature at first and they had some difficulty in raising him. It was at least two years before he seemed to get a better idea of what life was about and decided to make the best of it. He began finally to thrive. His mother had wanted him named for her father but Julian could not believe that any child, even one with such a slight chance of survival, should be burdened with the name of Bullstrode. A compromise was made in favor of a maternal uncle whose name was Titus, and so Titus Grace the boy became.

Mrs. Grace's indignation over the birth of a son to parents who were not married, and never would be, was heightened by the fact that her son arrived two days after the scion of illegitimacy in Vienna.

The fourth to put in an appearance was a girl. She was born in a small, damp house in Ireland and it was quite apparent that she had no prospects whatever. Unless, that is, something might be done for her by a relative in England. "It's Nell we'll be calling the child," said the father, who worked off and on for a horse breeder, "and when she's old enough we'll be sending her to her aunt in England who helps us with the bits of money now and then." The mother was agreeable, having already brought into the world and named six children and having thereby exhausted her stock of ideas; and so the child was christened Nell (not Helen) Groody. In four years she was just as pretty as her aunt (by courtesy, needless to state) had been and, in fact, showed signs of being the very image of that fabulous lady who had a large house and a shop and was as rich as rich.

All four survived the perils of infancy, thereby preparing themselves for the parts they were to play in life, which in every case would include a vital interest in the outcome of the Waterloo Tontine.

## 2

The years preceding the births of the four children had been a period of change in England. The age of reform was well under way by this time. Trade unions were becoming powerful and child labor was being strictly regulated. In spite of this, and to the surprise of many prominent men, trade continued to expand and already the Great Exhibition had been held to demonstrate to the world the power and extent of British industry. Railroad trains now roared over the rails beyond Maidenhead and it was possible to go to all parts of the kingdom. Rixby was on the main line to the north and was growing and becoming more of a model town, considered from the standpoint of the profits it poured into soft pockets.

After remaining six years in a French prison, Louis Napoleon escaped from the stone walls which had closed him in but had not prevented lovely ladies from visiting him, and returned to England. He remained there two years and made many calls on the Marchioness of Invermark, to the great indignation of her husband, who admonished her sternly in long letters from his castle in the Highlands. After returning as a peaceful citizen to France and getting himself elected to the Assembly, Napoleon the Lesser obtained the throne in 1852. He began soon thereafter to keep the international horizon black with storm clouds and the rumble of warlike thunder. Old Scratchy's brother-in-law Jimmy had many successors in the task of visiting the offices of the London *Packet* every weekend. It is not on record that the mysterious bag was opened on a single occasion.

Isabelle was not on good terms with her husband, in fact she was not on any kind of terms at all, and she never went to Kilmorlie Castle. The marquis visited London and appeared with his wife on special occasions. Otherwise they lived separate lives. Isabelle hunted and rode and swam and played golf and croquet and whist with as much skill as in her earlier years, and she flirted openly and continuously but never was convicted of stepping over the mark. She was still slender and many people considered her as beautiful as ever. Young Chip had become the Duke of Outland and his Amy had died, without leaving him children. The new peer was enraged at the refusal of the Marquis of Invermark to give his wife a divorce and he visited Isabelle frequently to discuss ways and means of forcing the hand of the stubborn Scot; but all to no avail.

The Admiralty retired Julian Grace on half pay with the rank of captain and he was sincerely grateful for the annual payments which reached him from the Tontine offices. "The only sound investment my poor father ever made," he remarked once. His mother died and the Fox wing was converted into a play room for Master Titus Grace, who had a temper as fiery as his hair and proved himself a difficult child to raise.

Helen Groody lived quietly in the Old Rectory and invested in many excellent stocks and so became quietly a wealthy woman. Letters reached her frequently from South Africa, sometimes from Samuel the Younger, sometimes from his wife Clara, and several times in large scrawls from their son Alfred.

Jonathan Bade had his share in bringing about the changes in conditions already referred to and managed also to do well for himself in private practice of the law.

## CHAPTER TWO

1

After his retirement the days were long and dull for Julian Grace. He insisted that he must pay half of the expense of upkeep at Three Gables, although his second wife's resources were ample to maintain a place several times as large. This left him with little money for his personal needs, even when the Tontine payments began to mount. He retained his membership in a nautical club in London and paid a visit there once a month. After a wholesome lunch he would read the periodicals and then he would summon a waiter and order a drink for such of his acquaintances as happened to be in the place. This done, he would say to himself, "There, my man, you've had your fling for the month." He ordered two suits of clothes a year and secured a lower rate of payment by agreeing to turn the old ones back. Being of a bookish turn, he had always subscribed to the *Quarterly* and the *Edinburgh Review* but he now discontinued them; and missed them very much indeed.

He received letters regularly from Ambrose Brinker in Jamaica. Since the abolition of slavery in all the western isles under British rule, there had been less need for the work which Mademoiselle Philline had returned to do. What happened to Reuban Dupuis and his group is not on record but the pretty woman who had held Brinker's devotion for so long finally came to her senses and married him. They moved to the bay on the north shore where Columbus had landed and built themselves a white house with wide porches well up above the water. Here they enjoyed the comfort of the trade winds which never ceased to rustle the leaves of the poinciana trees. It was clear from the cheerfulness of Brinker's letters that he was happy and reasonably prosperous.

To fill in the long hours, Julian undertook the care of the gardens, with a man to help him, and spent a great part of his time there. He did not work steadily, however. It was his habit to rest on a seat at the foot of the steps and to indulge in memories of the past, of the days when the garden had delight and magic because of the presence of Freddie; Freddie in working aprons embroidered with nursery rhymes and singing little bits from Jamaican songs. It was here that he read the letters which came from Timothy and Kit; for the latter had liked her very brief glimpse of Timothy's father and wrote to him regularly. He was secretly proud of the bold way they faced the world and the bravado of their extravagances. It never occurred to him to think that the hundreds of pounds they expended in entertaining a prince from the Far East or in purchasing a string of matched pearls for Kit would have done a great deal to relieve the monotony of his life. They were young and it was Timothy's great talent which provided the money. Let them spend it freely and get what pleasure they could from it.

Julian found little to stimulate him in the company of his wife. Esther was a visitor by inclination and was away a great deal, taking Titus with her. She always returned with ideas for changing the house, based entirely on what her relatives and friends were doing. She read the cheapest kind of novels and liked to have a box of sweets beside her as she consumed the pages; with the result that she was rapidly putting on weight. They quarreled often but not violently and, as they went to church together regularly, they were regarded as a model couple.

He was fond of his redheaded son but worried about him a great deal. Titus had an aversion to obedience and had sly ways of contriving to govern his own life. Esther worshipped the boy and thought him perfect. She lavished gifts on him and had a habit of opening her bag after returning from the city and counting her loose change, always ending with, "And here's a half crown for a good little boy." The father often wondered what Titus did with the money. As far as anyone could tell, he saved it; and Julian was convinced that his son had hidden resources sufficient to buy and sell him, his father, any day.

Titus was seven years old when word of a great tragedy reached them by way of the British embassy in Vienna. Timothy and Kit were both dead. They had been holidaying in Switzerland and had been caught in an avalanche which cut off one corner of a village and destroyed a whole inn. The ambassadorial communication added that their son was being sent to England in the care of a colored servant.

"He's not to come here," said Esther flatly, when an ashen-faced Julian placed the letter in her hands.

"But of course he must. Where else can he go, my poor little grandson?"

"Julian Grace!" cried his wife in a high and angry voice. "You have no right to bring a child born out of wedlock into this home, into contact with me, your own wife, and little Titus. It's never done. Homes are found for them with dependents or distant relatives or they're sent to schools and never come home for holidays."

"I know that such things are done, my dear, but it's in cases where the child belongs to the father of the family. I'm Julian's grandfather and so there's no embarrassment for you in having him with us. There's a great difference, you must concede."

"I concede nothing!" declared Esther tartly. "I won't have him here, living with my little son. Do you think I want my dear Titus contaminated? Unless, of course, it's your idea to let him eat with the servants and be a helper about the house, like a paid companion for Titus. Though naturally he wouldn't be paid."

"That is not my idea," said Julian. He had known for a long time that any affection he had felt for his second wife had left him. Now he began to dislike her actively. "The boy will live here with us, as my grandson should. He will be a member of the family and will be treated as such."

Esther flounced to her feet. "I'll leave you!" she declared. "And I'll take Titus with me. I'll never come back—at least I won't until you come to your senses."

She went upstairs and for an hour there was a sound of scurrying about from room to room and the opening and closing of portmanteaus and traveling bags. Finally she appeared in the doorway of the library where Julian was sitting, with the letter open before him and a look of complete misery on his face. She was wearing a traveling dress of brown material, trimmed most elaborately with velvet, and a small bonnet with a band around her chin. She held young Titus by the hand. The boy was attired in an Eton jacket and long trousers of blue velvet. His felt hat had a wide ribbon which hung down his back.

"We are going to my brother Singleton's," she announced. "And we won't return until you come for us and say you've made suitable arrangements for the keep of this boy."

Julian gathered up the letter and put it in a pocket. He rose to his feet and bowed to his wife. "I'm sorry we can't agree," he said. "My grandson and Noel will arrive sometime this week. I'm going in to London to be on hand to meet them. You can communicate with me at my club."

Esther stamped a foot and said, "You'll be sorry for this!" They left immediately, the carriage piled high with luggage. He heard Titus say, "How long will we have to stay away to make Papa sorry, Mama?"

Three days later Singleton Thwaites came to Julian's club in the city, where the latter was awaiting the arrival of the pair from Vienna. He was a portly man with a bushy blond mustache and hardly any hair on the top of his head. His coat was fashionably long and wide-lapelled and there was a broad braid stripe down the sides of his tight trousers.

"Now see here, Jule," he began, fingering his massive watch chain. "It won't do, you know. This sort of thing, you know, confound it, really. Bastards are bastards. You'd better come to your senses, old fellow, what! Esther's mad, this time. Hopping, by gad."

Julian had always entertained a mild liking for this brother-in-law, who was good-natured and quite devoid of the toughness of disposition which the rest of the Thwaites family had inherited from Sir Bullstrode. "I'm afraid Esther will have to stay mad, Sing," he said. "Do you think I'll put a stigma on my grandson by placing him in the care of strangers or bundling him off to a Yorkshire school? His parents were brave young people who sacrificed everything for love. It's my duty to see that the boy doesn't suffer for their sin any more than he has to."

"Esther said I was to pitch into you strong, you know. But what more can I say, by gad?"

"Sing, you've been positively brutal. I'll tell Esther—if I ever see her again —that I was in a damp perspiration by the time you got through with me. Now suppose we drop the matter and go in and have a chop?"

"Capital idea!" said the plenipotentiary. "You know, Jule, I saw the lady once. Castle's wife, you know. Gad, she was a topper! All she had to do was give her bustle a waggle and I'd have legged it with her to Timbuctoo."

2

When Julian saw his grandson far down the platform at Victoria Station, followed by a Noel who still held himself up straight but whose hair was white, he felt the first surge of happiness which had come to him since the letter had arrived. "I can see he's a fine little chap," he said to himself.

The boy looked foreign because of the clothes he was wearing. His cap resembled a mortarboard with a long tassel hanging over the brim, his coat was long and strangely cut and absurdly bedizened with braid. His trousers, which fitted him tightly over the knees, came a few inches only down his shanks.

Noel was wearing a long yellow overcoat which hung loosely on his frame because it had only one button, which was six inches wide and looked as though it might be silver. (Julian discovered later that it was the last of the silver set and that the rest had been cut off and sold one by one to pay the cost of their trip.) Under one arm he carried a large square package of a flatness which suggested it might be a picture. A conspicuously small bag was in his other hand.

"My boy," said Julian, holding out a hand to the small newcomer, "I am your grandfather."

"Yes, sir," said his namesake. He seemed tall for his years and he was thin. The blue of his eyes and the fineness of his features (he strongly resembled his mother) suggested that he was not particularly strong.

Julian turned then to the servant. "I'm glad to see you again, Noel. You've been away from me for a long time and I've missed you. Still, I was glad you were with Timothy and that you looked after him and his wife so well."

And then a curious thing happened. Noel answered with a clear enunciation quite different from the garbled bits of English he had always employed. Someone had taken him in hand, that was clear.

"Yes, sah," he said. "I'm glad to be back. But I'm full of grief besides, sah."

"Of course, Noel." Julian looked down at his grandson. "Now we'll go somewhere and have lunch and we'll take the afternoon train home."

The boy looked up with an expression which seemed wistful. "Yes,

Grandfather," he said. "My papa told about his room many times. It must have been a jolly kind of room. Will I have it, Grandfather?"

Reluctantly Julian shook his head. "I'm afraid not, young man. It's in use. But you'll have one just as good, and just as jolly, you may be sure."

The boy did not eat much at lunch. He seemed to have little interest in the chop his grandfather had ordered for him and he did not touch the pudding which followed. There was a suggestion of fear and uncertainty in his eyes and Julian found himself wondering if the insecurity of his parents' position had affected him this early. Was he concerned about how he would be received in his new home? How much did he know?

"My boy, would you like a glass of wine?"

"No, thank you, Grandfather. It has been a very nice lunch." The boy looked across the table then and asked a question which apparently had been in his mind and needed asking. "Is there another little boy living with you, Grandfather?"

"Yes. My son, who is just your age. His name is Titus. You will be the best of friends."

"Yes, Grandfather."

The tone in which the boy said this was somewhat lacking in assurance, however. Julian began to wonder if children in Vienna had been cruel enough to make him aware of something wrong about his family relationships.

When the local bus turned into the road which ran down to the river, Julian pointed out the roof of the stables above the fruit trees of the small orchard. The boy's interest was aroused at once.

"Where is the field where my papa played the cricket?"

"You can't see it from here. It's over there, beyond the trees. And it's cricket, my boy, not *the* cricket. It's a wonderful game and your father was very fond of it. At one time he wasn't sure whether he wanted to be a painter or a cricketer."

The boy was listening now with deep interest. "Oh, sir, wasn't it good he decided to be a painter! He was the best painter in the world, wasn't he, Grandfather? We brought one of his portraits, sir, and Noel carried it under his arm, so it wouldn't get damaged. It is of my mother, sir."

Later Julian learned that the creditors, who had descended on the household like locusts after the tragedy, had allowed the boy to select one thing to take with him. He had passed by his beautiful hobbyhorse and his complete set of lead soldiers of all armies to select the picture of his mother.

"Does the other little boy play cricket, sir?"

"Not yet. You are both too small for the game. Unless we had special bats made for you. But later, of course, you'll both play a lot of cricket. I've kept the crease in shape ever since your father grew up and went away, hoping that someday there would be little boys like you and Titus to use it. It will always provide you with a great deal of fun."

"But," said the boy wistfully, "I'm not very good at games, sir."

3

Grandfather and grandson spent a week together at Three Gables, with one maidservant to cook for them and Noel to see to all other needs. It proved a wonderful vacation for all concerned. Julian had loved his grandson from his first glimpse of him and his attachment grew with each hour they passed together. Perhaps adversity had tended to develop character in the boy early; at any rate, he proved himself unselfish and unassertive from the start. One of the guest rooms had been fitted up for his use and here he hung the portrait of his mother. It was a striking piece of work in Timothy Grace's very best style and a perfect likeness of the beautiful woman who had tossed her cap over the windmill. The boy asked no further questions about the room his father had used as a boy and, as far as Julian knew, he never went to look at it.

It was his first taste of life in the country and the boy took to it with eagerness and delight. He was outside all day long, discovering each moment seemingly some new and exciting thing about the ways of nature. He climbed all the trees and brought down aged birds' nests, one containing the skeleton of a spring egg. He tried to fish, unsuccessfully, in the river. He mourned the fact that both horses had been taken when Mrs. Grace left to visit her brother, and he spoke so wistfully of dogs that his grandfather sent Noel out to get one. Noel returned with a good-natured specimen which owed much to many breeds and answered to the name of Nark. Young Julian took the canine into his affections at once and the pair became inseparable.

Everything might be said, therefore, to be going well. For seven days the household lived in perfect content, with much excited romping on the greens and the cricket field between boy and dog, with good appetites for all meals, and always some exciting games of dominoes or Pope Joan between dinner and bedtime. On the eighth day Julian received a letter from Tontine head-quarters, out of which fell the yearly check. Apparently the lethal blade had been hard at work all year, for the check was a much more substantial one than he had received the preceding year.

Julian sat down in the library and studied that satisfactory slip of paper with a mind full of speculation as to the future. His pension and his participation in the Tontine would cease, of course, when he died. A heavy mortgage had been placed on Three Gables before his second marriage and he had not been able to reduce the principal to any considerable extent. What would happen to his grandson, therefore, in the event of his death? The boy would be left with almost nothing, for it was clear to the worried grandfather that the distaff side of the family would do nothing for him. After much thought, Julian decided that he must manage somehow to lay some part of each Tontine check aside for the use of the boy when that emergency arose. He had a banker friend in London who had been in the navy with him but had shown the good sense to get himself into something more lucrative as soon as the Napoleonic menace was removed. Almon Walters was honest and well informed and could be depended on to do the very best for the boy. With a satisfied nod of the head, Julian decided that he must arrange matters at once. He would go to London the next day and put things in the hands of his friend Walters.

He had just reached this decision when there was a sound of horses' hoofs on the road beside the house and he heard the excited voice of Titus saying: "Here we are, Mama! I'm glad to be back from that old place and that Cousin Eustace."

Julian went to the door in time to have his wife brush by him in a great hurry to get her maid started on the work of unpacking. Esther neither looked at him nor threw him a single word, but went straight to the stairs with a brisk rustling of silk skirts. He went out and found his son shying pebbles at some birds in the ivy which clung to the walls.

"Well, young man," he said. "I heard you saying you were glad to be back."

Titus regarded his father with a caution which suggested that he had been the recipient of instructions. "Well, I guess so, Papa. I'm glad to get away from that Cousin Eustace. He hit me with a cricket bat. A regular stinger. I hate Cousin Eustace."

Young Julian had gone on one of his futile fishing ventures in the neighborhood of the weir with Noel and Nark to keep him company. The steady barking of Nark was evidence that all went well in that quarter.

"Papa," said Titus, "is there a boy here? Is he smaller than me?"

"Julian!" called Mrs. Grace from the door, before he could answer his son. "I want a few words with you. Will you come in?"

The few words, which stretched into a full chapter by the time they had been said, were exchanged in the library. Esther seated herself on a sofa and spread out her skirts with a gesture which seemed aggressive.

"Now!" she said. "You did not write to me. You did not beg me to come back. You disregarded the urgent warning which my brother Singleton delivered on my behalf. You have behaved very badly; you've been rude and unkind and unfair. I am never going to forgive you for the way you've acted. I have—I have made plans." She raised her head and looked at him squarely for the first time. "Is that boy here?"

Julian nodded. "Yes, my dear Esther. My grandson is here. He has been with me for a week and I've found him a fine little fellow indeed. You spoke of plans. Are you ready to discuss them with me?"

"No! I am not ready to discuss them with you. They are *my* plans. I don't think I'll ever discuss them with you, now that you've been so stubborn and behaved in this way. Where is the boy?"

"He's fishing, I believe. Near the weir. Noel is with him. I'll give them the signal to come back."

"You have the colored man here too! Well, I see you haven't been giving a thought to my wishes or my rights at all."

"Yes, my dear Esther, I have. I've thought about you a great deal since you've been away. We have reached a situation which will require a great deal of thought on both sides before it can be straightened out."

"Then you're not prepared to do what I said must be done before I went away?"

Julian did not answer at once. He could hear the voice of his son calling out in some excitement: "What's the dog doing here? Mama, there's a big black dog in the yard!"

"I understood," he said after a moment, "from something Titus said that he didn't get along too well with Sing's boy Eustace."

"Eustace is a bully!" said his wife. "I'll never go to Singleton's again. Never as long as I live. Eustace struck poor Titus."

"I'm sure that Titus and my grandson will get along well, if it's part of your plan to stay here, Esther. Julian is not a bully. He's a fine gentle boy and will make a good companion for Titus."

The second Mrs. Grace regarded him with a suspicious air. "You seem to be taking it for granted that I'm going to forgive you after all."

"That is for you to decide, my dear Esther. It wasn't my intention to influence you."

"Where is the boy sleeping?"

"In the yellow room."

"H'm! I wouldn't have been surprised at all to hear you had moved all of my son's things out of his room and put your precious grandson in there."

"Titus is my son as well as yours. Why should I do anything like that to him?"

"I don't know. You're acting queerly, Julian Grace. I'm not going to tell you anything about my plan for the future but I'm not going away again. Not yet."

Julian looked up quickly and then dropped his eyes again. Had he been hoping that she was not going to stay and that the purpose of her return was to arrange for the removal of her belongings?

"We'll both have to be forbearing while you are here. I take it that my grandson and I, and poor Noel, and the dog, are on probation."

"I'm glad you realize that much." The second Mrs. Grace rose to her feet and walked out of the room and up the stairs. Almost immediately she returned to the landing and called over the railing in an angry voice: "What's that woman's picture doing in his bedroom? Julian Grace, have you taken leave of your senses, to allow such a thing? I won't have a picture of her in my house. I'm going to have it taken down at once."

Julian walked to the foot of the stairs and looked up. "Esther, he loved his mother and he brought the portrait all the way from Vienna. Understand this, once and for all. The picture is not on probation. It stays where it is."

4

Titus suspended his efforts to dislodge the birds from the ivy when he saw a face staring at him over the hedge which lined the road. A boy was watching him and Titus guessed at once who it was. He walked over toward the hedge.

"Are you the boy that's been living here?" he asked.

"Yes," was the answer from the other side of the hedge. "I'm Julian. Are you Titus?"

"That's my name and I live here. You don't. My mama says you don't."

"I'm living with my grandfather."

"My mama says he's not your grandfather."

"Of course he is!" cried Julian in a distressed voice. "He was father to my father and that makes him my grandfather."

Titus considered his enemy—for he already regarded Julian in that light —with an unfriendly and suspicious eye. "Look here," he said. "You better come in. I want a good look at you."

Julian accepted the suggestion by making his way through a gap in the hedge. He had a small fish dangling on a line, the first he had ever caught.

It was almost microscopic in size but he was intensely proud and had planned to suggest that it be used for a family breakfast. Noel was following slowly up the road with the poles over his shoulder and Nark, who had returned after his excursion around the grounds, pattering at his heels.

"I'm taller than you are," asserted Titus. "Well, if I'm not taller, I'm heavier. I'm going to fight you because you don't belong here. I bet I can beat you."

"I do belong here!" cried Julian. "I was sent to my grandfather and he met me and brought me here."

Titus decided apparently that the time had come to speak his mind fully. "Now then, boy," he said, "you haven't got a grandfather. You didn't have a father and mother. You haven't got a name by rights, except your first name. That's what my mama says, and she's always right. Don't you put on any airs with me because I know all about you."

Julian's face had gone white. This was not the first time that these charges had been leveled against him. He did not understand why. He had always lived with his father and mother and there had seemed no sense to what the other boys said, that he had neither. His name was Julian Grace. It had always been that. And yet boys like this redheaded Titus had jeered at him and said he had no name. He had hoped when his grandfather met him and brought him to this beautiful place and had been so kind to him that he would never hear again the strange things his companions in Vienna had shouted at him. But he had been wrong. Titus was saying exactly the same things.

"That's all a lie," said Julian, trying to remain cool. "My grandfather wanted us to be friends but I can't be friends with you if you say things like that."

"Friends?" sneered Titus. "We won't be friends." Then he suddenly became so angry that he could only sputter. Someone had left a hoe standing up in a flower bed. He took a firm hold of it by the handle. "If you say I'm telling lies, I'll crack you with this. You just say it again and see what I'll do! I won't take any lip from you!"

Julian was struggling to hold back tears, partly of mortification because it was all starting again, partly of anger. "Look here, Titus," he said. "We ought to be friends, my grandfather wants us to be. He said so. But—but you've got to stop saying things like that."

"You said I was a liar!" shrilled Titus, pulling the hoe out of the ground.

At this point he saw Noel coming up the road with the fishing poles over his shoulder and whistling contentedly. "Who's that?" he asked in alarm. "What's he doing here?"

"That's Noel."

"He's got no right coming around here and scaring people."

"Of course he has. He belongs to Grandfather. He's been with Grandfather nearly all his life."

"You send him away! Do you hear me, you Julian! And send that dog away too or my mama will have him shot."

"No one can shoot Nark!" cried Julian in sudden alarm. "He's my dog."

"My mama will have him shot. She'll do it in a jiffy. We don't want dogs here. Not black dogs in special."

Julian was now ready to fight this boy who was ready to destroy everything he had. "You listen to me, you Titus! No one's going to shoot my dog. My grandfather bought him for me. He won't let anyone touch Nark."

It seemed to Titus at this point that he had temporized too long, that words would no longer suffice in dealing with this invader with his black men and black dogs. The time had come for action. Just as Noel slipped through the hedge, and at the exact moment when Julian, attracted by the shrill boyish voices in the garden, stepped out from the house, he allowed himself to go berserk. Waving the hoe in the air, he charged at his enemy.

"Look out, Masta Julian!" cried Noel, dropping the poles and starting to run toward the antagonists.

Young Julian skipped to one side to avoid the upraised hoe. It struck the trunk of a nearby tree instead, almost throwing Titus off his balance. The next instant the two boys were pummeling each other with their fists. They clinched and went down on the ground where they rolled over and over in a flurry of flying fists and kicking feet.

The head of the family arrived in time to drag the two boys apart before any serious damage had been done. He hauled them to their feet, gripping each by the collar. His grandson made no effort to resume hostilities but Titus struggled and shouted madly at his opponent, making determined efforts to struggle free of his father's grip. It was at this point that Mrs. Grace arrived on the scene.

"What's this?" she demanded. "Julian, what's the matter with my little Titus?"

"They were fighting."

"And you are taking sides against your own son? Let him go at once!"

"Esther, you don't understand," said Julian, still retaining a firm grip on the collar of his wriggling son. "The two boys were fighting and Titus tried to hit my grandson with that hoe. I'm afraid he would try it again if I let him go."

"Titus, my son, come here to me," said Mrs. Grace. She was white with rage. "I'll take your part, never fear, even if your father *is* against you."

"Esther, I'm not against him. Can't you see that I couldn't let this go on?"

Titus, freed of his father's grip, ran promptly to his mother and burst into loud tears. "He called me a liar!" he cried. "That's what he did, he said I was telling lies!"

"There!" charged Mrs. Grace, eying her husband furiously. "My son was *not* in the wrong. He was fighting because he had been called names."

Julian turned to his grandson. "Is this true? Did you call Titus a liar?"

"Yes, sir." The boy gulped, expecting that summary punishment would be visited on him. "He said you were not my grandfather. He said I had no father or mother. He said I had no name."

"Yah, and I was telling the truth!" cried Titus. "My mama told me all those things. She said he wasn't your grandson, she said——"

"That will do, Titus," said his father sternly. "I think you had both better go to your rooms and get washed. Fortunately neither of you seems to have been hurt."

"Titus will stay where he is," declared Mrs. Grace. She glanced bitterly at her husband. "As for you, Julian, I want to talk to you. I have many things to say."

They walked to one side, leaving the two boys watching each other like a pair of belligerent tomcats. Julian said over his shoulder as he followed his wife, "If there's any more fighting, you will both be punished."

"Now!" said Mrs. Grace when they reached a safe distance. "I guess you'll agree that I was right. I told you it couldn't be done. I said we couldn't have this boy in the house, that it would lead to trouble."

"It seems," said Julian quietly, "that you made sure it wouldn't do. You filled our son's mind with—with all that malice."

"So!" cried his wife, her voice rising. "You're blaming me! You bring your son's illegitimate child into my house and then blame me when there's trouble about it."

"I didn't think you would go as far as this, Esther. But—you have, and now we face a problem. I don't know how we're going to settle it."

"I do. I know exactly how to settle it."

She walked away a few steps and turned to face the house. She called, "Carty!" After a few moments her maid appeared at one of the upper windows. "Yes, mem?"

"Carty, stop the unpacking. Pack everything up again. We're not staying. We're going back north."

The second Mrs. Grace turned then and faced her husband. "And now," she said in a triumphant voice, "I'll tell you about my plans. I bought a place when I was away, because I was sure something like this would happen. It's about twelve miles from Singleton's place. I can take immediate possession. I'm going to have all my things packed up and leave as soon as I can. I don't want to see you again or hear from you again—unless you send that boy away." She regarded him with an air of triumphant ill will. "And now what will you do?"

Julian was not surprised at this explanation of her purpose. It had been clear that she had returned to demand his surrender on her terms. The fight between the two boys had precipitated a crisis but it would have come to this in a short time in any case.

"Oh, I have plans too," he said. "I can take care of things rather well, I think."

"You'll get this place looking like a pigpen again!" cried his wife. "You'll starve, you and your precious grandson, and your Noel and your ugly black dog. Oh, don't try to tell me anything different! You were as thin as a plucked crow when I married you, Julian Grace!"

"I won't stay here, of course."

His wife looked startled at this statement. She regarded him with a shade less of assurance. "You won't stay here? Then what will you do?"

"I told you I had plans."

"What are these precious plans of yours? I insist on knowing."

"You'll find out in time."

He was thinking with a mingled sense of triumph and relief that he was in a very good position now to stand out against the wealth and security his wife represented. He had his half pay and his Tontine share, which was mounting fast. In a few years he would be drawing a handsome income from that source. While in London, waiting for his grandson to arrive, he had been asked to let this place on a ten-year lease. The rent offered had been enough to take care of the mortgage and the taxes and leave a fair margin over. There would be plenty to rent a comfortable flat in London for himself and his grandson and to keep Noel to look after them.

All that he told his wife was that he would put his own plans into effect as soon as she had left.

Esther did not like this at all. She faced him with even greater belligerence. "You can't drive me away, you know. I'll stay as long as I want to. I guess I can stand what that would mean as well as you can." She hesitated and then seemed to reach a decision: "Why should I rush myself to death to get all my things packed and out? I have a right to stay here as long as I want to."

"No one denies that, my dear Esther."

"Well, I'm *not* going to put myself to such inconvenience. I'm going to take my time. I don't like all this secrecy. What *are* you up to, Julian Grace?"

"You will find out—when I want you to and not before, Esther."

"I hope my being here will spoil all your plans."

"Not at all. But you must agree to behave sensibly and you must help me

in making it clear to Titus that he must not hurt my grandson with such
remarks. He must be made to behave as any decent little boy would. Is that
clear?"

His wife did not answer. She stamped her way to the front door, calling
to Titus to follow her. Julian spoke to his grandson. "Better go in and wash,
my boy. And don't feel too badly about this. I'm not going to let anything
or anyone hurt you."

## 5

The Fox wing was a one-story addition on the western half of the house.
There was a large sitting room with a good fireplace and bay windows on
each side. Behind this was a large roomy bedchamber which boasted a bathroom and, actually, a cast-iron tub. In the sitting room was an excellent copy
of a portrait of Charles James Fox, who had been the political idol of George
Ninian Grace. It was a sunny wing and had been ideal for Julian's mother
because it was secluded from the rest of the house.

Esther decided to make her quarters here while the work of packing proceeded; with, it must be said, a suspicious slowness. She did not put in an
appearance for the better part of a week but it was apparent that she directed
the preparations for departure like a general on a hilltop behind the field
of battle. Piece after piece of furniture (each of the period and therefore
ugly) was removed and strapped up for the long trip. Pictures were taken
down from the walls, hangings were removed, carpets were untacked and
ripped up. The bronze figure of a Nubian slave was carried out from the
hall and its unpleasantnesses concealed under a covering of canvas. The
work was done with an excess of zealousness which led to some things being
taken which did not belong to the distaff side. A Georgian wall clock which
Julian prized very much disappeared from its place beside the library fireplace. Several miniatures vanished at the same time. He delivered a note,
protesting the mistakes, to Carty for delivery into the hands of her mistress;
but no reply was forthcoming.

It had been the intention of Mrs. Grace to keep Titus secluded also but
he got out of hand after the first day. At any rate he appeared next morning
for breakfast and did not let the presence of young Julian prevent his making a good meal. The two boys did not exchange a word although the head
of the house, sitting between them, strove to make the conversation general.
Titus continued to protest the presence of Nark but contrived somehow to
be always around with the dog. He also reached a chatty basis with Noel
although he did not hesitate to make allusions to the servant's color and
station.

His mother observed these symptoms of weakening with alarm and summoned him to the Fox wing one afternoon. "Titus, don't you love your
mother any more?" she asked. "Are you going over to *them?*"

"I don't know what you mean, Mama."

"Titus, you don't have your meals with me always. You must like to have them *out there*."

"I like company, Mama. It's kind of dull in here."

"*Titus!* Do you find your mother dull?"

The boy did not answer this but confined his attention to scraping at the carpet with one toe.

"Do you like the company of that boy?"

"Nah, Mama. I hate him. If he says anything to me, I'll get that hoe again and crack him with it."

"Then why do you stay away from me? Don't you know that I'm lonesome without you?"

"You could come out to meals if you want to."

"Son, you were out for a walk with your father yesterday. What was he saying to you?"

"Ah, a lot of stuff. I don't remember, Mama."

"Was he saying he wanted you to stay? You and me?"

"He said he wanted me to remember him. That's all." The boy decided to ask a question himself. "Mama, are we going away?"

"It begins to seem so, my son."

"Then I want a dog. I don't like that fellow Nark. He's rough and he shakes himself all over me when he's been in the water. I want a white dog with a long nose."

"But I don't like dogs, Titus. You know that."

"He wouldn't be your dog, Mama. He'd be mine."

Apparently it entered her head at this time that she was playing a losing game, and that if she wanted to retrieve her fortunes she must act quickly. She instructed her son to send his father in to see her.

She had dressed herself with rather particular care in a magenta dress which, unfortunately, did not go well with her hair, when Julian presented himself in the Fox wing.

"Well," she said, ensconcing herself on a sofa near the east window. "The packing is completed and I'm going to send for the wagons to be here tomorrow. Unless, of course, you have come to your senses."

Julian looked very much distressed. He realized by this time that any affection he had entertained for her had vanished completely. But Titus was his son and it pained him to think of losing the boy.

"By coming to my senses, do you mean that I must be ready to send my grandson away?"

"That is what I meant and well you know it. I haven't changed my mind."

"Nor have I mine, Esther."

She raised both hands from her lap and waved them angrily at him. "So, you prefer this boy to your own son! Is that natural, is it fair, is it decent?"

"But it isn't a choice between them. I think Titus would be quite glad to stay here. It wouldn't take long for the pair of them to become adjusted. But you won't hear of trying it that way. You demand that I must turn Julian out of the house—this poor little fellow who has had so much sorrow already. You want me to condemn him to more years of unhappiness. He has committed no sin and so your reasons seem to me nothing but petty prejudice."

The light of battle had been mounting in her oddly placed eyes. "I think you are the most stubborn man in the world!" she stormed at him.

"I might with equal reason, Esther, say that you are the most stubborn woman in the world."

She sprang to her feet. "Very well. We'll have no more words. I'll send the message for the wagons. And I hope, Julian Grace, that I never set eyes on you again." She was now on the point of angry tears. "You know I can't give in. I can never change my mind once it's made up. You know that."

When it became certain that the rift in the family was beyond repair and that the second Mrs. Grace was leaving and taking her son with her, Titus began, in a quiet and secretive way, to wander all over the house. He dodged out of sight whenever he encountered anyone else. His errand, whatever it might be, took him also to the stable and down to the summerhouse. It was not until late in the afternoon that his father saw him vanish into the Fox wing with a well-filled bag in his hands. Julian understood then what he had been doing. Being afraid to hide all his savings in one place, he had been using nooks and crannies in all manner of holes and corners for the safe-keeping of the money he had accumulated; and he had been getting it to take away with him.

Julian was not pleased at this discovery. "This is wrong," he said to himself. "The boy's too young to have such a developed miserly streak. What kind of offspring is this that I've brought into the world?"

He had no further words with his wife. The wagons were packed the next morning (and he never laid eyes again on the wall clock or the miniatures or, in fact, many other things which belonged to him) and in early afternoon his wife departed from Three Gables, her bonnet strings framing a face which concealed none of the bitter emotions she was feeling. If she thought he would relent and send for her later, she was doomed to disappointment. She never set eyes on the place again.

But before leaving she had made a final tour. Julian found evidence of this soon after the vehicles had all vanished up the road. The portrait of Timothy's wife (he always thought of the lovely Kit by that term) had been torn down from the wall and thrown in a corner. The vigorous manner in which this had been done had damaged the painting beyond repair. A projecting point of wood had caused a hole in the face at the exact point between the two hauntingly lovely eyes.

## CHAPTER THREE

### 1

Nelly Groody arrived from Ireland to live with the lady she was to fall into the habit of calling her great-aunt when she was fourteen years old. She came by boat and by train and finally by coach, arriving in Oxford by the latter means of conveyance. Here she was met by Huruld Gladstone, who had started out from Little Shallow before dawn to reach the coaching station in time.

He watched the passengers alight, all of them so bundled up that they looked like grizzly bears disguised in greatcoats and shawls. All, that is, but a slender girl in a plain gray dress and with something on her head which resembled a man's cloth cap, who almost seemed to dance as she came down the steps. When he saw that she had blue eyes and black hair and was, in his opinion, the very image of his employer, he accosted her at once.

"You'll be the young leddy from Ireland," he said.

"Yes, sir, I am indeed." She began to recite: "My name is Nelly Groody and I come from Gilfoyle in Ireland. I am going to Miss Helen Groody, in the village of Little Shallow, Berkshire." Then she smiled at him. "And is it convinced you are now, sir? I've had to say my little piece eleven times. Father Hanley made it up for me."

Huruld had been growing ever since he was rescued from the slavery of Rixby but exclusively in one direction. He was not any taller but he had been widening steadily and rounding out to barrel-like proportions. While he thus put on weight, his face, as though unable to forget the hardships which had made up life for him for so long, had seemed to age. The wrinkles which had accumulated on his broad countenance gave him a sad look.

He grinned at the girl, who had stepped over to the horses and was patting their noses and saying things to them in a low and affectionate voice. "Do you like horses?" he asked.

"I think I love horses better than anything in the world," said the girl. "And why not? Isn't it from Ireland I come? Not," she was honest enough to add, "that I've ever ridden one. The Groodys of Gilfoyle didn't own any."

"These fellows are Al and Ben," said Huruld, by way of introduction. "You'll be seeing a lot of them, miss. And you're going to like it at Little Shallow. That you are."

"And will Miss Groody be glad to see me?" she asked anxiously.

"All she'll need, miss, is one look at you to see you're as much like her as two peas. She'll like you and she'll be out at the gate to welcome you. But get in, miss, get in. We've got a long drive ahead of us."

They had not gone a half mile when the girl asked to be allowed up on the box with him. She did not want to miss anything, she said. It was not necessary to stop the horses, for she climbed up beside him without waiting. In another half hour she asked in an offhand way if he would like to let her handle the reins. But Huruld drew the line at that. Al and Ben were a mettlesome team, he said, and he wanted to get her home in one piece. "Thanking you very much, miss," he added, "but I'll be keeping the reins myself."

The drive was long, as he had predicted, but there was much to be seen as they rolled along through the heart of Berkshire and finally worked their way down into the Vale itself. The passenger never stopped talking. Huruld said to her finally: "P'raps it's you should be called Glads'n. You are a great talker, now, ain't you?"

He had been right about his employer. When they reached the Old Rectory, Miss Groody was in front of the house and waiting for them. They took one look at each other, the loquacious young girl on the seat and the lady leaning over the gate, and both knew at once that they were going to love each other very much. Helen Groody helped her namesake to alight and took possession of her very small bundle of clothing, saying to her: "Anyone would know you come from Ireland, my dear child. Did you have a nice trip?"

"Oh yes, Aunt Helen. It's fine to travel, isn't it?"

Helen Groody smiled down at her new charge. "It's hard for me to say, Nelly. I've done so little of it. I've always preferred to stay here at home."

Huruld presented a note to his employer. "The village priest wrote it," he said. "Each one as looked after her handed her on to the next with this note."

It was quite brief, informing those who would be responsible for the care of a girl named Nelly Groody, daughter of Kevin Slaught Groody of Gilfoyle, Ireland, that she was going to a village in Berkshire, England, called Little Shallow to a Miss Helen Groody at the Old Rectory; and would they be especially careful of her and take whatever was needed for her fare out of the five-pound note attached? The good priest had added that he felt his Master would put a mark down in their favor if she arrived at her destination safe and sound.

The girl produced a five-pound note and handed it to her aunt. "It's the money you sent for the trip," she explained. "None of them wanted to break it, so I came over as free as a bird."

"How very kind everyone has been." Helen Groody looked down at this child who was to live with her, and smiled warmly. "I think they liked your looks, Nelly, to be so generous. Well, there's a nice tea ready for us, so I guess we should go in now. You will be hungry, my dear."

"We used up the two shillings you give me for lunch," contributed Huruld. "But the potpie was mostly dumplings, so I rather think she will be hungry, ma'am."

The newcomer was quite taken aback by the size of the house. She stood in the hall and gazed about her with awe. "I didn't hear you lived in a castle, Aunt Helen," she said. She was thinking apparently of her life at

home, where ten Groodys had existed in three rooms. "Does each one have
a room to theirselves?"

"Yes, my dear. And there's a very nice room for you, right next to mine.
I've had pink curtains put up and there's a pink coverlet. I think you'll like
it very much."

For the next hour the girl continued in a condition of wonder. She
touched a tall secretary desk and said, "Oooh, how grand!" The lamps held
her spellbound. She looked at her feet sinking deep into the carpet and
said to her aunt, "Could one go right through?" Her eyes became very large
and round when they saw the tea table. "Such grand food! Aunt Helen,
do you really have eggs for tea? And chicken! Are those lovely pink things
cakes? And such bee-utiful tay!"

She had never seen a cake with icing before and could not be contented
with less than three of the round pink ones. A slice of plum cake brought
an ecstatic light into her eyes. She was very full and very sleepy when the
meal came to an end.

"I think I'll send the five-pound note to that kind priest," said Helen
when the maid had cleared off the table. "It can be used whenever your
family needs it."

The child showed herself to have a streak of common sense at this point.
"It wouldn't do, Aunt Helen, for Himself to get the money," she said. "Harry
Boy Mulligan at the pub would have every penny of it in no time. And
the little mither would take it and hide it away against the bad times coming, and never a treat would the brothers and sisters get out of it. Yes,
indeed, the money should go to Father Hanley, who is very kind and would
put Himself in his place if it came to words between them."

From the moment of her arrival the girl took exclusive possession of the
name Nelly and her aunt was always thereafter spoken of by the more dignified name she had been given at her christening. Helen, to apply it at
once, looked at her niece with a broad smile. "I see that what they wrote
me about you was true," she said. "You were the manager of the family."

"Well, you see, Aunt Helen, the mither was always so busy with the new
ones that kept arriving that she couldn't do much about the house. So first
my sister Sheila sort of took things in hand. Then Sheila went out to service
and I took her place. Between us we'd even seen to it that Himself wiped his
feet on the mat and didn't tamp out his pipe on the tablecloth. We had a
very fine cloth," she added in a tone of pride. "Himself won it at a raffle
and it only cost him two shillings. Of course, Aunt Helen, we needed the
shillings at the time much more than we needed the cloth."

"They'll miss you, Nelly, I'm afraid."

"Not any at all, I'm thinking. My very most smallest sister, Mooneen, is
going to step right into my shoes. She's a manager, that one. You ought to
see her, no bigger than a whiffet, stand up to Himself when he comes home
with the stuff on his breath. She even tells Harry Boy Mulligan what she
thinks about him—which is a very great deal, Auntie, and none of it
friendly."

"And now," said Helen, "we'll all be off to bed. It's tired you must be, my child." She dropped an arm around the girl's shoulders. "I'm very happy that you are going to be with me now, Nelly."

2

Helen Groody was wakened next morning by the voice of her niece. The sound came from the stables. On looking out of her window, she was alarmed to see that the new arrival was standing in the open gable-end where the feed was taken up into the haymow. She was calling to Huruld and, just as her aunt leaned out of the window, she swung herself clear to the ground by use of the block and tackle, landing as safely and easily on her feet as a cat.

She came in to breakfast like a breeze and her eyes opened wide again when she saw what was on the table. "Eggs!" she cried. "And toast and oatmeal. What's this yellow stuff?"

"That's orange marmalade."

Nelly quite apparently had never tasted marmalade before. She liked it so much that she seemed to have neither time nor space for anything else. "Wonderful, oh, wonderful!" she said, watching her aunt and realizing quickly that it should be conveyed to the toast on the tip of a knife.

"And now, my child," said Helen as they sipped a last cup of tea, "we must consider what's to be done about your education."

"I was sure, Aunt Helen," said the girl in an alarmed tone, "that I was all through with it."

"I doubt that very much. Tell me how far you've gone at school."

It developed that Nelly's schooling had been of the hit-and-miss order. She could read a little and write a little but all other subjects were closed books. Helen was nonplussed when she made this discovery. "I could send you to a girls' school. It might be the best thing to do but not at once. I'm selfish enough to want to enjoy your company for a while. I think perhaps the best plan will be to have someone come in to give you lessons. There's little Miss Wilhelmina Tinkle in the village. Her father was a clergyman but he never got very far and didn't leave her much. She probably would be glad of a chance to add to her income, poor little Miss Willie. She's quite bookish and would know what you ought to be taught."

The girl sighed. "Schooling is a bother, Aunt Helen. I'm quick enough at it but I'm not thorough. That's what the sisters said at our school. But I'll tell you a secret. I could be thorough if I wanted to but I pretended I wasn't, so they wouldn't go trying to make a scholar of me."

"I expect that you and Miss Willie will get along quick enough, and thorough enough for that matter. You see, Nelly, a young lady needs a certain amount of education; just enough, of course, but never too much. To have too much is just as bad for a girl as having too little."

Nelly laughed happily at this. "Then I'll see to it, Aunt Helen, that I don't get too much." For a moment then she was silent. She sat quite still and looked at her new mentor and guide with a speculative eye. "I'm wondering whether I should say this. You see, they were at me all the time before I left. They kept dinning things at me. 'Now, Nelly, you mustn't say this,' and 'Now, Nelly, you must be very careful what you say and do or you'll be offending the old lady.' Oh, I *am* sorry. You're really not old at all, are you? You look quite young and *very* pretty. They kept telling me I mustn't speak until I was spoken to and all I must ever say was Yes or No or Please. They wanted me to be a mouse. But, Aunt Helen, I'm thinking it would be better if I'm just myself, if I act natural and say everything that comes into my head, which is what I like to do."

Helen leaned around the table and drew the visitor closer to her with an affectionate pressure of her arm.

"That's exactly what I want, dear child. I want you to be natural always. I don't want you to act like a mouse because it's so very clear that you're not one at all."

"But I ought to tell you," said the girl, "that when I act natural I'm likely to say things you won't like very much. They just pop into my head and then out they come. And I'm terribly curious. I ask questions."

"I haven't heard anything yet to make me want to change my opinion. What kind of questions do you ask?"

"Well, Aunt Helen, I might ask you why you've never married. You are *so* beautiful and they say at home you've got a great deal of money. It's *odd* that you never married."

"It's a long story, my child. Someday perhaps I'll tell you about it."

"Oh, I do hope you will. And, Auntie, why is there one streak of your hair white while all the rest is black? It's *very* attractive."

"You will have to ask a doctor about that, my dear. It just happened to turn white in one place. That's all I can tell you; except that all of it will be turning white soon, I expect." Perhaps to postpone the questions which she saw hovering on her niece's lips, she began to ask the girl about her needs. Her wardrobe would require augmenting, of course. Was there anything else she could think of which she required at once?

The girl shook her head. "I never wish for more than one thing at a time. When I want a thing, I want it very much and it's not until I get it that I can think of anything else."

"And what," smiling, "is the one great wish which fills your mind at the moment?"

"I must learn to ride," declared Nelly eagerly. "There's nothing in the world I could ever want as much as that. I love horses."

"That's a sensible wish, my dear. A young lady should be a good rider. Her Majesty is a great believer in going for a ride every morning. Now let me see. Neither Albert nor Benjamin will do. They're good carriage horses. I think, Nelly, I shall have to buy you a riding horse. Or perhaps you should start with a pony. What do you think?"

The visitor's eyes were shining with delight. "A horse!" she said. "I'm beyond ponies, Aunt Helen. Oh, to have a horse of my own! Aunt Helen, I don't think I'll ever have time to think of any other wishes."

3

One bright autumn afternoon, perhaps three months later, Samuel Carboy was driving at high speed in his Napoleonic carriage in the general neighborhood of Little Shallow. It happened that he glanced out of the window as they passed the junction point with a narrow road leading up into the low hills to the north and he saw a girl walking down this road with a pronounced limp. A second glance revealed the fact that she had suffered some damage to her clothing. Her riding skirt was torn and she was covered with dust. Her riding hat, moreover, was missing.

Carboy rapped on the front panel of the carriage. The driver, without hauling in the horses, opened a slot beneath his seat and squinted down at his employer.

"See here, Pound," said Carboy, "there's a girl on that side road who's had a tumble from a horse, I think. Draw up and we'll see if she needs help."

When the limping gait of the girl brought her to the junction of the two roads, the Colossus stuck his head out of the window and asked, "Are you hurt?"

"Not much," was the cheerful answer. "I put Brian Boy at too high a fence. The good fellow wasn't hurt himself and I suppose he's home by this time. I came quite a cropper. I'm all right, sir, but my leg is getting a little stiff with the walking."

"Do you live far from here?" asked Carboy cautiously.

"Not far. In the village. A half mile or less."

"Get in," said Carboy. "I'll take you home. I must say you show a pretty good spirit, my girl. No weeping or fainting or any of the usual foolishness." He looked at his passenger, who had seated herself beside him and had rearranged her torn habit to prevent a glimpse he might have had otherwise of one knee. She was a pretty girl with black hair curling crisply around her forehead. "What's your name and where do you live?"

"My name, sir, is Nell Groody, and I live with Miss Helen Groody in Little Shallow."

This brought him around on the seat to stare at her in real earnest. "So, you're the niece from Ireland I've heard about. Good gad, child, you look exactly like her! I mean like your aunt when she was a girl several years older than you are and her father was my coachman. Best man I ever had for the horses. She didn't wear a stylish riding habit like the one you're wearing but there's no missing the resemblance. You have the same eyes and hair and nose."

"You're Mr. Carboy," said the girl with the awe proper to such a discovery.

"Don't see how you happened to figure that out," he remarked, looking down at her from under his grizzled brows. He was beginning to show his years. His hair was scant and iron gray and deep lines turned his mouth and jaw into a sunken level.

"But you couldn't be anyone else, could you? Oh, I've heard so very much about you, Mr. Carboy. Even in our little village in Ireland people talk about you. Himself would come home——"

. "Himself?" Carboy regarded her with a puzzled frown.

"My father. He'd come home from Harry Boy Mulligan's and tell us all the things they'd been saying about you in the tavern. They said you were rich enough to buy out the queen and the whole royal family. Once Father heard you were worth *one hundred million pounds!*"

"Nonsense!" said Carboy. "No one man could ever be worth that much."

"No? Well, then, how much are you worth, Mr. Carboy? Fifty million pounds perhaps?"

"That's getting a bit closer—— See here, young lady, I'm giving you this lift home because you've hurt yourself and not to tell you all my private affairs."

"Oh, I'm so sorry, Mr. Carboy. I shouldn't ask questions like that, should I?"

"No. Children like you shouldn't ask any questions at all."

They had reached the Old Rectory and the coachman got down to help the girl alight while Carboy stamped ahead of them into the house. He had been carrying a curious-looking box on one knee during the course of the drive and unconsciously he had tucked it under one arm before getting out of the carriage.

He nodded to the maid, the same one who had admitted him years before although grown considerably stouter now, and walked in without announcing himself. "Is Miss Groody in?" he asked as an afterthought when he reached the hall. "Her niece was thrown off her horse."

"Yes, sir, we know," said the maid in a worried tone. "Brian Boy came home all by himself. The mistress has been fair distracted about it. Huruld has gone to search for her."

Hearing the voices in the hall, Helen came out from her office where she had been striving to keep her mind occupied until word came of what had happened to her niece. When Nell walked rather stiffly through the door the elder woman's face lighted up with relief.

"How glad I am to see you, child! I was afraid Huruld would find you badly hurt, or even killed, somewhere up in the hills." The afternoon light was waning and it was so dark in the hall that she now perceived Carboy for the first time. "Oh, I didn't see you. Please forgive me for such seeming rudeness. Did you find Nelly and bring her home?"

"I saw her coming down a small side road. She was limping, so I knew something was wrong."

Helen turned back to her niece. "Are you in great pain, my dear? I'll send for the doctor at once."

"I'm really not hurt at all, Auntie. I think I'll go right upstairs and have a hot bath. That will make me quite well again, I'm sure. There's no need for a doctor."

"Are you certain? Will you feel well enough to come down after and have tea with us? I'm hoping Mr. Carboy will stay."

"Glad to, ma'am," said the Colossus, suddenly realizing that this coincidental meeting was going to prove a pleasant one. "I haven't been here for—for quite a few years, have I? Gad, I've been getting old in the meantime!" Becoming aware of the box under his arm, he added, "This is a happy chance because I have something here you'll find very interesting."

They walked back into the library and he seated himself near the fire. When the maid appeared and held up a bottle of whisky for his inspection, he nodded with pleasure. "Most kind of you, I must say. Just a little water with it." He turned then to his hostess, who was sitting on the other side of the fire. "Have you been following all this investigating and inventing that's been going on all over the world about the making of pictures? Well, they're getting results at last. Look at this. It's called a camera. You point this at someone and press a button and then you take something into a dark room and out comes a likeness of the person on a piece of paper. I got so much interested in it that I sent one of these contraptions to Young Sammy in Cape Town. And will you look at what I got back from him a few days ago!" He fumbled in an inner pocket of his coat and produced a piece of stiff paper about eight inches square. This he held out to Helen.

She took it and looked at it closely for a few moments. Then she burst into excited speech. "Why, I believe—it is—it really is, a picture of Sammy himself, looking very handsome and important!"

"That's who it is. My grandson. And that's his wife with him."

"Yes, of course. I've had such nice letters from Clara. So friendly and sweet and understanding."

"She doesn't write to me," grumbled Carboy. "I expect you hear oftener from Sammy than I do."

"Isn't it exciting actually to see them like this! Clara is beautiful, isn't she?"

"I know some who are more to my taste, even though I am doddering along in the seventies," he declared. "It doesn't do me any good to say so. Yes, his wife is nice enough. And she's an heiress, you know. I could hardly believe they had so much money down there near the South Pole. And what do you think of the boy?"

"Sammy's little son!" said Helen in an awed voice. She studied the figure standing between the two adults and suddenly her eyes filled with tears. "Little Allie! I was so glad they named him that. And he's—he's exactly like the first Allie—your son, Mr. Carboy. He's going to be very tall and fair and——"

She could not go on. Handing the picture back to him, she began to dab with a handkerchief at her eyes. "What a wonderful thing! What miracles men are bringing about in this world. With the help of God."

"You're right. The boy is the image of my Alfred." Carboy began to feel that his own feelings were threatening to get the better of him and he placed the picture in a leather case and returned it to his pocket. "Did you notice the house in the background? Odd, wasn't it? All on one floor. No towers, no big windows. Nothing grand about it at all."

He stopped and stared down at his glass. It was plain that he was engaged in a mental struggle. Several moments passed before he spoke again.

"This taking of pictures is going to be a great hobby before long. Cameras like this will be snapping all over the country. There's money to be made in such things. This one is the best camera to come out so far. It's going to sell like sixty. Better put a few pounds in the company, ma'am."

A thought flashed through Helen's head. "Are you buying up the company?"

Carboy laughed, a hoarse kind of guffaw which did not suggest that he was very much amused. "Might have known," he said. "You're sharp, ma'am. Yes, I'm taking it over. The papers will be signed in a fortnight, perhaps sooner. As you've probably guessed, having a mind like a new-honed razor, the stock will go up as soon as it gets out that I own the company." The laugh he had indulged in turned to a rather rueful chuckle. "Look here, I hesitated about telling you anything. It goes against the grain with me. Even if you'd taken me up that time and become Mrs. Carboy, I'd have been unlikely to tell you about this. Might as well confess that I don't like other people making money on knowledge that belongs to me—and that would apply to a wife. I was more than half tempted to make you wait and pick up your stock after the sale had been made. Here, ma'am, is the name of the company. Get your stock quick and you'll have a pretty profit in a matter of three weeks—and you'll make plenty of brass on it as long as you live."

"I'm much indebted to you, Mr. Carboy. And much complimented that you decided to share your knowledge with me. I'll buy a block at once. I think I'll put half of it in Nelly's name."

"Eh?" Clearly this had startled him. "Now that's a silly and womanish sort of thing to do. Blast me if I expected you to be like the rest of them. This girl will come into some of your money in time. Why shower it on her now? Young people don't make the money, so let 'em wait."

"I want her to have a sense of independence. That's why I'm going to do it."

He was frowning as though regretful at having broken his rule in her favor. "Well, it's your brass. You can do what you like with it. But I expected better of you, ma'am." He broke off and stared up at the ceiling. "Who's doing that whistling up there? It's as clear as a bird."

"That's my niece. She must be feeling better again. She always whistles when she's dressing. That child springs out of bed as soon as she wakens, as though afraid she'll lose a few precious seconds of the day. Everyone says she looks like me and I hope she's going to grow into—well, into the woman I might have been."

A few moments later Nelly came down the stairs. In the short time she had been absent, she had transformed herself from a tomboy in a torn riding skirt into a young lady in the middle teens. Her vagrant curls had been bound up on the top of her head. This was the time when the crinoline was at the very peak of its popularity and the skirt she wore was wide enough to touch both the balustrade and the wall as she made her way downstairs. She seemed to glide into the room, without any motion of the skirt and with not as much as the tip of a shoe showing.

"Good gad!" said Carboy. "She's grown up in twenty minutes!"

## CHAPTER FOUR

1

When asked about his age Samuel Carboy had fallen into the habit of declaring himself in an offhand way as to be somewhere in the seventies. Pride perhaps dictated this casual clipping of at least ten years from the real total or it may have been a form of caution, that he did not want his partners and competitors to know how old he really was. He knew that potential successors lurked in every countinghouse and that at the first evidence of weakness on his part he would never again be free of the danger of palace revolution. When his grandson finally returned from South Africa, as will be related presently, he had reached the rather more than ripe old age of eighty-nine.

Although still active and maintaining a firm grip on every branch of his industrial empire, he suffered nevertheless from some of the infirmities of age. His memory was uncertain and it cannot be denied that he had become very absent-minded. His eyes played him tricks and he did not hear unless spoken to in loud and deliberate tones. As a result of these frailties it had become necessary for him at last to have a personal secretary to coddle him, to keep track of his mail and arrange his appointments, and, in fact, to lift as much detail as possible off his shoulders. The present incumbent of this far from easy office was a young man named Barry Coventry who had graduated from Cambridge into the offices of a Carboy mill in the eastern country and from there to the care of the great man himself. Coventry was of good family and he had no sense of humor. A Carboy witticism, never an airy or graceful morsel, did not win from him more than a wan and uncomprehending smile. His employer blamed him for everything, discharged him at least twice a day, developed a vocabulary of abuse at his expense, and paid him a very good salary.

It was December 21, St. Thomas's Day, and the weather was quite capricious. It would snow a little and then stop, and it would blow with considerable fierceness for a short time and then relent, and it seemed even to alternate between cold and warmth. The snow which came down was not heavy enough to give the ground a complete coverage but it filled all the low levels and decorated every staddle stone in Berkshire with a white nightcap. Traditions die hard in England, as slowly in Berkshire as anywhere else; and so this St. Thomas's Day had been looked forward to with the pleasantest expectations and it was hoped that the changeability of the weather would not be reflected in the attitude of the well to do.

During the morning Carboy was engaged in an inspection of the new wing he was adding at Beaulaw Hall for his paintings. He was looking at the freshly plastered walls and thinking that the added space would be used up in a very short time at the rate he was acquiring canvases. Coventry, wearing his habitual worried frown, approached him with a card in one hand.

"Linus Welstock to see you, sir," he said.

"You pitiful fool, you ought to know by this time that I don't want to be bothered with Linus Welstock," said Carboy in a sudden fury. "He never has anything but the work of these new fellows. I want names, Coventry, names. Ask Welstock if he has a Rubens or a Rembrandt and, if he says no, tell him to hop it back to London."

In spite of this declaration, the great industrialist, walking slowly and using his cane, followed his secretary back to the library where the London art dealer had been left.

"Welstock," he said in a loud voice, "there's no use telling me about your Martins or your Wilkies or your Turners. You know also that I despise the work of every member of the Clique—the Dadds and Firths and Augustus Eggs. Oh yes, I know the critics praise them but there's only one critic I go by and his name is Time. I won't buy a painting until Time has spoken and if you think I can be seduced by some bucolic Landseer, you are sadly wrong, my man. If you've discovered a new Holbein, for instance, that's a different matter."

There was a moment of pregnant silence. "I have discovered a Holbein," said the dealer.

"Come, come!" scoffed Carboy. "You're not going to palm off a fake on *me*. I'm too wise to be caught in any such mug's game as that."

"It's a hitherto unknown portrait and I know where it is," declared Welstock without any effort to conceal his sense of triumph. "It's genuine, I promise you, and I think it can be bought. Now, Mr. Carboy, if you will sit down and listen to me and promise not to roar at me or swing that cane around with your usual carelessness, I'll tell you everything I know about the picture."

"Why didn't that idiot of a secretary tell me you had something worth while!" exclaimed Carboy. "I almost refused to see you."

He seated himself, facing the art dealer, and said in an eager voice: "Well, speak up, man. Tell me all about it."

"It turned up near Basel. I'm told it has been in the possession of a small

German collection for several generations. I have a photograph of it which convinces me, and will convince you also, that it's genuine. I will stake my reputation on it."

Carboy looked at Welstock with one eye closed and the other brimming with suspicion. "See here," he said after a moment, "you're not telling me the whole story. The canvas is in London. It's been stolen and the thief, or his agent, has brought it to you to dispose of. Isn't that the truth?"

The dealer looked very much discomfited. "Well, partly. The picture *is* in London. I am told so, at least. I haven't set eyes on it yet and that's why I held part of the story back. I haven't been able to make up my mind about the honesty of the man who's offering it."

"Mark my words, it's been stolen. Where would that leave me if I should buy it from you? I wouldn't be able to acknowledge the ownership of it. I couldn't hang it with my other pictures. It would be necessary to keep it under lock and key in some closet where no eyes would ever rest on it but mine. And for this rare privilege, you are prepared, no doubt, to demand a fortune from me."

"You are right about the price," admitted the dealer. "The man offering it, a dealer from Antwerp whose reputation is a bit shady, is asking a staggering figure." He nodded his head dubiously and proceeded to explain another difficulty. "I must be honest with you, Mr. Carboy. If it *is* stolen, and the fact gets out, the purchaser will either have to send it back or face the certainty that on his death it will be found and he will be branded an accomplice after the fact. Do you know that there are many collectors willing to take that risk?"

"The buyer wouldn't need to be caught under any circumstances," declared Carboy testily. "Now, if I bought it, I would make arrangements with someone I trust as to its disposal after my death. Someone would be left with instructions to destroy it or, if that seemed too much of a vandalism, to hold it for a safe time and then deposit it on some doorstep. *Yours* in all probability. I would protect my reputation, I assure you." He paused as he conned over these rather depressing possibilities. "Have you decided what price you must get to compensate for your part in this little thievery?"

But he was not to hear the price then. At this moment Coventry returned with a look on his face which hinted at some impending calamity.

"Sir," he said, "an extraordinary thing has happened. Five carriages, actually five, sir, have turned in from the Oxford road and are approaching the Hall. At first I thought it a gypsy train but then I realized that was impossible. Your attitude toward them is too well known for any gypsies to come here. What it is, sir, I do not know and so I suggest that you come and judge for yourself."

"Five carriages? That rules out the butcher and the mailman. Are you sure you counted right?"

"Sir, in the first two carriages there is much loud talking going on and even laughing and waving of arms. I fail to see any reason for such hilarity."

Carboy got to his feet with the aid of his cane and with considerable reluctance. He said to the art dealer, "I'll have to look into this invasion of my property before we can finish our talk." He asked his secretary, "Will you follow me as you are or do you think it wise to borrow a battle-ax for self-protection from one of the suits of armor in the hall?"

The first carriage was turning in when they reached the front entrance. It was being driven by a boy in his middle teens, a tall fellow with light hair and blue eyes fairly sparking with excitement. In the space left over in the carriage, after piling the seats high with luggage of all kinds, sat a middle-aged man with an eye as blue as the youth's under a broad-brimmed felt hat. The second vehicle, drawn by a colored coachman, had dropped far back, perhaps because the two occupants were standing up and shooting at birds with long-barreled guns; and bringing them down, moreover, with uncanny skill.

After the second carriage came three curious vehicles of unusual size and rather extraordinary appearance. They traveled on wheels so high that the floor of each wagon was a good four feet off the ground; and they were six feet broad and fully five yards long. Each had a canvas tent which rose up to a peak, and the spaces inside were packed tight with furniture and belong-ings. The wagons would have looked completely in place on the South African veldt or the pampas of the Argentine, perhaps, but in the quiet countryside of Berkshire they looked so weird and out of place that the owner of Beaulaw Hall gaped with astonishment.

The broad-hatted passenger in the first carriage did not try to clear a way for himself through the luggage which girded him in but reached a hand over to the door and vaulted out. Running up the stone steps two at a time, he grasped Samuel Carboy by the hand.

"Grandfather!" he exclaimed. "I promised I would be away a few years only. I've stayed twenty-five. But here I am at last and I hope you're glad to see me."

"Sammy!" gasped the Colossus. "Is it really you? I'd given up hope of ever seeing you again since you got started on all this empire building." He turned with sudden fury and shouted at Coventry: "Why are you stand-ing there like a pillar of salt, you pitiful fool! Tell the butler he'd better get started on the fatted calves and such matters."

"This is my son Allie," said the homecomer, motioning to the youth who had descended from the driver's seat and was standing by with watchful interest. "Allie, this is your famous grandfather—no, your great-grandfather."

"I've boasted about you, sir, all my life," said the boy.

"You're the image of my Allie, your own grandfather," said Samuel Car-boy, studying the youth. "The very image. I'm glad, my boy, that you've come at last to see your ancestral acres. They're broader than they were when your father decided he wanted a new sky and a new set of stars. I've been adding to them and it's a tidy bit of land you'll come into someday."

"I decided to come home, Grandfather, as soon as my poor Clara died. I wasn't as happy in South Africa as I'd been. So I packed everything up and put the wagons on board ship, and came on home. I had been in touch with

your lawyers, Smythe, Boongrace and Curdle, but I warned them I wanted
to surprise you. They had a man at the dock to see us through—one of the
second-generation Curdles—and I was allowed to drive the wagons right off
the ship without as much as a cover being lifted."

"They're good enough, Smythe, Boongrace and Curdle," said Carboy.
"But sometimes, damme, I miss that preaching fool who walked out on me
without a word of thanks or a by-your-leave."

"I've lots of things to talk over with you, Grandfather, as soon as we
can get some time to ourselves. I've been having an exciting life, you know.
Business is war when you get your nose up as far as the Great Bushman
and north of the Zoutpansberg. I've brought with me two of my"—he
paused and grinned—"two of my neatest bookkeepers. Hey, Ride-All-Night
and Zulu, come over here and make the acquaintance of a truly great man."

The two occupants of the second carriage, still holding their long weapons, came forward at this. They wore wider felt hats than their employer,
and army belts, and they had long brown mustaches and mild brown eyes.

"This, Grandfather," said Young Sammy, motioning to the taller of the
pair, "is Geoffrey Blaney, who is better known as Ride-All-Night after a
South African song. The song's about a man who rides all night to see his
sweetheart in the morning on the other side of a mountain. Blaney's noc-
turnal rides have been to bring word of native troubles or new gold strikes."

"I've ridden a-all night to see sweethearts a-also, suh," said Blaney in soft
and slurring tones.

"And this one is William Pickledone, who's called Zulu because he's been
a great Zulu fighter. He can pick a Kei apple off the bough at twenty yards
with an assagai."

The second man grinned broadly and said, "But I was born in the mothah
country, suh, and learned the gentle a-art of self-defense out behind the
pubs, suh."

Servants had been arriving in considerable numbers and were grouped
near the door, waiting for instructions.

"Grandfather," said the leader of the invading forces, "I'm going to ask
you to let me put these wagons somewhere in the stables. They can't be
unloaded until I've found a home. We're back for all time, sir, Allie and I
and Ride-All-Night and Zulu, not to mention those black rascals doing the
driving. The first thing for me to do is find a suitable bit of land hereabouts
—not too big, you understand, perhaps a few thousand acres—because I
can't inflict this kind of a visitation on you for more than a few days."

"Well, you'll be ready to visit your rooms right away, Grandson," said the
old man. He looked around for his secretary. "Get your mighty mind to
work, you blighted idiot, and make suitable arrangements for my grandson and young Allie here, and Mr. Ride-All-Night and Mr. Zulu."

"I hope you haven't forgotten, sir," said the secretary, "that her ladyship,
the Marchioness of Invermark, is arriving this afternoon with some friends
for the holidays."

"Am I upsetting things for you?" asked the homecomer anxiously.

"This is your home, Grandson, as much as Isabelle's. Coventry, it's a case of first come, first served. You'll have to put my daughter and her friends into any rooms that are left. Now," he went on, "while you are getting yourselves settled, I'll finish an important discussion I was engaged in when you came riding home with carriages piled high with sheaves."

"And an odd million or two as well, Grandfather," said Young Sammy with a nod of pride.

2

"According to my calculations, Grandfather, you are nearly ninety years old," said the homecomer when the two of them had the library to themselves. "It's hard to believe but figures don't lie."

"No, they don't lie. That's my age. I'm an old gaffer, Grandson."

The old man had acquired a sunken look about the eyes, wrinkles by the thousands, seemingly, had invaded his face. His frame looked much younger; he was not stooped and his movements had still a hint of vigor. His cane was a convenience rather than a necessity.

"I conducted three annual meetings the last day I was in London," added Carboy proudly. "If they had the idea in their heads that I was losing my grip, they soon discovered their error. I demanded the dismissal of a top official in each concern, for sheer fatwittedness and a liking for winter vacations. Later I put them back, figuring they would be more valuable after such a scare than any new man I could put in their places. Was I wrong? Am I getting soft in my old age?"

"You're as sharp as an old fox, Grandfather, and there isn't a soft square inch on your hide."

"I insisted on a completely new policy for one of the companies. Gad, how they wriggled and fought me. They thought they knew better than I did, I soon took *that* out of them." He nodded his head several times and smiled fiercely. "I hold my liquor, Sammy, but I can't powder into food the way I used to. Of course my hearing is bad and—well, it's a fact, I don't see too well."

"Perhaps I've stayed away too long," said his grandson.

The old man seemed to have some difficulty in hearing him. He had cupped his hand behind an ear. "Too long? Yes, Sammy, much too long."

"It wasn't my fault, *oupa*." Words from the Afrikaans tongue slipped out occasionally through long usage. "My poor lovely Clara was ready enough to marry me, and I was mad enough about her. But she made one condition. She must never be expected to live in England or even go there on visits. You see, the Boers don't like us and Clara had been raised to hate and fear the English. But I was mad for her, my sweet *meisie*, and, as you know, she brought me a fine dowry. So I gave in.

"She never changed her mind about it," he went on after a moment. "Although she knew I was eager to get back, she always said, no, if I went

I must go alone, and that she would keep Allie with her. She was a resolute woman although she was so gentle, and I didn't know what was behind her no. If I came, would she refuse to take me back? I was *swakkerig* about it—I mean, I was afraid to take the risk. But I began making my plans years ago and corresponding with men all over the world. I have a dozen files, filled with information and ideas and figures. I have lists from all over—men who could be of value to us and those we would have to fight. I've brought everything with me, of course.

"My poor wife was wise enough to know what I was doing. When she fell sick last winter and knew she was not going to live, she said to me: 'My *liefhebber*, you must go to your England when I am not here. I have seen the longing in your eyes. And you must take the *seun* with you. He, my tall one, is more like his *vater* than like us. He will want to go.' He did, of course. After she had been buried, he agreed we should pack up everything and come. I had always seen to it that he read about England and I talked to him all the time. Yes, he wanted to come, though he loved the country out there."

"When you wrote me about her death," said the old man sharply, "you didn't say what she did with her property."

"She left it to me. All except the house and the farm, which were in her name. They were left to Allie and I think it's right he should have them. We rented the place to one of her brothers, Cornelius. A ten-year lease. For a lump sum."

Samuel Carboy had been sipping slowly from the glass in his hand. Now he sloshed fresh whisky into it and took a deep swallow. His eyes brightened.

"And now," he said, "we'll have your plan. What is this precious scheme you've carried in your mind so long?"

"This, *oupa*. I offer myself to you as a partner in a world trading corporation. I will put in everything I have and all that Clara left me. About two million pounds. Not bad for a young fellow, eh? I will assume all the work you are willing to let slip from your own shoulders." He began then to speak in a rapid and eager tone. "Out there they always speak of you as the richest man in England. I want them to call you the richest man in the world, and the most powerful. I want to see Carboy and Co. as well known in Paris and New York and Vienna and Shanghai as in London. It can be done. With our combined resources—you will be surprised when you know how advantageously my holdings are placed—and with the Carboy drive and resourcefulness, of which I've inherited my share, we can get a large chunk of the trade of the world in our hands. At first, of course, our foreign branches would be large trading houses. Then we would begin to buy in factories and large stores and get our hands on banks. You know the formula. It's your own, you invented it."

Samuel Carboy had been listening intently. "I'm nearly ninety, Sammy," he said.

"But your ninety is better than most men's forty."

"I don't want more money. I don't want more power. I've had more of both than I ever expected. But I still want a title. They've diddled me out of my knighthood a dozen times. It's always the same story. Opposition in high places, secret animosities working against me. I've never been able to get to the bottom of it. Who are these people who block it? If I knew for sure, I would crush them to dust! I would root them out, even if they tried to hide behind the throne, and I'd make them rue the day they picked me as the target of their weak spite!" He paused for a moment and when he spoke again it was in a different tone. There was a suggestion of eagerness, combined with a hint of supplication, in his voice. "Do you think they might give in about the title if we launched out as you suggest? If we had wires to pull all over the world?"

"Grandfather, if we accomplish what I have in mind, they won't be able to refuse you a peerage. Not to mention the foreign titles we could command. A duke, a prince—who knows?"

"Prince Carboy! H'm! Brave words, Sammy. But I've been disappointed too often to feel any real hope. I've offered donations. You would cringe if you knew how large. . . . Well—I'll think about it. We'll go over these notes together, and the correspondence you've brought."

"I was sure you would take that view of it. There's neither an Elba nor a Waterloo for the Napoleon of Industry!"

"If it looks good, I may be willing to—— We'll see, we'll see." His eyes had opened wide and they were filled with the old fire. "I'd enjoy showing them there's life still in the old hulk. It would send all the little curs shivering into their kennels if the lion came out of his lair and roared at them! We'll see, Grandson, we'll see!"

### 3

When Samuel Carboy discovered in the early afternoon that his grandson was loading his party into one of the carriages with the intention of paying a visit to the Groody household, he yanked at the nearest bell cord and said to the butler: "Have mine brought around, Bilson. I'm not going to be left out." The thought was in his mind that it would be more comfortable to be away when Isabelle arrived and found the best rooms in the Hall occupied. It was not the Napoleonic carriage which was sent for him but a dignified victoria; with, alas, no crest on the panels.

The vehicles created some interest on the main street of Little Shallow because of the strange broad hats worn by most of the party. Pitcher fell into a panic when she answered the summons at the front door. "Two Mr. Samuel Carboys!" she ejaculated. "Could it be the one as went to Austrylia?"

"South Africa," said Samuel the Younger, smiling at her. "I've been away a long time."

At this moment they heard the beat of horses' hoofs from the meadows behind the property. A girl riding on a small black horse came across the glebe lands, which were lightly covered with snow, and into the yard, not waiting to have the back gate opened but taking the low hedge at a casual lope. She sprang from the saddle and called in a clear, high voice: "Huruld! Here we are. I lost my hat again. It's back there somewhere on the meadows. Why can't I keep a hat on, Huruld?"

The namesake of the then prime minister of England came out from the stables and took Brian Boy in charge. "Perhaps," he hinted in a reproving tone, "you haven't any head to wear 'em on. You've lost three hats, miss."

Allie Carboy had not taken his eyes off the girl from the moment she came into view, racing across the meadow with her dark curls in the wildest of disorder. "Who's that, Great-grandfather?" he asked.

The old man squinted in the direction of the stable yard. "That's the niece, I expect. A wild young creature from Ireland. She's never off a horse, I hear."

The maidservant ushered them in and took them straight to the library where the mistress of the house was sitting in front of the fire. She took one look at the homecomer and her eyes filled with happy tears. Getting to her feet with some difficulty, she held out her arms to him.

"Sammy!" she cried. "My dearest boy, you've come back at last! Oh, what a wonderful surprise for Christmas!"

He took her in his arms and kissed her fondly. "This is a happy moment, Aunt Helen," he said. "I've thought about you so much all these years that I've been away."

"And you've become such a great man! How proud we've been of you. You wanted to win your spurs. How well you've done it!"

His eye had wandered toward the fireplace. "You have them there still, I see. My first pair of shoes."

She made an effort to walk to the mantel but, finding it too difficult, resumed her chair with a sigh of relief. "The little shoes I saw outside the door of the inn, Sammy. I loved you from that moment and before I had ever seen you."

"Aren't you well, Aunt Helen?" he asked anxiously.

"Oh, a touch of rheumatism. It's very bothersome because I don't get around as much as I would like." She paused and looked in the direction of the door. "And the boy? Isn't he with you?"

"I suspect he remained outside for a moment. Your niece arrived at the same time we did and he seemed rather interested in her."

"What's all this, ma'am?" asked Carboy, motioning toward a table which was covered with neatly wrapped parcels and a row of small silk purses.

"Why, Mr. Carboy, don't you remember that this is St. Thomas's Day? I'm all prepared for tonight. We'll have the mumping, you know. It's always a great pleasure."

"Pleasure, ma'am? Good gad, there won't be any mumpers coming to call on me, I can tell you. I sent them away with fleas behind all their ears the last time they tried it. That was quite a few years ago." He examined the parcels with a frown. "Do you mean to tell me that you're giving all this away? Is there money in those purses? Gad, ma'am, you'll spoil them. There's no poverty in the village or any parts hereabouts."

"But there is. You would be surprised if you knew how poor many of them are. If it wasn't for the mumping parties, they would have no Christmas at all."

Carboy shook his head stubbornly. "There's altogether too much fuss being made about it. Ever since that fellow Dickens wrote all that sentimental trash about Christmas carols or something of the kind, people have gone mad about the Day and the poor. They've taken to calling me Scrooge behind my back. I've heard them. Well, I'm no Scrooge and I don't expect to have a ghost in chains coming to *my* bedside; but I must say I resent this whole foolish business."

Allie's father had been right. The boy, realizing that no one was paying any attention to him, had not come into the house with the rest of the party. Instead he skirted around the side and made for the stable yard. Nelly was standing with her back to him, beating dust off her riding boots with the crop. She turned at the sound of his approaching steps.

"Good afternoon," said Allie.

It was only within the last year that he had been noticing girls at all. His life before that had been devoted to his education, to games with his few friends and, above all, to the great occasions when his father took him along on trips into the dark and strange lands of the north. It was on his return from the last of these dangerous missions that he noticed the daughters of their neighbors with a new eye. They were all very much alike, plump little chicks with apple-red cheeks and flaxen hair hanging in pigtails over their shoulders. They giggled a lot and gave him quick looks from their round blue eyes; but he had found them exciting.

This girl had blue eyes also—a most unusual type of blue, however, dark and clear and ringed with long lashes—and she had hair as black as midnight. He had never seen this combination before. "How wonderful!" he said to himself.

"Good afternoon," she responded. "I know who you are. You're the great-great-great-grandson—how many greats are there?—from South Africa."

"Yes, Miss Nelly. I'm Allie Carboy. My father and the rest of them have gone in to see your aunt. I—well, I thought they wouldn't miss me for a while, and I had seen you come in over the hedge——" He had intended to say something more but realized it was not necessary. He had made himself clear.

The girl said after a moment, "When my aunt saw the picture of you, she said you were exactly like the—the other Allie Carboy."

The youth nodded. "Of course my father never saw his father, so he had no way of telling. But my great-grandfather—one great will do—says I'm exactly like his son. The first Alfred Carboy was the one who knew your aunt Helen."

"Great-aunt," corrected the girl.

Her mind was busy as she spoke. She knew the whole story of the wrecked romance between Allie Carboy and Helen Groody. By dint of detailed and persistent questions she had gleaned everything about it that her aunt was willing to put into words. With eyes wide and lips slightly parted she had backed her aunt into mental corners like a lawyer in a courtroom. "And what did he say then?" and "How did he look, Aunt Helen, was he very unhappy?" and "What did he wear, and what did you wear? Surely, you had something besides that one old dress. Did you wear the shawl he gave you?"

She could recite the story now in the completest detail, with chapter and verse, and all the lapses and blank spots in the story filled in by her own fancy. She disapproved of the way her aunt had handled matters. "Why," she asked many times, "didn't you follow him to America and never let him out of your sight?" Once, with the moisture of tears in her eyes, she asked, "When you saw the little shoes outside the door at the inn, did something away down deep inside you tell you that they belonged to *his* son?" Her interest in the subject was never entirely appeased. She regarded old Samuel Carboy as an ogre who had wrecked her aunt's life. "Aunt Helen, if you hated that ugly old man—and I'm sure you must have—why is it you can speak to him now?" When told that time had an alleviating effect and that the bitterest feelings dwindled almost to nothing with the passing of the years, she said, "I'm sure I would never have forgiven him, never."

"They were very much in love with each other," she said now, for the benefit of this boy who bore such a resemblance to the recreant lover of half a century before. "Oh, very much. It was a beautiful romance, even if nothing came of it."

"I'm not surprised it was a great romance, if your aunt looked then the way you do now," declared the youth, growing bolder with the feeling that their acquaintance was ripening.

"If they had been married, he would never have gone to America and perhaps he would be alive today. So you see it was all very wrong and sad."

"But," said the second Alfred, "my father wouldn't have gone to South Africa in that case. In fact he wouldn't ever have been born. I wouldn't have been born. I wouldn't be here today, seeing you come riding in so beautifully over the hedge and now talking to you like this. And—and liking you so much." He paused after expressing this final thought, because it seemed to him he was going too fast. "Well, everything would have been upset, wouldn't it? At least, as far as I'm concerned. I've got to say I'm glad the romance didn't lead to anything. I feel that things have come out wonderfully."

"Aren't you being selfish?" asked the girl.

"Perhaps," conceded young Allie. Then he shook his head. "No. I've got a right to existence. I'm glad my grandfather married the actress in America. And I get really frightened when I think of how terrible it would have been if your father hadn't met your mother."

"Oh, Himself knew my little mother when she was just fifteen and he came back from trying to be a sailor. He didn't like it at all. I mean the sailoring. He liked my mother from the first instant he set eyes on her. There was never any danger of them not marrying. But there was real danger later. I was the seventh child. After the sixth arrived, poor little Jamesie who's not very strong, my mother said to Himself, 'There will be no more, Mister Groody.' But she changed her mind, bless her."

The back door of the house was opened and closed and the two adherents of the South African branch of the Carboy family came out stealthily. When they saw Allie, they grinned at him rather sheepishly.

"Lots of talk goin' on in there," said Ride-All-Night. "We didn't get the drift of much of it. Thought we'd come out for a breath of air, even if it ain't as good as the air of South Africy. You better sash'y back in and take our places." Then he spoke in a decided tone. "We'll be goin' back—when the tea's served."

Allie hesitated and then shook his head; he would remain outside a little longer. Then he regretted his decision, for Nelly had already disappeared inside the house.

The vehicles standing in front of the Old Rectory had attracted a few curiosity seekers. Their number grew when it was seen that two of the wide-hatted strangers had come out into the yard. The watchers became bold enough to encroach along the line of the hedge, observing closely everything that went on and listening with openmouthed avidity. Perhaps the presence of an audience had an effect on Zulu. At any rate, he suddenly threw back his head and emitted a high screech which sent shivers down

the backs of the villagers. They did not know it was the war cry of the Zulus but it was clear enough to them that it was something far out of their ken.

Zulu began then to stalk across the stable yard, moving his arms in front of him and raising his knees so high that they seemed to attain the level of his chin; the stalking gait, if they had known it, of that same warlike tribe. Reaching the carriage, he extracted from somewhere under a seat a long spear with a bulbous end and a sharp, glistening point, most festively adorned with feathers and red cloth. Returning to the yard, he stood motionless for a moment, the spear poised in the air above his head. Then he emitted another yelp and the weapon shot across the yard with the speed, it seemed, of lightning and struck on the other side of the enclosure. Retrieving the spear, the triumphantly grinning owner raised it in the air. At the end was a small, bloodstained bundle of fur.

"One less field rat to worrit you," he said.

The watchers, needless to state, were amazed. This was the most astonishing exhibition of marksmanship they had ever witnessed. Huruld, recovering his breath, asked, "Mister, can you do some more tricks like that?"

"More tricks like that?" Zulu spoke in an indignant tone. "Aren't you aware, boy, that you have just witnessed with your own eyes the most difficult shot that man born of woman can perform with the assagai? No one could do better than you have seen me do. Be content, my greedy friend, with what you have observed."

He began, however, to collect small stones from the ground, stepping about with a comic exaggeration of the stalking gait, and winking in the direction of Ride-All-Night. The latter in his turn went to the carriage and returned with his long-barreled gun.

"Now!" said Zulu, casting one of the pebbles high in the air.

Ride-All-Night waited until the pebble attained its maximum height and then raised his weapon casually to his shoulder. He fired and the stone broke into countless pieces. Zulu threw another a little higher and the process was repeated. This was done six times and the unerring marksman did not miss once.

The spectators were fairly dancing with excitement by this time and perhaps their applause went to Ride-All-Night's head. He turned to Allie.

"How d'ye feel, son?" he asked. "Reckless like? Ready to risk your blooming beauty?"

"I'm not afraid," answered Allie promptly.

The marksman produced a frayed cigar from a pocket of his coat. He licked the loose edges together and then struck a match. The lighted cigar was handed to the son of his employer.

"Don't go a-swallowin' of that juice, son," instructed Ride-All-Night, "or yuh'll be sick to yuh stummick. Just draw dainty like a bee on a hollyhock."

Allie took his station at the other end of the yard and turned sideways with the cigar in his mouth. The audience held its breath, not knowing what reckless feat was to be attempted next. The man with the rifle was singing in a careless monotone:

> "I'll ride, I'll ride, I'll ride, I'll ride,
>    I'll ride all night,
>  When the moon is bright, when the moon is bright;
>    I'll ride, I'll ride, I'll ride, I'll ride,
>  I'll ride all night;
>    I'll get there in the morning."*

Then, without any hesitation, he raised the rifle, sighted with outward carelessness and blew the lighted end off the cigar. Allie, a little pale, tossed away the fragment of tobacco which had been left in his mouth, and walked back across the yard. The spectators were too shocked to utter a sound but Ride-All-Night accepted their speechlessness as the highest kind of praise. He indulged in an exaggerated bow.

And then a stormy interruption occurred. Nelly had returned, having succeeded in that short time in getting out of her riding habit and into a proper afternoon dress. She had seen what happened but had not dared utter a word of protest for fear of disturbing the aim. Now she charged across the yard, seized the rifle from the hands of the surprised marksman and threw it across the yard.

"You terrible man!" she cried. "You might have killed him! What kind of a dangerous, unthinking, boastful creature are you, to take such a chance?"

Ride-All-Night retreated before the angry girl, his mouth falling open in surprise.

"Why, young leddy——" he began.

"Don't you young leddy me, you thoughtless idiot!" cried Nelly. "Why, you conceited fellow, you great clown, you might have disfigured him for life!"

"But, young leddy," protested the rifleman. "He wasn't in any dangah at all. I wouldn't nevah disfiguh him. Why, leddy, I just kain't miss."

Allie came forward with a suggestion at this point. "If you don't mind, all of you, I would rather you don't do any talking about this. If my father hears about it, he'll be very angry with Ride-All-Night—and he'll raise Old Ned with me too. So let's agree to keep it to ourselves."

There was an immediate agreement to this although Nelly, her cheeks still flushed with anger, and with lightning flashing from her eyes, was slow to give in. She remembered then that she had come out on an errand.

"Your presence is requested inside," she said to Allie stiffly. "I hope you are through risking your life to help this man do his silly tricks and that you'll go in now. You haven't seen Aunt Helen yet and she's *very* anxious to see you."

"I'll go in right away," he responded. Then he lowered his voice. "I wasn't afraid and I wasn't in any danger."

Standing at the youth's shoulder, Zulu said in a whisper: "That's a fine girl. That's a very nice girl."

Allie turned to him and whispered back, "I certainly agree with you, Mr. Zulu."

4

Helen Groody was still in her library when her niece brought Allie in to see her. She was sitting even closer to the fire, with a warm robe over her knees, and it was apparent in her face that she was suffering.

"I found him," announced the girl. "He was very busy outside, helping a galoot with a gun amuse the whole village." She stopped short at that point, recalling the agreement which had been reached.

The drawn face of the mistress of the Old Rectory lighted up and she held out a hand to him. "So you are Allie," she said. Her expression relaxed in a smile. "Your father was telling me a great many things about you. And now that I see you, I can tell for myself how much you are alike, you and the young man I knew who was your grandfather. I saw him first when he was about your age. Sit down with me, my dear young people. You can have your tea with me while the rest are in the dining room."

Loud conversation, reaching them from across the hall, made it apparent that the other men of the party were already deep in their meal. The boy looked at his hostess and asked, "May I serve you and Miss Nelly?"

"That would be very kind of you. I'm sure Daphne will be kept busy with the needs of our friends. I haven't been eating much lately and all I'll want will be a cup of tea."

He became much concerned at once. "Are you not well, Miss Groody?" he asked.

"The doctors have finally reached a decision," she answered. "I have rheumatism. It isn't news to me at all. I've been sure of it for a long time because I am the one who feels the pain. It has settled down at last. In one knee. It's a relief to know where it is going to be but this makes it hard for me to walk. I spend most of my time here by the fire." She turned and smiled at her niece. "If you serve Nelly also, you'll find her needs rather more exacting."

"I want a little of everything, please," said the girl. "But I had best go with you. If Daphne has lost her head, it will be hard to find anything."

Nelly was the first to return, carrying a tray and her aunt's cup of tea. As she arranged the tray on a side table, she leaned close and whispered, "Oh, Auntie, he's very nice. And he's very brave, so brave that he nearly got himself killed. I promised to say nothing about it but perhaps I can tell you later. Is he so much like the other one?"

"When he came in," said her aunt, "I could have sworn it was my Allie, come back from his grave."

"He's very handsome, isn't he?"

"He is, indeed. Do you like him, child?"

The girl nodded her head casually. "Of course. He's very easy to like."

The older woman sighed. "So was his grandfather. I, at least, was not able to resist him. You had better keep a close rein on your feelings, Nelly."

"I intend to, Auntie," said the girl. "We don't want a second broken romance, do we? But he *is* nice."

It developed in a few minutes that both the young people, even though a preliminary arrow from the rotund god had perhaps landed somewhere in their neighborhood, had healthy appetites. As they proceeded to make this clear, they talked without any hint of restraint and with much laughter. They all had a very pleasant time of it, in fact.

"Will you be going to college soon?" asked Helen, who had seldom allowed her eyes to stray from the boy's face.

Allie shook his head. "I'm not going to college. Which isn't very surprising, I guess, because none of the Carboys have ever gone, as far as I have been able to tell. They prefer to get into business early. *That* is what I want to do. I suppose I'll end up in the family business but at first I want to do what my father did. I want to make a start by myself."

Helen cried out in protest, "Oh no, don't tell me that. You mustn't do what your father did. He was sitting in that very chair and talking about his future with his grandfather and me. He said he wanted to win his spurs all by himself and that he wished to go to South Africa. He promised to come back in a few years. But he stayed away for twenty-five. You mustn't do that, Allie."

The boy shook his head. "No need to worry, Miss Groody. I want to get started in something right here in England. In fact I've got a plan in my head."

"My dear Sammy—your father—had a plan too. They came over to discuss it here. He was full of South Africa and nothing could budge him. I'm sure, Allie, that everyone will be very much relieved if you really mean to stay in England."

The boy was watching Nelly out of the corner of one eye. "I assure you that, if I had been thinking of anything else, I would have changed my mind today. I like England already. I like it here very much. And, as I said, I have a plan."

"Do you want to tell us what it is?"

He nodded his head eagerly. "I want to very much. Father heard before we left home that the building in London where Grace and Carboy did business has kind of fallen on evil days. It's being used as a storage warehouse. I want to buy it back and restore it. I want to have it as much as possible as it was before, and then to get myself started as an importer of Eastern goods. Wouldn't that be kind of exciting? Wouldn't it be a great incentive to becoming a good businessman like all the Carboys if I owned the old place where the foundations of the Carboy wealth were laid?"

Helen had forgotten her aches and pains. Her eyes were shining with an excitement which matched his own.

"Allie," she said, "I think your plan is wonderful. It would be kind of poetic, wouldn't it? Have you discussed it with your father?"

He shook his head. "No, Aunt Helen. I—I was afraid he might think I was being presumptuous. I know I'm too young to be thinking of running a business by myself. And I have a plan about that too. I'm going to take a position with some firm of Eastern importers—not a Carboy concern—and get to know something about it. As soon as I can get to London, I think I'll speak to Mr. Jonas Scanlon of Scanlon, Burns and Copbright. They seem to be a lively firm."

Nelly's plate was empty but when he noticed this and asked to be allowed to replenish it, she shook her head. "No, thank you. I'm more interested in what you're saying than in food."

Helen sighed and tossed the blanket from her knees. "I'm always too hot or too cold," she said. "It's so unpleasant to be tied down in this way. I like to be active and yet here I have to stay. I haven't been to the shop for two weeks and I'm sure everything is at sixes and sevens over there! But your plan is much more important and interesting, Allie, than my little worries. I have only one reservation about it. Wouldn't it be better to go to school for a few more years than to plunge right into business?"

The boy knew his own mind most emphatically on this point. "No more schools for me," he declared. "I can hardly wait to get out into the world where I'll learn something that will be useful to me." He indulged then in rather shamefaced smile. "I've been a terrible scholar. I forget Latin the day after I have a lesson in it. I couldn't be made to try Greek. I can write a fair business letter but I turn out a botch when I attempt a composition.

There's only one kind of history I like and that's the story of trade and commerce. No, a desk at Scanlon, Burns and Copbright is where I want to be for the next few years." He paused and then plunged more deeply into his confidences. "I want to buy the old Grace and Carboy building at once. Before anyone else can get it or it's decided to pull it down."

"That will make it necessary to go to your father, won't it?"

He became quite emphatic again on this point. "I don't want to ask him for a shilling. Not," hurriedly, "that he would be against letting me have anything I need. He's always been generous with me. But it's—well, I guess you would call it a matter of principle. Do you understand?"

"Of course."

"I have four hundred pounds of my own. From my mother's estate. I could buy the place with that much to put down."

Helen shook her head. "It wouldn't do to load yourself up with a mortgage. The better way would be to acquire a partner. A silent partner." She smiled at him. "Me, perhaps. I'm a partner in exactly thirty-seven concerns of one kind and another and no one, not even my lawyer in London, knows about all of them. I'm the most silent partner that's ever been known, I guess. I'm so quiet about my interests that I never go to board meetings, even though I control a few of the companies. I always know what's going on, of course. I have ways of getting my wishes attended to without stirring from this room. I'm such a silent partner that I think you could find me a very satisfactory one."

The boy looked up at her, his eyes glowing. "Say, I never thought of that. It would be a perfect arrangement for me. And we could keep it a complete secret if that's what you want. I'm willing to talk about terms right away."

"If you really want quick action, Allie, I can arrange to buy the old Grace and Carboy property next week. Through my lawyer in London. I will hold it for you until you are ready to make whatever arrangements are necessary to take it over. And, if you change your mind, I'll consider it an investment of my own."

"That's a perfect arrangement!" cried the boy. "I had no idea that deals could be made as fast as that! I suspect, Miss Groody, you're a very fine businessman yourself."

She smiled at this. "Your great-grandfather considers me one," she said.

CHAPTER FIVE

1

The party returned to Beaulaw Hall with an hour to spare before dinner. Samuel Carboy settled himself at a table with a whisky decanter at his elbow and said to his grandson: "Now's your chance, Young Sammy. Get your papers out and we'll have a look at this scheme of yours."

In half an hour the Colossus had gone rapidly through everything. He had glanced at the figures, had read some of the reports on trade conditions and, with rather more attention, had studied letters from men of proven stature. "Now give me everything," he said. "I've seen enough to convince me that it's worth while going into it thoroughly. I have a beastly habit of waking up at four in the morning. Tonight I'll get at it in earnest.

"There's one thing I like about it," he went on. "It would be breaking ground in countries where business is not so damnably handicapped by regulations and restrictions. I'm sick of labor unions and laws governing child labor and all this pother about sanitary conditions and hot water for the men to use before they start home. This is an age of coddling in England. It's my idea that there's only one thing to be coddled now, and that's dividends. It's impossible to make an honest shilling the way things are.

"Now look at the man I had with me, this Jonathan Bade. He's back in his own office and with his shingle out again. But does that stop him from going around the country to make speeches? 'Am I my brother's keeper?' is his slogan and wherever the fellow appears we have committees right away, snooping around the factories, getting into the jails, inspecting the work-houses. He attracts all these lunatics to him—these lank-jawed men and bitter spinsters. There won't be any profits or any of the old decency about business as long as this fellow is allowed to go on like this."

"In the East and South," interrupted his grandson, "we won't run into difficulties like that. But there are other kinds. We run into pleasant things like native uprisings and friendly little massacres and well intentioned burnings of plants. Why do you suppose I brought Ride-All-Night and Zulu with me? Because in places where I want to get established you need men like them who can shoot straight and aren't afraid to do it. I didn't dare leave them behind because I knew they would be hired out from under me. I suspect, Grandfather, they're the kind of coddlers you prefer."

Samuel Carboy did not respond for several moments. From the set of his jaw and the smoldering combativeness in his eyes, it was apparent that he was giving serious thought to the problems they faced. "If I were fifty, or even sixty, and had you with me just as you are," he said, "I would jump at this with the greatest eagerness. I would do it in the hope of accomplishing one thing: to become so rich and powerful that I could force my ideas on the country. That's not an idle dream, Grandson. If the wealth of the country rested in one pair of hands, governments wouldn't be able to do as they wish. These sickly creatures who pass laws telling us what we can do and what we can't do! They would have to toe the line. They would have to take orders!" •

"That's going a bit further than what I have in mind," said Samuel the Younger.

"It's what I would do if I had the time," declared the old man. "The bitterest thoughts I have are because of the opportunities I have let slip."

"The success we'll achieve with what I propose," said the grandson, "would remove much of the bitterness, I think."

Samuel sat for a long time in further rumination.

"My boy," he said finally, "we may be at the end of an era. What a century it's been! We licked Boney and that left us with the chance at last to use the power and the possessions which had come into our hands. We had an empire to play with. We used our power well. England became an industrial country as well as a maritime power. Our cities became huge. Our factories started to pour out goods for the whole world to buy."

He paused before continuing in a tone of deep bitterness. "I've done more than any single man to bring this about. I've created wealth for the whole nation to share. And what have I got out of it? I'm still Sam Carboy, criticized, hated, looked down on. And now I'm beginning to fear it's all over. The days have gone when a man can own a business and run it his own way. He has the government looking over his shoulder the whole time. He must do this, he must not do that. It may be that this new order is right. I don't pretend to know. But I tell you that I want none of it. I don't understand the new way. I'm getting reconciled to the idea of death because it will mean I won't have to endure these damnable changes. It's no longer the world I know and I've no desire to go on living in the new kind they're going to create."

"Business is given a freer hand in most of the countries I proposed to invade," declared the grandson. "Keep that in mind when you reach your decision."

They fell into such an earnest discussion on the ethics and difficulties of empire building that they paid no attention to the sound of carriages arriving in front of the Hall with much talk and laughter and shouting of "Merry Christmas!" Samuel Carboy was so absorbed, in fact, that he did not look up from the papers until a hand was laid on his shoulder and the voice of his daughter said: "Well! This is a warm welcome, I must say!"

The two men scrambled to their feet and Carboy gave her a fatherly pat on the cheek. "Well, Isa, you're here. What's that infernal racket out in the hall?"

"That," she said, her eyes beginning to blaze in a familiar way, "is being made by my friends. I brought five of them. I wrote you I intended to. They brought a carriageful of presents and the infernal racket you complain of is due to the unloading of them. Now will you come out like a decent host and meet them?"

This is a good time to make it clear that Isabelle, in spite of her age (she didn't concede sixty but she was quite a bit beyond it), was still a beautiful woman. Her hair had turned to silver but was as plentiful and as fluffy and had the same tendency to curl on her forehead as when she was a girl. If there were wrinkles on her face, she managed by some magic to conceal them. The voluminous skirts of the period made it difficult to judge her figure but her maids knew all about it and one of them had been heard to say, "Such slim legs and her such an old hand!" Perhaps it was because she still played golf and rode and walked. She was graceful and deadly on both the tennis court and the bowling green. Her friends said she would never grow old and her enemies declared ruefully that she was indestructible.

She was dressed with artfulness and quite a little dash in a gray polonaise and skirt of waterproof tweed with broad arrows of blue pointing boldly upward. The craze for trimmings which usually was expended on flounces had been employed with more skill to provide braid of a lighter blue to edge the arrows, and there were flutings of the same delicate shade at the neck; what little could be seen of the neck, that is, for she wore a large collar of fur in contrast to the diminutive muff she carried on one wrist.

The coldness of the air had put a natural glow in her cheeks and only an acquaintance of long standing would have thought of guessing her age at very much over forty.

"Isabelle," said her father, "this is your nephew Samuel. He arrived from South Africa this morning."

The daughter of the house had been against this nephew from the start, regarding him as an unwelcome and unexpected interloper in a field which had seemed all her own. She had been only too ready to embrace the belief that the minister who had married Alfred Carboy and Emmy Sweet in the wilds of America had been without any legal right to perform marriages. Something of this feeling could still be felt in the tone of her voice as she shook hands with the homecomer.

"I heard something in the hall about your arrival," she said. "Is this just a visit or for good?"

"For good!" cried Carboy. "I need him in my declining years and I'm not going to let him leave me a second time."

The expression on Isabelle's face made it clear that she had hoped they were making a brief stay. "Well," she said, "we're going to crowd the house, aren't we? I've talked to the butler and that wriggling worm of a secretary of yours, Papa—what is the silly creature's name?"

"Coventry," said her father.

"That's where you ought to send him, Papa, although I suppose dozens of people have said that to you. I discussed the situation with him and I'm afraid, Nephew Samuel, we'll have to accept some makeshifts. I'm putting you in the Wilmot room."

Young Sammy remembered the Wilmot room as a rather uncomfortable place with one window which gave a clear view of the kitchen midden. He smiled, nevertheless, in willing acquiescence.

"I'm afraid it's two turns and then up six steps to the nearest bathroom," said Isabelle, "but I expect you're accustomed to that sort of thing in the colonies. Your son and the two men you've brought with you who, I am told, take their weapons to bed with them—gracious, Papa, I do hope they won't insist on bringing their guns in to dinner!—will all have to put up with quarters on the third floor until after my guests leave."

"See here, Isabelle," said Carboy, beginning to scowl, "I think you're being a bit highhanded about this."

"Grandfather," protested Young Samuel, "we came without giving you any notice. We'll be perfectly happy with any arrangements Aunt Isabelle wants to make."

So they proceeded out to the hall without further discussion. They found it crowded with people who were standing in the midst of innumerable pieces of luggage as well as baskets, with the legs of turkeys sticking out over the top, and barrels of oysters and cases of wine. The strangers were introduced as the Baroness Belinbuttel, a statuesque blonde with an eye of the coldest blue, the Honorable Hermione Greevey, a small and talkative brunette whose husband had owned coal mines and had left them to her, and three men who were noticeably younger than the women and seemed to have been chopped out of one block. They were dressed identically and looked rather silly in long coats with huge buttons and hats which would be most extraordinarily tall when they had them on their heads. As none of the male trio will play any further part in this narrative, it seems superfluous to mention their names, except that the ladies called them Bertie, Prince and Dick-of-Ours.

The frostiness with which Isabelle had greeted her nephew left her when she greeted his son. Allie was most polite and smiled at her and said: "Why, you're a young aunt! I thought—well——"

"I know what you were told," said Isabelle, "and I appreciate the compliment you've paid me. You really are a pretty little fellow, aren't you? I declare, Papa, he's the image of poor Allie. It takes me back a long time——"

"I protest, your ladyship," said one of the male trio. "Not a long time, Marchioness, not really."

"I prefer my little nephew's compliment because it was much more spontaneous. I intended to sit at dinner between Papa and Dick-of-Ours but now I've changed my mind. I'm going to make it a family affair completely. I'm going to condemn Dick to outer darkness and have my sweet little nephew on my other side." She glanced at the tall clock in the hall and cried in alarm: "We must hurry if we're going to dress. Upstairs, everybody. Mr. —er—Bantry, will you see that my guests find their right rooms?"

2

Dinner proved a most interesting occasion. Over the roast veal, which was beautifully brown and crisp and rich, Ride-All-Night came out of his shell and told stories of adventure on the veldt which caused the visiting male trio to listen with drooping jaws. The baroness, having learned that Samuel the Younger was both a millionaire and a widower, leaned her white bosom over the table while listening to the story of his discovery of a gold mine. Carboy himself, having been warned that he must eat lightly and having to content himself with one small lamb chop, was so unhappy about it that he injected comments into the conversation like an apothecary distilling drops from a bottle of acid. Isabelle was an attentive hostess but she managed nevertheless to keep an eye continually on her nephew. There was something assured about him which worried her.

When the time came to leave the men to their wine, Isabelle rose and paused for a moment at her father's shoulder.

"Don't be too long, Papa," she said. "Ermintrude and Hermione and I will be at each other's throats if we're left alone together for more than half an hour. Besides, I have something to say to you."

In half an hour Carboy rose stiffly to his feet. "Gentlemen," he said, "remain as much longer as you like but, with your permission, I am leaving. I've reached the miserable stage of existence when a short nap is needed to keep me on my feet for the rest of the evening. I may add that the speed with which you young men keep the wine circulating has made me dizzy."

In another half hour the Colossus was down again and looking refreshed. His grandson joined him at once and was taken on a tour of the picture wing. It was the old man's custom to pay a visit there each afternoon but on this day, as need hardly be explained, he had been otherwise engaged. His usual way was to stand in front of each of the canvases in turn as he made his way up and down the new gallery, which was devoted exclusively to historical portraits. Sometimes, when his feelings were stirred, he would address the subjects. "Ah, Villiers, you were a poor creature but you had a handsome face," or "Cromwell, Old Noll, you're still the bogeyman of English history and always will be. The French are more sensible about their Bonaparte."

When he discovered that his grandson's interest in art was so slight as to verge on the impolite, he led the way back to the library. "I'll have another old master to add to my collection in a matter of weeks," he said.

In a few minutes all thoughts of art had been brushed aside and they were deep in discussion of Samuel the Younger's plan. Around eleven o'clock Isabelle left the drawing room to her two feminine guests and the inebriated trio and paid a visit to the library.

"I am going on an errand tomorrow, Papa," she said, "which will take a good part of the day. I'll have an early breakfast, at seven, and so I mustn't rob you of your coachman. I've spoken to Allie and he seems pleased at the prospect of driving me. None of the three in there will be capable of an early start. In fact I hardly think you'll see them before noon and they'll be blotchy and loathsome even then."

"You'll find Allie has a good hand for the horses," said the boy's father. "I'm sure he's quite proud to have the chance."

"A word of warning," said Isabelle, looking at the homecomer. "The baroness, bless her marble heart, is prepared to make a conquest of you. Keep clear of her tomorrow when I won't be here to lend protection."

"Which one is the baroness?"

"The taller one."

Samuel frowned. "I didn't notice there was any difference in their sizes."

"Pht! I can see you're in no danger whatever."

Isabelle then seated herself in a chair between them, a Chippendale with

a ribbon back and dolphin feet. She had dressed herself quite well for dinner in a white gown with trimmings of black velvet which were so deft and
unobtrusive that they seemed to play hide-and-seek when she moved. A
gorgeous bracelet was the only jewelry she had donned for the evening. She
studied the glitter of the diamonds against their base of black French enamel
for several moments and then raised her eyes.

"What's going on here?" she asked.

"Business," answered Carboy shortly. Although he was proud of his daughter's realistic approach to things, he still held to the conviction that anything
concerning finance was man's sole prerogative.

"Oh, I was sure of that. Whenever men get that look in their eyes, it's
business or horses; and I know it's not horses with you. But I am curious. I
suspect that my clever nephew, with South African laurels all over his brow,
is laying some proposition before you, Papa."

"Quite right." Carboy intended to give his head one short nod but it developed into a succession of them. "Sammy has a Plan. We are discussing it."

"As your largest single shareholder, Papa, am I not entitled to know something about it?"

Carboy indulged in a puzzled frown. "My largest single shareholder?
What are you talking about, Isabelle?"

"I think," she said in a voice as still as the waters which are supposed to
run deep, "that I've described my position accurately. In addition to what
you have settled on me, I have invested with you all of what came to me
from my husbands' estates."

"But," said her father in a tone not far from quarrelsome, "a very large
part of your holding is what I have put in your name."

"What you gave me, Papa."

"Say it any way you like but it was my money, Isabelle."

"Yes, dear Papa. But now it is *my* money. I could sell the shares, couldn't
I?"

Carboy gave this suggestion a few moments of unwilling and awkward
thought. "I suppose you could. But you wouldn't, of course."

"What's more," she persisted, "I could vote the shares. I never have, because you prefer to have proxies handy for any emergency. But I *could*.
Why, Papa, I could even vote against you."

"Just try it, my girl!" growled Carboy.

There was a moment's silence. Samuel the Younger had not felt disposed
to enter the conversation but he had been watching his handsome aunt with
the fascinated interest which can be aroused by the spectacle of a cheetah
creeping through the underbrush. He waited anxiously for her next word.

"As I am your largest shareholder," said Isabelle when the silence had
been maintained for exactly the right space of time, "I desire to say again
that I'm entitled to hear about this mighty Plan."

"If you have no objection, Grandfather," said the homecomer, "I'll be
quite happy to explain what I have in mind."

"Go ahead," said Carboy, reaching for the decanter.

Samuel proceeded to outline his plan to extend Carboy and Co. into a world-wide concern. He talked well, so very well, in fact, that Isabelle had to concede to herself that she had never heard better advocacy. The Plan took form as he talked and he made the future glow with prismatic effect.

Isabelle asked a few questions which were readily and satisfactorily answered. Then a silence fell on the room. The advocate of the plan, watching his female relative with intense interest, knew what position she intended to take.

"I am against it," she said finally.

"Why?" demanded the old man. "I find myself strongly disposed to favor it, and I'm not easy to convince. One final play, the most daring of all, before I die!"

"That's why I'm against it, Papa. You are getting close to ninety years old."

"Am I showing any signs of old age?"

"None yet, as far as your mind is concerned. But what of next year? What of the year after that? What of all the years while this big combine is being built up?"

"If I should die," grumbled her father, not relishing any hint of the approaching end, "there's Sammy here to carry on. Are you discounting him after his remarkable record in South Africa? Tell her what you've got down there. And all on your own efforts."

"I had a gold mine," said the homecomer. "A trading and importing house with six large branches. A clothing mill, a hat factory and half a dozen smaller concerns. I had a controlling interest in a bank and I owned twenty-eight thousand acres of land. I've sold some of it but I still hold the mine, the trading company and the control of the bank. What I got out of the factories and land is in cash."

The old man said in an accusatory tone to his daughter, "No one has ever done as well as that in such a short time."

Isabelle nodded her head calmly. "Quite true. But has your grandson that extra quality which made you what you are, Papa? I'm going to repeat what a friend of yours said once, 'Samuel Carboy has every quality you'll find in any leader in trade, plus an infallibility of judgment which makes him a genius.' That, Papa, was said by Jonathan Bade. It was his opinion that only two other men ever possessed it. One was a Frenchman. Jonathan called him the Great Moneyman. The other was a banker in Vienna named Fugger." She turned and looked straight into the eyes of the grandson. "How sure of yourself are you? Do you think this great quality will be found twice in one family?"

For the first time Samuel the Younger showed traces of feeling. He flushed resentfully. "I made no mistakes in judgment in my twenty-five years abroad," he declared.

"But are you prepared to build this empire you talk about step by step as Father did? And as you probably did yourself?"

"How much of it would I live to see if we did it piecemeal?" demanded her father. "I'll have you know, my girl, that we have the resources and the will to do things on a large scale."

"I see you've been listening to your grandson, Papa. I've never heard you talk like this before."

Another silence fell on the room. Samuel the Younger began to gather up the papers which were spread out on the table. He worked slowly and did not look again at Isabelle.

"See here, my girl," said the old man. "There's no need for you to get so excited. Nothing has been decided. Sammy and I will look at this thing from every angle before we invest as much as a shilling."

She said in an ominously quiet voice, "I don't want a shilling of my money invested in it."

"Your money!" cried Carboy in a sudden rage. "Must I remind you again that I gave it to you? I was generous enough to allow you the use of it right away, instead of making you wait for my death. Am I to be penalized for my kindness? Is this the way you are going to repay me?"

Isabelle got to her feet. "If you decide to go into this I'll fight you. I'm giving you advance warning, Papa. I'll take it to court if necessary."

## CHAPTER SIX

### 1

Perhaps it had snowed more heavily in the vicinity of Outland Park than elsewhere. Allie and his passenger had breakfasted sumptuously at seven o'clock on chops and sausage and kedgeree. They had been under way by eight. It had been a difficult trip, because of the snow. The hoofs of the horses kicked it up in feathery clouds and the wheels dragged and groaned at being forced to churn through the drifts on the road. It was nearly noon when they reached their destination, and a leaden sky still carried the threat of more storm.

The windows of the gatehouse were blank and it was clear that no ruddy-faced custodian had stood guard at the wrought-iron gates for many a long day. Nevertheless Allie broke into loud praise as he turned the horses into the drive which was as white as the fields of the Park.

"I love all of this!" he exclaimed. "The snow and the great estates and the fine stone houses. I love the men you see in the pubs in their funny smocks. I love my grandfather and my beautiful aunt Isabelle."

"Young flatterer!" said Isabelle, who was snuggled down under the rugs so that little could be seen of her but her eyes.

"And I think I love that pretty Irish girl at Miss Groody's."

Isabelle sat up very straight at once and gave him a sharp and reproving look. "Just because your name is Allie Carboy," she said, "you don't have to fall in love with some girl whose name happens to be Nell Groody. We had enough of that the first time. Just keep a cool head, Allie, and I'll produce plenty of girls of the right sort for you."

"She's different from any I've ever seen," he asserted stoutly. "And she's nicer."

Outland Hall, when they came within sight of it, looked like a picture of the last house on earth after the last man had died. There wasn't a footmark in the snow, not as much as a rabbit track. Silence brooded over the place and not even the raucous note of a crow greeted them from the woods. Curtains were drawn over all the windows and, if any eyes looked out through them, they were undoubtedly ghostly eyes.

"Has it been closed up for the winter?" asked Isabelle in a tone of distress.

"No," said Allie suddenly. "I can see the faintest trace of smoke above one of the chimneys."

So they hallooed loudly and were rewarded by the appearance of a man muffled up to his eyes in something knitted of red wool. He took the horses in tow.

"Better walk right in, sir and ma'am," he advised, his breath freezing into a nimbus about his head. "They don't seem to hear the bells any more."

So they walked in and found the Duke of Outland huddled over a fire in the hall, with a newspaper in his hands and piles of other papers on the floor about him. He got to his feet and stared at them as though he could not believe his eyes.

"Issy!" he cried. "What a dashed wonderful surprise! I didn't think anyone would venture out on such a monstrously bad day as this. You are looking toppish, my love. But then you always do."

He was not looking toppish himself. It seemed that he had been shrinking with the years. His eyes, which had always been large and bold, looked still larger now in a face which had not retained its fine round pattern. It had to be conceded also that his trousers were decidedly on the baggy side.

"I came over with news, Chip," said Isabelle. The number of the periodicals surprised her because he had never been a reader. "Whatever are you doing with all those papers?"

"I read 'em," declared the duke. "It's got to be a kind of hobby with me. I get 'em from all over. Old or new, it doesn't matter. It fills in the time now that I've given up riding."

"Given up riding!" cried Isabelle, with as much horror in her voice as if he had said he was giving up breathing. "You can't. I won't hear of it."

"It's all a matter of blunt, brass, oof—whatever you prefer to call the wonderful stuff. I've none of it. The mumpers came around last night and took every shilling I had left."

"Chip!" cried Isabelle. "Have you gone insane? You hand money to those cadgers and don't keep enough to pay your butcher. Have you any food in the house?"

"Very little," he said cheerfully. "Things are right back where they were when Old Sheppy was alive. Amy didn't leave me anything. Hadn't anything to leave, poor soul, out of all that fortune. I went through it. And now, as a punishment, I have to pig along the best way I can. Did you say you bring news? Is it good? All the news I ever get is bad. Has the Sawney come to his senses at last?"

Isabelle said to Allie, who had been looking with proper awe at the high pillars of the hall and the marble ceiling: "Wouldn't you like to go around and see everything?"

"Yes, Aunt Isabelle. It's a—a remarkable place, isn't it?"

"Keep bundled up," advised the peer. "The wonderful place is full of the most abominable drafts. It's a good deal like a tomb but somewhat less cheerful."

When the boy had started off on his solitary tour of inspection, Isabelle looked up at Chip with a sober expression. "Yes," she said, "he's come to his senses at last."

"You mean—Isabelle, is he dead?"

"Perhaps. Just as I was leaving, I received a letter from Margot, his daughter. She said he had been given up by the doctors and couldn't last until Christmas. It was a very stiff note; she hated me almost from the first. I wasn't asked to go up. In fact she made it very plain that they didn't want me. Perhaps I did wrong, Chip, but I didn't say anything about this to the guests I brought down to Beaulaw Hall. There was nothing for me to do, and I didn't want to put a damper on the festivities."

"Quite right. Issy, should I do the decent thing and express my regrets? I don't feel any. He didn't do the right thing for you and I've hated him for years. I'm sure if I had ever seen the fellow I'd have hated him more." Suddenly, feeling the first full impact of her news, his face lighted up. He placed both hands on her waist and raised her above his head. "Issy, Issy, this means we can get married at last. Damme, I'm glad I stuck to my guns and fended all those wealthy widows off. I could have had my pick but it was you I wanted, my girl." Wrapping one arm around her waist, he lowered her slowly to the floor, kissing her resoundingly when her face was on a level with his and then giving her an enthusiastic slap with his free hand.

She stamped her foot when she was free. "How dare you! Do you think I'll allow such liberties?"

"Come, Issy!" he said cheerfully. "I've wanted to do that for thirty-five years."

"I suppose you've slapped others in that vulgar way."

"Thousands of 'em," he acknowledged with a broad grin. "But I've never found it so pleasant before."

"And another thing," said Isabelle with a hint of sharpness in her voice, "I will not be called Issy. It's vulgar. It makes me feel I ought to be behind a bar with a wet cloth in my hand. I'll thank you, Your Grace of Outland, to call me Isabelle."

He had now become very happy and with a tendency toward noisiness. "Isabelle it is. From now on. How soon can it be? Next week? Next month? When?"

"Is this a proposal?"

"Of course it is. I've been proposing to you all my life, haven't I? I must have popped the question a dozen times at least."

"But it never counted before. Either you were married or I was. If you ask me now, I can take you up on it, you know. You had better consider carefully before you say another word."

"Do you remember the time I proposed to you first?" There was a sentimental tear in the corner of each of his eyes. "It was back there in the first sitting room. Old Sheppy was feeding us corned beef sandwiches and you were pretending to like them. I was about fifteen and I was furious because you were going to marry Tib and I was too young to do anything about it. Well, it's been a long haul, my love, but at last that stubborn Sawney is throwing in the sponge and I'm going to have you." He came to a sudden stop. A comic expression of doubt took possession of his face. "You haven't changed your mind, have you? Good gad, have you?"

They were standing so close together that Isabelle was able to reach up and give his cheek a light pat. "I've always wanted to marry a duke," she said, "and you seem the only one available. I think I'll take you, Chip."

"Whoosh!" cried the peer. "Three cheers! Hurrah! A tiger, as the Americans say! There's going to be no tiffling this time. Isabelle is going to marry me at last!" He repeated the performance of a few minutes before, raising her up in the air, kissing her as she passed on her way down and ending up by making her the recipient of another sound slap. "No objections, if you please, Your Grace. You belong to me now, you know."

Isabelle did not raise a single objection. She looked at him and smiled. "*Your Grace!* Those words have a sweet and wonderful sound. I'm going to enjoy hearing them for the rest of my life, Chip."

2

"And now," said Isabelle, "is there a servant in the house? We need some good rousing fires built."

"There's a man and a girl somewhere," answered Chip vaguely. "They're probably a quarter mile away. In the kitchens or the stillroom or the scullery. They probably have a good fire for themselves. They always look so rosy and comfortable when they happen to hear the bell and come to see about it."

"Let's ring bells until they come," suggested Isabelle with a shudder. "I'm going to take you out of here for Christmas, Chip, because you might die of pneumonia. And I must make a tour of inspection of this snug little home of yours. You see, I have plans. I have a great deal of income, all my own, and I'm willing to spend every farthing of it on reviving the glories of Outland Park."

"Horses?" asked the peer hopefully.

"Of course. But no betting on them. Unless I do the picking. I'm lucky."

She paused and fell into a reflective mood. "We won't throw the money away. We'll make every coin count. You see, Chip, I'm going to be the greatest hostess of the day." Her eyes began to fill with enthusiasm. "Outland Park is going to swarm with guests. Titles, wealth, coats covered with orders, uniforms, cabinet members with dispatch cases, all the beauty and chivalry of the empire. It will be an honor to be seen here."

"Good girl, Issy—I mean Isabelle. This is going to be a great lark."

"Yes," she answered. "We're going to enjoy it. But make no mistake, Your Grace of Outland, it's going to be war to the hilt at the same time."

Allie turned up a moment later with a red nose and an air of bewilderment. "I got lost twice," he said. "Please, sir, how many rooms do you have here?"

The duke pondered the question. "My boy," he said, "I don't know. I don't believe anyone has ever known. They never were counted, not even by the builder fellows. They were so busy adding on wings and running up towers and leaving spaces for silly quadrangles that they didn't have any time for counting. Even Old Sheppy built on something in his day; and he never counted them! I haven't even added a root house. A lot of silly swank, it always seemed to me."

"Swank?" said Isabelle in a happy tone of voice. "My dear, innocent, unsuspecting Chip! You have no conception of the swank we're going to put on here now that——" She looked at Allie and stopped. "We'll go into that later."

Isabelle then led the pair of them on a quick tour of inspection. They went from one end of the vast pile to the other. Allie began to count rooms but gave up at a hundred. Isabelle took a long-handled bed warmer and dislodged an indignant bird from the top of the tester bed in the Queen Elizabeth room. She looked at the kitchens and shuddered. She shuddered again when they found that a broken pane of glass had allowed snow to drift over the carpet in the library. She was awed, however, by the magnificent proportions of the Great Hall and by the long series of reception rooms and studies and strawberry parlors and such.

"It will take a regimental band to provide the music when these rooms are filled with guests," she said.

Furniture seems to thrive in cold and ancient houses, so the fine things that the Outland dukes had collected about them in more prosperous days were in remarkably good condition. The carpets and the hangings, however, were so old and worn that Isabelle fell into a shocked state of mind when she strove to calculate the cost of replacements.

They came back to the entrance hall where the manservant had succeeded in building the fire into a roaring fine blaze.

"Can you give us lunch?" asked Isabelle.

"I think there's the remains of a meat pie somewhere but I mustn't promise. We rather cleaned things out for the mumpers last night. Of course, there's plenty of bread and some cheese. Or," doubtfully, "is there? They jolly well waded into things. Still there's a good bottle of wine, I'm sure."

"That will help. Let's have it right here in front of the fire. Then we'll take you with us and be on our way before it begins to snow again. I'll be much obliged, Chip, if you and Master Allie will get started on some absorbing male talk without dragging me into it. My mind is filled with figures and calculations and plans."

"Before you get too preoccupied, I've something to show you," said the duke.

They sat down in front of the fire and Isabelle raised her skirts almost an inch to get the benefit of it. The peer produced a letter which he had been carrying in his pocket for days apparently. It looked a little yellow and dog-eared.

"Did you ever see inside Outland House?" he asked.

Isabelle shook her head. "I was a small girl when it happened. I wanted to go and see it the day after all the shooting occurred but Mama put her foot down. About all I can remember of Mama was the way she used to put her foot down every time I wanted to do anything. Allie—your grandfather, my boy—couldn't do anything wrong in her eyes. I couldn't do anything right."

"I saw it," said Chip eagerly. "The day after the shooting."

Isabelle turned and stared at him with fully aroused interest. "How exciting! Tell us about it."

"Well, I walked over to Grosvenor Square—I couldn't have been more than nine years old—and there were two police officers keeping an eye on things and chivvying the people off the premises, particularly boys. 'Stand back, boy,' said one of them to me, 'or you'll feel this club across your rear acres.' 'My grandfather owned this place,' I said to him. 'He's the Duke of Outland.' 'Is that so,' says the officer, in a different tone of voice entirely. 'Then you're the one they call Young Chip.' 'Yes, sir,' I said, 'I'm Young Chip.' So he told the rest of the crowd to jolly well stand back and he let me in. He even went along to make sure I didn't miss anything. I saw the bullet holes in the walls and the windows and doors."

"Were there many holes?"

"Dozens of them. A big chandelier had been hit and the broken crystals were all over the floor. The fourth duke, who was hanging over a fireplace, had one eye drilled out. It improved his looks, I thought. I saw the little room where Hark Chaffery blew his brains out."

"Was there any blood on the floor?"

"All over the place. And I saw the spot where the Frenchwoman was killed. The officer said she was a thorough bad one and had made a practice of poisoning husbands."

"It must have been exciting, Chip."

"I had bad dreams for weeks after. But it was worth it."

"Who was Hark Chaffery?" asked Allie. Having lived so far away, he knew nothing of the great men in the past of the metropolis.

"The king of the crooks in London," answered the duke. "He was an amazing chap. Had 'em all working in harness and bringing the take in to him. The most popular game among boys for a long time after was called Outland House and all of them wanted to play the part of Hark Chaffery." He paused before adding, "He bought the house from my grandfather."

"Every time I see the place I feel sorry for it," said Isabelle. "It looks ashamed of itself, standing there so shabby among all the great houses. It's nearly always empty and it always needs paint. It can't live down its past."

"The letter," said the duke, "is from a man who sells property. He offers me a chance to buy the place. I had a good laugh when I read it."

"Let me see the letter," said Isabelle. Her interest had been suddenly aroused.

She read it carefully and then gave her future husband a steady and calculating look.

"Chip," she said, "at the figure he quotes, it would be the biggest bargain in all London."

The peer gave his head a shake. "But no one will buy it, even at that price. It's been sold half a dozen times, with the figure dropping always. The people on the square have snubbed all of the owners and made them pretty miserable. And think how much it would cost for repairs."

"The people of the square wouldn't snub the family who built the house and lived in it for generations until Old Sheppy had to get rid of it. The price is too high for anyone else. It's a great bargain for you, Chip."

The impoverished peer looked at her with an uncertain frown. Then, slowly, the truth began to dawn on him. "Good gad, yes! The Duke of Outland will be welcomed back. And it didn't occur to me at once that"—with a cautious glance in Allie's direction—"that there's going to be unexpected funds in the family."

"Let me keep the letter, Chip," said Isabelle. "When I return to London, I'll drop in and see this man. I'll bring him down on the price. You can be sure of that."

The duke looked as though he wanted to break into cheers again. "You know, it'll be grand to spend the season in the old town. Ah, to stroll in the square, to go to my club for lunch, to take in the theaters, to go to parties in an honest silk hat and a proper frock coat!" Then he nodded to her. "This means I can give up newspapers. I'll have no time for reading."

## CHAPTER SEVEN

### 1

Jonathan Bade had his offices on a narrow street within a stone's throw of Lincoln's Inn. There was a brass sign in front which shone with a hint of prosperity and there were clean curtains in the one window. Inside there was a narrow hall and a good-sized room containing a long flat-topped desk for his own use and a smaller one at which sat an assistant who combined the duties of clerk and bookkeeper. There was another room behind this, to which no doubt the assistant would betake himself when clients came in to discuss their private affairs. From the second room came a steady thumping, as though someone was hitting a metallic surface with a hammer.

There was nothing Scroogelike in the size of the fire when Isabelle paid a visit there immediately after Boxing Day. It was burning so well that all parts of the room were comfortably warm. She took a chair on the other side of the desk and placed her muff on the surface in front of her. She was wearing mourning.

"This is the third time you've seen me in weeds, Jonathan," she said. "And now I'm going to be married again."

He looked downcast at this, as though he had hoped she was through with matrimony for all time. It was not that he entertained a vision of presenting a winning case in the court of her favor with himself as client. But he might see more of her unmarried and that would mean much pleasure.

"May I venture a guess as to the lucky man?" he asked. When she nodded, he said, "The Duke of Outland."

"Yes, it's Chip. We must wait awhile, of course. Everyone knows that my husband and I had been separated for years but it's best to observe the proprieties. The marriage will take place, I think, in midsummer."

"I was responsible for your marriage to the marquis," said Jonathan. "At any rate I threw you together. I regret that it turned out so badly."

"He wasn't happy away from Kilmorlie and I couldn't be happy there. Well, it's over now and I'm inclined to think I'll get along well with Chip." She smiled. "He's been my perennial suitor."

"You're going to attain your great ambition, Your Grace. I can remember when you announced your purpose. It was in the Tontine offices and you swore that you would never consider anyone under the rank of duke. You were most deadly earnest about it."

"What I've come about is to ask you to take things in hand for me in connection with my late husband's estates. You've always seen me through my widowhoods so easily and successfully." She paused. "I'm sure I'll do badly in the will and that we'll have to fight for my rights."

It was clear that he was surprised. "I thought, my dear Isabelle, that you had put yourself in the hands of Smythe, Boongrace and Curdle."

"I may be on the other side of the fence from them. You see, I'm at odds with Papa and likely to remain so. In spite of my warning him against it, he's decided to support his grandson in a plan to carry on the Carboy operations all over the globe. I want to talk to you about that too."

She told him then of the Plan and the efforts she had made to keep her father from participating in it. "Every shilling I possess is invested with Papa," she added. "If they went smash I'd be a pauper. I consider it a crime to gamble like this when things are going so smoothly. Can't I sue for an injunction to prevent Papa from doing it?"

Jonathan gave the question considerable thought, drumming on the desk with his knuckles and looking across the room with partly closed lids. "A shareholder can always ask protection of the courts," he said finally. "Provided mismanagement can be proven or some doubt established as to the ability or probity of the corporation heads. I've been studying the statements of Carboy and Co. and there's no handle for you there. It's as sound and strong as the Rock of Gibraltar. Do you want to go into court in an effort to prove your father incapable of continuing at the head?"

"He's close to ninety years old. And if anything happens to him we'll have to depend on the grandson. How can we be sure he has the capacity to handle a world-wide corporation?"

"He scored a spectacular success in South Africa, making himself a millionaire several times over by his own unaided efforts. Could the court be convinced that he lacks the strength for such a great effort?" Jonathan gave his head a negative shake. "I'm afraid you couldn't make out much of a case. What you should do is to sell a good part of your holding in the Carboy interests. It's a great mistake to have all your eggs in one basket under any circumstances. My advice would be to sell two thirds of what you hold and invest in other directions. You must not leave yourself in a position to lose everything."

"But that's impossible!" she exclaimed. "I need the income. Every shilling of it. If I sell my shares and put the money into consols, my income will shrink to a third. No, I must hold my shares and that is why I'm so disturbed over what Papa is doing."

Jonathan made a frowning calculation on a sheet of paper. "I don't understand this, Isabelle. You're a very wealthy woman and your income is enormous. Why do you think you can't get along with a lower return from some part of your holdings? You would still be able to live like a queen. Or a duchess, if you prefer that."

"I must put Outland Park into proper condition and the cost of renovations will be staggering," she said, making it clear that she resented the need of explanations. "I'm providing the money to buy back Outland House on Grosvenor Square. It's being offered at a low figure but it will have to be renovated from top to bottom. We intend to entertain at both places on an elaborate scale. I tell you, Jonathan, I'm going to need every shilling of my present income."

"There are other companies which pay high returns."

"But none as high as Carboy and Co."

Jonathan allowed a note of urgency, even of exasperation, to show in his voice. "Isabelle! You can't have your cake and eat it. You must take some of those golden eggs out of the one basket. You should have done it long ago. It's plain common sense. You *can't* risk losing everything."

"Oh, I don't know what to do!" Isabelle was almost at the point of tears. "I know exactly how much all this is going to cost me and I can't see any way of reducing it. Everything must be done right. I will *not* consider drawing on my principal. It must be paid out of income; and so I can't sell a single share in Carboy's. I tell you, it's impossible."

"Since you've done me the honor of consulting me, I feel a real sense of responsibility. I implore you to curtail these ambitious social plans. Curtail them enough, at any rate, to make it possible for you to sell some of your shares and invest elsewhere."

"How much can I anticipate from my share in the Tontine?"

"It's still a mere bagatelle, as far as you are concerned. Last year the amount paid was about six hundred pounds. There will be an increase each year, of course. If you are anxious to know how things stand, we could drop in and consult them. It happens that the Tontine offices are just around the corner."

The metallic thumping from the inner office had come to an abrupt end. A young man with a mop of red hair stuck his head through the door.

"Mr. Bade, sir," he said. "It won't run. It's gone and got itself broke again."

"What's wrong this time?"

"Mr. Bade, sir, I don't rightly know. It just stopped. I think it's pure stubbornness, sir. It acts just like a pig at a gate."

"Send to Bradden Brothers and tell them what's happened. They must get a man down at once to repair the machine.

"It's one of those letter writers," explained Jonathan when the assistant had drawn his head back into the rear office. "It isn't very practical yet because it's always doing this and you can only write in capital letters with it. Still, it's fast for copying, and that's why I keep it. I suppose in ten years they'll have it so improved that all correspondence will be done on machines." He looked inquiringly at his client. "I presume Carboy and Co. own the concern making these Pratt machines?"

Isabelle shook her head. "You ought to remember that Papa doesn't believe in taking a risk on the initial patents. He buys in subsidiary patents, the ones which make money from the start. He owns some which have to be used in making any kind of writing machine. I heard him say one of our companies makes the keys."

Jonathan sat in deep thought for several moments. "Isabelle," he said, "I'm deeply concerned over your situation. I must have some days to think it over so I can give you the best advice—and then convince you it *is* the best. This much I'll tell you now: put the idea of a suit out of your head; you would get no good out of it and you would create enmity in the family." He got to his feet, and struggled into a long topcoat. Taking down a fur hat from a peg behind him, he nodded to Isabelle. "And now let's drop in at the Tontine offices and talk to them there."

It was a sunny as well as a cold afternoon and Jonathan paused to look about him as they emerged on the street. The thoroughfare to the north was a busy one at this hour. Hansom cabs and four-wheelers rolled by endlessly, twisting and weaving in and out around the slower and more stately victorias and private coaches, the cheerful cries of the drivers filling the air. This was the London he loved, busy, noisy, exuberant, bobbish.

"The eternal clack-clacking of that machine in my office," he said to his companion, "has filled me with disturbing thoughts. Can you conceive of London without hansom cabs? Of course you can't; it would seem unfriendly and alien without those odd, tipsy things with the driver's head up in the clouds. And yet we'll come to it, just as we're coming to writing letters by machinery. The horse will vanish in time from the streets of London.

"There's no denying," he went on, "that the hansom is a contradictory affair. This is the age of the chaperone but there's no room for a chaperone in one of them. In fact it's a bit snug for two. I suppose you've ridden in them, even if you do have your own carriage."

"Of course I've ridden in them," said Isabelle. "Yes, they are quite snug. That's considered the best thing about them. I'm in no position to judge; I've only ridden in them with husbands, you see."

Jonathan sighed. "Some of the savor of life in London will be lost when we have no horses on the streets. The horseless carriage—that's what we'll come to—will be faster but still a poor substitute."

Perhaps this is a good place to record the fact that Jonathan Bade was looking his years. No one seemed to know exactly how old he was but there was no question that he was somewhere late in the seventies. He had grown thinner. His features had always had something of the hawk about them and now they had sharpened. He looked like a prophet from Holy Writ; a prophet who had fallen foul of despotic law and been branded ferociously.

He was doing little public speaking, although huge crowds turned out whenever he made an appearance.

"I'm going on to my little mission when we get through with the Tontine people," he said. "Would you care to walk over with me and see what goes on there?"

But Isabelle thought not. Her mind was too full of other things. Someday, she said, she must give him a donation for the mission. "But not now," she added hastily. "I can't spare a shilling."

2

As they approached the entrance to the Tontine offices, the door opened and a man came out with such abruptness that Isabelle had to step aside to avoid being shouldered into the gutter. He was tall and wore a long coat buttoned up tightly under a pair of most luxuriant gray whiskers.

"I think I've seen that man before," said Jonathan, staring angrily at the receding back of the stranger.

"It's Sir Seymour Grim," said Isabelle. "I danced with him once. At Beaufort House, I think. It was several years ago. He held me so tight in a waltz that I had to breathe through his whiskers."

"I wonder what he was doing in there."

They found out immediately on their entry. The manager nodded to Jonathan and asked, "Did you see that old dandy who just went out in a great huff? He's one of the shareholders and he gives me more trouble than all the rest put together."

"I have brought you a shareholder who has never given you any trouble at all," said Jonathan. "The Marchioness of Invermark. Your ladyship, this is Mr. Baird, who is our manager."

The manager bowed almost to his waist and began to stammer in his surprise. "Ha-happy to be of—of service to your ladyship. Great honor, I'm sure. What does your ladyship desire to know?"

"I would like to know what I am to receive on the next payment."

He fished nervously under a pile of papers on his desk and brought out a slip of paper. "As of the present moment, seven hundred and forty-eight pund, six shillings, your ladyship. It will be more than that when payment day comes. Some are certain to kick—well, er, pass away in the meantime."

"I hoped the increase over last year would be larger," commented Isabelle.

"Well," said the manager in an attempt at lightness, "it's this way. We can't hurry them along, much as we might—ha! ha!—like to do it. We've got nothing but the tough old birds left now—the gouts, you know, and the livers, and the ones too mean to die." He stopped with a horrified look on his face. "I *do* beg your pardon, your ladyship. Didn't mean it that way at all. Don't know what gets into me, saying such things."

"I'm sure what you meant to say, Mr. Baird," declared Jonathan, coming to his assistance, "is that those who live this long are likely to live longer."

"Exactly, Mr. Bade, that's what I meant."

"I'm sure also that your reference to the way they manage to survive their ailments is quite true. But in all respects you realize that her ladyship is the beautiful exception to prove the rule, and that she is going to live most gracefully to a very ripe old age and enjoy a very large income from this office."

"That's it, Mr. Bade! I've got my twenty quid up at even money on her ladyship. I'm backing her through thick and thin. Let 'em bring on their butchers and their musicians, I still say it's her ladyship against the field. And now that I've seen her, I'm disposed to give odds."

"I'm sure it's very kind of you," said Isabelle. "Do you recommend a diet of oats for me? And a gallop every morning at four o'clock with clockers on the rail? This has been most educational, Mr. Baird."

"It's been a surprise," interjected Jonathan, "to find that Sir Seymour Grim has a share."

The manager frowned. "His father, old Sir Bodley Grim, put his three sons in. The other two went early. This one's supposed to be a wealthy man but I know some things about him. Wisselthorpe Grange is mortgaged to the hilt and there's a tenant in with a ten-year lease. Sir Seymour's supposed to live at Claridge's but he has a single room nearby and pays the clerk two shillings a week to accept mail for him at the hotel. He spends most of his time here, trying to badger me into giving him advances against the next payment.

"Would you believe it, your ladyship and Mr. Bade," he went on, "that, out of the forty-odd still in the race, only six are independent? The rest depend on the money we send 'em. They're always up to tricks to get loans on their prospects. I spoke of butchers, though it goes against the grain. The butcher we've got has sold a half interest in his chance to be the last for two hundred pounds a year. He's sold his business and lives on the fat of the land. He never misses his ten quarts of ale a day, and thrives on it.

"If anyone drops off before the date of a payment, they lose their share for that year, and it's my guess that some banks are going to be caught one of these days. They're making loans and charging a high rate of interest."

He was warming to his subject. Isabelle, interested in spite of her desire to be along about other matters, helped herself to a chair and sat down to listen.

"The last one to slip off the roost," said Mr. Baird, "was a widow in the north country. It's an odd thing but nearly all of our survivors are women, your ladyship; at least thirty-five of the forty-odd. The relatives of this one were so angry because she dropped off that none of 'em went to her funeral. They've put in a claim for this year's money although she only lived three months into it. There's another one up there still—a widow also and a tartar if there ever was one. She sold her place years ago and goes around visiting relatives, and telling each one to expect an especially generous cut of what she leaves when she gets the boot. She takes a carriage and pair, a coachman, two dogs and a cat with her, and demands the best of everything. I happen to know she's made a will, cutting them all off. It's just a little trick with which she amuses herself in her old age. She's a contender, that one; as tough and bony as a stewing hen."

Jonathan had been conscious of a lack in the office and now he realized what it was. The stool in the corner was empty.

"What's wrong?" he asked, inclining his head in the direction of the bookkeeper's desk. "He's never been away before to my knowledge."

"You mean Old Scratchy? Perhaps he's away for good, Mr. Bade. On Christmas Eve—he always worked right up to seven o'clock, you know—he closed the ledger, wiped the pen, sighed once, and fell right off the stool, hitting the floor with a thump. He didn't get conscious for two days and all he does now is hobble around. Part of him seems paralyzed."

"Apoplexy," said Jonathan.

"That's what the doctors say."

"I'm sorry to hear it. It doesn't seem right here without him. I always associate this office with the sound of his pen, going scratch, scratch, scratch, over the pages of the ledger."

The manager shook his head solemnly. "It's an odd thing but he almost got into this himself. This class of the Tontine, I mean. His father was a coal merchant in a small way. So small he knew he wouldn't have much to leave. So he went around to all his friends and customers, scraping up money to put his son in. He got ninety guineas but couldn't get his hands on another shilling. He tried to convince them it would be safe to accept the ninety and put the ten on the slate. They said, No, one hundred or nothing.

So all Scratchy got out of it was a post on the staff. It must have cut him a bit to think when he sends out the checks that one might have been going to him. Fate does odd things, your ladyship, odd indeed."

### 3

Isabelle had been right in anticipating trouble over the will of her late husband. He had left her practically nothing and a suit was pending which promised to be bitter and hard-fought. Until the will could be probated, she remained in stubborn possession of the London house, which stood, rather small and unpretentious but substantial, on a corner just off Berkeley Square.

Early in the afternoon of a very blustery day a young man approached this corner. He had a good head, with plenty of black hair and a pale face in which intensely dark eyes hinted at deep and bitter feelings. Perhaps his feelings had to do with the surroundings in which he found himself, for he looked about, with what seemed like hostility, at the tall houses which bespoke wealth and privilege and luxury. Reaching the number he sought, he gave the bell a vigorous pull. His eyes seemed charged with even deeper feeling when a very tall footman in a livery of black velvet with gold facings opened the door.

"I am here to see the Marchioness of Invermark," said this rather disquieting young man. "By appointment."

"Who shall I say?" asked the footman.

"Mr. Fawkes. Alexander Fawkes."

Shown into the small sitting room on the ground floor which Isabelle used as an office, Alexander Fawkes bowed briefly and somberly, and said, "I received your letter and have come in response."

Isabelle shook hands with him and regretted it. His palm was soft and somewhat moist.

"Yes, Mr."—she found it necessary to glance at a note on the table to refresh her memory—"Mr. Fawkes. It is good of you to come."

"I'm sure," he said, "you are wondering about my name. I am, it so happens, a descendant. Yes, ma'am, a descendant of the traitor, Guy Fawkes; by the left hand, as far as we can tell. May I add that, although I have no sympathy with those who believe in tearing down governments by force, I am not ashamed of my lineage."

Isabelle looked at him in puzzled dismay. She was finding him very strange and disturbing. For a moment she wondered if she had addressed her letter to the wrong man.

"You are a partner in the firm of Smythe, Boongrace and Curdle?"

The unpleasant young man bowed in assent. However, he added in amendment, "A junior partner."

"May I ask if you are—entirely contented with your arrangements there?"

"Ma'am, junior partners are never contented."

"Mr.—Mr. Fawkes, I am in need of some special assistance. Of a legal nature. I made inquiries in certain quarters and your name was given me. I value the opinions of my informants but I am beginning to wonder if you are the kind of lawyer I need. May I ask you some questions?"

"Assuredly, ma'am."

"You began as a practicing lawyer with your own office. In Norwich, I believe."

"In Norwich. I hung out my shingle there."

"There was some difficulty, I believe, which led to the shingle being taken down."

"I left Norwich under a cloud," declared the visitor with a willingness which surprised his questioner. "I may tell you, however, that the situation which made it necessary for me to leave—or shall we say, advisable?—had nothing to do with my ability or my conduct as a lawyer."

"I was told that." Isabelle was becoming more doubtful with every word exchanged. There was a brooding look in his eyes which made her uncomfortable. She decided, in spite of this, to proceed with her questioning. "You next came into notice in a town in the north where you secured the acquittal of a man charged with murder. It seems to have been a sensational trial. I read about it in the newspapers at the time with great interest and I was surprised at the verdict. I understand that your conduct of the case brought you to the attention of the firm with which you are now connected."

"Yes, that is so."

She had seated herself behind her desk and he had taken a chair on the other side of it. She studied him with a questioning frown.

"Would you be interested," she asked finally, "in undertaking a service quite apart from the work you do at the office? For a suitable fee?"

"I'm not supposed to. But—I am badly in need of money, ma'am."

"I believe you are not married."

"Your information is correct. I have no wife. As I have the habit of speaking with frankness, I may tell you that I don't approve of the institution of matrimony."

"I'm beginning to think, young man, that there are many things of which you don't approve."

"Many things, ma'am."

"Perhaps you don't believe in wealth."

"That above all else, ma'am."

"But you are willing enough, I judge, to accept as much as you can get your hands on for yourself."

"Quite. When I see people with more wealth than they should have, I consider it a service to humanity to separate them from some of it."

"You *are* being frank, aren't you?" Nevertheless, she had made up her mind to tell him what she wanted. It was natural, she thought, that a man selected for the purpose would have qualities which she might find undesirable and even obnoxious. This young man, at any rate, had a curious degree of honesty.

"Let me come to the point," she said. "My father is planning to widen the scope of his interests. You know of this?"

"Naturally. It is, and will continue to be, the main preoccupation of the offices of my firm."

"I," she said, watching him closely, "am opposed to the plan. I feel it unwise to take the risks entailed. My father's companies are doing very handsomely as it is."

The visitor's expression at this point indicated that he thought the Carboy interests were doing very handsomely indeed.

"Your firm will continue to handle all the legal work for my father. What I want is to have someone—someone in the offices of Smythe, Boongrace and Curdle—who will look after *my* interests."

"Secretly, ma'am?"

"If it was known, you might not be able to act for me. I want to know——" She stopped and her eyes began to burn as much as his with the intensity of her feeling. "I want to know what is going on. They won't tell me. I'm a big shareholder and I'm entitled to know. I want to be in a position to judge of the success, or otherwise, of this great gamble they're taking. I want to know in time if things don't go well. It's maddening to be kept in the dark this way."

The junior partner had shifted his position in his chair so that he no longer faced her. She noticed that the cuffs of his coat were frayed. Apparently being a junior partner was not too remunerative.

"It could be done," he said. "I have heard of cases. But it must be done with great care."

He continued to stare at the opposite wall but Isabelle was watching his face with the closest absorption. She was beginning to believe that he was, after all, the man for the purpose. She decided on one more question.

"I'm still curious about that murder case. Most people thought your man was guilty. Did you think so?"

He nodded. "Oh, of course. I had no doubt of his guilt. But he had put his life in my hands and I did my best for him." He paused and then swung around in his chair to face her. "I got him off by the application of a theory. Would you care to hear what it is?"

"Yes." Her interest was really aroused now. "I would like to hear about it very much."

"I acted on the supposition that there were only thirteen people in the courtroom—the twelve jurors and myself. Whenever I questioned a witness, I got the eye of one juror and made him feel that I wanted him to understand, that it was a matter of the utmost importance for *him* to follow what I was doing. I took turns with them in that way. In my summing up, I addressed myself to each of them in turn. Before they left the box, there was a bond between me and each of the twelve." His eyes came around and fastened themselves on hers, as though she were a member of the panel. It was clear he possessed a power bordering on the hypnotic. "I am inclined to think they paid little attention to the strictures of the judge in his charge.

They seemed little concerned with the prisoner himself. Each of them felt that he knew something about the case which the others didn't understand and which was very important."

"I think you hypnotized them." She brought the conversation back to the question of her proposal. "There's more to what I want than I've told you yet. If anything happens which might give me a weapon to use——"

The lawyer gave his head a nod which had a touch of slyness about it. "I see. A case of Two-on-Ten."

Isabelle looked puzzled. "Two-on-Ten? I don't understand what you mean."

"It's a saying, ma'am. From the vulgar tongue, I'm afraid. It's short for Two Eyes on Ten Fingers. Do you see? It's used when there's need for watchfulness—such as occasions when a shopkeeper suspects there are thieves around. Forgive me for using the expression."

Isabelle hesitated. "Well, in a sense it does convey what I have in mind."

His mood became confident and brisk again. He nodded his head. "If they ever take steps which seem unlawful, you want to know about it."

"That is what I meant."

"To get you the kind of information you want, I would have to obtain access to confidential documents and correspondence. If I should try it and fail—well, it would be a very costly matter for me. You are asking me to risk my whole future in the profession. Would the reward be sufficiently large to justify taking such desperate risks?"

Isabelle produced an envelope and laid it on the table. "Payment would be made in bank notes," she said. "This would be in the nature of a retaining fee."

Alexander Fawkes had no hesitation in reaching for the envelope. He broke open the flap with an eager thumb and then began to count the contents. He counted slowly and deliberately. At the finish he looked up but kept one hand on top of the rather deep pile of notes.

"This convinces me that you are in earnest. I believe we can come to an arrangement. I warn you that I won't be easy to deal with. There is a serious flaw in my character, ma'am. I am covetous. Hating wealth in others, I am miserly as far as my own share is concerned. Ma'am, it comes down to this: I am ready to do what you wish."

HISTORY was repeating itself. It was a Thursday afternoon and the east drawing room in Miss Bordley's School for Young Ladies was in readiness for receiving, and already rather better than half full. Miss Bordley herself was studying one of the young male callers, who had just arrived, and trying to get him placed in her mind.

It must be explained at once that this was not the Miss Bordley who had suffered, on an occasion some half century before, the indignity of being kicked on the shins by Isabelle Carboy. That estimable lady had been in her grave for most of the years since. On her death the institution had been taken over by a company and it had been considered wise to retain the school name because of the well-earned pre-eminence it had attained. One of the new owners had then been struck by another thought: why not have the headmistresses assume for scholastic purposes the name of the founder? This had seemed to all of them a rather neat and ingenious idea and there had been since some six or seven Miss Bordleys. Whether or not this little stratagem had been in any degree responsible, the fact remained that the school had continued popular and profitable.

It may have been a part of the policy of the school also that headmistresses should be shortsighted; this latest incumbent was, at any rate. She looked at the card of the tall visitor and fumbled ineffectually for her eyeglasses.

"I'm sure everything is quite right and proper, young man," she said. "You—er—seem to have your card, so I assume you wrote me about it in the first place. But I don't seem to—er—recognize your name."

"It's Carboy, Miss Bordley," said the youth. "Alfred Carboy."

"Ah!" exclaimed the head of the school with a sudden unchaining of affability and acceptance. "You are Mr. Carboy. Of course. I received your letter and I was very happy indeed to send you the card. It's Nelly you desire to see. Our dear Nelly who comes from Ireland but who lives, I believe, with an aunt not far from that delightful city of Oxford. We had to strive to understand her at first but now she's a great favorite with everyone. I'm speaking of Nelly, of course, and not—ha-ha!—her aunt."

So Nelly came forward, wearing a charming frock which was not of magenta. This was most unusual. Ever since the Empress Eugénie in France (Louis Napoleon's beautiful young wife) had expressed her liking for that rather difficult color, English fashions had inclined to it almost to the exclusion of other shades. It might have been said, in fact, that the east drawing room had broken out into a magenta rash. Nelly's dress was a simple one

of sapphire blue which went well with her dark hair. It was conventional
enough, however, in all other respects. The skirt was looped up by a hidden
combination of cords and pulls so that a triangle of lighter blue underskirt
showed on each side. Instead of billowing out in all directions, as it would
have done in the days of the crinoline, Nelly's skirt was drawn back over
something which might be termed a juvenile version of the naughty bustle.
It looked very pretty and just sufficiently daring.

"Good afternoon, Miss Groody," said Allie, bowing. He was arrayed most
properly in a swallow-tailed coat with a deep velvet collar. His trousers were
quite tight and were strapped under his boots. His snowy cuffs were turned
back over the sleeves of his coat and he carried in one hand a cane with a
green tassel and a pair of yellow gloves.

"Good afternoon," responded Nelly, with a curtsy.

"It's a pleasure indeed to have you with us, Mr. Carboy," said the head-
mistress, turning toward the door, which had opened to admit more guests.
"I trust you and my sweet Nelly will have a pleasant tea together. You must
visit us again next term, Mr. Carboy, you must indeed."

They were escorted, and this comes under the heading of coincidence
without a doubt, to the same corner table where Julian Grace had taken tea
with Winifred Ballard so many years before. Tea was brought to them at
once, and a profusion of plates containing the very thinnest of sandwiches
and a bewildering array of buns and cakes and tartlets.

"Hallo, Irish," said Allie in a low tone of voice.

"Hallo, Afrikaner," she responded on the same cautious level of speech.

"Your Miss Bordley needn't have worried. I'm going to have a most pleasant tea with you. At least I'm going to have a most pleasant talk. Not light,
casual, silly talk, mind you. I'm too earnest a man for that kind of thing. I
shudder when I look at the weak, simpering faces of the youth surrounding
us here——"

"What's making you so earnest and serious all of a sudden?" asked Nelly.
"Is it because you have your position with Scanlon, Burns and Copbright?
There *is* a sort of business air about you. Have you made a million or two
already?"

Allie grinned at her. "I'm earning a salary of ten bob a week," he said.
"You can hardly say I've made a start on my career. But I'm learning a lot.
I'm sure I've done the right thing in beginning at the very bottom of the
ladder." He took a quick sip of tea and replaced the cup. "I am serious today
because I want to talk to you about a subject which is quite serious. In a
sense."

"In what kind of sense?" she asked.

"The matrimonial sense."

"You Carboys don't believe in losing any time, do you?" Nelly was remembering the story of the first Allie Carboy's courtship of her great-aunt.
Then she replaced the sandwich she had been on the point of raising to her
lips and looked at him with a sudden expression of dismay. "How unfortu-

nate!" she said. "Miss Beaverwick doesn't begin her course on courtship and matrimony until next term."

"Why is that unfortunate?"

"Because I can't listen to any talk that's meant in a matrimonial sense until I've completed the course. Why, Mr. Carboy, I wouldn't know what to say or how to behave. You must see for yourself that I would be completely at a loss."

Allie looked at her in some doubt for a moment. Then he began to smile. "Thanks," he said. "You've set me right. No sense riding point-blank at the highest fence the first time. A fellow ought to work up to it, I suppose. Very well, no more of that. I'll try to talk most soberly and sensibly from now on."

So they talked, if not soberly and sensibly, at least without any mention of such thrilling topics as love and romance and marriage. They made a splendid tea, finishing all the sandwiches and making serious inroads on the supply of gooseberry tartlets, an item for which Miss Bordley's was famous. It was not until the time came for young Mr. Carboy to take his leave that he began again on the subject which, clearly, was very close to his heart.

"I must see you again at the earliest possible moment," he said. "See here, Nelly, I've been dealt a terrible blow. School breaks up for the Christmas holidays next Friday, doesn't it?"

The girl nodded eagerly. "We're counting the hours," she said.

Allie frowned darkly. "If a fat corpse is found floating in the Thames in the next few days—well, it will be my handiwork. That 'Buttons' Scanlon! He's the son of the senior partner and he's always up to some nice little trick like deciding the office must keep open full hours on Friday. I'll have to take the Saturday morning train. I don't suppose you could stay over and take the same train?"

"Certainly not," said Nelly. "Well, there is one way. I could take sick." They looked at each other with a shared appreciation of the gravity of the situation. Then, suddenly, she began to smile. "Miss Micey will be furious. She's second to Miss Bordley. She's a mean little creature about as large as a good-sized doll but stuffed with vinegar instead of sawdust. If I take sick, it will be Miss Micey who'll have to cope with the situation, even if it means staying over an extra day herself. She'll be perfectly livid about it. And it will be worse the next day when I recover miraculously."

"Nelly," said the youth enthusiastically, "we'll take the Great Western together on Saturday and I'll pray that it gets in hours late. *Ek het jou lief*. Don't ask what that means. I won't translate it for you. Not yet. But soon, my pretty *meisie*, soon."

2

"Your recovery, you aggravating child," said Miss Micey, hovering over the breakfast table where Nelly was eating oatmeal porridge with an excellent appetite, "is very sudden and *very* suspicious."

The teacher, who lived up to Nelly's description of her, was dressed for the street in an enormous cloak and the type of hat known as a pork-pie, which was rapidly going out of style. It was evident that she was in the worst of humors.

"I'm feeling quite recovered, Miss Micey, thank you," answered Nelly.

"If it hadn't been for you," declared the teacher in a tragic voice, "I would be in my home this very instant. At the Brush House, East Tabby, Herts."

"I'm very sorry, Miss Micey." Nelly's voice belied the words. It was thoroughly cheerful.

"Your sickness was all made up, you provoking girl; for some reason which I don't understand. You had no fever. You had no rash. You didn't throw up. You slept like a top and you looked as rosy as a babby. Would that you were one," cried the teacher, "so you could be trounced as you deserve."

"I was terribly sick, ma'am."

The teacher whisked away the plate of toast and the marmalade jar. "I'm not going to sacrifice another day to your silly whims, my girl. One of our old teachers is in town and is returning to Reading this morning. You will travel in her care. She will take you on to your destination and then return to Reading. She is married but her husband is not a good provider and she will be glad of the five shillings you must pay her, my girl, as well as all her expenses. Is that clear?"

"As far as it goes, Miss Micey. But where will I meet her? And what is her name?"

"Oh dear, what *is* her name? There is so much bother to getting all you provoking girls off for the Christmas holidays! I think her name is Hazelrig. No, that was her maiden name. Betsy Hazelrig. She taught music, I think. Or was it needlework? I really can't be more explicit and it doesn't matter anyway because I'm taking you to the station and putting you in her charge."

But things did not go as smoothly as both of them hoped. When they arrived at Paddington Station, there was no sign of the onetime teacher of music, or was it needlework? The train was at the starting platform, the engine was puffing and heaving in readiness for an immediate start, the head of the engineer protruded from the window of the cab to catch the guard's signal; but with the exception of the pair of them there was not a female of any description in sight.

The little teacher stamped her foot and squeezed a tear of annoyance out of each eye. "Now what are we going to do? This is a nice how-d'ye-do, this is! I will *not* take you myself. I refuse, I positively refuse, to waste another day on your whims. And it will never be said that one of Miss Bordley's girls was allowed to travel in a railway train by herself. The heavens may fall but that is a rule we do *not* break."

"But, Miss Micey, it's a short trip. Just to the Wantage Road Station. Nothing can happen to me."

"No words from you, miss! If this stupid woman doesn't arrive, I'll take you back to school and leave you there. And you'll spend your Christmas holidays with the orphan from Jamaica and the one from India."

"But, Miss Micey——" began Nelly, on the point of tears.

"There are no 'buts' about it, you provoking child. You brought this on yourself and I'm going to wash my hands of you. Oh dear, I believe they are getting ready to start and that stupid woman isn't here!"

An elderly gentleman had been standing near them on the platform, prepared to board the train at the last possible moment, it was clear. He had been a burly man in his day but now his shoulders were slightly bent under his coat of burgundy broadcloth. His trousers were white and without the slightest hint of crease. In fact he was squirely in appearance even in such details as the silk bandanna he wore instead of a cravat, the massiveness of his watch chain, and the stoutness of his gaiters. It was apparent from the sympathetic look in his eyes that he had listened and was sorry for the dilemma in which Nelly found herself.

"Will you pardon me, ma'am," he said, addressing the teacher, "if I make a suggestion? It's clear someone has failed to turn up and this nice young lady is going to be condemned to spend the holidays in an empty school —a dashed bleak prospect, I must say. Now, ma'am, I've been nearly everything in my time but I must confess to you that I've never been a chaperon. Still, ma'am, I'm going beyond the station where the young lady is getting off and I'll see she isn't molested on the way and, what's more, I'll put her safely into the hands of her people."

"Sir!" said Miss Micey, drawing herself up indignantly.

"Come, come, ma'am. There's no time to be lost, so don't stand there striking silly attitudes. I have no evil designs."

"How do I know what designs you have?" cried the teacher. "You may be a highwayman for all of me. You may be the dreadful murderer who killed that poor woman with a butcher knife. And we have our rules at Miss Bordley's and I must see——"

At this point the guard called to the elderly man: "Better get on, Your Grace. We're off now, sir." He waved an arm in the direction of the cab and the head of the engineer disappeared.

Nelly clutched at the teacher's arm. "Did you hear what that guard said? He called him, 'Your Grace.' I know who he is now, Miss Micey. He's the Duke of Outland. I saw him riding through our village once."

"Oh, if I could be sure!" wailed Miss Micey.

The girl said desperately, "I'm going anyway!" and made a dash for the train.

"Watch the doors!" shouted the guard. "Train leaving!"

The Duke of Outland—for Nelly had been correct in her identification of him—waited for her. With an approving, "That's it, my girl," he took her arm and helped her up the steps, getting on himself just as the train started to move.

The coach was crowded but a compartment had been kept for his sole use. The guard escorted them to it, unlocked the door and let them in, with a nod and a "Close work, my lord!"

"Thanks, Durdson," said the peer. As a matter of habit, he did not offer a tip. The dukes of Outland had been impoverished so long that no one expected a gratuity from them under any circumstances. Then, recollecting the change in his financial position, he called: "Durdson! Here's a little Christmas gift for you, my lad," and handed him a whole pound.

"Sit at the window, my brave girl," said the duke, helping himself to the opposite seat. "There! Now we're both comfortable. I judge you're from Miss Bordley's from what I heard that silly little creature say. It's a good school. I've had sisters and nieces and so on and so forth there. And my wife was a Bordley girl. In fact, by gad, all my wives were."

"Her Grace is very beautiful," said Nelly. "I've seen her several times."

A smile of deep pride lighted up the face of the duke. "By gad, yes! She's the most beautiful woman in England. Always was. And," smiling at his companion, "you're pretty trim yourself, you know. What's your name?"

"Nelly Groody, my lord. I live at Little Shallow."

His face showed recognition at once. "You're the niece, the Irish girl. They say you've a fine hand with the horses. Well, since we have an interest in common, we can sit here comfortably and talk horse until you have to get off."

At this point he noticed a look on her face which suggested she had been on the point of asking a question but had decided reluctantly not to do so.

"Out with it," he said.

"I don't think I should. I've always been told I shouldn't ask questions, that it's a bad habit of mine. But I *am* curious. I'm curious by nature."

"And what is it you're curious about now?"

"Well, my lord, why did you take so long to marry your beautiful duchess?"

"Now that *is* a long story. My girl, if you knew the answer to that one, all the ins and outs, all the difficulties and the disappointments, all the hesitations, why you could write a story in twenty installments which would knock this Dickens fellow all hollow." He grinned jovially at her. "Any other questions bothering you?"

"Oh, so many, my lord. I'd like to know if you enjoy being a duke and having trains held up for you, and compartments locked for you, and everybody bowing and touching their hats to you. I really don't believe I would like it myself."

"Then you had better be careful, my girl. Some young fellow with a title is likely to set eyes on you and see what a fine, pretty little bargain you are and snap you right up. And then you'll be in a nice fix!" He lowered an eyelid in a partial wink. "I won't deny it has its advantages. But if I had to do it all over again, I really believe I would run off to sea instead."

"That's what I thought!" said Nelly in the pleased tone of one who has had a notion confirmed.

"By the way," said the duke, turning in his seat to look in the other direction, "there's a young hoddy-doddy standing out there in the corridor as still as a lamppost. He's never taken an eye off you for a second. Do you suppose he's an acquaintance of yours?"

Nelly looked in that direction and nodded her head. "Yes, it's Allie Carboy."

The duke took a longer look at the motionless figure in the corridor. "So it is. He's a nephew of my wife. She's very fond of him; and so am I for that matter, though I didn't recognize him at that distance. My eyes are not what they used to be. Does young Allie know you?"

"Oh yes. He knows me."

The duke began to see the light. "And you know him?"

"Oh yes."

"Did the fellow know you were going to be on this train?"

"Yes, my lord. He knew."

"And that means you knew he was going to be on the train. See here, my girl, I begin to suspect something. I'm going to be the one to ask the questions now. Did you plan to see each other on the train, by any chance?"

"Why, really, my lord——"

"Come, come. Be honest about it."

"Yes, my lord, we did."

"Did you perhaps delay your leaving school in order to be on the same train?"

"Oh, this is not fair! What makes you think such awful things of me, my lord?" She hesitated for a moment and then nodded her head. "Yes, all the other girls went home yesterday."

"Then," said the duke accusingly, "I've been thinking things about that absurd teacher which she didn't deserve. You were the one at fault, my girl. The silly creature *was* in a predicament, wasn't she?"

"Yes," said Nelly in a contrite tone. "It was all my fault."

"Under the circumstances," said the duke, "I really think we ought to invite the young man to come in and join us for the rest of the trip."

### 3

The two young people got off together at Wantage Road Station. The Duke of Outland, watching from a corridor window, saw a stout fellow with a whip in his hand greet Nelly and escort her to a carriage on the north of the tracks. He saw Allie Carboy wave a hand to the girl before mounting a horse, which a groom held for him, and turning south in the direction of Wantage. Convinced that everything was in order and that he had fulfilled the duty he had taken upon himself, the peer returned to the compartment and, with an air which had a suggestion of secrecy about it (for the beautiful wife of his autumnal years had turned an emphatic thumb down on his old habits), he drew out a bundle of newspapers from the one bag he was carrying. He remained deep and content in his reading until the train reached his station where a new and handsome ducal carriage was waiting.

Samuel Carboy the Younger had found an ideal site for his home in

England. It was high up in the Lambourn Downs, a hill surrounded on all
sides by ones of equal height. It had an advantage which none of the others
shared, a flattening out on top which provided a plateau of nearly a quarter
mile in every direction. Here, at very great expense, he had erected a stone
house of one story only, a rambling structure somewhat reminiscent of his
old home near Table Bay. It had a wealth of doors and many large windows
facing every point of the compass. The rooms were large and blessed with
high ceilings and enormous chimneys which drew furiously.

Ignoring his grandfather's heated protests, he had given no consideration
to the beautiful English furniture of the preceding century and had filled
the house with all the beloved possessions he had brought with him. He
had ignored also his son's almost pathetic pleas for a tower. Allie had been
tremendously impressed with the high stone keeps of England and he had
wanted the feeling of the past, the mystery and the power of them. "I want
a very tall tower, with a secret room and dungeons and archery slits in the
deep walls," the boy had said insistently. Samuel the Younger, who had a
fine appreciation of architectural standards, had brushed this idea aside.
"Allie," he said, "you would soon get over such boyish fancies. Just to please
you for a year or two, I'm not going to construct a monstrosity to stand on
this sky line for generations."

It had been necessary to cut a road up to this hilltop site, and it dipped
and rose and wound in and out and spanned many little streams which
meandered uncertainly and indifferently down to the plain where, like companies falling into the Carboy maw, they would unite with other brooks
and rivulets and becks and become in time broad and busy rivers. No such
thoughts, however, filled the mind of the young clerk from London. He
could think of nothing but Nelly. He saw her everywhere, in the grays of
the sky, in the depths of the woods, in the pattern of the hills. He heard her
voice in the murmur of the aforementioned streams, he detected her laugh
echoing back to him in the Yuletide efforts of birds sheltered in the trees.

"Oh, Nelly, I love you so much!" he said to himself with a sense of complete happiness and assurance. "It's a fortunate thing that I am cutting out my own path. I can do what I like, and when I like. I can marry the girl I love and no one can say no to me; and you, my Nelly, with your lovely eyes, and your sweetness and your gaiety and your courage, are the only one I want!"

He said to himself then that his love for her was a rare example of the poetic belief in justice. It went further than that, he believed; he and this high-spirited girl were simply carrying along from the point where the original lovers had left off. It had been inevitable that Alfred Carboy should marry Nell Groody, even though the happy ending had to be delayed two generations. He would marry her as soon as he was earning enough to support a wife and in that way provide the last act in this protracted love story.

Before the house came into view he heard the sound of a gunshot from the hills somewhere above him, followed by two more sharp discharges in quick succession. He drew in his horse and listened but there were no more shots.

"Must be old Ride-All-Night," he said to himself with a grin. "Keeping his eye in. Guess he finds life pretty dull back here in England."

As he topped the final rise of the road he was surprised to find his father standing on an edge of the plateau and gazing raptly off into the distance across the wide acres he had acquired for himself. Allie put his horse to a gallop, pulling up in front of his parent with a spattering of gravel.

Samuel the Younger turned toward his offspring with a pleased smile. He waved a hand to indicate the line of hills which ringed them in on all sides.

"I couldn't have found a better place," he said, "if I had searched a lifetime. It's just like home, isn't it? It almost makes me wish to go back. A passing fancy only, my boy; I'm too busy in reality to think of such things for more than a few minutes."

"When did you get back from Paris?" asked the boy. "The last word I got from you was that you probably wouldn't arrive until after Christmas."

"I arrived this morning," said the father. He was thinly clad for outdoors and was finding it necessary to flail his arms about to restore circulation. "I was so anxious to get back that I took a night coach out of London. I found, son, that I couldn't bear the idea of spending a Christmas in France. I was only too certain that I wouldn't be wakened up by carol singing in the streets and that there would be no happy prospect of a plum pudding for dinner. The French aren't as sentimental as we are and at this time of year I find their matter-of-factness hard to accept. So here I am, and happy to be home where I can shout 'Merry Christmas!' to strangers without being suspected of lunacy."

They went inside where Allie was taken aback to find the entrance hall monopolized by a huge Christmas tree. His father explained its presence with pride. "I cabled ahead about it. I said I wanted the damnedest largest tree which ever sprouted from English soil and that from Christmas Eve on it had to blaze with candles and fairly droop with trinkets and gifts. I must say that Prodger caught the spirit of things and has done us proud. We had some fine trees when our dear Clara was alive, but nothing to equal this."

He seemed in the very highest spirits. Taking his son by the elbow, he directed him into a room off the hall which was filled with mementos of their life in South Africa.

There were assagais on the walls and war shields and native ornaments. On the owner's desk, serving as a weight for papers, was a large piece of quartz shot through with the unmistakable yellow of gold; a reminder, no doubt, of the mine he still owned.

Seating himself under the long and rather solemn head of a hartbeeste, he began to talk of the results of his French trip.

"Allie, my boy," he said, "the plan is taking hold. We have shops in Paris and four other cities in France; and the novelty of the goods we offer has been loosening the reluctant purse strings. Our French manager, a Monsieur Paul Dulain, is the very man we want—keen, hard, full of ideas. Is he completely honest? I wish I could be sure. For the time being we have him under a form of observation; the first false step, if he makes one, will be noticed, and we'll know what to do, of course."

He reached into the drawer of a ponderous desk and drew out some papers. "The New York office is a success already. I'm sailing sometime next month to look it over but it's largely a matter of form. This man we have in charge, Mr. Philander J. Budge, is like my own blood brother. I understand him and he understands me. It was reported to us that he was a ring-tailed squealer—the exact words—at making a business hum; and, by gad, that's exactly what he is! Getting settled in our quarters on the Bowery was a small expense. The money's rolling in. Actually we could declare a dividend if we felt so disposed. The banks are only too happy to give us every accommodation but we'll have a bank of our own in no time at all."

Allie was listening with the closest attention. "What's the next move?" he asked.

"Hong Kong or Shanghai. We'll be in both places in quick order. I'm working on plans already. Got to find employment for these two rascals we brought with us. Zulu is getting morose and Ride-All-Night is depleting the hills of birds."

They were interrupted by the entrance of one of the native servants. He had been a very tall man, well over six feet in height, but the advance of the years had bowed his spine and rendered his head a little heavy for his skinny neck to sustain. There was little in the way of flesh on his bones; and an old suit of clothes, which had belonged originally to Allie, hung on his frame like the trappings of a scarecrow. A pipe made of marrowbone was in his mouth and he was puffing at it furiously and shivering at the same time.

"Tatab," said Samuel sharply. "No smoke here. Tatab told many times."

"Baas," said the native in a high whine, "Tatab no smoke, Tatab freeze."

"Tatab wear more clothes, Tatab no freeze."

The old man scratched his pate, which was covered with thick gray hair.

"Baas," he pleaded, "take Tatab home. See sun, no freeze." He gave a nod with his seemingly insecure head. "Food ready, Baas."

Father and son proceeded down the hall to another room which looked out to the north. The crest of White Horse Hill could be seen, although the horse himself was on the hidden slope. Here they were joined by Ride-All-Night and Zulu and they sat down to share a steaming platter of beef stew, a loaf of bread and a bottle of red wine. They had made minor inroads only when the buttery hatch swung open and another native appeared. This one was younger than Tatab but he had the same attenuated frame and the same leathery brown skin. His name was Hobe, which meant "lazy" in the Hottentot tongue, and he acted as cook for the household.

"Baas," said the cook, "you like? Stew good?"

"Stew no good!" cried the master of the household. "Too much pepper. Too much spice. Three times Hobe told, less pepper. Hobe no listen."

"Can't the blasted old fraud cook anything but these infernal stews?" asked Ride-All-Night.

"As you know, he burns roasts and broils chops to charcoal. Stews are monotonous but at least we can eat them."

"This is the fourth day in a row that we've had one shoved at us."

Hobe understood the tenor of these remarks and he broke into a loud and indignant gabble of words, directed at Ride-All-Night. The latter did not reply but shoved his plate away in disgust.

"What's he saying?" asked Samuel.

The marksman grinned. "He's commenting on my ancestry."

"Hobe!" said the master with increased sharpness. "No talk. What else you got?"

"Berries, Baas. Stewed."

Zulu joined in the criticism at this announcement. "More berries! How many bushels did this stinking rascal do down to poison us with? It's berries, berries, berries all the time."

"He can't get the materials he's used to, you know," commented Samuel. "I've told him not to try pie crust again. The last lot landed in my stomach like coal rolling down a chute." He turned to the cook. "No berries. You got cake?"

"No cake, Baas."

"What have you got, you lazy rascal?"

"Berries, Baas."

As there seemed no prospect of further food, the two South Africans took chairs in the north window where they puffed their pipes in silent discontent. Allie, with the not too discriminating appetite of youth, was still making headway with the stew but he pricked up his ears in immediate interest when his father began to speak again of their French venture.

"There's a man in France who may be of great interest to us. And this is a matter which concerns you."

Allie hazarded a guess. "Jacques Plessis, the banker?"

"I don't know how you managed to arrive at that conclusion but you happen to be right. Jacques Plessis. A most remarkable fellow. His father was an army contractor under the first Napoleon and naturally he left a solid fortune to his only son. Jacques is the great banker of France today. It's said he backed Louis Napoleon's coup d'état with financial aid and that the little emperor can't deny him anything today. When I reached Paris he was the first man who came to see me, the great Jacques Plessis himself, with his long black beard and his high black hat and his eyes gleaming like two fiery coals." Samuel nodded his head with intense satisfaction. "He had sensed what brought me and he wanted a share in it."

Allie contributed one nugget of information on the subject of the great Gallic banker. "In the City they call him the Black Bonapartist."

"He did something quite unusual for a Frenchman, he invited me to his home for dinner," continued Samuel. "It was a lesson to me how this man lives. He hasn't one of those large estates in the suburbs, with great parks and lakes with gondolas on them and stables full of horses. He lives quietly but with a hint of almost Eastern comfort on two floors of one of the oldest houses on the Left Bank. I was told that D'Artagnan had lived in rooms on one of the floors while he was the king's lieutenant, and it's easy to believe. The rooms are large and rather moldy and there's a rich arras in every one of them, and they're packed with priceless furniture of the reign of Louis XIV. I expected to hear the ghosts of the immortal musketeers rustling about."

The boy had finished his meal and was listening now and not missing a word.

"He's a widower and just before we sat down a beautiful lady arrived, an actress from the Opéra Comique who's known only as Lucette. She's his——" Samuel paused doubtfully and then decided to go on. "Well, you're growing up, son, and I expect you've heard of such things. She's his mistress. I'm sure she's kept by the company for her looks because she can't be much of an actress. She didn't get into the conversation at all; just an occasional, 'Oui, Papa' or 'Non, m'sieur.' But what an eye she has and what a fine pair of white shoulders; and her manners were very dainty and pleasing. She was dressed in black, not due to any sorrow but because the color becomes her most, and she wore a scarf embroidered with violets. The insignia of the Bonapartists.

"Jacques Plessis has only one child, a daughter," continued Samuel. "She put in an appearance before dinner for a moment, bowed prettily and re-tired. He tells me she's fourteen and that he named her Hortense Alphon-sine. Well, my boy, she's a regular little beauty. She's as dark as he is and she's got a pair of melting eyes, and she's small. I swear her foot is no longer than your hand. The little Hortense Alphonsine will be one of the great catches of Europe when she's old enough to marry." He was not looking at his son at this stage but was keeping his eyes on the window where the line of the downs could be traced in detail. "We talked about that, Plessis and I."

Allie was startled. "About what?" he asked.

"Well, about the little Hortense Alphonsine. And her marriage in two or three years."

"Father," said the youth, "I see what you're driving at. And I must tell you I'm not interested."

Samuel swung around in his chair at once. "So! You see what I'm driving at and you aren't interested! Why do you jump to conclusions in this way? How do you know you're not interested?"

"Well," said Allie, "I suppose you meant that someday I might marry the daughter of Jacques Plessis. Was that it?"

"I may tell you that Jacques Plessis is thinking that very thing. You ought to feel honored instead of sitting there and bristling like a young porcupine."

"I guess I do feel honored," conceded the youth. "But just the same I'm not interested in the idea. I want to shape my own life. I want to do the things which interest me. And certainly I intend to select my own wife."

It became evident at this point that the two marksmen, who had been carrying on a conversation themselves, had nevertheless been hearing every word said. Mr. Zulu got to his feet and came tramping over to the table.

"That's the way to talk!" he cried enthusiastically. "No marriage of convenience for you. You'll wait until you see the girl you want and then you'll take her. That's the English way."

"By God!" cried Samuel, springing up and pounding the table with his fist. "This is more than I can stand! Ever since my dear *moekie* died, this household has been turning into a damned male free republic. Everybody says just what he wants to. That cook serves us slops because he's too lazy to learn anything else. And now this master of the assagai comes blundering into a private conversation and tells me to my face that I'm wrong!"

"You are wrong," said the assagai thrower easily. "This little French girl is likely to be sly and mean and all hopped up with perfume. Why do you want to force her on a fine, upstanding lad like your son?"

"I'll have no more advice from you, if you please. And now, young man, I expect to hear you tell me that you've already picked the girl you want to marry."

"Yes, sir. I have."

"And who, may I ask, is the paragon of beauty and virtue you want so much that you're ready to throw over the chance to combine the two greatest fortunes in the world for yourself?"

"Sir," said Allie, "I can't mention her here. It would be like discussing her in public. Anyway she's as likely to say no to me as yes. It's all on my side so far. If she turns me down, I'll be willing enough to discuss your plan. And not before. Can't we leave it that way, Father?"

"For the moment only. I certainly don't want to say anything more while two pairs of long donkeys' ears are listening. But there's something I am going to tell this pair of deep thinkers. Things are going to change around here. The republic of free speech is going to go back to a despotism of obedience and respect. Tatab isn't going to come into my presence smoking his rank tobacco and Hobe will be put to work with mops and brooms instead of taking it easy in the kitchen. These two bright young men will be expected to keep their tongues between their teeth. As a first step I'm going to ride into Wantage this afternoon and find myself a good English-woman to do our cooking—someone who'll make us a plum pudding and mince pasties for Christmas and who knows that sweets are no good unless they have plenty of suet in them. You'll come with me, Allie, and we'll continue this conversation. I've got to know more about this infatuation of yours. Who the girl is, and how far you've gone, and what we have to do to drag you back to shore before you sink."

4

The Duke of Outland had been away for ten days. There had been some matters to attend to at the town house, newly reacquired and in course of repair; and also he had been getting so much in the way that Isabelle had been glad of an excuse to see nothing of him for a short spell. Returning now, he discovered at once that miracles had been wrought in his absence. The drive was clear of snow and sounds of continuous activity could be heard from the stables, the smithy, the pimping shed and the root house. The great sprawling pile which people spoke of with awe as one of the stately homes of England was fully alive again. Smoke rose from scores of chimneys and none of the windows was muffled. Young Chip (no one thought of calling him anything else) smiled with deep satisfaction. "My wife," he said to himself, "has been at it. What a relief it is to leave things in her hands!"

Isabelle greeted him in the Great Hall with a triumphant smile on her lips. The Hall had been transformed. The stone walls had been scraped; the large tapestry, showing a knight in full panoply sallying out for some presumably brave adventure, had been so artfully repaired that the casual eye could detect no evidence of what had been done; the pennons which had been rotting on the bog-oak beams of the roofing had been still more radically attended to by skillful hands.

"They've gone!" she announced. "The carpenters, the painters, the over-seers, all of them. I gave them three o'clock as the last possible moment to be through with everything; and I looked my last on their honest, if some-what stupid, faces at exactly two fifty-three." She gazed then at the clothes in which he had traveled down from London. "My sweet, if sometimes stupid, spouse, you look like Honest Giles or Piers Plowman or a Yorkshire squire. What a spectacle you are!"

The duke grinned appreciatively. "This is easy and comfortable like. I'll strip the things off if you say the word."

"I do say it. Most emphatically."

"There's plenty of time. When will the guests begin to arrive?"

"In two hours. Everyone is coming. You must read the pleasant notes of acceptance they all sent. I tell you, Chip, they were keen to be among the first to taste the new hospitality of Outland Park. Did I say all? Well, we drew one blank. Dizzy can't come. But he sent the wittiest note and expressed the most abased regrets. I'll get him next time, you'll see."

"Who you talking about?"

"Mr. D'Israeli, of course."

"Oh, that fellow. We can get along without him. I take it that Archie and Sir Bere Roke and my best-beloved Nancy Roke will be among those present."

"Of course!" cried Isabelle. "And Derek and Constance, and Willie and his duddy wife, and the Terror and the Creature, and the Sweet Young Thing, and Sir Acton Ferrers from the Foreign Office who *will* have a dispatch case with him *and* a guard. Tosti will be here for one day. In uniform, of course."

"Here's the first of them arriving now," said the duke as the sound of carriage wheels reached them from the drive.

"Oh no! It can't be!" cried Isabelle. "I was most specific about the directions and the time with all of them. What am I going to do?"

Fortunately it was not a guest. It was Samuel Carboy the Younger, looking quite ill at ease. He and his ambitious aunt had not been on speaking terms for a year.

The visitor was ushered in and bowed to Isabelle and then nodded and smiled at the duke. "Sorry to do this," he said. "I'm sure it's the worst possible time, just as you're hoisting the flag for the whole world to see. But there's something I must discuss with you, Aunt Isabelle. Will you condescend to speak with the villainous and conniving scoundrel that you consider me to be?"

"Sit down. We'll forget our differences—for a day, at least—over a cup of tea. I'm sure it's something pressing or you wouldn't have come to *me*."

She pulled a bell cord and in a trice a footman appeared in response. The duke smiled with delight at this proof of the new day which had dawned in the home of his ancestors. When the duchess ordered tea, he caught the man's attention and made a motion to indicate that something a bit stronger might be introduced into his cup.

"And now," said Isabelle, addressing her nephew in a tone quite devoid of affection, "which one of my prophecies of disaster has come true?"

"It's nothing in that line. We're doing rather well, as it happens; and by some miracle, of course. It's something that I feel is out of my line. Allie, in fact."

Isabelle's interest was aroused at once. "What has my sweet boy been doing?" she asked. "Women, I'm sure."

"Well, yes." Samuel began to tell them of his meeting with Jacques Plessis and of the suggestion which the French banker had made, and then of the obstacle which had arisen. Isabelle proceeded to ask questions.

"Is the Frenchman as wealthy and powerful as they say?"

"His resources have not been overestimated. That much I can guarantee. An alliance between the houses of Carboy and Plessis would be an event to shake the whole fabric of international trade. I don't need to tell you that the soundest basis for such a merger would be a match between the two young people."

"What is the girl like?"

"As bright as a button. And very pretty. There's a hint of the East about her but it adds to her beauty, in my opinion. You know there's a brown ancestor somewhere on the Plessis family tree."

"All the better," declared Isabelle. She was deeply concerned over the problem. "We've reached a point where the family must acquire a title. All the big houses of the past saw the value of nobility patents. The Fuggers, for instance. And today the Rothschilds and the Barings. It may be easier to move into the peerage through Allie than any other way. You know how hard Papa has tried. I've had several girls in mind for the boy. From the very best families, all of them, and not bad-looking either. But it may be that the Plessis plan is better. An alliance on that level would bring titles tumbling down on us, I'm sure."

A new note was introduced into the discussion when the duke spoke up for the first time.

"It won't do," he said.

Isabelle turned on him with a slight hint of sharpness in her voice. "May I ask why not?"

"I don't believe in foreign marriages. If you had been with me that morning, Isabelle, up on White Horse Hill, you would agree with me. I saw then how wrong it is. They're a different breed of cats, my dear. We mustn't tie the boy up for life with one of them."

"Chip, actually!" said Isabelle. "I don't appreciate your bringing *that* up. French people can be perfectly charming; and I don't see any reason why Allie couldn't be happy with this nice child." She looked questioningly at her nephew. "What are you going to do about it?"

"What do you advise?"

"You must be firm. I suppose he thinks he's in love with someone else."

"Naturally. And it's most awkward. It's the Groody girl."

Isabelle nodded. "I suspected that." Her voice took on a deep note of umbrage. "Why do these Groody women have to be so pretty in their cunning little Irish way? Why do Carboy sons, the great oafs, always go and fall in love with them? It's annoying, to say the least."

"I'm more concerned with the awkwardness of it. I must go and speak to poor Aunt Helen. I dread it, I don't mind confessing. She's so sweet and understanding and I owe her so much. But—it must be done. I must wound her pride by telling her that her niece isn't good enough for my son. I must ask her to help me in preventing them from seeing each other."

"You must," said Isabelle in a suddenly demanding tone.

They had left the Great Hall and were sitting together, the three of them (although Young Chip had remained silent and did not count for much), in a small apartment which had become known over the years as the Signing Away Room. It was here that the dukes of Outland had on many sad occasions affixed their signatures to papers of one kind and another, all unpleasant and all involved in measures of financial expediency. The only space of any consequence on the walls was occupied by a portrait of the second duke, who had started all the trouble back in the days of Good Queen Anne by his wild extravagance. There was an expression on the painted floridness of his face which hinted at a wry sense of amusement. The free-spending ancestor seemed almost on the point of indulging in a sardonic chuckle over the difficulties he had bequeathed to his unlucky successors.

"I'm glad you came to see me," said Isabelle. "And you can take that as an indication of the interest I have in the future of young Master Alfred, because there has been no other time in the past year when I've wanted to see you or would even consider speaking to you. I'm still bitterly opposed to what you are doing. Oh, I know the first ventures have seemed to be successful——"

"They have gone better than we dared hope," declared Samuel with a slight degree of heat as well as pride.

"I am glad to see you today because it gives me a chance to speak seriously about this matter. You must be firm with the woman. Don't let your sentimental feelings get the better of you. She must *not* be pampered. Tell her it must be stopped, that it won't do under any circumstances."

Samuel nodded his head somberly. "I'm entirely aware of the need for taking a firm attitude. I'll do it but it will be the most difficult task I've ever had to perform. You needn't worry. Allie is my son and I can't allow him to make such a mistake at this stage of his life." He paused and shook his head. "I'm going there at once. An unpleasant duty should never be postponed."

The duke shook his head sadly. "Damme, Isabelle, and you also, Samuel," he said. "You're making a great mistake, between you. You have all the brains, you two, but you're not using them this time."

After Samuel's departure Isabelle spent some time with the housekeeper, Mrs. Skurry, making certain that the sixteen extra bedrooms needed for the holiday guests were ready. She checked over certain points she had jotted down on a paper pad. Were the proper writing materials on the desks? Clean pens and fresh ink? Had the beds been aired and made up with the best linen? Were the fires laid? Were the warming pans ready? She was concerned also about the preparations for the incoming servants. Were their rooms in readiness?

"Our staff is small, Your Grace," said Mrs. Skurry. "We are getting along with no more than thirty-two. Inside, that is. It is not adequate. But Your Grace felt the need to economize and so we are doing our best."

"Are you, Mrs. Skurry? I hope so." The duchess was checking carefully from another list. "At meals, now. Who will sit on your right, at lunch and dinner?"

The housekeeper showed a slight tendency to bridle. "I have gone over the seating with the utmost care, Your Grace," she said. "I will have beside me on my right the gentleman of His Grace of Hurlingforth and on my left the gentleman of my Lord Crame. The steward, Your Grace, will have the respective ladies on his right and left. The rest will be seated according to established custom. I am, I may tell Your Grace, a positive stickler for form. If any mistakes were made, I would positively die of shame."

"I hope so, Mrs. Skurry."

A footman entered with a card on a tray. "Y'Grace," he said. "If y'plise."

Isabelle glanced at the card and then hastily took it from the tray and found a receptacle for it among the papers she was carrying. "Where is he, Grindle?" she asked.

"In the library annex, Y'Grace. I thought it better as the guests will be here soon."

"Quite right, Grindle."

It was Alexander Fawkes who rose from his chair, reluctantly no doubt because his aversions included all social amenities, and bowed to her. The annex was dark and, as no one was ever expected to visit it, little care had been taken to give it a share of the renovations. The books were moldy and all the old furniture had been left, some of it badly in need of repair.

"I am sorry to disturb you, ma'am," said the descendant of the man who had given gunpowder a permanent place in English annals. "As it happened I was sent on office concerns to see your father and a Miss Helen Groody who lives not many miles away. It occurred to me that I should take advantage of the opportunity to see you also. There are some things to tell you which, I am sure, will prove of interest. I prefer not to entrust such matters to the mails."

"A preference which I share, Mr. Fawkes," said the duchess. She seated herself on a horsehair sofa and turned to him with an expression of extreme interest. "What have you found?"

The junior partner glanced about him as though from habit and then drew some papers from an inner pocket. Selecting one at a time, he began a series of explanations in low tones. Isabelle leaned closer to him and listened with the closest attention, sometimes asking a question in an equally guarded voice. At the finish he gathered the papers together and replaced them in his pocket. He did this with an air of satisfaction and even triumph.

"That is all so far, ma'am," he said. "And I rather think we have something which will prove useful. If the necessity ever arises."

Isabelle's face was flushed. She kept her eyes down for fear he would read in them the full sense of satisfaction and even of power which his information had given her. "Well!" she said. She was thinking that the weapons supplied as a result of his prying in the letter presses at the offices of Smythe, Boongrace and Curdle would indeed be most useful if the necessity arose; and she was certain that sooner or later the need to intervene would come up and she would then confound her confident and resourceful nephew with some unpleasant truths. "Well!" she repeated. Then she looked up and gave her accomplice a smile which conveyed no sense of warmth. "You are doing exactly what I wanted. Have you a brief summary on paper of all you have told me? With the dates, so things can be traced back? I think I would like to have it. Oh, I understand the trouble we would both be in if such a paper came to light. Be sure of this, Mr. Fawkes, I will keep it so securely that no other living eye will ever rest on it."

"I prepared such a summary, ma'am. It's not necessary for me to add any words to what you have said about the need for the utmost care."

"You spoke of visiting Miss Groody," she said. "Is she concerned in some business deal with my father?"

"Indirectly," answered the lawyer. "It is a matter of calling in some preferential stocks. Your father, ma'am, and Miss Groody happen to be the largest holders. It had all been settled by mail and my responsibility did not go beyond getting the necessary papers signed."

"What did you think of her?"

He gave his head a shake. "Most intelligent and well versed in business matters. But she's a very sick woman. Rheumatism, I think. I happen to know that she's a shareholder in the Waterloo Tontine but I don't believe she'll remain a competitor very much longer."

"She has a niece. Did you see her while you were at the house?"

"I had two glimpses of her. She came dashing into the house in riding clothes and then came down in a very few minutes from her room where she had changed into a dress—a very becoming dress, I must say. She called a greeting to her aunt and then closed herself into another room where, according to Miss Groody, she would spend several hours deep in a book. Some novel, called, I think, *Edwin Drood*. I thought her unusually attractive."

Isabelle nodded unsympathetically. "I haven't seen her but she seems to make the same impression on all men."

At this moment pandemonium broke loose outside the house. There was a sound of carriage wheels on the gravel of the drive and a horn sounding forth a sketchy rendition of a Christmas carol. A clamor of voices threatened to drown the music out, feminine voices as well as masculine. There was also a loud ringing of bells which caused the horses to stamp and neigh. It became apparent almost at once that not only had the domestic staff mustered at the entrance to add to the welcome and take care of the baggage but that the outside help had rallied to join in the greeting. This meant the staff from the stables all the way down to the humble steel boys who spent their lives furbishing bits and polishing bridles, and all the gardeners who pottered the winter months away in a mysterious region known as the bothy, and the ax-wielders who made fagots for the almost countless fireplaces (there was a somewhat sly tendency at this particular moment to call fagots by an early Anglo-Saxon name, "pimps") and, of course, the lordly coachmen. All were out in full force and cheering their heads off in an excess of Yuletide exuberance.

The voice of the Duke of Outland could be heard declaiming: "Merry Christmas! Damme, if it isn't pleasant to see all your familiar and dull old faces again."

The chatelaine of Outland Park sprang to her feet. "My guests are arriving," she said. "Do you mind, Mr. Fawkes, if I go out at once?"

"Not at all, ma'am. I have nothing to add. At the moment."

"I hope you have a merry Christmas. Although I don't suppose you condescend to enjoy anything so sentimental. You probably regard Santa Claus as a malefactor who ought to be arrested and you think his reindeer should be seized and put in the nearest pound. I'm sure you consider the giving of presents as a form of domestic bribery."

"Quite. I have no family, ma'am, and I expect to spend Christmas Day at a meeting. I belong to a society in London—made up very largely, I must confess, of foreigners who bring enlightened ideas to this country. The time will be spent in a serious discussion of ways to—well, to better our forms of government."

Isabelle was already on her way to the door. "It all sounds most ominous. I have a feeling I should notify the police, Mr. Fawkes."

As she walked to the entrance hall her mind was not on the guests or the festivities ahead. It was still with business problems. "Things may seem to be going well," she said to herself, "but I'll get him out of there! I'll bide my time and not strike until the right moment. Papa's getting too old. He's losing his grip. I notice he's more concerned to have a whisky decanter beside him than with what's going on in Paris and New York. Will it come to the point of getting him declared incompetent?"

5

"Have you nothing to say, my dear?" asked Helen Groody, looking with deep concern at her grandniece, who was sitting on a stool beside her and saying nothing. This was so unusual with the girl that the elder woman had every reason to feel disturbed.

"Yes, Aunt Helen," answered Nelly. Her face was flushed and it was apparent that she had been restraining herself with difficulty. "But I'm afraid to start for fear of going too far."

"You mustn't be angry." Helen Groody's voice seemed strained and sad. The scene through which she had passed with Samuel Carboy the Younger had left her in such a weak condition that she had remained in her cumbersome wheeled chair in the middle of the floor without any effort to propel it back closer to the fire.

"You have every reason to feel upset, dear child, but—well, the less said the better. You are young and you are becoming more attractive by the minute, it seems to me. All you will ever have to do is to crook a little finger or give the swain of your choice a smile. You mustn't think that Allie Carboy is the only man in the world."

"He isn't, Aunt Helen! What makes me angry is that his father would dare to come to you and say such things. You, to whom he owes everything! You saved him from being taken back to America to live with his actress mother. What would have happened to him if you hadn't seen his shoes at the door and offered to keep him?"

"I suppose Samuel Carboy would have come to his senses in time. But the boy was like a son to me and I confess, Nelly, that I am very much hurt. I had done nothing to—to trap his son. Nor had you. He was attracted to you and he came of his own free will."

The girl gave her head a defiant toss. "You mustn't think, Aunt Helen, that my heart will be broken. I liked him and I enjoyed being in his company. But I wasn't in love with him. And I've made up my mind about one thing: I'll never see him again. Never! Not as long as I live. Not if he should come and beg to be forgiven."

"But the boy has done no wrong," said the elder woman, in a haste to set this point right. "Samuel told me that Allie didn't know he was seeing me. He said the boy would be furious when he found out."

"Well," said the girl in a voice which showed she was ready for battle, "I'm angry with the whole tribe of Carboys. They're crude, selfish, stuck-up. Allie has always been nice but he has Carboy blood in him and he'll get like the rest in time."

"I'm not sure of that, child. But they'll be at him. They'll wear him down and in the end he'll give in. Just as his grandfather did. That's why I say you are right, my dear, in deciding to see nothing more of him. It will be best in the long run."

"I ought to thank his father," declared Nelly, stifling a tendency to tears, "for ending things like this. He's saved me from being disillusioned later."

The tired woman in the wheel chair looked at her with anxious eyes. "You speak of being disillusioned, dear child. Are you sure you don't love him?"

Nelly did not even hesitate to take stock of her feelings. "Yes!" she cried. "Any feeling I may have had for him has gone. This has changed everything."

"Oh, I do hope you mean it. I don't want you to suffer, my very, very dear one."

"I do mean it." The girl's eyes were flashing. "I wish I could face the whole family and tell them my opinion of them! Aunt Helen, I can't get over that man daring to come to you and say such things. I would like to scratch his eyes out!"

Helen Groody had tossed off the cover from her lap while they talked but now she motioned to her niece to retrieve it. "Please," she said. "A few minutes ago I thought I couldn't bear the weight of it on my knees and I was burning up. Now I'm freezing. This is the strangest disease. You never know what to expect."

"My poor little aunt Helen," cried Nelly, wrapping the cover about the thin frame. "I think you should take a nap. Close your eyes and forget all about that great lord of creation and what he said to you. When you waken we'll both be feeling better and we'll have a laugh together at their expense, these almighty Carboys of Beaulaw Hall. While you sleep, I think I'll take a walk. I need to cool off."

The fear that she might meet Allie Carboy riding over to explain himself caused her to turn her steps up a path through the glebe lands behind the Old Rectory. She walked slowly. The first feeling of resentment was wearing off. It was not Allie's fault; she was sure of that. "But he's a Carboy," she said to herself, as though that were a crime in itself. She did not walk far. In fact she had barely reached the cover of the trees when her feelings overcame her. Seating herself on a low stump, she began to cry.

"I didn't tell Aunt Helen the truth!" she confessed to herself. "I *am* in love with him. I'm so much in love with him that I don't know what I'm going to do. I could never hate him, no matter what he did. But I've got to act as though I do. Because—because I don't want to have the kind of life that Aunt Helen has had. Somehow I must manage to forget him. And in the meantime," she added to herself, taking out a handkerchief and applying it to her eyes, "I must remember the promise I've made her. I must never see him again."

When she returned from her unhappy stroll through the snow-covered trees, Nelly had made up her mind on one important point. Her aunt had wakened from her late afternoon nap and was very glad to report that she had some appetite for tea, a most unusual thing.

"Perhaps emotional scenes are good for me," she commented with a patient smile.

The girl had paused by the library table, which was piled high with periodicals. Helen Groody had grown into a great reader and she took the more serious reviews, such as the *Fortnightly* and the *Contemporary*, as well as popular magazines, *Blackwood's* and the *Cornhill*. Prominently displayed was the latest issue of *Punch*. Nelly reached for a copy of the *Women's Suffrage Journal* and held it up before her aunt's eyes.

"Are you interested in this?"

The older woman nodded emphatically. "Every woman of any intelligence believes we should have the vote," she declared. "Some of them don't acknowledge it. They're afraid it would make them seem cranks or mannish. Many are afraid of what their husbands would say. But down in their hearts all women know they could use the vote at least as well as men."

"One of the teachers at Miss Bordley's is a suffragist," said the girl thoughtfully. "She gives us history and sometimes when she speaks of democracy and the right to vote, her eyes get like stars with excitement and she begins to speak—well, just like a prophet. Once I had a moment alone with her and I asked why she felt so strongly about it. She didn't answer right away and then she smiled at me and said: 'Let's put it this way. Whatever brains there are in my family, I happen to have. I have three brothers, and I love them all, but they haven't an ounce of sense between them. All three vote.'"

"Very well put," said Helen Groody. "Mr. Spudsby, the butcher in the village, can't write more than his name and he enjoys killing animals. He has the vote. Florence Nightingale hasn't."

"Aunt Helen," said the girl, "I did some thinking while I was out walking. I don't want to go back to Miss Bordley's."

"Nonsense, my dear," protested her aunt. "One more term and you'll graduate. It would be foolish to stop now."

"But Allie will be in London and he'll be trying to see me, I'm sure. It would be easier for me not to be there."

"But, my dear child, what would you do with yourself? Riding and going to tea parties isn't going to satisfy you. I understand you pretty well and I know you'll need something to occupy your mind and give you a chance to use up that astonishing energy of yours."

Nelly was still studying the suffrage periodical and turning the leaves slowly. "This is published in Birmingham," she said. "I think, Aunt Helen, I would like to see if there's any work I could do for them. That would keep me occupied."

There was a long moment of silence. Helen Groody sighed and shifted about in her chair. She could never be comfortable in one position for more than a minute at a time.

"I think, my dear, you may have hit upon the very best thing to do. It would be stimulating work and useful. Women are going to have the vote someday although the opposition of men like Mr. Gladstone will delay it. I must say I'm very much disappointed in him. He's positively pigheaded about the vote. Well, what I want to say is that I know Miss Lydia Becker who edits the *Journal*. She's a remarkable woman, the greatest we've had since Florence Nightingale. I'll drop her a note. You would find working with her a great privilege."

She sighed again as she thought of what this would mean, the lonely days when the house would seem empty again. "I've fallen in with your idea, Nelly, because I realize we must consider Allie as well as ourselves. He and I are partners, you'll remember, in a certain little deal which only the three of us know about. I've never had a partner who seemed fairer or more enthusiastic. Someday perhaps he'll make a lot of money out of that venture he has in mind, for you and me as well as for himself. I owe him some consideration. And now look at it another way. Allie doesn't know yet what his father has done. He'll be very angry when he hears. He'll say he loves you and that he isn't going to let them dictate to him. Of course, he may give in to them later, and because I realize it's possible, I think you will be wise to break off with him. But suppose—just suppose, my dear—that he has the resolution to stand out against his family. Suppose he insists he is going to run his own life—and choose his own wife?"

"I've thought of that," confessed the girl. "It's been in my mind ever since I heard his father had been here. But, Aunt Helen, how do we know? I can't waste my life waiting to see if he's going to be steadfast."

"That's why I think you would be wise to go away for a time. If you get into work for the suffrage movement, you'll be fully occupied. You'll be so busy you won't have any time for personal troubles. Also you can keep free of other romantic entanglements—if you want it that way. You are so very young, my dear. It won't hurt you to forget all about men, including Allie, for a few years. That will give him a chance to show how deep his feeling for you goes." Helen nodded her head with a certain air of satisfaction, as she reached this reasonable conclusion. "And now, let's have tea."

## CHAPTER TWO

### 1

In his declining years Julian Grace was rediscovering music. As a boy he had been kept chained to a harpsichord while a mincing little music teacher had counted out the time in a high and squeaky voice. He had not disliked it as much as most boys of his age who were compelled by maternal insistence to take lessons. For some reason, however, he had not followed up his early instruction. Life in the navy had given him no chance and, after getting back ashore, he had made no attempt to master any instrument. He had continued a lover of music and a frequent attendant at concerts, sitting in rear seats which could be purchased at low prices.

And now here, on the day before Christmas, he sat at a square piano, a Broadwood no less, in the parlor of his flat on Lowndes Street, playing, with the use of fewer fingers than qualified musicians are likely to employ, an air from a slender bit of nonsense that two promising young men named Gilbert and Sullivan had produced under the title of *Trial by Jury*. He was able to achieve no more than the air itself but the result pleased him immensely and he went through it several times, humming to himself, "I said to myself, said I."

It was in the middle of the third rendition that Noel came into the room. The old servant was younger than his employer by a matter of three years but he looked much older. His back was bent and he hobbled rather than walked. In one hand he carried a cup of tea with a buttered muffin perching precariously on the rim of the saucer.

"Sir," he said, "you will like this. I put brandy in tea, sir." The improvement noticeable in his speech on his return from Vienna had continued to a remarkable degree.

Julian took the cup and nodded in approbation. "A good thing for both of us. We're not as young as we used to be, Noel." He gave his head an eager nod. "I'm expecting the boy any minute. It's a long trip down from his school. A full night and a day on the train. He was due in"—he reached for his watch with his free hand and consulted the time—"two hours ago."

"I got everything ready, sir."

The train had not been late, however. Noel's comment was almost drowned out by the opening and vigorous banging shut of the door of the flat and a loud juvenile voice raised in demands for information. "Merry Christmas! Where are you, Noel? Where are you, Grandfather? My arms are full of presents."

Julian the Younger entered the room a moment later, making it clear at once that he had not exaggerated about the parcels and packages with which he was loaded down. He had been growing rapidly over the years and was now threatening to achieve the almost majestic height of his handsome, white-haired grandfather; and it could not be denied that he had his full share of the good looks which had been handed down in the Grace family.

"You seem most remarkably well, Grandfather," said the youth, depositing his bundles on the table. "How do you fend off all the plump widows with large property who must be chasing after you? I would have been here sooner but I kept stopping the cab to get off at shops along the way and picking up these things. There's something there for you, Noel, but I'll skin you alive if I catch you unwrapping it before tomorrow! I'm fairly bursting with news, Grandfather."

"So am I, my boy. Which one of us shall begin?"

"You," said the boy promptly. "Your news will be more important than mine, I'm sure. So, if Noel will hurry me up a cup of tea and two or three— or four—of the muffins, I'll sit down and listen."

"My news," said the older man, when the cup of tea and the muffins had been supplied, "is both good and bad. Which kind do you want first?"

"The good," said the boy.

"Very well then. The good news is *very* good. Sir Hammond Avery from the Admiralty was in to see me a few days ago. You know that island midway in the Atlantic called Bermuda? The Admiralty is anxious to improve it as a naval base and make it more useful for commercial shipping. It has a fine natural harbor but the entrance would have to be blasted out considerably to make it really useful. They're building a floating dry dock at Sheerness to be towed out to Bermuda and anchored there."

"I read about it the other day," said the boy.

"Well, it happens that during my last fifteen years or so at the Admiralty I was engaged exclusively with dry-dock facilities and I had a reputation—not really deserved, my boy—for knowing quite a bit about it. Sir Hammond's call was to tell me they would like to yank me out of retirement and send me over there to keep an eye on things. I told him it would be a pleasant break in the monotony of retirement and that I would be happy to go. It has been arranged. I'm to go back on full pay for the term of service and Sir Hammond whispered to me that there was a possibility—no more than a possibility, mind you—of a knighthood in it for me."

"Hurrah!" cried the youth, putting down his saucer and doing a good imitation of a hornpipe. "Sir Julian Grace! It has a fine harmonious sound to it. Stand out for a baronetcy, Grandfather, so the title will come down to me." He stopped and a look of flushed dismay took possession of his face. "No, that wouldn't do, would it? Silly idea, I must say. I beg your pardon, Grandfather, for saying such an absurd thing."

"Another piece of good news," went on Julian the Senior, to bridge over the awkwardness. "Jeff Wilkes, who's had the lease on Three Gables for so many years, is going to move over to one of the Channel Islands. He wanted to get out of the rest of the lease and I, my boy, was delighted to agree. Do you know why? Because we're going back to the old place ourselves."

The youth's face lighted up. "Are we really, sir? Say, that will be absolutely spiffy! I've always loved it beyond words and it will be really great to live there again. Are you quite sure, Grandfather, that we—that we can afford to do this?"

Julian the Senior drew a pad of paper from one of his pockets and picked up a tuning fork from the top of the piano to point out some figures he had set down. "I've gone into it carefully, Julian. In addition to my pension *and* the money I'll get for the assignment in Bermuda, I have an ever increasing annual payment from the Tontine. Have you any idea what I received this year?"

"A thousand pounds?"

"A modest guess. It was well over two thousand of the best. I've heard that a number of us have died recently and the payment to survivors next year will be close to three thousand pounds. I've been laying quite a bit of the Tontine money away, my boy, so you won't have to start out in life with empty pockets exactly. It's gone into sound investments. All in all, it comes down to this: I'm getting positively rich in my old age and there's plenty of income for us to settle down again in our beautiful old place on the Thames where your grandmother and I lived so happily—so many years ago."

There were tears of happiness in the boy's eyes. "Grandfather," he said, "I can hardly believe it! It's wonderful news!"

Julian the Elder conquered a tendency in the same direction but it took a quick whisk of a handkerchief to accomplish it. "And now, are you ready for the bad news?"

"I hope it's not very bad."

"Julian, my wife is dead. I had word of it four days ago. Her brother Singleton wrote me."

"Oh!" said the boy. He had no pleasant recollections of the second Mrs. Grace but custom asserted itself and his face assumed a solemn expression. "I'm sorry to hear it, sir."

"Singleton said she had not been particularly happy of recent years. He didn't lay the blame on me for that and I wouldn't have accepted it if he had. Titus didn't write me, although I fully expected he would. From reports I had, he didn't seem to do well at Harrow and left without finishing. Perhaps it was just as well because he was with his mother all of the past year. I'm sure that was a great consolation to her."

Julian the Younger had heard stories of Titus Grace at Harrow which he had never repeated. They had not redounded to the credit of the son of the second marriage. He made no comment now, however.

"Singleton said in his letter that Esther left everything to Titus. That was to be expected, of course. He hinted in his letter that it was an even more considerable estate than anyone had anticipated."

"She left nothing to you?" The youth's face showed surprise over what seemed to him a summary disposition of the property.

"On the contrary," answered his grandfather, "she disclaimed any such intention in a stinging reference to me. Perhaps I deserve it. There can be no doubt that some of her unhappiness was due to our separation. The truth is, Julian, that the marriage was a great mistake. We were not suited to one another and, I suppose, I was too old to change or to knuckle under. She was a jealous woman and that made it harder—jealous even of the past. I should never have sought her hand. That's very clear to me now."

It should have been equally clear to him, for his memory was still active and faithful, that he was less to blame on the final point than his words indicated. Esther Thwaites had made up her mind that she wanted to marry the handsome widower and, if the gossip of the neighborhood where the Thwaites family reigned supreme was to be believed, he had found it impossible to escape her.

If he realized this, he did not give any hint of it. "I've thought about the failure of our marriage a great deal since getting Singleton's letter," he went on in a grave tone, "and I feel my shortcomings deeply. Well, so much for that. Poor Esther is dead and nothing can undo what has been done. My greatest regret is that they didn't get word to me in time so I could attend the funeral. I would have liked to pay her that much respect but I suppose they didn't want me there. She may have left them instructions to keep me away. At any rate, they didn't go to the expense of telegraphing me. That's their usual gait; there's a close strain in the whole family."

After a moment he added in a more cheerful tone: "Perhaps I'll see something of Titus now. I can't understand why he didn't write me. He's old enough to know that I would be expecting to hear from him. I wonder if Esther set herself to alienating his affections completely from me? Well, I must see; I must write him at once." He turned then to his grandson. "And what, my boy, is your news?"

"It's mostly about my ideas for the future," answered Julian the Younger, glad to get onto more cheerful ground. "Grandfather, I'm going to give you the surprise of your life. I want to go into business."

The older man did not disappoint him. He *was* surprised and a little puzzled as well. "Just what do you mean? Do you want to get involved in manufacturing things or, perhaps, importing goods the way Grace and Carboy used to do?"

"Yes." The grandson gave his head an enthusiastic nod. "That's it exactly. There's nothing wrong with business, is there? Some of the earlier Graces were good businessmen, I'm sure. Not, of course, as far back as anyone can remember. My father was a portrait painter and you were a naval officer. I don't know what your father's bent was but everyone seems to say he was *not* a businessman in any sense. On the other hand, the Carboys have always been keen in that line. Look at old Mr. Carboy and his grandson from South Africa and the fortune he made out there. Now I hear there's a great-grandson employed with an importing firm in the City. He's learning to be a businessman by starting in at the bottom of the ladder." The youth nodded his head again. "I've got a feeling I should follow his example. I want to do something that will bring in money, so we can all be comfortable. It would be a great surprise, I think, if a Grace really waded into things in the City. It might make the Carboys sit up and take notice."

Julian was still puzzled over his grandson's attitude. "But, my boy, what makes you think you would like it? Why do you think you might be a success?"

"Well, there's nothing else I want to do. I can't paint like my father and I don't want to go into the navy. I'm sure I wouldn't like it in the Church and I would be a flat failure as a lawyer. On the other hand, I'm really interested in business. I read about it in the newspapers; all about dividends and patents and bankruptcy proceedings. I find it fascinating. It may be that something's coming out in me that's been missing in the Grace family for generations." Then another thought occurred to him. "My mother's father was a greengrocer in Bermondsey. Perhaps that's where I get it."

"I don't want you turning into a greengrocer, in Bermondsey or anywhere else," said Julian in great haste. "I prefer to think this strain in you comes from your Grace ancestors. Well, why not? If it's business you want to get into, I expect it could be arranged easily enough. I'm rather in the dark about such matters but I have a friend who's been investing the Tontine money. I could speak to him."

"Grandfather," said the youth with sudden earnestness, "I've already done something about it. Perhaps I should have waited to speak to you but I—I felt the need to get started when I heard about this Allie Carboy going into the offices of Scanlon, Burns and Copbright. I wrote to another firm, Johnstoun, Ward and Seeley. They're in competition with Scanlon, Burns and Copbright."

Julian was frowning again. This kind of thing was rather out of his understanding. "You wrote to the firm? Really, my boy, should you have rushed in this way? What did you say to them?"

"I told them who I was and what was in my mind. I said I would like a berth with them and that I was prepared to start at the bottom."

"You did? I wonder if they'll think you rather—well, impetuous or even, shall we say, brash? What are they going to say about it?"

"I know exactly what they'll say. I've had an answer, Grandfather. They've got a place for me!"

"Good gracious, boy, you have taken things into your own hands, haven't you? What kind of post does this firm—of whom I've never heard, I must confess—offer you?"

"They don't say. A humble one, I'm sure." His manner sobered a little at this point. "They won't be paying me much, Grandfather. Eight shillings a week to start. Can I live on that in London?"

"No, you can't live on such a pittance," said his grandfather emphatically. "Some people do, no doubt, but I wouldn't allow my grandson to grub along that way. If you take this position——"

"I have the letter written and right here in my pocket, saying that I will."

Julian the Older rubbed a hand across his forehead as though he found such precipitancy beyond his comprehension. "Perhaps you *are* intended to be a man of business. You certainly don't allow any dust to collect under your feet. This means you have given up all idea of going to Cambridge?"

"Quite." The boy's manner changed. "I wouldn't be happy there. The story of my birth would soon get around and they would make me feel it. I hope it's going to be different in business, that they won't pry into such things."

"Well," said the grandfather hastily, "there won't be any difficulty about money matters, my boy. I'll give you a sufficient allowance to go along with the eight shillings a week. You must never forget that you're a gentleman. You must live in accordance with your station in life." A dismaying thought took possession of the older man's mind. "Now that I'm moving back to Three Gables, I was counting on seeing you down there a great deal."

"You will, Grandfather, you will! I'll come down every Saturday night and go back on Sundays. That will be oftener than you'd see me if I went to Cambridge."

Julian began to regard the idea with less distaste. "That is true, my boy. I'll be in London often and will have a chance to see you there. The plan seems to have some advantages after all. But we'll have to think it over and talk about it at some length before we decide."

"Grandfather!" said the boy anxiously. "The letter of acceptance is written and dated. We must act quickly, like real businessmen. They've offered me this sit but we must take it before they change their minds. Strike while the iron's hot. That's a motto I believe in, Grandfather. It's a good business motto."

2

Julian Grace was fond of any kind of atmospheric disturbance. He liked to walk in the rain, without hat or galoshes or umbrella. The first fall of snow each season would send him out to roll in it enthusiastically and shout like a schoolboy. He liked above everything, in fact, to go for long strolls when snow began to fall, and the harder it fell the better he liked it, so that sometimes when he had gone too far he had difficulty in plowing his way homeward through the gathering drifts.

A month or so after Christmas the first real storm of the winter arrived, giving him an opportunity to indulge in this taste. When he arrived back in sight of Three Gables (to which he had moved a fortnight before) he found the roof of the house taking on a pleasant semblance of cotton batting and the limbs of the trees already beginning to bend a little from the weight of the snow. It held him in a momentary spell, staring at the iron rooster atop the stables whose comb had turned white and at the summerhouse which seemed now to resemble a pagoda which had made the mistake of getting itself located in Norway or Siberia.

"Winifred," he said in a low tone, "this is so beautiful that I'm sure you come back at times to see it again. I believe you're not far away right now, my dearest one. Can you see me? Do you want to see me after the way I've treated our home? Letting it run down so badly and then bringing another wife here and finally leasing it for so many years? Perhaps you understand about everything and have forgiven me. God grant that you have, for there must be no rift between us when I get my release at last."

At this point he became aware of something happening in the region between the house and the stables. He was conscious first of voices and then he saw that the stable doors were open and that an alien carriage was drawn up in front. He clambered through the hedge and began to climb the path to the house, getting additional impressions with each step. The carriage was a decidedly "dandy" equipage, being smart of line and as spick and span as new paint could make it. It was an open one and piled high with luggage which, needless to state, was now as white as the trees and the ground. The horses were chestnut and handsomely accoutered.

A tall young man in a greatcoat of tan over a blue suit and with the most fashionable of high green hats on his head was standing beside the carriage and speaking to Noel in a strident voice. Coming a few steps closer, Julian discovered that under the green brim the visitor had hair of the brightest red. He realized then what had happened. His son Titus had arrived.

The latter confirmed his identity as soon as Julian had made his way to the vicinity of the stables. He came forward with his hand stretched out.

"I'm Titus," he said. "Your son. I hope you're glad to see me." His voice was strident even in conversation. He spoke, in fact, in what might be termed an aggressively affirmative style. "I got your letter. I want to tell you that I decided to come down at once. There was no longer any reason why I shouldn't see you. And I'm very glad, I am indeed, to find you looking so well. I want to tell you that I expected to find an old man boggling over a fire. From the looks of things, you'll draw your Tontine share for a great many years. And a fine, sound idea it is, I must say."

"Titus, my boy!" said Julian, with a lump in his throat. "I'm very happy to see you. It's been a long time, hasn't it? You were just a little codger when the—the break occurred. I've often thought of writing you or even going to see you. But it didn't seem wise and so I didn't."

The tall youth shook his head. "There would have been an unholy row if you'd tried it. When the mater got an idea in her head, she held on to it like glue. Nothing ever changed her. If I had said I wanted to see you, there'd have been a jolly storm, I can tell you. Hysterics, whew! I believe, I honestly believe, she'd have cut me out of her will. And that wouldn't have done at all."

Julian was studying his offspring with an eye which threatened to mist over, partly because of the emotion he was feeling and partly, perhaps, because the flakes were now coming down as though the celestial weather-maker was in a hurry and had taken to shaking them out through his screen with both hands. Titus, he saw, was handsome in a rather pronounced way. His eyes were a bright blue, his complexion was decidedly ruddy and his chin, although sharp and assertive, was neatly cleft.

"I think, my boy," said the father, "that you're on the Grace side of the fence."

"I'm glad, I'm positively overjoyed, to hear you say it. The Thwaiteses are a dumpy lot and they don't run to one straight pair of legs in a dozen. I want to tell you in confidence," went on the youth in a voice which had enough penetrative quality to be heard far up the road, "that I'm fed with the other side. Uncle Singleton is an ass. Uncle Gandrel is an oily scoundrel. Cousin Eustace is a beast." He glared angrily. "I want to tell you, they held a meeting to discuss the mater's will. They were enraged because everything had been left to me. They actually talked of bringing suit to have it set aside. They told me so to my face. I told them some truths myself, you may be sure. I said to them, 'Why should she leave money to you vultures and wolves?' "

"My son," asked Julian, "was it wise to quarrel with your mother's family? You are close neighbors, are you not?"

"I couldn't take a pot shot at a crow in any direction without hitting a

Thwaites. But there's no need for worry, Pater. . . . Do you mind if I call you that?"

"Not at all, my boy. I'll enjoy it. I sometimes called *my* father pater."

"I've cut my cables," declared Titus. "I sold the place last week. At a reasonable figure. I sold every stick of furniture, every bushel of grain, every bale of straw. I sold my mother's things. I've decided I must see something of life and so I'm going to set myself up in London. A tidy little flat, a valet and perhaps a cook, and there I'll be, a regular man about town. I'll meet people, not just clods. I'll meet the right kind of young ladies. Perhaps an heiress or two. You ought to see the ones who pass for heiresses where I come from!" He continued in a brisk tone, nodding his head. "And if you'll have me, I'll run down here often over a weekend. You know, I always liked it here. I said to myself as soon as I had your letter, 'It'll be splendid to see Three Gables again.'"

"There will always be a warm welcome for you here, my boy. The door will be wide open. And I think you're making a wise move. You must see something of life and meet the right kind of people. London is the place for you decidedly."

After dinner, while the two men went through the motions of passing the wine although neither of them drank very much, Titus began to talk. It had been apparent to his father almost from the first moment of his arrival that he had something to say. Squaring his elbows on the table, he leaned forward in a confidential pose.

"Pater, do you believe in frankness?"

"Why, yes. Of course, I do. Up to a point, that is."

"Then," said Titus, "I should like to ask you some frank questions. I want to ask you about your will."

Julian laughed easily. "My will? I have so little to leave that my will is a small matter. A very small matter indeed."

The heavy reddish eyebrows of his son drew in together. "Small?" he said. "I am not sure I agree with you there. This is a valuable piece of property and I happen to know that you've cleared off the mortgage."

Julian looked up over the rim of his glass with considerable surprise. "How is it you know that?"

"I had inquiries made. And I've kept track of the amounts you get out of the Tontine. One way and another, Pater, you've got a very decent income. A very handsome one, in fact."

"Well, I'm in easier circumstances now than for many years," conceded his father. "But it takes a good deal to keep this place going. I save very little."

"I think I could make a shrewd guess about what you save." The bright blue eyes under the red eyebrows were alive with interest. "Pater, what are you doing in your will? I mean, what am I going to get out of it?"

His father was so taken aback by the suddenness and unexpectedness of the question that at first he could do no more than stare at him.

"Why, my boy," said Julian finally, "you are a very rich man, having the

whole of your mother's estate. I haven't made any inquiries—considering it
none of my business—but I am certain you are in possession of more than
you'll ever need. Under the circumstances you can't expect any part of the
few pounds I can manage to lay aside."

"Why not?" Titus spoke sharply and looked his father intently in the
eye. "Why shouldn't I have a share? Why shouldn't I have it all? What I
have now comes from my mother and has no bearing on the case. It's mine,
and it's all tucked away, and my having it doesn't interfere with my rights
where your property is concerned. I am your only living child. No one can
say any different from that. And now that we're on the subject, and speaking
frankly, this property is worth a lot. It's a very desirable location and it gets
more valuable all the time."

"This property," declared his father with equal sharpness, "goes to my
grandson, of course. It was acquired by Timothy Ballard and was given as a
wedding gift to my wife. When she died, she left it to me with the understanding that it would pass to Timothy, our son. As Timothy is dead, it goes
to his son."

"His son is illegitimate. He has no right to the property at all. Oh, I've
looked into that, you may be sure. He couldn't enter any claim to the
property. Why, damnation, Pater, under the French law *you* wouldn't be
allowed to will anything to him."

"We don't live under French law, Titus. And a fortunate thing it is. I
can dispose of my property as I see fit. You must be aware that fathers dis-
inherit their sons all the time. If I desired to, I could leave this property
to a society for the care of sick cats or for penniless illegitimate children.
What I do with it is my business. My will is my business. Is that entirely
clear?"

Titus said nothing for several moments. He was staring angrily into his
glass. "I know my rights," he said finally. "And I'm going to stick up for
them. Mark my words, you'll have to make me your heir."

"Titus, was it to say this that you came here today?"

The son flushed. "Partly. I believe in getting things straightened out. I
rather expected you would take this stand, and I want you to know that I
consider you are being rankly unfair and prejudiced. Apparently I can't expect
any fairness or decency of treatment from my own father, unless I go to
law about it. This is a regular Jeremy Diddler of a deal! I won't stay under
this roof another minute if you don't promise to reconsider."

"My son, if I live long enough, there will be a fair share for you in my
will. A few years of saving out of the Tontine funds will make a great difference. But I can't give you any promises. You should be reasonable and
realize my position."

The young man's face had flushed an angry red. "How can I be reasonable
when I'm being robbed of my birthright!"

He got to his feet in such a hurry that he spilled his wine on the tablecloth. He stood still for a moment, glaring at the silent figure at the head of
the table.

"I'll order the horses and be off, storm or no storm. I can't breathe the air of a place where such injustice is being done me. I'll never return, until I hear from you that you've come to your senses!"

"This is all so familiar," thought Julian, staring unhappily at the board after Titus had stalked from the room. "He is exactly like his mother." The boy would not be foolish enough, he hoped, to carry out his threat of driving on at once to London.

But in less than half an hour he heard sounds of departure from the direction of the stables and Titus calling peremptory orders to Noel.

3

Julian Grace walked into the law offices of Jonathan Bade and looked about him with curiosity, wondering on what scale this spectacular character was conducting his legal firm since leaving Samuel Carboy. He was surprised to hear himself addressed at once by Jonathan who was seated at his desk in a corner of the main office.

"Good morning, Captain Grace," said Bade.

Julian smiled and held out a hand. "I didn't expect to be recognized. I desire to have some legal papers drawn up and executed. It has always been my intention to leave my place of residence to my grandson, who bears my name. Something has transpired, however, which makes me think it wise to transfer it to him at once. I discussed it with him and he is insisting that we draw up as well a lease on the property in my favor, to run as long as I live and desire to remain in residence there. He was against having any rent and gave in only when I pointed out the wisdom from a legal standpoint of putting things on a purely business basis."

"Decidedly," commented the lawyer. "Possession for any length of time without any payment can be used as grounds for a claim of ownership. Do you propose to make it a token payment?"

"I would prefer to pay him a proper rent. Because of my share in the Waterloo Tontine, I am in a position to afford it. The rent could serve in lieu of an allowance which I now make him."

They discussed the details of the transfer and Bade took down the necessary notes. "It will not take long to get these papers prepared and ready for signature," he remarked. "I can wait upon you with them whenever you find it convenient. Or would you prefer to come here and bring your grandson with you?"

"We'll come here. My grandson has a position in London. With the Eastern exporting company of Johnstoun, Ward and Seeley. He entertains the idea that he can make a businessman of himself. If he succeeds, it will be the first time in the history of the Grace family. I'm quite proud of him, I may say. He's working very hard and refuses all the indulgences which youth so often demands." Julian rose to his feet and gathered up his gloves. "I'm leaving in a month or so to take up quarters at Sheerness and after that I shall be absent for some time in Bermuda. I'll be grateful if the papers can be signed and the whole matter cleared up before I go."

"Sheerness and Bermuda. I don't want to seem inquisitive but the association of those two names indicates that you are concerned with this great floating dock being built at such enormous cost for the island."

"It will be the most complete and the most expensive operation of the kind ever undertaken." Julian decided after a moment's consideration that there would be no harm done in explaining something of the part he was to play. No secret seemed to have been made of it in Admiralty circles. "You see, Mr. Bade, I became something of an authority on dry-dock facilities when I was at the Admiralty. To build the Bermuda dock here and then tow it more than halfway across the Atlantic is taking a tremendous risk. The Admiralty has been under criticism already. Some authorities think it would be wiser to send it out in parts. Others take the view it should be built on the island itself. The Admiralty heads are convinced they are taking the right course; and I may say that I am completely in accord with them. They are bringing me back from retirement for as long as it will take to get the operation finished. I am telling you this in confidence, of course. I am to keep an eye on everything that is done and to report to the Admiralty whenever it seems advisable. Most particularly I will be in a position to support them if the controversy should continue after the dock has been delivered and placed in the camber at Bermuda."

"It seems to me that a very high honor is being paid you, Captain Grace."

"I'm happy, at any rate, to be in harness again. The idleness of retirement is sometimes very trying. By the way, I heard you speak here in London a few weeks ago. It was a most impressive performance, sir, and I left the hall convinced it was a matter of duty to take some part in the cause you preach. I have already made a donation to the fund."

"I knew you had, Captain Grace, and it was my intention to thank you before letting you get away. It was a most generous check and my associates and I are grateful. These things move slowly, my dear sir, and so we are always in need of financial support."

"Don't you ever become discouraged?"

Bade shook his head. "Not any more. There were many times when I felt I was wasting my efforts but gradually I came to see that far down underneath the mills were actually grinding; though ever so slowly. Whenever I still feel a tendency to discouragement, I can raise my spirits by watching something which happens on the street above us here." He drew out his watch and snapped back the lid. "Ah, how fortunate! In exactly two minutes you will be in a position to see with your own eyes. Would you care, Captain Grace, to step to the front window and fix your gaze on the street which crosses a block up? At five o'clock sharp a man passes there every Friday evening. He never fails. You will know him by the fact that he carries a satchel in each hand."

"There he is!" exclaimed Grace suddenly. "He has a bag in each hand, as you said. He's walking slowly and seems much concerned over what is going on around him."

"He's following orders. It's assumed that someone might take an unwarranted interest in the contents of at least one of the bags. What type of man should you say he is?"

Grace continued to study the passing pedestrian. "He's in trade. Or he might be a banker."

"You are right on the second guess. He's a banker."

"He's wearing a hat which was once a good one but has lost most of its nap from long usage; but he keeps it neat and well brushed. The same applies to his coat. I judge him to be an employee in a bank who has to keep up an appearance of respectability on a small wage."

"Quite." Bade joined his companion at the window just in time to see the bank employee, with his two bags, his worn but respectable hat and his once impeccable coat, vanish from sight. "He comes from a bank a half mile or so away and he goes to the office of the *Daily Packet* two blocks north of here."

"That seems odd. What do you know about him?"

"About the man himself? Nothing. He's the fourth man I've seen carrying out this errand."

"You mean that this has been going on for a long time?"

Bade nodded. "It has been going on for more than thirty years, my dear Grace. And I expect it will continue much longer. Will it surprise you if I say I know what his errand is but that the man himself doesn't?"

"It would indeed. If this man doesn't know what he's supposed to do, how can he carry out his orders?"

"He receives no orders, other than the instructions given him when he begins this service. I doubt if anyone at the bank knows today what he's supposed to do and the same applies to the people he sees at the newspaper office."

"I think, Mr. Bade, you are trying deliberately to confuse me. I make no sense whatever out of this."

So Jonathan told him of the experience of his friend on the occasion when Louis Napoleon made his futile gesture at invading France and of the furor which ensued in the *Packet* offices. "My friend is now the editor," he explained, "and I'm sure he would recall the circumstances if he discovered that his office still has this weekly visitor. I doubt if he has been informed of the fact. It's taken for granted and never discussed."

Julian Grace shook his head with a certain degree of exasperation. "My dear Bade," he said, "this is the most absurd story I've heard in many a long day."

Bade nodded in agreement. "I've called it to your attention because it has a bearing on what we've been saying. We have here a prime demonstration of the solidity of English customs. It has been the rule for over thirty years for a member of the banking staff to go each week to the newspaper office. Now neither his going nor his arrival is questioned. It has always been done;

ergo, it should still be done. There is something absurd about this incident —but also something admirable, a blind and unquestioning adherence to tradition." He turned and walked slowly back to his desk. "The advocate of change should always remember how wholeheartedly we cling to tradition. When I get discouraged over the slowness of public reaction to open wrongs, I go and stand at my window at five o'clock of a Friday and watch my bank clerk pass, as prompt as Big Ben, as infallible as death, doing his duty blindly. It teaches me not to expect quick change. It bolsters my courage with the certainty that when reform comes it will be accepted as completely as the condition which preceded it, that we'll stand by the new order as zealously as we stood by the old. We are not a flibbertigibbet nation, ready to seize a gun and bellow for change at a moment's notice." He indulged in a smile like the sudden illumination which comes with the swing of a beacon light. "Do you realize that the improvement in child labor has become a permanent one? Those who fought against it would now fight for it!"

## CHAPTER THREE

### 1

It was a beautiful day. A warm sun was lending to the Island of Cedars an even larger share of magic and romance than it usually had; for the waves, which buffeted a coast of jagged rocks, interspersed with beaches of blinding white, were of a blue which few on the convoy had ever seen before, a translucent shade which might only be expected if celestial water lapped the walls of paradise.

Spanish Point was not black with people as it had been the day before, when it had been expected that the huge dock would be brought in to its permanent home, but there were plenty of people risking the loss of another day to see what would happen. The heads of the horses which had brought the spectators out in carriage and surrey were resplendent with plumes, and the bandannas of the colored girls were of every gay color known. The bay was covered with small craft and it had taken the full exertions of one of the gunboats to keep the ambitious amateur pilots from getting into the Narrows.

The *Bermuda*, which had been built to such new specifications that it could claim to be the largest floating dock in the whole world, was behaving well after its performance of the day before, when it had ripped up anchors with abandon and broken hawsers with nonchalance in a determination to set off on its own for Halifax. There it lay, close to the camber where it was to remain for all of its life span. The curtain had been removed and it looked, with its huge rounded sides riding high above the water, so much like Noah's Ark that the people on shore might reasonably have expected to see the animals start coming out, two by two as they had gone in, or perhaps six by six, with the dove displaying the olive branch above them.

Julian Grace was in a high state of exultation. The experiment had been a great success. The dock had been towed across the Atlantic and had been brought in, to the complete confounding of the critics. His report on all this was in his cabin, written in a hand which was neat if not quite Spencerian, and couched in tones which sometimes rose above the level of pedantry and took on overtones of exuberance. The lords of the Admiralty had been right. All that remained now for him to do, in order to establish their complete rightness for all time, was to survey the islands and get the necessary evidence in rebuttal of the suggestion that the dock could have been built here in the first place. From what he had already heard, he had no doubt that it would be easy to make a case. Two weeks would suffice and he would then catch the first ship back to London.

As he stood by the rail he could read fatigue in the back of the admiral who was standing above him on the quarterdeck, from which he had not absented himself all the night before. There was fatigue also in the pose of Eben Rufus Culpepper, who shared the rail with him. Mr. Culpepper had been in London on business connected with his small chandlery shop on Front Street and had been granted passage back with the convoy through some influence.

"Ah, Captain Grace," said the merchant, "the great exploit has been brought to a successful conclusion. But I, sir, cannot share this enthusiasm manifested on every side. I, to come straight to the point, am in no end of trouble."

Julian glanced down at him and saw that his face was a picture of deep worry. "I'm sorry to hear it, Mr. Culpepper," he said.

"You see, Captain Grace, I am a bachelor. I know it is generally supposed that bachelors are carefree fellows with all the time in the world on their hands. You will perhaps not be surprised to hear that no one hesitated to give me commissions when it was known I was going to England. I was entrusted with verbal messages for friends in odd corners of the kingdom. I was asked to pick up little items obtainable in only the most damnably out-of-the-way places. Sir, I have failed to carry them out almost without exception. I am wondering how I shall face the charming ladies who depended on me, when I return with such a record of failure."

"They'll be no worse off than they were before," suggested Julian.

"Sir, that is not entirely true. There is one exception. Which involves not only the chagrin of friends but the loss of cash, hard cash, sir, to the value of four pund ten. I was asked by no fewer than six young mothers to purchase shoes for their offspring, and the money to pay was entrusted to me. Had I been wise, sir, I would have left this errand until the very last minute. But one day quite soon after my arrival, finding myself in the proximity of a good shoe shop, I bought all six pair in the sizes specified. Then began a series of most unexpected delays. I was held back by one thing and an-

other, I was chivied about and neglected and cozened by this one and that,
I was beguiled by promises never kept and perhaps never meant. Captain
Grace, as a result of all these vexations it is three months since I purchased
the shoes. Sir, each of the six children, who are all most unnecessarily healthy,
have grown out of them long before this!" There was a long pause. "And I
fear that the loss of the four pund ten will be mine!"

Before Julian could find any suggestions for Mr. Culpepper in his dilemma, a steward appeared at his elbow.

"The admiral's compliments, Captain Grace, and could you step up for a
word with him?"

He found the commander of the convoy in a relaxed mood. "Ha, Captain
Grace," said the great man in a tone which he probably regarded as a whispered confidence but which allowed all about him to hear, "I'm inclined
to think we've shown them, these doubting Thomases, these self-made experts who thought they knew better than we did! The experiment has been
a success. The half million pounds it cost have not been wasted. There she
lies, without a scratch on her sides, big enough to swallow a whale, and as
quiet now as a canal barge. I hope, Captain Grace, that the full measure of
our triumph will be reflected in the report you are preparing."

"I'm inclined to fear, sir," answered Julian, "that a definite note of pride
has crept into what should be a cut and dried record. I'll undoubtedly have
to do some pruning before I place my report in the hands of the great men
at Whitehall."

"Make the pruning light, sir, make it light!" prompted the admiral.
"We've had to swallow a lot of guff and civilian jackassery over this matter.
Now that we've proven our case, it won't hurt to blow our bugles a little."

The admiral's eye turned in the direction of the floating dock, lying as
docile as a scow beside the camber, with its two wooden bridges and its
binnacle and steering apparatus, all of which would soon be removed. His
eyes lighted up with affection and pride.

"She's as broad in the beam as a waddling widow," he said, "but, damme,
Captain Grace, I've taken a liking to the faithful old gal. She got a bit skit-
tish once or twice, but what could you expect when her ribs were new and
she was plastered with paint from bow to stern? I'm positively fond of her.

"You'll go ashore with us, sir," continued the admiral. "I imagine you
won't mind putting your legs under a table which doesn't heave and roach,
and dining again off a plate which knows enough to stay on its own bit of
tablecloth."

2

A week later the report had been completed and the weaknesses in the
theory that the dock might have been built in Bermuda had been thoroughly
exposed. Julian Grace decided to celebrate his release from the ardors of
composition by taking in the races at Shelly Bay. He lunched on a fine white

fish and a slice of cold chicken and hired a carriage to take him out to the course.

The Hill was crowded with those who preferred to watch at an outlay of a shilling. Julian produced his four shillings for the grandstand and found one seat only unoccupied. This, it developed, placed him beside a lady he had met once before, a Mrs. Beltrade. She turned her fine dark eyes on him and said with a welcoming smile, "Why, Captain Grace, I didn't expect to find you doing anything as frivolous as this."

Julian was glad that he had dressed himself with particular care, selecting an immaculate cravat and brushing his hat and coat assiduously before starting. He was glad also that in the brief glance he had given his mirror in the course of dressing he had found reason for believing that he did not look his age. His forehead was unlined and the hair which crowned it, although silver in hue, was as ample as ever.

"Good afternoon," he said. "I've completed my labors and so I confess that I feel in a frivolous mood."

He seated himself beside Mrs. Beltrade, to whom he had been introduced at the Admiralty House dinner to celebrate the success of the great undertaking. She was a widow who had lost her husband, a wealthy American, a few years after they had settled on the island and purchased one of the oldest and finest of the houses.

"After the large racing tracks in the United States, you must find this one small enough to be described as quaint," he said, letting his gaze take in the half-mile course and the meager space provided for spectators.

"Oh no, not at all. I come out every Thursday. I love horses and I'm devoted to the sport. And I'm not an American, Captain Grace. I met Mr. Beltrade in Jamaica, where I was born. I've never been in the United States."

Julian understood now why he had been interested in her at once at the Admiralty dinner. She had been separated from him by almost the full length of the table but there had been about her something that reminded him of Winifred. This had been no more than a passing reflection but now that he knew she came from Jamaica he gave her a quick glance and saw that she indeed possessed the same smooth black hair and dark-lashed eyes he remembered with such undiminished affection.

"I was in Jamaica once," he said. "That was a long time ago. You will know how long when I tell you that I was on my way to join Admiral Cochrane in the South American War of Independence. I was left waiting in Kingston for a month but it was because of the delay that I met my wife. How fortunate it was!"

His companion looked up at him at once with aroused interest. "Of course! My memory must be getting poor or I would have known as soon as I heard your name. I remember hearing as a small girl—quite a small girl, Captain Grace, because a lady must protect herself in such an important matter as her age—well, I remember my mother saying that Winifred Ballard, who had been sent to a fashionable school in England, had married a naval officer. I believe it was said to have been an elopement."

"There were circumstances which made some people think we had eloped. I assure you, however, that all the details of our wedding were arranged by my wife's father, who had come to England to look things over. What a splendid man Timothy Ballard was!"

"I met you at the Admiralty dinner also, Captain Grace," said the lady on the other side of Mrs. Beltrade, "but you don't seem to remember, even though I too am a Jamaican by birth." She was a lady of uncertain years and equally suspect blondeness whose name, he now recalled, was Miss Violet O'Malley and who lived with Mrs. Beltrade in the capacity of companion. "I'm older than Sue and I remember all about your wedding. It was the sensation of the day in Jamaica, Winifred Ballard being such a great heiress." This was skating on thin ice, in view of what happened later to the Ballard fortunes. Sensing this, Miss O'Malley lapsed into silence.

A colored man in scarlet shirt and jockey cap came out from the stable enclosure and made his way to the judge's stand. Here he blew a bugle for the first race, doing it so thoroughly that his cheeks seemed on the point of bursting. It was a finely rounded performance, *Taran-taraw, Taran-taraw!* Six horses, with jockeys up, came out on the track and the spectators tensed with sudden interest.

Julian's eyes settled on a rangy gray. "I like that fellow," he said.

"That's Epsilon," explained Mrs. Beltrade. "He's certain to be the favorite. It seems you have a good eye for the horses, Captain Grace."

"I don't know anything about them at all. I just happen to like the easiness of his gait. Still, I feel disposed to risk a few shillings on him. How do you go about laying a bet?"

"Friends make wagers among themselves. And over on the Hill I believe they have pools." She glanced up at him and fleetingly touched his sleeve with a hand gloved in black lace. Her voice fell to a whisper. "Of course, it *is* said that if one goes around behind the grandstand there's likely to be a man there named Harty who offers odds on all the horses. I've never done that, of course, because this Mr. Harty, who is called Holy Joe, I'm told, has no right to be there. In fact he would be arrested if he were caught at it. But it's a funny thing that the police never think of looking behind the grandstand."

Julian nodded gravely. "I see. It is strange."

"This is all hearsay, Captain Grace, but if you were to go up to him and put in his hands, say, ten shillings or even a pound, and whisper 'Epsilon' to him, he would give you something which, I believe, is called a ticket. You can't be mistaken because he always wears a yellow vest, no matter how warm it is."

Julian smiled down at her. "I'm going to pay a visit to this Holy Joe Harty. Could I—ahem—place a bet with him for either of you?"

Miss O'Malley had been listening and at this point she shuddered. "Oh no, Captain Grace. I never gamble. But dear Sue is much more wicked about such things. She's a positive *plunger.*"

"Which one would you like to plunge on this time, Mrs. Beltrade?" he asked.

The pretty widow was watching a small black mare which had just gal-
loped easily past the grandstand. "That's a new entry," she said, consulting
her list. "And a new owner. Agnès Sorel. H'm. I rather like the little lady."

"She's kind of small, isn't she?"

"She's good for the distance." Mrs. Beltrade gave her head a convinced
nod. "I like the way she carries her head. Look at the darling! She has courage and the will to do her best. Do you know, Captain Grace, I'm going to ask
you to place ten shillings on Agnès Sorel for me. You see," giving him a quick
smile, "I'm not such a plunger after all."

"Are you sure you want the mare? The gray has a fine easy gait and you say
yourself he's the favorite."

"I suppose it's silly of me but I still want to bet on my little Agnès Sorel."

He located the yellow-vested Holy Joe Harty and placed the bets. Harty
whispered in a husky voice, "I'll be generous wid ye, seein' as ye're a stranger,
and give ye nine to one on the mare."

When Julian returned the horses were lined up for the start. Epsilon went
out in the lead but, turning into the stretch, the black mare passed him and
came tripping home a full two lengths ahead. Julian looked down at the
widow in wonder. "You are the one who seems to know the horses," he said.

"I'm sorry you were so stubborn about the gray," she answered. "If you
hadn't been so determined to bet on him, you might be ninety shillings
ahead too."

"Oh, I am," smiling. "I changed my mind, not being as stubborn as you
think. Your reasoning convinced me and I bet on the mare."

This became the fixed order of the afternoon. He would see a horse he
liked very much and exclaim about it, and generally it proved to be one of
the favored entries. But his companion would be watching one of the others
and would finally say, "I like that one."

"Come. Come, Mrs. Beltrade!" he would protest. "Not that scrawny roan!"

"Yes, the scrawny roan. There's something about his eyes, Captain Grace."

There was always something about the horse she favored, and always he
gave in. They won five times in the first six races. When he returned after the
sixth, his pockets bulging, and dropped a handful of notes into her lap, she
looked at him with a guilty air.

"I'm beginning to feel most awfully selfish, Captain Grace. Aren't you?"

"Not a bit," he answered cheerfully. "This is the only time I've ever made
money on horse races. It's averaging up for me ever so little."

"But——" She stopped and frowned doubtfully. "But I don't know anything about this Mr. Holy Joe. Suppose he's an honest man with a wife and
family to support? Are we taking the bread out of the mouths of his poor
children?"

"Spare your doubts and sympathies, ma'am. Holy Joe wears a ring on one
finger with a diamond large enough to keep a hundred families, if he had to
sell it. I watched every time he forked over the money and the stone seemed
to glint at me balefully." He paused to make a mental calculation. "We are

each ahead a matter of fifteen pounds ten. I'm the one who should feel guilty. I've been battening on your superior judgment."

"Ah, if I had only been brave enough to do the same!" sighed Miss O'Malley. "But I can never get my courage up to risk my own money."

Mrs. Beltrade carefully deposited her winnings in a pocket concealed under one of the seven flounces on her skirt of blue taffeta. "Come along, my good friends," she said. "Don't you think we've had enough of this? And I've thought of a perfectly gorgeous way to ease my conscience."

"I hope it's more sensible than some of your ideas, Sue," said Miss O'Malley.

"I'm going to give every penny of it away."

"No, no!" cried the companion. "Unless you're going to give it to me!"

"I'm going to give it to those who need it."

Julian got to his feet at once. Mrs. Beltrade settled a scarf of black Maltese lace over her shoulders and Miss O'Malley, still protesting and bewailing her lack of luck, gave a perfunctory touch to a curious form of collar she wore which resembled a stock. They edged their way down through the crowded grandstand seats and reached the ground.

"Have you a carriage?" asked the widow.

He nodded. "I hired one to bring me out."

"Then pay him off, if you please. I want you to help me with this scheme of mine."

"Take my advice and go home, Captain Grace," said the companion. "You don't know what kind of trouble this scheme of hers will get you into."

Julian was looking into the melting black eyes under the long curled lashes. He thought to himself, "I wonder!"

"Don't listen to Vi," said the owner of the eyes. "There's nothing very unusual or strange about the idea at all. I just happened to think of someone who needs the money."

As they walked up the hilly path to the enclosure where the carriages were waiting, she explained what she wanted to do.

"There's a wonderful character on the island, a colored woman named Victoria Regina Shand. When she was young she had a gorgeous voice and she was small and, they say, quite beautiful, with large sad eyes. That was before I came to Bermuda. When I saw her, she had grown very heavy and she couldn't sing at all because her husband had tried to throttle her in a jealous rage and had damaged her vocal cords. . . . She still speaks in a low and husky voice.

"I'm very fond of her," she went on. "Being deprived of her voice, she's started a free school for children of her own race. She teaches all day and earns her living at night by making the most exquisite dresses. They have figures embroidered on them in perfect color combinations. I'm going to turn my earnings over to her."

"A capital idea," said Julian. "I'll give mine too."

Mrs. Beltrade leaned forward as she walked to glance up at him around his rather massive shoulder. "I so hoped you would," she said. "Why, between us, we'll give her clear sailing for a year. How very nice you are, Captain Grace."

"Where will we find her?"

"She has a little stone cabin not far from here, facing the east. It's on top of a high slope and she tells me if all the hills and the trees could be cleared off she would be able to see Jerusalem. She doesn't believe the world is round. The Bible doesn't say so, and she knows it can't be true."

As they climbed, a fine equipage had detached itself from the rest and had come out to await them. The colored driver, holding in a spirited black team, grinned broadly at his mistress.

"Miss' 'Trade, you win t'day?" he asked.

"I was very lucky, Zebulon," she answered. "But every shilling goes to Victoria Regina. If you expect to get any of it, you'll have to convince *her* that you deserve it."

"No chance a *that*," said the driver in a disappointed tone of voice. He brightened up, however, when Julian caught his eye and winked reassuringly.

3

The house which faced Jerusalem was reached by perhaps the steepest climb on the island. The grade was so extreme, in fact, that they had to leave the carriage and climb the last hundred yards on foot. At the top they found, in addition to the tiny stone cabin which served as school and home for the teacher, a cluster of even smaller and ruder habitations. As none of the owners could afford as much as a candle, they had already finished their evening meal and were sitting about in the twilight in attitudes of complete relaxation. When they saw the trio of white visitors plodding slowly up the winding path, their eyes grew large with curiosity. One of them, who had been strumming on a crude form of banjo, suspended his musical efforts and stared with the rest.

"Oh dear, the dirt is ruining my shoes and this is the first time I've worn them," said Mrs. Beltrade. She held one foot out in front of her to demonstrate that the neat black cloth shoe with buttons up the side, of the same shade of blue as her dress, was covered with white dust.

When they reached the top Julian remained outside with the companion while Mrs. Beltrade vanished within the half-opened door. They heard a voice raised in throaty welcome, and a moment later the small light of a single candle appeared in the dark interior.

"See how they watch us!" said Miss O'Malley in a whisper. "Look at that one with the scar on his cheek! I'm sure he's a bad lot. I'm all over goose flesh."

"But their eyes are friendly," contended Julian.

It was clear from the tone of the voices inside the little stone house that the news they brought had delighted the schoolteacher. In a few minutes she appeared in the doorway, a squat figure in calico with a red bandanna bound around her head. Her dark eyes seemed thoroughly alive as well as hauntingly tragic.

"Sir," she said, addressing Julian, "you and the sweet lady of Crosswick are an answer to prayer. We have been in the greatest straits and today I had the class recite an appeal to the good Lord up there behind the stars to grant us a boon. He has heard our prayer."

Julian bowed to her. "I'm happy that Mrs. Beltrade's idea is going to prove so helpful to you."

"Captain Grace, your name suggests kindness and beneficence." He was quite taken back by the cultured voice and by her choice of words. "I seem to remember something about you but it eludes me. What have you done so unusual that word of it might reach our ears on this side of the world?"

Julian shook his head. "I've done nothing, I assure you. I've lived a very quiet and uneventful life."

"If I saw your hand I might find the answer. Also I might find in it something pleasant to tell you as a slight return for your wonderful gift. Do you care?"

Mrs. Beltrade had now left the house and, at the mention of palm reading, she almost ran across the brown and much-scuffed sod to join them. Her bouffant skirt swayed about her and the petticoats under it announced most unmistakably that they were made of silk. "You must find nothing but pleasant things to tell him," she admonished.

Julian held out his hand and the head in the bright bandanna bowed over it intently in the rapidly gathering dusk. "You will never lack again for money," she said at once. "You will receive more and more of it as long as you live. And it makes me very happy, Captain Grace, to see that you will live for many years. More years than you perhaps expect. You are going to live far beyond the threescore and ten that the Lord in His wisdom allotted to us. But"—she had begun to frown as she strove to make out the meaning of something she saw in his palm—"there is something here I don't understand. There are people who do not wish you well and that surprises me very much, sir. There are many of them."

He nodded. "That is quite true."

"I can see now that there are twelve of them who share this unfriendly feeling. This is very strange. Can it be a conspiracy?"

"You have named the exact number! But rest easy, it is not a conspiracy and none of them can harm me. Do you know what a tontine is?"

She looked up at once. "Of course. That is it. I had heard of the great Tontine in England. The twelve are those who survive with you and would divide your share if you died. It is greed with them and not malice." She gave her head a positive nod. "Little good it will do them, Captain Grace. I can read here that you will outlive most of them at least."

"And what pleasanter picture could you give him of the future than that?" said Mrs. Beltrade.

"I knew Captain Grace was one of them," declared Miss O'Malley. "I read everything about the Tontine that I can find in print. It's becoming quite a fascinating speculation, isn't it? Why didn't Terry O'Malley, my beloved but improvident father, put me into something of the kind?"

"You were born too late. The Waterloo Tontine was the last one of any size to get started. There's been talk, as you doubtless know, of stopping this one because of the gambling side of it. But there's nothing they can do."

They retraced their steps down the sloping path and ensconced themselves in the carriage. Miss O'Malley, with a tact which had grown out of long habit, took the front seat with her back to the horses. The lovely widow, who seemed to Julian to get lovelier with every moment spent in her company, smoothed out her skirt and settled back contentedly beside him on the other. "Do you know," she asked, "that I'm taking you home for supper?"

"I hoped you were," he answered with a smile.

"We have a full hour's ride ahead of us. I'm going to use it to the very best advantage by asking you all manner of questions, Captain Grace. About yourself. I confess freely that I am one of the most curious women in the world."

It was very warm, and whenever the carriage passed behind a stone wall or a thick cover of trees or, more particularly, when it was engulfed in the canyons of coral rock through which the roads had been cut, the air was uncomfortably close. Julian would feel prickles of perspiration on his brow at once. But such moments of discomfort were brief, for they would soon bowl briskly out into the open and feel the benefit of the steadily blowing breeze from the sea. The most delightful sense of coolness succeeded the heat. Julian was not yet accustomed to such sudden changes and he looked with surprise at Mrs. Beltrade, who seemed to feel no effects whatever. Her face was still visible to him, perhaps because of the magnolia whiteness of her skin. She seemed to him as coolly beautiful as the cameo brooch which hung at her throat on a rope of fine gold chain.

The conversation which ensued revealed more about Mrs. Beltrade herself than about her guest. It developed that she had been a widow for eight years and that she expected to remain one. She lived in a house with considerable acreage just over the parish line in Pembroke and could see Government House from her bedroom window. She went to London and Paris every second year and returned with trunks filled with clothes.

The information she had intended to acquire about him ended when he stated he was leaving in another week. She made no effort to suppress a sigh on hearing this. "That's *such* a short time. Must you go so soon? Can't the Admiralty wait for this mysterious report you are preparing?"

"I'm afraid not. I'm under orders, you see."

"Then you must come back. In fact I don't see why you don't settle down here. It's the one perfect place to live, I assure you. No fogs, no cold, no hail, well, very little. The air is as soft as a caress. And, to get to practical matters, your money goes much further here."

"I agree with everything you say, Mrs. Beltrade. But I have a place on the Thames which I love. It's filled with memories. There's a cricket field behind the stables where my son Timothy played with his friends. He's dead now but it's not hard for me to close my eyes and hear their voices when I sit outside of an evening. And my grandson Julian is employed in London and comes down to be with me every weekend. He couldn't do that if I lived in Bermuda."

"How can a mere island of sunshine and peace compete with that!" Mrs. Beltrade shook her head in defeat and turned to another subject. "It was kind of you, Captain Grace, to go with me to see Victoria Regina. She has a great imagination and I would like to hear her tomorrow, telling her pupils about the tall Englishman who came in answer to their prayers. She'll give you wings and a great golden horn like Gabriel."

Miss O'Malley entered the conversation for the first time at this point. "Did you say your son was named Timothy?" she asked.

"Yes. He was named for his grandfather, Timothy Ballard." Detecting a look of curiosity in the companion's eye, he gave his head a grave nod. "I expect you are recalling what happened to him. Yes, Miss O'Malley, he was the Timothy Grace who ran away with another man's wife. Who gave up a great career for the woman he loved."

Mrs. Beltrade made no comment but her eyes had become aroused. Perhaps she was wondering if the romantic spirit of the son might be wakened again in the cool, silver-haired father who sat so straight beside her.

They had stopped before a pair of stone gates from which a flagstone walk seemed to stretch endlessly into the darkness. The roof of a tall house was black against the sky. The driver scrambled down from his seat and opened the carriage door.

"This is Crosswick, Captain Grace," said Mrs. Beltrade.

4

When they had climbed several levels of the flagged walk, he found that the house was wide and spacious, and that its coral walls were white instead of the prevailing pink. The Welcoming Arms, beginning at the top of the entrance steps and spreading outward as they came down, were a perfect demonstration of the meaning of the term. A dim suggestion of light showed in the long front windows.

"What do you think of it?" asked Mrs. Beltrade.

"It has an immediate feeling of peace and seclusion," answered the visitor.

She nodded to him gratefully. "I have always thought so. I enjoy that feeling of peace whenever I come home. The outside world ends at these steps."

Julian was shown to a bedroom on the ground floor by a colored servant. Answering Julian's question about the supper hour, he pouted out his lips. "Half hour, suh, an hour, suh. Mo', I thinks, p'raps, suh. When Mist'us claps she hands, not befo'."

So he found himself with plenty of time to fill and he employed the idle moments in a survey of the reception rooms. There were three of these across the front of the house, a high center hall, a sitting room with a knee-high chimney and cedar paneling which had been polished and oiled by generations of careful brown hands until the wood was as dark as mahogany, and a library filled with massive volumes. Through all of them there was a pervading odor of cedar which he found as grateful as it was unusual. All of the rooms, he thought, contributed to the sense of peace he had felt on his first glimpse of the mansion.

Behind the entrance hall was a room of equal size from which the staircase rose, a spacious flight of wide steps and graceful balustrade. Here there was space for the display of venerable furniture: a William and Mary escritoire, an odd-sized cabinet with a handsome hood for bibelots, and a tall grandfather's clock with a tick which sounded cheerful rather than ominous. Behind the library was a book-crammed annex, some of the volumes much used and weak of back, and a ladder for getting to the top shelves which was not as ancient as Jacob's but must have been a contender for second honors, and a table covered with periodicals with more of the same in a canterbury beside it. This, he decided, was the chatelaine's room. The chimney was a neat little affair and clearly capable of providing a fine, crackling fire, and the hangings were of a cheerful chintz.

The dining room was on the other side of the stairway, a most imposing apartment with a tray ceiling and a hearth which, in contrast to the knee-high structures in the other room, was almost waist-high. This room had the glitter and more than a smack of the elegance of London. A large chandelier of amethyst crystal had sconces for a hundred candles, or so it seemed, and the table was of mahogany and capable of seating at least a score of guests. The chandelier, however, was to play no part in the evening's supper. Not a candle had been lighted in the midst of its glittering forest of prisms. At each end of the board there was instead a massive candle under hurricane glasses two feet high which provided enough illumination for the white napery and the beautiful old silver and china.

There were no portraits on the walls, which might be accepted as an indication of the owner's honesty. The Beltrade family tree became like a guttering candle beyond two generations and soon went out in total darkness. Perhaps it was just as well, for only the hand and the brush of genius can redeem the human face after memories of the subject fail.

Julian found the rooms so much to his liking that Sue Beltrade had taken two or three steps from the foot of the stairs before he turned. He saw at once that she had used the long interval to the fullest advantage. Her dress was black with touches of green, and cut square and low at the neck, a style infinitely becoming to one with such perfect shoulders to display. She looked so different that he stared at her for several moments in a state almost of disbelief. Had this slender creature heard talk of the wedding of Winifred Ballard and Julian Grace? A hasty consideration of dates established her as at least fifty on that understanding. What was the magic which made it possible almost to believe her still in the magic span of the thirties?

"Am I a stranger?" she asked when he continued to stare at her and failed to find his tongue.

"My dear child," he said, "you fill me with strange thoughts. Bold thoughts and presumptuous and—and very absurd."

"We'll rule out the mention of absurdity. But it will be interesting to explore what you mean by boldness and presumption." She took possession of his arm. "Shall we go in? Or would you like a glass of sherry in the library first?"

Violet O'Malley, looking rawboned and leathery even with a lace shawl over her shoulders, had followed her employer down the stairs. "Oh, bother the sherry, Sue," she said. "I'm famished. And Anastasie tells me we have sole and a really splendid leg of mutton." She fell into step with them as they turned toward the dining room. "Put Captain Grace at the head of the table, Sue," she suggested. "It will be pleasant to see a man presiding in the house for a change."

Mrs. Beltrade looked a little put out. "Must you anticipate all my little plans, Vi?" she asked. "Of course Captain Grace shall sit at the head. With a respectful partner on each side."

Nothing daunted, the companion took the conversation in hand at the start of supper. She seemed to be filled with curiosity about the Tontine. "I think that woman knew there were only thirteen of you left in," she said.

"That's possible, of course. There have been many items in the newspapers about it and a great deal of talk. But, somehow, I don't believe she knew."

"I've read everything I could find about it. It's a positively fascinating thing. Do you know any of the other contestants?"

"One only. The Duchess of Outland."

"That woman is amazing, isn't she? I've followed her career for as long as I can remember. Why should one woman have four husbands while some of us can't even catch one? Is she as beautiful as they say?"

"Yes, Miss O'Malley. I've known her ever since she was a very small girl and so I'm in a good position to judge. You see, her father and mine were partners."

"Do you mean to tell us that your father was the partner of this fabulous Samuel Carboy who has so many millions?"

"Yes, equal partners in a business known as Grace and Carboy. They broke up more than half a century ago. Violently. The two families were always bitter afterward but I remained on the best of terms with Isabelle and her brother."

Mrs. Beltrade asked in a studiously low tone, "The *best* of terms, Captain Grace?"

He turned his head to her side of the table. How much should he tell? After a moment's consideration he decided that no harm could be done by a full confession at this late date.

"We eloped," he said. "At least, we tried to."

"Oh no!" cried Miss O'Malley ecstatically. "Oh no! I can't believe it. I can't! Captain Grace, this is wonderful. To know that such a thing happened in the life of the beautiful Isabelle Carboy and that you are actually sitting here to tell us all about it."

"I don't believe that Captain Grace wants to tell us all about it," said the widow.

"But he must. I want to hear everything. I don't believe I've ever been so excited in my life."

"I think, Vi, we should accept the fact that it was all very beautiful and romantic, and leave it at that," declared Mrs. Beltrade rather coldly.

"It was the most cruel experience of my life," he declared. "Isabelle's father followed us and she went back with him willingly enough. I—I was left to suffer alone. Particularly when she became Lady Gardiner so soon after. It was a sad blow to my pride."

"But you got over it," said the widow. She was toying with her food, in contrast to her companion, who continued to attack the sole, even in the midst of her transports of interest.

"Yes, I got over it. After a year, during which I earned a reputation for being a thoroughgoing misanthrope. I suppose I came in time to rather enjoy my misery."

"Winifred Ballard?"

He nodded, sensitive to the fact that the limit of confession had been reached. "When I saw Winifred again I forgot Isabelle at once."

"But," persisted Miss O'Malley, "I must hear more about this fascinating woman. Why has she always married older men? Apart from the fact that at least three of them were rich and all had titles?"

"Isabelle is selfish and ambitious. I can say that without being guilty of any degree of malice because I'm sure she would be the first to plead guilty on both counts. I think the pattern of her matrimonial career can be explained that way. Men of her own age, most of them being selfish and ambitious themselves, could generally read her correctly. Older men could never resist her. Every time she came into a room, every pair of eyes under white eyebrows got a gleam in them. And as for boys, they fairly wept because they had been born too late to have a chance."

Miss O'Malley was still avid for information. "I wish you had known some of the others. The coachman's daughter, for instance."

"Miss Groody is a charming and clever woman, from all I hear. I have sometimes thought of paying her a visit, just to say that if she should win I would have no hard feelings at all; or feelings of any kind for that matter. But, somehow, I never seem to have had the chance."

"Who do you think will win?"

"Isabelle, of course. I don't think she's ever had a serious illness in her life. She still plays golf and can hit a stout ball."

"How lucky you have been, Captain Grace," sighed the companion. "What a romantic and exciting life!"

Julian looked at her in genuine surprise. "Do you think so? There were many times when I thought myself the most unlucky man in the world. And, I believe, with good reason."

"But you eloped with Isabelle Carboy, you married a great heiress, you fought in wars, you're one of the final contestants in the greatest of all tontines! And there you sit, looking like a man of middle age, and quite as handsome, I'm sure, as you ever were. Women must run after you in droves, Captain Grace. Just think of our little Sue, when she saw you coming into the grandstand, arranging things so there would be a vacant seat beside her——"

"Leave me out of your schoolgirl vaporings, if you please, Vi," said the widow hastily. "I think the time has come to change the subject."

The subject was changed for them by the appearance of the colored butler. "They's here to see you, ma'am," he said.

"Who are here, Hannibal?"

The butler drew himself up with the disdain he felt. "De woman dat cooks at Miss' Loudon's. De man doan' say anything, ma'am. He just stand by hoss."

Sue looked at her companion. "Be a dear, Vi, and get me the envelope. I'll go out and talk to her. Now don't look at me like that. I know you disapprove. But I've given my word."

When the butler opened the door for his mistress, a woman was found to be standing just outside it. She was wearing a bonnet tied tightly around a stolid face. It was evident she had been listening, for there was a belligerent lift to her chin.

"Oh well, come in, Mary Tindy," said Mrs. Beltrade, frowning with annoyance.

The woman walked into the dining room, planking her feet down firmly and looking quickly and suspiciously at each member of the company. She was rather more than plump and her hands, encased in white gloves at the end of bare wrists, were large and, undoubtedly, capable.

"I've come for it, ma'am," she said. Her voice was aggressive and had a grating note to it. "And I'm not the cook for Miss' Loudon. I'll have you know I've removed myself and my belongings elsewhere."

"I'm sure that's a relief for all concerned. I wasn't expecting you tonight."

"Lowfoot had a load of blocks to deliver and he brought me, ma'am." Her dress bore this out, the skirt being covered with fine white dust. "My passage has been took and so Lowfoot and me'll be married the day afore the boat sails."

"Then everything seems to be arranged."

Violet O'Malley returned to the room at this point with an envelope in one hand. "I most certainly do disapprove of this," she said. "You're being very silly, Sue. I'd send her about her business if I had the say."

"Indeed and would you, now!" said the visitor, bridling. "But you don't have the say, do you?"

"Come, enough of this." Mrs. Beltrade transferred the envelope to one of the white-gloved hands. "Where is your young man, Mary Tindy?"

"He's not young, ma'am. He's a sight older than I am but he's all the better for his years. Settled and sober and knows his own mind, ma'am."

"I'm glad of that. I've never seen him, coming to think of it."

The visitor shook her head emphatically. "No, ma'am. No one ever sees

Lowfoot. He's not sociable, ma'am, and he's not a talker. If you was to meet him, sort of unawares, he wouldn't raise his eyes from the ground, being that unsociable, and the most you'd get out of him would be a grunt. But, ma'am, though he ain't sociable and he ain't a talker, he's a thinker. You'd never believe the schemes he thinks of to get orders for cut stone. When we gets to England and buys this brickyard, which is what takes him back, then he'll show 'em. He'll make brick, Casper Lowfoot will, and he'll sell brick." She looked at the envelope in her hand. "How much is it, ma'am?"

"Why, the amount you said, of course. One pound, three and six."

"No more? I was hoping, ma'am. You having so much and me having so little."

"Mary Tindy," said the mistress of the house, with a frown which indicated much inner annoyance, "you should be glad of what you're getting. What with your future husband's thinking and your asking, I'm sure you'll soon have plenty. I hope you get along well with him."

"I'm United Saints of Shiloh and he's Brothers and Sisters of Love and Piety and we won't ever change. But we'll get along. And we'll move up in the world, ma'am. The day will come when we'll have help in our own house. If you lived in England, ma'am, you'd have me calling on you, friendly and sociable. But not Lowfoot. Money will never make him sociable. Get it and keep it, and never say anything to anybody; that's his way, ma'am."

When the visitor had retired, with more than a hint of flounce, Sue Beltrade had to put a hand over her mouth to keep from laughing. "You must be wondering what all this is about, Captain Grace. Hannibal, you may bring in the mutton. Well, Mary Tindy has been cook in the household of a very good friend of mine, Matilda Loudon. Matilda wanted a white cook and so Mary was brought out with the usual understanding that she would pay off so much each month out of her wages. There was still one pound, three and six to be paid but Mary decided she wanted to return and Matilda was certain she wanted to get rid of her. But the one pound, three and six was a stickler. Mr. Lowfoot contended it wouldn't be right for him to pay it because it would be the same as buying his wife. Which would be heathenish and wicked, according to the beliefs of the Brothers and Sisters of Love and Piety. And then Jack Loudon got up on his high horse and said the money had to be paid or she wouldn't be allowed to leave the island. When we found that it wouldn't go against their religious beliefs to accept the money from an outsider—well, to put it in a nutshell, I agreed to pay the one pound, three and six."

"You're indulging in one pound, three and six of foolishness, Mrs. Beltrade," said Julian.

"That's what I've said all along," declared Miss O'Malley.

"I suppose your Mary Tindy will now marry her Mr. Lowfoot and that they'll spend their honeymoon on the voyage back," remarked Julian.

"Well, no, it's not quite that way. Mary had ideas about that also. It seems she was very seasick on the way out and she's sure she'd be just as ill on the way back. She didn't feel that Mr. Lowfoot should be expected to pay for a honeymoon which won't be a honeymoon at all. Mr. Lowfoot, needless to state, agreed with her."

"And are you paying her passage?"

"No, Matilda is doing that. Out of her personal savings, and without Jack knowing it. Anything to get Mary off the island."

"I think," said Julian indignantly, "that you've both been taken in by a pair of very sharp people with the most convenient of religious beliefs."

"I suppose you're right. Don't become sociable with them on the ship, Captain Grace, or Mary Tindy will find some way of getting money out of you."

5

Julian Grace was disturbed about the spending of his last evening in Bermuda. He had been seeing a great deal of the charming chatelaine of Crosswick. In fact of all his evenings had been spent in her company and even some of the afternoons. He had enjoyed every minute of the time and he was aware that his feeling for her had been mounting to a point which seemed dangerous. How pleasant it would be to hear her voice and her low-pitched laugh at Three Gables, to have her at his side, to be able to look down his dinner table and always see her at the other end! Could she be persuaded to live in England? He was inclined to think she would not be averse to the idea.

"There's no fool like an old fool," he would say to himself, each time that such thoughts rose in his mind. But they persisted in coming back.

He was convinced that he should not marry again. It was true that he was in excellent health and in a condition of unusual preservation. But he was probably twenty years older than Sue Beltrade and that was much too great a disparity in years. The memory of Winifred was of even greater importance. More and more as the years passed he had been finding her a bulwark against loneliness. Had he any right to put another woman in his first wife's place? Esther had not counted. But Sue—so agreeable, so sympathetic, so infinitely desirable—was quite a different matter.

His trunk had been packed and sent down to the ship, which was sailing at midnight. He sat alone at a table in the hotel for his last dinner in Bermuda and wondered if it would not be better for both of them if he went aboard at once. It had been understood between them that he would go out to Crosswick to say good-by; but if he went, would it be possible for him to stand by a sane and sensible resolution? He did not underestimate the attractions of the lovely widow.

He decided finally that he must not be a coward, that the engagement he had made must be kept. "Somehow," he said to himself, "I must find the strength of will to keep away from personal topics."

It was still light when he finished the meal and he decided on a last look at the town. He strolled down to Front Street and decided after one glance at the crowds that never before had he seen so much activity and gaiety and color at this time of day, the hour sacred to the evening meal. There were two large vessels tied up at the docks, the Cunard mail ship on which he would travel back to England and one which had just put in on its way to the West Indies. The people of the town, of all conditions and shades of color, had come out to have a look at what was going on.

He saw naval officers, looking very smart in their uniforms and glad of the chance to catch their shore legs for a brief hour and to see female faces and to hear the laughter of pretty girls. Sailors from the southbound ship were enjoying an early taste of shore leave and some of them had been doing themselves rather well at the taverns.

Beyond the second of the great ships there was a handsome yacht of American ownership which had come in a few days before. Three carriages were lined up in front of it and the guests of the owner, an elderly man who had made a fortune in the California gold rush, were piling into them with much delighted talk. He heard enough to know that they were driving over to one of the ocean beaches for a midnight swim and that the costumes they were wearing under their long silk dressing gowns were rather extreme. Knee-length, he gathered. Whew! That was not only extreme, it was positively revolutionary!

"What will come of this sort of thing?" he asked himself.

And yet they seemed rather nice, young for the most part, and pretty, and decidedly gay; he could hear their voices and their laughter as he turned up from Front Street to Reid. "Just youth," he thought. It was going to be an adventure for them and they were looking forward to it.

He paced slowly around the business section, Front and Reid and Queen and Burnaby streets. He visited the bookshop where he had been getting newspapers from London and New York, and bought some reviews for reading on the long run home. He looked in on the bespectacled little tailor who had made him a splendidly fitted pair of trousers at a very low cost. The emporium where he had shopped for many articles, including a woolen garment which was being called by the far from euphonious name of "sweater," was closed for the night; he regretted this, because he had enjoyed several long talks with the proprietor on life and letters and ships that sail the sea. Everything about the island had pleased him; he had found it friendly and easy and without too much in the way of artificial barriers.

For his use in getting about the town and countryside, he had rented a bicycle at one of the shops on Front, being lucky enough to find one of the type he had been using at home. It was called a "phantom" and the wheels were almost of the same size, which made riding less hazardous and a much more pleasant experience than on the high kinds in use earlier. He had become quite an ardent bicyclist, in fact, and had even thought of joining a London organization known as the Pickwick Bicycle Club.

Crosswick was no more than two miles from town and he decided to use the machine in getting there. He took his bicycle from the rack in front of the hotel. It would be a pleasant way to see this beautiful island for the last time.

He rode slowly. The grades were steep and, as the sun had gone down, the road was dark in the coral defiles and in its tortuous turnings through groves of cedar trees. A breeze blew in from the sea with an invigorating insistence, however, and he did not regret his decision to travel on his own power. He looked about him as he rode and wondered about the white houses which stood well up above the road, with lights twinkling in the windows. How fortunate the people were who lived in them! Sometimes he could hear voices, cheerful voices always, and quite as often the twang of stringed instruments.

It was a perfect evening, even for an enchanted island where most evenings were close to perfection. He was aware, as he rode slowly along the twisting, up-and-down roads, that in his mind there was a remembrance of something which had happened many years before. When was it that he had started on a journey with the stars blotted out continuously by a moving rack of cloud although the moon came fitfully through at intervals and lighted the trees and the water to the midnight blue of sapphires? Then he remembered. It was his last night on the island of Jamaica when he and his great friend Cymric Forster had rowed out into the sea to take the ship to Santiago, and Constance Ballard had watched them go with tears in her sad eyes.

"Poor Cymric!" he said to himself, feeling a threat of tears in his own. "Poor Constance!"

And then he smiled as he recalled the very youthful voice of Constance's young sister Winifred reaching them through the blackness. "I'll be more grown up when they come back again," she had said, not realizing how far the voice could carry, "and Mr. Grace may want to marry me."

He had not gone back but Winifred had grown up and had come to England, and he *had* wanted to marry her.

His feet on the pedals moved more and more slowly. Should he turn back?

He passed many groups of colored people along the road and never failed to get a friendly greeting from them. They were generally singing and his progress past them would interrupt them for no more than a minute or so. There was nothing sustained in their songs, nothing of the serious note of the spirituals of American plantations. Mostly they were two- or three-line catches, sung to airs of their own making, the words very often sly bits of doggerel supplied by their white employers.

He heard one group ahead of him singing,

> "*Spread yu' nets while t'others sleep,*
> *Catch all de fish in Granaway Deep.*"

After he had passed them they swung into another, one of their own, he was sure. They rolled it out with a hint of relish, keeping time with their bare feet.

> "All the way to de Ducking Stool,
>    De Ducking Stool, de Ducking Stool;
>  We'll see white thief go splash in Stool,
>    To wash his sins away!"

When he came to the tall gates of Sue Beltrade's home, he lifted his bicycle over the stone of the wall which edged the flagged walk and behind which there stood a solid row of Bermuda cedars. There was a corner here devoted to the flowers which grew only in Bermuda and he was careful to place the machine against the trunks of the trees where it could do no harm to the fragrant white snowberries, the purple bloom of the wild bean or the vivid yellow of the St.-Andrew's-cross, coaxed from its home in the marshlands to a more cultivated background and more sedate companionships. Here somewhere, he knew, there was a solid mass of a pleasant blue flower which was generally called "sailor's choice." Sailor's choice! Here he stood in the fragrant dark, a sailor who had seemed to have a difficult choice ahead of him but who had finally made up his mind that it was not a choice after all.

When he reached the end of the walk and could see the white stone of the Welcoming Arms, he heard a welcoming voice from a screened corner of the wide front porch.

"My dear Julian!" said Sue in a low tone. "My new friend who will be leaving me so soon! I was beginning to think you were not coming after all. And I was feeling very sad and, I'm afraid, rather sorry for myself."

"Sue," he said, letting himself into the secluded corner, where they had spent much time together on other evenings, and taking a chair beside her, "I rode over slowly because I had so much to think about. So very much." He sighed deeply as he became aware of the dark beauty of the gardens lying below them, from which came the rich mingled odors of a thousand lovely blooms. "This place is quite matchless. I'm really sure, Sue, that your home is the most beautiful in the world."

"But," she thought, "it can't be reached by a grandson on his weekends! And could I take the place of the memories in your mind, my very dear Julian?"

Their conversation after that was punctuated by long pauses, and sometimes it seemed to have little continuity or purpose. Once they heard wheels turning some distance up the road and that always arresting sound, the *clip, clop* of a horse's hoofs. The air was so still now that they could hear a masculine voice say: "We're passing the property of the richest woman in Bermuda. Mrs. Beltrade. You'll see the gates in a second. She's a handsome woman too."

A woman's voice responded, "I think, Chester, you would love me more if I had been born rich. And it's not hard to look well when you have a personal maid and can take things easy."

Sue was amused. "It's true," she said with a light laugh. "I *am* rich. My husband left everything to me. I think I've been a good custodian, because it's grown a little since."

A moment later, with seeming irrelevance, she began to speak of the house. "I love it here. I love my home. And did you know that it even has a ghost? Or perhaps it's a party of ghosts. At any rate, whenever a daughter of the house has been married a crash is heard that night. A great, resounding crash, as though all the family glasses had been broken at once. There is an immediate rush downstairs, of course, but there's never anything to be seen. Every glass is in its place, nothing has been disturbed or broken. It's happened every time there has been a wedding, although the last occasion was more than thirty years ago."

"An odd way for a ghost to behave, Sue."

"I think," she said after a moment, "that the ghosts are friendly. I think they like the family and are delighted that one of the daughters is being married. They're so pleased about it that they get together to drink a toast; and then, so there will be no heeltaps left, they follow the old custom of breaking their glasses on the hearth."

"But didn't you say that nothing is ever broken?"

"They use ghostly glasses, I suppose." There was another pause. "I wonder if it would happen if I were married here?"

Julian laughed confidently. "Of course. I'm sure they are sensible fellows, these ghosts, with an eye in their heads for a beautiful lady. They've had enough time to get to know you and to acquire a liking for you. It will be an especially loud crash when you are married."

Some time later she asked him a question. "You still grieve for the loss of your son, don't you? I feel it whenever you speak of him."

He nodded his head slowly. "I've never been able to get over it. He was such a wonderful little chap. Always my right-hand man in trouble. We seemed to have a great deal of it in those days. When he grew up he showed a real touch of genius. His portraits had something different about them. He not only painted perfect likenesses but he seemed as well to get inside the sitter's mind. I have often thought I would like to have one of those he did in Vienna, when he was at his very best; but somehow I haven't gone about it yet."

"Did you like his—his wife?"

"Thank you, dear Sue. That is what I always called her. Yes, I liked her very much. I only saw her once but she wrote me many long letters. I got to understand her through them. You know, of course, that she was quite extraordinarily beautiful. I tried to convince Timothy that he shouldn't take her away but I suppose I knew all the time that he would. They were very much in love."

"How old is your grandson now?"

"He'll soon be twenty. The elopement of his parents made it very hard for him. Boys can be cruel to each other. When he came home to me after the tragedy, he didn't want to go to any of the large public schools. He knew the other fellows would never let him forget the irregularity of his birth. I sent him finally to a small school in the north and for a time he seemed to get along well with the rest. Then they found out and they began to call

him Julian Fitzgrace. He begged me to take him away and finally I gave in and let him follow his own bent. He's taken a position in the City, in business. And, oddly enough, he seems to be doing very well."

They were conscious as they talked of the issue unresolved between them. Once he touched her hand and said, "Sue!" She turned quickly in the darkness and looked up at him, making no effort to withdraw her hand. "That fellow driving by was guilty of a serious understatement. You are *lovely*. I can't help wondering why you have remained unmarried so long."

"For a variety of reasons," she answered. "All of them having to do with the candidates who offered themselves. Oh yes, there *have* been candidates."

When the time came for him to leave, they rose together and walked hand in hand to the front steps. He pressed her fingers tightly.

"Good-by, Sue."

"Good-by, Julian." There was a moment's silence and then she burst out impulsively, "Isn't there anything else you want to say?"

The light of the moon was completely obscured by a heavy cloud and she could not see that he nodded his head. "Yes, there was something I wanted to say. But I—I knew that I shouldn't." He realized then that he should speak with complete frankness. "I wanted to ask you to marry me. But it wouldn't have done for—for a great many reasons. The chief being that I would love you too much."

"Julian, Julian, I don't understand. I think you'll have to explain this to me."

"I'll try to make myself clear. But it's going to be hard. I'm not clever with words, my dear." He paused and cast about in his mind for the right way to express himself. "You see, I was very much in love with my wife. It's true that I married again but that was a matter of necessity. I was at my wit's end. My income wasn't enough to keep up the place and it was running down badly. The marriage didn't work out well at all. I'm sure that Winifred understood about it and that she didn't hold it against me. But if I should propose to you, and if you should say yes——"

"I might, Julian. Yes, I might. It's been such a short time that you've been here but I like you. I'm afraid I've made no effort to conceal it."

"If we married, my dear, it would be a far different matter. There would be nothing of the marriage of convenience about it. I would love you very much and—and, of course, Winifred would know how I felt about you. She

often seems very close to me, even though it has been so many years since she died. She would go away. And she would never come back. I am certain that I couldn't have you as my wife for the rest of my life and find her waiting for me in the next."

"But you have been tempted?"

"Yes, my dear. The temptation has been great."

There was a long moment of silence. "I understand," said Sue finally. "It's a conflict of loyalties. And you have decided which one you should obey. I suppose you are right. At any rate, my dear friend, I am in no position to attempt persuasion against the course you are taking." She paused and then added in a burst of genuine feeling: "I am sure you are right. Your loyalty to the memory of your wife is something quite rare. I don't believe I've encountered anything like it before. But I know it is honest and fine and I should have known it would be the way you feel—I'm sorry, of course. I'll never see you again. And I'm certain now that my house will never resound with ghostly heeltaps for me."

He walked slowly down the steps. The Welcoming Arms had ceased to be anything but railings of white stone.

"Good-by, my dear," she called after him.

He may not have realized that he had closed a door on more than romance, that what he had done was to turn his back on life itself. His feet, carrying him down the lowering levels of the flagged walk, were taking him into a new land, the land of Borrowed Time: where men yielded at last to the pressure of the years and rather suddenly became old men, suffering strange new aches and pains, growing stiff in movement and slow in mind, finding comfort in slippered idleness before open fires, dwelling much in the memories of the past—and waiting.

## CHAPTER FOUR

### 1

Grosvenor Square had been the scene of a serious congestion. Carriages, carriages and more carriages had been driving up to Outland House all through the latter half of the afternoon, leaving their much beribboned and befurbelowed ladies and their stiffly erect gentlemen in Prince Albert coats at the entrance to the town house of the duke and returning later to take them away. It had been a very special occasion, without a doubt. Most of the residents of the square had been among those in attendance but there were a few who had not been invited; just enough to make it clear that the once not exactly notorious but certainly spectacular Isabelle Carboy, who had progressed upward through the lower branches of nobility to become a duchess at last, had not forgotten certain things which had happened to her on the way.

Isabelle saw the last guest depart and retreated at once to the small room on the ground floor which she used as an office. There had been much tearing down of walls and rearrangement of the ground plan with the result that no one seemed to remember just exactly where it was that a certain Hark Chaffery had blown out his brains. The architect was convinced that the desk of the duchess was on the very spot; but he knew when to keep his mouth sealed. The room as now constituted had more space and plenty of room on the walls for tall mirrors, so that the occupant was never at a loss for an appraisal of her own face; a fact which possibly indicated a new tendency on Isabelle's part to worry about the ravages of time.

When a woman has been notably beautiful and has retained in her later years a good share of her looks, it is customary to say that she is as lovely as ever. This is what people said about Her Grace the Duchess of Outland but it should be set down at once that this was an exaggeration. Isabelle was still a handsome woman, with lively brown eyes under silver-white hair, and she was active and seemingly in remarkable health; but the fact that she had crossed the border of the seventies was evident in the sudden clustering of lines around her eyes and a crease or two in her neck.

She seated herself at her desk, pushed back the satin sleeves of her beautiful black afternoon frock and said to a footman, "Bestery, have Miss Trounceman come in."

When her secretary joined her, she said, "Well?" on a rising inflection of tone.

"A great success, Your Grace," said Miss Trounceman. "Really remarkable. Afternoon teas are generally pretty tame affairs but none of them will ever forget this one."

"Am I or am I not the most talked-about hostess in England?"

"You established yourself at the very top by your entertainments this summer at Outland Park, Your Grace. There never have been weekends to equal yours. Today's function has—well, it has added to your laurels."

"I'm hungry," said Isabelle suddenly. "I've been so busy all afternoon, Trounce, that I didn't have a chance for a sip of tea or a single crust of bread. Send around to Marie's Pastry Shop—two blocks west, one north, front painted green—and get me one of her cherry puff pastry squares."

"But, Your Grace," protested the secretary, "there are scores of pastries left over in the house. And little cakes, and muffins, and ices and the most delicious sandwiches."

"There's nothing in the world I like better than puff pastry, and Marie's squares are divine. What if I do get an upset stomach once in a while? It's worth it. Send someone over at once. And, Trounce, you might as well order a double square while you're at it."

It would have been a diplomatic error to warn Her Grace that people over seventy must start at last to be careful of their diet, so the secretary sent a footman out on the errand. She returned then for further instructions.

At first the duchess seemed disposed to gossip about the happenings of the afternoon and to savor her triumph. "I suppose you noticed that Lady Swiveller didn't come. I've marked that down in the ledger and the old battle-ax will suffer for it, even though Swiv did come himself. He's an old lamb. And will you tell me, Trounce, how in the name of everything holy and righteous does that Abberbrook woman always manage to get such stunning clothes?"

"She has a good figure," commented the secretary.

"H'm!" said Isabelle in a tone which implied, You ought to see *mine*. She paused then for a moment's thought. "Trounce, I have another task for you. I want you to take the earliest train tomorrow for the Park and keep an eye on His Grace. He *must* appear for the dinner that D'Israeli is giving on Friday. If he doesn't come, I won't be able to go either and Dizzy will have to fill in with another couple at the last minute. Now that I think about it,

Trounce, you had better bring him back yourself. Sweeten him up, if it's necessary, by letting him have as many newspapers to read as he wants Even let him read some bits out of them to you. That always pleases him. And be very careful on the train. He has a cute way of getting on and then slipping off at the next station, and going back home to his reading."

"Very well," said the secretary in a resigned tone. "I'll produce His Grace, with his evening clothes, in plenty of time for the dinner."

At this moment there was the sound of a furious voice in the drawing room and then something fell with a loud crash on the floor.

"What's that?" asked Isabelle, springing to her feet.

The secretary hurried from the room and returned in a few minutes with a disturbed look on her face. "It's your father, Your Grace," she said.

"Do you mean that Mr. Carboy is here? I didn't expect him. And whatever has happened?"

"He's angry, Your Grace."

Samuel Carboy was indeed angry. His daughter found him standing beside a delicate French table and glaring about him in a rage. It could have been that the mere fact of the table being French had thrown him into a fit of anger, he having no respect or liking for the French school. It was a vase, however, which had suffered the consequences. The pieces were lying on the floor after contact with his cane and he was glaring about him as though seeking some other suitable object. A newspaper was spread open on the table and it seemed likely to Isabelle that something in it had been responsible for his sudden wrath.

"Papa!" she cried. "What's the meaning of this? I want you to know this isn't a tavern bar. And neither is it your office where you're free to behave like a wild bull if you like. This happens to be my home. That vase was my property."

She was feeling sorry for him even as she blamed him. Samuel Carboy was showing his years most unmistakably. His back was bent and his face was so wrinkled and sunken that he might have passed for a Cagliostro approaching his final stage.

"Don't talk to me, my girl!" he quavered. "I had good cause to be upset. Will you look at that paper? Ninny Grace's cub of a son is to be made a knight! Just because he wrote some stupid report about a floating dock. How does that strike you, my girl? I've made England a wealthy, industrial nation and in what kind of coinage have I been paid? Contempt, scorn, opposition. No title for Samuel Carboy but a knighthood for a dull fellow who shined his trousers on a desk at the Admiralty all his life! When I saw he had been commanded to appear at Windsor tomorrow to be knighted by the queen, I lost control of myself."

"Come, Papa, sit down," said Isabelle sympathetically. "Why should you care about such a trifling matter? It isn't a knighthood you deserve. You should be made a peer, Papa. An earl, perhaps. And you'll get to be one before long, the way this enlargement of the business is going. They must appreciate you now. Come, Papa, sit down. You'll tire yourself out."

Samuel Carboy scowled about him at the servants who were standing at iscreet distances or peering around doors.

"I didn't come here to sit down, Isa, my girl. I came here to attend to an nportant matter and I need your help. We must go——" He paused and a lank look came over his wrinkled face. "Thunderation, girl, I've forgot hat it is! Now what could it have been?" His look became even more lank. "*Sir Ninny Grace, Sir Ninny Grace!* Is that the cub's name, Isa?"

"No, Papa, his name is Julian."

"So it is. A silly name, it always seemed to me. Just the kind that fool artner of mine would pick. What was the matter with names like George nd Thomas and Samuel? *Sir Julian Grace!* I've a notion to demand an nvestigation of the Admiralty over this."

"Papa," said Isabelle in a tone of rising impatience. "Never mind this nighthood business. What brought you to town?"

"Something very important, my dear. Let me see." He buried his head in is hands and fell into deep thought. Finally he got up out of the chair into hich he had subsided. "I have it! I remember. Get your bonnet on and e'll be on our way."

"Papa, tell me what it is so one of us at least will remember. You'll let it o out of your mind in another minute, I'm sure."

He responded rather eagerly. "A good idea, child. I *am* getting absent-ninded. We're to go to a warehouse I own. In the east end."

"But is it so important that we can't go tomorrow? I don't see why we nust set out this very instant. Don't you realize that I've had a very im-ortant tea here this afternoon and that I'm tired?"

"Thunderation, Isa, you're never tired. I bet you could go out and play a ound of golf. Get on your bonnet."

"You see, my girl," he said as they emerged on the street, "it's something hat has to be done right away. One of these days they'll be tucking me in ith a spade, you know."

"Papa! How can you talk about such things and in such a casual way? I efuse to think about it. It frightens me. It—it almost drives me crazy hen anyone speaks of it." She looked at him with fear in her eyes. "I won't ie! I'm going to go right on living. Death is only for people who are sickly nd I'm still as healthy as I ever was. I won't give in. Papa, I won't!"

"Easy, my child, easy. I wanted to go right on too but as you get older ou get kind of tired of it all. That makes the prospect a little easier. I'm lmost reconciled to it."

"I never will be! And now, Papa, I want you to promise never to mention uch a thing again."

They took a hansom cab to save time and drove down in the direction of he City. The cabby did not seem to sense the importance of their errand, or he let his horse trot along serenely until, in a sudden rage, Samuel Carboy ounded on the roof of the cab with his cane.

"We want to get there before the end of the century, you blasted fool!" e bellowed.

Thus urged to action, the cabby whipped up his horse and had them a their destination in no time at all. It was in close proximity to the missic but Isabelle did not recognize the dilapidated building before which the stopped. It looked as though it had not been in use for a long time. Th door was locked and bolted and all the windows were covered with met shutters.

"What place is this?" she asked, frowning at her father.

He did not seem to know. Standing stock-still on the sidewalk, he looke up at the gloomy structure with a puzzled frown. "Isabelle, child, why an we stopping here?" he asked.

"I wish I knew." Her voice had more than a hint of exasperation in i "You brought me here. You said there was something you must show me

The frown on his wrinkled forehead cleared slowly. "So there is. So the is."

2

The warehouse was filled with an odd assortment of discarded office equip ment and furniture from Beaulaw Hall which the Colossus had gradual discarded as he got better pieces. Isabelle recognized many things, includin the bed in which she had slept as a child and a rocking horse she had re ceived once at Christmas.

"Gracious, Papa, why are you keeping all this old stuff around?" she aske

"Couldn't get decent prices for any of it," he grumbled. "It's against m principles to give anything away, so here it is. Doesn't cost anything to kee it here."

She reached suddenly and grasped his arm. "Someone has been in here

"Nonsense. You saw yourself how well the place is closed up."

"Someone, in muddy clothes, has slept in that old bed of mine." Sh shuddered. "How awful it looks! I can't believe now I ever did sleep in it

"Must have been a tramp," said Carboy, looking at the condition of th bed. "One of Bade's pets, no doubt. I'll have to take a look around and se how he got in. By the cellar, most likely."

Isabelle's only thought was to get through with the errand which ha brought them there and leave this depressing place. "Hurry, Papa. I war to get out of this."

The old man, with something in the nature of a smirk on his face, le the way to the rear. Here he pointed to a sagging screen which covered large part of one wall.

"Look behind that," he instructed.

When the screen had been folded back, Isabelle found a tattered an damp tapestry covering the stained wall. This she removed on her father instruction.

"There's a room behind," said the old man, with a wink. He drew a ke from one of his pockets. "See that lock on the wall? This will open it."

Isabelle took the key and turned it in the lock. A section of the wa swung inward, providing entrance into a room of some size but without a window save a square of plate glass in the ceiling. This provided sufficient light to reveal that the room contained nothing but a large armchair and a portrait on one wall.

"The Holbein!" said Carboy. His eyes were shining with excitement. "It was stolen. Do you remember? A few years ago, from some place in Germany. I bought it after it was smuggled into this country. And I may tell you, my child, that I paid a pretty penny for it."

Isabelle was recalling the incident of the theft as she studied the picture on the wall. "I seem to remember there was a great deal of talk about it," she said. "It's a wonderful picture. I can understand why you couldn't resist buying it." Then she began to realize the full significance of the situation. "Papa, if they ever found it here, you might be sent to jail."

"Exactly." Carboy's excitement was mounting as he studied the canvas. He was breathing hard. "I knew that when I bought it. I was willing to accept the risk in order to own it. This, my dear child, is Holbein at his best. Look at the mastery shown in the brush strokes. And the composition! It's perfect in every respect. Business doesn't bring me to London any more. I come up only to gloat over this." He remained silent for a moment and then turned to his daughter with a serious air. "If it should be found here after I die, I would be branded a thief. I'm depending on you, Isabelle, to prevent that happening."

"I? Heavens, Papa, what can I do about it?"

He handed her another key. "That's a duplicate. When I die, come here at once. Bring a servant with you, one whose honesty you can be sure of. Have the picture packed up—there's a cover ready on that other wall—and take it away. If the situation seems to warrant it, have the canvas destroyed. There's a better plan than that, however, if you want to risk it. Here is the name and address of the dealer who sold it to me. He'll probably be able to sell it again. To some collector as eager for it as I was. There are plenty of them in the country, I assure you. In that case, you would get a price for it to knock your eye out."

"How much?"

"Well, that would depend on how firm you were with this dealer fellow."

"If you expect me to look after this, you mustn't hold anything back. How much did you pay for it?"

He hesitated. "Well, I suppose you ought to know. I paid seventy thousand pounds."

His daughter gasped in astonishment. "You paid a price like that for a picture you have to hide away in a filthy warehouse? Papa, I think you were insane."

"Of course I was. All collectors have a streak of insanity in them."

With impatient movements of her hands, Isabelle put the key and the slip of paper with the address away. "A pretty kind of a mess, this is."

"The kind of mess out of which you might get better than fifty thousand of the best. I know you well enough to be sure you wouldn't sell for less than that."

"Why do you entrust this to me? Why not your grandson?"

"He's away too much. When I come to the end of my days he may be in Johannesburg or Shanghai or New York. No, child, I must put my dependence in you. Do you give me your promise?"

"But—but, Papa, why don't you sell it back to the dealer now? It would be the easiest way."

An almost fanatical gleam had taken possession of Samuel Carboy's eyes. "I can't bear to part with it as long as there's breath left in my body. Damme, child, it's the first thing I think of when I waken in the morning. It took a bit of will to decide not to risk making a place for it at the Hall. I wish I could come here every day."

At this Isabelle surrendered. "Very well. Put your mind at rest, Papa. I'll take care of it. And the fifty thousand, if I sell it for that much, will be mine."

"Of course. The fewer who know about this the better."

The chair was one of the kind invented by William Morris, the poet, and named after him. Carboy ensconced himself in it and studied the portrait with a rapt eye.

"Whenever I come into town I sit here for an hour or so," he declared. "The face repays all the attention you want to give it. I think the subject was a merchant, perhaps the head of one of the great Flemish guilds. D you notice the light in his eyes? He was keen, courageous, calculating. There's determination in the mouth too. The nose is full of character, a fine conky one. Always look at noses, my child. They make a face or spoil it. A weak nose, a weak character." He sighed deeply. "I wish I knew who he was. It would be a gratifying thing to have him traced. I'm sure he was a man of rare parts. A thorn in the side of the Spaniards."

He remained silent after that, his eyes fixed on the painting. Finding the dead cold of the place hard to bear, Isabelle drew the shawl she was wearing more closely about her neck and walked out for another look at the disorderly mass of stuff in the other room. When she returned he was still sitting quietly in his chair but he was staring up at the glass in the ceiling and his eyes were filled with tears.

"Papa, what's wrong with you?"

He paid no attention. "I'll never forget the look on his face when I said we must break up the company," he muttered to himself. "Poor Georgie! He never knew a thing about business. Or anything else, I guess."

"Don't waste any sympathy on him," she commented sharply.

He did not seem to be aware that anyone had spoken or, for that matter, that he had company in the room. After a moment he went on in stumbling tones. "I wish I hadn't said what I did that day. I might have known it wasn't safe with those two listening. That Stacker and that Gabriel Wilkins. A tough pair, always looking for a chance to get ahead. I saw the look on each of their faces when I said it. Calculating. Figuring they might make capital with me. I should have stepped in right there and then. I should have said, 'I didn't mean it.' I should have said, 'We'll let the do-gooders alone. What does the lion care if jackals yap at his heels?'"

"Papa!" cried Isabelle. "Do you know what you're saying?"

He still did not seem to hear. "Poor George! He should have died in his bed. With three nurses in the room and twenty different kinds of medicine on the table. That was *his* ticket, the demanding old coot. But he didn't. I talked with my beautiful daughter. Might have turned the world upside down, that one, if she'd been born a few centuries ago. But she wasn't. We talked——"

"Papa!" Isabelle's voice held a frantic note. She took him by the shoulder and gave him a vigorous shake. "Come back to your senses! Do you know what you're saying?"

Carboy rubbed a hand over his eyes and then blinked at her. "What was I saying?"

Isabelle gave him another shake. "Pull yourself together. You were talking to yourself. And saying things out loud which might get both of us into trouble." A sudden fury took possession of her. "Didn't you know it? Papa, what a dreadful habit. Are you holding something back from me? Are you sure you said nothing that day except what you told me?"

He raised his eyes to hers and then allowed them to drop. "I'm afraid, my child, that what I said was—a little more to the point."

"Those two men, Stacker and Wilkins. I haven't heard you mention them for a long time. Where are they?"

"Stacker's dead. Wilkins retired five years ago. He's living near Bath."

"What kind of man is he?"

"Hard. As hard as a piece of ice chipped off the North Pole. They wouldn't get anything out of him."

"Has he money?"

"A cool million, I expect."

"Papa, if the police knew what you said to those two men, what would happen?"

"Well, it was a long time ago but it's possible they would try to reopen the case. I don't think they would get very far with it."

Isabelle shook her head. "We can't be sure. I know one thing, we've got to find some way of putting a check on that tongue of yours. Any more muttering about what we said to each other and we'll be in a pretty fix. Perhaps you should live with me so I can keep an eye on you."

"No," he said flatly. "I'll stay where I am. I like my own bed. And I couldn't take my pictures with me. I guess the best thing for me to do is to hand in my papers."

Isabelle reached out a hand to help him up. "Let's get out of this tomb or it will be the end of both of us. But we'll talk about this after dinner. You've got me frightened to death, Papa."

### 3

When they reached Outland House there was a visitor waiting for Isabelle, one who should have been apologetic for arriving at such an hour but who did not seem to reflect that feeling at all. It was Alexander Fawkes and, as a popular saying of the moment went, he was dressed right up to the nines. His coat, which was buttoned almost to his neck and had the narrowest kind of collar, was of a rich green cloth. His waistcoat, showing only around the waistline, was of fawn and piped with brown braid. He had placed his tall hat on the carpet beside him and had made it a receptacle for his gloves and a rest for his gold-knobbed cane. His shoes shone, his face had been barbered elaborately. He was, in fact, a perfect picture of prosperity.

"Mr. Fawkes!" said Isabelle, coming into the room with a frown. "This is a surprise. Has something happened? Something I should know about at once?"

"Well," said the lawyer, who had moved up several notches at the offices of Smythe, Boongrace and Curdle and could no longer be called a junior partner, "well, yes and no. Something *has* happened. But in view of the general prosperity which pervades the Carboy enterprises and the booming condition in our own offices, you may not feel that it requires more than passing notice."

Isabelle seated herself at a distance and regarded him with an air almost of distaste. It seemed to her he was wearing on his back the retaining fees she had been paying him.

"You had better tell me what it is."

The lawyer gestured largely with his right hand. "First, I wish to point out that the term 'the Midas touch,' once in general use, is being changed in the City to 'the Carboy touch.' And quite properly so. The prosperity of Carboy and Co. is being felt in every capital of the world. You will soon have tangible evidence of this in the size of the dividends you will be receiving."

A thought occurred to Isabelle. "Have you, by any chance, been gambling in Carboy stocks?" she asked.

He gestured even more largely and grandly. "I have. I acknowledge it openly. I have been, to paraphrase the Bible, plowing with the Carboy heifer. In short, I've been actively in the market—buying, selling, buying again, making profits at every turn. Ma'am, I have been doing very well for myself."

"Well," she said reluctantly, "I don't suppose there's any reason why you shouldn't. Anyone who chooses can go into the market. I'm sure all your partners have been doing equally well."

"My partners," he said, "are literally rolling in pelf."

"Do you attend any more of those meetings in Soho for the purpose of making the world over?"

"Ma'am," said the lawyer, "I was shocked to find that my sudden prosperity was being noted by fellow members and that I was expected to share it with them. This I considered unjust, illegal and absurd. I have—well, to answer your question—I no longer attend the meetings."

"That seems sensible, Mr. Fawkes. And now what is it you have to report?"

"This, ma'am. Your nephew has been receiving bonuses from all of the company branches as compensation for his services. I have heard no criticism of this. It is generally believed, in fact, that he has earned a reward. But he accepts the bonuses and is turning them over to a new concern which he has started in South Africa. It seems to me that he is dropping a strong anchor to windward."

She rose to her feet. "Thank you," she said. "This is the kind of information I need to know."

## CHAPTER FIVE

### 1

Jonathan Bade had been living in the Land of Borrowed Time for a good many years. He had given up his offices and his practice and now dwelt in rooms above the small hall near Shadwell which he had selected for his mis-

sion so many years before. He no longer went on speaking tours to spread
the particular gospel in which he believed so fervently. But he managed to
keep himself very busy.

One evening in the early fall he put a shawl around his shoulders (for
men were wearing shawls as much as women in these days), placed a tall
and rather solemn hat on his head and started out on a walk which took
him in the direction of the river. He seemed to be in search of someone; at
any rate he looked closely at every man he passed, particularly those who were
shabby and down at heel. The nearer he got to the river, the more men he
passed who answered to this description in some degree. But none interested
him sufficiently to make him stop and enter into conversation until he
reached a street of one crooked block ending at a dismantled warehouse
against which the waters of the Thames lapped restlessly. Here he saw an
old man sitting on an upturned crate. The stranger had his coat collar turned
up close to his ears and a disreputable hat pulled down so far that little could
be seen of his eyes. There was despair in every line of his stooped figure.
Jonathan, convinced that he had found the type of man he sought, seated
himself on the other end of the empty crate.

After a spell of silence during which Jonathan studied his neighbor
closely, he asked a question: "My friend, are you ill?"

The stranger turned his eyes slowly in the direction of his questioner. He
had not shaved for many days nor made the acquaintance of soap and water
for an equal length of time; but there was something about his features which
made it clear he had known better days.

"No, worse luck. I'm not ill. I wish I were so ill that I might count on
being through soon with this sorry existence."

The voice in which he spoke was hoarse but it was evident that he had
been well educated. Jonathan was now convinced he had made the right
selection from among the many derelicts he had encountered on his slow
stroll.

"Do you mind if I ask you some questions?"

"No," answered the other, turning his eyes back to an aimless survey of
the passing water. "I have no pride left. I will answer any questions provided
it leads to a shilling in the end. Or enough for a meal and a bed tonight in
some verminous dive."

"What is your name?"

"My name?" The man turned and looked suspiciously at Jonathan. "Is
that necessary? Are you an investigator of some kind? Do you want to put
me in a report?"

"No, my friend. I want to help you. I have every intention of helping you
if you'll assist me as much as you can. But first I must know who you are."

"My name is Bryce. Richard Donovan Bryce."

"You went to college, I think."

"Oh yes. I was at Oxford. And I read for the bar. I passed my examina-
tions and practiced for some years. Most unsuccessfully. I have been unsuc-
cessful in everything all my life. I went into business. I tried to sell on

commission. I was a failure. My wife died and I was unable to manage her small estate with any success. It was soon gone. For the last few years I lived with a married daughter. She grew so tired of supporting me, although I kept as unobtrusively in my attic room as I could and curbed my appetite at meals, that she finally turned me out. She said she never wanted to see my face again."

"How long ago was that?"

"In the spring. Since then I haven't had a decent meal, a bath, or a bed in which any self-respecting man could sleep." Jonathan saw now that tears were streaming down his face. "God have mercy on me! I am one of the unwanted old."

"Mr. Bryce," said Jonathan, "civilization has failed in many things. One of its most cruel failures is its inability, or its unwillingness, to do anything for old men without means or homes or work. I've been trying for a very long time to call attention to this and have something done about it. With this much success only: all over the country there are charitable people who agree with me and have pledged me a certain measure of support. I devote my time now to finding old men who need the help. I think, sir, you are one of them. If you'll come with me, I'll see that you have all the assistance now that we are in a position to give."

The man made no move to get up. The tears continued to flow, making dirty streaks on his cheeks.

"Come. Come with me, old man. I mean what I say. I can help you."

The derelict reached for a stick on the ground beside him and made use of it in standing up. "Sir," he said in broken tones, "I've needed help all my life. It's not that I'm lazy or indifferent. I've never been able to do things well. God help me, sir, I'm a failure even as a beggar! How many times—even now when I'm old and more useless than ever—have I cried out to my mother to come back to life and lead her unfortunate son by the hand!"

Jonathan took him by the arm. "I think perhaps she has heard you, my friend," he said. "Perhaps my steps were directed down this way. All I can do for you tonight is to see you have a hot meal, a bath and a warm, clean bed. After that I'll see what permanent arrangements can be made for you."

When they reached the little mission Jonathan opened the door and called, "Jacko!" A man who had once been a sailor, from his gait, came down the hall in response to this summons, carrying a lamp in one hand.

"Jacko, this is Mr. Bryce," said Jonathan. "He will be a guest of ours until we can arrange something better for him."

"Bub and grub?" asked the man Jacko.

"Plenty of grub but we'll go easy on the other as usual, Jacko. I'm sure Mr. Bryce is as anxious to avoid drink as we are to have him do so. Still, he needs a little stimulation. One finger, Jacko."

"One finger," said the old sailor. "My own portion, sir."

"Yes?"

"One finger and no more, s'elp me bob."

Jonathan turned back then to the new guest of the mission. "Where were you born, sir?"

The derelict had lost all of his early reluctance to answering questions. "I was born in Bath and practiced law there."

"Where does your daughter live?"

"In Windsor."

"And her name?"

"Mrs. Thaddeus Tipton. Her husband is a builder of carriages. In a small way."

"Thank you, Mr. Bryce. Now, Jacko, if you'll inquire as to our guest's preferences, you will get him some supper."

The ex-sailor looked at the unfortunate Mr. Bryce and said, "I could fry you some ham."

Richard Donovan Bryce raised his head. "Ham, did you say? Sir, when I am particularly hungry I dream always of ham—ham sizzling in a frying pan. Nothing in the world would suit me better."

An hour later the man Jacko made his way to the small room at the back of the mission where Jonathan Bade was writing a note by the light of a kerosene lamp suspended from the ceiling.

"I've looked after him, sir. He's had a bath, and a hearty meal, and now he's sound asleep and snoring like a whole band of kettledrums. I've picked out clothes to fit him and they'll be on a chair at his bedside when he wakens in the morning. His own clothes has been burned and, if you'll allow me the liberty, sir, I've never seen human raimint which needed burning more."

"What do you think of him, Jacko?"

"Sir, he's one of our kind. A poor helpless old coot if I've ever seen one."

Jonathan sealed the note he had been writing and held it out to the ex-sailor. "If you please, Jacko, I would like this taken at once to Mr. Griggson. I hope he will start his inquiries in the morning bright and early."

When the man had departed with the note, whistling cheerfully, Jonathan took a book from a shelf behind him and began to run his eye down a long row of names printed in columns by one of the new typing machines. Finally he paused and suspended his pen over one of the names.

"Mrs. Arthur Barnes Hawley," he said to himself. "I remember Mrs. Hawley. A widow of considerable means. Lives outside Buxton. She has a large manor house called Diamond Crest."

The more he thought about Mrs. Hawley the more convinced he became that she was the one into whose hands he should entrust the fate of Richard Donovan Bryce. She was a kindly woman and had been one of his most enthusiastic converts. It surprised him, in fact, that he had never called on her before. She lived far enough away from Bath, moreover, to avoid any complications rising out of the man's old associations.

He decided to write to Mrs. Hawley as soon as he had the reports from Griggson.

2

A week later the new guest at the mission was asked to step into Mr. Bade's office. He found the latter in a smiling mood, with a railway ticket held between finger and thumb.

"Well, Mr. Bryce," said Bade, "it's all settled. Mrs. Hawley has agreed to act as your sponsor and to bear all expense. She doesn't say what she proposes to do but there are three methods. Perhaps I had better explain."

Bryce had just finished a very good breakfast of two boiled eggs, two pieces of toast, marmalade and tea. The inner man, therefore, had been looked after well but he was still unable, it seemed, to realize the full extent of his good fortune. His manner had something of the unhappy mongrel dog who slinks about and hides behind bushes, living always in expectation of being kicked. Jonathan noticed that he was sitting on the extreme edge of his chair and that the hand which kept his new cap on his knee was tightly clenched. He suspected that the unfortunate man's tongue was ready to pour forth a string of eager affirmatives to anything which might be suggested.

"Many hundreds of people have pledged themselves to take the responsibility for one man who has fallen on evil days. I have sent well over a hundred such to people in all parts of the country. The plan has been most successful. Only in six cases have we had failures; and the failures have always been due to drink or drugs.

"Usually the sponsors use one of the three methods I spoke of," continued Jonathan. "Sometimes they take their charges right into their own households. In cases where they have large estates they are likely to assign a cottage for his use; not much more than a badger box, you understand. He gets his meals at the hall. More often they arrange to board him with respectable people who are glad of the chance to have additional revenue. The third method, and the best whenever it can be applied, is to find employment and so give him a chance to get back on a self-supporting basis. Which of the three would you prefer?"

The old man fumbled nervously with his cap. "I don't know," he said after a long hesitation. "What happens, sir, if the lady gets tired of me and doesn't want me around any more? Will I be turned out again?"

Jonathan shook his head. "Of course not. If that should happen, there would be a report sent to me and I would make other arrangements for you."

"People get impatient with me," muttered Bryce. "I do so many things the wrong way. I'm a clumsy dick, you know. I played the piano well when I was a little fellow and perhaps that was what I was cut out to be. I've never been able to get the hang of anything else. I think, sir, there would be less chance of Mrs. Hawley wanting to get rid of me if she didn't have to see anything of me at all."

"Mrs. Hawley is a very kind woman and you needn't have any fear about her. But if you prefer the boarding plan, I'll write her to that effect."

"No, no!" cried the old man in sudden alarm. "I don't want her to think

I'm picking and choosing. She wouldn't like it, Mr. Bade. She might send me about my business right away."

"Well, then, we'll leave it to her."

"I'm willing to work." Bryce was desperately anxious, it was clear, to get started on the right foot. "But it shouldn't be at anything where I can have breakages. I'm always unlucky that way. If I'm carrying a teapot, someone is sure to come up behind me and bump it out of my hand. If I'm set to weeding in a garden, I pull out the flowers and leave the weeds. I did that several times at my daughter's. I guess I would be best at something like pitching hay or shoveling muck."

Jonathan shook his head. "You're not young, Mr. Bryce. I believe Mrs. Hawley will think it best not to find employment for you. At any rate this is your ticket. Jacko will accompany you to the station and see you off. You will be met at Buxton."

"I'll be met? Do you mean they'll go to the trouble of sending someone to get me?"

"Of course. It's a good five-mile ride to the hall."

"I won't have to walk it? I'm to be driven?" For the first time he seemed to be realizing fully the change in his status. "Mr. Bade, they shouldn't go to so much bother for me. I'm a good walker still." Then his eyes lighted up. "It's most kind of the lady. I can tell now that I needn't have any fear of her. It's a great relief, sir. You get out of the way of expecting things like this." He paused to rub his eyes with a clean handkerchief. "I'm most grateful to you for all this, Mr. Bade. I'll be eternally grateful."

3

"A leddy to see you," said Jacko, later in the day. "A young leddy. A very beautiful young leddy."

"To see me?" asked Jonathan. "It's a long time since a beautiful young lady wanted to see me. In fact I'm not sure it ever happened before. Show her in, Jacko."

The young lady who was ushered in a moment later was undeniably beautiful. Having no knowledge whatever of fashion, Jonathan did not know that the black velvet cloak she wore was of the kind called a Maintenon but even that useful piece of information would not have added to his conviction that it was most becoming. Her hat was small and pert. She did not come into the room with the mincing gait which was the fashion but with a free step which, he was sure, was the result of much healthful walking on country lanes and wide moors. When she seated herself on a chair beside his desk he saw that she was wearing neat shoes of black cloth with red buckles. A quite pleasing young lady in every way.

"Sir," she said, "I have come to see you as a test."

"Indeed?" Jonathan was convinced that she resembled someone he had known quite well but he could not determine who it was.

"I belong to the Votes for Women movement," went on the caller, "and we have been confining our efforts to get readers for our magazine to women. It's now felt that men of intelligence, who take an interest in progress, might be equally interested. That is why I have come to see *you*."

"My child," he said, "the choice was not a wise one. I am an old man and I have withdrawn from any part in public affairs. All my time is devoted to this little mission."

"But everyone knows how active you were. I've heard all about your campaign against child labor. I've heard the story many times. I know everything that happened to Rixby and how you got the better of the factory owners. I know about Sadie Coaster and Boisterous Billy Isbester and the parson who thought the end of the world was coming."

"That was long ago, my child."

"But you believe that women should have votes," said Nelly Groody; for, of course, she was the visitor.

"Why are you sure?" Then he gave the matter a moment's thought and nodded his head. "Actually, I believe I am."

"Then you may want to give us your support. To the extent, at least, of subscribing to the *Women's Suffrage Journal!*"

"Who are you, young lady? I feel I ought to know the answer without being told. You resemble someone I know. Most unmistakably."

"You'll find out my name when I sign the receipt for your subscription, Mr. Bade—*if* you decide to take it. I would rather not take advantage of a connection with you."

"And how much is it?" he asked, smiling.

"A guinea."

He produced a pound note and a shilling and, when he saw the name she wrote on the printed acknowledgment, he nodded his head and smiled. "Of course. Miss Groody's niece. You are very much like your aunt, my dear; and no one could think of a better compliment to pay you. Your aunt is my most generous and consistent backer in the maintenance of this mission. If it were not for her donations I don't believe we could keep our doors open. Is she in better health?"

The girl shook her head rather solemnly. "No, Mr. Bade. Aunt Helen suffers a great deal from the rheumatism and it seems to me she's becoming very frail. I worry about her a great deal."

"It's an odd thing that my work now depends so much on the help I get from two of the few survivors in the Waterloo Tontine. Your aunt, of course, and Julian Grace, who was knighted the other day. Sir Julian is not a wealthy man but he sends me five pounds every month without fail. Generally his money reaches me at a time when I am finding it rather difficult to make both ends meet." He regarded his visitor with a smile which carried a suggestion of quickly aroused liking. "Have you received many subscriptions, Miss Groody?"

Nelly nodded briskly. "Yes, Mr. Bade. It isn't really hard. I've taken in many hundreds, all from London. I found out early that it was useless to approach the wives of prominent men. Instead I went to women whose husbands were of no special consequence; even, by preference, men who were dull or even stupid. It's surprising how many there are. When I asked the wives if they didn't think they were as capable of voting intelligently as their husbands, I would always see a gleam in their eyes. They generally paid down their money without another word."

"I see that you are holding a meeting here tonight."

"Yes, Mr. Bade. Miss Becker has come to London and will be the principal speaker. Would you honor us with your presence? Ah, if we only had speakers like you, sir!"

"I may be able to attend." Jonathan saw that his visitor, with his money safely stowed away in a neat purse, was ready to leave. He delayed her departure with a question. "Why did you decide to work for the cause of woman suffrage?"

Nelly allowed her eyes to drop with a hint of unease. "There were good reasons, sir. I felt I should be doing *something*. I didn't want to devote my whole life to riding and pouring tea. And there was a personal reason also."

When she had gone he sat for a few moments in deep thought. "I remember now," he said to himself. "I think I heard something about her and this great-grandson of Sam Carboy's. Allie Carboy and Nelly Groody! Good gad, is it happening all over again?" Then he smiled with an air of satisfaction and began to write a note. "Jacko!" he called when he had completed it. "Take this letter at once to a young man named Alfred Carboy in the offices of a firm called Scanlon, Burns and Copbright. I believe they are not far from here."

"Three blocks west, two south," said Jacko confidently. "Have it in the young gemmun's hands within the quarter hour, sir."

CHAPTER SIX

1

It had been decided to hold the meeting at which Miss Lydia Becker was to speak on Lincoln's Inn Fields. This decision was reached on the sound military principle of keeping a line of retreat open, in this case the house just outside the Fields which belonged to Mrs. Chillingly-Wick, who was heart and soul with the cause. In the event of trouble (the advocates of woman suffrage always expected plenty of it), they could abandon their platform and their flaring gas lamps and make a quick exit down the area steps which led to the Chillingly-Wick kitchen and to safety.

Allie Carboy, arriving on the scene as a result of the suggestion made in the letter he had received from Jonathan Bade, was not aware of this circumstance and he wondered anxiously what the outcome of the evening's proceedings would be. Miss Lydia Becker was speaking, a lady with a fine face and a sound grasp of her subject but little sense of showmanship. It was clear that she was failing to hold her audience, which filled most of the open space. People were beginning to heckle and at the edge of the crowd one 'Arry Carson, known to the fancy as the Battersea Basher, was keeping up a constant flow of insults.

"There's going to be trouble here," said Allie to himself. "This fellow's a thorough bad one." He looked anxiously about for Nell Groody. She was not on the platform. She was not a member of the hopeful little orchestra which earlier had striven to please the public with madrigal and stave. She was not to be seen anywhere, in fact. He had just about reached the conclusion that she had stayed safely away when the trouble he had expected began to make itself apparent.

"Come on, nah!" cried the Battersea celebrity. "Tell us why a lot o' bleeding femiles should get the vote when none uv us 'as it, men in good 'ealth and sound mind, the backbone and pride uv old England? Go back where ye belongs, in the kitching and the scullery, ye draggle-tailed mords!"

"We'll have no more interruptions of this kind!" said Miss Becker, glaring down into the crowd.

"It's no more h'interruptions, is it!" cried the pugilist. He began to dance about and shout, going through the motions of rope skipping and bag punching and keeping up a steady flow of remarks. "Preach at us, will they, the old flipflaps? If they caggs at us like this afore they has the vote, what in bleeding 'ell and Tommy will they do if they gets it? That's what I wants to know."

At this point Allie Carboy saw Nell making her way along the edge of the crowd in the direction of the voluble pugilist. He had not seen her in several years but it was clear to him at once that his love for her had not diminished; his heart had leaped wildly throatward at the first glimpse of her beautiful blue eyes under the trimmest of black bonnets. He wanted to disregard everything including all the proprieties, by rushing out and clasping her in his arms. Then his mood changed to one of alarm. There was such evidence of set purpose in the way she carried herself that he hurried in her direction in the hope of reaching her in time.

"The pride of England!" he heard her say, placing herself in front of the capering Carson and eying him with bitter scorn. "We're conducting a public meeting and we're entitled to a fair chance to state our case. If you have any sense of fair play you will reserve your comments until the proper time."

"I makes my comments as they comes into my 'ead, young leddy," said the Basher. "I says the vote comes to the men uv England afore it's to be 'anded to a lot uv tea-swilling old maids."

"The vote should be universal!" cried Nell. "Why do you want to keep it away from us when we want you to have it?—even if you do think a Whig is something to wear on the head."

The crowd roared with approving laughter at this. "That's right, miss," cried a cockney voice. "The Basher don't know the difference. He don't know enough to keep his blarsted shoulder blades off the canvas!"

"Any more lip outa you, young leddy, and I'll be laying ye across my knee!" said the thoroughly enraged Mr. Carson.

Allie had reached the scene of the trouble. He hastily brushed Nell aside with one hand and faced the pugilist with arms raised in the approved fashion.

The Basher's answer to this was to let loose a blow of the variety known as an uppercut. Allie got his jaw out of the way in time but the rush of wind past his ear was warning that Mr. Carson from Battersea was a dangerous customer.

"'Ere's one uv 'em!" shouted the pugilist in delight. "'Ere's a voter. 'Ere's a young rooster as has the right to walk up and say 'oo he wants 'lected. And why, I asks? A'cause this young rooster 'as propitty." He was motioning with his arms and at the same time gazing at Allie with the delight of a dog which has cornered a cat in an alley. "Stand back, all on ye, and make a ring. I'm goin' to fix this young fancy bloke so he won't be doin' no voting for quite a cun-sider-bull time."

"Police! Police!" cried a good half of the crowd. But the other half had turned away from the reasoned discourse of Miss Lydia Becker and were milling over to the edge of things in the hope of seeing a good fight. "Make a ring!" they cried. "Fair play! Give them both a chance."

Allie had taken boxing lessons and rather fancied his skill. Against anyone of his own weight and experience he could handle himself well. He knew how to keep his head out of danger and how to adapt his tactics to circumstances, and to shift and dodge and weave. But this was different. It was all very well for him to get his arms in the way of the flailing blows the Basher was raining on him but they lacked the strength for resistance. It was like trying to fend off a steel battle-ax with a stage property shield. Sometimes the blows he blocked refused to stay blocked and reached his shoulders and chest and head with deadening weight.

"Knock 'im into a cock-and-pinch!" roared the crowd; which meant they would like to see him knocked into a beaver hat. They were delighted that a well-dressed antagonist was getting the worst of it from a cove in a workman's smock.

The Basher was thickset and his shoulders and arms were so hard that Allie felt his few counterblows were landing on a granite headstone. His only chance was to get in a lucky blow and to land it before he tired. But the unshaved jaw of the angry Basher looked capable of resisting any swing he might land there. It was, he realized, a lost cause. All he could do was to sidestep and retreat, and avoid as much punishment as possible. He had no hope of resisting long.

"I say!" cried a cultured voice from somewhere in the crowd. "This won't do, you know. The big fellow has two stone the better of the boy. This isn't fair play!"

"He arsked for it, didn't he?" demanded another voice, the owner of which was well pleased obviously with the way things were going. "He's as thin as a barber's cat but he stuck up his blooming dukes, didn't he?"

A general cry of "Make cold meat out of him, Basher," seemed to express the feeling of the crowd. What right had a fancy bloke to come "messing in" where he didn't belong? Let him pay the price since he had asked for it.

Allie was paying a high price. His arms were numb, his head rang with the blows which had landed on it. His nose was bleeding copiously. The chief regret he felt, however, was that Nell was seeing him beaten in this decisive way.

The Basher had enough knowledge of ringcraft to realize that there was little resistance left in his opponent. His method of finishing a bout was to cut circles in the air with his left arm while waiting for the chance to bring the heavy ammunition of his right into play. This method of attack he now started.

Allie's eyes followed the circling left arm of the Battersea pugilist with an absorption which verged on mesmerism; and it was not long before the inevitable happened. The right came up with the suddenness of a cobra's head and the force of a piston, catching him on the jaw. The blow, fortunately, had bad direction and landed more on his cheek than the vulnerable point of the chin but even at that the recipient felt his senses leaving him. The vestige of strength left in his arms deserted at once, his knees buckled, his head dropped. He lost his balance and fell back against the solid dike of spectators banked behind him.

Allie was aware of excitement all about the ring, of shouting voices and waving hands. He could see the left arm of the Basher still inscribing circles and the deadly right cocked for a finishing blow. For the first time he was aware that the lower lip of his enemy had fallen, revealing a glittering mouthful of teeth. His last coherent thought was that the other man in the ring looked like nothing so much as a straw-yard billy goat. At that moment darkness settled over him.

When Alfred Carboy regained consciousness, he found that he was lying on the grass with his head propped up on someone's coat. The someone, a young man of about his own age, was swabbing his face with a handkerchief dipped in cold water.

He tried to raise himself into a sitting position and immediately the gables of the houses began to do somersaults.

"Take it easy," said the Good Samaritan, giving him another cold sousing with the damp linen.

A voice issued from a forbidding upright figure which he realized represented authority. "How did it start?" demanded the voice.

"I saw everything," said the Good Samaritan. "The other fellow——"

"Do you mean the Battersea Basher?"

"I don't know what he's called. But it's easy to believe he has earned some such nickname as that. Well, the Basher—if that's who he is—was interrupting the speeches in a way which could be described conservatively as not gentlemanly. The young lady——"

"This young lady?" It became apparent that a girl was standing beside the policeman. Allie raised his head a few cautious inches to see her but had to drop it to stop the world from the giddy gyrations it began to perform.

"Yes, that's the one. She came over to protest about his conduct. To tell him to shut up, in other words. It seemed to me she was as polite as the circumstances permitted but the Basher threatened to take her over his knee. At this point my friend here—he isn't really a friend but I hope he's going to become one—went into it to save the young lady from suffering the indignity the Basher was promising to inflict upon her." He made a gesture with one arm. "The rest, as someone has said, is history."

The officer had taken out his notebook. "And now, young lady, what is your name?"

"My name is Nell Groody."

This was not unexpected but Allie struggled to sit up. He did not succeed.

"And where do you live?"

"My home is in Little Shallow, Berkshire. For the past year I've been in London. I have been staying in the home of Mrs. Chillingly-Wick."

"The old lady who lives in the first row of houses?"

"Yes, Officer."

"Are you one of these Votes for Women agitators?"

"I'm in favor of votes for women. But I don't consider myself an agitator."

"And you came over to protest about the carryings on of the Battersea Basher?"

At this point the world returned to normal for Allie Carboy. His head cleared and he was able to raise himself to a sitting position without any accompaniment of dancing gables or skies filled with shooting stars.

"How are you feeling?" asked the young man who had befriended him.

"I'm all right again. I've got a bit of a headache but otherwise I don't seem to have any bad effects."

The officer left Nelly and came over to the two men. He looked down at the seated figure of Alfred Carboy.

"Feeling better?" he asked.

"I'll be as right as a trivet in a minute or two, Officer."

"But not quite bang up to the elephant, eh? Not quite perfect, in other words. They tell me you took a good solid clout on the jaw. The Basher is no great shakes as a boxer but he has a wicked right. Name, please."

"Alfred Carboy."

The strange young man drew in his breath in surprise. "Carboy?" he said. "Did you say, Carboy?"

The officer wrote the name down. "No connection, in course, of *the* Samuel Carboy?"

"He's my great-grandfather."

The policeman whistled. He broke regulations by indulging in a slang exclamation of surprise. "Dog bite my ears! Now this is something, isn't it? I'll bet the Basher didn't know *that*. He wouldn't have been so eager to flatten you out. Going to lay a charge, Mr. Carboy?"

Allie shook his head. "No. Let's forget the whole incident, Officer. No harm seems to have been done."

"Someone *has* been harmed a bit. Take a look at the young lady."

Allie could now see that Nell was looking rather limp. She was holding a hand over her right eye and the hat she had worn earlier in the evening was gone. It seemed she had been in the fight also.

He got to his feet and walked unsteadily to where she was standing.

"Nelly!" he said. "What happened? Has your eye been hurt?"

"A little." She smiled and extended the hand which was not occupied in covering up the damage she had sustained. "I'm very glad to see you, Allie. It's been a long time since we had that pleasant chat on the train, hasn't it?"

"We'll go into that later. What matters now is about your eye."

"I'm rather afraid it's going to turn black. It isn't regarded as proper for a young lady to get herself a black eye, is it?"

"But how did it happen?"

"I can answer that," said the strange man. "When the Basher had landed the one blow on your jaw and was ready to give you another of the same, this young lady rushed in and took hold of his mighty right arm. The Basher, fine gentleman that he is, seemed to resent this interference and he was rough in shaking her off. It was then she acquired the injury to her eye."

"Nelly," said Allie in an awed tone. "What a wonderful thing to do!"

Before he could say anything more to indicate how deeply he felt about the matter, the officer interrupted them. All the facts had at last been jotted down in the official book and he was prepared to take whatever action seemed necessary.

"I'll report this at headquarters. The Basher seems to have made himself scarce but if any of you want to lay a charge against him, we'll have him in to answer it in a matter of an hour or so." He looked at each of them in turn with a hopeful air. "It would be a pleasure."

But no one seemed anxious to do anything about it. The officer, regretfully, closed the notebook and put it away in a pocket. "If you change your minds," he said, "just get in touch with me at headquarters. The name is Officer George Floyd. At your service always." He turned away reluctantly and stalked off down the street.

"You know my name," said Allie to the young man who had come so wholeheartedly to their assistance. "Do you mind telling me yours?"

The stranger indulged in a smile. "I wonder if you'll think I'm pulling your leg? At any rate you'll find this rather hard to believe. My name is Grace. Julian Grace. I was named after my grandfather."

"Julian Grace!" cried Allie in astonishment.

"It is quite a coincidence, isn't it?"

Allie held out his hand. "Alfred Carboy desires to convey his thanks to

Julian Grace. It was sporting, if not downright noble, of you to come to my assistance in this way. But when you spoke of it as a coincidence, you didn't know the full extent of things in that direction. Doesn't the name of Nell Groody mean anything to you?"

"When I heard it," said Julian, "it seemed familiar. But I haven't been able to discover why."

"It's a long story," said Allie. "With the kind permission of the bearer of the name, I'll tell you about it after I've escorted her home and seen to it that a piece of raw beefsteak has been applied to her eye. In a matter of fifteen or twenty minutes, Mr. Grace, I'll join you at the Mutton Chop and Bitters. Do you know it? It's not more than two blocks away. We'll moisten our clay and get ourselves a cutlet. Then we'll have a long talk."

"Right!" said Julian. "I wouldn't be surprised if we found it worth while to bury a very old and rusty hatchet."

2

"I'm going to throw myself on your mercy, Nelly," said Alfred Carboy as they began to make their way across the now almost deserted Fields. "I have a long explanation to make and a thousand apologies to offer; and I'm going to ask you to let me state my case before heaping reproaches on my bloody and slightly bowed head. It may be, of course, that your aunt Helen has kept you advised of events. In that case it will be easier for me to explain."

"I have no intention of reproaching you, Allie. Especially after the way you came to my rescue tonight. But Aunt Helen has told me nothing. What was there she should have told?"

A serious frown settled on his face. "In that case I must start from the beginning. I didn't know my father was going to speak to your aunt that day. If I had, there would have been a dust raised between us. I threatened to leave home when I *did* find out and it was your aunt who persuaded me not to do it. In fact I've been acting on her advice right through these long and painful years. She didn't want any repetition of what happened to her and so she felt I should stay away long enough to let each of us find out how we felt. I've been bombarding her with demands that the term of consideration be considered over as far as I'm concerned. I know exactly how I feel and I know I'm never going to change. I'm properly done over with. I'm all wrapped up and ready to be delivered."

"Do you go to see Aunt Helen?" asked the girl, looking at him as intently as possible with only half of her usual equipment in working order.

"Of course. There's no counting the number of times I've seen her since I saw you last. In between visits I've written her."

"This begins to sound like a conspiracy," said the girl.

"There had to be a conspiracy. I had to know whether your fancies had started to stray in wrong directions."

"And," said Nelly in an ominously quiet voice, "I presume Aunt Helen has reported to you that no competition has developed apart from that lawyer from London who bothers us so much."

Allie sensed danger at once. He turned an anxious eye in her direction. "Look here! Has she been overlooking something? Have her reports been based on insufficient evidence?"

"Perhaps."

"This will have to be looked into at once."

"Doesn't it occur to you that it may be too late to be looked into?"

The Carboy jaw, wearing on this occasion a black bruise from contact with the fist of the Battersea Basher, came very much into evidence. "If I thought that, I would do two things," he declared. "First, I would call out this robber, this Jack Nasty, this snake in the grass; and I would strew his mangled remains over the landscape. Second, my sweet one, my beautiful one, my beloved one, I would take you by the ear or by your long tresses, and drag you before a parson. I would see to it, moreover, that you answered nothing but 'yes' to all his questions."

There was a long pause. "It's been such a long time since I've seen you," said the girl. "And in the meantime it's been generally believed that you are going to marry a French girl. The daughter of your father's partner in France."

"Oh, *that* one," said Allie gloomily. "My ill-advised parent is in favor of the match. They've been talking about arranging a meeting between us for a long time. Something has always turned up providentially to prevent it."

"You mean that you've never seen her?"

"Never. But I'm afraid that weakness in the plan is going to be corrected soon. Monsieur Plessis and his daughter are going to visit Beaulaw Hall before long."

"You'll fall in love with her," declared Nelly. "They say she's beautiful. And, of course, she's such a great heiress!"

"Nelly," he said after a moment, "I don't believe it's a good thing to have such a lot of money. My father is killing himself trying to get more and more of it. He's worked himself into a nervous state. He doesn't enjoy his food and he sleeps very little. It's nothing but business with him all the time. I've decided I don't want to be a great industrialist. In fact, Nelly, seeing you again, black eye and all, I've reached a definite decision. I'm not going to let that father of mine, or Aunt Isabelle, or anyone, tell me what I am to do. They can cut me out of all their wills and it won't bother me.

"In other words," he went on, "I'm going to run my own life and I'm going to choose my own wife. I don't mind telling you that I have a young woman in my mind who suits me perfectly."

"A word of advice. Wait until after the visit of the French family. She may prove to be the right one for you, after all."

Allie laughed scornfully. "There's no danger of that."

Nell decided that the stage had been reached when she should state her own case. "When you and Aunt Helen reached this decision between you, that we should be kept apart until we were able to know our own minds, you did it without consulting me. Didn't it occur to either of you that my mind might have been made up then? I'm not saying that it was; and, of course, there was reason to fear the pressure that the Carboy family could bring to bear for the second time. So it's possible you were right in deciding what you did; although I still think I might have been consulted."

"I was in unwilling agreement with the idea," declared Allie.

"As a result of what you two decided, I've had a long time to think things over," the girl went on. "I've made some discoveries in that time—about myself and about life. I've found that having a career, even as humble a one as mine, is very satisfying. I'm heart and soul with the movement. I like going out into the city and selling subscriptions to the magazine. I'm not saying that romance isn't important but there are other things in life. It might be that I could go right on with my present work and not be too much disappointed if romance passed me by. Did anything like that ever enter your mind?"

"No," answered Allie. "I'm incapable of imagining anything so unnatural and dreadful."

"But you thought of the possibility that I might have become interested in some other man. In other words, you see a limited horizon for a woman. Courtship, marriage, children, a settled life; nothing else, no career, no active interest in politics and affairs. Well, Mr. Alfred Carboy, you're quite wrong. I'm not content with such limitations, I'll have you know."

"Nelly," he said earnestly, "you can't quarrel with me on this point, even if I am lacking in imagination and can't see these—er—new horizons you talk about. I'm not concerned about them. You can go on with your career —after we are married. You see, I'm willing to take you on any terms."

They had reached the doorstep of Mrs. Chillingly-Wick's tall and austere home. Allie rang the bell and waited until the door opened.

"Good night, Miss Groody. I hope the injury to your eye won't prove too serious. And when you see your aunt Helen, tell her I've decided to work direct from now on."

"I think that will be the better way."

"And I want you to know also that two great ideas have come into my head this evening. You know what one of them is. The other is about *my* career and it's a blazing fine idea. I think there will be millions in it. It concerns you, of course, and it also concerns my new friend, Mr. Julian Grace. I'm on my way now to discuss it with him."

## CHAPTER SEVEN

1

Being a knight made little difference in the life of Julian Grace. People paid more attention to him, of course. Invitations for dinner, for lunch, for tea, for croquet began to pour in on him. He was always recognized in the villages and on the roads when he drove out or went for one of his long walks. "Goo' day, Sir Jul'n," the country people would say, reaching up to the forelock. Gentlemen he had never seen before bowed to him.

It made some small changes in his home life. He had to be more particular about the supplies in his wine cellar, because there were many callers now. He had to insist that Noel wear a clean collar every afternoon.

His grandson had been unable to contain his delight when the summons came from Windsor and it is probable that he talked about it quite a little in the offices where he spent his long hours of labor. He made a habit of bowing very low to his grandfather and addressing him in full. He said once, "No man ever deserved it more than you do. I've made that clear to the boys at the office. I certainly sing your praises."

It was in the spring of the following year that Young Julian came down for the weekend with an air of excitement wrapping him about as self-consciously as a new topcoat.

He was beginning to look very much like the first Julian. He had, at any rate, the same poetically high forehead and the loosely curling mane of black hair. He was filling out and his shoulders were as broad as a grenadier's. In the handsome head of the homecomer there was news for his grandfather which was strictly confidential and could not wait.

"Sir," he said when they had taken seats at the foot of the garden where they could see the swollen weir as they talked, "I'm going into business. With a partner. It's all settled if I—well, if I can raise my share of the stumpy."

"The *what*, my boy?"

"I'm sorry, Grandfather. It's a term we use in the City. Stumpy. It means cash. Same as *rowdy*, sir."

"Silly words. But then, Julian, it does seem to me that all this modern slang is silly."

"Oh, I'm not so sure. It's kind of expressive."

There was a moment of silence. Sir Julian seemed to be engaged in mental arithmetic. "How much of the stumpy will you need, my boy?"

"It hasn't come down to exact figures yet," said young Julian eagerly.

"Let me tell you first about the plan. We're both young, sir, my partner and I. We acknowledge that we need a bit more experience before we launch out. So we're going to wait a year. In the meantime we'll keep our eyes open and pick up our stock at bargain prices. My partner has the building we'll occupy. He owns it already."

"What line of business are you going into?"

"Why, the Eastern import trade, of course. Just like Grace and Carboy did in the beginning."

"I'm glad to hear that. It sounds natural, doesn't it? And now tell me about your partner."

Young Julian began to laugh. "You'll think I haven't all my buttons on when I tell you. You won't believe it, Grandfather. My partner is Alfred Carboy."

"What!" Sir Julian sat up straight on the bench and stared at his grandson as though he actually did fear the latter was lacking his full share of the buttons of reason. "Do you really mean it, boy? Gad, where did you meet him? How did the pair of you ever get around to such an unbelievable proposition as this?"

"We're friends. We're the very best of friends. I like to be with him all the time." Then he began on an explanation of the circumstances which had brought them together. Sir Julian found the story rather hard to follow because of the references to the girl and the speaker and the Battersea Basher and the police officer. Finally, however, he began to understand how the meeting had taken place.

"What is young Allie Carboy doing?" he asked.

"He's been in Eastern export for several years and already he's got to be an expert. Grandfather, he's going to be a turkey merchant just like old Sam. That means top grade."

"That doesn't surprise me at all. The Carboys have always been—er—turkey merchants." Sir Julian was beginning to look thoroughly bewildered. "My boy, I'm too old to take this all in at once. I think we had better go up to the house and have Noel get us some sherry. It may clear my brain."

They started back up the sloping path. Even with so many strange things to occupy his thoughts, the old man was happily conscious that spring was upon them. A robin chirped at them from the oldest of the oak trees in the garden and its mate hopped along close to the path with no trace of fear. He stooped to pick a snowdrop and a purple crocus from the edge of the grass.

When he straightened up he was smiling. "I'm just realizing what all this you've told me is going to mean. Julian, my boy, it's a capital idea. I'm sure all the Graces and the Carboys of the past are sitting together up there and clinking their glasses in approval of what the two of you propose."

"I was sure you would come around to it at once, sir."

"Did you hear," asked the old man, "that Mrs. Harriet Overall died in Norwich two days ago? She was quite a character, it seems, and everyone called her Old 'Arriet."

"Who was she?"

"One of the survivors in the Tontine. Her death means that my yearly income from it will rise to more than four thousand pounds. Peace to her ashes, poor lady, but because she has been doubled up this way, I suspect we'll be able to lay our hands on enough of the stumpy when the time comes."

After lunch Sir Julian Grace and his grandson drove out to a village in the neighborhood on a matter which had been under discussion between them for some time: the building of a brick wall where the property touched the water. The demise of the lady in Norwich, with the increase in revenue it would bring, had led them finally to an affirmative decision.

"We're going to St. Wilfrid's because it has a brickyard," explained the head of the family as they reached the main road to the west. "But I'm realizing that by some curious chance I've never been in the place. It's the only village hereabouts which I haven't visited at some time or other. I'm interested to see what it'll be like."

It developed that St. Wilfrid's was different from the other communities in the sense of being, on the surface at least, a one-man concern. The greengrocer shop had a sign which read,

LEW STAIN
PROP.

Across the road there was a repair shop with the same information on a sign of somewhat less imposing size. Farther up the road they found another mercantile establishment with several entrances and the same proud statement of ownership over each. The doors led into the community feed and grain shop, the barbershop and an insurance and undertaking establishment. Lew Stain, it was apparent, was prepared, even eager, to provide any service the villagers might desire. It was not until they had passed a short distance beyond and had come to a brick-walled space of some size filled with a score or more of circular brick kilns with domed tops that there was any variation from this form of declaration. The small shed which served as an office bore a new sign reading:

LEW STAIN AND CASPER LOWFOOT
BRICKS

"Here we are," said Sir Julian. "This is a comparatively new place but I'm told they make a good red brick, the kind you find in all genuine samples of Tudor houses." He stopped and looked at the sign with a concentrated frown. "Casper Lowfoot. Unless I'm mistaken, this man and his bride returned home from Bermuda on the same ship with me. I never set eyes on him."

He could not be sure, after a brief talk with the occupant of the office, that he had yet laid eyes upon him. Mr. Lowfoot was seated at a rickety table with a plan of some kind spread out upon it and he was so busy following the printed instructions it contained with the aid of a quill toothpick (which he applied at intervals to its regular use) that he never looked up.

"Mr. Lowfoot?"

"Oo ay. Lowfoot's the name."

"I want to buy some bricks."

"Bricks," said the joint proprietor, still following the lines of type. "Oo ay. We make 'em."

He got to his feet, keeping his eyes glued to the floor, shuffled to the rear door, opened it and let himself out. A moment later they heard a bell ring. It did not ring as loudly as the kind used, for instance, to summon pupils to school, but it brought Mrs. Lowfoot over promptly to wait upon them, while Mr. Lowfoot himself vanished into one of the drying sheds and never did return.

The lady, who first appeared on these pages under the name of Mary Tindy, had not changed in any respect. She still wore the same dress. She was very businesslike.

"Bricks?" she said. "What for?"

"A wall," explained the caller. "Along the bottom of our property where it touches the river."

"Ye'll need a stone foundation, then," said the lady briskly. "Who's your builder?"

"I haven't done anything about that yet."

He detected an alert gleam in her eye at this point. "Then Lew Stain's yer man. He does building and bricklaying and excavations and sich. I'll send ye to him. Yes, Lew Stain's yer man for almost anything under the sun." Her eyes had been darting about as she talked, coming back always to rest on Sir Julian's face with frowning concentration. "I've seen ye afore, mister. But where, I don't know."

He supplied the information. "It was in Bermuda. At the home of Mrs. Beltrade."

"In course," she said. "And may I inquire like as to yer name, sir? Seeing as we're like to make a deal."

"I'm Sir Julian Grace."

"Oh, *him*. Proud to hev made yer acquaintance again, Sir Grace. And where is it ye has yer residence?"

"At Three Gables. It's on the river about six miles from here."

She nodded her head. "I know it." She was the very opposite of her taciturn spouse, for her eyes never left his face now. "Did ye have much of a talk with Lowfoot?"

Julian shook his head. "The shortest and least satisfying talk I ever remember having. We had hardly said a word when he dived out the back door, rang that bell and disappeared."

Her air took on a note of satisfaction. "That's Lowfoot for ye. He leaves the talking to me. And he never looks at anyone. Not him. When we was joined in the holy bonds, he didn't raise his eyes once to the parson. He didn't even look at me. But make no mistakes, Sir Grace, he's a smart one and he sees everything. Oh yes, indeed. He'll come popping out as soon as ye leave and he'll tell me all about the pair of ye, even to the number of buttons on yer coats and the color of yer neckerchers. He'll say whether ye'r sharp or slack about business and he'll have ye measured to the last penny we can expect to get out of selling ye bricks. It won't be big, in any case, 'cause our profits is low, sir, and allus must be reckuned in no higher than shillings and pence. Oh yes, he's a smart one, that Lowfoot."

"He may be a smart one," said Sir Julian to his grandson as they drove away, "but he has all the earmarks of a rascal. I wish we had someone else to deal with but this is the only yard within reasonable distance."

"I'm sure this Lew Stain is a moneylender on top of everything else and charges a high interest," said the grandson. "He was pointed out to me once at the station in Windsor. He has a small head on a huge body. People are afraid of him. They call him the Anteater because he has such a long nose."

"They seem like a charming pair, or rather trio. Well, we'll let them build our wall and then we're through with them. And now, my boy, let's discuss your business plans while we're free from interruption. I want to know everything about what you're going to do."

2

There had been two deliveries at the house during their absence. The first was a letter, addressed to Sir Julian Grace.

He opened it at once and discovered that it was from Titus in London. There had been other communications from his son, all of them distinctly unfriendly in tone, although occasionally Titus had forgotten his grievances as he mentioned his activities and his successes as a man about town. There was nothing friendly about this letter, however. Titus had just found out about the transfer of the property, by what means he did not explain, and he had sat himself down in a towering rage to express his feelings.

This is the end [he wrote]! I will never forgive you for this monstrous thing you have done. This is to tell you that you will never hear from me again, except in the form of legal communications from my attorneys. I consider you have been most damnably unfair and I hope never to lay eye on you again. And if I ever meet that grandson of yours, so called, I will take great pleasure in giving him a horsewhipping.

You must not think that I am accepting this theft of my rights. The matter has been placed with my lawyers and you will hear from them in due course. ᐱ

Sir Julian folded the letter back into its envelope with a hand which trembled. His grandson saw that he was disturbed and refrained from asking questions. As they walked together into the house, Julian referred to the contents of the communication very briefly.

"It was from Titus. He knows about the transfer of the property and is threatening legal fire and brimstone on me. It may be his lawyers will talk him out of any hasty action but we can't count on it." He smiled ruefully at the equally unhappy face of his grandson. "I don't like quarrels, particularly in families. Legal troubles always give me an empty feeling at the pit of my stomach. I won't enjoy it if Titus precipitates an open breach."

The other was a pleasant surprise, however, a large square canvas which his grandson studied with excited eyes. It was the portrait of a redheaded young officer with a blond mustache and a monocle, wearing the white dress uniform of the Austrian army.

"My father painted it," said young Julian in a rapt voice. "I remember when he did it. The officer was killed in a duel afterward. My, he was handsome!" There was a pause while they studied the picture side by side. "I think it was one of the best things my father ever did. Don't you?"

"It's a gorgeous piece of work, Julian. But how does it happen to be here?"

"Mrs. Prouty says it came this afternoon. Direct from a dealer in Vienna. There was no letter but one will follow, I suppose. Oh, what wonderful luck! To have such a splendid specimen of his work! Who do you suppose sent it, Grandfather?"

The explanation had come suddenly to Sir Julian. Sue Beltrade had heard him say he would like to have one of his son's paintings from his mature period in Austria. As he had never expressed this desire in the hearing of anyone else, it clearly was her work. She had set negotiations under way which had resulted in the sending of this remarkably fine canvas.

He examined it with eyes which had become moist with tears. It was a truly rich example of the portrait painter's art. The handsome auburn-haired officer in his white tunic, covered with decorations, had been depicted against the background of a superb sapphire-blue curtain. It was a gift beyond price.

"A friend has sent it, Julian," he said. "A friend for whom I have a very deep regard."

CHAPTER EIGHT

1

It was Monsieur Jacques Plessis who first uttered in England the words which soon came to be on all tongues, "Hard times are coming." He expressed this opinion in the course of a conversation with Her Grace the Duchess of Outland.

It was some time after the last events recorded and it was at a very elaborate dinner given at Outland House on Grosvenor Square as part of the entertainment of the long-deferred and often-postponed visit of the great French banker. Monsieur Plessis was not seated at her right, however. In order to make the event a memorable one and to impress the visitor properly, Isabelle had at her table a duke, two earls, a viscount and a variety of lesser nobles, as well as two cabinet ministers and a smattering of assorted artists, writers, actors and businessmen; and, of course, the wives of all of them. It was one of the most distinguished companies ever assembled around a private board and, as the law of seniority had to be observed, the black-bearded and dramatic banker sat some distance from his hostess.

He enjoyed the meal nevertheless. Not only had Isabelle imported a French chef several years before but she had succumbed completely to the Romanesque ideas about food which industrial prosperity had introduced into England. The artistic menu at each plate, printed most expensively in three colors, was almost a foot long. It included caviar, pâté, ptarmigan on toast, things out of season brought over packed in ice from North Africa such as asparagus and strawberries and peaches, a variety of rich soups, a large baked salmon, Dover sole, a haunch of prime beef, Cotswold mutton, Westmoreland ham, a twenty-five-pound turkey, capons roasted with links of sausage draped over them like bay leaves on a victor's brow, salad, puddings and tarts and a wonderful ice in the form of a medieval castle with Italian chestnuts sticking out of its sides. The wines were choice and carefully selected.

It was not until the gentlemen rejoined the ladies in the drawing room that Isabelle had an opportunity to get Monsieur Plessis to herself. He was one of those who grew pessimistic when stuffed with rich food and the effect of Isabelle's bountiful hospitality had been to plunge him into depths of gloom. With a deep sigh he gave vent to the expression quoted at the beginning of the chapter.

"Hard times are coming?" said Isabelle, frowning uneasily. "Do you mean that business will suffer? That dividends will be cut?"

"Dividends!" The banker indulged in a snort. "We are forgetting the word in France. Of course," he added, "we have the cost of the war with Prussia to pay and the unbelievable indemnity they have demanded of us."

"Do you think," asked Isabelle, "that we are going to have hard times here in England?"

Monsieur Plessis considered the point with a reflective frown. "As to that, I don't know," was the conclusion he finally reached. "You have no war indemnity to pay. In fact, my dear Duchess, you profited in this country by the war. It may be that you will continue to sit in prosperous isolation and see the Continent writhing in want."

Isabelle raised the point then which had leaped into her mind as soon as he spoke. "What of our companies in France?"

Monsieur Plessis gestured with both hands. "What can we expect? We are losing money, of course. It is to discuss it that I come to England. That, and the matter of our young people."

At this point Alfred Carboy put in an appearance. He had not been invited for dinner, there being just so many seats available, but Isabelle had laid a strict injunction on him to come as soon after as possible. Hesitating in the arched entrance to the drawing room, he looked very young in his first evening clothes, with long tails and a white vest and a high starched collar. Catching his eye, the duchess motioned him to join them.

"Good evening, Aunt Isabelle," he said, bowing over her hand. "And my respects to you, m'sieur."

Isabelle was seated on a couch and Monsieur Plessis occupied a chair in stiff-backed discomfort beside it. She invited Allie to sit beside her and patted his hand affectionately when he obeyed. He was the only person for whom she thus displayed open affection.

"And what have you been doing today, my dear boy?" she asked.

Allie looked at her dubiously and then transferred his glance to the spade-bearded visitor with an equal degree of apprehension.

"I've been very busy and I don't think you are going to approve of what I've done."

"Indeed! And what is it you did?"

"I made final arrangements for starting in a new business."

An orchestra began to play in the wide reception hall and for a moment the hostess gave her attention to the music. In a few minutes the program she had arranged for the evening would begin. It included a soprano of great note (but, alas, not Jenny Lind, who had not been tempted by the large sum Isabelle had offered), a violinist from Spain and a comedian named Bert Sloper straight from an east end variety stage. Whatever was to be said would have to be said quickly.

"You are so unpredictable, Allie," declared the duchess. "What is this business you are starting? Something to occupy yourself in your spare time?"

"No, Aunt Isabelle. It will take all my time, I assure you." The youth looked at the dignified figure in the chair. "I'm getting my hand in, m'sieur. Trying my wings, you might say."

The banker nodded. "That's understandable and, I think, perhaps, commendable, young M'sieur Carboy. You are following in your father's footsteps."

"Yes, m'sieur. In a way." He hesitated, knowing that the rest of his news would not be well received by the duchess. "With this difference. I have a partner."

"A partner!" said Isabelle sharply.

She would have interrogated him if there had not been at this point a stirring in the long room which arose from the fact that the soprano had appeared. Isabelle said in a whisper, "We'll go into this later. Find Ma'amselle Plessis and apologize for your late appearance." She then hurried forward to introduce the singer.

Monsieur Plessis also spoke in a whisper. "You'll find my little Hortense Alphonsine in the conservatory. The younger members of the party are there."

Allie did not linger in setting out to find the pretty daughter of the French partner of the house. Hortense Alphonsine had already made quite an impression on all members of the family, being not only lively but as delicately lovely as a camellia blossom. She had become a little less fragile perhaps than when Samuel Carboy had first seen her in Paris and it might have seemed to critical eyes that in time this tendency would become more rapid and pronounced; but now, certainly, she was as alluring as any little beauty in direct descent from Eve.

From the door of the conservatory, he saw that she was seated between two young men and quite obviously had not been missing him at all. The interlopers had vanished, however, when he reached her side.

"'Allo, M'sieur All-ee," she said, smiling.

"'Allo, Ma'amselle Hortense Alphonsine."

"You are ver' late. I was thinking you were not coming."

"I wasn't invited for dinner. But Aunt Isabelle told me that, if I were a good little boy, I might come in later."

The girl looked up at him from under her long black lashes. "Then you 'ave been the good little boy, 'aven't you?"

"Not exactly. My aunt Isabelle is going to be furious when she finds out everything about today and the new business. Your father, I think, is going to approve."

"Oh yes, I 'ave talked much to my good little papa and he thinks well of it." She regarded the very snug fit of his swallow-tailed coat with an approving eye. "You are quite 'an'some in a tall, clean kind of way."

"And you are much more than 'an'some in that white frock and that pretty little ermine muff and those tiny white slippers. In fact you are positively devastating—in a small, dainty kind of way."

"I am in love," she said softly. "But not, of course, with you, dear All-ee."

"No. I understand. It's not with me."

"With my sweet René. For whom my little papa has such very small regard. And you are in love too."

"Yes, dear Hortense Alphonsine. I'm very much in love. But——"

"But not with me."

"But not with you, ma'amselle."

She sighed. "What a pity that I didn't meet you before I fell in love with my René. I think it might have been you in that case. And what a pity also that you didn't meet me before you got to liking this Irish girl so much. Perhaps you would have picked me instead. And that would have made my papa and your papa and that beautiful old Aunt Isabelle very 'appy. As it is——"

"As it is," said Allie grimly, "they are not going to be very happy at all. In fact they are going to be very damned angry."

The soprano was singing something from Donizetti's *The Daughter of the Regiment* and her sweet voice filled the house. There was a pause of several moments between the young couple, who now had the conservatory to themselves.

"We must let them know," said Mademoiselle Hortense Alphonsine finally. "It is not right to delay any longer. I have been thinking about it a great much and I think we must tell your papa and my papa together. We must present the—what is it you say?—the united front?"

"Yes. We must present the united front, my sweet Hortense Alphonsine. We must be firm."

"Oh, very firm. As firm as rock. We must make it clear that we have made up our minds to be married—but not to each other."

"The fur will fly," he predicted gloomily.

The soprano completed her number and a raucous voice reached their ears instead. It was apparent at once that the inimitable Bert Sloper was in good form, for waves of loud laughter came back to them.

"I think, All-ee, it must be done tomorrow," whispered the fair visitor.

"Might as well get it over with," he whispered back. "Keep your head up, little horsie."

When the young couple emerged from the cover of the potted palms and the calla lilies in the conservatory, Allie observed the Duke of Outland pacing slowly down the hall by himself and looking rather distrait. Another young man in the white and black which had become recognized as the proper garb for dress occasions carried Hortense Alphonsine off and Allie joined the lonely peer.

"I have to keep walking, Allie," said the duke, "in order to stay awake. I'm so sleepy in the evenings that I get to snoring in a minute if I sit down. This way I can just manage to keep my eyes open." He uttered a sudden exclamation of alarm. "That blasted fiddler is going to play now. That will do it for me! The sawing of a fiddle will send me to sleep on my feet."

"Let's put on cloaks, sir," said Allie, "and go out to the garden for a stroll."

"Capital idea, my boy. The fresh air will revive me. Gad, how I hate this gay social life. But, of course, it's meat and drink to your aunt Isabelle. She's doing it up proud tonight, isn't she?"

When they reached the gardens the duke looked about him cautiously to make sure no one else had been struck with the same idea. "My boy," he said, "I'm glad of this chance. Look here, now, you mustn't let them talk you into anything. Stick to your guns and refuse to marry the girl. Oh, I acknowledge she's a trim little filly, and it would be a most convenient kind of a match. But, my boy, that one I took home on the train, that little Irish girl, she's the one for you."

"Did you hear, sir, that she waded into a fight to help me and got a black eye for her pains?"

"Did she? By gad, no, I didn't hear it." The duke looked most tremendously interested in the episode. "Well, that settles it. Any girl who will risk a black eye for you is the wife you want."

"Would you believe, sir, that she looked lovely, even with the black eye? Well, I'm going to take your advice. I'm going to marry her. If she'll have me."

"There's another matter too, my boy. Damme, they mustn't be allowed to talk you out of this starting your own business I've been hearing about. They'll be at you, the whole pack of them, arguing and protesting and threatening to cut you off. Don't listen to them."

Allie laughed. "It's too late for them to do anything about *that*," he said. "We signed the papers today."

"Splendid!" said the peer. "You seem to know your own mind, my boy."

"I have the knack, sir, of seeing what I want very clearly. I don't believe my father and Aunt Isabelle quite understand that. They think I can be swung around like most other people. Well, I can't; and they're going to find that out soon."

"That damned singer is squawking again," said the duke. "Why do they always have to sing this Italian guff instead of things you can understand like 'Annie Laurie' and 'Let Me Like a Soldier Fall'? Still, I'm afraid we should go in now."

2

Isabelle's mind had been too filled with other things to take in the full meaning of what Monsieur Plessis had said about business conditions. It came back to her later in the evening, however, and she began to realize the seriousness of it. She spent an almost sleepless night. If the world was facing a period of depression, it might lead quickly to a diminution in the profits she received. It might mean that the expansion of the company into foreign fields would cease to be as successful as it seemed. It might even mean heavy losses abroad.

She rose early the next morning. The first person she met on going downstairs was her social secretary, looking grim with the responsibility of restoring order in the household after the activities of the previous evening.

"Trounce," she asked, "what do you make of the way business is going?"

The secretary looked up from the pile of mail she was opening. "Business?" she said in a somewhat blank tone. "Business is going on, I suppose. It had better, the way we're spending money here." Then she frowned thoughtfully. "Coming to think of it, I've heard whispers that hard times are on the way."

"Why? Why?" demanded the duchess in strident tones. "I've heard nothing of the kind. Why should people suddenly begin to talk this way? Hard times are coming! How do they know? Why are they so pessimistic?"

The secretary did not seem very much concerned over the business situation. "I'm sure I don't know. It's just a lot of talk, I suppose. By people who don't know anything about it, to begin with." She held up a letter. "Another begging note. A Frenchman. You must have known him once. Rather well, if we can believe what he says. He's living in Antwerp and he begs his 'dear little Belle' to take pity on him and save him from starving to death."

"What's his name?" asked Isabelle, pausing on her way to the small room overlooking the gardens where breakfast would be waiting for her.

"Claude something," said Miss Trounceman, turning back to the letter to make sure. "Yes. Claude de Launy."

Isabelle held out a peremptory hand. "I'll take it," she said. She intended to say nothing more but after a moment it seemed wiser to explain. "He's the man who killed my first husband in a duel."

Miss Trounceman's mouth fell open in consternation. "Oh! I didn't know. I'm very sorry, Your Grace."

The duchess gave the matter a brief moment of thought. The duel and its fatal consequences had not entered her head in many years. She had almost forgotten what her first husband had looked like and the memory of him was very vague. Claude de Launy had been a selfish coward. She took the letter in both hands and tore it vigorously into many pieces before dropping it into the wastebasket beside the secretary's desk. "He doesn't deserve a penny," she said.

Half an hour later, dressed most becomingly in a sealskin paletot over a Pekin velvet dress and with a tiny hat on her snow-white hair, the duchess stepped into her carriage and drove away in the direction of the City. She drove direct to the mission near Shadwell where her arrival sent Jacko into a splutter of excitement.

"She's a-gettin' out," he said to Jonathan Bade. "It almost sent me over on my back seam when she stopped here, with a coachman up in front and a tiger behind, and a spanking team of blacks."

"Who is it?"

"She can't be anything less than a duchess," declared Jacko.

Jonathan was prepared, therefore, when Isabelle walked in, her cheek flushed from the brisk March winds she had encountered on her drive through the town. He pulled out a chair for her.

"There's trouble in your eye, my dear Isabelle," he said.

"Jonathan!" said Isabelle. "Do you believe hard times are coming?"

Jonathan's years had overtaken him at last. He was as thin as a lath and his face had become so bony that he looked more than ever like a Roman leader. The change was even more noticeable, however, in his manner. He had become quiet, even subdued. When he spoke it was in brief sentences and no longer with the flowing style of a speech in the House of Commons.

"Well," he said, taking off his spectacles but putting them back again when he found that she was no more than a blur when he lacked them. "There is some evidence of recession in other countries. France isn't prosperous, what with the war and the trouble in the vineyards. Even Gambetta, that wonderful patriot, doesn't seem capable of doing anything about it. There's sheep rot in all the wool-raising countries and the herds are diminishing. But actually the real trouble is in America."

This was something quite new and it opened up terrifying prospects. "In the United States? But—but our companies there are doing so well."

"All companies over there were doing well. When the Civil War ended the Americans started to open up the West and to build railroads across the prairies. I suppose they allowed themselves to overbuild; an American habit by the way. At any rate the boom is over. The rate for a bushel of grain from Chicago to New York is only twenty-two cents. It used to be thirty three cents. I saw that interesting piece of information in *The Times* this morning. Then a company went broke, an important one headed by a man named Jay Cooke. The whole business world has been terrified ever since."

"But we're still making money there," she persisted, unwilling to accept anything but the rosy picture which had led her into such extravagances.

"Are you? I would make sure on that point, dear Isabelle."

"What should I do?"

"Go to your father. Make him tell you the truth. And no matter what he tells you, get rid of a great deal of your Carboy stocks. That is plain common sense."

"But, Jonathan, there are no signs yet in England."

The forensic mood, which had been so marked in Jonathan before, came back. He gestured with a very thin white hand. "A discerning eye might see on the horizon a cloud hardly as large as a man's hand. There's been the merest hint of trouble. It hasn't had any effect on business in England yet. But if the rest of the world is hit we can't expect to sell our manufactured goods abroad. And *that* is where Carboy and Co. would feel the pinch."

This kind of talk was what Isabelle had dreaded to hear. She was convinced now that things were not as prosperous as she had so blithely believed; but she could not yet accept the idea of any degree of weakness developing in the great empire her father had built. All her life she had been accustomed to thinking that the world revolved around Carboy and Co. It had been like the Rock of Gibraltar. Nothing could hurt it. To sell any of her shares was unthinkable.

"I'll see Papa at once," she said. "Unfortunately he's at Beaulaw Hall and I'll have to go there. I hope I can catch him on one of the days when his mind is clear. He's into his middle nineties now, you know, and some days he doesn't remember much." There was something she had never told him about the stock. She had no legal right to sell any of it, except to her father. This stipulation had always been made when she acquired shares.

She noticed then for the first time how old Jonathan himself was looking. His face was gray and his hands, which were folded in his lap, trembled perceptibly.

"How are you feeling, Jonathan?"

"Dear Isabelle, I am an old man and I have most of the infirmities which old men must expect. My mind is clear; that much I *can* claim but there's little else I can say for myself on the credit side. I eat very little. I don't believe I've dared take a slice of roast beef for five years. How tired I've become of thin soup and anemic little puddings!"

Isabelle's eyes filled suddenly with tears. "We're old, all of us, Jonathan!" she cried. "We're old, old, old! Isn't it dreadful?"

He tried to give her a reassuring smile. "I never expected to hear you say that. I knew that all of the rest of us would grow old. But you? Never!" He leaned over and touched one of her hands. "Isabelle, you still go regularly to church, don't you?"

"Of course I do. I drive to church every Sunday morning."

"Do you listen to what is said?"

"Oh yes. Well, some of the time."

"Do you believe what is said?"

She became indignant at this point. "Of course I believe. I'm as good a Christian as you are, Jonathan Bade."

"I'm glad to hear it, Isabelle. When we get old it is a great comfort to have the belief. It helps to compensate us for some of the things which old age brings; and it gives us peace and happiness. But, Isabelle, it isn't enough to believe. We must prove ourselves in all the things we do. Our faith must be shown every day of our lives. I wonder—— Well, I've done enough preaching. Please convey my kindest sentiments to your father. I hope he has forgiven my desertion from the all-conquering ranks. I've always hoped he would finally give up his interest in material things and allow himself a concern in matters of the spirit."

"He will die in harness," declared Isabelle proudly.

"I suppose he will; and it may be that such is the divine plan for him. I've known him to do many generous things. I must not presume to judge him. It is possible that in the final measuring by the tape of the gods what he has done to make a new industrial world will weigh more than my puny fight for what I believe. Who are we to guess at such things?

"But, Isabelle," he went on, "I hope you are going to be sensible. Put your house in order so you'll be ready for anything that may happen."

CHAPTER NINE

1

Mrs. Chillingly-Wick's butler admitted Allie and escorted him to a parlor which contained portraits of a formidable-looking woman, probably Mrs. Chillingly-Wick herself, and of a man with dull eyes and a strong jaw who might have been the late Mr. Chillingly-Wick. The whole establishment seemed to the visitor cold and orderly and completely lacking in ease and charm.

"Exactly the kind of place you would expect of a woman who's out for the vote," thought Allie. Then he checked his fancy sharply. "Won't do to be thinking that way, young fellow. Not if you expect to find favor with a certain young party who also believes in votes for women."

There was a light step on the stairs and Nelly came into the room. She was looking very bright and pretty, and very smart as well in a coat of some blue material. She was carrying a copy of the suffrage magazine and a businesslike case in one hand and a gray umbrella in the other.

"I was on my way out," she said cheerfully and casually. "To sell a very large number of subscriptions, I hope."

"Sit down and give me a few minutes before you resume your attack on the established order of things. I have something important to say to you."

There was a solemnity in his manner which she could not fail to notice but she decided to ignore it for the time being. "Why don't you stroll along with me?" she suggested. "You could tell me about it then."

"This," he said emphatically, "is not the kind of thing to be discussed while strolling along the streets of London. Nor, for that matter, with two such unfriendly faces staring down at us from the walls. However, here we are and what I have to say won't wait any longer. Please take a seat beside me here on this sofa where we can talk comfortably."

But Nell chose a chair instead. She sat down and fixed her eyes on the floor while she traced patterns on the pink roses of the carpet with the tip of her umbrella.

"My father is cutting me out of his will," began Allie. "My aunt Isabelle, who was planning to be very generous with me, has decided to leave me nothing at all."

Nell looked up at him, her eyes filled with sudden commiseration.

"Oh, Allie!" she said in a whisper. "I'm so sorry!"

He did not seem at all concerned himself. "I'm not to be taken into Carboy and Co. My own business is being started at a time when clouds of dark depression hover over us. I've spent almost my last shilling in getting things ready to start, all of mine and all of my partner's. In other words, I'm a poor man with a fight on my hands and no prospects for the future. Except what I may be able to make for myself. Nelly, my darling, will you marry me?"

She looked up quickly. "This means that the match with the French heiress has been broken off," she said. She lowered her eyes again. Her cheeks had flushed a rosy color.

"It's smashed into a million pieces, into fearful and complete flinders," he affirmed cheerfully. "By mutual consent. She loves another. I love another. Oh, Nelly, how much I love the other!"

"And things are as bad as you say?"

"My affairs have reached a truly desperate pass."

There was a short pause.

"Then," she said, "if they are really quite desperate, I am very happy to say yes."

In a moment, it seemed, they were standing together and he had taken her into his arms and was kissing her with the pent-up ardor of years of separation and waiting. Her arms went up around his neck and she found herself returning his kisses and laughing and crying at the same time.

"Oh, Allie!" she whispered. "At last I can believe you mean it! You have sacrificed everything for me. My dear, my dear!"

"Don't think of it as sacrifice. I'm glad to be in this situation. It's—well, it's inspiring. Now I can do everything for you myself."

"Yes, Allie, yes!" Her voice was now as eager as his. "The only thing I fear is that you will be cut off from your family. Will there always be this breach? Will your father ever forgive you?"

"Of course he will. At first he favored the French match because it would have been so advantageous from a business standpoint. As soon as that fell through, Aunt Isabelle began to talk about marrying into some noble family. Titles and crests and all that. My father agreed with her. But he'll come around before long. He likes you. He thinks you are beautiful and intelligent." He stopped talking and stared intently into her face. "There's no sign of the black eye left. I'm sorry in a way that there isn't. It would be so much more important than a crest."

"I'll be—well, a kind of an heiress myself someday. Do they know that?"

There was another long period when the chance to look into each other's eyes seemed much more important than anything else. Once he said, "Of course I know you'll be an heiress and that's why I'm marrying you, really." It did not seem necessary to make any response to that; Nell, at any rate, made none. It was again Allie who finally resumed the conversation.

"She caught me that time," he said.

Nell looked up in surprise. "Why, what do you mean?"

"There's a lady pacing up and down the hall," he explained. "I suppose it's your Mrs. Chillingly-Wick. She looks in every time she passes this door. She went by just as I kissed the tip of your pretty Irish nose."

"That means I'll have to tell her the news, so she'll understand why I was letting you kiss me."

"Tell her, by all means. It's my fervent hope that the whole world will ring with it in the course of a day or so." His mood sobered as he began on some explanations. "We're going to be very busy the next few days. First, I must get the marriage license. The next step will be to see the owner of a beautiful house out in the west end—well, it's a house, even if it is small and has the tiniest garden in all London—and get the key and put down the two pund six to bind the bargain. Finally I must send a telegram to your aunt, to whom I paid a visit over the weekend——"

"Alfred Carboy!" cried Nelly, the quick temper of the Groody family (which had missed her aunt, of course) showing in her eyes. "What is the meaning of this? Are you inventing it or did you really take me so much for granted that you talked to others before you even came to me?"

"Nelly, my beautiful future bride, I couldn't afford to wait. The landlord wouldn't agree to hold the house. And of course I had to ask your aunt for her consent to my—well, to my popping the question. That was part of the agreement between us."

Nell looked even more stunned at the rapidity of everything. "But, Allie," she said finally, "why are you plunging in this way? After all, we can't be married for weeks. Even months."

He drew a paper from his pocket which seemed covered with penciled data. He studied it carefully. "We can be married in exactly four days. I would prefer to cut that down but then it wouldn't be possible to get the sticks of furniture moved into the house."

"I'll have you know, Alfred Carboy," cried Nell, "that I must pass on every stick of furniture that goes into the house!"

"And then," he persisted, "I'm afraid your aunt couldn't get down under four days. She must travel slowly and make two overnight stops."

Nell took him by the shoulders and gave him an angry shake. "You seem to think I can be moved in at a moment's notice although the sticks of furniture can't! And it seems that Aunt Helen feels the same way. Well, I'll have you know that I'm going to have something to say about this——"

The scuffling sound of a cautious slippered foot could be heard in the hall. Allie waited until the anxious Mrs. Chillingly-Wick had passed. He took Nell's face between his hands and gazed raptly into her eyes. "It's nearly sixty years since Allie Carboy first made love to Nell Groody," he said. "It's time we brought the courtship to a happy ending. Your aunt has agreed to start her long journey to London as soon as I send her the word. We mustn't lose another minute so I'll draft the telegram while you break the news to the curious lady in the hall."

When Nell returned he handed her the draft of the message. It read:

The Lord Mayor has ordered bunting on all the shops in London and the trained bands are marching. Fireworks tonight at Buckingham Palace to top things off. In other words the lady has said yes. Start at once. Love from both of us.

2

Alfred Carboy had been correct in his calculations. The wedding took place on the fourth day.

Helen Groody was at the church, looking pale and weak from the fatigue of her long drive. Her eyes shone with a warmth which might be attributed to what the happy groom had said, that this was in reality the culmination of a romance which had started sixty years before. The delicate old lady, looking very pretty in spite of her ailments, in a butterfly bonnet and a quiet velvet dress with white ruching at the throat and wrists, was partly convinced that it was the girl she had been who made the responses in a clear, high voice and that the man beside the girl was the Allie Carboy who had won her heart. At any rate she sat very still through the ceremony and during the extending of congratulations and the rather general kissing which followed, and her eyes, moist with tears, had a faraway look in them.

There were two unexpected witnesses in the dark church. Allie's partner had found it necessary at the last minute to go away about some business of the new firm (if he had not gone, it would have been necessary for the groom to absent himself and that would hardly have done at all) but he was represented by his grandfather, Sir Julian Grace. Beside the tall and robust figure of the new knight sat Jonathan Bade, who had received a hint of what was afoot in a note from his onetime partner in reform. The two men exchanged comments in low tones and seemed very happy indeed over what they were witnessing.

The party then adjourned to an imposing hotel in close proximity to the church where a very fine wedding breakfast awaited them. If little attention was paid to the food, it was not the fault of the groom, who had planned it with particular care. He and his bride were in the customary deliriously happy frame of mind and were scarcely aware of what was placed before them. The older members of the party had passed the stage where it was safe to indulge much in sole smothered in such pleasant accessories as shrimps and oysters and mushrooms, with boiled eggs wrapped in table napkins to keep them warm, and thick slices of ham, not to mention toast and muffins and marmalade. The chief responsibility for eating the food fell, therefore, on the formidable Mrs. Chillingly-Wick, who did her best to make up for the feeble efforts of the rest.

It was somewhere about halfway of the meal that the bride, looking suddenly apprehensive, whispered something into the ear of the proud young man beside her. It must be understood, she said, that it was not in any sense a national custom, in fact it was purely local and she doubted if it was even known in any other part of Ireland. It did happen to be the thing to do in the village where she came from, perhaps as a deterrent to hasty and ill-considered marrying, and so she supposed they would be expected to comply. She had not mentioned it before because—well, she had feared it might prove such a handicap that it would be necessary to postpone the wedding, a development which (and what a confession this was!) she could not have faced. But now that they *were* married, she saw no way out of meeting the issue.

"Well, Mrs. Alfred Carboy," said Allie, quite casually and without any hint of concern, "what is it we must do? Join hands and leap over a blazing log, or something like that?"

"No, no," she answered. "We wouldn't have minded that, would we? But this—in view of the *terribly* high cost of weddings and of getting started in the business—this is much worse, dear Allie. It's the custom when a man marries into a family to present a pound to each unmarried child."

"Well, chip me off!" whispered Allie, taken back rather seriously. He began to do some mental arithmetic, concerned with what small shreds of capital he would have left after paying for the sole and the ham and the eggs, tipping the waiters and engaging a hansom cab to reach the beautiful little house in the west end into which the carefully selected sticks of furniture had been carried the evening before. "How many unmarried Groodys are there?"

Nell swallowed rather hard. "Nine," she said.

"Nine!" The groom's face took on a stricken look. "Why in thunder, my sweet wife, did your parents feel it necessary to have such a large family as that? And—and if the rest of them are anywhere near as beautiful as you, why are they all still lingering on the shelf?"

"Allie," said Nell in a tone which pleaded with him to be patient, "it just happens that we have picked the worst possible time to be married. Three of the girls are engaged and two of the boys are walking out. In another year they will all be married, except the young ones, of course. Himself says that very soon he will have no family about him at all."

A hint of the crisis spread around the table, however, and there was an immediate searching in pockets and wallets and purses and in a matter of minutes it was found that not only had the nine pounds been loaned (Allie insisted it must be done on this basis) but that they were four pounds over. It was suggested that they might better the custom by giving the balance to Himself and the Mither but Nell put her foot down on that. It was finally decided that the four pounds should be turned over to Jonathan Bade for his mission. He accepted it gladly and announced that now he would be able to deck out in unusually fine style two derelicts he had found the night before.

Jonathan Bade sat beside Helen Groody at the table and noticed with alarm how little she was interested in the food and the wine in which the toasts were drunk.

"Life has settled down for both of us," he said at one stage. "I suppose it's inevitable and sensible. I tire very easily and look forward to my bed with longing. We can't run around the country, stealing children from factories and the like, when the years have climbed up on our shoulders."

"My life is very quiet in a sense," said Helen. "But I must be frank with you, old friend, and add that it isn't pleasant. The pain is always in my joints and sometimes it becomes almost unbearable. If it hadn't been for the need, and the desire, to see my niece safely launched into the right kind of life, I would have welcomed the chance long ago to see the end of it."

Jonathan studied her with a sympathetic eye. "I didn't know it was as bad as that. Your letters are always cheerful. And while we are on the subject of your letters, I want to thank you for the success you've had in placing men for me."

"They are doing well, all three." She smiled and it was clear at once that the mention of the interest they both had at heart had done her good. "Such grateful old fellows they've turned out to be! Simon Barney insists on working and he's first-rate with chickens. He has only one fault, he likes to over-feed them, and sometimes their blood gets too rich and they die. Poor Mr. Pancho, who is a gentle old lamb, sits in the sun and chews on a twig of slippery elm. He does a lot of speculating about other old men he met and he shakes his head and wonders what became of them."

"I'm afraid it's too much to hope that we found them. Does he mention their names?"

"No. His mind isn't very clear. He sometimes comes out with their nick-names. Old Twitch and Phil the Fag and Poor Charlie. My third man, the Spaniard, pronounces his name differently every time I see him—or so it seems—and he spends his time watching the sky. I think he's waiting for something or someone." She paused before adding as an afterthought, "I had a letter last week from Buxton, from my old friend Charlotte Hawley. She speaks well of old Mr. Bryce, although he mystifies her by disappearing whenever he sees her coming. I suppose the fear hasn't left him yet."

"Ah, if we only had all the money we need and a hundred workers to go along with it!" said Jonathan Bade. "I fear that when I die the movement will die also. And we haven't done more than make a start!"

Later she turned and spoke to Sir Julian, who sat on her other side.

"I expect," she said, "that a few people in England would be glad if both of us became fatally ill from eating these shrimps and things today."

He nodded and his eyes twinkled. "It's getting down pretty fine, isn't it? Just seven of us left. I suppose it's natural enough for some of the survivors, and those who depend on them, to take the race seriously. I hope to live a few years longer in order to lay aside a bit more for my two boys. Julian, at least, is going to need it."

"It has never seemed very real or important to me," she confided. "And I feel the same about the money I've been able to accumulate over the years. I suppose I've a mind of limited dimensions. At any rate my little shop has always seemed more important than all the rest because I can see it and work in it. It's real and substantial. I built it myself and it will always be there."

"The Tontine money comes in very handy for me," declared Sir Julian. "I'm on half pay, you know. But I assure you that I'm content with things as they stand now. I want to go on living for a while longer but all of the rest can live at least as long as far as I'm concerned."

"Do you get letters?" asked Helen.

"All the time. I suppose they come from friends and dependents of the others. They are generally quite bitter. They tell me openly that I should do the decent thing and hop off the twig. Do you get them?"

She nodded. "They come every so often. And they bother me. They make human nature out to be so selfish and cruel."

Jonathan Bade joined in the conversation from her other side. "You are all very much in the public eye and I have something to say to you both. You happen to be my most reliable supporters and it would be a downright calamity if anything happened to either of you.

"The older I get," he went on, "and I'm a bit older than either of you, the more convinced I am that life is a conflict between good and evil. There are other kinds of conflict also but underneath everything the great struggle goes on and the great forces clash. It may be that I am getting soft, now that I stand on the threshold of eternity and am trying to look far beyond the stars. Certainly the belief is strong in me that in the end good wins. Not necessarily of its own strength. I believe it is God's plan for the good to prevail.

"If there's any truth in that, then surely both of you will survive for a very long time," he concluded. "I pray for each of you every night. It's a selfish prayer, perhaps. I happen to need you so much."

Through all of the lively conversation carried on throughout the rest of the meal, Helen Groody remained silent. The happiness on the faces of the bride and groom was sufficient, however, to take the bitterness out of her memories. "Time has made up for all I suffered when Allie died," she thought. "How wonderful they look, my two young people! They have all of life ahead of them and they will live it together. Perhaps it is better this way."

3

When the rest of the company had disappeared and only Helen was left with the young couple, the point came up as to how the rest of the day was to be spent. Allie had an idea at once. "Let's see our offices," he said.

The idea appealed to the visitor. She did not mention that it was her money which had made it possible to buy the old building and it is doubtful if the thought entered her head. "It was a pretty gloomy-looking place when I saw it last," she said.

"That was when we went to look it over," supplied Allie. "We had to make sure it was worth the price they were asking before we invested your money in it, Aunt Helen. It wasn't worth the price, having stood empty so long, and we had to beat the owner down considerably. The place is different now. It's all painted fresh and the bricks have been scraped and new panes put in the windows. And there's a new sign over the door. It's quite fine, I think. Red on a white background. That was the original color combination."

Helen Groody was worried in spite of his enthusiasm. She said to herself: "But how is it worded? That is so important, so very important. Has he been generous about it and made the firm name Grace and Carboy? If he hasn't—"

When they came in sight of the building the old lady's eyes went first to the sign. It was as fine as Allie had said. The paint had been spread on lavishly and there was a hint of confidence in all the letters, and vigor too, and honesty and a proper regard for tradition; or so she thought. It read:

## GRACE AND CARBOY
### EASTERN MERCHANTS

"Oh, Allie!" cried the old lady. "I hoped you would! But it's generous of you, and very, very farseeing. If you had made it Carboy and Grace, as you could have done in view of the size of your respective interests, not to mention the value of the name Carboy, it would never have seemed quite right to your partner. I'm sure he's grateful for what you've done."

"We never discussed the point. I ordered the sign myself and I didn't say a word to him. But I noticed there were tears in his eyes when he saw it first. Aunt Helen, it had to be this way. After all, we're reviving the old business, aren't we? It was Grace and Carboy then, and Grace and Carboy it must be today."

"What will your father think about it?"

"Well, I haven't been in his confidence lately. In fact I haven't heard from him since I issued my ultimatum. But I'm pretty sure of one thing, he'll approve of the firm name. He's understanding about such things."

"And what of your aunt Isabelle?"

He grinned at that. "She'll be as mad as hops and turkeys."

At this point the old lady noticed something else and let out an exclamation of delighted surprise. She raised her parasol and pointed in the direction of a tall bronze object, obviously old and very much in need of attention, which stood at the entrance.

"It's Old Taku!" she cried. "Allie, Allie, where did you find it?"

He nodded his head with equal delight. "It was Julian found it. We made up our minds it should be used and he and Nell searched everywhere."

"It was you thought of it, my retiring, unassuming, take-no-credit-for-anything husband," said the young wife, who had been hanging proudly and possessively on his arm ever since they issued forth.

"Well, yes, I suppose it was. I don't think Julian would have brought the point up, because it was Samuel Carboy who got rid of it. Where do you suppose the old fellow was?"

"Probably in some junk yard," suggested Helen, eying the bronze figure, which looked much less like a god than it had ever done before.

"Let me tell it!" cried Nell. "I hadn't much to do and so I was helping Julian in his search. Someone told him about seeing it in a back yard in Bermondsey, but just where they didn't know. We searched all over Bermondsey, peeking into yards and snooping down alleyways and having housewives bark at us, 'Naw, then, what're ye up to, ye yong divils?' It was Julian saw it first. Would you believe that it was being used to attach clotheslines to and that there were eight red flannel shirts and two night-gowns and an assortment of baby's things hanging out that very day? There was such an odd expression on Taku's face. It was as though he wanted to say: 'Honestly, you know, I'm a god. I've fallen on evil days, it's true, and I can't expect to have incense burning in my stomach and dishes of rice laid at my feet. But surely there's a limit! These dreadful damp clothes! Diapers, *really!*' So we bought him for ten shillings and paid twelve to have him moved back where he belongs. Taku's expression changed at once. I'm sure he was saying, 'Well, here I am where the boys can pelt me with stones and the pigeons can get at me. But now I'll be a London landmark again and so I ought to be content.' "

"Sir Julian's face was a study when he saw it," declared Allie. "He stood and talked to Taku for several minutes. I didn't hear what he was saying."

Helen Groody was not yet fully satisfied. There was an alertness in her eyes when they moved in to inspect the offices and she kept looking about her with an air which suggested uneasiness. It came to a head when she saw that the large central office was still intact.

"Come in," said Allie, leading the way, his wife still clinging to his arm.

Her fears left the old lady as soon as she stepped through the door. The space was evenly divided and there were two desks instead of one. She was able now to laugh.

"I'm *so* relieved," she said. "I was afraid that one of you would have it alone. That wouldn't have done, you know. It would be an excess of gen-erosity if you had given it up, Allie. That caused trouble before and in the end it would have come to the same thing. *This* is the proper way. Now the firm of Grace and Carboy is on a proper basis at last. I'm sure it is going to grow and grow and grow. I'm certain that both of you fine young men are going to be quite wealthy because of it."

Nell, still in possession of her husband's arm, shook her head at that. "We don't care about money, Aunt Helen. But we do want to succeed. And we're going to. Orders are beginning to roll in already. Aren't they, Alfred dear?"

"Yes, Mrs. Alfred Carboy, but the orders aren't really flooding in, knock-ing their heads together and tramping on toes and all that sort of thing. Still, they've started. Perhaps, as they *have* started, we should have a sort of celebration. Julian will be back and his grandfather is remaining in town. We could all have dinner together and then come here and crack a bottle of wine over the rear seam of Old Taku, and declare the firm of Grace and Carboy duly launched."

"Tomorrow night," said Nell firmly. "Tonight Mr. and Mrs. Alfred Car-boy dine all by themselves."

## CHAPTER TEN

### 1

Helen Groody made a call the next morning. Samuel Carboy the Younger had moved into the offices which his grandfather had used on the upper floor of the once light and glossy quarters of the bank. She was ushered in to see him at once.

She found him at his desk, a long flat table reputed to have come out of one of the Gilbertine monasteries. Whether this was true or not, the scars on its surface could not have been made by the humble bowls of the Gilbertine monks and so obviously they were the work of time. Samuel Carboy was a stout believer in system and dispatch; the great table was bare save for a magnificent inkstand made of elks' horns and a solitary pile of letters neatly arranged in an illuminated leather cover.

They had not met since the day he had visited her to say that the romance developing between his son and her great-niece must be stopped. There was a consciousness of this in his manner as he rose to greet her.

"Sammy, my dear boy!" she exclaimed, holding out her hands with a warmth which showed there was no feeling on her side. She was studying his face with anxious eyes, noting that he looked thin and worried. "You're working too hard. You haven't the iron constitution of your grandfather, you know. I'm sure you're under too great a strain."

"I'm a little tired at the moment, Aunt Helen." He held her hands in his and studied her face in turn. "You are not well yourself. Although I haven't seen you or heard from you in several years, I've kept a check on you. I've known about your rheumatism and what the doctors say."

"How good of you, Sammy! There is no cure for it nor any way of getting relief."

He drew out a chair beside his own and they sat down. A large plate-glass window faced them, against which large flakes of snow were falling in their leisurely and erratic descent.

"I'm afraid," she went on, "that I'm to suffer these horrid pains as long as I live; and having said that, I'm not going to add another word about it." She hesitated, looking at him doubtfully from under the rim of her poke bonnet. "I bring news that you won't like."

He was silent for a moment, then from the letter portfolio he drew out one that bore a foreign stamp. This he spread on the table before him.

"I think I know what your news is," he said. "It's about my son and your niece. Are they married?"

"Yes, Sammy. They were married very quietly yesterday morning."

"I expected it." He picked up the letter. "This is from Jacques Plessis and it announces the marriage of his daughter to the Frenchman she was in love with. It's written in a pleased vein as though he had favored it all along. When I read it, I said to myself, 'I'll be hearing news of Allie very soon.'"

He paused. "Perhaps it's all for the best, Aunt Helen. They seem to have known their minds from the start. Well, it's done now and I begin to see that I've behaved badly about them. Will you forgive me?"

"There's nothing to forgive, Sammy; not as far as I can see. It was easy to understand why you were against letting them marry. You're an intensely ambitious man. You want the world in a bandbox, don't you? And, of course, you wanted your son to make a dazzling marriage."

He smiled in a somewhat shamefaced way. "I expect that was how I felt. Well, if you'll forget the past, we can work together for the well-being of these two young people of ours. Do you suppose they'll have a welcome for the hardhearted father if he calls on them, carrying an olive branch and belated gifts and perhaps a cabful of supplies from the best greengrocer in town?"

She smiled at him eagerly. "You'll make them very happy if you do." Then her manner changed. The hardest part of her errand was accomplished but she still had something to say which was not going to be easy. "Sammy, you've been generous enough to defer to my opinion in some matters, so you must think me worth listening to, at any rate. What do you think of business conditions?"

He frowned uneasily and repeated the stock phrase: "Hard times are coming, without a doubt. In fact they're here already in a degree."

"Yes, hard times have come. You can feel it in the air. You can see it in the shops. People aren't buying as they did before. They haven't the money to spend. I hear that men are out of work already."

He nodded in agreement. "I've been watching things. We can catch the first indications of a business recession." His smile was rueful. "I've been catching it from my aunt Isabelle. She's been in twice, railing at me and demanding that I do this and that. After a visit from her yesterday, I felt like a dunce in a corner. She was demanding that I close all of our foreign branches and bring our money back."

"Aren't you prepared to do that?"

Samuel brought his eyes back from the snow-splattered window and faced his visitor. "Dear Aunt Helen," he said, "what would you think of an army which ran away from the field of battle at the first whiff of gunpowder?"

This was difficult to answer but she was not entirely unprepared for it. "A good general fights battles at times and places of his own choosing."

"You think well of my grandfather, I'm sure. What would Samuel Carboy do under these circumstances?"

"I'm hardly in a position to judge of that."

"Do you think he would close up shop and take his losses because of conditions which are bound to be temporary? I don't believe he would. Samuel Carboy was a fighter. He raised himself to the top of the heap when everything was against him." His voice was full of confidence now.

"My grandfather began his daring expansion in the face of the worst depression England ever knew. It was during the years following the defeat of Napoleon and the debts of twenty years of war were piled up like a cross on the back of trade. In telling me about it, he has always said that any man—any fool, he sometimes put it—can make money when things are booming but that the real gains are made when times are at their worst."

As they talked, they were continually interrupted. A very important young man, with a high starched collar and cuffs which protruded two inches from his sleeves, kept breaking in from a rear office, without as much as a knock or a by-your-leave, and laying letters and cables and reports on the desk before the head of the company. Sometimes he would whisper in Samuel's ear and point out something in the communications. Each time he came in, he bowed so low to Helen that the starch in his shirt crackled. There was also a dumbwaiter which kept rattling from floor to floor and sometimes came to a stop behind the president. Whenever this happened the important young man would rush in, seize the contents of the basket and carry the papers out with him, making a hissing noise with his teeth as though protesting such disturbances.

Helen had heard Samuel Carboy talk as his grandson was doing. Once he had told her about the day when he walked into the Stock Exchange and bought while the market was in a panic because it was feared that Napoleon had won the Battle of Waterloo. He had never been afraid. But a supreme degree of good judgment had been back of his courageous moves; and now, she knew, he was lost to the business, a hollow shell, incapable of any sustained coherence of thought.

"Think about it, Sammy," she urged. "I'm insisting on retrenchment in the companies where I have large holdings. Things look bad to me. The sky is very black."

Some of his confidence had deserted him. "I respect your opinion, Aunt Helen. You're as shrewd in your way as my grandfather. I've already put up the danger signals. Our companies are being directed to move cautiously. You may rest assured that I'm doing as that—that good general you mentioned would do at a time like this. I'm drawing back to shorter and stronger positions all along the line."

"I'm sure you are doing everything that needs doing, my boy. Forgive an old lady who happens to have your best interests very much at heart."

The important young man, bowing even lower, came in and said to Samuel, "Sir, *they* are here."

Samuel got to his feet. "The accent wasn't on the *sir*, which means that he isn't trying to help me get rid of a persistent caller but that some people have come about a most important shipping deal and that I really must see them at once."

"Don't buy any more ships, Sammy!" she exclaimed. "I think I've heard something about this plan. It's no time to be expanding."

He smiled down at her. "I'll go into the meeting with them, clad in the armor of caution. And if you should see Allie today, warn the young rascal that he's going to have a caller tonight. I'm going with my arms full of peace offerings. I hope that pretty wife of his will find it in her heart to forgive me. And I want you to know, Aunt Helen, that I never did cut him out of my will. I threatened to do it—but I never even talked to my lawyers about it."

2

Samuel Carboy the Younger had not been entirely frank. It was not to discuss the shipping deal that he had interrupted his conversation with Helen Groody. A quite different group awaited him in the long and gloomy board room, with its enormous chimney and its collection of solemn portraits, that of the organizer of the company at the head of the line and that of the long-defunct Mr. Plumbottom at the end.

There were six in the group and they shared one thing in common, an air of gloom and unease. Five were presidents of Carboy subsidiaries, men of the Carboy stripe and kidney; vigorous, rough, able, not too scrupulous perhaps. The sixth was a handsome man with a fine head of snowy hair, a fine nose, a pair of twinkling brown eyes and a neatly trimmed beard. This was Lion W. Colter, one of the leading attorneys in the City.

"Samuel," said the lawyer, who was acting as spokesman for the group, "something's got to be done. We've got to get to grips with the old man about it. Time is getting short."

"Is it about the stockholdings?"

"Yes, the bone of contention on which we've been gnawing so long. The bargain your grandfather made with my clients was too exacting, Samuel. He must release us on that one clause."

Samuel the Younger was studying the long row of austere portraits of the men who had played leading roles in the Carboy saga, as though seeking silent support or guidance. Finally he said: "When my grandfather allowed all of you to buy substantial blocks of stock in the parent company, it was quite in order for him to protect himself as he did. He did it by stipulating that you must never sell any shares, except to him or his heirs. Wasn't that entirely reasonable? He didn't want to find himself someday in the position of having outsiders voting the shares against him."

The sparkle in Lion Colter's eyes became somewhat less noticeable. "Conditions have changed, Samuel," he said sharply. "Business, as you must concede, is bad. We are still paying dividends here in England, although our losses abroad are beginning to worry all of us. Inasmuch as we are still showing a robust front here, there is a chance to—to lighten the cargo, as you might say. We are none of us as wealthy as you are, Samuel. We feel, all of us, that it may become necessary for us to have anchors to windward; to sell some part of our stockholdings, in other words. People will snap it up like hungry pikes and so the unloading can be accomplished without seriously affecting our position on the market. *If* we act at once. But the clause stands in the way. We are not allowed to sell a single share."

"I'm in the same position that you are," stated Samuel. "I got my stock on the same terms that you did." This was not an entirely honest statement, for old Samuel had been easier with him than he had been with his subordinates. "I paid the same low price for it and the payment terms were easy. But I had to agree not to sell any of it except to him. My aunt, the Duchess of Outland, is bound also by this provision. Gentlemen, as I am in the same boat with you, I am able to see that the clause is a—a trying one. But my grandfather has been adamant on the point. As you know, he has been emphatically against any change in the arrangements. He has felt that any desire to sell partakes almost of—well, of treason. What makes you think he might give a different answer now?"

"Samuel," said the lawyer, "we think he should take a different attitude because conditions are different. There's no sense using blinders. Hard times have come. Even Carboy and Co. may find it impossible to go on paying dividends. You see, most of my clients have all their eggs in the Carboy basket. I understand your grandfather criticized one of us because he has a butler wearing knee breeches and silk stockings——"

"That was me," interposed one of the hard-visaged group. "It was my wife's idea. I wouldn't have the fellow around the place, if I had my way."

"The point is this," went on the lawyer. "Mr. Bennett here assures me that if he's not allowed to get some of the profits on his stock, while there is still time, he may not have a butler, with or without silk stockings. He may not have a house in which to keep a butler, or himself for that matter. Benny isn't the only one in this position. All of my clients face the same danger."

"You seem to be taking it for granted that the value of Carboy stocks will go down. I disagree with you. I think we'll weather this storm without any difficulty."

"That, Samuel, is a matter of opinion. But you must allow that things are looking black." The lawyer made a circular motion with his arms to take in the whole group. "We are all in this together. It's a family matter, in a sense. The well-being of the parent company is the first consideration with all my clients. But they feel—and surely they can't be blamed for it—that they are entitled to this much protection. We all know that the matter could be taken to court with the certainty that the decision would be in our favor."

"Why are you so sure?"

"Similar cases have been tried," declared Colter with a confident air, "and the decision has been that, after offering the stock to the company and being refused, it can be sold for whatever it brings."

"Very well!" said Samuel sharply. "You go to court. You get your decision. What does my grandfather do then? If you don't know, I will tell you. He will be quick, ruthless, merciless. He will throw you all out of the organization. You won't be able to go to court about *that*. It comes down, then, to a choice. You can sell your stock and lose your positions or you can keep both."

"Samuel," said the lawyer, "we're well aware of what would happen. We know the old man as well as you do. And so we've come to you with this suggestion. We would like to try him once more, and we hope to have you with us, lending us your support."

"It will be wasting time if you expect him to buy the stock back at the market price. The price now is three or four times as much as you paid for it. That's why he's got his back up. He can't see why he should pay you three or four hundred per cent profit."

"We'll be reasonable about the price. Up to a point. Well, if he still says no, as loudly and emphatically as he's always done, then we wait. We wait until you become president. It won't be a long wait. The old man is very ill."

"And suppose I also say no?"

"We don't believe you will. You are going to need us. We keep our ears to the ground, you know, and rumors reach us of little dissensions in the family. What you hold won't be enough to assure you of control after the old man dies. The Duchess of Outland will have as many shares as you do. But with the shares we hold, you would have control. Wouldn't you like to have us on your side?"

"But you can't vote your stock if you sell it now."

"A few weeks won't matter. We don't believe Mr. Carboy has more than a short time to live. You hold a meeting to elect his successor immediately after his death. We stand behind you and make your choice certain. Then each of us sells as much of his stock as he desires."

There was a long moment of silence. Then Samuel the Younger asked, "When do you want to see him?"

"At once. There's no time to be lost. I propose that we select a committee of four, say, and take the first train down tomorrow morning."

Samuel thought it over carefully for several minutes. When he had made his own deal with his grandfather, he had struggled to be free of the restriction on selling. Old Samuel had been as firm with him as with the others. He felt certain that whatever the old man left him in the will would carry the same clause. There was little or no hope that his grandfather would change his mind and for that reason he was certain a final appeal to him would be futile. There was, however, the future to be considered. If Isabelle came out into the open and fought him for control, he would need the support of these smaller stockholders.

Samuel rang a bell and sat back in his chair. The important young man, his cuffs seeming more starchy than ever now that he was appearing before the top men of the company, entered in response.

"Wilbert," said Samuel, "what appointments have I for tomorrow and the day after?"

The secretary began to recite the list from memory. At each name, the acting head of the company waved his forefinger back and forth as a signal to arrange a postponement. At one name, he held the forefinger upright. "Who's that?" he asked.

"Davis. Ardmore Davis. He's coming in about the telephone. You've had several long letters from him."

"Give him another date as soon as possible," directed Samuel. "Put him at the head of the list. Monday, if possible. I'm eager to talk to him." He let his gaze wander over the rather glum faces in front of him. "The telephone is going to be more important, gentlemen, than the telegraph. It seems just about ready for commercial use. Yes, Wilbert, get this man in to see me Monday. Some of us are going down tomorrow to consult with my grandfather. You had better stay here but arrange for either Fiddler or Wibling to go with us. To take notes."

"May I ask, Samuel," said the lawyer, after the secretary had withdrawn, "what stand you are going to take?"

"Gentlemen," said the acting head of the great amalgamation, "I am going to support you. And in return you are going to support me."

## CHAPTER ELEVEN

### 1

Snow had been falling lightly for three days in London, melting quickly, and then falling again. By way of contrast, the sun had been a steady visitor in the country of the Vale, and when the deputation stepped off the train the air was most pleasantly warm. The members did not notice that the grass was showing solid patches of green and that the vanguard of spring flowers had debouched in scattered ranks because the business which brought them down had driven all other thoughts from their minds. The only remark made came from one of them who happened to be a golfer. "I must oil my clubs," he said.

When they reached Beaulaw Hall there was a carriage with armorial bearings standing on the drive. Samuel the Younger frowned in exasperation.

"It seems," he said, "that the Duchess of Outland is visiting her father. I think, gentlemen, we must postpone this discussion until she leaves."

Isabelle had arrived half an hour before and the footman who opened the door, although short and round and rather comic-looking generally, had greeted her with an expression of settled gloom. "Ah, Your Grace," he said, "he's took to his bed."

A tall man in a salt-and-pepper suit was sitting at a small table outside her father's bedroom and making a hearty lunch of lamb chops while keeping an eye on the door. He stood up and bowed to her, table napkin in hand.

"You are the Duchess of Outland, I presume. My sincere respects, Your Grace. I am Dr. Saulter. From Oxford. I was called in because I specialize in mental cases. You must be prepared for changes, Your Grace."

Isabelle had received no intimation of a turn for the worse in her father's condition and she felt resentful that a medical attendant had been summoned who was unknown to her.

"What is wrong with Mr. Carboy?" she asked stiffly.

"Chiefly, that he's ninety-eight years old, Your Grace. I very much fear he won't know you. His mind has become clouded and much of the time he's close to a condition of delirium. I regret to tell you that he doesn't know who he is. He denies that he has anyone near and dear to him."

Remembering how wildly her father had talked in the cold and the isolation of the hideaway he had created for the stolen Holbein, Isabelle became alarmed. Striving to maintain a casual tone, she asked, "Has he been talking much?"

"He never stops, Your Grace. The nurses tell me he goes from one thing to another but that he talks most of old friends."

Isabelle felt now that her worst fears were going to be realized. "Why didn't I come back with him?" she asked herself bitterly. "I should never have let him get into the hands of strangers!"

"Is his mind clear when he talks?" she asked. "I mean, can you always tell what he means?"

A new voice joined in the conversation. "Very seldom, my lady." It was Coventry, the secretary, who had come up the winding stairway. She was surprised to see that he looked most unhappy. "I'm very much disturbed. About him; your father, I mean. I can't get used to it. Why, Your Grace, I haven't been discharged once in two weeks!"

When Isabelle entered her father's bedroom, she found him propped up with pillows in a huge tester bed. His face was ashen in color and his gray hair was rumpled. There was a glass on the serving table beside the bed but it contained medicine instead of the customary whisky. This was proof he was very ill indeed.

The sick man said, staring belligerently at the doctor, "King Billy had an oncommon high head."

Isabelle was still confident she could bring him back to a normal condition. "Now, Papa," she said, trying to speak cheerfully, "they tell me you've been giving them all a scare. This won't do, you know. You must keep a tighter hold on yourself. This is Isabelle, Papa."

Samuel Carboy stared at her without any hint of recognition. His eyes, in fact, seemed to ask who this presumptuous female was who addressed him so familiarly.

"They're always at it," he muttered in a husky voice. "Always trying to get at me." He looked about him and shook his head with its long, uncombed hair. Then he added in a whisper, "They want my money! The letters they send, and the nice little notes. All perfumed. They come to the office in 'ansom cabs. Don't I remember them? Please, I need this much or that much. Dear Mister, Dear Grandfather, Dear Papa! One thing or another all the time." The sick man repeated the name Isabelle three times as though trying to reach some recollection of it. Then he shook his head again, this time with a touch of anger. "Don't you Isabelle me. I don't know you, ma'am. Go away." He glared about him and his eyes focused on the form of the doctor. "Who are you? Standing there, staring at me. I don't like you. If Sam Carboy was here, he'd boot you down the stairs." His roving eye came back to Isabelle. "Who is this old woman?"

Isabelle, shaken to the core of her being, caught the doctor's eyes. He nodded gravely. It was clear he wanted to say, "What did I tell you?"

The sick man never stopped talking. He spoke in an unnatural tone and the little coherence he had shown at first had deserted him. It was clear that his sick mind was full of his long years as the head of Carboy and Co. It was hard to follow him but the listeners caught references to board meetings and stocks and bonds. He mentioned names, often with open hostility. There was also involved talk about such matters as power and engines and wheels and sprockets. At intervals he would address one or the other of them, saying in the same unfriendly tone, "King Billy had an oncommon high head."

Once he straightened up in bed and indulged in a hoarse laugh. "Sam Carboy will catch you!" he exclaimed. Then a puzzled tone came into his voice. "Who am I? Where am I? Where's Sam Carboy? He must have died by this time." He laughed and cried and whispered of this and that, jumbling his sentences and sometimes even his words, his head tossing continuously on the pillows. Finally he repeated several times in a parrotlike manner, "Sir Samuel Carboy, Sir Samuel Carboy, Sir Samuel Carboy!"

And then what Isabelle had dreaded happened. He settled down into his pillows and his expression lost all of its hostility. A nurse had entered the room and had stationed herself beside the bed.

"Poor Georgie!" he said in a low voice. "He died, poor Georgie did. A long time ago. I said——"

The duchess went hurriedly to the other side of the bed and laid a hand on her father's forehead. "Come, Papa," she said. "You mustn't worry your head about anything. Stop all this talking and see if you can't get to sleep."

"It's best not to disturb him but just let him wander on," declared the nurse, who seemed to resent what Isabelle had done as an infringement of her authority. "He'll soon settle down, ma'am, if you'll just leave him be."

Isabelle had been certain from the first that this woman was not to be trusted. She had an unpleasantly lumpy figure and her face was moist and complacent. "I wonder if he's said anything that could be picked up," Isabelle asked herself. "If he has, this creature will be a hard one to deal with."

She brushed away the restraining hand of the nurse. "I think I understand my own father best," she declared, frowning as she glanced about her. "I would like to be alone with him for a while."

He seemed to settle down when the room had emptied and he became less disposed to talk, rousing himself only once to mutter, "I shouldn't have said it, I shouldn't have said it."

"Whatever it was you said, Papa, was the right thing to say. Get that into your head and—and don't talk about it again. You must get some rest now."

He became antagonistic again at this. "Who are you?" he demanded angrily. "Go away. Go away, I tell you!"

When she left the bedroom some moments later, she found that the doctor had not yet completed his lunch. She paused beside the table. "Get rid of that woman!" she said. "Get her out of the house at once. I've decided to stay beside my poor father every possible minute. I'm going to have a couch moved into the room." She was watching his face as she spoke. "How long has he to live?"

The doctor hesitated. "He hasn't taken any food for two days. It won't be long, Your Grace."

"A week?"

"No, not nearly that long. Two days, Your Grace. That, at least, is my opinion."

The butler appeared at the head of the stairway. "Mr. Samuel Carboy, Your Grace," he announced. "And four other gentlemen."

Isabelle felt a moment of panic. She had been certain it would be hard to keep her father's dangerous babbling from being noticed with so many people in the house. With her nephew, and the men who had accompanied him, added to the rest, it might well be impossible. Her face lost some of its color.

"Ask Mr. Carboy to leave his friends downstairs for the time being," she directed. "Show them into the library and provide whatever they may need in the way of refreshment. And ask Mr. Carboy to come up alone."

Samuel the Younger came upstairs immediately with a worried look on his face. "What is it?" he asked. "Has he taken a bad turn?"

Isabelle nodded with a frown. "Dr. Saulter fears the worst," she said. "He will tell you himself but first I would like a word with you alone."

The doctor had finished his lunch. He dropped his napkin on the table and betook himself elsewhere.

"Samuel, who are these men with you?"

"You know them all." He proceeded to name them. "It's the old story. The stock arrangements. They've come down to make a final plea."

"They've come too late," she declared.

She walked to the open door of the bedroom and looked in cautiously. "His mind is unsettled. He doesn't know anyone. The doctor gives him two days. No more. I think, Samuel, you had better send the others away. They've had their trip for nothing, I'm afraid."

The sick man had started again to toss and turn. His voice was raised querulously. "Yes. It's the truth, it's the truth, I tell you. I know something about Sam Carboy. But what—what is it?" He muttered about other things, generally in a tone which expressed puzzlement and wrath. Then he came back again to the point from which he had started. "Did he tell me? No, I told him. Perhaps it isn't Sam Carboy I talk to. Perhaps I'm Sam Carboy myself. Which is it?"

Becoming conscious of the faces at the door, he turned over in his bed to stare at them. "Who are you? What are you doing there?"

"This is Samuel, Grandfather," said his grandson. "I've come to see you."

The old man continued to give him the benefit of a hostile scrutiny. "King Billy——" he began. Then, instead of proceeding as he had before, he repeated the name over and over, "King Billy, King Billy, King Billy!" After the briefest interval of silence, he cried out with a sudden surge of anger, "Go away! Don't stand there staring at me! Get out of my sight!"

The grandson looked at Isabelle. "I'll talk to the doctor and see what he thinks should be done."

"I can tell you what should be done," she exclaimed. "First of all, send those men back to London. It won't do them any good to stay. You've seen for yourself. And they'll be a great nuisance if they do stay. They can go back on the late afternoon train."

"I'll speak to them. But I'll have a word with the doctor first."

Isabelle's nerves became taut. "Send them away! Never mind about the doctor. I don't know who he is. I don't even know who asked him to come here. Did you?"

Samuel shook his head in dissent. "Certainly not. I haven't been consulted at any time."

"Perhaps old Dr. Carraway felt he needed help. I'll find out. And now, Samuel, get those men out from under our feet."

She went back into the bedroom and closed the door after her. Standing beside the bed, she asked herself: "What am I going to do? He'll say something to start them talking, and I'll be left to bear the brunt of it. Why does he keep harping on it this way?"

She decided that she must never under any circumstance leave her father's bedside. Summoning a maidservant, she arranged to have her meals in the room and to sleep there on the couch. She sent off a note to her husband, asking him to come at once. "I'll have to get some sleep," she thought. "Chip will be the safest one to stand guard while I do."

Half an hour later there came a light tap on the door. Then it was opened and Samuel the Younger put his head into the room.

"Dr. Saulter says it's just possible he might have a lucid moment before the end," he said in a tone a little above a whisper. "When they heard that, they decided to stay. It's very important for them to see him."

Isabelle lost her temper. "I told you to get them out of here!" she raged. "Have they no sense of decency? Why do they want to stand around and watch him die? Samuel, if you don't send them off on that train, I'll go down and attend to it myself."

But when a maid brought her a tea tray in the middle of the afternoon, she delivered a message from the cook. "Mrs. Tarble says, Y'Grace, she thinks it better be oysters and roast beef for dinner. She says men like that best."

Isabelle's face turned a furious red. "Are those men still here?" she asked.

The maid nodded. "Indeed an' yes, Y'Grace. They're all down in the

library and it keeps the butler a-running, it does, to supply them with
drinks."

2

The lucid moment did not come and at the end of the second day the
disappointed heads of the Carboy companies departed together, convinced
that they must now depend on the promise of Samuel the Younger, who
remained at the Hall. The sick man had rarely stopped his rambling talk
and had come back time and again to King Billy and the death of George
Grace. No one seemed to pay any attention to it. Fearing, nevertheless, that
he might at any moment indulge in more dangerously clear confidences,
Isabelle hovered over him continuously, breaking in on his soliloquies and
preventing him from going too far by applying sponges to his hot forehead
and popping medicine spoons into his mouth, or busily rearranging the
bed clothing. She kept the new nurse in the background, finding duties
for her which kept her in the kitchen or the pantry and as much as possible
out of the sickroom. Although her very much disturbed husband had answered her summons and was always on hand, she had not slept a single
moment. Her eyes, for perhaps the first time in her life, had deep circles
under them. Her cheeks looked pale and wrinkles began to show themselves.

The old man clung to life in spite of what all the doctors said. There were
plenty of them around the place now, including a group of specialists from
London. These stony-faced experts in life and death knew very well that he
would pass away in a matter of days or hours but they held solemn consulta-
tions and talked at great length about him and, in fact, strove to earn the
large fees each of them intended to collect.

Another class of specialists began to appear, the gentlemen of the press
from all the large cities of England where the name of Samuel Carboy had
been a potent one for more than half a century. They were all over the
countryside, getting bits of information about the life and habits of the
great man who would soon be no more. One of them, a sharp individual
who could have been either a young old man or an old young man, was
known to other metropolitan penny-a-liners as Plowman Stamp, because he
got himself well plowed at regular intervals. This one even went to the
extent of questioning the Duchess of Outland.

He had been admitted through the judicious expenditure of a few half
crowns and he encountered Her Grace in the Great Hall. At first he did not
recognize her because she looked like an old woman. The lightness of step
and grace of carriage which had always been characteristic of this beautiful
and spectacular climber were no longer in evidence. There was no hint of
the onetime sparkle in her eye.

"Your Grace," said Plowman Stamp, "I would esteem it a great honor if
you would answer one question."

Isabelle recognized him at once for what he was. She had always been sensible enough to treat the press well and by so doing had made herself a favorite with them. She stopped by force of habit.

"I think I know you," she said, peering at him with eyes heavy from loss of sleep. "You are—of course! Your name is Stamp."

She had made a friend for life. The newspaperman beamed all over his sharp and inquisitive face. To be recognized and addressed familiarly by the notable Isabelle Carboy! This was indeed a taste of fame.

But Isabelle was having more to say. "I remember something else about you, young man. You wrote a piece about my marriage to—to my present husband. It was an impertinent piece."

"No, no, Your Grace!" cried Stamp. "I've always liked you. I may have taken a liberty or two in that bit but the fact that I *did* like you stood out in every sentence!"

"Well," she admitted, "I think there was a certain friendliness about it as well!"

"Your Grace," he said, plunging hastily into his present needs, "let me tell you first that I'm gathering information for an article about your father. I'm picking up wonderful stuff and I think—indeed, I'm ready to swear—that out of what I have there will come a real flesh-and-blood portrait. I'm thinking of heading it 'Old Ironsides of Industry.'"

"Where are you getting all your information?" she asked, interested in spite of her fatigue; and quite aware that it might be profitable to make friends among these avid creatures who buzzed about like flies on the edge of all great events.

"I got much of it from the people hereabouts. The rector, the curate, the sexton, the owners of the pubs, the servants here at the Hall."

"Most of it will be prejudiced," commented Isabelle sharply. "I hope you're not going to put too much reliance in the gossip of the countryside. They don't like my father."

"In a sense they don't," responded the newsman. "And in a sense they do. Not one of the lower orders—the old dadas in the pubs and the sheepsheads who doze in the sun—have ever had a shilling out of him——"

"My father has never believed in the unearned shilling," declared Isabelle. "He has always paid well for proper services but he doesn't hand out money for a pull at a greasy forelock."

"I had a long talk with the rector, Your Grace. He admires Mr. Carboy very much but he told me a story which I'm afraid I must use even though you may object to it. It seems the reverend gentleman——"

"Dr. Parker Godby?"

"Dr. Parker Godby himself. He says he has had one great ambition in life. He wants a new tower on his church. One with chimes. But not only did Samuel Carboy refuse to contribute, he killed the project with one hasty phrase. When approached by the reverend gentleman, he said, 'Be damned to this stinking foolishness!' Someone else heard it and no one after that wanted to be considered in favor of something which had been pronounced a 'stinking foolishness.' Now, was it really foolishness to want the sound of chimes ringing out over the Vale on Sundays, this beautiful green Vale, Your Grace? In some ways I can see that it's rather a farfetched idea. Old Godby needs more money than this little country parish can be expected to produce. But there's another side to it as well."

"I agree with my father. I don't want to be quoted—and you know enough to keep a confidence, I'm sure, Mr. Stamp—but Old Godby has never had any other idea in his head and he talks about nothing else. He has buried his idea by boring the whole countryside with it."

"There were tears in his watery old eyes when he spoke to me."

Isabelle had had enough of this. "What was the question you wanted to ask me?"

"This, Your Grace. Everywhere in the neighborhood I heard your father spoken of as Old Staddle. I had picked up a dozen names for him—The Oliver Cromwell of Trade, Old Ironsides, Cast-iron Sam, The Fifth Horseman of the Apocalypse. But never Old Staddle. Why do they call him that?"

"I don't know," said Isabelle. "I've never heard it used before. It seems rather silly to me."

"No, not silly, Your Grace. I'm going to find out what they mean by it."

He found the answer when he paid a visit to Helen Groody at Little Shallow. The slender woman, muffled up in blankets in her wheel chair, gave him much useful and dramatically colored information about Samuel Carboy (with not a single trace of spleen or ill nature) and finally answered his question about the local nickname of the dying titan.

"I've heard it applied to him for many years," she said. "It originated around here, I suppose. And it always seemed to me a perfect one."

The newspaperman gave his head a puzzled shake. "But why? I've never even heard the word before."

Helen thought this point over before answering. "I believe," she said finally, "that 'staddle' means foundation. Around here we speak of staddle stones or rick staddles, which means the stone foundations on which the hayricks are built. To keep the rats out. Haven't you ever seen a staddle stone? They are wide at the top. Surely you've noticed that there's a row of them along the drive at Beaulaw Hall."

"Oh. Those things. Yes, I saw them and I wondered what they were. They're shaped like toadstools."

She indulged in a brief smile. "Yes. Now that you mention it, they are. But they represent security and strength. They keep the harvest safe. And," with a nod of her head, "that's why the name seems a perfect one for Samuel Carboy."

"I see your point. Yes, it's a good name for that extraordinary man. I think I'll lead off my article with it."

Two days later the article came out in the *Packet* under the heading,

## THE TWILIGHT OF ONE GOD
*Called by his neighbors Old Staddle,*
*Samuel Carboy lies at death's door*

It was quoted extensively and almost immediately men in all parts of the country began to speak of Samuel Carboy by that name.

3

The two days given to the dying man by the doctor from Oxford kept lengthening out and became in time two weeks. Late in the afternoon of the last day of the second week, when the sun was so strong and so high in the heavens that it must have broken through the great clouds of smoke he had created over the Midland towns, Samuel Carboy called in a voice which sounded normal again, "Isabelle!"

The long watch she had kept had almost worn her out by this time. She had lived in a daze, her one purpose in life to prevent him from indulging in wild and random statements in the presence of others. The sound of his voice was always enough to draw her from the deepest sleep, of which she got very little, and to bring her to her feet like a fire horse at the first sound of an alarum.

She had been lying down on the couch. Getting to her feet in an almost sodden condition, she walked slowly to his bedside, wondering why his call had seemed so urgent.

She found him staring up at her with eyes in which she read recognition. He seemed no more than half his normal size. His hands, which were out on the richly quilted counterpane, were thin and blue.

He began speaking in a low tone, with pauses between words as though his strength did not permit of a more sustained effort. "Isabelle, this—this is the end. I have—only—a little time—left. I would like—to see the boy——"

"Do you mean Allie, Papa?"

The head on the pillow moved slightly in assent. "Yes—yes—Allie."

"He's here, Papa. I sent for him as soon as we knew. He's married, you know."

There was a hint of surprise on the drawn face at this information. "Married?"

"Yes, Papa. To the niece of Helen Groody."

Samuel Carboy seemed to smile. "He—he stuck to his guns—didn't he!"

"Yes," affirmed the daughter. "He stuck to his guns. He's as stubborn as his great-grandfather."

There was a long pause. "It's just as well. One of them—was entitled—to have his own way." The tone of voice seemed to have recovered some of the old determination. "Get him back—in the business. . . . There must always be—Carboys to run it. . . . No one else—will do. . . . You must not—sell your shares, Isabelle. . . . You—you stick to your guns too, my girl."

There was such a long pause then that she would have thought he had paid his final farewell except that his eyes denied this. They told her he had other things to say, if he could find the strength.

"Remember—the Holbein," he managed to enunciate finally, in the husk-

iest of whispers. "They will—carp—at me. . . . The newspapers. They'll say
—good riddance. . . . But I won't read it—I won't even know—about it. . . .
That's some consolation."

Isabelle was sure that he had not much time left. She said in an urgent
voice: "They're all here, Papa. Allie and his wife. And Samuel. They want
to see you. They've been waiting for the chance. Shall I bring them up
now?"

The dying man opened his mouth to answer but did not succeed in making a sound. He nodded instead.

Isabelle hurried in her satin bedroom slippers to the head of the stairs.
She saw Allie striding up and down in the entrance hall, his hands in his
pockets and his eyes puckered up in an intense frown.

"Allie!" she called.

He stopped and looked up. "Yes, Aunt Isabelle?"

"He wants to see you. Get your father and your wife. And come up, all
of you, at once."

Samuel the Younger came out of the library at a run, his spectacles on his
forehead and a newspaper in one hand. He paused at the foot of the stairs
to ask, his face almost comic in its dismay and fear, "Is it—is it . . . ?"

"Yes. I think so."

"This newspaper quotes two of the doctors as saying——"

"Never mind the newspapers. Come at once."

They mounted the stairs together, Samuel first, still clutching the paper,
Allie and his wife following, hand in hand. They climbed as rapidly as they
dared, striving to muffle the sound of their heavy leather heels. But they were
too late, because the lucid moment had passed when they reached the bedroom. Samuel Carboy had slipped back into the shadows.

There was a portrait of him on the wall facing the bed. All through these
last days he had seemed to be disturbed by it. His mind, traveling along un-
familiar and uneven paths, had seemed to pause at intervals and come back
to this likeness. Once he had said: "Who's that? It can't be Sam Carboy.
Sam's a plain fellow. None of your damned frills for him. He wouldn't sit
still while some fellow dabbed away with his brushes. That's not Sam's way.
And it don't look like him! All prettied up."

He was staring at the canvas when they reached the room and he did not
turn in their direction.

Isabelle said: "Papa! Here they are. Sam and Allie, and his wife."

It was evident that he had not heard her. He continued to stare at the
picture. "Not Sam Carboy," he muttered. "Some blasted stranger!"

Isabelle motioned to Allie to draw closer to the bed but this failed also.
The figure under the coverlet did not move.

The titan spoke only once again in the half hour of existence which was
left to him. It was not in the natural tone he had found so briefly for his
last messages to Isabelle. His voice seemed to come from far away. "Blasted
idiots! . . . When I'm gone—they—they'll spoil everything."

When the doctors finally convinced her that her father would never speak again, Isabelle looked at them with doubtful eyes. "Are you sure?" she asked. She placed a hand on her forehead as though something pained her there. "I—I don't know what it is. I can't seem to think. My head aches. I've never had an ache like it before." She removed her hand and stared anxiously about her. "Do you mean my father's dead?"

"Yes, Your Grace. Your father is dead."

"Then," she said, "I can sleep. I haven't really slept for two weeks. My head keeps going around. Perhaps I'm going to be ill. If someone will—will send for Porter, my maid, she can help me to my own bed."

## CHAPTER TWELVE

### 1

The will was read immediately after the funeral party returned to Beaulaw Hall and it had to be done without the presence of the Duchess of Outland. Isabelle, suffering her first real illness, had sunk into a mental condition not entirely dissimilar to that of her father in his last moments. The doctors spoke of complete exhaustion and one even shook his head and made guarded references to the possibility of brain fever.

To make up for her absence there were present a most unexpectedly large number of the deceased man's business associates, quite a few titles, some members of Parliament, and surviving relations from every branch of the family; all of the latter eager to learn of the disposition of the great man's incalculable wealth and hoping, undoubtedly, that in a mood of generosity he had thought of them. There were so many on hand, in fact, that it was found impossible to accommodate them in the library. Extra chairs were moved into the drawing room and all of them had occupants when Mr. Percy Boongrace broke the seal of the huge envelope in front of him, cleared his throat and began to read.

Allie Carboy and his wife seated themselves at one side of the room and in the next chair was someone who turned out to be related in a rather nebulous way. He was a man of perhaps fifty and an air of gloom hung about him.

"It will be a bad will," he whispered to them. "I feel it in my bones. It will be a selfish will. I won't be mentioned. My wife won't be mentioned. My children won't be mentioned. Don't tell me anything different. I know that's how it will be."

Allie, who had never seen him before, asked who he was. "I," said the man in an accusing tone, "am a cousin of yours, Cousin Tristram Chepe of Ipswich. I am a stationer with limited capital and so we are a one-joint family. Do you know what the means? I buy a leg of mutton at the auction Saturday night. Sunday, roast mutton; Monday, chops; Tuesday, warmed up; Wednesday, Thursday and Friday, mutton stew; Saturday, tripe and mackerel. If by some miracle, in which I refuse, I positively refuse, to believe, Samuel Carboy has left me a matter of, say, one hundred pounds, I could take on new lines. In time we might aspire to roast beef on Christmas and chickens on family birthdays. But," darkly, "that is asking too much. There was not that much generosity in the man."

"I'm in the same position," confided Allie. "I don't expect to be mentioned."

"Because you married that girl?" asked Cousin Tristram, leaning forward to stare at Nelly.

"Yes," said Allie. "Take a good look at her. Have you ever seen anyone as sweet and lovely as she is? I don't mind telling you that she's worth the price several times over."

It was conceded by everyone, after the will had been read, that it was the most fair and thorough will ever drawn. Samuel Carboy had forgotten nothing and it was clear that a great white light of benevolence had played about him as he decided on its terms. A new hospital at Rixby was provided for, there would be new schools in three other manufacturing cities and a park in still another. More bronze plaques in public institutions would bear his name than that of any other private individual. All of the Carboy presidents had been remembered. There were bequests to his servants and his office staff, including a round and most unexpected thousand pounds for the much-derided Coventry. There were neat little sums for many neighborhood characters and even a substantial donation for the church chimes, "if or when sufficient other financial support is found to make the project a practical possibility." (The rector sniffled loudly at this point.) Even a valuable Etruscan vase was left to Jonathan Bade, and a pound, ironically, to the Sadie Coaster Memorial.

Every relative had been remembered, no matter how far removed; fifty pounds here, one hundred there, two hundred in exceptional cases. When the name of Tristram Chepe, one hundred and fifty pounds, was read out, the stationer from Ipswich broke into tears. "Samuel Carboy," he said aloud, "was the most generous, thoughtful, kindly, Christian man that ever trod this earth."

The stock in Carboy and Co., held by the maker of all this wealth, was divided equally between his daughter and his grandson. Fifty thousand pounds was left to his great-grandson, Alfred Carboy, with the provision that it could be used, in part or in whole, in the purchase of treasury stock, for which arrangements had already been made. The Duke of Outland was left a legacy of such generous proportions (with the provision also that it could be used in taking up stock) that his lower jaw dropped in amazement. "I have not built this widespread business," read the will, "for strangers to acquire and carry on. It is my wish, as I lay down my control of it, that there will always be a Carboy at the helm. For that reason I make the stipulation that none of the stock given to my three chief beneficiaries is to be sold outside the family for a matter of twenty years from the date of probate of this will."

The pictures at Beaulaw Hall went to the National Gallery, the Hall itself to Samuel Carboy II. A shooting and fishing lodge in Scotland, which he had never occupied, went to Isabelle, as well as a commercial property in London being used temporarily as a warehouse.

Samuel Carboy looked happy when the reading had been completed and the more or less contented visitors had filed into the dining room where a remarkably fine cold collation awaited them. He walked over to his son and daughter-in-law.

"Well, Allie," he said. "And you too, Nelly, I'm happy that you came off so well, in spite of—of expectations to the contrary. The will was drawn, Nelly, before you came into the family and so nothing could be done for you. I doubt if Grandfather knew anything about the wedding. You won't have to take up the stock unless you wish to, my boy. You can use your fifty thousand pounds for any other purpose. But I strongly recommend taking the stock."

Allie turned to his wife, who though properly subdued for the occasion could not conceal the fact that she was a bride. "What does Mrs. Carboy think about it?"

"Oh *yes*," said Nelly. "We must use the money to get the stock. It was his wish."

"That settles it," said the young bridegroom to his father. "I'll talk to you about arrangements when we get back to London. I might hold out a little of it for use in my own business."

"Don't you realize that you're to come into Carboy and Co. at once? He expected that also."

"Well, not immediately," said Allie. "We'll have a talk about it, Dad, when we get back to London."

"Let's travel together," suggested the father. He patted Nell on the shoulder. "I'm getting very fond of this young lady."

This expression of liking for the new member of the family was in the nature of an understatement. Samuel had found it necessary to carry on the business while waiting at Beaulaw Hall for his grandfather to die and this had brought him into constant contact with Nell. She was always down as early as he was for breakfast, which was quite early indeed, and always the possessor of a hearty appetite. She fussed over him like a mother hen and got him into the habit of eating more. He found that he liked cracking the top off a second boiled egg and hearing her say, "That's the way, Papa Carboy, that will start you off right." He had kept one of the assistant secretaries with him and even the important young man with the starched cuffs came down twice with papers in folders and envelopes and tin boxes, and maps and charts, together with two copyists and enough paper to supply the Home Office. There was so much rushing about and conferring and sending of telegrams and cables that Nell's curiosity was aroused. Having little else to do, she had made a practice of slipping into the library, where all this hullabaloo centered, and asking questions of her father-in-law.

"Why do you do that, Papa Carboy?" she would ask when something in articular had caught her eye. Or, "Why is it necessary to send so many ables to the Akhound of Swat?" Or, "What do you keep so secretly in those oxes?"

Her youthful curiosity not having abated in any degree, she sometimes sked more personal questions: "Why do you always wear that old mulberry oat? Why do you always drink coffee and never tea? What are you thinking f when you look out the window with that positively frightful frown on our face? Are you thinking of gobbling up some poor innocent little competitor? Isn't it about time you were thinking of getting married again?"

Samuel rather liked this evidence of interest in his affairs and he never ailed to give her an answer. He would say, "Well, it's this way, young lady," nd would then enter on what generally proved to be a satisfactory explanaion. Gradually he grew to feel so much partiality for her company that he emanded her presence beside him at tea. This meant sharing the sandviches which were brought in to him and which he ate at his desk to save ime. He never saved any time in reality, because it became an occasion or much chaffing back and forth, and much laughter. On one occasion when llie had been allowed to join them (it had required diplomacy on his part o get the invitation), his father indulged in a sudden shaking of his head.

"What a narrow escape it was," he said.

"Whatever are you talking about, Papa Carboy?" asked Nell.

"Well, I was thinking I wouldn't have liked that Ma'amselle Hortense lphonsine as much as I like you. So, having *not* got her and having on the ther hand got *you* as a daughter-in-law, I consider it was really a very narrow scape."

"You're just trying to make the best of a bad bargain, Papa Carboy. But 'm pleased to hear you say it just the same."

Lion Colter had been present at the reading of the will. He sidled up to amuel the Younger, who would no longer need that distinguishing appellaion, and suggested a brief conference.

"It will be well to have the board meeting without delay," he advised in a vhisper.

Samuel nodded. "Yes, the election of officers should take place at once. I ope the duchess will be well enough to attend. It might seem rather—shall e say, cavalier?—to hold it without her."

The lawyer let his voice fall. "Samuel," he said, "let's be candid about his. I know how things stand. The illness of Her Grace is nothing short of a olden opportunity. You can hold your meeting and get yourself planted rmly and officially in your grandfather's shoes before she recovers. It will ave you a fight—a hard, bitter struggle for control."

After a moment Samuel nodded in assent. "You're right. She would have ontested it."

It developed that Isabelle was too ill to be told about the will. In fact it vould be quite a time before she could be told anything.

## CHAPTER THIRTEEN

1

It was two weeks later that the Duchess of Outland opened her eyes to realization that she was alive and in her old bedroom at Beaulaw Hall. Th sun was creeping around in the west and invading her privacy over the lo slate roof of the household offices; by which she was instinctively aware tha it was late in the afternoon.

"Have I slept long?" she asked, in the hope that someone was within hea ing. She was surprised, without a doubt, to find so much difficulty about th simple matter of speaking. Her voice sounded as faint as that of a child's.

There was a sound of movement in a chair beyond her immediate rang of vision and a heavy foot coming down on the floor.

"Thank God and Billy Pitt!" said the voice of her husband. She coul hear him crossing the floor and then had a glimpse of his tired old fac staring down at her. "Isabelle, have you come around? Are you feeling bette at last?"

She struggled to raise her head from the pillow and finally had to give it up

"Chip!" she cried. "I don't feel like myself at all. I feel tired and weak How long have I been asleep?"

"A little matter of two weeks," he replied, in a tone of contentment grow ing out of her return to reason.

"Two weeks! I don't believe it. Is this one of your foolish jokes?"

"No joke at all, Isabelle. It's God's truth. You've been lying there for tw weeks, tossing about and talking to yourself, and scaring the everlasting soul out of everybody." He grinned. "Welcome back, my dear."

Isabelle felt a sudden tug of anxiety. "Chip! Bring me a looking glass At once, if you please."

"Very well. But a little word of warning. You'll see a difference in your self. The doctor's had to cut your hair off. I think it looks kind of cute th way it is but there's no denying it's a lot different. And you've lost weight my dear. It wouldn't do to give you a cobb on the behind now. Might brea you off at the middle."

"Bring me the looking glass!"

She took one glance at herself and then dropped the mirror with a scream "Chip! I'm a skeleton! My face is so thin I look like a scarecrow. Ugh! Tak it away. I'll never want to look at myself again." An exploring hand unde the sheets brought further proof of her reduced condition. "There's nothing left of me! I'll be a sight! I won't dare get out of this bed!"

"Easy on, my girl," said the duke. "Two weeks of stowing away plenty o good food will bring you back to where you started from in *that* department. Perhaps it'll be an improvement. You were getting just a bit droopy in the middling, you know."

One of the doctors came in at this point, followed by the nurse. The duke was banished from the room and did not see his wife again until the next morning. He was at work on a breakfast kipper when the word reached him that the invalid was awake and desired his presence. He took one last glimpse at the newspaper propped up beside his plate and walked up to the bedroom.

"Well, well, well!" he said cheerfully. "Welcome back from wherever you went to, my dear. It's capital to have you here, I must say."

"Sit down, Chip," said Isabelle in a voice which delighted him with its closeness to normality. "Nurse, you may go. I want to talk to His Grace."

When they had the room to themselves Isabelle began to speak in an urgent tone. "I'm frightened about what may have happened since I took sick. I haven't dared ask a question. Chip, did Papa die?"

He nodded his head. "Dead and buried, my dear. The old boy had a fine funeral and a rousing send-off from the press all over the country. Leaders with black lines and plenty of praise. One of them said he should have had a title. *That* would have pleased him no end."

"Chip, what about the will?"

He proceeded to tell her the terms of the will. Apparently she was satisfied, for she nodded her head.

"About what I expected," she said. "I'm glad he remembered you, Chip. We'll have to figure out some fine investments for all that money, won't we?"

"Point of fact, I've already found a fine investment for it. Now don't get all excited. It's something for you. Something to help in bringing your health back."

She began to breathe hard and it was apparent that she had been thrown into a panic by what he had told her.

"Chip, if you've gone and thrown that money away——"

"Nonsense, my dear. I've got myself a remarkably fine bargain. It's—well, Issy, I might as well out with it. I've bought a yacht."

"A yacht! Chip, Chip, what folly have you committed? Why, a yacht costs——"

The duke interrupted her with a shrewd twinkle in his eye. "They cost almost as much as renovating an old county house in order to entertain lavishly. But not quite as much. I bought it because I knew it was the perfect thing for you. As soon as you're strong enough, we'll go for a long cruise and you'll come back in perfect health again—with color in your cheeks and your eyes sparkling."

"I'm never going to get out of this bed!" cried Isabelle. "Never as long as I look my age—or within twenty years of it! You've thrown your money away. I'll never be able to sail on your yacht." Her eyes turned toward him accusingly. "How much did you pay for it?"

"Ten," he answered.

"Ten what? Ten thousand pounds?"

He nodded. "Of course it's going to need some overhauling and refitting and that will run the cost up. I imagine I can do it on what I get out of the estate. It's the *Semiramis*. They built her, as you may remember, my dear, at Wivenhoe for Freddie Sackstone. It's been laid up since Freddie died. Oh, Isabelle, she's a beautiful thing! She sails as light as a bird."

Isabelle was too weak to give full vent to her indignation. Feeling utterly inadequate to handle the situation, she asked, "Has it steam power?"

"No!" cried the duke. "Would you have us drummed out of every club in the United Kingdom? Of course it hasn't steam. That's one of the fine things about it, I can take a hand in the navigating. You know, Isabelle," with a delighted smile, "this is like a dream. I've always wanted to be a sailor."

"You've bought it for your own pleasure and not for my health," charged Isabelle.

The truth of this was not hard to perceive. The purchase of the *Semiramis* had made a new man of the Duke of Outland. He seemed to be holding himself straighter and the old gleam could be detected in his eye. No longer an old potterer, with outdated newspapers under his arm! He seemed now like the Young Chip of an earlier day, who owned race horses and ran blithely through the money his wives had brought him.

"It's for both of us," he conceded.

Isabelle roused herself to ask another question. "Have you paid for it?"

Young Chip nodded briskly and proudly. "I arranged with the executors to get a bit of my money right away. I've paid down four thousand. The balance can be cleared off when I get the rest myself."

Isabelle began to cry in sheer bodily exhaustion and the exasperation of spirit created in her by his impetuosity. "Why did I have to be sick this way? You take advantage of me by going out and squandering all your money on a yacht. My nephew, I'm sure, has stolen the business from under me while I lay here unconscious." She paused and then demanded in a tone which had become sharp again, "Has that conniving fellow called a meeting of the directors yet?"

The duke nodded, glad obviously to have the subject changed. "He lost no time about it. They met a few days after the funeral."

"Did he have himself elected to all of Papa's positions?"

"Every one."

Isabelle lapsed into more tears. "I knew it. I was sure he would lose no time. I couldn't think of anything else all last night. I'm sure he made a bargain with the rest of them. They agreed to support him and he paid them off by promising to remove the restriction on stock sales. I'm sure that's what happened." She stifled her tears a second time and looked at her husband with anger and frustration in her eyes. "I intended to fight him for control. I had talked to many of the largest shareholders and they promised to support me. I would have thrown him out and closed up all the branches in foreign countries. And now it's too late." Her voice rose to an almost hysterical pitch. "Or is it? Perhaps I can still win over enough shares to outvote him at the next meeting. If I can only get my strength back! Chip, when will I be strong enough to get out of this bed?"

"The doctors agreed it would be two weeks. But you won't be able to do much for a long time. It may be several weeks more before I'll be allowed to take you home. As for getting out and starting a fight for control of the company—well, that's impossible. At least, for a long time. You must realize, my dear, that you've had a tough bout of it. We weren't too sure about you for a few days."

A sudden change came over Isabelle. He could read a hint of panic in her eyes. Her hands clutched at the edges of the counterpane. She had just remembered the Holbein and the promise she had made her father.

"Chip!" she cried. "I must get up this instant! There's something I must do. Something very important. Bring the doctors in at once. I must make them see that this won't wait. They must know of some way to get me well quickly. I must go to London, Chip. I must go at once."

"I don't know what all this is about," said the duke, "but I do know that you won't stir out of this bed for a fortnight."

Isabelle almost screamed at him. "I must! I must! There's something that has to be done and no one else can attend to it but me."

"Come, come, if you go on like this, I'll find some way to get you on this yacht of mine and take you far away. What is this important matter which must be seen to in such a damnable hurry?"

"Chip, there was an old building in London which Papa owned. It was a sort of warehouse in the east end. Was it mentioned in the will?"

"Yes, my dear. It was left to you. I didn't speak about it before because it seemed of no importance. Not worth more than three or four hundred pounds, I suppose."

She felt like crying out, "Three or four hundred pounds! It may be worth fifty thousand pounds to me!"

She felt somewhat relieved, however. Since the property belonged to her, it was unlikely that anyone had gone to inspect the place. She still had time, in all probability, to follow her father's instructions about the stolen masterpiece. But it was a matter of the utmost urgency. Her hands were trembling and she was finding it almost impossible to restrain her tears. This made it abundantly clear to her that she could not attempt to go to London until she could muster sufficient strength. Could she delegate the task to someone else? Her eyes rested speculatively on her husband as this thought entered her mind.

"Chip, I must ask you some questions. They mean nothing, of course; I'm just trying to get something clear in my mind. Suppose an object of great value had been stolen and had come into the possession of a man of good reputation."

The duke did not wait to hear anything more. "In a case like that," he declared, "the man of good reputation would turn it over to the police at once. And, what's more, he would jolly well see to it that whoever had been guilty of the theft was laid by the heels." He looked at his wife anxiously.

"You're talking too much. You mustn't tire yourself out this way. Here, have a drink of this rum and sweetened milk. The doctors said you were to take it every hour."

Isabelle took a few sips of the liquid. "I feel dizzy and there's a pain in my back. Isn't it terrible to be sick? I never realized what it was like."

The rum and sweetened milk seemed to have given her back some of her strength. In a few moments she resumed the questioning of her spouse.

"But if this stolen article was of great value. Oh, *very* great value, and the man who had it had paid a fabulous sum for it, not being sure that it *was* stolen."

The duke still possessed no doubts as to what should be done under these circumstances. "He must turn it over to the police at once. As soon as he's sure it's been stolen. And he must give them all the information he has about it."

"But if he did that, he would lose what he paid for it."

"That's bad luck of course. But there's no other course open to him." Isabelle was finding his rigidity of opinion hard to swallow, but she felt, nevertheless, that she must probe further. "Let's suppose, then, that he has put the stolen article in the hands of someone else. What does this second man do?"

"Why, he goes to the police about it, of course."

"Even though the first man is a friend and will be considered to have broken the law and so be subject to punishment?"

The duke's opinion was not shaken at all. "He should be punished. He's broken the law."

"But suppose the second man decides to send the article back to the original owner, the one from whom it was stolen? Wouldn't that be the best way? The wrong would be righted and everyone would be satisfied."

"But not the law." The duke shook his head stubbornly. "All the parties to the transaction would be guilty of breaking the law and would have to be punished. No, my dear, there's only one way to handle a thing like this and that's to go straight to the police."

Isabelle screamed at him: "The police! The police! Can't you think of anything else to say? Why must you insist on going to the police? It's a nauseous idea to begin with. Policemen are always stuffy creatures and their quarters smell frightfully. Why are you so obsessed with the need to go to them about everything?"

"It's the law," he declared. "Someone has been guilty of an offense and must be punished. It's my opinion, Isabelle, my love, that *all* of them should be punished."

"Well," said Isabelle to herself, "it's clear I can't ask *him* to get the Holbein out of that dreadful building for me. He would take it under his arm and go straight to the nearest police headquarters. He would be ready to have me sent to prison because of his silly law. But what am I to do?" It had never entered her mind that she should follow his advice. There was her father's reputation to be guarded, and there was also the fifty thousand pounds she might get out of a sale. "Can I lie here," she asked herself, "and take the chance of someone stumbling into that place and discovering the picture? Is there anyone I can trust?" She thought of Jonathan Bade but dismissed that possibility. Perhaps Jonathan would share her husband's obsession about rushing to the nearest police headquarters and turning everybody concerned over to summary punishment. Who else was there to call upon in this emergency?

2

The equipage of the Duchess of Outland proceeded slowly through the streets of a mercantile district which believed in open and rather lavish display. There were on all sides shopwindows of plate glass, filled with costly goods, and flamboyant signs, and doormen in livery who could spot a likely customer by instinct and be at the carriage steps in a trice. But by way of contrast there was almost a hint of secrecy about the place where the carriage came to a stop: a door which needed paint and had a brass plate at the bottom of a row of such plates which said no more than "Linus Welstock."

Inside, she walked up a steep and dark stair, because there was nothing else to be done, and on the floor above she saw more plates on the wall, including one which showed the first inclination to consider the feelings of prospective clients by announcing, "Linus Welstock, next floor." When the second floor was reached there was a positive outburst of candor, a plate which said, "Linus Welstock, Art Gallery," and a hand painted on the plaster (and quite badly painted, considering its purpose) which pointed down the corridor.

The offices of Linus Welstock might be hard to find but, once inside, it became apparent that he was conducting a busy establishment. Isabelle caught glimpses of rooms filled with framed paintings and she heard enough voices to convince her that there were many customers in the place. Her name gained her immediate admission to the office where the owner of the gallery conducted his affairs, and she found herself facing a man with a florid face and a high, dead-white bald head.

She came to the point at once. "Mr. Welstock, you are aware, of course, that my father is dead."

"Yes, Your Grace. Mr. Carboy's death is a great loss to the country. A great loss indeed."

Isabelle's face was still thin but her manner had become quite normal again. Her voice had all of its customary assurance.

"Mr. Welstock, you sold my father a painting."

He became immediately wary and reserved in attitude. After one quick glance at her face, he turned his gaze to the window. "Your Grace, I sold Mr. Carboy many pictures. I am happy to know they will hang for all time in the National Gallery."

Isabelle frowned. "Is it necessary to play with words? I mean *the* picture.

Papa told me about it a short time before he died. He let me see it. And—he left it in my hands. To dispose of as I saw fit."

Welstock's small dark eyes could not conceal the fact that their owner did not know just what he should do. He remained silent for the space of a full minute and then asked in a casual voice, "What is your purpose in coming to see me?"

"There are two courses open to me. I can destroy the picture. Or I can allow you to sell it on my behalf to some other collector."

"I dón't believe I understand. You speak of one particular picture. I think I should have someone with me to hear your explanation. Unfortunately our Mr. Purdy does not seem available at the moment. Perhaps you could come back another time, Your Grace."

Isabelle looked him squarely in the eye. "You are being rather absurd, I think, Mr. Welstock, and *quite* transparent. I'm certain you are too wise to take anyone on your staff into your confidence, Mr. Welstock. Not in a matter like this. I'm not sure you even have a Mr. Purdy. You seem to think women can be deceived easily." She tossed her head. "I've just this one thing to say. I came in to discuss the Holbein."

"The Holbein?" He frowned as though trying to understand. "I don't know what you mean."

"The Holbein you sold to my father, Mr. Welstock."

The dealer indulged in a laugh. "Your Grace, what a wonderful dream! To have the chance to sell a Holbein and to Samuel Carboy of all men! No, it never happened. I don't know how you got that idea but, alas, dear lady, that great good fortune was not mine."

It was clear now that he had no intention of acknowledging any part in the transaction which had brought the stolen masterpiece into her father's possession.

"Then you are not interested in making another profit."

"Your Grace, I am a dealer and I am always happy to make a profit. But I'm at a complete loss to understand what you mean. I think your father must have secured the picture through another dealer."

"What can I do now?" wondered Isabelle, keeping her eyes on the floor. "This man is a thief and a liar and there's no way to get anything out of him. What is my next step?"

After further consideration she got to her feet. "I expect I should send it back to the museum from which it came in the first place."

Welstock smiled blandly. "Your Grace, I am hardly in a position to advise you in a matter which is new to me and which you have not explained."

"I'll have no hesitation about explaining it, Mr. Welstock, if the necessity ever arises," said the duchess, making her way to the door.

Welstock got slowly to his feet and bowed. "Dear lady," he said in a low and mocking voice, "I am quite sure that the time will never come when the making of any such explanation will seem expedient or—may I say?—sensible. Good morning, Your Grace."

Welstock remained in silent thought for several moments. Then he got to his feet, took a hat from a peg on the wall behind him, pulled it down over his eyes and sallied out into the street. A short walk took him to a dingy series of law offices behind a large brass plate marked, Smythe, Boongrace and Curdle.

"I desire to see Mr. Fawkes," he said.

Alexander Fawkes received him in an office little more than a cubicle in size, with a fireplace in which a fire was burning and from which smoke belched out at intervals. The art dealer seated himself as far away from the fire as he could manage.

"You attended to that matter?" asked Welstock in a low tone.

"I attended to it. Successfully."

"Glad to hear it. She was in this morning. Asking questions. All set to make a deal. I was put to it for a minute, not knowing how much she knew. So, she knows nothing. She's on her way over there now, I'm sure."

The lawyer, who acted for the Duchess of Outland in his odd and unaccounted-for hours, nodded his head. "She'll think it an act of God when she sees the place. All evidence was carefully committed to the flames. Except, of course—it."

Welstock frowned over the top of his walking stick. "Be careful what you do with the money. Don't seem too damned prosperous all of a sudden."

Alexander Fawkes smiled knowingly. "I'll tell you what I'm going to do with my share, my good and esteemed partner in crime. I'm going to buy Carboy stock."

Welstock looked up in surprise. "Are you, now? That's interesting. I noticed it had been sliding off a bit lately."

Fawkes looked about him to make sure that no one was lurking near his door. "Some of the directors are selling. You see, Cast-iron Sam wouldn't let them sell while he was alive. The grandson has loosened up on it and the boys are busy converting some of their shares into cash of the realm. Just to be on the safe side, you know. That's what has been bringing the stock down. It's as good as ever. It's just like the Rock of Gibraltar. It's survived business depressions before and it has a record of half a century of unvarying success."

"H'm," said Welstock. "I may pick up some shares myself."

3

When Isabelle returned to Grosvenor Square, after visiting her property in the east end, she found the duke most handsomely accoutered in a blue coat with brass buttons, trousers of white flannel and a peaked cap which he was wearing at a jaunty angle. He performed a very good imitation of a hornpipe in the entrance hall and came to a stop in front of her, his face beaming.

"Everything's ready!" he announced. "Anchors aweigh! The overhauling of the pretty little lady is complete and she's slick with paint fore and aft.

I've got my wardrobe ready and my will made. I've laid in enough in the way of wines and liquors to last our guests——"

"Our guests?" Isabelle's voice conveyed the impression that the cruise would get away to a stormy start. Her husband did not notice this, however; he was too full of his plans.

"Yes, my dear. I took it on myself to invite three or four friends to go along. Well, seven, to be exact. Must have enough for two tables of whist, you know. They're all packed up and ready."

"Chip!" said Isabelle, her lips trembling. "I've had a great blow. I went to see that property Papa left me. Chip, it's gone! It's burned to the ground! A week ago some terrible old man got in to sleep there and he set fire to it. At any rate, they found his bones in the ashes afterward."

The duke looked at her with a surprised air. "But, my dear, what's so bad about that? The building didn't amount to anything. A wormy old warehouse, filled with discarded junk. What would you have done with it if this old fellow hadn't got in and finished it off?" He began to laugh in a thoroughly hearty and nautical way. "By gad, were you thinking we should sell this place again and move out there? Come, come, my girl, forget all about it and start to pack. The sea is calling us. Old Whatchemacallem has chucked his trident and is holding out both finny hands in welcome!"

Isabelle burst into tears. "What could I have done? I thought it was enough to write that lawyer and instruct him to see that the place was safely locked up. Should I have hired a night watchman?" She began to wring her hands. "Why didn't I do something! Fifty thousand pounds thrown away! A fortune lost through my carelessness! Oh, I'll never get over it. I'll never forgive myself."

Chip had stopped fidgeting about and indulging in single dance steps. He stared at his wife with eyes rounded in surprise. "What's this about losing fifty thousand pounds?" he asked. "Are you going to be sick again? Are you all right up here?" He touched his forehead with one hand. This served to remind him of the imminence and importance of his own plans. "Now, come, pull yourself together. Don't you realize that we're leaving tomorrow? At nine sharp. I don't know how many bells that is but I'll read up on it and find out. Yes, the others are coming by to join us here——"

Isabelle dashed the tears from her eyes. "Do you think I can be bundled off like that? I can't go on a cruise! I've never heard of anything more absurd. I haven't any clothes——"

"I've thought of that too. We'll cross the Channel first and spend a week in Paris, where you can buy everything you'll need. Then we'll start out on the long trail."

Isabelle was staring at him with hostile eyes. "Fifty thousand pounds thrown away! All your money sunk in a yacht! A fortune spent to stock it with wines for your friends to guzzle! And there you stand, gabbling about starting on a cruise. I think, Chip, you must be insane. You've got a wild look I don't like at all."

Her husband became completely serious at once. "No, I'm not insane.

I'm doing a very sensible thing, as a matter of fact. I'm taking you away from all this trouble, all these little molehills which seem so big to you. All you'll do will be to sit on a deck and let the sun make you well again. You'll be a new woman in no time at all. I've decided what we are going to do. Tomorrow morning, whether you like it or not, we get on a train and set out for Portsmouth. Is that clear?"

## CHAPTER FOURTEEN

### 1

The little cloud which had risen out of the sea like a man's hand was now making the heavens black with wind and a great rain. Men no longer said, "Hard times are coming," because hard times had come. Factories had closed, and shops were empty of customers, and the streets were filled with the unemployed. Directors went to board meetings in silk hats and came away grumbling over the necessity of passing dividends. Questions were being asked in the House of Commons.

Samuel Carboy the Younger got off the train at Wantage Road Station. He looked tired under his black bowler hat and he was so deeply immersed in thought that he let his topcoat blow open in the sharp wind without making any effort to button it up. The secretary who accompanied him, with a well-packed dispatch case, was too busy blowing on his fingers to notice what his employer was doing. They climbed into the carriage in a mutual silence and it was not until the coachman turned onto the south road that the owner laid aside his preoccupation sufficiently to say: "No! North to Little Shallow. The Old Rectory."

The doctor had just left with a parting admonition to Helen Groody: "I don't like your pulse. It's got a fast, jerky movement. Bad, that—very. Well, compresses on your knees. Don't take anything but beef tea and a little arrowroot. A tablespoonful of brandy, if you get faint." Passing the new arrival at the door, the doctor frowned. "A sick lady, Mr. Carboy. I wish I knew some way to ease her pain."

She was sitting most uncomfortably in her wheel chair when the tired man entered, after depositing his bowler hat in the hall. Her eyes lighted up when she saw him.

"Sammy, this is most unexpected," she said. "And most pleasant. You seem a little disturbed. Are things going badly?"

He managed to smile. "I've come to pour out my troubles," he said. "Into ears which, I trust, will be sympathetic."

"Always that, Sammy."

He gave his head a rueful shake. "There's little but trouble these days. I sometimes wish I had stayed in South Africa. Ah, how wonderful it would be to have my own little business again! With no fat, greedy directors hectoring me and badgering me and telling me what to do and what not to do. Directors are a low order of creation, Aunt Helen, and I wish they could be abolished. When I found I had to come down about the sale of Beaulaw Hall, I decided to pay you a visit and weep on your shoulder."

Helen opened her eyes wide at this. "You are selling the Hall? I'm sorry to hear it. I think it was your grandfather's wish that you would settle down there and that Allie would follow you."

"I have a good reason which I'll come to later on. In any event, I'm not intended to be a country squire."

He was pacing about the room, kicking at the corners of rugs, gesticulating with his hands, and in fact giving every indication of being mentally much upset.

"I hoped this depression would be a short one," he said. "But it goes on and on. In fact it seems to be getting worse. They're having a bad time of it in the United States and the French are rooting around on a low-tide flat. My directors are screaming at me to close factories and lay people off by the thousands. That would be an easy way to weather the storm. If I kept only our key industries open, those which manufacture staple goods, I could get through easily enough. But I don't want to do that. Decency seems more important to me than the feelings of a red-faced director. My duty isn't to protect the investor only. I've been on a tour of the country and I talked to the men in the shops as well as those in the front offices. They're frightened, Aunt Helen, all these overworked people who just manage to live on what we pay them. Most of them were afraid to talk to me at first. I made a discovery: as head of the company I have a responsibility to the men we employ as well as to the shareholders. I can't turn them out to starve."

This was a new Samuel Carboy. Since his return from South Africa, Helen had known him only as the bold innovator, the ambitious industrialist who aimed at controlling world markets, the man who would be content with nothing but the top. Now he was showing a human side. She watched and listened with a sharply aroused interest.

"Grandfather didn't lay off one man during the Napoleonic depression. I would like to follow his example. But they're making it hard for me. Dividends, dividends, dividends! It's all they ever think of. And I have to acknowledge that I've made two serious mistakes. I should have closed the foreign offices as soon as the trouble started. They became at once a severe drain on the parent company. But I had started them and I was too damned proud to give in at once. I held on and now they have to be closed after all. I'm afraid that the damage has been done. They've cost us too much."

After a moment's silence he sighed deeply. "Yes, my pride has cost us heavily. I acknowledge my fault. I acknowledge it most humbly."

"What was the other mistake?" she asked.

"I removed the ban on the sale of shares held by our own officers. They've taken advantage of it to dump most of their holdings on the market. I'm sure you've noticed how sharply our shares have declined. The public hasn't known what to make of it because Carboy and Co. has always been like a barometer. If our stock declines, then conditions must be very bad. It was a serious mistake; and I resent the way they've taken advantage of it."

Then his mood seemed to change. He threw off his depressed air. "You mustn't think that I'm seriously discouraged. We'll come through it. There's magic still in the name of Carboy. And I'm prepared to pay for the mistakes I've made. That's the reason I'm selling Beaulaw Hall."

Helen shifted her position in the chair and then adjusted the coverings on her afflicted knees. She sighed with the discomfort of it. "I think I know what you are going to do. And I don't see the necessity of it."

"Some of our difficulties are due to this foolish pride of mine," he declared. "I must be prepared to pay any price that becomes necessary. When I got this offer for the Hall, I decided to take it. The price is fair, considering conditions. I'm going to sell all the furnishing as well, even the antiques he collected. I'm bringing back the funds I sent to South Africa. At first I thought of supporting our position in the market by taking the shares the rest of them are dumping but that would have been like putting money in their pockets. Instead I'm issuing more of the treasury stock and I'm going to buy as much of it as I can myself."

"You haven't sold any of your shares?"

"Not one."

"Do you mind telling me what Allie has done with the money he was left?"

"I advised him to find other uses for it. But," proudly, "he refused. He put it all into Carboy stock. He said that was where it came from in the first place. Your niece agreed with him. I tell you it was an encouraging thing to see two young people display as much faith and courage as that. I was proud of both of them."

"I think," said Helen Groody with a smile, "that you've changed your opinion of my little Nelly."

He nodded emphatically. "I almost made a third mistake there. It would have been the most costly of the three. But I was saved from making it and I'm very happy about the way things have worked out." He relaxed for a moment into a smile. "That lovely child! I grow fonder of her every time I see her."

This lighter mood soon deserted him. He took to his pacing again about the room. "There's a whispering campaign going on around the country," he said. "All independent companies are against us. They're afraid, of course, and think someday we may be powerful enough to gobble them up. There isn't one of them with anything but hate for us. They are saying now that only the genius of my grandfather made such a combination possible, and that it's illegal anyway. A word has been coming into use just the last year or so—the word 'trust.' They apply it to us, although I'm sure they would prefer to speak of us as a mis-trust. Well, they are whispering it about now that this is the time to attack us. They say I lack the strength of my grandfather and that, if they exert themselves, they can destroy us. Oh, I hear it everywhere. When I go on the Floor of the Exchange, I can see them nudging each other, and nodding their heads and grinning."

He stood for a few moments at the window, looking up toward the cross-roads of the village. "You can have real peace here, Aunt Helen," he commented. "I've forgotten what it means. I'm all alone. I even feel now that I can't trust our own lawyers. I can never be sure of anything they do. They overlooked some points of French law which has resulted in our shouldering every franc of the losses in that country. Jacques Plessis, that wily fellow, did not bear any of the loss, although he was a full partner. Sometimes I wonder if it wouldn't be wise to entrust our legal affairs again to Jonathan Bade."

She shook her head. "He's too old now to assume such a load as that. I'm certain he wouldn't consider it."

"I know that some of the partners at Smythe, Boongrace and Curdle are speculating in our stock all the time. I don't like it. If those fellows ever began to sell Carboy shares, the whole country would rush in to attack us. One of them, a scoundrelly fellow named Fawkes, is in and out of the Exchange every day. I hear he's been operating with considerably more capital lately."

Helen motioned to him with a hand that was startlingly thin and white. "Sammy, please draw up a chair. And try to calm down a little. I want to talk to you, and I can't as long as you keep pacing around like a caged lion. There! That's better. Now I have something to say to you."

There was a long moment of silence between them. She was looking into his eyes with so much love in her own that he began to realize the extent of the hold he had on her affections.

"I have no right to feel that you belong to me," she said finally. "But I do. It was your small shoes I saw outside the door of the inn that night in London. It was you my father taught to ride. It was you who left school and traveled alone to Yorkshire when you heard I was in trouble. You have always seemed like my own son."

"I have always felt that I belonged to you, dear Aunt Helen."

"Then, my boy, you must never think that you stand alone. I can be of great help to you in this trial you face. I hope you'll call on me if the need ever arises. I have money, you know. It's all invested in one form or another but I could get my hands quickly on much of it. It's nothing to compare with your grandfather's great fortune; but enough perhaps to turn the tide if you found yourself in a tight financial corner. I want you to know, my boy, that I'm willing to entrust it to you. I would do it willingly, gladly, lovingly. You must never hesitate to ask if you need it."

"I don't believe I would ever have had the courage to come to you," he declared. "Not after the things I've done."

"I agree with you wholeheartedly that it's as much your duty to continue giving employment to your men as to earn dividends for your investors. I'm willing to risk everything I possess to help you do it." She added hastily:

"Everything but my shop. *That* I could never risk losing. To me it's more important than all my other possessions."

He seemed reluctant to put into words the question which was on the tip of his tongue. Finally he asked, "How much might I count upon if—if I ever find myself with my back to the wall?"

"I think I can promise you one hundred thousand pounds."

He gaped in astonishment. "One hundred thousand! Aunt Helen, you've been nothing short of a genius. You started with nothing! There isn't a bank in England today which would advance me that much at the moment— except on impossible terms. I know—because I've been to many of them, and they all want to get both feet and both legs inside the Carboy door."

"It is yours if you need it, my son." She paused then and smiled. "I have some confidence in my way of handling money. I might come to London to give you a hand."

2

Carboy looked at the important young man with the starched cuffs and indulged in a wry smile. "Wilbert," he said, "there's going to be one hell of a fine rumpus in there. I would like to get it over with as quickly as possible. When I touch the bell, come in at once and distribute the envelopes."

"Old Barney Bagby is going to roar about it," said the secretary. "He'll be the worst, sir."

"You're right. Old Barney Bagby will be the worst. Old Barney Bagby has always been the worst. Because he started as a boy with my grandfather and because the old man grew accustomed to him and babied him, he has got the idea that he's indispensable around here. He has patronized me from the very start. And what's more, Wilbert, there isn't a loyal bone in Old Barney Bagby's frame. If we rendered down all the grease and suet in his carcass, we wouldn't get as much as an eggcupful of honesty and decency out of it."

They were all in their places when he walked into the board room. Because Carboy and Co. was the result of so many amalgamations and mergers and deals of one kind and another, and because it had so many subsidiary concerns, the board was a most unusually large one. The president blinked a little as he took his seat, finding it very difficult to make out many of the faces in the very dim light Nature was providing on this particular day. He said to himself: "A damned disagreeable lot of faces. And they'll get much more disagreeable when they've heard what I'm going to say."

"Gentlemen," he began, "there's been a disposition among you to favor a wholesale reduction in our payrolls. I have something of that kind to propose today, one which will save the parent company, and a number of our subsidiaries, a rather substantial amount." He paused and those who sat nearest him saw that his face had turned red with what seemed to them like indignation. "But before we go into that I must refer to another matter.

This, gentlemen, is a matter of honor and loyalty—or, rather, the lack of it.

"Some months ago," he went on after a moment, "it was decided in this room that members of the board who held shares in the company on the terms which had been set by my grandfather were to be allowed to sell a certain percentage of them on the market or by private treaty. It was stipulated in the resolution that the selling must be so managed that the position of our stock on the Exchange would not be adversely affected. It was stipulated that, for the time being, no one was to be allowed to sell more than a third of what he held."

There was an uneasy rustle along the board and some of the faces, which he had mentally catalogued as disagreeable, became decidedly more so, because fear and uncertainty had been added to the inner qualities which made them unpleasant faces in the first instance.

"You all know what has happened. There has been such a rush to sell shares that the market has become unsteady and our stock has dropped rapidly. Incalculable damage has been done to us. People are beginning to wonder. I have means of checking on what has been sold and even the blind deals some of you have made—where the sale is not immediately recorded—and I have all the figures here. Gentlemen, it is hard to believe; but of the eleven directors who have availed themselves of the privilege granted to them unwisely—and I am taking all the blame for that—three have sold every share they possess, three others have sold up to seventy-five per cent, the rest over half."

He stopped speaking and reached under the table to touch a bell. The door behind him opened with a suddenness that made it clear the summons had been expected. The young man Wilbert, starched cuffs and all, came in with a sheaf of sealed envelopes in one hand. These he distributed to eleven of the apprehensive men seated about the board.

"These, gentlemen," said Samuel the Younger, "are letters of resignation. You will oblige by signing them. You will note that you are resigning, not only as directors of the company, but that you are relinquishing as well the positions you hold with us. The separation terms are fair but not generous. Generosity, gentlemen, would be impossible to justify under the circumstances. And this, I may add, is the economy measure I referred to at the opening of the session. The eleven very large salaries we will cease to pay will constitute a great saving indeed."

There was a roar of indignation from the far end of the table. A bulky figure had risen and was shaking a fist in the general direction of the presiding officer.

"This, sir, is an outrage! I'll have you know, sir, that I was your grandfather's right-hand man. I have played an important part in the success of Carboy and Co. I have served this company with all my ability and with every grain of loyalty I possess for fifty-seven years. I will not be forced to resign by a whippersnapper who has insinuated himself into the control of this great organization. I refuse to resign, sir! I throw this infamous demand on the floor, sir. If you try to take other action you will not be able to withstand the storm of opposition I am in a position to raise!"

It was such a very dark day that it was hard to see the face of the speaker at the full distance of the long mahogany table.

"I believe it is Mr. Barney Bagby speaking," said the president.

"It is indeed, sir."

"I thought so from the voice and from the nature of the sentiments expressed. Yes, Mr. Barney Bagby, you have served Carboy and Co. for fifty-seven years and you have become very wealthy in doing so. I am sure you have served us with all your ability but there may be differences of opinion as to the proportions of your share of that desirable gift. I am equally certain that you have served us with every grain of loyalty you possess but I am compelled to add, Old Barney Bagby, I find the grains so infinitesimal in size as to be invisible to the naked eye. You, moreover, are one of the three who sold every share of stock."

"Intending to buy it back later!" roared the old man in the shadows at the end of the board.

"I have only this to say to you. If you don't sign the resignation form I have a letter ready to be handed you at once, discharging you from the offices you hold with us. The terms in the letter will not be found as favorable."

After a very great deal of stormy discussion, and much pounding of fists, and much uttering of threats of various kinds, the eleven papers were signed and collected. The eleven signers rose from their chairs and turned without exception in the direction of the president to predict he would rue this day, before stamping out.

When the last indignant footstep had died away and silence had descended on the board room, Samuel the Younger said: "Gentlemen, I desire to express my regret that this had to happen. We have much work to do today. Among other things, I desire to put through a general, and rather steep, cut in salaries. As of this morning I have taken myself off the payroll. Shall we proceed?"

"Wilbert," said Samuel when he returned to his office after the adjournment of the board, "we have made a few enemies today. But somehow I find it rather inspiring to think that they *are* enemies and that we can deal with them openly. I hope Old Barney Bagby won't have a stroke on the way home."

"There are a few matters which, sir, I very much fear you won't find inspiring," said Wilbert. "There's been word from Lloyd's that the two ships overdue are definitely lost. The larger of the two, sir, which you'll recall came to us in the Barnaby Mercantile and Shipping deal, carried little insurance, as we suspected. It was in Mr. Bagby's department and it seemed he overlooked it. At any rate, nothing was done."

A stricken look took possession of the president's face. "We can't stand losses like this," he said. "It's deplorable that it had to happen at this particular moment and that Old Barney Bagby, exercising all his ability and calling on every grain of his loyalty, has let us down so badly."

"And," said the secretary, "we've had a fire. At Arkworthy Woolens, sir. The power plant was burned out and the plant will have to close."

The countenance of Samuel became white at this information. "One of our most profitable concerns," he muttered. "This is fully as bad as the loss of the ships. It's really damnable that it happens at just this time. I'm beginning to wonder, Wilbert, if an impression exists somewhere, say up there in the clouds, that I come from the land of Uz and that my name isn't Samuel Carboy but Job."

He sat so long at his desk, saying nothing and doing nothing at all, that the important young man became very much worried. The latter bustled about the office and rustled papers and did other things to attract attention without any results whatever. Finally he cleared his throat and said, "Your pardon, sir, but there are papers to be signed, if you will be so good."

Samuel the Younger brushed a hand across his eyes as though hoping to clear away the visions which had been disturbing him. "Very well," he said. "Bring the papers, Wilbert. But before you do, what word has been had of the *Semiramis?* Have we had any response yet from the letters and cables we've sent?"

The secretary shook his head. "The word is that they cleared from Gibraltar before receiving any of your messages. It's thought they may be sailing for the Canary Islands but so far there's nothing to confirm it."

"See that every possible effort is made to get in touch with the duchess," said Samuel earnestly. He was thinking, "She hates me and will be a continual worry if she comes back. But I must get word to her so she can save some of her holdings if—if it becomes necessary." Aloud he added, "She must be kept advised or she'll think we've done it deliberately."


3


Samuel knew it meant trouble as soon as Mr. Hugh Daddleson was announced. The president of the Keyston Bank was a power in the world of money; a ruddy, stoutly built individual who looked as though he would be addicted to hunting and fishing but whose sporting proclivities were limited to an occasional game of cards at his club.

"We can get this settled in no time at all, Carboy," he said, settling down in a chair beside the refectory table. "You persist in saying you must have time to make the final payment on your purchase of the India and Singapore Shipping Lines. Well, here it is: we can't give it, we won't give it. We want our money."

"Then what do you propose?" asked Samuel, stiffening. This, he knew, would be the hardest problem he had yet faced.

"This. Let us take it off your hands. We can refinance it and operate it independently again. In fact we are ready to make an immediate start. If I leave your office this morning with an agreement in my pocket, we will be in business by noon."

"Twenty per cent of the purchase price remains to be paid. What will you give us for our eighty per cent?"

"Stock in the new company. Preferred, if you like. Common, if you fancy going along with us."

"We would have control," said Samuel, regarding his visitor with a far from friendly eye.

"Don't be absurd." The banker threw back his handsome, graying head and laughed heartily. "You'll have a chance to get your money back and nothing else. We intend to recapitalize and to spend millions, not immediately of course, in new ships and improved facilities. Your share in this could not, under the most favorable circumstances, exceed forty per cent."

"Do you think it likely we will permit you to trample on us like this?"

"Well, Carboy, we want our money. That's the starting point of this discussion, and perhaps that's where it will end." The banker's face had lost all of its joviality. "Have you, then, a proposal to make?"

Samuel did not answer at once. He was studying the visitor with an equal lack of cordiality.

"I have sensed a feeling of hostility at every stage of our negotiations, Daddleson," he said finally. "Has it been fancy on my part or have you been happy in the chance to force this issue?"

"Carboy," said the banker, swinging around in his chair to face the industrialist, "in matters of business I am a banker, first, last and always. The man in me is never allowed to show. In answer to your question, let me say this: if the man *had* been allowed to show, there would unquestionably have been an element of ill will in our talks. You see, Carboy, I am a grandson of Ernest Plumbottom."

"Whose portrait hangs in the board room. Plumbottom and Hook started this bank and did business in this building before my grandfather took it over and renovated it. I see. You are Ernest Plumbottom's grandson. I didn't know it."

"There has always been a feeling in my family that my grandfather was treated badly. Your grandfather decided he wanted this bank and he forced Plumbottom and Hook to sell by methods which were nefarious, to say the least. I am, perhaps, enjoying a sense of justice in being the instrument of a returned compliment."

"You are very frank, Daddleson. Much franker, I think, than a banker can afford to be. It may interest you to know that we have a promising young man on our staff whose name is Peter Hook. He's a great-grandson of the Hook who was your grandfather's partner. When Samuel Carboy bought the bank he did it with the full approval of Hook's widow. Mrs. Hook, and the other four partners as well, felt that the bank had fallen on evil days because of the stubbornness and stupidity of Ernest Plumbottom. They wanted to get free of that blustering autocrat and they practically begged to be taken into the Carboy fold."

"Very interesting. Shall we get back to business?"

After several moments of intense concentration Samuel began to speak. "Suppose we agree to your proposal. We'll get similar proposals from many quarters. All independent companies seem to be antagonistic to us. Other concerns, on which we still owe some small part of the purchase price, might come forward to claim emancipation on the same terms. Do you realize this?"

"Of course. But it's no concern of ours."

"Daddleson, I have no intention of letting my grandfather's organization be dismembered while I stand by."

"It seems to me, Carboy," said the banker, lighting a cigar with a quick flick of a match, "that you are allowing personal pride to come between you and a practical view of your difficulties. You see, we know all about the position you're in. But at the same time we realize that the blame doesn't rest on your shoulders. What is happening was inevitable. An organization like yours is bound to disintegrate, to break up, to go smash. If Sam Carboy was alive and sitting in that chair, I would be sitting here and saying to him the same things I'm saying to you. I would be saying to him that he had made a mess of things and would have to knuckle under."

For several minutes a heavy rain had been falling and at this point there was a loud clap of thunder. The banker looked startled.

"Thunder?" he said. "I didn't know it was raining."

Samuel smiled. "It may not have been thunder. It seems likely to me that the noise we heard was the result of my grandfather's reactions, wherever he is, to the things you were saying about him. Daddleson, if my grandfather sat here, you wouldn't dare say such things. He would blast you right back to the little countinghouse where you belong." The smile left his face. "You are trying to commit us to a policy which would lead to destruction by creeping paralysis. I'm sure Samuel Carboy would consider me a weakling if I gave in. Still, I'll think it over. You'll have your answer in twenty-four hours."

"No hurry." The banker got to his feet, still puffing at his black cigar. "Take two days if you want it."

Samuel had been sitting in silence for a full quarter of an hour, during which time he had not glanced once at the pile of correspondence in front of him. He was gazing out of the window, which was still streaked with the falling rain, when Wilbert entered the office.

"Mr. Carboy, a lady to see you. A Miss Helen Groody. She came in on crutches."

A change came over his thoughts. "Aunt Helen here? This is more than a coincidence. If I had any superstition in me, I would think she came on the winds of the storm." He turned his head from the window and motioned to the secretary. "I'll go out, Wilbert, and help her in."

When she entered the room a few minutes later she was clutching his arm with one hand and manipulating the crutch with the other. It was clear enough that she found walking painful but she was smiling and seemed to be happy.

"I had a feeling in my bones, Sammy, that it was about time for me to pay you a visit."

He seated her beside his desk and arranged about her knees the rug which Huruld, now waiting in the anteroom, had brought for her.

"You were right, Aunt Helen," he said, seating himself. "My back is to the wall."

4

News gets around quickly in the world of business. In a matter of days it was known in the City that the evils of overextension were showing in the joints and limbs, perhaps even in the heart and lungs, of Carboy and Co. Even when the last payment on the purchase of the India and Singapore Shipping Lines (this had been one of Samuel the Younger's deals) had been duly paid and a luncheon held to celebrate the event with bigwigs from the political world to make speeches, the conviction that trouble lay ahead was not shaken. Whenever a group of men got their heads together on the Exchange, it was safe to assume that the Carboy situation was under discussion.

One thing the rumormongers did not know was that Samuel went every afternoon at teatime to visit a little old lady in rooms above a draper's shop on the edge of Soho and that the two of them talked at some length about business matters. No one knew that it was the little old lady who had suggested cleaning off the shipping-line indebtedness and making capital of the event, even though it was hard to scrape up the funds for the purpose. If they had known, they would have applauded her good sense, for it was agreed it had been a shrewd stroke. In fact no one would have known who she was, or practically no one; she had always been one of the most silent of silent partners.

Helen Groody's health was so bad that she never stirred out of her rooms but sat at a window in her wheel chair and marveled at the lustiness and noise of London's streets. She herself had no idea of the dubious conclusions reached by the doctors who came in to pass on her condition.

That the head of Carboy and Co. now had a silent partner was quite well known in the establishment of Grace and Carboy, where a cheerful hum of activity was to be noted and where the balance at the bank, although never plethoric, was always sufficient for their relatively small needs. Early one afternoon Allie Carboy looked up from his desk, which was almost bare because he did not let himself get immersed in detail. He whistled a bar from *Trial by Jury*, and called to his partner: "Julian, I had an interesting talk with Jonathan Bade last evening. As the beautiful bride can't go out very well, he came over to visit us."

Julian Grace, who was deep in invoices, said, "Yes?" in a detached voice and reached for another sheet.

"The old boy is following the battle closely," went on Allie. "He says the fight they're putting up is quite—I think the word was Homeric, whatever that means. In fact he says it reminds him of Napoleon in 1814 when the Emperor with a small force held all the continental armies at bay, attacking first one and then another and winning all sorts of battles."

Julian dropped the letter he was holding. He was a Napoleonic student and the comparison interested him.

"Allie," he said, "I know it's none of my blooming business but you *did* put all the money left you into Carboy and Co., didn't you?"

"All but a small bit of it. I'm still holding that out in case a certain thriving young concern reaches the point where more capital is needed to keep it thriving."

It was clear that Julian was disturbed about the situation but that he did not know what to say. "Are you content to have it that way?" he asked.

"Yes, I'm content. I may lose it all. I know that as well as you do. But, Julian, my father needs every bit of support I can give him. My feeling for him is much greater than my regard for fifty thousand pounds."

Julian was still shaking his head. "If it wasn't for those two colonial railways! They seem to be getting in worse shape all the time and I don't suppose anything can be done about it."

Allie's mood had now changed over into gravity. He nodded his head. "I have nightmares about those ill-begotten roads. Father has tried too hard to keep them alive. He knows it now." To change the subject, he asked his partner to pay a visit to the house in the west end into which more sticks of furniture had been moved recently, if a cradle and certain accessories could be considered as coming under that head. "Nell thinks you're neglecting us. Come in for a bite of supper tonight. She can't get out much, you know."

"Can't," said Julian regretfully. "I'm seeing a lady from Jamaica who's visiting here with a daughter, or a niece or something. My grandfather knows a Mrs. Beltrade in Bermuda and these people are relatives of hers. The old lad is laid up at the moment, so I'm going to do the grand in his place."

Allie was very much interested at once. "Do you suppose this is another case of history repeating itself? A young lady from Jamaica! Is she an heiress? Is she pretty?"

Julian brushed this aside. "My very dear fellow, I'm not interested in this girl. I shouldn't need to tell you that I can't afford to be interested in girls for a matter of two years at least. Has it slipped your mind that we reached a decision not so long ago that one of us would go to the Far East to make connections and establish agencies? Well, you can't be the one. Not in view of the imminence of a certain very important event. So I must go; and I assure you that I'm looking forward to it, even though it means that romance must wait until I come back. If this Miss Sue Steven—which happens to be her name—turns out to be a ravishing beauty and rich as rich, I must still regard her with a cool and dispassionate eye."

"Well, I don't know. The East might be the perfect place for a honeymoon, you know," said Allie.

"Now," said Julian, becoming serious again, "about that comparison. It's true that Napoleon did a masterly job with his long boots on, marching, countermarching, catching them unaware, beating large armies with small ones. But in the end one of the large armies left him to his marching and went straight to Paris instead. When they took Paris, Napoleon was beaten and they bundled him off to Elba."

"I know." Allie had become equally serious. "I'm frightened about it, old fellow. I'm afraid they're headed for a smash. I don't care about *my* money being in it. It's other people's money that bothers me. What will happen to my aunt Isabelle? They can't locate her. The yacht's somewhere in the Greek islands and out of communication. The Dodecanese, or somewhere a long way from a cable. And I don't like to see Nell's aunt throwing all that good money after bad. Well, it's not quite that; and certainly she's doing it cheerfully. By the way, your grandfather isn't in it, is he?"

"I think he has a few shares. He doesn't like to sell because the price is so far below what he paid. And I think the dear old boy has scruples about selling."

"Great God!" cried Allie. "This gets worse and worse. Jonathan Bade has a bundle of shares and he depends on the income from them for that mission of his. I know all sorts of people who have a few shares tucked away. God help all of them if these blasted railways fall into the hands of the bondholders, which I'm told may happen! Why in hell and Tommy do colonies think they need railways!"

They looked at each other in mutual dismay. "I hope, my dear fellow," said Julian, "that all this doesn't bother Nell too much. A bad time for *that*."

"Not at all. She felt as I did about the legacy. You'd think we were agreeing to give away sixpence to a crossing sweep. And whenever she gets herself all bundled up and pays a call on her aunt, she comes back quite bucked up and full of confidence. I may tell you, my old cove, that her aunt is a remarkable woman."

"Well," concluded Julian, "all we can do about it is to keep the flag flying here."

## CHAPTER FIFTEEN

### 1

The news of the failure of Carboy and Co. fell on the public on a damp and gloomy day, a sodden, hopeless sort of day to begin with, and it had much the same effect as if the Bank of England itself had gone into a receivership. Men looked at each other with panic in their eyes, as though to say, "If Carboy's has gone under, then watch for the earth to heave up and swallow all civilization." Gradually, of course, they had second thoughts and the same thing was said all over London, "It wouldn't-a happened if Cast-iron Sam had been alive." All the blame was laid on the bowed shoulders of the grandson. The crowds collecting outside the building kept repeating with rising hostility: "It's his work. He's the one what's lost us our money and thrown us out of work. Why didn't he stay in South Africa and not come back here to do us in like this!"

Men who had been brushed aside, or swallowed up, or trampled underfoot by the Colossus came to the front again in all parts of the United Kingdom to voice their delight. "The nightmare is over!" they chanted in interviews with the press. "The freedom to do business in one's own way is restored. Despotism has been destroyed and democracy has asserted itself again in the world of industry." In Rixby, Boisterous Billy Isbester, long since retired, emerged from his slippered and gouty ease, to gloat. "I have only one regret," he declared. "That Old Sam did not live to see this day." Banker Daddleson, bested on the India and Singapore deal, had a great deal to say, none of it complimentary to the passing order.

The newspaper editorials were better considered and more judicial in tone. "It may prove a good thing in the end, even though such a spectacular failure, coming at this time of crisis, is certain to have a disrupting effect and may even lead to disaster," stated the *Packet*. "The idea of a trust is not in keeping with British ideals and perhaps we can afford to risk the danger of even blacker days if we can be certain that in time we will become again the nation of little shopkeepers which forced the great Napoleon to his knees. . . . But this must also be said: Samuel Carboy was a genius, a great and dynamic figure, and the vigorous way in which he shook up the stagnant bottle of business has had a permanent effect. More than any other man, he was responsible for turning Britain into an industrial giant."

It was assumed that all men employed in Carboy enterprises, and that meant many hundred thousand, would find themselves out of employment. The afternoon papers carried hope, however, that the shutdown would not be permanent and perhaps even of short duration.

They carried interviews with Samuel the Younger in which that unhappy man assumed all the blame. "I was too confident," he said. "I didn't think any storm could disturb the second Rock of Gibraltar, for that's what Carboy and Co. seemed to all of us. It was our foreign commitments which led to the trouble."

The news writers asked him what he intended to do. "As soon as possible I shall return to South Africa," was the answer. "To make another start. Perhaps young Mr. Cecil Rhodes will be in need of a very humble assistant."

2

One of the very few places in London where the failure of Carboy and Co. was not the main, in fact the sole, topic of conversation that afternoon was a small sitting room in a family hotel not far from Berkeley Square. It contained a table, laid out for an elaborate tea, and two ladies who hovered about and waited.

"I'll have you know, my child," said one of them, a middle-aged woman whose figure had widened through long years of interest in teas such as this, "that the guest we're expecting is well worth your consideration. He's Sir Julian Grace's own son and he has a fine fortune left him by his mother. A very great deal of money, I hear." She lifted the lid of one dish and emitted an exclamation of delight. "Poached eggs! What splendid teas they serve here! I don't want my egg to get cold, so I hope young Mr. Titus Grace arrives on time."

"Aunt Tiffy," said the other, who was young and slender and quite pretty, "I'm sure I'm not going to be interested in him at all. They say he's conceited and a most unpleasant young man."

"No one with seven thousand pounds a year is either conceited or unpleasant," declared the aunt, replacing the cover over the platter of eggs. "I hear he's downright handsome. Red hair and blue eyes. The kind we lost our hearts over when I was a girl."

The niece seemed little concerned. She seated herself at some distance from the table and drew a long sigh. "Do Grace men always behave the same way, Aunt Tiffy? They are so very handsome and so very nice that they make you like them very much. And then they turn around and go away. That was what happened to poor Aunt Sue in Bermuda, wasn't it?"

"Sir Julian Grace had the good sense to know that he was too old for your aunt Sue."

"But now *he* is leaving soon, I mean the grandson, and he'll be away for two years. *Two years*, Aunt Tiffy! I'll never see him again. My nice, tall, wonderful, handsome Julian!"

The older woman regarded her niece with surprise. "Do you really feel as deeply about him as that?"

"Yes, Aunty, I do; oh, I do, I do!"

Aunt Tiffy reached the conclusion under these circumstances that she would have to take steps. "Do you know all about him?" she asked. "I can't put it into words, my dear, but there's a reason why a young lady like you should not be interested in this grandson of Sir Julian Grace. In fact I'm surprised he arranged for the boy to call."

"Aunty, I know all about *that*. He told me himself the first chance we had to speak alone. He said to me then that he wanted to come back and see me but that he shouldn't. And then he explained the reason." The girl, who was pretty enough to suggest that someday she would be as attractive and charming as her aunt in Bermuda, raised her head defiantly. "I told him it didn't matter. It *doesn't* matter to me. It isn't his fault, and besides, he's sweet and gentle and—and wonderful!"

A waiter put his head in at the door and said, "Mr. Titus Grice, m'em." The door opened wider and the Thwaites heir made what might conservatively be termed an entrance. Certainly the hero in a provincial melodrama could hardly have done better. Pausing for a long moment on the threshold and bowing low over his tall silk hat, Titus said: "Your servant, ladies. I am Titus Grace. I believe my father has spoken of me. It is kind, it is *most* kind, of you to let me come."

"Come in, Mr. Grace," said the older woman, bustling across the room to greet him. "I am Margaretta Smedley, from Washington, D.C. And this is my niece, Sue Steven. Sue, take Mr. Grace's hat."

Although Titus bowed so low again that his throat seemed in jeopardy from the steel-like palisade of starched linen, his bold blue eye did not leave the figure of the girl for a moment. It was quite apparent that he approved of her most thoroughly. "You must not go to any trouble," he said, although he surrendered the hat. She was dressed in blue merino and her Indian shawl was not used on her shoulders but had been draped instead across her slender hips.

They seated themselves in a window embrasure while a waiter proceeded to serve them their tea. Titus, feeling every moment more favorably disposed to Miss Sue Steven, began to monopolize the conversation, telling about the social life of London as though he himself moved in the very highest circles. He described the balls, the assemblies, the routs, the receptions, in glowing terms. "You will find this hard to believe, and perhaps you will disapprove of me because of it," he said, "but it's the truth that I'm out so late every night that I haven't risen before two o'clock once in the past year. I've forgotten, positively, what mornings are like. The streets were very crowded today but I came straight through, not asking a question and not wishing to be late by as much as one minute."

"Yes, there's been a great deal of excitement today," said Miss Smedley, who had been listening to him with every evidence of interest and admiration. "It's caused by the failure, Mr. Grace."

"Failure? A business failure?" He gestured carelessly. "I take no interest in matters of business. None at all. Oh, I suppose that later I shall find it necessary, as responsibilities pile up on my shoulders. But at the moment my money is well invested." He paused and then seemed to feel a sudden twinge of interest. "Who has failed?"

"That great company we've heard so much about. They say it's a very bad smash. People will be ruined all over England. They were weeping on the streets when I went out this morning. It was Black Friday all over again; but perhaps worse."

The assurance with which Titus had been carrying himself began to leave him. He looked anxiously at Miss Smedley.

"Who is it? In God's name, ma'am, who is it?"

"Carboy and Co."

"Car-boy!" Titus uttered the first syllable almost in a shout, a shout of dismay and horror, but the second issued from his lips in a hoarse whisper, as though his capacity for speech had deserted him. "Carboy has failed? Ma'am, it's impossible. You are mistaken. You must be!"

"No, Mr. Grace. I assure you it is only too true. I read it in the newspapers. Yes, indeed, they've gone completely smash."

Titus got to his feet slowly. His face was white and his eyes seemed to have the glassy look of the prize fighter's who has fallen to the boards. He stumbled to the side table where Sue had deposited his hat, placed it on his head back to front, and then made his way to the door.

"Ladies, Miss Smedley, your pardon. I'm very ill. I must—I must go." He reached the door, opened it after fumbling inertly with one hand, and started down the stairs. They could hear him saying in hoarse tones: "Carboy and Co.! Failed! Impossible! It's a mistake."

"Well," said Miss Smedley, looking at her niece. "What very strange conduct! Why should he be taken ill so suddenly? He had barely eaten a thing. I must say I think it very queer. Do you suppose he's drunk?"

"It's my opinion," answered the girl, "that he had money invested with Carboy and Co."

"Perhaps you're right. His behavior might be accounted for that way. He certainly began to act queer as soon as I mentioned them. Well, Sue, we must keep our eyes open. If he's had heavy losses, we must be careful about seeing much of him. If you are going to marry an Englishman, he *must* be a man of property."

The girl said, with a spirited toss of her head: "I wouldn't be interested in Mr. Titus Grace if he had all the money in the world. I didn't like him. He was so sure of himself and so *very* fashionable."

Aunt Tiffy drew up a chair to the table. "Well, there's one advantage to all this. I'm going to have his poached egg as well as my own."

The dishes had been removed and Miss Smedley had retired to her bedroom for a nap. The niece remained in a chair by one of the windows, watching the life of the streets below rather listlessly. She was so preoccupied that a rap on the door had to be repeated before she called, "Come in, please."

The door was opened by Julian Grace. He did not enter the room but stood on the threshold with his hat held diffidently in his hands. He stared at her with eyes which were round and serious.

"I shouldn't have come, Sue," he said. "When I left yesterday, I never expected to see you again. Everything seemed so hopeless! But this failure has made a difference and I thought—well, here I am."

"I'm glad you've come back," said the girl. "I'm very happy about it. Don't stand there looking so guilty. Come in and sit down. Here, in this chair beside mine. What is it you've come to tell me, Julian?"

He took the chair she had indicated but still seemed very much disturbed and uncertain. "It's the failure, as I said before. You see, Allie Carboy, my partner, would have been expected to go back with his father at any time. But now, of course, there's no business for him to go back to. We've talked it over and decided we must go ahead full blast with our little business and the first step will be for me to go East. On the earliest boat." He paused and looked at her solemnly. "Sue, it won't be easy. All the ships are small and the cabins cramped and hot. There's no comfort to be found anywhere when the hot season's come. It's not the kind of life for a girl raised in luxury." He paused again, searching for words. "But—but—if you—if we——"

"Julian," said the girl, leaning toward him, "will you take my hands and hold them tight, very tight? So tight that I'll know you don't want me to get away from you." She looked at him steadily with dark eyes under long black lashes. "And now tell me what it is you have in your mind."

3

Allie Carboy had known the night before that the end had come and he had reached the little house in the west end in a depressed mood. He told his wife the news but they had exchanged few comments; there was very little worth saying in the face of such a catastrophe. There was even less said through dinner and, when he rose and announced he was going in to see his son, his voice seemed almost perfunctory.

"If Little Dan knew what his father had done to him," he remarked, "he wouldn't have a smile for me."

The son, now nearly three months old, had been named with some difficulty. At first it had been in the young father's mind that one of the time-honored Carboy names should be chosen, Samuel or Alfred, but Nell had objected. "You, my love, are all the Alfreds there should be in the world," she urged. "And as for Samuel, I don't care for it, and never have. Let's give our son a name all his own."

When a name is to be chosen more or less at random from the vast conglomeration which time has assembled, useful and otherwise, decorative and plain, high-toned and vulgar, it becomes a trying task indeed. In the end they called the boy Edward after the Prince of Wales and Daniel after the rather genial Irishman who had founded the Groody line in England. It was understood that Edward would be the front-door name, as it were, to be used in signing letters and writing checks and making wills, to appear in newspapers and to be sonorously declaimed by the footmen of dukes and ambassadors (assuming that he ever got into such high reaches of society), while Dan would be the boy's name at home.

"You just watch and see the smile my little man will have for you," said Nell, leading the way into the ground-floor bedroom where the cradle was kept. But Daniel had no smile for his father. He was sound asleep.

Nell was wakened at some hour of darkness that night by a feeling that things were wrong. She felt the place beside her where Allie slept and discovered it to be empty. She got out of bed, moving cautiously for fear of wakening the offspring, and made a tour of the house. The master was nowhere to be found.

An hour later, when she was on the point of arousing a neighbor and sending him to the nearest police headquarters, Allie returned. He had been walking, he said. Walking? But where? Nowhere, was the answer, just walking. And wrestling with his guilt.

They went inside and sat down together, and then he began to talk.

"What a careless, senseless, stupid fool I've been!" he said. "The will didn't state I *must* put the legacy in the treasury stock. It suggested that I do it. I shouldn't have rushed in so casually and easily to buy shares. Nelly, my darling, if I had that fifty thousand pounds now, there would be no problem for any of us. We could pay back some to your aunt Helen, we could stake my father to another venture in South Africa, your future would be secure, and that young fellow in there, sleeping so soundly and not knowing his father has done him in, would be a young man with prospects and not a pauper."

"Little Dan is not a pauper!" declared Nell. "His prospects are exactly what he would ask for if he had anything to say about it."

"Well," said Allie, beginning to take off his shoes, "I thought a walk might clear my mind but it hasn't. I feel exactly about things as I did when I went out. I've been a triple-blasted idiot and nothing will ever convince me to the contrary."

He returned home the next evening in a mood of the deepest depression, having spent the day watching the Carboy empire go up into smoke and then settle down in ruins. Saying nothing to his wife, he sat down in a chair and looked about the comfortable room in which Nell had succeeded in creating a feeling of peace and even beauty with the few sticks of furniture.

After a few minutes he tossed off a remark in a disinterested tone: "Julian's going to be married."

Nell, who had the matchmaking instinct which is either active or dormant in all women, and who had kept an almost proprietorial eye on her husband's partner, dropped the spoon with which she was beating up cream to go over the pudding, and almost charged across the room.

"What did you say? Julian going to be married! I don't believe it but, if I did, who would the girl be?"

"That girl," answered Allie listlessly.

Nell came close to shaking him. "What girl? What girl? What girl?"

"The one who came over from Jamaica or Bermuda or America. Or somewhere."

"Oh, that one. I haven't met her yet. What does Julian mean by going behind our backs like this?"

"He's happy about it." Allie at last became slightly communicative. "He came back to the office and did a handspring over his desk, knocking off a pot of glue on the floor. He danced and sang. She's going to sail with him next week. He's as happy as a dickeybird."

"When," demanded Nell ominously, "is he going to condescend to let me see the bride he's picked out for himself?"

"As soon as he can. Julian can hardly wait to waltz the paragon over here and show her off." Then his interest sagged. It was in a tone of the greatest discouragement that he finally volunteered another piece of information. "Titus Grace lost money. In the—in the crash."

"That," commented Nell, "is a matter of complete indifference to me." Then she roused her courage to ask a question. "How is your father taking it?"

"Bravely," answered Allie. "He smiles and keeps busy but you can see his pride piled up on the floor like shavings, waiting to be swept out with a broom. He dreads meeting people." Then he got to his feet. "Well, I'll go in and pass the time of day with the little pauper."

Nell followed him indignantly into the bedroom but had nothing to say for fear of rousing the child.

"He's asleep," said Allie. "It seems to me he's always asleep. Is it right to be that way? Is it natural? Sometimes I wonder, Nell, if we've brought a hoddy-doddy into the world."

"Now you're going to listen to me, Allie Carboy," cried his wife, her outraged feelings driving away all sense of caution. "In the first place, he isn't a pauper. I have a little song I sing to him which I made up myself and which begins, 'Dan, Dan, the lucky little man.' There! I've wakened him up! And see him smile, with his beautiful blue eyes. He smiles exactly like you. You can work out for yourself whether that makes him a hoddy-doddy or not."

"He's kind of a cute little codger at that," conceded Allie.

"Do you know what he's thinking, you unnatural father? 'My mama is right,' he's saying to himself. 'I'm a lucky little boy,' he says. 'Supposing I haven't got fifty thousand pounds? I've got a father,' he says, 'who's going to be the best businessman in the world. And besides that,' he says, 'I've got a mama who can go out on commission and sell subscriptions like sixty. And what's more,' he says, 'I'm a very healthy little boy and that's the most important thing of all, that is.'"

Allie's mood lifted at this. He laughed and drew his wife close to him. They stood shoulder to shoulder and looked down into the cradle. And Master Edward Daniel Carboy was delighted to see them, and he grinned, and kicked his heels and waved his plump hands at them. They stood there in silent worship for a long time.

"You're right, Mrs. Alfred Carboy," said Allie finally. "Let's forget all about the fifty thousand pounds I tossed so casually into the nearest flue or rathole, or wherever it went. We'll make a lot more than that for young Master Frumkenned here."

"I don't know what that means but I'm in favor of the sentiment."

"Frumkenned? It means First-born. Taken from the Something-or-other. Well, Mrs. Carboy, I believe now I could enjoy a little supper."

His appetite proved quite good under the circumstances but it deserted him once during the meal. Laying down his fork, he looked soberly at Nell. "The *Semiramis* is due in tomorrow."

Nell's appetite took wings immediately. "Now there will be trouble!" she said. "Poor Papa Carboy! Would he consider it too undignified to go into hiding for a while?"

4

On the return through Gibraltar the Duchess of Outland had found a great accumulation of mail awaiting her. There had been urgent letters and alarming cablegrams and chits left by other vessels; and the trend of all the communications had been in one direction, she must dispose of some part of her holdings before it was too late. Isabelle, needless to state, was very much disturbed. She read everything with a flame of indignation in her eyes, mentally charging her nephew with all of the blame. She was not sufficiently disturbed, however, to send off an order (it would have been too late in any event) for the disposal of such shares as she could sell legally at market quotations. There was in her, inasfar as the stock of her father's business was concerned, a combination of obstinacy and faith, born of the long years of tumultuous prosperity and the uninterrupted flow of the dividends. Not even as weak a man as Samuel the Younger could wreck a structure so soundly planned and raised. Carboy and Co. might suffer losses but, in the end, there it would stand, strong and unshakable.

It was not until they reached the Estuary that the word of the failure reached the *Semiramis*. Isabelle heard it with a stony face and then rushed to her cabin, slamming and locking the door after her. The duke, quite as much alarmed over his wife as the news of the disaster, tried to gain admittance to the cabin. He stood patiently outside the door, pleading with her to be reasonable and not take things so hard. Finally he heard her say in a suppressed voice, "Go away!" which relieved his mind because it was clear she had not done away with herself in sheer desperation. He returned to his own cabin then and did not see her until the next morning.

Isabelle had found North Africa and the isles of Greece new and strange and exciting. She had even taken to buying oriental fabrics in rich colors and entrusting them to the hands of native tailors who believed in free and flowing effects. She had been dressed in one of these startling costumes when the word reached her; with bangles and bracelets and huge earrings which jingled as she moved, convinced no doubt that she bore a close resemblance to Balkis progressing regally to Jerusalem. She was still in this far from correctly Victorian garb when she emerged from her cabin next morning; looking, it must be said, very much more like a Jezebel than a Balkis. It was clear that she had not been in bed.

The ducal carriage was waiting for them when they went ashore and Isabelle seated herself bolt upright therein, not deigning to say a word to anyone. They had traveled some distance through the City, in fact, before she could bring herself to talk.

"I suppose," she said to her husband, "that you realize what this means?"

The genial duke, well tanned from the long and happy months he had spent in helping to sail and navigate the yacht, sighed deeply. "It means, m'dear, we'll have to pull in our belts," he said. "I guess we won't be able to take any more little fliers on the hosses. And we'll have to sack a few grooms and a maid or two. And go without savories at dinner, of course."

"Chip!" protested Isabelle indignantly. "It's clear you haven't the faintest idea of the full extent of this horrible disaster. We'll have to lease the Park and Outland House and the shooting box in Scotland. Fortunately they're in good condition and we'll be able to get good rentals."

The duke's jaw fell open. He had not indeed realized the full extent of the disaster. The knowledge that they would be so hard put to it as this made him feel very apprehensive of other possible retrenchments.

"We'll have to live in that little house you own. The one given to you by the father of your first wife."

"You don't mean the one we called the Cullender because the roof always leaked?" cried the duke, distressed beyond measure. "That dull, mean little house that looked cross-eyed for some reason or other? Just under White Horse Hill?"

"Yes," said Isabelle grimly. "In that dull, mean little house—and I can think of worse things to say about it. We'll have to live on our land rents and what's left over from the rents of the two houses, won't we?"

"Will we?" asked the duke, who had not gone into the mathematics of the situation at all.

"First, of course, we'll have to sell the yacht."

Young Chip emitted a sharp yelp of dismay. "No! Not the yacht! Isabelle, I couldn't part with it. I tell you, I've been happier since we started on this cruise than I've ever been in my life. I couldn't live without my yacht."

Isabelle looked at him coldly. "Then we'll have to live *on* it. How would you like to exist through an English winter in a damp little tub full of drafts

nd without running water or comforts of any kind? I tell you, Chip, the
acht *must* be sold at once. It can't be allowed to eat its head off a day longer
han necessary."

"But—but——" The duke was too shocked to find any words to defend his
iew of the situation. Finally he managed to get out: "But, Isabelle, the
'ontine, the Tontine! You get eight thousand pounds out of that each year.
nd it's bound to grow larger."

She turned and looked at him with eyes which were not only cold but bit-
erly resentful. "I didn't believe my papa when he said the time would come
vhen the Tontine would be the most important thing in my life. I laughed
t him. And now it's come true. The Tontine money is all I have left of my
wn! What a calamity! What an unbelievable trick time has played on me!"
he seemed to be on the point of tears but no gentle liquid caused by grief
ould get through eyes which burned as furiously as hers without dissolving
n the way. "Chip, I won't permit the Tontine money to be used for
leasures. I am reserving every pound of it, every shilling, every penny, for
ne purpose."

"What purpose, my dear?"

She stared at him stonily for several moments. Then, in a deep voice, she
aid, "For revenge!"

Young Chip had not intended to pursue so painful a subject any further
ut at this he was forced into a stammering question. "Isabelle, I don't
nderstand. What do you mean?"

"I mean what I said. Revenge!"

"But what—— Come, m'dear, revenge? Really, do you plan to burn down
he Stock Exchange? Or pay fellows to carry placards around the House of
Commons?"

"I mean," declared Isabelle, "to have revenge on that treacherous, lying
reature, that Uriah Heep who came here from South Africa and wormed his
vay into the confidence of my papa! That bungler who turned the Rock of
Gibraltar into a house of cards! Who threw all our money away in wild
chemes. That's what I mean, Chip. I'm going to devote my life to it. I'm
going to see him in jail, branded as a thief and a swindler!"

"Isabelle, actually, you astonish me," said her husband. "It's plain you
nean Young Samuel but how can you send him to jail? He hasn't done any-
hing dishonest."

"I'll have no difficulty in proving him dishonest," declared Isabelle. "As
oon as my poor papa in his dotage gave in to this conniving scoundrel, I
ired a lawyer to protect myself. He was in a position to keep an eye on what
vas going on. He brought the evidence to me. Oh, he found plenty! I'll
ave chapter and verse to offer the courts when the case comes up. I'll show
ll the sharp corners he turned and the underhanded things he did, not to
mention the way by which he took all the cream from the top for himself.
He'll go to prison for this if I have to fight the case all the rest of my life and
pend every penny I possess. Now do you see why I can't use the Tontine
money for any other purpose? Do I make myself clear?"

The duke sighed. "Yes, m'dear, you make yourself clear. Most unfortunately clear, I'm compelled to add."

"But that's not all!" exclaimed his wife, fixing him with what, in his disturbed condition, might safely be termed a hypnotic eye. "I'm going to make a final effort to get at the truth of what happened in America. I've never believed that my brother Allie was legally married to that dreadful actress. And if he wasn't, what does that make his son? Papa's will left Beaulaw Hall to his *grandson*. When you're illegitimate, you're not a son or a grandson or a nephew. You're nothing, and you've got no rights at all in a court of law. If I can prove it, it will mean this thief had no right to the Hall under the terms of the will. As he has sold the property, he'll find himself in a pretty position, won't he?" She paused for breath. "I intend, Chip, to devote the rest of my life if necessary to seeing that this impostor spends the rest of *his* in jail."

She said nothing more for most of the long trip but poor Chip, stealing occasional glances at the unbending profile of his spouse, knew that her mood had not relaxed at all. His own thoughts were sufficiently unpleasant to keep him thoroughly occupied. Was it really going to happen? Was he to be forced to sell his beautiful yacht? If it came to that, he would not care whether he had much longer to live. Certainly his existence would be sadly humdrum if it consisted of living in the Cullender where there were saddle rooms (he had given up riding) and a billiard room (his eye had lost its cunning) but only one tiny and distinctly inadequate toilet. The good duke had grown to like the luxury of toilets with tile floors and heated towel racks and that sense of security and confidence which comes only from lack of competition.

"What's the fellow's name?" he asked after a very long silence.

"What fellow?"

"This lawyer who's been muddying up the stream, and scrouging around and stealing papers out of confidential presses, and all that sort of thing?"

"You've never heard of him," said Isabelle sharply, "and so it won't do you any good to know his name."

But this reference to Alexander Fawkes had set her to thinking. Could she trust the man any longer? On reviewing the events of the fatal day when she discovered that the Holbein had been lost forever, she had reached several definite conclusions. She was certain that Mr. Linus Welstock had the picture in his possession when she called on him or that he had already disposed of it. Why otherwise would he have been so cavalier with her, denying all knowledge of such a picture and swearing he had sold nothing of the kind to Samuel Carboy?

It was equally clear to her that the burning of the warehouse had been deliberate. It had been set on fire to cover up the fact that the masterpiece had been stolen. And who besides herself had known that the precious painting had been concealed there? The only person who might conceivably have guessed the truth was Alexander Fawkes, who had been sent while she was too sick to stir from her bed to make sure the building was securely locked and safe. His instructions had not gone beyond an outside inspection but suppose he had become curious? Suppose he had forced his way in and had found the masterpiece in its hidden niche?

She had no real doubt that he had been responsible for the theft of the Holbein and that he had shared substantially in the price Linus Welstock had secured for it. Her proper course of action would be to summon him to her, confront him with her knowledge of his guilt, and then cast him into outer darkness. She could not take any steps to punish him, for the Carboy possession of the picture had been illegal and she herself would be involved in the consequences of any legal action which might be taken.

She was fully conscious of this: that Fawkes was the only one who could provide her with the evidence on which she proposed to have her revenge. He had found it in his surreptitious searchings of the records at Smythe, Boongrace and Curdle. He still had most of the papers in his possession. Distrust him as much as she liked, she must continue to employ him, and pay him handsomely, if she hoped to bring her much-hated nephew to a degree of ruin more complete than he had already brought down on himself by his carelessness with the pillars of the Carboy temple. It was a distressing and paradoxical situation. She must set a thief to catch a thief and pay him for doing it, even though she knew that the one had been as guilty as the other.

When they came to Grosvenor Square and she saw Outland House in all its fresh paint and general resplendence, she felt a new emotion. She began to experience a sense of personal deprivation.

"How will I do without our wonderful town house?" she asked herself. "Here I have established myself as the most successful hostess in the country. Here I have entertained royalty. How can I give it up!"

Nevertheless she walked straight to her office and issued a summons for her secretary. Miss Trounceman appeared promptly, dressed for the street and with a sheaf of notes in one hand.

"Your Grace, how can I tell you how badly I feel?" she said.

"Trounce, I'm sorry to tell you this. I've got to do without you."

"Expected it," said the secretary. "I've spent the last two days making everything shipshape. I could walk out this minute if you wanted to be rid of me as soon as that."

"No, Trounce, there's no hurry at all."

"I'm not expecting any quarter's notice, Your Grace."

Isabelle was in a mood to grasp at any economy, no matter how small. "Most kind of you, Trounce," she said. "I don't suppose anyone else will be kind to me. I'm anticipating endless vexation and trouble." Then she made up her mind suddenly to burn a certain bridge behind her. "Trounce, please send a message to Mr. Fawkes at the law offices. Have him told that I must see him at once."

5

Although the Duchess of Outland refused to give out any statement, the newspapers made a great deal of her return. The *Packet* by some means had secured accurate information about her holdings in Carboy and Co. She had been, the paper pointed out, the largest single shareholder. In addition to the huge blocks of stock given to her by her father over the years and in his will, she had invested in the company all of what she received from the estates of her three previous husbands.

"It is conceivable," concluded the *Packet*, shrewdly, "that as a result of the failure Her Grace will be very grateful for the income she will continue to receive each year from the Waterloo Tontine."

A daily periodical of less importance spoke of what had happened as another demonstration of what it called Outland bad luck. No matter how much property the heads of that ill-fated line might bring into the family by rich marriages it had a curious knack of dissolving in their hands. "It looked," stated this paper, "as though the present duke had been more successful than any of his predecessors in marrying the beautiful though aging daughter of Samuel Carboy with the seemingly unlimited wealth she commanded. But fate, acting along entirely new lines, has struck again."

One of the more staid of the metropolitan dailies concluded a brief report of the return of the Duke and Duchess of Outland, and the difficulties they would face, with a brief dispatch from a small place in the North Riding called Brendan Wood.

Today a prominent citizen of this town passed away in the person of Mr. Oliver Bertram Strike. His prominence was not due to any special achievements, for the late Mr. Strike was of a quiet turn of mind and for many years, since retiring from a modest post with a textile concern, had occupied himself solely with his garden. It was due entirely to his being one of the final survivors in the last, and greatest, of all tontines. Mr. Strike's death, at the age of eighty-one, leaves only three holders of Tontine shares to compete for the honor of being the one to possess finally the full income. The three remaining in the race are:

Her Grace, the Duchess of Outland.

Sir Julian Grace, of Three Gables, Windsor.

Miss Helen Groody of the Old Rectory, Little Shallow, Berkshire.

# BOOK VI

## *The Good Idea Leads to Much Excitement and Some Violence*

1

THE TRIP to London to see his grandson start off on the long journey through the East with his newly acquired wife had taxed the strength of Sir Julian Grace. He leaned back in his comfortable deep chair in the Fox wing and closed his eyes at intervals, and the voices of his visitors sounded far away. It was safe enough for him to disregard them in this way. A committee from the church had descended upon him unexpectedly, a bevy of ladies organized to meet the pressing need for repairs to the organ. The good ladies already had his guinea, and now they were relaxing over the scones and tea which Mrs. Hiddledy had provided. Their talk flowed on without any help from him at all and with little consciousness of his presence.

There was a fine crackling fire in the chimney piece and the warmth was most grateful to his feet and shins. Whenever his eyes opened they rested on the sample of his son's work which, through the kindness of Sue Beltrade, was hanging over the mantel. It was vastly comforting to look at it, and think of Timothy laying on the paint with sure and skillful strokes, with perhaps his beautiful auburn-haired Kit sitting at one side and watching as he worked. How he would have enjoyed being with that gallant pair!

Mrs. Hiddledy came to him and said in a discreet whisper, "Sir, there's someone to see you."

Sir Julian sat up in his chair. He took a quick survey of the room but saw no addition to the ranks of the busy ladies. "Where, Mrs. Hiddledy?"

"Outside, sir. He saw as how the leddies was here and decided not to come in, sir."

Sir Julian struggled stiffly to his feet, bowed in an absent-minded way in the general direction of the chattering group and left the room.

"Now who is it?" he asked in a lowered voice.

"The rector, sir, as is off on his holidays tomorrow, sir. And he deserves a rest, sir, if any human being ever did."

When Julian walked out into the grounds he saw no sign at all of the Rev. Gilbert Tranmer. Then a hand was raised from behind the stables and he turned his steps in that direction. The rector was ensconced in a narrow space, largely filled with shrubs, between the stables and the vine-covered wall bounding the cricket grounds. He was holding his bicycle by the handle-bars.

"What's all the mystery, Gib?" asked Sir Julian, very much puzzled.

"I've come to say good-by, my very dear fellow," answered the rector.

"But why didn't you come in? A committee is in there, the one to raise funds for the organ."

"Dear old friend, it was because the dear ladies were in the house that I decided to stay out. You see, there was a gathering at the Rectory last evening to say farewell to me. I felt that—that there was no need to go over it all again."

The Rev. Gilbert Tranmer was a stoutish man of advanced middle age with a large round face, free of all hirsute embellishment save for a small clump protruding from a mole on his chin. He looked a little on the order of a Chinese god, a good-natured one, for there was generally a twinkle in his eyes. With the monotonous passing of the years he had become a little untidy about his clothes. Certainly his coat was a shade on the rusty side, and the less said of his gaiters the better.

"Sir Julian," went on the rector, "I am going to take you into my confidence. I've worked with committees for over forty years. The real reason I'm taking this six weeks' vacation in Italy is because I feel the need of a rest from the dear ladies." He gave his head a reminiscent shake, thinking back no doubt over the long succession of busy committees who had labored with him. "Last evening, Sir Julian, I got out a pencil and started to do some figuring. I reached the conclusion that, starting with the birth of the Established Church in the days of bluff King Harry, there have been at least seventy million active committee members, not counting churchwardens. From England alone, mark you. They're all up there in heaven now, and what a lot of convening and voting and electing and organizing of garden parties and so forth is going on!" He sighed. "It's an astonishing figure, isn't it? But there, I've provided the recording angels—all ex-committee members without a doubt!—with a really startling item for the books today." He looked closely at Julian. "My dear old friend, you are not looking well. You are tired. You are the one who should be off for Italy tomorrow, from the look of you."

"I'm just back from London and I found the journey a little fatiguing, I confess. A delightful occasion took me to the city. The marriage of my grandson and the departure of the very happy couple for the East."

"Of course! I made a note to ask you about it but it—it went right out of my mind. I believe I was told it would be your first glimpse of the bride."

Sir Julian's face lighted up. "Yes. And I liked her immensely. The fact that she came from Jamaica was enough to incline me in her favor."

"Of course, of course. I was a very young fellow, living with an aunt near Swindon, when you came here first. I remember your wife so well. I fell violently in love with her and worshiped her—from a distance, of course."

"Will you believe it, Gib, that Julian's young wife is much like my Winifred? She's very much like her in appearance and she even has some of the same traits. Ah, yes, it's going to be a happy marriage. I have no doubts on that score."

"And an heiress, I believe? We must never be so concerned with the purely personal side of things as to overlook that little point, eh, Julian?"

"I suppose you could say she's an heiress. Her mother was an American who married a Jamaican. There's quite a bit of money on both sides but there are six children to divide it. Still, little Sue shouldn't do badly. She's accustomed to colored servants, of course, and took a great fancy to old Noel. If I hadn't put my foot down, I believe they would have spirited him out from under my very eyes and taken him with them. But Noel is getting quite feeble and he wouldn't be able to stand a trip as rigorous as the one they're planning. I had to protect the old fellow."

"I'm glad you did!" declared the rector. "Do you know that Noel is my very best listener in church? Indeed yes. I look around when I am in the midst of my discourse and I see polite inattention everywhere. Then my eye travels to our good Noel, sitting so humbly back there in the last pew. I can see in his eye an intense interest in every word I'm saying. It does me a world of good. I assure you, old friend, that Noel is an inspiration to me. I don't believe I should be able to deliver a good discourse at all if I didn't have him to—to spur me on, as it were."

From the front of the house came the sound of many feminine voices engaged in speeding their own departure. A look of concern took possession of the broad expanse of Tranmerial face. The rector opened the side gate and threw one leg over the bar. "The dear creatures must *not* see me," he said. "That would be nothing short of catastrophic under the circumstances. Farewell, old friend, and may God be with you always." He stopped, one leg on the ground, and felt hurriedly through his pockets. A letter was produced which he handed to Julian. "Met the mailman on the road coming down and he asked me to deliver this to you. He was late and in a bit of a hurry. He's always late, that man!"

Having attained the shelter of the road where arching chestnuts lent concealment, the clergyman pedaled rather frantically away.

Sir Julian saw the good ladies off at the main gate, engaging them in more conversation than he had intended in the interests of the fat gaitered legs making their retreat up the road. It was not until they had gone, all eight of them crowded into two dogcarts, that he opened the letter.

He read it through with an expression which hinted at deep concern and fear. Then he hurried into the house.

"Mrs. Hiddledy!" he cried. "Where are you? I have very bad news."

The plump housekeeper, who had been with him for many years and expected to remain many more, came hurrying out from the pantry where she had collected the tea things.

"Lor', sir! What is wrong?"

"My son is very ill. This is a letter from a doctor who's attending him in London." Sir Julian crumpled up the note and put it away in a pocket. "I knew, Mrs. Hiddledy, that he had lost some of his money in the Carboy smash but now it seems all his inheritance had been put into Carboy shares. Every shilling that he possessed! The blow has prostrated him. The doctor says he's a very sick young man and advises me to get there at once."

"Not tonight, sir!" said the housekeeper firmly. "It would be snuffing of yourself, sir, it would indeed. Why, sir, it's getting dark already. If you has any thoughts of starting out now, go to the looking glass, I beg you. You're as white as a ghost."

Julian gave the problem some thought. "I'm afraid you're right. I do feel a bit overdone. But I won't have a moment's peace, thinking of the poor lad so sick and with all that trouble on his mind."

"You'll feel better, sir, when you've waded into the broiled trout I'll have for your breakfast, with some crisp bacon to go along with it. Get to bed early and you'll waken up as fresh as a blessed babby, sir."

Before making up his mind definitely, Sir Julian went down to the kitchen in search of Noel. The old servant, whose head now resembled nothing so much as a ball of cotton batting, was sitting before the open fire. His back was stooped and his legs seemed no more than skin and bones.

"Noel, I'm driving to London tomorrow to bring Mr. Titus back."

The old man sat up at once. "Yes, suh. Us have to make early start, suh."

"Noel," said Sir Julian with deep regret, "you're not strong enough to do this. I'll get young Abel from the village. Now don't look offended, old friend. You've done more than your share of long drives and now the young people can take it over. I hope you'll get up in time to see me off. Mrs. Hiddledy will have some broiled trout for you, if you do."

"Yes, suh." Noel's voice was sorrowful. "Old dogs got to take any bones young dogs doan't want."

"You'll always be top dog around here, Noel, but it's your turn to take it easy."

2

They started out at eight o'clock the next morning, Sir Julian with cushions and blankets inside, and Abel, a lad from nearby, with two topcoats on the box.

They had not gone more than half a mile when Dr. Henry Sandilands overtook them on horseback, his manner bristling with indignation.

"What in thunderation are you driving out for at this time of day?" he demanded of Sir Julian, glaring into the carriage.

"I'm going to London——"

"To London again? Absurd! Confound it, man, don't you know you're on the ribs"—a racing term, much in use to designate poor health—"and shouldn't stir out of the house? Good gad, Sir Julian, do you want to kill yourself?"

"I must go," declared Julian. He was feeling weary already and had a longing for the comfort of the chimney piece and his deep chair in the Fox wing. "My son, who lost all his inheritance in the Carboy failure—every shilling of it, I'm sorry to inform you—is seriously ill. Keep this between us but he has no money in the house and is getting poor attention. I'm on my way to bring him home."

"You seem to think, you quixotic idiot, that you'll cure his illness by getting most damned infernally ill yourself." When the mounted physician saw that he was having no influence on his old friend he took another tack. "Haven't you any local pride, then? Let me tell you this, the people of the district are proud of having one of the final contenders in the Tontine living in their midst. They go around throwing out their silly chests, saying, 'Just look what a healthy part of England this is, and what fine, rugged specimens we all are.' They're sure you are going to outlive the others and some of them are betting money on it. Well, if you go this way, you won't be in the running long; and that will be a blow to the whole Thameside country." Then he gave a disgusted grunt. "Who am I to be talking this way? Here I am, so sick that I can see two of you sitting in that carriage, and I'm starting off in this raw weather to lance an abscess in the jaw of a fat old woman who has never paid me a shilling in the whole of her life."

It was in the darkness of early evening that they reached London. Titus lived in a good neighborhood, his flat backing on a long and narrow piece of open land. This made it possible to look through the rear windows into the gardens of a row of fashionable houses with slate roofs and high chimneys and an extravagant tendency to light up from basement to garret as soon as dark fell.

This form of illumination did not apply on the side where Titus had his diggings. The upper halls were so dark that it was difficult to read the cards and Julian had to strike several matches before reaching the right door.

The flat was locked and the knuckles of Sir Julian brought no response although he thought he could hear a voice calling from inside.

"There must be a key somewhere about," he said finally.

He turned up a corner of the rug and there it was. He found himself in a dark flat and heard a querulous voice asking, "Who is it? Who is it?"

"Titus!" said Sir Julian, crossing a large sitting room and pausing in the door of the bedroom. "It's your father. My poor boy, I'm afraid you've been having a pretty bad time of it."

When he managed to get a lamp lighted and carried it to the bedside, it was apparent that the once dashing Thwaites heir had indeed been sick. He was thin and much of the high color had been washed out of his cheeks. His red hair was in a touseled mop from much tossing and turning.

"Now, my boy," said Sir Julian, seating himself by the side of the bed, "I've come to see that you get well quickly. And then I'm going to take you home to Three Gables."

Titus began to shed tears through sheer weakness. "I'll be glad to go back," he said. "I always liked it there. It will be a relief to go, Pater. I've found that city life doesn't suit me. I haven't made any friends here."

"It will be a good thing all around, my boy. You see, I'm all alone. Julian has been married and has gone on a long trip through the Far East. It may be two years before he gets back. And I'm a pretty old party and I get lonesome."

Titus sighed, and it seemed to his father that it carried a note of relief.

There was a return of anxiety in his voice, however, when he spoke again. "Pater, I've been a great fool. I was so convinced that I didn't need advice about investing my money. I liked the fat dividends from the Carboy shares, and I said to myself, 'If it's good enough for some of my money, why not for all of it?' So I came a cropper. Yes, I caught a complete zig."

"A zig? Isn't that a racing term? Titus, were you gambling on the horses?"

"Yes, Pater. I might as well tell you everything. I was betting on the horses—and getting well scrubbed every time."

There was a moment of silence. "Well, my boy, don't talk any more. We mustn't exhaust your strength, you know."

Sir Julian rose to his feet. "I will go out and do some foraging," he said. "Just lie still while I'm gone, my boy. And remember this, I'm going to look after you, and you'll be on your feet in no time at all. And as for the future, I'll do something about that too."

"I haven't any prospects, Pater," said Titus in a weak voice. "I guess you'll have to change your will after all."

"I think it will be only right and fair to do it now."


Sir Julian had slept on a couch which was hard and lumpy and he wakened in the morning to find his head heavy and his bones aching. It took an effort to throw off the covers and sit up.

He could hardly believe his eyes when he glanced about him. He seemed to be surrounded by drums. They were hanging on the walls and even from the ceiling, they were piled up in corners and they perched on the tops of tables. There were army kettledrums and large bass drums from Turkey, and elongated specimens used in parts of France, as well as tambourines and Grecian dulcimers and many strange instruments from the dark continent of Africa, the steppes of Asia, and the wilds of South America. Some of them carried cards. Julian, stepping warily over the cold floor, lifted one card and saw that the inscription read: "Carried by drummer boy Ewan Fitch through three years of the Peninsular War. Fitch was killed by cannon ball at Albuera." A card on a very old type of drum read, "Found on field of Bosworth, close to body of Richard III."

He walked to the door of the bedroom and looked in. Titus was awake, and it was apparent that the resilience of youth had been at work. His eyes had lost their haggard look and a trace of color, slight but unmistakable, showed in his cheeks.

"You're better, my boy. I can see an improvement already."

"Yes, Pater. I think I *am* a little better. Have you been admiring my drums?"

"Well, I've been looking at them. What's all this about? Are you a musician? I haven't seen so many of them at one time in all my life."

"It's been my hobby. I've been collecting them since I came into my money. Had to pay a pretty penny for some of them. My collection is close to being the best in all England."

"I suspect," said his father, "that it's rather valuable."

"Rather! I've been intending to sell it since I lost my money. Now that you're here, perhaps we can do something about it."

"An excellent idea, Titus. You'll need money now more than drums."

Titus sat up with the intention of reaching a drawer in the occasional table beside his bed. His strength was not equal to it, however, and he sank back on the pillow, breathing hard.

"There's an address on a card in the drawer. An agent who would come on the hop, skip and jump if he knew I thought of selling. Will you look for it? Yes, that's it, I think."

Sir Julian read out from the card he had found: "Sylvester Frame, Antique Instruments. Is that your man?"

"Yes. His place is not far from here. Send over a note, inviting him to call."

At three o'clock a squat individual in a light green coat and buff trousers put in an appearance. "I'm Sylvester Frame. Sir Julian Grace? I had your note. Glad to get it. Your son's collection is a fair one. Not good, mind you. Nothing very rare in it."

"You lie, you oily scoundrel!" cried Titus from his bed in the other room.

The dealer looked startled. "Your son's voice, I think. Why doesn't he come out?"

"My son has been ill, Mr. Frame. He asked me to get in touch with you and discuss the matter of his collection. He's leaving town and may find it necessary to let some of this go."

The dealer began to walk about the room, eying the drums which filled it with quick and wary eyes. "H'm, a Mashonaland tom-tom. I've seen other specimens. Better ones, I think. Well, well, a sacrificial drum from the Mayan country. Now I wonder how he got that?" After a quick turn he came back and faced Sir Julian. "Does your son want to deal with me?"

"He's not strong enough to get up yet. I'll represent him."

The dealer named a figure. "For the lot, Sir Julian. It's generous. I'm taking into account that he's been sick. Don't want to take advantage of a sick man."

"Robber!" cried Titus from the bedroom. "You'll have to triple that figure."

"Ha ha!" The dealer indulged in a grating laugh. "We'll never get together. Good day, sir."

Sir Julian nodded and led the way to the door. "Sorry to have bothered you, Mr. Frame."

The dealer did not take a step across the threshold. "Wait! Isn't this being hasty? You can't expect to post the blue on an assortment like this, you know. Still. I may have been a little low in my estimate. Suppose I say twenty quid more."

"Say five hundred quid more and I'll still call you a robber!" shouted the sick youth.

Mr. Frame raised his eyebrows. "Pretty bouncy for an invalid. Don't like all this calling of names. Good day, Sir Julian."

"Good day, Mr. Frame."

The dealer got as far as the door again. He paused there and, after a moment, turned.

"Fifty quid above the first offer."

"Five hundred," shouted Titus.

"Do you call that playing the gummy? Come, come. Sixty-five!"

"Four hundred and seventy-five."

The parties to the transaction called back and forth in voices which became harder and more acrimonious as the gap diminished slowly between them. Left out of it, Sir Julian smiled at the vehemence with which his son countered venom with venom, sharpness with equal sharpness. "I suppose," he thought, "this is the Thwaites coming out in him."

At four hundred from Titus, the dealer paused, gulped painfully and said in a strained voice, "Done!"

"Guineas!" cried Titus from his sickbed. "Not pounds, mind you. Guineas!"

The dealer raised both arms in the air and called on his gods and his ancestors to witness that his life's blood was being drained off, drop by drop. "Guineas it is," he said.


3


A day had been set for the return to Three Gables and the afternoon before it looked as though the positions had been reversed and that it would be Titus taking his father home. The drive to London had drained Sir Julian's vitality to such an extent that he had not recovered from it. He rose in the mornings looking pale and tired and by nightfall had barely enough strength to crawl to his uncomfortable couch. It did not seem to occur to Titus, who was up and about and displaying quite a little of what the drum dealer had called bounce, to install his ailing father in his own bed.

Late in the afternoon a ring came at the door. Titus was slowly sorting out his clothes (he had enough of a wardrobe for any three young men about town) and did not stir, so his father put down the glass of port he had decided to take instead of tea, and went slowly to the door. A distinguished-looking man with handsome side whiskers and a spruce bowler hat was standing outside.

"I think you must be Sir Julian Grace," said the visitor. "My card, sir."

The card bore a name only, Guy Chasson Batson. The visitor launched into an explanation. "It's considered advisable for me to use my name only, because of the nature of my work. If you'll turn the card, sir, you'll find that I've penciled something on the back."

Sir Julian turned the card and found the words in a really Spencerian hand: "From the Home Office. On a confidential matter."

"Come in, Mr. Batson," he said, stepping aside to admit the Home Office man.

They took seats in the living room, which was now relieved of the drums and was, as a result, quite charming and comfortable. Mr. Batson placed his hat and cane and gloves on the floor beside him and adjusted the black pearl in his cravat. He was most fastidiously attired.

"Sir Julian," he said, "this Tontine, in which you have such a considerable interest—ha ha! a very important interest, I should say—is causing us some concern. You see, the large tontines have been out of fashion for a long time. If the man who started this one, Hark Chaffery—a most remarkable fellow, Sir Julian, even if he did come to such a bad end. Well, if he hadn't thought of playing on the sympathy and patriotism aroused by the victory at Waterloo to raise funds for the veterans, this one would have turned out much the same as all the others which began at about the same time and which didn't stir up much interest. But here we have it and we—I'm speaking for the government now, sir—and we're rather disturbed over what the consequences may be. I may tell you in confidence, sir, that Mr. Gladstone is very much upset and wonders if there's any way of putting a stop to it. There isn't, I assure you. It's been running over sixty years and this is no time to question its legality. The Home Office is convinced there's no law to give us an excuse for stepping in." The well-manicured hand of the visitor was raised in a sly gesture. "On the other hand, sir, we are aware that Mr. D'Israeli is both interested and amused. I know for a fact, sir, that good old Dizzy has laid a wager on the result."

"Indeed. May I ask which of us he prefers?"

"Come now, Sir Julian, he's been an acquaintance and admirer of the Duchess of Outland for many years. I've heard it said that he repeated what the ladies are saying about her—that she's indestructible. His guinea is on her."

"May I take it, then, that the purpose of your visit, Mr. Batson, is to assure me that the Tontine will go on?"

"No, Sir Julian. It's something rather more important." Mr. Batson drew a scented handkerchief from a pocket and gave both hands a perfunctory rub. "You see, now that it's down to three of you, the public interest is going to mount fast. When betting starts, you can't keep it out of the hands of the odds-players. You may know that books have already been opened on the outcome. It's to keeping matters in hand that we must apply ourselves. I've just come from a strange interview with Mike and his chief aide, a greasy little dealer in figures known as Herb Biler."

"Mike?" said Sir Julian, frowning in a puzzled way. "And who is Mike?"

"I'm afraid, Sir Julian, you've been living a secluded life. Mike is a great figure in London. Here in the city we take a real interest in our masters of crime, the modern equivalent of the Upright Men of the past. I remember myself the days of Silk Finucane and Common Jack. Since then there's been Ghost Molineux and Chiseling Charlie. Now we have Mike. His name is a long foreign one, full of consonants, and it's been cut down to plain Mike. He concentrates on controlling the books."

"Then I assume that Mike is the one who'll be taking an unhealthy interest in the race in which I'm lucky enough, or unfortunate enough, to be involved."

Mr. Batson nodded his well-groomed head. "Exactly, Sir Julian. I was ushered in to see him in a grubby hole behind a tobacconist's shop which he was using as his headquarters. He keeps on the move, it seems, to make things hard for the police if they should desire his presence. No doubt he's already ensconced in some other moldy little dive as a result of my visit. When I told him who I was and the purpose of my visit, he said that the Tontine was a small matter compared with the daily traffic in betting on horses and that he wasn't bothering about it himself. Well, he turned me over to Mr. Herb Biler. Herb said: 'Gorbasteme, it's true that the Tontine is small tawties and that's why it's been turned over to me, governor.'"

Sir Julian was beginning to feel both interested and amused now. "I wish I'd been with you, Mr. Batson. Mike and Herb Biler sound like charming people."

"I endeavored to throw some fear of consequences into Herb. I made it clear that if any form of violence developed we would hold him responsible, and Mike as well." The visitor nodded emphatically. "And now I want to lay a warning on your doorstep, Sir Julian. You must take no chances. You see, if the books begin to fatten up, and I'm quite certain they're going to, feelings will run high. You are probably wondering what might happen. Let me give you one illustration. A big bookmaker finds that most of the fancy are putting their money down on Sir Julian Grace and that a relatively small amount is being bet on the ladies in the case. He stands to lose what they call 'a wad of feathers' if you outlive them. It's conceivable that he might not be above protecting his interests by having you put out of the way."

Sir Julian was startled. "I don't believe they would go that far, Mr. Batson."

"That," declared the visitor emphatically, "is where you could make a very great mistake. It's been done before, I assure you."

"But I won't be the favorite, I'm sure."

"Ha!" said the Home Office man triumphantly. "That's where you are wrong to begin with. At the moment you *are* the favorite. The duchess would have been a long way out in front but that sickness she had took the edge off things. What do you suppose Herb Biler said to me? 'Good old Issy is beginning to bust out at the seams.' Of course no one thinks much of the chances of poor Miss Groody, all crippled up with her rheumatism and ready to tear up her ticket at any minute. She's bound to be a long shot. The odds are twenty to one on her already. And on top of all this, it happened that the first reports on you were very good. This strong old man, as straight as a poker and going out for a long walk every day and still handsome enough to make the widows and spinsters wonder about him, looked very much best of the three. Well, the early money has been going down on you, Sir Julian." The visitor paused. "If they saw you today they might change their minds. You don't look at all well, sir. I'm sorry to say it but I think you'll have to take better care of yourself. I advise a period of rest."

"What is the warning you came to deliver?"

Mr. Batson raised two fingers in the air. "First, the matter of food. Be sure that all your provisions come from a reliable source. Be certain you can depend on your cook. And allow no one else in the kitchen."

Julian smiled. "I would like to see anyone try to bribe Mrs. Hiddledy into putting poison in my food."

"Trust no one completely," urged Mr. Batson earnestly. "If your cook has a weak streak anywhere, they'll find it. And now for the second point. Have a watch kept in the neighborhood. If any strangers come around, particularly if they can't explain why they've come, send word to me at once, sir."

"What steps would you take then?"

"Guards will be sent down at once, sir. They'll see to it that no strangers ever set foot on the premises."

Mr. Batson retrieved his belongings from the floor and stood up. "I think that is all, Sir Julian. You must not hesitate to call on us and to report the smallest thing which seems suspicious to you."

"It has been most kind of you to take so much interest in me, sir. I appreciate your desire to protect me from the dangers of my position."

The Home Office man turned on his way to the door and smiled broadly. "Don't you find it all rather exciting?"

But the Tontine participant could not oblige him with any degree of enthusiasm. "No, Mr. Batson. I'm afraid that I don't."

## CHAPTER TWO

### 1

The weather had turned raw and there was a wind blowing in from the west when they started out next morning. Long before they were clear of the city they found themselves driving in the teeth of a sleet storm. They made slow progress as a result.

Sir Julian was well wrapped up in blankets and shawls but the wind got in through the front of the carriage, where Abel sat shivering in his two greatcoats, and there seemed to be a perpetual draft playing about the ears of the old man. He had been subject to colds for many years and, as they always left him miserable and weak, he knew that the homeward trip would do him no good. "I hope," he said to himself, "that we can get there before I catch pneumonia."

It never occurred to him to think that he should have stayed at home in the first place. His son had needed him and he had never questioned his duty under the circumstances. Titus himself seemed quite unaware of the risk his father had taken. Fully recovered from his indisposition, he had muffled himself up in a handsome tan greatcoat and seemed not to be minding the weather at all. He was, in fact, in a cheerful mood and disposed to talk.

"Pater," he said, "I've been doing some thinking. About my prospects."

Sir Julian did not realize he was being addressed, the shawl being wrapped so securely about his ears.

"Great Scott, Pater, how can I talk to you if you get yourself buried away like that! I was saying I would like to be looking around for some way to make money. What's more, there's no time to lose about it. I'll have to walk my chalks right away."

His father loosened the shawl over his mouth sufficiently to say: "Quite right, my boy. You'll have to find some suitable occupation. Have you anything in mind?"

"Well, yes. I've been thinking about the old firm. Grace and Carboy. Why not buy me a partnership there? A strictly family affair, eh?"

The suggestion disturbed Sir Julian, knowing how little sympathy there had been between his son and his grandson. He turned an anxious eye in his son's direction and was amazed to see how comfortable he looked. Titus had regained his high color and he seemed actually to be enjoying the trip. "Young bones!" thought the old man with a trace of envy.

"Well, my boy," he said finally, "I don't know about that. Frankly I have doubts. Julian and young Allie Carboy seem to be getting along very well together and the business is doing nicely. I'm not at all sure they would care to have a third partner, upsetting the even balance of their holdings."

"It's a young concern," said Titus confidently. "I'll lay you ten to one they could do with a bit of capital."

"But what would you like to do in the business? I mean, what part of the work would you care to undertake?"

"Well, Pater, I'm not sure I would want to take off my coat and wade in. I thought of it, rather, as an investment. I could be a silent partner. No chance for friction that way."

"No!" said his father sharply. "There was a silent partner once in Grace and Carboy. And what happened? The silent partner, my father, was thrown out. If you had an interest in the concern and did nothing else to earn your share of the profits, the same thing would happen again. There would be trouble and the partnership would drift on the rocks."

Titus did not seem to take this too much amiss. He gestured carelessly. "Well, it seemed like a good idea. You see, Pater, I've never had any experience at working. I probably wouldn't be good at it and I'm not sure I want to try my hand. But I must have some way of building up an income for myself. Even though you've promised me to change your will, you won't be able to leave me enough so I can live on it. It's a problem and we'll have to square up to it. Three Gables has been practically stolen from me and I won't even have a roof over my head if anything happens to you."

"My boy," said Sir Julian after considerable thought, "I was quite impressed at the way you stood up to that dealer in London. That Mr. Frame. You seem to have a gift for bargaining. How about getting into that kind of thing?"

"Low," said Titus promptly. "It wouldn't do, Pater. It's all right to chaffer with them when they're trying to take a bite out of your ear. But as a way of spending my life? No! It's low, very low. In fact, Pater, it's downright vulgar."

His father had no further ideas to put forward so the conversation ended there.

Because of the unfavorable conditions, they were lucky to get as far as Windsor by nightfall. They put up at an old inn almost under the walls of the castle. It was undoubtedly a charming place in the right seasons but it was not well adapted to weather such as this. The room to which Sir Julian was shown was large and dark and drafty. The bed, a great solemn four-poster, looked as though it had not been slept in for months and had not been aired once in that time.

"Where will you have your supper, sir?" asked the porter.

Titus had vanished almost as soon as they arrived, with a chipper "I think I'll have a bite later in front of that fine fire in the common room." The old man had no appetite, however, and the only thing he desired was sleep.

"I'm going straight to bed," he said to the porter. "Bring me a brandy and hot water. A long one. And warming pans, if you please. I'll probably need more covers on the bed."

"Right, sir," said the porter cheerfully.

"And put some life in the fire. It's just succeeding in not going out. This room is like a morgue."

"Right, sir. Good fire it is, sir."

The lusty application of a poker and the addition of a few coals seemed likely to extend the life of the fire but did little to add to the comfort of the room. Sir Julian felt thoroughly chilled when he crawled between the covers in the gloomy bed. The brandy helped a little. It succeeded, at any rate, in sending him to sleep.

He woke in the morning with a feeling that he would never be able to summon the energy to stir from bed. The weather had turned to a sharper cold during the night and the windows were frosted over. They admitted only the faintest light. The fire, dead many hours before, was a mass of uninspiring ashes.

It is doubtful if he would have made the effort to get up at all if the prospect of reaching home had not appealed to him so strongly. As his efforts to win the attention of the servants by pulling at the bell beside the bed had produced no results whatever, he finally emerged from between the covers, trembling in every muscle. The cold in the room seemed to seize him with icy fingers and he came close to the point of tears in his frantic efforts to don his clothes. Finally, however, he was dressed and he managed somehow to navigate the drafty halls and the almost endless twistings and turnings of the stairs to reach the dining room on the ground floor.

Here he found Titus sitting down to a solid breakfast of broiled kidneys on toast and a mutton chop. The young man looked up when his father came to the table and fumbled with chilled fingers at the back of a chair.

"Gad, Pater, you don't look much like a lifter this morning," said Titus, a lifter being a horse much given to rearing and plunging and violent kicking. "We had better get out of here as quickly as we can. If you can manage your packing as soon as you've got outside of a bite of food, we'll be off at once."

"I don't feel like eating," said his father, shuddering at the sight of the food. "And as for the packing, I'm afraid you'll have to manage that for me, my boy."

Titus shoved back his plate and faced his father with an air of determination. "Now see here, Pater," he said, "I know that I've come a cropper and that I'm going home like the prodigal son. But I've no idea of letting myself be used as a valet because of it, you know."

"Titus, Titus!" said the old man. "I may never ask you to do another thing for me. But this morning I don't seem to have any strength. We'll leave the things here, if that is how you feel about it. I can't face those stairs again."

"Well, I believe in having things out, clear and aboveboard. If my feeling about this is understood and duly accepted, I'll see what I can do about tossing your stuff into a bag."

He grumbled some, nevertheless, as he climbed the stairs and he took considerable time over the packing. As a result it was noon when they got away. The wind was worse than on the previous day and it had grown dark when they reached Three Gables.

For the first time in the history of the Grace occupancy it seemed to hold out no welcome. There were two windows in the front in which light showed but the Fox wing was dark.

"This is strange," said Sir Julian. "Mrs. Hiddledy has never done anything like this before. I sent word we were coming and I was sure she would have the place blazing with light and that there would be fine fires in all the rooms, not to mention a good dinner ready and waiting."

Titus got out of the carriage and stared at the house. "Not much of a home-coming, I must say," he declared. "No trace of the fatted calf about this, Pater."

2

Three men were standing in the partial gloom of the large sitting room when they entered. They were in a row and at first they neither moved nor spoke, and their eyes were fixed on the newcomers with what seemed an uncanny intentness.

There was an ominous note about the presence of these strangers which was not to be explained in any casual way. What were they doing in the house, so alien and aloof and watchful?

Then one of the trio took a step forward. "Sir Julian Grace?" he asked. "Yes. Who are you?"

"I am Dr. Colfax. The coroner. There has been a death here and I came to investigate."

Julian glanced with a feeling of dread at the other two men, wondering what duties had brought them to the house. Had there been troubles in his absence about which he had not heard?

"Who—who is dead?" he asked, although he had no doubt as to what the answer would be.

"The colored servant, sir."

Julian's heart sank at this confirmation of his fears. Noel was dead! They had been together so long that he knew life could never be quite the same again. The old man had always been beside him, filled with readiness to aid, cheerful, hopeful, amusing. Added to his natural feeling of grief, there was a desperate uneasiness in his mind as to what there had been in the manner of his passing to bring the coroner and these other men, neither of whom was at all prepossessing.

"Poor Noel!" he said in a voice which threatened to break. "This is sad news, Dr. Colfax. He has been with me almost all of my life. He was a member of the family. I dread to ask this but—was there any violence?"

"I think not. He was alone in the place, so no one can do more than guess yet as to how or when it happened. A boy from the neighborhood noticed late this afternoon that there was no smoke rising from any of the chimneys and he decided to look around. He happened to look in one of the kitchen windows and there was your servant lying on the floor. There was no fire in the chimney. All fires in the house, in fact, had been out for at least a day."

Sir Julian's mind was filled with regrets and self-incriminations. Noel had been left alone in the house and had come to his end in this sudden and perhaps tragic way, with no one to lend him a hand.

"You say he was alone. Where was my housekeeper?"

"She was called away. There was a note she had left for you on that round table in the corner. I opened it in my investigation and I've kept it to present at the inquest, if it is deemed necessary to have one. I'm beginning to feel sure it won't be necessary." The coroner opened his wallet and produced a sheet of paper which he smoothed out with one thumb. "Here it is. You will see she had word that a daughter in Basingstoke was expecting a child, her sixth, and needed assistance. Mrs. Hiddledy seems to have anticipated a hard time for the daughter. She expects to be away for some time."

A new and disquieting thought had taken possession of Sir Julian. He asked, "Was there food in the house?"

"Plenty, Sir Julian. The housekeeper had baked a good supply before leaving. There was a plate on the table in the kitchen which he had used. The mice have been at it since and have strewn it all over the place."

"Then what was the cause of his sudden death?"

The medical man gestured to indicate that it was still a guess. "Old age, perhaps. Or failure of the heart. I would say to look at him that he had attained to ripe years for one of his race. I'll know better when I've had a chance to examine the body thoroughly."

Julian sank into a chair with a deep sigh. "I'm sure the poor old man was very unhappy at being alone in the house. He was always afraid of the dark. I suppose he stayed down in the kitchen for the comfort of the fire and because he didn't dare go upstairs alone to his room. Surely the housekeeper could have done something about it before she left! Someone from the neighborhood would have been willing to stay in the house with him. But she was always impatient with the old fellow."

"Your solicitude does you credit," said the coroner. "Well, we mustn't stay longer than is necessary. This is Dr. Cass Hoard, Sir Julian." One of the other men bowed. He was young and prematurely bald and had an owl-like look about him generally. "He's down from London to see after Dr. Sandilands' patients until our good friend can get on his feet again. He's a very sick man himself. And this, sir," indicating the other, who was quite enormous, with huge shoulders on which his rather small head seemed entirely inadequate, "is Lew Stain, the undertaker. I instructed him to come and see about the body."

"I'm acquainted with Sir Julian," said the undertaker. "I have served him in several capacities. Never before in this."

The blow he had suffered had deprived the head of the Grace family of the small store of strength he had retained after the ordeal of the journey home. He looked about for Titus but his son had been utilizing the services of Abel to get all the clothing moved to a room upstairs. Their footsteps could be heard in the room above. "I must get to bed at once," he thought. Rising slowly to his feet, he said to the watching trio, "I have been using the wing here on the ground floor and I think I must retire at once."

The coroner gave him a quick appraising glance. "You don't look well, sir," he said.

"No, I am not well. Not well at all."

He started to walk toward the entrance of the Fox wing but his strength was not equal to the task. He staggered and instinctively put out a hand for support. The coroner hurried to his assistance, taking one of his arms while the owlish young doctor took the other.

"We will need a lamp," said Julian.

He could hear the lumbering Mr. Stain moving clumsily about in efforts to find and light a lamp. Having succeeded finally, the undertaker followed on their heels into the sitting room of the wing, the light in his uplifted arm making it possible for them to see that a fire was laid in the chimney piece. Sir Julian sighed with an intense relief. He was home at last. True, it was a sad home-coming and it would be a long time before he would be able to take any satisfaction in life with Noel no longer beside him; but the familiarity of everything about the room, with the portrait of the Austrian officer looking down like an old friend from above the chimney, brought him a warm sense of security and relief.

"If someone will be so good as to touch a match to the fire," he said.

"Thank you, Dr. Hoard. I think I shall stay right here for a time before going to bed. With my chair pulled up close to the fire, I shall be very comfortable. Ah, it is not easy to travel when you are old!"

He looked up from the ease of his friendly chair and saw all three pairs of eyes fixed on him with curiosity and speculation. It made him feel uneasy. "They are like vultures," he thought. "They look ready to pick my bones." The coroner might be a little officious but otherwise he seemed quite decent. The same could not be said for the others. The undertaker's face was heavy and predatory and the young doctor was as cold as a fish straight from the water. The intentness of their gaze made him feel uneasy.

"Do you think Dr. Hoard should remain with you?" asked the coroner. "I'm sure he would be glad to do so."

"No, no," said Sir Julian hastily. "There's nothing wrong with me that won't pass away when I have rested."

He heard them leave the room and in a few minutes there was a sound of turning wheels on the drive. The unwelcome company had gone. For several minutes he indulged in the luxury of perfect restfulness, with the warmth of the crackling fire about him.

His mind turned then to Noel but his thoughts had ceased to be filled with regret. Mostly they had to do with the earliest days and particularly of his arrival in Jamaica when the colored lad assigned to him had smiled so pleasantly and said: "I'se Noel. I'se yu' boy." He remembered the mornings when Noel would be at his door as soon as the sun came up over the mountains and while the air was still fresh and cool, asking about his wants for breakfast, telling him whatever news there was and full of suggestions for the day ahead of them. Noel had been his boy nearly ever since and he had never been mean or ugly of mood.

Then his thoughts went much farther afield. Noel had been dead for at least twenty-four hours and there had been plenty of time for him to reach the home in the skies where all people as good as he had been were destined to go. Was it not certain that those who reached heaven watched hopefully for the ones who were to follow? Then Winifred most certainly had already welcomed the new arrival. She had seen him coming, with his head bent and his footsteps slow, stumbling a little even in his course through the clouds (would he say "I'se Noel" when he reached the Gate, confident that he would be admitted?), and she had held out her white hands to help him. It was a wonderful thought.

He began to smile. "Freddie, Freddie!" he thought. "I've heard that time means nothing where you are. That it is hard to keep track of worldly things because of it. Well, you have seen Noel and you have realized how old he has become. I am older than he is and you know that very soon I will be following up the same path. You must be waiting for me, my dear, and holding out your hands to help me along too. It won't be long now. Not—not very long at all."

3

Two hours later Mr. Lew Stain returned, puffing on a long black cigar. He pounded once on the back door, then turned the knob and walked in. He waited for a few seconds only and then called, "Hallo!"

Titus came down the front stairs in response. He had changed into an elaborately frogged lounging jacket and was wearing a fez with a long gold tassel.

"Oh, it's you," he said. "What brings you back?"

"Business," replied the jack-of-all-trades. "About the body and what's to be done in the way of a funeral. And how much is to be spent."

"I suppose you'll have to speak to my father. He's sound asleep in there in front of the fire. I went in about an hour ago to see if he wanted to join me in a bite. He didn't stir, so I decided he was more interested in sleep than in food."

Mr. Stain rolled the cigar around in his mouth. "He should be going to his bed anyway," he said. "Let's wake him up and have a word with him first."

Titus walked into the Fox wing. There was a long moment of silence and then the air was split by a piercing cry of alarm. The son of the house came running out into the sitting room, his cheeks white, his eyes distended with fear.

"He's dead!" he cried. "I touched him and he was cold. He must have been dead when I was in before. Oh, what am I going to do now? What am I going to do?" When the undertaker made no response but simply stared at him and puffed out clouds of smoke, the distraught Titus seized him by the arm. "Don't you hear me? He's dead, I'm telling you. He's gone and died, and left me alone to face things. There is a smile on his face as though he was glad."

"Well," commented Lew Stain, "he was an old man and it had to be expected almost any time. But it's bad that he couldn't hang on a little longer and collect more of the Tontine money. I grant you that."

A few lumbering steps took him into the wing. He leaned over the recumbent figure in front of the fire for a time, and then straightened up.

"You're right," he said. "He's dead. He went easy, I can tell you that. But it *is* bad about the Tontine."

An additional reason for grief suddenly occurred to Titus. He let out a screech of rage and despair. "He died without changing his will! He promised me. We talked it over. It was all settled. And here he's dead before he could do anything about it!" His eyes were burning furiously in his pale face. "And he's smiling. He's smiling about it!"

"Sit down, young fellow," said the undertaker. He took a chair himself and gave the cigar another reflective roll. "Sit down, I tell you. And stop all this noise. This may not be the end of everything, you know. I've got an idea in my mind. I want to turn it over." Apparently he kept the idea and the cigar working in concert in the turning-over process, for the weed between his heavy lips was never still. "I get ideas about everything, where money's concerned. When the time comes that I've got no ideas, I'll know that I'm due to be going myself. And there won't be a smile on *my* face when that happens."

"I don't know what you're talking about."

Lew Stain gave his head a satisfied nod. "It can be done," he said. "There's risk, of course, but the stakes are big. Certainly they're big enough to make it worth while. It will depend on you, young fellow. Whether you have the right stuff in you. Whether you're good strong ale or just plain foot rot. I don't know. I haven't made up my mind about you."

Titus had sunk back into a chair and was resting his head on his hands. If he had heard what his companion was saying, it had made no impression on him. Grief was playing no part, however, in his attitude. He was giving no thought to anything but the effect this catastrophe would have on himself. And he was angry. His cheeks had become red again, a fiery red.

"Do you want to gamble with me, young fellow?" asked the undertaker finally.

Titus looked up. "Gamble with you? What do you mean?"

"Just what I said. A gamble for a good stake—a jingling, fine big stake. All that Tontine money. We can scoop it in, after all. At least it will be evens in the field. But we'll have to work together, you know. I'll need you and you'll need me. What about it?"

"I don't know what you mean!" cried Titus in a tone of intense exasperation. "How can we get any of the Tontine money now that he's dead?"

"You know he's dead. I know it. But no one else needs to."

Comprehension of the plan finally dawned in the distracted mind of the son of the house. "You mean—that we'll pretend he isn't dead at all?"

"Exactly."

"But how can it be done?" Titus remained silent for a short spell, thinking the idea over. Then he burst out in decided negation. "I think you must be out of your mind. There are a dozen reasons why it can't be done."

"Name 'em."

"Well, the body."

"I'll take care of that. My business, you know."

"Do you mean you'll take it away and dispose of it?"

"That's what I mean."

"But supposing you were seen taking it from the house?"

"That's easy, that one. I'm burying the colored man. If anyone sees me moving this one, I tell 'em it's *his* body."

Something in the nature of agreement with the plan was beginning to sprout in the completely selfish and callous son. "But how could we explain his absence?"

Lew Stain took the cigar from his mouth, looked at what was left of it and lighted another. "Simple," he said, puffing hard to get it started. "He won't be absent. He'll be here. Walking about. Being seen every now and then. At a distance, of course."

"You mean that we—that we could get a substitute for him? Someone to play the part?"

"That's it, young fellow. I have connections in London. I know three men offhand who might be able to do it. They would be willing to try, I'm sure."

The new eagerness in the face of Titus subsided. He shook his head. "It's impossible. Where could we get an actor good enough to deceive all my father's friends? They'll be around here thick." Then a new thought took possession of him. He stopped and pondered. When he turned again in the direction of Lew Stain, his eyes were filled with a newly aroused excitement. "There was a man from the Home Office in to see the Pater before we left London. He said every precaution would have to be taken, because efforts might be made to have him killed. Well, couldn't it be given out that my father has had to go into seclusion? That, because of this danger he's in, he can't have anyone allowed on the premises? Sometimes he could take a turn in the garden and if anyone came along he could wave at them."

The jack-of-all-trades removed the cigar from his mouth in the excitement this suggestion had aroused. "That settles it!" he exclaimed. "No one is allowed in and we keep a guard around the place all the time. A strong fellow who meets all visitors and says no to them."

"But wait a minute!" cried Titus. "We can't have two. A guard as well as someone to play *him*."

"One and the same. Don't you see? They're never on view together. When the guard is about, the sick man is in his bedroom. When your father makes his brief appearances in the garden, the guard is nowhere in sight. And, what's more, I know the man to do it. Oh, this is good! This is the cheese that drops the skittles! There's one man in London capable of doing this, and he's a bosom friend of mine."

"Who is he?"

"A gentleman, to begin with. There was some little trouble. An attempt to forge a will, I'm inclined to think. At any rate, he was thrown out and took to the stage to make a living. He had a fine voice but somehow there was always more trouble and in time he drifted into what seemed easier ways of getting along. In other words, he became a crook. His name is Selwyn Geist and he's called by his intimates 'Sell'—a rather descriptive name."

Titus was looking doubtful. "But does he look enough like my father to be mistaken for him?"

"That's quite simple. He's tall, has an ample pair of shoulders and a wide brow. There are differences, of course, but make-up can take care of that. A few lines on the face and a good wig. Besides, no one is going to get a close look at him. Not when he's playing your father. When he's playing the guard, he'll make up with a mustache, perhaps, or even a beard."

"Why are you sure he'll be willing to try it? And how can you get him down in time?"

"He'll arrive tomorrow night. I'll see to that. I'll go up myself and bring him back."

Suddenly Titus threw his arms in the air. "I knew it," he said. "I was sure there would be a reason why it wouldn't work. The housekeeper. She'll be coming back in a few days. And your Mr. Selwyn Geist won't be a good enough actor to fool her."

The organizer of the scheme was not at all disturbed. "Naturally we can't have that woman around. You must sit down at once and write her a letter in behalf of your father. Make it clear to her that he is bursting with indignation because she left the old colored man alone. Pitch it strong. Tell her he doesn't want to see her again, that her clothes will be sent on to her and her pay for the next quarter. That will settle her."

"But we'll need someone to run the house for us. I have no intention of turning housekeeper and cook."

Lew Stain had already worked out the solution to this problem. "My partner's wife will take it on. Mary Lowfoot. She was a cook before she went out to Bermuda and met Lowfoot there. The Lowfoots are always ready to earn some extra money."

As the plan thus kept taking on more definite form with each point raised, Titus could not help feeling like a fox caught in a trap. He wanted to reap the full benefit of the plan but he could not avoid the conclusion that a fatal error would develop somewhere in the calculations.

"Are we going to take this Mrs. Lowfoot into our confidence? It can't be done any other way; and that means her husband will be included. The secret will be shared by too many."

Lew Stain nodded. "They'll have to be admitted as partners. Junior partners. You and I will split the Tontine money evenly after we've provided for the others. A thousand pounds for Sell Geist. That's more money than he's ever had his mauleys on before but there won't be any use offering him less. Not when he knows what we are gunning for. I think half of that will satisfy the Lowfoot family. When is the next yearly payment?"

"In six weeks."

"Then let's start the wheels turning. You write that letter at once and then help me load my wagon out there."

Titus still found himself in a state of indecision. What would be his fate if the plan failed? He might escape, of course. But if he were caught it would mean a long term in prison. "Still, it seems," he said to himself, "as if everything has been contrived to help us. Julian away in the East. The housekeeper away. Noel dead and the undertaker here. This actor available to play the part. That call from the Home Office man to serve as an explanation. It all fits in. And how else could I get my hands on so much money?"

"There's another thing for you to do," said the versatile undertaker. "Practice up on signing your father's name."

### CHAPTER THREE

1

Titus Grace did not sleep well that night. He could not get out of his ears the sound of the crunching wheels of Lew Stain's wagon on the gravel of the drive as he went away with the body of Julian Grace. He could not escape from a prophetic vision of police officers coming to take him into custody, charged with nearly every crime on the calendar from fraud to murder. It was not remorse which prompted these thoughts. It was nothing but a selfish fear. Having committed himself to this violent course, he was doomed to live in dread and apprehension for the safety of his own skin.

He fell asleep about three o'clock and did not waken until a full hour after his usual time. Sounds reached him from the kitchen. Someone was down there and quite busily engaged at various tasks. He could hear the tap, tap of heels and a clatter of saucepans. A most delicious aroma was finding its way up the stairs and into his bedroom. He got up, donned a dressing gown and went down to investigate.

A woman was in the kitchen, bending over the stove. She was quite plump and, when she turned around to stare at him, he saw that she had a square and rather plain face.

"Who are you?" he asked.

"I'm Lowfoot, sir," answered the woman. "Lew Stain brought me. He said it had been arranged, sir."

Titus felt his spirits sink. Then it was not just a bad dream, it had actually happened. His father was dead and Lew Stain had taken the body away. A strange scheme of deception was about to begin, in which he, Titus, would be involved and which might end—where might it end? In prison, perhaps, even on the gallows. It might also end, he hurriedly assured himself, with his pockets filled with gold and a big bank account in his name.

"I come from these parts," volunteered the woman. "Most knows me as Mary Tindy. I got married in Bermuda. To Lowfoot. He has the brickyard."

"Your Lew Stain doesn't lose any time," said Titus.

"No, sir. Not Lew Stain. He's a fast 'un, he is. Lowfoot allus says, 'Wait and see.' Lew Stain says, 'Pitch in.'"

She had prepared exactly the kind of breakfast he liked. There was oatmeal with cream, a slice of ham, a boiled egg, toast and marmalade. Titus laid his fears aside for the time being and began to eat with the appetite of youth aided by convalescence.

When he had finished, Mrs. Lowfoot paused by the table to say: "I knew your father, sir. Oh, what a fine, handsome man he was! I saw him in Bermuda. At Mrs. Beltrade's. Everyone on the island was saying he was going to marry her. But he didn't. He came back and got hisself made a knight. But if he'd stayed and married that lovely, rich Mrs. Beltrade, he'd be alive to-day."

Titus had heard no more than a whisper of his father's visit to Bermuda and he began to question the woman. The information he received left him with cause for speculation. It seemed clear that this lady, who was so attractive and so rich, had been in love with Julian Grace. Someday he might be able to turn this to account. If he got into trouble she might come to his assistance. If he had to cut and run for it, as a result of Stain's machinations, he might go to the island and throw himself on her mercy.

The day passed slowly. Lew Stain had gone to London and a careful study of the timetables made it clear that he could not possibly get back until the middle of the evening. In any event it would not do for him to arrive in daylight with the stranger he expected to bring with him. But the hours hung heavily on the hands of young Mr. Grace and his mind was filled continuously with the liveliest fears.

Titus spent the day looking over his father's effects. He went through the house from top to bottom, examining every article of clothing and every personal possession, mentally setting a value on each. "Whatever isn't left in the will to someone will come to me," he said to himself, his jaw setting in a tight line. "I'll jolly well see to that!"

He left his father's desk until the very last. It was after his lunch that he came around to this most important phase of the search. "It's too much to hope that he's kept his will with him," he thought, seating himself before the old mahogany escritoire in the Fox wing where Julian Grace had kept all his papers. "It'll be in the lawyer's office. That fellow Bade will have it. But it's just possible he kept a copy here."

A minute search, which included much measuring of the depth of drawers and knocking of knuckles on partitions in the hope of discovering secret compartments, confirmed his first impression. The will was not there, nor was there a copy of it. Nevertheless, he examined and read every letter, every bill, every scrap of paper, with the utmost concentration, his head bent to his task, his eyes sharpened to pin points by the avidity of his mood. One item which he perused with the most complete absorption was a letter from Sue Beltrade. He read it through twice, in fact, and then gave his head a satisfied nod. "She was in love with him," was the conclusion he reached. "It sticks out all over. All he had to do was twiddle a finger and she'd have come a-running. Well, *this* is something to remember. I'll have a chance someday to turn it to advantage."

He was on the point of closing down the lid of the desk when a slip of writing paper on which his father had begun a letter caught his attention for the first time. It had been caught between some account sheets and so had eluded his eye. With an eager nod, he saw that it was addressed to Jonathan Bade.

Since our last talk about the will [his father had written], I have given the matter considerable thought. I realize that my son Titus is a rich man. From some information which reached me the other day, unsought and unsolicited, I know that his yearly income is in excess of double the full amount I would have to leave if I should die now. I am convinced now we were right in the conclusion we reached with reference to his share. It cannot be as large as I had hoped to make it, although it is my intention to increase it if I am permitted to live long enough to enlarge my capital to any considerable degree. I am hopeful of balancing things up later.

The letter had not been finished. Titus read it a second time with a scowl on his face. "Well!" he said aloud. "It was just as I expected. He's fobbed me off with some miserable pittance. That's paternal affection for you! That's how my own father considered *my* interests!"

He happened to turn the partly covered sheet and saw that the other side contained some hastily inked figures. They were notes, obviously, which his father had jotted down while his mind wrestled with the problem of the disposal of his worldly goods.

500

100 (to be paid on a weekly basis)

25

It did not take long for the sharp mind of the son to work out the meaning of these figures. The small item, which undoubtedly stood for twenty-five pounds, was what his father was leaving the housekeeper. "He can be pretty damned generous and free and easy with his money when he wants to be!" thought the angry son. The hundred was a sum to be set aside for the maintenance of Noel if that faithful servant should survive his master. The five hundred was what he, Titus, was to receive!

He slammed down the lid of the desk. His eyes had drawn close together, his color had risen to a burning red.

"This is a pretty thing!" he said to himself. "This shows me where I stood. That bastard grandson was to have everything and I was to get about as much as he would have left to an old family butler or for the care of a superannuated saddle horse! Now that I know, I can go into *this* with an easy conscience."

It was eleven o'clock that night when the sound of wheels on the drive announced the arrival of someone. Titus sighed with relief when he heard Stain's voice saying, "Here we are, Sell." The back door opened and the jack-of-all-trades came in, followed by a tall man in a long black cloak lined with white and a high silk hat. "He refused to dress like a human being," said Stain to Titus. "But I wasn't with him on the train, so I guess it did us no harm."

A sense of dismay had taken possession of Titus at his first glimpse of the stranger. "He won't do!" he exclaimed. "I tell you he doesn't look any more like my father than you do."

"Hold your horses, young fellow," cautioned the undertaker. "Just wait a minute, will you, before you go blowing off like that. This is Mr. Selwyn Geist, a very great actor in his day. And this impatient young man, Sell, is Mr. Titus Grace, who will be a partner in our little affair."

The stranger said, "How do you do, Mr. Grace," in a deep and melodious voice, holding out a hand to be shaken.

"Hold on!" cried Stain. "Don't take it, Grace. He has a grip like a python. He'll mash your fingers to pulp."

Titus hurriedly withdrew his outstretched hand and the actor laughed, a rich cachinnation. "I'm descended from a line of Teutonic knights," he said, "and I've inherited some of their strength. I'm afraid I was always a little rough on the stage when the play called for wrestling or fisticuffs or laying on with a property sword. The swords I've broken in my day! And the heads, too."

The undertaker was showing signs of relaxing now that he had his man safely delivered at the scene of the deception which was to be played. He brought out a cigar, bit off the end and spat it unerringly at the fire. A quick flick of his wrist and it was lighted.

"Now, Sell," he remarked, puffing contentedly, "we must allay the young man's fears. He don't think you look like his father. We must have a demonstration." To Titus he said, "You must have a picture of the old man somewhere about the house."

Titus produced a photograph which had been an especially good one. The actor reached out a large paw and studied the picture carefully. Finally he gave a nod of satisfaction. "Fine-looking, your father," he remarked. "Still, it won't be too hard. I brought my make-up kit with me. Where can I go?" He pointed in the direction of the Fox wing. "In there?"

"Yes, that will do," said Titus.

"I'll help myself to a suit of his clothes," said the actor.

Selwyn Geist retired to the wing and closed the door after him. He must have been a rapid make-up because in less than a quarter of an hour the door opened and he stepped out.

Titus gave vent to a gasp of dread. He thought he saw his father standing there!

"What did I tell you?" said Stain, emitting a cloud of smoke in his delight. "Won't this be a story to tell your grandchildren, eh? You ought to see him made up for *King Lear*. Or *Richard III*."

The actor had donned a wig and had marked a few lines on his face, and the result was a complete transformation. He looked urbane and even kind, and very much indeed like the deceased man. Seen at closer range, the illusion vanished to some extent but at a distance it was remarkable. It was clear that he could play the part.

"What about the voice?" asked Stain anxiously.

"He speaks more slowly than my father did," said Titus. "More like an actor on a stage."

"Try it the other way, Sell. Just as though you were talking in a room."

The actor tried many modulations of voice and finally reached a way of speaking which promised to pass muster. After half an hour of this practice, the instigator of the plot got to his feet with a satisfied nod of the head. "He'll swing it on," he said. "We'll all collect our dibs. Get to bed now, Sell. You've had a long day. And mind you, no scammering."

"Never a drop," said the actor, nodding his leonine head.

The next day passed without anything happening to disturb the conspirators. Selwyn Geist proved to be an interesting companion. He liked to talk and he entertained Titus with stories, first of his stage days and later of experiences since he had taken to living by his wits. Those in the second category proved particularly fascinating to the listening novice. Titus laughed heartily over the success Geist had achieved in a daring scheme to sell a church, St. Martin's in the Fields, to a visiting tinman to be converted into a huge draper shop, and with equal gusto over an almost successful effort to convince a young squire that Dusky Dorcas was an heiress from Barbados. "That's nothing," Geist would say airily at the end of each anecdote. "Just listen to this one."

In the afternoon the actor made himself up with a fair mustache and a reddish wig and went out to patrol the grounds. His presence there attracted a certain amount of attention. A delivery wagon arrived with supplies and Mrs. Lowfoot called to Titus from the kitchen, "Here's a young 'un, sir, as wants to ask a question."

Titus went back and was greeted by the greengrocer's boy with "I say, sir, 'oo's the cove soodling ar'und in ta garden?"

Glad of the chance to start the explanation into general circulation, Titus told of the visit paid to his father in London by Mr. Batson and of the warning the latter had given.

"You picked a strong 'un to guard 'im," said the delivery boy. "'E'll keep strangers off the place, 'e will. And 'ow's Sir Jul'an, sir?"

"Not well, not well at all," declared Titus. "The trip to London tired him out. He won't be able to see anyone for quite a time, I'm afraid."

The face of the driver clouded over. "Not going to scratch out on us, is 'e?" he asked anxiously. "I've got me ten bob up on 'im, you know."

"You needn't be afraid," Titus assured him. "My father will be up and around soon."

"Is 'e going to post the blue for us?"

"He expects to. He's the favorite in the race, you know."

The imposture might be said, therefore, to have started in a most auspicious way. Not a ripple of suspicion seemed to have stirred in the Thames-side country. The dignified guard patrolled the grounds at regular intervals, swinging a heavy cane and keeping a watchful eye on anyone who came within sighting distance of the house.

After a fortnight a passing neighbor was rewarded with a glimpse of Sir Julian himself, muffled up in his tweed greatcoat and walking slowly up and down in front of the house. He was leaning on the arm of his son.

"It's jolly good to see you again, Sir Julian!" shouted the neighbor.

The old man responded with a friendly salute of his cane. Titus added a verbal reassurance. "He'll soon be himself again."

"Glad to hear it. My five-pound note feels a bit safer."

The news went over the countryside like wildfire that the favorite in the Tontine was on his feet again. He was no longer the favorite on the books in London, however. Reports of his illness had reached Herb Biler and others of the same stripe, and his price had dropped. The Duchess of Outland was now the favorite.

2

One morning there came a knock at the door which from the inside seemed to smack of authority. The deception had continued, with apparent success, for a month but this had not instilled any degree of confidence in the partners to it; they still trembled inwardly at the sound of an alien step on the drive and of knuckles applied to the portals.

Mrs. Lowfoot answered the summons and found on the front stone steps a small man in a pea jacket, a variety of overcoat worn mostly by sailors but also by landsmen of penurious mold, because its abbreviated length made it most economical. In this case, it reached no more than an inch or so below the wearer's waist, thus exposing to view a pair of extremely slender legs in very tight gray trousers.

"Ma'am," said the man in the pea jacket, "my name is Glossop. William Wordsworth Glossop. I desire to see Sir Julian Grace."

"He sees no one," answered Mary Tindy shortly. "If ye'd inquired at any of the pubs, they'd told ye that. He's not in good health."

"He'll see me, ma'am," declared the visitor. "I assure you that he'll see me."

Without further parley the small man put out an arm to prevent the closing of the door in his face and brushed by the angry woman into the entrance hall. He took off his gloves and stuffed them into a pocket of his coat. Then he looked about him with open interest.

"And now, ma'am," he said, "I'll tell you why Sir Julian Grace will see me. I come from the offices of the Waterloo Tontine. I am the inspector, ma'am. Do I need to say anything more?"

Mrs. Lowfoot knew what this meant. It meant at the best a critical situation, at its worst exposure of the deception. The little man was standing in a self-satisfied attitude which seemed to say: I dare them to prove to me, William Wordsworth Glossop, that all is right and proper and aboveboard in this household.

"If you please, sir," she said in faltering tones, although Lew Stain had coached her in what she should say and do when this situation arose, "I'll —I'll speak to him and see if he *will* see you."

"Do so, ma'am, do so."

Sometimes, quite frequently, alas, good fortune seems to sit on the shoulder of iniquity and to speed the execution of plans of nefarious design. Despite the woman's obvious trepidation, the visit of the inspector could not have been better planned from the standpoint of the conspirators. For no reason whatever, Selwyn Geist had decided on rising that he would step at once into his disguise as the master of Three Gables. He had donned a baggy suit of clothes in which Sir Julian had been most happy on his daily rambles. He had put on the wig with the greatest care, he had applied the necessary make-up to his face. And, while the colloquy was carried on in the hall, he was sitting in a deep chair from which he could look down over the sloping gardens and see the river. Sir Julian's knobby stick was in one hand and his one ring, a handsome piece of sardonyx, was on one finger.

Without further words, Mr. Glossop strode into the room where the actor sat. Perceiving a head over the back of the chair, the inspector crossed in that direction.

"Ah, Sir Julian, I am glad to see that I don't intrude on you at a bad time. You are up, in good health and spirits, I trust, and ready to receive visitors. At least, sir, I assume that you are ready to receive an inspector from the offices of the Waterloo Tontine."

If Selwyn Geist felt any contraction of the muscles of the heart at this announcement, he did not show it. He turned and employed his most successful imitation of the deceased knight, which consisted of an urbane smile and a nod of the head.

"Sit down, sir. Sit down. What is your name, sir?"

The visitor told him. Glossop began then to say, "I have never called on you before——"

Geist realized at once that this might be a trap. If he agreed that they had never met, the inspector might cry out triumphantly, "But we have, sir; and so I perceive that you, sir, are a fraud." He decided to step with the greatest care.

"Haven't we, Mr. Glossop? My memory is not what it used to be but it does seem to me, sir, that both your name and your face are familiar."

"Sir," declared the inspector in positive terms, "I have never done myself the honor before. In fact, Sir Julian, the officials of the Tontine have never felt it necessary. You have been so much in the public eye, in a sense. The calls you made at your club and less frequently at the Admiralty were sufficient to make any concern about you unnecessary. But now, Sir Julian, things are different."

"Indeed, yes, Mr. Glossop. Quite different."

"You have retired to the quiet life of your lovely home. And the sums involved are so large, so very large, that the utmost caution must be observed. You appreciate our position, I trust?"

"Of course, of course." Geist was at his histrionic best, genial, smiling, anxious to assist in everything. Underneath he was seething with hostility. This kind of man annoyed him excessively. He was saying to himself: "This simpleton, this meticulous little nonentity, this ill-bred booby coming into the home of a gentleman with his questions and putting his pipestem legs into a chair!"

"When did you come back from Chile, Sir Julian?"

At last, a question designed as a trap. The actor felt an instant need for caution. "My dear Mr. Glossop," he said, "I'm not sure that I shall be able to fix the date. When you reach my age, you know, things begin to desert you. Dates, most especially. But I think we'll be able to arrive somewhere near it. I was taken off the active naval list immediately after Waterloo and soon after that I was on my way to join Thomas Cochrane in the fight for South American freedom. I went first to Jamaica and stayed there quite a time—ah, sir, I must tell you that story before you leave. It was in Jamaica, you know, that I met my wife. She lived with her parents on the fabulous Ballard plantation." He was now Sir Julian Grace to the life. His face had lighted up, his lips were parted in a heartfelt smile. Years seemed to have lifted from his slightly bowed shoulders. "You know, Mr. Glossop, if you asked me what I was doing a week ago at some specific hour, I wouldn't have the faintest idea about it. Life has become such a matter of small detail that my mind refuses to retain much of it. But ask me of the campaigns of Cochrane, ask me about the time I spent on the Golden Isle, and I will pour out a story, sir, complete in every detail."

He proceeded to talk about the victories Cochrane had won (having read about them on Lew Stain's specific demand) and went from there to his subsequent courtship of Winifred Ballard. The little inspector sat rigidly in his chair and listened with the deepest attention. He was thinking: "I shall have a story for my friends. How I heard all this from Sir Julian's own lips."

It was as fine a performance as Selwyn Geist had ever put on for the benefit of an audience. At the finish William Wordsworth Glossop rose slowly to his feet. He bowed to the old man in the deep chair.

"I shall have the honor and pleasure of calling on you once a year, Sir Julian," he said. "It will always be a short time before the annual payment is due. I trust, sir, that there will be many such calls to make." And then, quite suddenly, remembering no doubt the essentials of his work, he pointed a finger at the bent figure and hurled a question at him: "How much did you receive from us last year, sir?"

Geist was prepared for this question. He laughed. "You can't catch me there, sir. I remember the exact amount because—well, Mr. Glossop, this has always been an important matter to me, being on half pay. I received, sir, seven thousand eight hundred and ninety-one pounds, ten shillings and sixpence."

"That is exactly what you received, sir. But tell me this, if you please. Did you say in your report to the Admiralty on the transporting of the dry dock to Bermuda that the admiral in charge had called it 'a clumsy old trollop'?"

Again luck was perching on the shoulder blade of criminal intent. Stain had procured a copy of the report and had insisted that the actor read it from beginning to end.

Geist wrinkled up his forehead in deep thought. Finally he said: "No, sir. I didn't so report the admiral's remark. His exact words were, if I recall my statement accurately, to the effect that on one occasion she behaved 'like a filthy old scow.'"

"Forgive me, Sir Julian," exclaimed the inspector penitently. "I had to ask these questions. It was demanded of me at the office. You see, I had never set eyes on you; and we have to be very, very sure."

When the visitor had departed, the actor walked to the bedroom in the Fox wing which he was using and looked at himself in the mirror. The work he had done on his face was beginning to show. "Five minutes more of that little monkey's prying," he said to himself, "and the show would have been over. He'd have twigged I was made up for the part."

3

The bent figure which had hobbled rather than walked into the bedroom was Sir Julian Grace. It was Selwyn Geist who emerged a few minutes later. A new Selwyn Geist. His eyes seemed to have drawn together and they were sparkling with animosity. A side of his character which he had managed to keep hidden before had taken full possession of him. He pounded on the floor with his cane.

"Here, Mrs. Lowfoot, Mary Tindy, whatever your name is! Come a-running, woman! And where is that little whippersnapper, that cringing, unnatural son who sold his own dead father's body? I want you both."

They came in response to this demand. Mrs. Lowfoot looked thoroughly frightened. Titus was apprehensive, watchful, but angry as well.

"Now then. I want you to know that I carried it off. Damme, I was superb! I sent him away without a doubt in his Peeping Tom of a mind. No actor on the stage, no diplomat in any chancellery in Europe ever equaled it." He looked at Mrs. Lowfoot. "And now I need a drink. I know you've been told I'm not to have it but you two swipes had better produce a bottle of gin without any more urging or—well, I'll come to that later."

Stain's warning had been urgent enough but he had not been explicit on one point; he had neglected to explain that the actor was a periodic drunkard and that sooner or later the urge would take control of him.

"I'm going to get drunk," Geist told them. "As drunk as a broken wheelbarrow. You, young fellow, you have the keys you took off the body. Go down to the cellar and bring me up a full bottle of gin."

Titus was frightened but he knew the danger of obedience. "No, Mr. Geist. You're not to have anything to drink. We've had our orders on that."

They had all experienced something of the strength in the actor's hands but Titus was now due to realize the full power. Geist reached out suddenly with both arms and took him by the shoulders. Titus felt what a lamb must feel when the steel claws of an eagle are sunk into its frame. He could not move. All he could do was to hang inertly in that crushing grip and pray to be released.

"Go down and get me that bottle," ordered the actor.

Titus obeyed. It took him a long time because he had to try many keys before he found the right one. Geist clutched the bottle from his hands when he finally appeared.

"Now," he said, "I like company when I'm in my cups. Good, gay company. Can you manage to be gay, either of you? You had better try. I don't like dull, frightened faces around me. I'm a blithe spirit myself. You, Mary Tindy, my ducky, would you like to join me in doing justice to the ambrosial contents of this bottle?"

"No, sir. Not me. I'm United Saints of Shiloh. I've never took a drop of the stuff."

The actor turned to Titus. "What about you?"

"I never drink. And someone here will have to remain sober."

"Then sit down at this table with me." Geist poured out a small glass of the opaque liquor and tossed it off without as much as a facial grimace. He then repeated the feat. A third went the way of the first two. His expression began to change, to take on an almost maniacal gaiety. Seeing that Titus had one hand on the table, he clutched slyly at his cane and then suddenly swung it in the air and brought it down on the exposed knuckles. Titus cried out in pain and sprang from his chair.

"Sit down!" said the drunkard ominously. "I switched you on the hands like a schoolteacher, did I? Watch yourself, my fine young fellow, or I'll break the cane over your back. I don't happen to like you and I would enjoy doing it."

Titus felt his hand gingerly to see if any bones had been broken. He found the pain almost unbearable. But automatically he obeyed the order. Another quick splash of gin went the way of the rest. Geist's mood began to mellow. "I like singing when I drink," he said. "You, Mary Tindy, oblige me with a song."

Too frightened to protest or disobey, she began to quaver out a hymn which was a favorite with the United Saints. Geist heard one verse through and then shut her off. "I don't want hymns. Weak, slavering pap. Did you hear what I said? Slavering pap. You," turning to Titus. "You sing something."

The first sharpness of the pain was beginning to pass. Titus pulled himself together and began on the first song that entered his mind.

> *"Johnny used to grind the coffee-mill,*
> *And he mixed up sugar with the sand.*
> *Johnny, our Johnny—"*

"Stow it!" ordered the autocrat. "I know that song and it's a silly one. Anyway it ends up with Master Johnny going to clink and that's not the kind of song for *us*. Try something else. And make it livelier."

Thus pressed, the angry but submissive Titus began on something he had heard his Thwaites relatives sing. It began:

"*I'm Yorkshire Sam, that farming man,*
   *Hurrah, hurrah, hurrah!*"

This pleased the fancy of the drunkard. "That's the ticket. That's got a swing to it. Good old Yorkshire Sam. Sing it again, and keep on singing it, Master Grace. I like it."

So Titus sang it over and over while Geist drank steadily, sometimes waving his glass in time to the music. When the bottle was better than three quarters empty, the actor got to his feet, grasping it by the neck. "I'm going to—to bed," he said thickly. "I'm going to—to take bottle with me and finish in peace. I'm going to drink my success in fooling inspector."

When the door of the wing closed with a loud crash behind him, his two unwilling companions sat for several moments in dazed silence. Mrs. Lowfoot's mouth had fallen open and she had suffered such a shock that she couldn't summon any coherent words. Titus was angry. The steady pain in his hand was a reminder of what he had been forced to endure. Finally he got to his feet.

"It would be a pleasure," he said bitterly, "to go to the police and tell the whole story. Just to see him standing in the dock at the Old Bailey."

4

When Lew Stain arrived at Three Gables and learned what had happened, he found a wooden tub in the cellar and filled it with cold water. This he carried to the Fox wing.

"Get up, you drunken fool!" he ordered.

As Selwyn Geist continued to snore stertorously, the jack-of-all-trades dragged him out of bed. Forcing the inert actor to his knees beside the tub, he proceeded to immerse his head in the cold water. The actor spluttered and struggled but the ducking continued until he was wide awake, with some, at least, of the liquor fumes released from his brain.

Geist got to his feet and began to express his opinion of Stain in a fluent and eloquent stream of profanity until suddenly the full torrent of his great voice dwindled to an insignificant trickle of words.

"I'm going to be sick!" he said, and threw himself across the bed.

Stain returned to the sitting room, motioning Titus and Mary Tindy to join him.

"This has been a narrow escape," he said, frowning. "Suppose this inspector fellow had come while he was in this state? I tell you, we can't risk exposure any longer through the weakness of this great lubbering fool. I'm going to London on the first train and I'll bring back a man who can keep Geist in order. I wish we could get rid of this drunkard but he has been seen and a change would be noticed. And he plays the part well. I judge he put on a great performance when the inspector came this morning."

"We have only his word for that," declared Titus, looking bitterly at his swollen knuckles.

"No, Mary Tindy tells me that when she saw the inspector to the door he was fairly bubbling over with praise of that wonderful man, Sir Julian Grace. It comes down to this: we'll have to keep him but we'll provide a safeguard. A man who can take him in hand when the need arises. Oh, I know, I know! You're thinking it means another in the secret and another to split off a share of the profits. But we have no choice. We're in this. We can't quit, we can't back up, all we can do is go straight ahead and meet any emergency, no matter how costly it may be." He rubbed a hand over his unshaven jaw as he gave the problem some thought. "I know the right man. If I can find him and persuade him to share our risk."

"Where," demanded Titus dubiously, "can you find a strong enough man to handle Geist?"

"Oh, the man I have in mind isn't strong. As a matter of fact, he's quite small. But I've seen him put the fear of the devil in better men than Selwyn Geist. He's a very odd and frightening fellow."

"Is he an actor too?"

"No, he isn't anything. I've never known him to do a lick of work but he's always around when action is needed. I don't even know his name. Everybody calls him Pint. Just Pint, nothing else. And that's all you need to know about him at this stage."

## CHAPTER FOUR

### 1

One of the largest auction sales the country had ever seen was being held at Beaulaw Hall, where the antique furniture gathered with such discrimination and at such great expense by the late Samuel Carboy was being sold for the benefit of his grandson's creditors. Allie Carboy had come down from London to attend, partly with the idea of reporting later to his father, partly because there were some items, one in particular, which he hoped to pick up at sufficiently low prices to suit his slim purse. He was shocked to find the fine long rooms of the Hall overrun with wary-eyed dealers and pushing, insensitive buyers. They went everywhere as though the place belonged to them. They poked into corners and opened clothes closets, they plumped themselves down heavily on eighteenth-century couches and slammed the delicate doors of Chippendale cabinets. He began to resent them before the sale began and his gorge rose as he listened to the haggling over bids and the crude comments on the wonderful things which had been secured through the impeccable judgment of Old Staddle.

He also resented the auctioneer, an excessively facetious individual named Crandell Spong. Mr. Spong had endeavored at first to run the sale on the Dutch method, which was to ask for more than an object was worth and come down gradually, the first buyer to cry, "Yes!" becoming the purchaser. The crowd had protested that this was too hard on their nerves, too chancy, too much in favor of the seller. They clamored for the old system of competitive bidding and Mr. Spong had finally given in. The auctioneer had an irritating habit of saying things like, "Yes, leddies and gent'men, this is the very chair Cast-iron Sam sat in when he put away his seven solid courses of a night," or "If you buy this footstool you'll own what Old Staddle rested his feet on as he concocted his little schemes."

The sale moved from room to room, beginning with the important apartments on the ground floor. As Allie followed the crowd, keeping well in the rear, he found himself wondering about one of the buyers, a lady of advanced years who was decidedly familiar. Finally he found himself close to her and saw after his first quick glance that she had once been a beautiful woman but had yielded to the advance of the years to the extent at least of using no cosmetics and dressing simply. Her plain silk mantle was worn although obviously expensive. Then he saw her eyes, which were dark and fine and still full of life.

"Aunt Isabelle!" he exclaimed.

She had not noticed him, for she turned abruptly on being recognized and gave him the benefit of a quick smile.

"My dear boy!" she said. "I'm so glad you came. It shows a proper interest in the background of the family even if we are seeing the final act of our downfall today." She studied him with affectionate eyes. "You're looking well, Allie. Probably the only one of us who does. I'm surprised you recognized me; no one else has so far. My years have overtaken me, Allie. I'm an old woman, and the odd thing about it is that I don't seem to care much. I can't afford to buy expensive clothes any more, so I wear whatever I like. Look at this old thing I have on! And, do you know, it's quite satisfying to the pride. I say to myself, 'I'm the Duchess of Outland and I don't have to be well dressed.' But I suppose that's the philosophy of an old woman."

Allie had been watching the play of her eyes as she talked, and he said with complete candor: "Now that I see you like this, I can tell you don't need fine feathers to be beautiful."

"How nicely spoken, Allie! Are you here to suffer at the sight of the disposal of the Carboy treasures?"

"No. There are some things I would like to pick up if I can. There's that bracket clock, Robert Burfield, 1702. I always liked the sweetness of the chimes and the fineness of the wood. And when I stayed here there was a chest-on-chest in my bedroom which I took a fancy to—a William and Mary, I think, with the quaintest design and beautifully matching wood. Do you remember? It came from a vicarage in the Cotswolds and the last vicar to

ave it pasted numbers in each drawer. The junior Carboys need a good chest
f drawers and I'm going to bid on it. Besides, I would like to have one thing
rom Beaulaw Hall to leave to my son."

"I remember the chest," said Isabelle. "It's a very good piece. I'm afraid it
ill go rather high. I had a small hope that one of the pictures which don't
o to the museum could be picked up at a bargain price, the one called
*Muscovy Wedding*. I got in two bids and then they trampled over me like a
tampede of cattle. I hoped to get it around sixty guineas but it went for
early five hundred."

"You should come and see us," ventured Allie. "My son is a great little
ellow. A Carboy to his finger tips, though there are some touches of the Irish
1 him as well. I left him with his mother at Miss Groody's and came on here
lone."

"What a sentimental idiot you've been, Allie. I read something the other
ay about your Hortense Alphonsine. She's a comtesse now and is one of the
eading political hostesses of the day."

"And is probably worrying over the first signs of a mustache," declared
llie. "I'll have you know that Mrs. Alfred Carboy, nee Groody, is entertain-
ag no one at this stage but her son; and her husband is very happy to have
t so."

The duchess had not allowed her eyes to leave his face for more than the
ccasional moments needed to keep on the move with the noisy bidders. She
ame to a stop as they reached the library doors and heard the voice of Mr.
pong beginning: "Now here, leddies and gent'men, we have a set of Surtees,
ound in honey-brown leather and in perfect condition. What am I bid for
t?"

"Allie," she said, "I've always been a selfish creature, I suppose. My affec-
ions have been bound up in myself instead of in others. I despised my
nother. I admired Papa and could get along with him. We understood each
ther, Papa and I. I didn't care much for my brother and I hated your
ather. But, you, dear boy, I've always loved. I should have had a son like
ou. It might have made a difference if I had. But even though I do love
ou I'll never come to see you and so I'll never see *your* son. Because"—she
esitated—"because I'm going to do something that will make you hate me."

"Oh, come, Aunt Isabelle," said Allie, grinning at her affectionately, "I'll
ever hate you, no matter what deviltry you may be up to. And I don't
uppose it will really be so very devilish."

"Allie," she said solemnly, "I'm going to follow a course which will make
ou despise me. I know the effect it will have and yet nothing can stop me.
won't tell you what it is. You'll find out soon enough and, when you do,
ou'll never speak to me again."

"Then why do it?" he asked, still smiling skeptically.

"I can't help myself! I don't care if it makes the whole world feel the same
ay about me. I have a debt to be collected." She leaned over and touched
is sleeve and he was surprised to see that there were tears in her eyes.

"Good-by, Allie, I won't see you again. I hope you get your chest-on-chest."
Then she turned and made her way into the library.

It became apparent to Allie Carboy early in the sale that his father's creditors were going to make a good thing of it. The bidding was sharply competitive and the prices went sky-high. He began to doubt if it would be
possible to buy the chest. After careful calculations and some discussion
with Nelly, he had decided that twenty-five pounds was the limit to which
he could go for the piece. When they reached the small bedroom which he
had occupied on first arriving in England, he found that the chest in question
was coveted by many people. The bidding started at twenty pounds. He held
on doggedly until it reached thirty-five and then, figuratively, he threw in
the towel. He could not afford a shilling more.

"To hell with it!" he said to himself. "Master Edward Daniel Carboy,
that fine little rascal and complete pauper, will have to struggle through life
without any mementos from Beaulaw Hall, the home of his immediate ancestors."

The chest-on-chest was sold for fifty-two pounds finally. Soon afterward,
Allie found his horse among the many tethered on the lawn, and started off
on the long ride to Little Shallow.

2

Allie was a little shocked when he arrived at the Old Rectory and found
Helen Groody bundled up in shawls and sitting close to the fire. She looked
thinner and much paler than he had ever seen her.

"I hoped to find you better, Aunt Helen," he said. "Is it trying on you to
have two such active people here as my wife and son?"

"Allie," she assured him, "it is going to break my heart when you have to
take little Danny away from me. What a child! Will you believe that he sat
up this afternoon? And him not more than four months old."

"Did he really?" The young father's eyes lighted up with pride. "He's a
one, that Danny Carboy. He'll be walking and talking in no time."

"It's hard to believe," she said with a glow in her eyes. "You know the
story of the pair of boy's shoes I saw in the corridor of an inn in London.
They were your father's, my boy, and they were so small that I knelt down
beside them and wept, thinking of his father and what poor prospects there
were for the boy. And now we have little Danny and he is the grandson of
*that* boy. How time flies!"

Nelly came in from the room where the object of all this praise was being
persuaded to go to sleep, and disappeared for a moment into her husband's
arms. "I'm an old married woman," she said, "but I have to confess that I
missed you. Did you get the chest-on-chest?"

He shook his head. "Damnation, no! It went for fifty-two pounds. So
we'll have to struggle along without it and the little pauper won't be able to
show it with pride to his grandchildren."

"How many times must I ask you not to use that dreadful word, Allie Carboy!" cried Nelly. "We're as good as any other generation of the Carboy family and we don't need to inherit our wealth."

A loud outcry from the next room resulted in the latest scion of the Carboy family being wheeled in. As his great-great-aunt had said, he had mastered the difficult feat of sitting up in his perambulator and it was easy to be seen that he was as proud as punch of himself. He waved his pudgy arms about and chortled loudly.

"The little nipper certainly knows his own farver," declared Allie. "How are you, Stick-in-the-mud? You get to look more all the time like old Putty Dunnett, the village ne'er-do-well."

The baby crowed delightedly at this insult and uttered a succession of sounds which caused his mother to say, "I wish I knew what he's trying to tell us."

"He's not trying to tell you anything," declared his father. "This is a conversation we're carrying on between us."

"If you know what he's saying, you might tell me what it is," said Nelly scornfully.

"Of course I know. But I'm not going to tell you. You're a woman and this is man's talk. Man to man, straight from the shoulder. In fine, virile Saxon words, fit only for masculine ears."

"He talks to me too," said the old lady almost timidly. "Not about anything special, of course."

"I saw Aunt Isabelle at the auction," volunteered Allie. "There were some things she wanted to buy but I don't think she got them."

"How was she looking?" asked his wife with more than a hint of hardness in her voice. She did not have any affection or pity for the once great Aunt Isabelle.

"Old," he answered. "Sometimes she seemed to me quite plain, if you can believe that. But sometimes I saw a trace of her former beauty clearly enough. And do you know, she seemed to me more human than she's ever been before." After a moment he added another piece of news. "I've had a letter from Julian. Mailed back from Singapore. He's getting things done, that partner of mine. He told me everything he's seen and said and accomplished. They're both well and they love the East. In a postscript he said that he didn't intend to bring home any bronze gods."

"I hear his grandfather is in bad health," said Nell soberly. "Won't it be dreadful if he dies before Julian gets back!"

The Carboy family having departed, the next morning was a quiet and rather doleful one for Helen Groody. Shortly after noon, however, there was a change for the better. The maid came in and announced that two men had arrived in "a fine carritch." One of them was a gentleman with "sich whiskers," the other—well, the less said about him the better, in the opinion of the rather prim Daphne.

"What kind of person is he?" asked Helen.

"Well, ma'am, he seems to be a ricing person." It developed that her guess was based on the fact that he was small, wore a cap, and preferred the side of his mouth for purposes of elocution.

Daphne proved to be right. The small man, cap in hand, came in alone. The gentleman with the whiskers, it appeared, had been escorted into the parlor and would remain there until his presence was requested.

"Name of Tope, m'em," said the little man. "Joe Tope, m'em."

"Yes, Mr. Tope. And what can I do for you?"

"M'em, I'll come straight to the pint. I works for Herb Biler. I scrubs and chalks mostly."

"You scrub? What are you—a special kind of footman?"

The little man seemed to be pleased by this demonstration of her ignorance on a matter of such importance. "I marks the board. When prices goes up or down, or when Herb, f'r instance, wants to give the punters some stick. Then I sponges the board and chalks in the new prices. But I works too, m'em, on the Tuntine. Herb's sent me here with a bigwig. From Orstrer."

After asking a number of puzzled questions, Helen learned that Mr. Tope's senior, Mr. Herb Biler, took a deep interest in her health. Such a deep interest, in fact, that he had secured the bigwig, who was a great surgeon from Austria, and sent him down from London to see what could be done about her rheumatic condition. All she had to do was to say the word and the bigwig would come in from the parlor, where a sense of ethics kept him in the meantime, and see what could be done.

Helen Groody could not understand this at all. Why, she asked, did this Mr.—er—Biler take an interest in her state of health? The answer she received was that she was not being given much of a play on the books. All the money seemed to be going down on the Duchess of Outland or Sir Julian Grace. Now if she could be coddled along—Mr. Tope's own expression—and turned into a skinner (a winner which had not been backed), everybody under the big mush (the bookie's headquarters) would be happy and prosperous.

"But I've seen many doctors and physicians, Mr. Tope," she protested. "Some of them have been—er—bigwigs too. I'm afraid this gentleman can do nothing for me that they didn't do."

"No harm trying him, m'em."

"But I'm afraid he'll be very expensive. They always are, Mr. Tope."

She must not give the expense of it a thought, declared Joe Tope. Everything was paid for in advance by Herb Biler, who, after all, stood to benefit most. The fee would be a "thumper" but that was Herb's lookout. "Ye've nothink to lose, m'em," concluded the amiable scrubber and chalker.

"Ah, if he could only save me from some of this dreadful pain! Well, as I have nothing to lose, you may bring him in, Mr. Tope."

"Your heart, madame," said the specialist, after completing his examination, "has been touched. So far, I am happy to tell you, the attack has been confined to the outer parts but you must realize that nothing can prevent the disease from penetrating to the heart itself. Madame, there is no cure. The penetration may be slow or it may be rapid but it is sure. All I can do is to warn you that it must be aided in every possible way. You must lighten its labors, this very vulnerable heart of yours. Do not permit them to cover you with too much bed clothing——"

"They insist," she said. "Every doctor I've ever had. It makes me so hot that I suffer. But if I say so they scowl at me. They ask if I am trying to teach *them*. They are really very angry with me. So, of course, I always give in."

The foreign specialist frowned. "Let them scowl. Let them get angry. It is your life, dear madame, that is at stake. Promise me, I beg of you, to withstand them, these so-sure-of-themselves little country doctors."

"I promise. Gladly."

"And insist as well, dear madame, when they give you an injection, that the limb is covered with medicated cotton wool. Over that, of course, the covering of oiled silk. That will relieve you of the pain. For a time at least.

"And now a final word. Your heart will behave best if you avoid all exertion. It must be put to the least possible strain. And you must keep an easy mind. Do not worry. Let your heart fill up with love if you so desire but no other emotions. Fear, annoyance, jealousy, no! I beg you to realize that any of them might mean the end."

When the doctor had made his exit, smiling and bowing to her in the most courtly way, Mr. Joe Tope came back to have a final word with her alone.

"M'em," he asked, "what did the sawbones do for you?"

"He gave me some very good advice."

"Will he have you walking about easy and sociable in a few days' time?"

She smiled. "No, Mr. Tope. That can never be. But he told me many things which will help me."

The scrubber made a gesture of disgust. "I knew it. What does a furriner understand about curing English people? I knew as he wouldn't do wonders for you. But," giving his head a mysterious nod, "I can."

"You, Mr. Tope?"

It developed that he was sure he could make her the beneficiary of a miracle. With much shaking of his head, and glancing about the room, and placing of a forefinger on his lips to enjoin caution, he explained that there was a healer who could perform the much-desired miracle. He himself had been to see this mysterious person with a brother-in-law who had been a cripple for years. The Healer had a little place high up in the Cotswolds, not more than an hour's drive away. The Healer, who looked like a heavyweight champion (Mr. Tope's description), had worked on the brother-in-law with great powerful hands and had promised that a few more treatments would effect a partial cure, at least.

"Now, m'em," he said, with more cautious glances and shakes of the head, "that's the ticket for you. He'll take the pain out of yer j'ints. Will you go and see him if I comes back to show you where?"

"This all seems very strange, Mr. Tope," said Helen, drawn to the idea in spite of an inner conviction that it would prove a hoax. "Why does he hide himself in the hills?"

"So's he don't fall foul of the law, m'em. The doct'rin' perfession 'ud have him up as a quack and h'impostor and it 'ud mean a carpet for him. Three months at the least, m'em." More nods of the head followed in an effort to impress on her the need for secrecy. "M'em," he whispered, "you should see the crutches. I counted 'em. Twenty, m'em. Left by them he had cured."

The upshot of it was that she promised to pay a visit to the secret quarters of the Healer at some time in the near future; as soon, in fact, as Mr. Tope could return to act as her guide. It would be necessary, he explained, to stay over at least one night, so she must travel in her carriage and take her maid with her.

"M'em," was the final word from the mysterious Mr. Tope, "he can cure you if anyone can. Go to him and we'll shoo you in the winner. And it'll be Joe Tope as done it, not Herb Biler and his bigwig from Orstrer. Don't ever forget that, m'em."

3

A few days after the young Carboys had returned to their little house in the west end, a van drew up at the front door and two husky men began to unload a large piece of furniture well covered up with mover's rugs. They had it at the front door when Nell answered their ring on the bell.

"Here it be, leddy," said one of them. "Not a scratch on it. A nice, ship-shape job, I calls it. Paid in advance. But, leddy, there's a *very* nice pub down the road *if* you feels these two lab'rers is worthy of their hire."

"We're not expecting anything of this kind," said Nell, looking dubiously at the tall article.

"Name's Carboy? Alfred?"

"Yes, this is the home of Mr. Alfred Carboy. But there must be some mistake."

"No mistake, leddy. Instructions ex-plicit. Where you want it?"

When the movers took off the coverings and she saw that it was a chest-on-chest, young Mrs. Carboy was sure she knew the explanation. Allie had bought it in after all and had planned to surprise her in this way. So she produced what would be needed to let them prove their worthiness of hire at the pub, and then spent some time in an almost ecstatic survey of the piece of furniture.

"What a beauty it is!" she said. "But I'll certainly have something to say to Mr. Alfred Carboy for playing a trick like this on me. In fact I'll have a great deal to say to that young gentleman."

Then she began to open the drawers and in the one labeled 3 by the meticulous clerical ex-owner she found a note which she had read before she realized it was not intended for her. It ran:

When I saw you had dropped out of the bidding, dear boy, I carried on in your behalf. I was sure you didn't notice, for all I was doing was to give my fingers a twiddle for the benefit of the auctioneer, so perhaps this will be as pleasant a surprise for you as I want it to be. Please accept this small gift from your ·

*Aunt Isabelle*

In an excess of candor the word "aunt" had been crossed through and the word "great-aunt" written beneath it.

## CHAPTER FIVE

1

The house in which the Duke and Duchess of Outland now lived, sometimes called the Cullender, was far from pretentious. Seen in daylight, and not in the dark as Sir Theobald Gardiner and his second had seen it when they arrived there the night before the duel, it was a rather lopsided structure, with sharp gables and windows of mean dimensions and doors which seemed secretive rather than welcoming. There were two things only in its favor; one, a pleasant stream of no great size which meandered through a meadow on the east side of the house and had splendid trees along the whole of its tortuous course; and, two, a clear and complete view of the White Horse.

In a short time the yearly installment of the Tontine money would arrive but this cheerful fact was failing to raise the spirits of the duchess. She walked into a small cubicle, heavy with the odor of leather, which was called the Saddle Room, where she knew she would find her husband. He was there, lolling comfortably in the wreckage of a morris chair and almost submerged in newspapers.

"Chip," she said sharply, "I've come for a final word with you."

The duke dropped the paper he had been reading and looked at this third wife, who had been so beautiful that he had wanted her all his life, and who was now showing her age as everyone else had to do in time. Isabelle had reached that stage much later than anyone else, however.

"Yes, m'dear," he said.

"You must get over this stubborn streak, Chip. About the yacht, I mean. It must be sold. I've been going over the figures and there's nothing else to be done. It would be different if one of the others dropped out. Or both. It would give us all we really need. But they persist in hanging on and so we must take that offer you got for the yacht. Twelve thousand pounds will put us right on our feet. At least it will take care of our most pressing problems and enable us, perhaps, to move out of this mean little rookery and into someplace where we can be comfortable."

"Well, m'dear, I'm all in favor of getting as far away as we can from this beastly hole. But we'll have to find some other way of paying for it. Isabelle, I won't sell the yacht."

"You must. You must, I tell you." She was on the point of tears. "Oh, Chip, why do you have to be so stubborn, so difficult? Why can't you be sensible and give in? You must, finally, you know."

"Not a bit of it," he responded cheerfully. The duke thereupon got to his feet and stood at a window looking out over the lush green lands which led to White Horse Hill. "Look at that fellow up there, Isabelle. That foolish horse has been galloping madly for centuries. He's been fairly tearing up the sod in his anxiety to be away about some horse business or other. And he never progresses by as much as an inch. That's the way we are about this matter of the yacht. We talk about it all the time and you pull one way and I pull the other. And in the end we're exactly where we were when we started. We might as well stop."

"The time has now come," declared Isabelle, "when we aren't going to stop at talking. We're going to act. Chip, I *demand* that you agree to sell the yacht. In fact I've drafted a letter to those rich Italians who want it, accepting the offer. All you have to do is sign it, and the matter will be settled once and for all."

"How very kind of you, m'dear, to want to save me all that trouble. But as it happens the matter has been settled already without any signing of letters at all. I am not going to sell. It's my yacht. I bought it with my own money——"

"Which came to you from Papa's will!" she reminded him bitterly.

"But it was my money, m'dear. The point is this. I love the yacht. I don't care a jot about leasing the Hall and the town house. We're better off without 'em. All I ask is two months of cruising each year. And I've fixed it so that's what we'll have. I've signed two leases on the yacht, my love. One for the winter, and one for the spring months. I like to be in England through April, May and June. Capital months, all of them. Yes, m'dear, I've put my signature down on both papers and we'll get enough out of it to pay all the expenses of our summer cruise. Even," he added, "if we do things up brown. And I'm all in favor of that."

Isabelle looked at him with smoldering eyes. She found it hard to believe that he had actually disregarded her wishes for the first time. It was a frustrating situation. She had worked so hard on her study of their financial position and had arrived at the conclusion that they could get along nicely if they had the money from the sale of this great white elephant. But Chip, who had never resisted her before, had actually taken the bit in his teeth and gone against her.

"Everything is wrong!" she thought. "If I were still beautiful I would be able to twist him around my fingers as I always did. But I'm an old woman now and he looks at me as though I'm a broken-down housekeeper or an ancient dependent relative. What am I going to do about things now?"

The duke came back to his chair and ensconced himself comfortably again in the midst of his newspapers. "This fellow Gladstone gives me the willi-waws," he said, falling deep into his reading.

"Chip!" exclaimed Isabelle sharply. "Have you no manners left? Don't you realize I'm still here? I want to explain that I'm expecting that lawyer today."

Chip frowned as he glanced up at her. "Do you mean that poisonous fellow who's writing you letters? I thought you were through with him."

"I thought so too. But I've had another letter, saying he intends to call on me. He's in need of money, I am sure, and he may be going to make some demands on me. I want to see him. I have some things to say to *him*."

The duke got up from his chair and walked over to her. "See here, Isa-belle, I won't have the fellow bothering you. I'll talk to him, this anarchist, this blackmailing hound! I'll send him away in a hurry, I promise you."

"No, Chip." Isabelle gave her head a decided shake. "It's very sweet and comforting that you are willing to see him in my stead. But I'm afraid I must be the one. I must find out what his purpose is. Perhaps later I'll call on you."

"It would be a great pleasure to kick him off the place, m'dear."

2

An hour or so later Alexander Fawkes stepped off the first train from London and was met by a lumbering big man in a greatcoat of the cheapest cloth who was driving a buggy behind a single horse.

"You're Fawkes?" asked the large man, peering at the arrival in a short-sighted way over a long black cigar.

"Yes, my name is Fawkes. And if you're this Mr. L. Stain, I had your letter. I'm on my way now to see the Duchess of Outland. I must see her at once but I'll get over to your office later."

"Better see me first. It's important. And rather pressing. Tell you what, I'll drive you to where she lives now and we can talk on the way. Nothing like a spin on a country road for privacy. No one listening at keyholes or watching through cracks in doors, eh? Well, what do you want to do?"

"I'll drive with you."

"I've been picking up information about you, Fawkes," said the jack-of-all-trades as soon as they were out of the station yard and benefiting from the privacy of which he had spoken. "It seemed to me we ought to get together. For our mutual benefit perhaps. Now let's see. You were a partner in Smythe, Boongrace and Curdle but you ain't any longer. I hear they got you out after the Carboy crash when they discovered you had been peddling information to the duchess. How do I know? There are other leaks in that office. I happen to know someone there very well."

Fawkes made no comment. He had been in a bad case since his connection with the law office had been severed. No other firm would consider hiring him and, since he had lost everything in the crash, he lacked the means to hang out his own shingle again. He had been living precariously since, writing briefs, even falling as low as copying. His clothes were shabby, he looked undernourished, he was becoming careless and had given himself no better than a hurried shave.

"There is a way to make a great deal of money hereabouts," said the local man after a suitable pause. "I thought you might be interested."

"I'm in need of money," said Fawkes. "I grant you that much."

"It's the Tontine. By an odd quirk of things, all three survivors are living around here. That's kind of fortunate. It draws the whole thing together, you might say. I'm for Sir Julian Grace myself. I believe he'll be the one to last it out. I'm so sure of it that I've bet heavily on him. I've taken so big a chance that I don't want to see him lose."

A small light began to flicker in the mind of the lawyer from London. He believed now that he saw the trend of his companion's thinking and could be sure of what was coming. The bitter and almost desperate look which had shown in his eyes when he stepped off the train gave way to one of alertness.

"I'd better explain what I've got in my mind. Something queer has been happening. There's a fellow named William Hust who's always called Badger Bill. He's a poacher and a thief among other things. He seems anxious to talk to the Duchess of Outland. He's been seen dodging around the place, peeking over the stone fence and sometimes even coming into the grounds. Once he tried to speak to her and she threatened to have him sent to jail. Well, he did speak to the personal maid of Her Grace. This girl, name of Dossie Smith, is pretty sharp. She can see a shilling for herself a mile off. She came to me."

"And you saw the poacher."

"Finding it interesting, eh? No, I didn't see the poacher. I saw him hanging over the fence at the brickyard and once he was loafing outside one of my shops. When I tried to speak to him he vanished like a scared jack rabbit. He seems to be as shy as a wild animal, but I suspect he's got plenty of animal cunning. That's all I know but I have my own ideas. If it's what I think it is, you can take it for granted that it's as hot as buttered rum."

"I suspect the hangman's noose is suspended over this poacher fellow," said Fawkes.

"Well, this is why I'm telling you about it. I happened to know you were going to see Her Grace today—might as well tell you, I heard it through the girl—and I thought you might be able to find out something more definite. The girl seemed scared to death of me but she might be persuaded to talk to you. And somehow there should be a shilling or two in it for us."

"You think it has something to do with the Tontine?"

The jack-of-all-trades gave him a quick glance out of the corner of one eye. "Did I say that? I dunno. It might be any one of a dozen things."

Silence descended below them. The creaking buggy was bowling along now at a fairly steady clip through country of great beauty, the Vale below the line of the hills.

"What do you know about the girl? The maid?"

"Dark. Neat. Rather pretty. And smart in her way. She's out to get what she can. I don't trust her too much but she's the kind can be used in things like this."

"It may be necessary for me to stay overnight. Where do you suggest I go?"

"There's an inn at St. Wilfrid's, the Golden Beetle. I own it. Better go there." He hesitated and then committed himself with obvious reluctance. "Free of charge."

"Will you come and pick me up when I'm through? About four o'clock."

"I'll send someone for you. Better for us not to be seen together."

They had come in sight of the sharp gable of the present ducal house. "Get out quick when we reach the gate," instructed Stain. "I'll drive right on. Before anyone sees us."

3

The maid who answered his ring bore out Stain's description to the letter, dark, neat, kind of pretty.

"Are you Mr. Fawkes? I see, thank you, sir. Will you come in? Her Grace is engaged at the moment but she expects you. Lunch has been set out for you, sir, if you are hungry."

"Well, yes, I am rather hungry. I had to catch an early train and had no breakfast."

"Then come this way, sir." She turned and walked briskly ahead of him. "Yes," he said to himself. "She *is* neat. A very nice ankle. If I had the time now——" She led him to a small room reserved for breakfast where a single place had been set.

"Her Grace is upstairs at her correspondence."

"Thank you," said Fawkes. He was gaining additional impressions of the girl, Dossie Smith. "Sharp as a tack. Out for everything that will help her. Not immoral, not much at least. Too concerned about other matters to let herself get into trouble that way."

As he dealt with the substantial lunch laid before him, the lawyer caught glimpses of His Grace sitting in solitary state in the dining room, with a newspaper propped up in front of him. He could hear the grunts, the chortles and the harumphings with which the duke was expressing his reactions to what he was reading.

"He wouldn't demean himself to sit at the same table with me," said Fawkes to himself. "He's the Duke of Outland and he wouldn't condescend to look down his conky nose at me. There we have the kind of thing which will go out someday. It will go out in blood and thunder and smoke and destruction." Since misfortune had returned to claim him as a victim, Fawkes had gone back, a thoroughly embittered man, to the meetings in Soho which he had attended before. "I hope I have a hand in pulling down the pillars in the temple of privilege and letting the roof fall in on snobbery."

When he had finished his meal the maid returned and treated him to a quick bob of her neatly frilled cap.

"Her Grace is ready for you, sir."

The duke had finished his lunch by this time and had left the dining room, his arms filled with newspapers. For the moment they had the place to themselves.

"You are Dossie Smith?" he asked.

"Yes, sir. That's my name."

"I've been hearing about you. It seems you spoke to someone—whose name needn't be mentioned—about a friend of yours who had a plan in his mind."

"No friend of mine," she said quickly and even sharply. "He came to me. That's all I know."

"Good. That's sensible. I'm sure that's all you know about it, my dear. But about this man. He *has* ideas, I believe."

"I don't know, sir. He wanted to talk to me but I wouldn't listen. I don't want to get into any trouble, sir."

"You're much too nice and pretty a girl to get into any trouble. And much too clever, I'm sure."

The lawyer paused to consider what he was going to say. He had to be very careful, as she was almost as shy about getting down to matters as the skittery poacher himself.

"Listen to me, my dear. You went to Mr. L. Stain, intending to tell him—whatever needed to be told. But you didn't. You kept your little potato trap closed. You didn't like his looks. He frightened you. Isn't that so?"

"He did frighten me but you mustn't go supposing things——"

"Are you frightened of me?"

For the first time the girl looked him straight in the eye. Fawkes realized he had seen other eyes like hers, direct, cold, hard, sometimes in people he had encountered in prisons, often too on witness stands. They had something of the quality he often saw in the Soho meetings: a willingness to face danger for reasons of gain, to go through with things connected with definite purposes. But she was new to this sort of thing and that made her very cautious.

"I guess I am frightened of you. Some."

"Do you trust me?"

This brought a sulky response. "I trust no one. It's not safe."

"I see I've got to talk straight out," he went on after a moment. "You've heard of something. From this poacher fellow. You see a chance to do yourself some good. I'm not asking you to tell me what it is. Not yet. I'm just trying to make you see that sooner or later you've got to trust someone. You can't handle it all by yourself."

There was a moment's silence. "No," said the girl. "I can't."

"Then do this much. Send this Badger Bill to see me after supper. I'll be at the inn in St. Wilfrid's, the Golden Beetle. He mustn't come to the inn. At nine o'clock I'll go out for a stroll. He must be around. Tell him to whistle something when he sees me come out. A bar from some song. Very low. Are you willing to do that?"

Another pause. "Yes. I'll do that."

He shot a question at her with calculated suddenness. "How much does he want?"

"How—how should I know?"

"I think you do. There's a reason why I must know. I must have money in case he demands something down."

The girl's dark eyes rested intently on his face for several moments. Then she began to whisper. "One hundred quid down. Not a check. Cash. Four hundred pounds later."

Fawkes nodded with satisfaction. "I'll see you tomorrow. Or I'll get word to you somehow. To let you know what's been done."

"Don't send any messages here. I'll have to find some way to see you."

"I leave that to you then."

The maid laid a hand on his arm and looked steadily into his eyes. "I haven't talked to you. I've told you nothing. There's nothing to tell. It's that way, mister."

"It's that way."

She raised her voice. "Her Grace is ready to see you, sir."

"Tell Her Grace I'll be up in a few minutes. Say I haven't quite finished my lunch. I've got some things to get settled in my mind before I talk to her."

Alexander Fawkes went to a window to do his thinking. If he had been interested he would have been able to see the White Horse from there but his mind was too busy to be concerned at all with that strange outline on the crest of the hill.

"This Badger Bill has a scheme in his head to get one of the Tontine contenders out of the way," he said to himself. "That's what all this mystery is about. What else could it be? They wouldn't be asking five hundred quid for anything less.

"It can't be the duchess," he went on, "or he wouldn't be trying to have words with her about it. I don't suppose it's Grace. He lives too far away. It's the Groody woman who's to be shoved into the rail and put out of the race. He has it in mind, perhaps, that she could be rather conveniently shot through a window of her house. He must be a crack marksman to make a living by poaching. Or he may be thinking of burning the house down. Being an invalid, she might not be able to get out in enough of a hurry."

After going over the matter from every angle he found that no other solution fitted the facts. It must be that the poacher had it in mind to reduce the race to two and to benefit thereby himself to the tune of five hundred pounds.

"If one of them did drop out and the field was narrowed to two, there would be more than ten thousand pounds a year extra to be divided between the two survivors. I could get a slice of that for myself from the duchess. She couldn't refuse any demand I made on her. There should be enough in this to give me a clean, fresh start somewhere. Australia or Canada or South Africa. Is it worth the risk?"

After the most careful consideration he decided that it was worth the risk. Had he any alternative? This led inevitably to the very important matter of protection in case things went wrong. Fawkes had no desire to be found out and made to pay the penalty. A scheme of such diabolical neatness occurred to him at this point that his face became pinched up into something resembling a smile. "We must make it seem that Her High and Mightiness is in it. There's been a good start in that direction. The fellow's been seen slinking around here. The maid probably has some grievances and would be willing to swear to things. If I could persuade the duchess to give me the hundred pounds in the form of a check—the undertaker fellow would cash it—she would find it difficult to prove her innocence. I would get the benefit of any efforts made to cover things up in her interests. They couldn't protect her without protecting all of us. It's a very tidy idea."

He nodded his head and walked out into the hall where the maid was waiting for him.

4

Isabelle received him in a small sitting room on the floor above. He had not seen her since her return from the cruise and the change in her appearance was so great that he stared at her for a moment in a state of almost shocked surprise.

"I had your letter," she said. "It had been my intention not to see you again. But you were so urgent about it that I allowed you to come. Will you sit down, please."

"You are aware," he said, surprised at the cold finality of her greeting, "that I have been thrown out as a partner in Smythe, Boongrace and Curdle. It was done because of my activities in your behalf. It's not necessary, I'm sure, to explain how difficult this is making it for me."

"I am aware of that," said the duchess. "I am aware of other things also. This, particularly: that you made a great deal of money at my expense." She paused to study him with a decidedly unfriendly eye. Then she leaned forward abruptly and asked him point-blank, "How much did Linus Welstock pay you?"

The lawyer was taken off guard for a moment. "Your Grace," he said with a suggestion of a stammer, "are you referring to the art dealer of that name?"

"I am. I think you turned over to him something which belonged to me. I think you both made a handsome profit out of it. From what I hear, Mr. Fawkes, your share of it went in the crash. That is one of the few things in connection with that dreadful event from which I have been able to take some satisfaction."

"Your Grace, I am at a loss to understand what you mean."

"I will speak plainer then. I am certain, Mr. Fawkes, that you removed a painting from that warehouse I sent you to inspect before the building was so conveniently burned to the ground. I am convinced you took the painting to Linus Welstock and that he paid you well when he sold it to another wealthy collector. Don't go to the trouble of denying it. It couldn't have happened in any other way."

"I am hardly in a position, Your Grace, to defend myself against such an ill-considered and wild charge."

"Let me leave it at that for the time being. Your letter said you had certain suggestions to make. What are they?"

"Your Grace, my present desperate situation is due to my serving you. I come to ask what you propose to do about it."

"I propose to do nothing about it. I am prepared to pay you such sums as you may earn in connection with the suit. I am in the strange and uncomfortable position of having to make use of your services, even though I have no doubt you stole that valuable piece of property from me." She seemed to become aware for the first time of the seediness of his garb and the evidence in his appearance of what he had been through. "You don't look well. Has your conscience been at work?"

"You can best judge of that," answered the lawyer, a flush coming into his cheeks, "by looking into your own. And may I say that you don't seem to realize how much you still need my services."

"Explain yourself, please."

"What evidence do you have for the suit you propose to bring?"

"I have kept all the notes you prepared for me from time to time. The evidence is there."

The lawyer hesitated as though he knew the plunge he proposed to take would be into troubled waters. He did not look at her but studied the tips of his fingers.

"With the material in your possession, madame," he said finally, "a lawyer, or a staff of lawyers, could develop a case, without a doubt. But it would entail going over the records of years, all the records of the company, in fact, for there's nothing in your notes to make the search an easy one. No dates, madame, no specific references as to where or when certain things happened. It would take a long time, a very long time. And to begin with, of course, it would be necessary to obtain court sanction for the search."

Isabelle's manner had changed, almost with the first word of this explanation. "It was my understanding," she said in a hard and even tone, "that these notes were complete. You said you had given me chapter and verse. Your exact words, Mr. Fawkes."

"That is quite true. I used those exact words. I can supply chapter and verse. But to get this more detailed information, I would have to consult certain notes which I've retained in my own possession."

Isabelle turned in her chair and regarded him with a steady and hostile eye. "I haven't had anyone else go over this material you gave me. I think I had better do it right away. I lack the legal knowledge to judge it myself."

"It might be a good idea, Your Grace, to consult your family attorney. Although I can understand your reluctance to do so."

"This is, of course, an effort to extort money from me."

"I think it would be fairer to put it a different way. I have taken this means of protecting myself in case you should suddenly decide to cut me off with no compensation for the loss I have sustained. Which is exactly what you have announced your intention of doing."

"You acknowledge," she said in a fiercely accusative tone, "that you are holding back information you have been paid to obtain."

"I acknowledge more than that. I discovered certain other things of which I have given you no inkling at all. Things which would be extremely useful to you. These facts, for which I have chapter and verse, would strengthen your case considerably—if you were in a position to produce them in court."

"You've come here today to put a pistol to my head!" she exclaimed. "I knew it would be something like this when I had your last letter. You are the most dishonest man I have ever known!"

"My dear lady," said the lawyer, "you know the old saying, Least said, soonest mended. If you had met me fairly, if you had professed a willingness to compensate me, even though I might have felt your offer small, I wouldn't have fallen back on my last line of defense. I would have produced whatever you need. I think you must realize now how wise I was to hold something back. You would have thrown me out otherwise, without a shilling in my pockets, to eke out an existence as best I could."

"I said you would be compensated for any work you might be called upon to do."

"And I am doing no more than take you up, my dear lady. Except I'm seeing to it that there's plenty for me to do. The service I can render you is of such importance that I can dictate to you the nature of the compensation."

Isabelle remained silent for a considerable time, turning over in her mind the possibilities that confronted her. She was so angry that she found it hard to remain calm and not burst out in angry denunciations of him.

"I don't believe," she said, "that you would have turned everything over to me under any circumstances. You would still have held something back as a safeguard. You see, I know how your mind works. How much are you going to demand from me?"

"That seems to me a matter for negotiation."

"Then let us begin. You must first tell me what you have withheld so we can arrive at an understanding of the value."

"No, no," he said. "You must accept my word for its value."

"Do you mean I must pay in advance for something which may prove to be of little use?" cried Isabelle. "This is truly absurd. Your word, sir, is worth nothing at all!"

"And yours, madame? And yours?" he asked softly.

When it seemed that she had no intention of breaking the silence which fell between them at this point, the lawyer rose to his feet. He gave the briefest inclination of his head which could be construed as a bow.

"It seems we have reached an impasse," he said. "You need time, perhaps, to think things over. I shall be at the Golden Beetle in St. Wilfrid's tonight and for some hours tomorrow. I can be reached there if you care to reopen these matters."

At the door he turned and came back. "Had our talk today brought us to a mutually satisfactory basis, it was my intention to mention another matter. I know of a way by which you could make a great profit, Your Grace. Enough to pay for the tremendous expenses you will face if you commence this litigation. I can offer you no inkling of the nature of this—this transaction. You would have to take my word for it; and you've already made it clear you don't value my word. This much I can tell you and nothing more. If you could persuade yourself to advance a small sum—no more than one hundred pounds—you would be in a position to make"—he paused and then continued, accenting each word—"*a very great deal of money.*"

"You think poorly of my intelligence," she said, "if you believe I could be interested in any such mysterious nonsense. What do you propose to do? Steal the crown jewels from the Tower? Rob the Bank of England? Cause a panic on the Stock Exchange by some cock-and-bull story?"

"The little matter I have in mind is much simpler, Your Grace."

"Then tell me about it."

He shook his head. "Is that necessary? I think you know what it is. You are a shrewd woman, as I have many reasons to know. Give the matter a little thought and you may suddenly see the light."

"I have no intention of giving it any thought at all."

He bowed to her curtly. "If you should decide to reopen these various matters with me, send word to the Golden Beetle. If you have decided to put a bit on this flier I've mentioned, enclose a check with the note. Nothing more, no explanations. If I don't hear from you I shall return to London and the matter will be closed. Definitely and finally."

5

His Grace the Duke of Outland had driven himself in the dogcart to a neighbor's for tea and it was getting quite dark when he arrived back. He found his wife in what passed as the drawing room of the establishment. Dressed in something quite old which had been rather handsome in its time in a crimson and gold and black way, she was seated at a rather decrepit escritoire looking over some letters with a distrait air.

"Confound it, my mind is as full of leaks as the roof on this horrible house," said the duke, taking a chair. "There's been something I've intended to say to you for a week. When we spent the weekend with the Pitt-Ransoms it occurred to me that we were within a few miles of Little Shallow and I said to myself, 'Chip, here you are and you ought to pay your respects to the Groody lady.'"

"Chip, you absurd creature!" exclaimed Isabelle. "You didn't follow that silly impulse, did you?"

"Of course I did. Here we have a race. Just three people in it. The whole country talking about it. Stands to reason there should be good feeling between the contenders. In the interests of good sportsmanship, I had to go. I knew there was no use saying anything to you, m'dear. You'd not only refuse to go yourself but I was quite sure you would bullyrag me out of it."

"You don't consider me a sportsman. I see your point."

"That's all right, m'dear. I love you for your faults as well as your wonderful good qualities. Well, I went and it was really quite pleasant. There she was, this poor little woman, in the very worst of health and suffering pain, but she talked with me and laughed and I think she enjoyed it."

Isabelle was interested in spite of herself. "Is she really very ill?" she asked.

"I'm afraid so. Rheumatism doesn't kill people by itself, not unless it goes to the heart or the brain. I got that straight from a doctor once when I felt a twinge or two in my toe. It hasn't touched her brain yet, for she's still as bright as a new-minted sovereign, but from the symptoms I'm sure it has attacked her heart. I'm sorry to say it but she doesn't look to me like a long contender for the Tontine money."

"Why are you sorry to say it? Come, Chip, don't look so shocked. We've got to be realistic about this."

"But we don't want the poor lady to die. She knows how serious it is, but she's very hopeful that a man she says is a friend of hers, a Mr. Joe Tope, is going to be able to do something about it."

"A Mr. Joe Tope?" Isabelle began to laugh. "And who is this friend of hers who can perform miracles?"

"Well, he's what they call a scrubber and chalker, if you know what that means."

"I suspect it has something to do with horse racing."

"That's exactly what it means, ducky."

Isabelle became most distinctly annoyed at this point. "I've told you before, Chip, that I don't like being called these vulgar names that you picked up around the tracks. Ducky! It makes me feel unclean. And what's more, you can see what kind of a woman this Helen Groody is when she calls a man like that her friend. Once a coachman's daughter, always a coachman's daughter."

"Not at all!" said the duke emphatically. "I'm sure from what she told me I would like this Joe Tope as much as she does. He seems a pleasant sort of fellow. If I had to make my living in the world I think I would enjoy doing it as a scrubber and a chalker. Just think: the sun shining, the gee-gees running and me standing up on my stool and posting the odds! Capital, really!"

"Well," said Isabelle, "if she's putting her case in his hands, it's clear she hasn't any brains for the rheumatism to go to."

"Oh, he just knows someone he wants her to see. And, by the way, she must have been dashed pretty in her day."

"And way," commented Isabelle. She jumbled all the letters together and tossed them into a drawer. "No use answering any of that lot. Now, Chip, seeing that you felt urged to make a fool of yourself in this way, you might as well go on and tell me about it. Did she know how to behave?"

"She was more like a lady than any lady I've ever met. She wasn't flustered, if that's what you mean. It was too early for tea and she asked me if there was anything I would like to drink. When I said I could do with a liqueur, what do you suppose she produced? Benedictine and chartreuse! The best of both. I looked around and saw she had good books and magazines. Even the woman suffrage thing. You don't believe in votes for women——"

"Chip, why do you assume you know what my opinions are?" cried Isabelle. "Of course I believe in votes for women. I've had ample proof in the course of my life that women have more brains than men. But I can't support the movement while such impossible creatures are running it."

"Well, I enjoyed the visit very much." The duke seemed on the point of subsiding but then realized that he had left the one important thing unsaid. "Damme, there I go forgetting again. Isabelle, you never told me of the nice thing you did, sending that chest from the Hall to young Allie. M'dear, I was ready to burst with pride when she mentioned it. I think it was the damnedest, finest thing you ever did in your life—except, of course, marrying me."

Isabelle seemed puzzled that he should consider the gift a reason for such praise. "Why, I'm very fond of Allie," she said. "He's the only one of my relatives I've been able to like. Why shouldn't I send him a gift? Particularly as I'm planning to attack his father."

"Quite," said the duke, sighing. "And that brings me to another point. I wish you had gone with me to the Lansburys' this afternoon."

"Such dull people. I wouldn't think of it."

"One of the other guests had some very interesting things to say about lawsuits. A lawyer himself. A bigwig, Sir Harold Ashley."

Isabelle looked up with a hint of annoyance in her eyes. "What got the discussion started? Were you asking questions?"

The duke shook his head. "I was just a bystander as usual, m'dear. They were talking about a case when I went in. Some Johnny up north sued the directors of a company, claiming they had mismanaged things. Sir Harold's point was that all the information about the profits of the company were brought out and that the public was bound to get unsettled. He said that where great profits had been made the fact should be kept bottled up. No use stirring up class conflict. Then, with an eye on me, he said, 'Suppose someone got ideas about the Carboy case and had the books brought into court?'

"Well, this lawyer chap, who's really quite keen, pointed out that the profits in Carboy and Co. had been enormous. He said if the books had to be produced in court and discussed and hashed over, the whole world would know about it. That sort of thing, he said, leads to social troubles. Discontent, strikes, mobbing of people on streets and burning of jails and churches. He pointed out that so many people had lost money in Carboy shares and through the closing of the factories that a scent of trouble is all that's needed to get the whole country stirred up."

"Most interesting. I suppose you agree with it?"

"Absolutely, m'dear."

Suddenly the duchess began to weep. She laid her face in her hands on the table and her whole body shook.

"I don't want to spend all our money," she said in muffled tones. "It would be much easier to forget about the failure and what caused it. But I can't change my mind! I must go on with it. I won't have a moment's peace if this great bungler goes unpunished. How can I stay silent when I think of him coming back home where everything was going along so smoothly and well and convincing Papa to back his wild schemes? I fought hard to keep Papa out of it but I was talked down. And now the business is ruined and we are all so poor we have to live in mean ways like this. All because he thought he was good enough to run the world!"

"My sweet, you do feel strongly about all this, don't you?" said her husband.

"Yes. I wish you understood me better, Chip. You would see then why I do."

She raised her head and gave her eyes the benefit of a quick rub with her handkerchief. Her mind went off on a different slant. She began thinking about the proposition made by the lawyer at the close of their talk. It had never been out of her mind entirely since. "How could he make all that money for me? How? I think I know what he meant. By getting me a larger share of the Tontine income. How else?" She found herself thinking of the death of George Grace and the events which had led up to it. "Was I responsible?" she wondered. "All I did was to speak to Papa about breaking up the reform meetings and he repeated what I said to some of his men. They took him seriously about it. But it was a pure accident that George Grace was killed. No one could be blamed for *that*. It was the last thing in any of our minds. But it was in poor Papa's mind to the end of his days." She sat for a long time in deep thought. "If I gave this man the hundred pounds, would I be responsible for what he did with the money? I can only guess what's in his mind. He refused to tell me."

Far back in her own mind, however, she had no doubts. If he did what she thought he might, it was natural that the two—George Grace's death and this scheme of the lawyer's—should seem to her to be connected. Would she again be to blame for someone's death?

"It's all nonsense," she said to herself finally. "He isn't planning to get rid of anyone. Why did I ever think of such a thing? All he's trying to do is to get some money out of me. He's in desperate straits. Well, supposing I play generous with him once——"

Reaching for a sheet of paper, she wrote a note and addressed it to Alexander Fawkes at the Golden Beetle. Then, after more thought, she made out a check and enclosed it in the envelope.

6

During the second night Isabelle slept badly. She wakened half a dozen times and lay in the darkness of her room, oppressed by a sense of impending trouble. There was nothing tangible in this; it was, rather, a dull conviction that things were going wrong. Once she got up and fumbled for matches in the dark in order to see the time. The solemn clock on the small blackened chimney piece informed her that it was a few minutes after four. She went then to a window and looked out into the darkness, and immediately the fear which had kept her in uneasiness took definite form. Off to the east a small section of sky showed red.

"There's a fire," she said to herself.

As she watched it seemed that the fire was increasing in size. The glow against the sky was covering a larger area and growing more ruddy.

She returned to her bed but found that sleep had deserted her. There was no reason to connect the fire with the mental unease from which she had been suffering but somehow it had become a part of it. All the vague dangers seemed to have been brought into definite form and were summed

up in that growing blaze in the eastern sky. She got up again and visited the window. There could be no doubt about it: the fire area had enlarged in the interval.

Her husband heard her stirring about and came into the bedroom, wearing a tattered scarlet dressing gown. He was carrying a lamp and his tousled hair lent an almost comic touch to his appearance.

"What's wrong?" he asked. "Are you ill?"

"Look," said Isabelle.

He went to the window and stared out. "It's a big one," he reported after a moment. "Not just a cowshed or a barn. It's a long way off."

"Where do you suppose it is?"

He looked off into the dark, studying the position of the blaze. "Just about due east, or perhaps a bit north," he said. He named a few villages which seemed likely under the circumstances.

Out of her instinctive fears, Isabelle asked, "Could it be at Little Shallow?"

"It might be." She saw his head nod in the dark. "See here, you had better tumble back into bed. We'll find out all about it in the morning."

The duchess could not get to sleep at once although she tried hard to compose herself. Half a dozen times she got up again, to stare into the east, her mind filled with uncomfortable speculations.

She dozed off finally and it was broad daylight when she was wakened by her maid coming into the room to draw back the curtains of the bed, the inevitable cup of tea in her hand.

"Smith," said the duchess, sitting up without any of the usual struggles, "there's been a fire. Did you see it?"

"Yes, Your Grace." The girl's tone was completely lacking in its usual briskness. It seemed to Isabelle that she also was uneasy in her mind.

"Do you know what it was?"

"No, Your Grace. The cook says it may have been Mr. Packingham's place."

Isabelle felt a momentary sense of relief. God grant that the cook was right!

When the maid returned later with breakfast on a tray it was easily to be seen that she was not herself. She looked pale and her eyes avoided those of her mistress.

"Was it Mr. Packingham's place?"

"No, Your Grace. Someone drove by and told Burkey"—naming the gardener and man of all work about the place—"that it was at Little Shallow. The Old Rectory, Your Grace."

"The Old Rectory!"

"Yes, Your Grace."

Isabelle needed no further proof. This was the lawyer's mysterious plan, then: to put one of the Tontine survivors out of the way so that the share would be divided. No wonder he had been so evasive about it. He had not hinted at what he might claim as his share of the profit on the transaction. That, she realized now, had not been necessary. He had been well aware that all he would have to do was to name the figure he wanted and she would be forced to comply.

Far back in her mind she knew that she had half expected this, that she had sensed the nature of the plot. And knowing what he meant to do, she had still given him the money! It had been a sense of guilt she had suffered from these last two days. Despite this she had not gone to him and demanded that the conspiracy be stopped.

"If she is dead," she said to herself, her thoughts on the destruction of

Helen Groody's home and the probable fate of its owner, "then I am guilty of her death! As guilty as any of them."

She pretended to be interested in the food on her plate. "No loss of life, I hope."

"They don't rightly know," answered the maid. "The man who told Burkey said the fire was still burning and they hadn't been able to search yet." In a low voice she added, "They fear the worst, Your Grace."

An hour later another carriage came along and stopped in front of the house. Peering out from behind the curtains ("Like a villain in a play!" she said to herself), Isabelle saw that the driver was in conversation with Burkey. They talked for several minutes and then the traveler picked up the reins, gave a flick of the whip and drove off. The gardener turned at once and hurried to the house, a bearer undoubtedly of news.

Not waiting for the maid to assist her, the duchess dressed herself in the first thing her fingers encountered in the wardrobe. She hurried to the door, intending to go downstairs, but checked herself before leaving the room. "That wouldn't do," she thought. "I mustn't appear anxious."

When the maid came next to the bedroom she made no comment on the fact that her mistress was dressed, although this was an unprecedented departure from the daily routine. The girl was white of face and her fingers seemed clumsy as she arranged the dishes on the breakfast tray. At first she did not speak.

"The place was set fire to," she volunteered finally. "Leastways, Your Grace, there was a man seen hanging about late last night and he's been taken in. On suspicions, more or less."

"What man is it?"

"He lives near here, ma'am. A poacher."

Isabelle's heart began to pound. "Do you mean the one who was here a few days ago? The one who tried to speak to me?"

"Yes, Your Grace." The maid's response was spoken almost in a whisper. "That's the one."

The duke was shaving in the next room. Isabelle opened the door and looked in. He was standing in front of a cheval mirror and his face was covered with lather. In a cheerful mood, he was humming as his fingers plied the brush. All the songs he liked had a low strain about them, in her opinion, and this one had to do with a certain "Bill Sloggins."

"Chip," she said, "they've arrested a man in connection with the fire."

"So I heard before I came up. That poacher fellow. Well, I'm glad he's been laid by the heels. A nasty, dangerous fellow, that one."

She had half made up her mind to take him into her confidence. In fact she had given some thought as to how she would phrase the explanation. "Chip, I'm in trouble. I've done nothing wrong—just something very foolish. I gave money to that lawyer. A check for one hundred pounds. He said he needed it and I didn't ask any questions. But now I'm dreadfully afraid that it had something to do with this fire and—and Miss Groody's death, if she is dead. Chip, what can we do?" This was more or less what she would have said.

He began to strop the razor. "I heard something else. Pretty dashed suspicious, I would say. The fellow had money in his pockets. They were fairly stuffed with bank notes. Now how would a poacher and good-for-nothing get so much money? Take my word, m'dear, he'd been paid to do it."

She recalled now how he had reacted when she talked to him about the Holbein, how convinced he had been that in any kind of trouble there was just one thing to be done, to go straight to the police. He had been so clear in his mind that any kind of wrongdoing should be punished.

"If I tell him," she said to herself, closing the door so the maid could not hear the rest of the conversation, "he may even insist on taking *me* to the police." It now seemed to her unwise to confide in him, at least not at this stage. Instead she asked, in a voice which she strove to make casual, "But who would give him money to burn down the house?"

"That's not hard to answer," declared the duke in a robustly cheerful voice. "Someone who would benefit by the poor lady's death. In the matter of the Tontine, I mean."

"Such," she said in an effort to appear amused, "such as—I?"

"You! Good gad, no, m'dear. I meant some of the fellows running the books. Although now I think of it, that's no answer. *They* wouldn't want poor little Miss Groody out of the way. They'd be more apt to pick on you, my sweet. You're the favorite in the race."

Isabelle returned to her room to find it empty, the maid having gone downstairs. The latter returned soon after with a note which she produced from under her apron.

"A man came with it," said the girl, who seemed quite as much perturbed as her mistress. "He saw me and motioned me to go down into the garden. It's from *him*."

"Him! Who do you mean?"

"That lawyer, Your Grace. Mr. Fawkes."

There was no address on the outside. Isabelle was so disturbed that she spread back the flap with a finger which trembled, without waiting for the girl to go.

You must understand we are in this together. If the poacher squeaks, and he's certain to, there are several of us who'll be drawn in up to our necks. Better start pulling whatever strings you can, because only influence will help us now. Don't think a denial will do you any good. Where would I get a hundred pounds? I'm making myself scarce. There is one place, fortunately, where I can hide with some hope of not being found. For your own sake, pray God they don't find me. Destroy this at once.

"This is the end!" said Isabelle aloud, too absorbed in the terror of her position to care about the presence of the maid in the room.

"Is it—is it bad news, Your Grace?"

Isabelle turned on her sharply. "Why are you still here?" Then she walked
ver closer to the girl. "I'm beginning to suspect that you've had a hand in
ome things that are going on."

"Oh, my lady, my lady!" wailed the maid. "I've done nothing wrong. I'd
wear it on a stack of Bibles."

"He was here. Fawkes, I mean. He brought this note himself."

The maid did not attempt to deny it. "Yes, Your Grace. He brought it."

"I must see him. At once."

"Oh, my lady! He's gone. He was off like a shot as soon as he handed it
o me."

"You might as well confess. You've been in it. You've known what they
vere planning to do."

"No, no, my lady! I swear it. All I did was send him, the poacher, to this
awyer—this dreadful, scheming, lying, cruel lawyer!"

"Keep your voice down!" said Isabelle. "Do you want everyone in the house
o hear you?"

"Oh, Your Grace, my lady, I'll need your help. They won't be easy on the
ikes of me."

Isabelle could see now how simple it was going to be for the police to
nake a complete case out of what had happened. Perhaps even a case against
ier! She had given Fawkes the check and he, without a doubt, had given the
oacher the money found in his pockets. She felt for a few moments like
ushing into the other room and crying to her husband, "Oh, Chip, save me!"
ut then she regained enough of her courage and common sense to realize
hat she must not give way to her emotions. She must remain cool and
letached.

A thought came into her mind and she motioned to the maid not to leave
he room. Seating herself at a small mahogany desk, one with a marquetry
id in which her name was spelled out in large yellow letters, a gift of the
luke's, she wrote a telegram to Jonathan Bade, asking him to come out as
he desired very much to see him.

"This is to a lawyer friend of mine who may be able to help you," she said.
I'm asking him to come down. See that Burkey takes it to the village to be
ent off at once." She looked closely at the white and frightened face of the
,irl. "If you're thinking of running away, put it out of your head. You can't
un away from the law. If you try it and are caught, it is accepted as an
cknowledgment of guilt. Better stay and face it out—whatever it is you've
lone."

"As if you didn't know!" said the maid with a return of her impudence of
pirit.

Isabelle took her by both shoulders and gave her a shake. "Be careful
vhat you say, my girl. Be careful even what you think. I know nothing about
ny of this. I may suspect some things but that is all. Do you understand?"

"Yes, Your Grace."

"Don't talk to any of the other servants. Keep yourself busy with your
vork. I'm making you a promise to help you in every way I can."

During the balance of the morning carriages went by the house in considerable numbers and some of them stopped. Isabelle watched each with fear and trembling but did not go downstairs to learn if anything new had been heard. At noon the duke came upstairs.

"Why are you moping here?" he asked. "You look kind of pale, m'dear. Aren't you well?"

She shook her head. "Not very well, Chip."

"Funny business, this," he said. "They've searched the ruins but haven't found any trace of bodies yet. Perhaps they were burned right to ashes. It was a furious fire, they say. And another thing, the fellow they've nabbed had a gun with him. A couple of shots had been fired. Now they think he may have shot the poor lady first and burned the house to cover up the crime. But that would mean he shot 'em all, the maid and that stableboy she kept. The police seem to be a bit puzzled. They can't get a thing out of Badger Bill. He just sits there and snarls at them."

"I want to ask you a question. The law is always impartial, I've been told. But is that true?"

"Of course it's true."

"But—well, let us suppose you had been the one to give this man all that money. That you had paid him to do this. What would happen to you?"

"You mean if I had planned to have the poor lady killed? In order to get more of the Tontine money for you at once? Gad, Isabelle, what an idea! That's too farfetched for words. But I'll tell you what would happen to me. I would be tried, convicted and jolly well hanged."

"That," she said, "is what I thought."

7

Isabelle had been aware for some time that her health was far from good but she had spoken to no one about it. After a lifetime of perfect health she did not like to acknowledge that she was beginning at last to show signs of old age. The trouble, she was sure, was with her heart. She found it hard to breathe at times and she suffered severe pains, starting in her left shoulder and continuing down her arms, but only on the left side. Her feet were showing a tendency to swell; and this disturbed her more than the pains and what might be causing them. Not to be able to use the small, trim shoes she had worn all her days was more than she could bear. To have her ankles swollen out of all recognition was an indignity that time was visiting on her which she resented bitterly.

The early hours of the afternoon passed slowly. Jonathan Bade, of course, had not arrived. He could not be expected to put in an appearance much before the dinner hour under the most favorable circumstances. She knew this but the hours became harder to sustain without someone on whom she might lean. "He always told me he would know when I needed help," she said to herself. "Why, then, hasn't he come of his own accord?"

Once she rang her bell and after a long delay the cook came waddling slowly and painfully up the back stairs. She stood in the door and looked inquiringly at her mistress, brushing the hair back from her moist forehead.

"Midge," said the duchess, "I don't want you. I rang for Smith."

"She's not here, m'leddy," said the cook. "She's gone, the hussy. Haven't seen hide or hair of her for hours."

"What do you mean, Midge? That she's left for good?"

The cook nodded her head. "She's took French leave, m'leddy. Just packed her things and went. And a fine thing it wur to do, leaving me to look after everyfink."

"Never mind then. Go back to your work. I'll attend myself to what I had in mind."

After the heavy step of the goddess of the kitchen had completed the return trip, Isabelle sat for some time in a somber study of the situation. So the maid had succumbed to her fears after all! This, she knew, was one of the worst things that could have happened. The girl might not have been under suspicion up to this point but now attention would be focused on her. Isabelle knew that it might bring the police to a belief earlier that she herself had been concerned.

If the police traced the girl and put her under arrest she would tell everything. Isabelle had no doubts on that score at all. She would tell of the two visits Fawkes had paid to the house. The most damaging bit of evidence would be the hasty call he had made that morning to deliver the note for her. The police would pounce on that and demand to be shown the note. This she would be unable to do; she had promptly destroyed it. What explanation could she give them? What message could she say it had contained?

"Why, oh, why did I send him that check!" she asked herself a dozen times, in an increasing agony of fear.

In her calmer moments she knew that her connection with the case was slight and that she might succeed in convincing the authorities that her relations with Fawkes had been limited to the legal work he was doing for her. If she had the conviction of innocence to lend her courage, she might establish this belief. But she lacked that conviction. There had been in her mind from the start a half understanding, never really acknowledged to herself, of what was afoot.

Her thoughts, traveling in an almost dizzy circle, always came back to one point. "I won't let them take me. Ugh, to be put in one of those dreadful cells! I couldn't face a long trial, being stared at in court and the newspapers full of the case—and what might follow!"

The climax came at four o'clock that afternoon. This was the time when ordinarily she would be indulging in her afternoon nap but she had been unable to settle down. She was spending the slow-moving minutes instead in pacing up and down her room, turning matters over and over in her head and running to a window at the first sound from the road. She heard a galloping horse and quickly reached her observation point behind the curtains in the front window. She knew at once that her worst fears were being realized.

The rider was in uniform. He turned in at the gate and came at a walk up the drive. A moment later he was pounding at the door.

Isabelle went out stealthily to the landing and stationed herself at the head of the stairs. She heard a heavy foot in the hall and her husband' voice asking, "Well, sir, what brings you here?"

She then heard a deep voice begin on a detailed explanation. "I'm Office Gray, Your Grace, on orders from Mr. Batson of the Home Office. We were sent down from London as soon as the news came. Five of us, Your Grace The others are working on different lines. My orders are to remain here un til Mr. Batson comes himself. He'll be here in an hour, Your Grace."

Apparently the duke was very much disturbed. "But, see here, Officer," she heard him say, "isn't this quite unusual and—er—arbitrary? I mean, fo the Home Office to be taking steps like this?"

"I heard Mr. Batson explaining that the whole country will be talking about the case and that people will be stirred up over the killing of the lady They'll be demanding action, Your Grace. It's no time, Mr. Batson says, fo half measures."

"I see," said the duke. "But I must say I'm surprised that your Mr. Batson thinks it necessary to go to such lengths as this. What possible information can he hope to get here?"

"I don't know, Your Grace. He said nothing about that to me. All I know is I have orders not to allow anyone to leave until he arrives."

A moment later the officer asked the question which the listener on the landing above had been dreading. "Is Her Grace here, sir?"

"Yes, Officer. She's upstairs. She hasn't been feeling very well today. I must say this intrusion isn't going to do her any good."

Isabelle waited a little longer, expecting to learn if either Fawkes or the Smith girl had been apprehended. The conversation ended at this point however, and she heard the officer turn and leave by the front door. He would, no doubt, begin a patrol of the grounds to see that no one tried to leave. She returned to her bedroom on tiptoe.

For several moments she stood near the foot of her bed in a state of in decision. The light outside was waning and the room was becoming dark What a dreadful place it was! Even in the disturbed condition of her mind she gave a disapproving look about her. It was dull and poorly furnished and without a vestige of charm; so much like Chip's first wife, Amy, whose father had bought the property for them. "I won't be sorry to leave this place," she thought.

"I am tangled in the web," she said aloud, in a low voice. Unhappy thoughts began to crowd her mind. Things had always gone her way but now it seemed as though fate was determined to balance the scales. Was this to be her punishment? There was her first husband's death. Poor Tib had died because of her conduct. And there was what she had said about her father's former partner, George Grace. "Poor Papa was sorry about his death," she thought. "It was on his mind right to the end."

She was conscious of a new pain at this moment. It was a strangling, terrible pain, as though someone were trying to crush her breastbone, to force it against her spine. She found it impossible to breathe for a moment and dropped exhausted on the side of the bed. Even with this to distract her attention, she was aware of the heavy tread of the police officer in front of the house.

"Is there anything left in life that's worth while?" she asked. The pain seemed to be getting worse. Panting for breath, she reached a resolution. "I told that girl she—she mustn't run away. I said no one—can escape—from the law. And now I—I am going to run away myself. But—but I *will* escape from the law. This terrible law!"

She rose with difficulty to her feet and walked to the bathroom. It was small and uncomfortable and unattractive in every way. There was a cheap medicine cabinet hanging on one wall. "I'll never have to use it again!" she thought. She looked inside the cabinet. Since the pains in her shoulder and arms had begun, she had been taking sleeping pills. The bottle she had been using was empty but there was a full one beside it. With the new bottle in one hand and a glass of water in the other, she made her way back to the bedroom.

"I never thought I would run away from danger," she thought. "But I never realized what danger can mean."

## CHAPTER SIX

### 1

Jonathan Bade arrived on the scene a full hour before he could have been expected if he had managed to catch the late morning train. It seemed to him that he had been directed to the wrong place when he reached the house where the duke and duchess were making their home. He stared at the ungracious lines of the relatively small building and at the restricted and unkempt grounds. It was hard to believe that Isabelle was living here.

Mr. Batson from the Home Office was in the house when Jonathan was admitted. He was looking subdued and a little lacking in his usual assurance when the newcomer introduced himself.

"Jonathan Bade!" he said, shaking hands effusively. "Ah, sir, you have been an ideal of mine. As a young fellow, with visions of a political career, I admired you immensely. I heard you speak many times and I may say, sir, that you quite carried me away. Now, alas, my dream of sitting in the House has been destroyed. I see no future for myself but to continue my work in a purely administrative department."

Jonathan had been aware as soon as he entered the door of a subdued air about the place. People moved as silently as possible and spoke in lowered tones. He had spent the night in Reading to arrange homes for several of his derelicts, and in the early afternoon he had felt an impulse to drive north and see Isabelle. It had seemed to him during the long journey that this might well prove to be the last chance. This was not because he had any fears on her score; it was his own capacity to hold onto the last phase of a long life which he doubted.

Now, however, he began to wonder, "Have I come too late?"

"Mr. Batson," he said, "has there been trouble here? I seem to sense something of the kind."

"Trouble?" said the Home Office man. "Yes, Mr. Bade, serious trouble. Her Grace is dead. The end came two hours ago."

Jonathan did not make any response for some time. It did not seem possible that Isabelle could be through with life. She was too young, being more than ten years younger than he was, which made her seem almost youthful. She had been full of life and the will to go on, and too ambitious, to give up the fight so soon, even though things had been going against her. There could be no mistake, of course; but how could such an unforeseen tragedy have come about?

When Mr. Batson found the silence becoming uncomfortable, he proceeded to talk about the tragic event at Little Shallow and the part he was playing in it. Jonathan listened with increasing disbelief. He had heard hints in London that the narrowing of the Tontine field might lead to trouble of some such kind but he had not believed them. Violence over shares in an annuity? In the England of good Queen Victoria? It had seemed to him impossible enough to verge on the absurd. And yet it had happened. Helen Groody was dead, the first victim.

"My dear sir," he managed to say finally, "I am so distressed at what you tell me that I am without words!" After a moment, however, he managed to phrase a question. "But what are you doing here, sir?"

"There's a side of the case which has to be examined," said the official. He raised a cautioning hand. "Mind you, no one thinks Her Grace was concerned in any way with the tragedy but the fact that the villain in the case seems to be a shady lawyer named Fawkes from London and that he had been employed by her—still is, we believe—seemed to make an inquiry necessary. Then when I found that Her Grace had died from an overdose of sleeping pills——"

Jonathan's mind became decisively clear at once. He turned in his chair and stared aggressively at the man from the Home Office. "Sir!" he said. "Are you telling me that the duchess ended her life by taking opiates?"

Mr. Batson pursed up his lips. "An unpleasant idea to accept but—well, that *was* the cause of death, sir."

"I don't believe it," declared Jonathan. He got to his feet. "I don't know what His Grace is doing about this but I assure you that I intend to take certain steps if he hasn't already done so. I knew her too well to believe such a thing possible."

"The evidence, sir, seems clear enough."

Jonathan had been weary from the long drive when he arrived. His features had seemed paper-thin, his skin almost transparent. He had moved with great difficulty, his back bowed, his knees stiff. But now he seemed to come to life.

"Where is the duke?" he asked.

"He went to lie down a short time ago. He seemed completely exhausted, sir."

"What steps have you taken?"

"The body is being held for an official examination. An autopsy will be held, I expect."

"Is the body in the room where she died?"

Mr. Batson shook his head. "No, Mr. Bade, it has been moved to one of the other rooms, pending the examination. Not," hastily, "that we moved it until a thorough study had been made of the room and its contents."

"What is the evidence which points to the taking of opiates?"

"Her personal maid is not here but the cook tells me that Her Grace has been taking sleeping pills because she had serious pains in the region of her heart. The supply in one bottle had been exhausted but a fresh and un-opened bottle was in the medicine cabinet this morning. It can't be found now."

"Has the whole house been searched?"

"Not as thoroughly as it will be after the first shock passes and we can have complete possession."

Jonathan felt a fury growing in him that this dandified official from London had jumped to conclusions on such hasty evidence as this. "You act, sir, as though you are not aware that Her Grace the Duchess of Outland was a very great person. One of the loveliest women England has produced and one of the most gifted. Do you feel that her memory should be tarnished in this way until you have positive proof of what you are saying?" He stared bitterly at the now somewhat discomfited Mr. Batson. "Will you please take me to the room?"

The Home Office man led the way upstairs, full of explanations of his conduct of the case and voicing his belief that there would be new and un-expected developments. Jonathan did not pay much heed to what was being said. He was finding it hard to keep his mind clear and active, with this heavy burden of grief which had descended upon him. That Isabelle might die before he did had never occurred to him as a possibility and he had not been prepared for the shock of it.

His first reaction to the room where she had slept through the last unhappy phase of her life, and in which she had died, was one of pity. He looked about him and thought, "Is it possible that this drab and dreary place was the best they could afford?" It was indeed a depressing room. The furniture was old and in need of repair, the hangings were tawdry, the wallpaper a repellent sand color. The chimney piece was small and inclined to smoke, judging from the blackened condition of the bricks. Through the door of the bathroom he saw a square zinc bath and a single mat on the floor.

"My poor Isabelle!" he said to himself. "How unhappy she must have been in this place!"

The examination which had been made of the room must have been of the most hurried and perfunctory kind. Almost on his first glance about, while Batson held up a small oil lamp to assist him, his eye caught what seemed a gleam of glass under the tattered taffeta skirt of the dressing table. He went down on one knee and picked up a bottle from the floor. After studying the label, he turned and handed the bottle to the official.

"The new supply of sleeping pills," he said. "You will see that the bottle is unopened. Her Grace may have felt the need of something to ease the pain but it is clear that she either changed her mind or—was not allowed the time. Certainly she did not kill herself with an overdose of pills as you so rashly assumed!" He made a peremptory gesture as he allowed his voice to rise. "Sir, I would advise that you take immediate steps to undo the terrible mistake you have made! Call in everyone who may have heard the story and then make a statement which will leave no doubts in any mind. Tell them frankly that what you had accepted as fact was completely wrong and that it would have been a great injustice to the memory of a brave woman!"

Batson held the bottle in one hand and mopped his brow with the other. "It shall be done at once, sir. Luckily, sir, no one has left the house since we were told about the sleeping pills. The mistake will be corrected at once."

2

Feeling that he had not covered himself with glory in this phase of the investigation, Mr. Batson was glad to take to his carriage and return to Little Shallow. Before leaving, he had a final word with the Duke of Outland and Jonathan Bade.

"We'll have our hands on this fellow Fawkes in no time at all," he said. "A description has been sent all over the country by telegraph. He'll be recognized wherever he shows his face. Yes, we'll soon have him and then we'll get to the bottom of all this. And by the way, he left the inn at St. Wilfrid's in such a hurry that he didn't take a bundle of notes. I've had no time to study them carefully but they seem on a quick glance to deal with business meetings and transactions."

The duke, who had been sunk in a chair in a deep silence, looked up at this. "I know about those papers," he said. "It was some work he was preparing for my wife. It has no—no bearing on this case."

"I'm sure you are right, Your Grace, but they'll have to be studied," said Batson with a return of his official manner. "The material seems to consist mostly of disconnected notes. Undoubtedly the man intended to use them in the preparation of a more coherent statement."

"When you have looked them over and convinced yourself that what I've said is true, I'll appreciate having the stuff." The duke's manner took on some of the stiffness it showed on such occasions. "I suggest, sir, that you complete your study quickly. Fawkes will agree, I am certain, that the papers should be sent to me. When I have them"—he paused and looked at Jonathan out of the corner of one eye—"I shall know what to do with them."

When they were alone the duke sighed with relief. "I am very grateful to you, Mr. Bade," he said, "for removing this stigma from my wife's name. I didn't know what to do about it, although I was certain it was all wrong. I became so angry with that fellow Batson that I couldn't remain in the same room with him."

"The truth was bound to come out. That bottle was certain to be found in due course." Jonathan, who was looking very worn and tired, nodded his head slowly. "I think I must relieve you of the inconvenience of a guest at this time and so I'll drive over at once to Wantage. But before I go I would like to say a word about Isabelle. I seem to have known her all my life. The day that Samuel Carboy first spoke to me about joining his forces, he came into court where I was on a case and brought his daughter with him. I thought her quite the most bewitching and fabulously beautiful child I had ever seen. She created quite a stir in court, I assure you."

"She created a stir the first time I saw her," contributed the duke. "As far, at least, as I was concerned. I was a grubby boy of about fifteen but I proposed to her on the spot. I didn't see any reason why she shouldn't wait a few years while I grew up. And I kept on proposing to her until I finally got her, by gad!"

"I saw her many times, of course, and occasionally under rather extraordinary circumstances. You know that she went to France on that rash expedition of Louis Napoleon's. She eluded the French authorities and returned to Dover, disguised as a governess in the household of the Marquis of Invermark."

"I heard the bare outline of the story only. I am of a possessive nature and I never liked to talk to her about her other husbands. I had the lowest kind of opinion of that damned French comte. And as for Invermark, I can still get myself into an apoplectic condition by thinking of him."

"What you probably don't know is that I was in Boulogne that day. The whole scheme was such a silly, paste-and-paper business that I knew it would blow up quickly. I didn't want to see Isabelle in a French prison so I convinced her she must get off that absurd excursion steamer they had rented. Then I took her to the marquis and she got out of the country with his household."

The duke was watching him closely. "Odd thing that you were there at just that time."

"Yes, it was odd. But very fortunate, the way things turned out."

It was clear that a suspicion was beginning to grow in the ducal mind. "I shouldn't go prying into your feelings, Bade," he said. "Isabelle spoke of you often and I've known you had a very special place in her regard."

"I'm glad to hear you say so, Your Grace."

"It never occurred to me before but I begin to think you may have shared my feeling for her."

Jonathan looked up quickly. No one had yet thought of bringing in a light and the room where they sat was in partial darkness. The duke nodded his head as though something had occurred to him to confirm his suspicion. "She depended on you in so many ways. I would hear her say, 'I wonder what Jonathan would think' or 'I must speak to Jonathan about that.'" He paused and gave his head a rather rueful shake. "I don't suppose any woman ever had so many men in love with her as Isabelle. I used to get angry with them as individuals but when I considered them as a whole I always felt kind of proud."

The improved health and the jauntiness of spirit he had shown after the long cruise in the *Semiramis* had been largely lost. He seemed stooped and his face was thin and hollow. Bade's face was thin also, to the point almost of transparency. It was not hard to imagine the officials on a certain Gate watching the approach of this unusual man on his last journeying and one of them saying: "There's no mistaking that kind of face. It's rather wonderful, don't you think, for a worldling?" And another one adding: "Wasn't it just the other day that we sent a chariot of fire down to bring one back who looked very much the same?"

Finally Jonathan nodded in agreement with what the duke had said. "Isabelle is dead and it's all over now. Perhaps it has become permissible to talk about such things. Yes, Your Grace, I was in love with her. It was all on my side, of course. A silent and never declared form of devotion. She may have known it but I was never quite sure."

"Of course she did," said the duke. "Depend on Isabelle for that."

"Well, then, you know that I never had a chance and realized it from the start. There was always an old man around with great wealth and a title. And you in the offing, Your Grace."

"Gad, how she kept me waiting! But it was partly my own fault."

"I was a useful busybody who could always be depended on and might even be expected to turn up in moments of need. I was happy to be of service to her, and proud. I became used to that role over the years and I even believe that I became content with it. No, not quite. You never get too old for dreams."

Jonathan rose slowly to his feet. "I must be on my way. I'm afraid I will never get used to—to knowing that Isabelle will never need me again."

The two old men, their eyes brimming with tears, shook hands slowly and solemnly.

"Life is going to be pretty damned dismal without her," said the duke. "Look here, Bade, you must come and see me. We'll talk. We'll talk about Isabelle."

"I'll take you up on that, Your Grace. I think it will do us both good to talk about her. You'll hear from me quite soon."

## CHAPTER SEVEN

### 1

Six people had gathered for a conference in the square main room at Three Gables, sitting in a semicircle near the corner where the curving stairway opened. There were the four who might be called the regulars, Titus, Lew Stain, Mary Tindy and Selwyn Geist. Casper Lowfoot had come to join in the discussion and was sitting beside his wife with his eyes fixed on the fringe of a rug at his feet. The last member was a newcomer, the Pint of whom Stain had spoken. He was a small fellow with a round face in which eyes of the color of a deep fog never seemed quite able to focus.

It had been decided that there would have to be a quick exodus from the house when the money was received from Tontine headquarters two days thence. Titus was to deposit the check in the Wantage bank his father had used and at the same time he was to draw out two thousand pounds in cash, to pay the expenses of taking his father to Switzerland where, it was hoped, his health would improve. The money would be divided at once according to the agreed basis of sharing. Titus would remain abroad and over a matter of six months he was to draw on the bank for various amounts, never addressing them from any one place twice, until the whole sum had been withdrawn. The division of the money was to continue until the final withdrawal. Lew Stain and the Lowfoot family had already declared their intention of staying at home to look after their local interests.

At this point Lowfoot raised his eyes from the floor for the first time, revealing that his face was almost as brown and warty as a toad's back. "Supposing the young man gets the money and never sends us our shares?" he asked.

Pint had said little in the course of the discussion. Now he spoke up in a thin, high voice. "He'll send the money," he promised. "I'll always be with the young man."

"Will you go to the bank at Wantage with him?" asked Lowfoot.

"Oh yes. I'll be right at his elbow."

Titus had been listening with a growing sense of resentment and frustration. These people, who had gathered to dispose of money which he considered to be all his own, had never consulted him. They made decisions and settled on methods without as much as a "What d'ye think, Mr. Grace?" or a "Well, do *you* agree?" It seemed to him, besides, that he was always elected to take the risks. He must go to the bank with the fraudulently endorsed check (his handiwork, moreover), he must draw out the two thousand pounds, sustaining the scrutiny of the banking officials, he was the one who must forge check after check, laying a trail by which he might be traced, while these five obnoxious strangers shared in the proceeds. And now they were openly questioning his honesty.

"See here," he said, the color rising in his cheeks, "I'm the one who's taking the risks and if there's anyone questions how they'll get what they claim is their share, I say let 'em walk out now. As far as I'm concerned, it will be a case of good riddance."

Selwyn Geist grasped the handle of the cane he was holding, Julian Grace's favorite cane, as though he would enjoy laying it across the youth's shoulders. "Listen to the young cock!" he said. "Does it occur to this seller of his father's body that we can get along without *him?* If his fine gentlemanly pride has been hurt, let *him* do the walking out, I say. Let him go to the police and see what good he'll get out of that."

Pint turned his almost opaque eyes in the direction of the actor. "Stow your gab, Sell!" he ordered.

Geist's fat, white fingers tightened on the cane handle but he accepted the little man's advice. He closed his mouth.

"Now that all's settled in a proper friendly spirit," said Lew Stain, who would have been glad to be rid of all of them so that the profits would remain intact in his great grasping paws, "I've a piece of news for you. Last night Helen Groody's house burned to the ground and she did not get out."

Five pairs of avid eyes turned in his direction. Selwyn Geist was the first to regain his breath. "That means," he exclaimed, "that I get fifteen hundred quid instead of the thousand!"

"Nothing of the kind!" said the undertaker sharply. "You were hired to do a job of work at a fixed sum. An outrageously high sum. What happened last night doesn't affect you at all."

"This once I agree with the play actor," said Lowfoot, addressing the rug at his feet. "Mrs. L. and me gets *our* share of this windfall and make no mistake about that!"

Lew Stain winked at his partner as though to say, "You fool, I'll take care of you later!" but the Lowfoot eye could not be reached. From the flush on Mary Tindy's face, it was apparent that she too was prepared to do battle for a full share of the extra money.

For a few minutes the amiable group raged at one another. Titus bit at his nails and said to himself, "Listen to these buzzards, fighting over *my* money!" Pint, who was sitting on a sofa and could swing his feet without touching the floor, seemed content at first to let them thresh it out among them. Finally, however, he grew tired of the repetitious abuse they were bandying back and forth.

"Will you all listen to me for a minute?" he asked.

The others suspended the argument. The little man's curious gray eyes, which had the effect of creating a chill about him, seemed to loom larger than ever in his moonlike face. "Mr. Stain, I am ashamed of my colleagues," he said. "I don't agree with them at all. I apologize for them, Mr. Stain." He paused and his eyes followed a slow orbit from face to face. His voice grew more restrained and gentle. "They are asking too little, Mr. Stain. Oh, very much too little, Mr. Stain!"

"I'll have you know——" began the organizer of all this deception. But the opaque eyes were fixed on him. He rolled his black cigar nervously in his mouth and left the sentence unfinished.

"In the first place," said the little man, "the death of Miss Groody increases the risk. It narrows things down. Most certainly it makes it difficult for us to succeed in our ingenious and laudable design. My thought is that the increase in the financial return—a matter of better than five thousand pounds—be shared equally among us." He looked at the tip of the semicircle where the Lowfoot family sat. "Five shares, the Lowfoots having one between them. Five even shares."

"You robber, you thief!" cried Titus. The way things were going, he would emerge from this nightmare of risk with a sadly shaved share.

"The codling is angry," said Pint. "He says things he doesn't really mean. For his own sake, I hope he doesn't mean them. The codling will be wise to remember that our need of him will grow less all the time. And who knows what might happen to him when we find we don't need him at all?" Reaching to a table at one end of the sofa for pen and ink, the little man wrote something with an easy flourish and handed it to Titus. "Do you think you're the only one who can do a passable imitation of your father's signature? My fine young gentleman, how does that impress you?"

Titus gasped. It was a better imitation than he had been able to achieve.

"I might have known, Pint," said Stain bitterly, "that this sort of thing would happen. All you got to do is wedge one foot inside a door and right away you're not content until you have the title deeds in your pocket. You'll never be content with afters, you want the whole blasted dish!"

"For the first time," said Geist, grinning at the others, "I see some sense to having Pint in this."

For some minutes a distant sound of voices had been heard from the road. Now the sound grew and it became uncomfortably clear that a considerable number of people were approaching. The six parties to this amiable discussion sat in a sudden, uneasy silence.

"They're coming here!" said Stain in a tense whisper. "I don't know what it means but it's going to be a test. Sell, get into your make-up. You may have to put in an appearance. I mustn't be seen here, or you, Pint, or you, Lowfoot. We must get upstairs into clothes closets or the House of Commons, or any dark hole we can find. We'll be cold meat if we don't step lively."

2

Titus was sent out by the insistent Pint to face the visitors. There were a dozen or more of them, all middle-aged and upward, and all more or less men of substance. Their carriages had been left farther up the road, for it became narrow and rutty as it neared the river, and they had walked the last hundred yards or so. In the lead was Dr. Henry Sandilands, who had recovered sufficiently from his own illness to venture out.

It was the old doctor who first saw Titus waiting for them by the side of the house, and waved to him exuberantly.

"Are you the son?" he asked. "Young Titus? I remember you as a nipper, my boy, before—well, before your mother went back to Yorkshire. I'm Dr. Sandilands. No mistaking that hair. When I brought you into the world, your father felt the way William the Conqueror did when they showed him his son William Rufus. Well, my boy, we've come to congratulate Sir Julian. These are all old friends of his. We want to be the first to shake the winner by the hand."

Titus found himself at a loss. "What do you mean, sir?"

"Haven't you heard? Well, that's easy enough to understand. You are rather cut off down here, aren't you? Titus, the Duchess of Outland died of a heart attack this afternoon. Miss Groody was not able to escape from the bonfire that rascal made of her home, so your father is the only one left in. The Tontine has been won by our entry and the whole neighborhood is in a state about it, I can tell you. They'll be flocking down here by the hundreds. Everyone had a bit on the race and they're pretty happy about it."

Panicky thoughts were running through the head of the son of the house. "There's no way out of this!" he said to himself. "Someone is sure to twig what's going on. What can I do? What can I say?" Keeping pace with his anxiety was a deep sense of regret. "Thirty thousand pounds a year! If the Pater had only hung on a little longer, it would all be ours. I would be set up for life. Why did he have to die?"

Then he saw the obvious way to save the situation for the next few days at least.

"My father is not well, Dr. Sandilands," he said. "It's nothing more than complete exhaustion, following his last trip to London."

"I saw him starting off. I warned him. I said to him, 'Sir Julian, you stubborn fool, if you insist on this, it will be a miracle if you survive it.'"

"He hasn't wanted to have Dr. Hoard in to see him, preferring to wait until you were well enough to come down. But I'm afraid he can't see anyone today. Perhaps not for another week. The exertion might be too great. Nothing must happen to him—you'll understand, I'm sure—before that check comes."

"I'm sure everyone agrees with that," said the doctor. His voice, however, carried a heavy measure of doubt. It was clear that he was puzzled and not well pleased with the situation. "We've all got a bit up on the Tontine; and every shilling of it on your father, my boy. But—" he paused and frowned— "I don't think I quite understand you. You say he's so ill that he can't see anyone. Not even his doctor. Now I wish to point out, young man, that this is quite absurd. If he's as ill as you say, he shouldn't see visitors, but there's all the more reason for him to see me."

Titus shook his head. "I'm repeating what he said himself."

"Yes, I know what a stubborn old coot he is," declared the medical man. "He hates to concede that he's ill enough to need me. I know him. From long experience. I've had to force my attentions on him all these years because he doesn't take kindly to doctoring. Do you know what I caught him doing one day? Pouring the medicine I had left down a drain. He acknowledged he had intended to let me think he had used it all up. Yes, I know Julian Grace through and through and up and down. And under the circumstances, I think I'll just go in and see what's wrong with him."

Titus said desperately: "He's asleep, Dr. Sandilands. He just dropped off a few minutes ago and I'm sure he mustn't be disturbed yet. He—he hasn't been sleeping well."

The doctor hesitated. "Well, in that case, perhaps I'd better come back later on. I'll come alone, my boy, so you needn't have any fear that I'll bring a party of serenaders with me."

Titus was thinking fast. "I'll tell the pater you called, Dr. Sandilands, as soon as he wakens up. And I'll send you word about coming just as soon as the money has been received."

The medical man looked at him as though a new train of suspicion had been aroused by this hint of delaying the call. Titus expected to hear him say: "There's something wrong here, boys. Let's go in and investigate." But after a few moments' thought the doctor took him by the sleeve and led him aside.

"My boy," he asked in a whisper, "are you in trouble here?"

"Why—why, what do you mean?"

Dr. Sandilands was frowning now with deep uneasiness. "Somehow I don't like the look of all this. Mrs. Hiddledy gone and that great fat slut of a Mrs. Lowfoot in her place. Was she your father's choice? Honestly, son, I can't believe he wanted her to look after him. Do you find her satisfactory?"

"So far, sir. She—she's hard-working and she's clean about the place."

"And that great muscle-bound ox of a guard. Who is he? Where did he come from? And why do you think you need him? Oh, I know the explanation that's been given. That he's needed to guard the premises while the race is on. But I don't like him and he doesn't look to me the kind of man your father would want."

"He's here on orders, sir. Mr. Batson of the Home Office said we must keep someone on the place. That my father's safety might depend on it."

The doctor nodded his head reluctantly. "But what I don't see is why you had to import a man from outside. There are plenty of good strong fellows in the neighborhood who would have taken on the work gladly and guarded your father with their lives."

"We talked it over, sir. With Mr. Batson. He recommended getting an outsider. A local man might be taken in by friends, he said."

The doctor rubbed his nose reflectively. "Well, he might have a point there. But I still don't understand why you had to get someone as aggressive and unpleasant generally as this man. When I was in the United States I heard a word used which describes this fellow perfectly. Plug-ugly. That's exactly what this man is, a plug-ugly from the criminal world of London."

"He's not a bad fellow, Doctor. And he's very strong."

The doctor made a gesture with his hands. "I may be getting suspicious and nosy in my old age. But I do think I am justified in wondering if your father, Titus, is getting proper care in this strange new household. What did he have for lunch today?"

The mind of Titus was moving with more agility. "Soup, sir," he said. "Soup and toast. He didn't want anything else."

"Tea?"

"Oh yes, tea."

"Well," grumblingly, "that's sensible enough. Everything may be going on properly, but I still must say that I don't like to think of my old friend at the mercy of a pack of strangers. Titus, I want a promise out of you: that you'll let me know as soon as I can come back. And if I don't hear from you pretty soon, I'll come anyway. Get that into your head, young fellow."

### 3

When the visitors had departed and silence had settled again over the road to the river, Pint came down and took possession of the main room. Standing beside a table, he gave it a loud thump with an Indian club which he took from the wall. When Stain looked in to see what it was all about, the little man said, "Call 'em in, Stain, call 'em in."

"What for?"

"A discussion. This news brings us new problems. And get this into your head: I'm in charge here from now on. I'll be giving the orders. Now don't go skying a copper! I'll have no arguments about it. I'm running things."

Each member of the party was aware on entering the room that a change had come over Pint. He was no longer quiet and self-effacing. His eyes seemed as incandescent as a cat's, even in the daylight. His manner carried authority.

"Now you'll all listen to me," he began. "We've won the Tontine. There will be a check sent here two days from now for over thirty thousand pounds, drawn to Sir Julian Grace. That money is ours and the size of it means we must change our whole idea of what's to be done. Stain, you've got a mutinous look on your face so we'll start off by asking you what you think should be done under the circumstances."

"Done?" said the undertaker. "There's nothing to be done that we haven't already decided. We've got more to collect and we'll have to be a lot more careful. I grant you that."

"Has anyone got anything to add to that? No? Well, that shows what a narrow lot you are. You, Stain, have been a village factotum so long that you've got a village outlook." The strange eyes of the little man went around the circle of faces. There was a touch of scorn for them in his expression. "We've got to get ourselves a new Sir Julian Grace. We must have a permanent one. Someone who will look so much like the original that everyone will be fooled. He's going to live openly in considerable state on the Continent for as many years as we can get out of him. A French seaside resort will be the best place. And we're going to collect our thirty thousand pounds each year. That's the new plan as I see it."

"He thinks he can pufform miracles," said Casper Lowfoot. "Listen to him talk! Where's he going to get this new man who'll look so much like the real Grace?"

"Every man in the world has at least one double," said Pint. "There's a man in St. John's Wood, a bank clerk, who's the living image of me. I've talked to him. Even his voice is like mine. I could move right into that house of his and no one would know the difference. Well, somewhere there's a double ready-made for the late deceased Sir Julian Grace and all we've got to do is find him. That will be part of Mike's job."

Stain looked up with a start. "Mike!" he said. "What's Mike got to do with this?"

"My dear Mr. Lew Stain," rebuked the little man in an even gentler tone of voice than usual, "you don't think we can keep Mike out of this, do you? Thirty thousand pounds a year makes this a regular board-room go. We might as well give him our invitation because he'll walk in anyway and make himself right at home.

"Very well," he went on. "Mike is in and it's his responsibility to find the permanent double and get him thoroughly trained in the part. This is the kind of thing he likes to play around with and he'll come through with terrific results. It's to be hoped the double he finds is a few years younger so we can get good long use out of him. Mike will have to find some way to create a feud with the grandson who's in the East because it won't do for them to get together. Fortunately this bothersome grandson won't be back for more than a year and by that time Mike's lawyers will have such a breach opened up that the grandson won't want to see the old man. The codling here may be able to help us on that. Perhaps it'll have to do with the deeding over of the house; undue pressure, something of that kind. As far as the establishment on the Continent is concerned, it will be all open and above-board. No hiding like this. Our new Sir Julian will live rather well but quietly, of course. You," turning the shallow gray eyes on Titus, "will live with him. On the fat of the land and with a fine fat allowance. The rest of you will be sent so much a year. I reckon about half of it will remain in Mike's hands; and that's not a bad percentage for the expert job he'll have to do."

The little man remained silent for a few moments, waiting for comments. The others looked at each other out of the corners of eyes and fidgeted about in their chairs. It was clear that the same thoughts occupied their minds: resentment, dissatisfaction with the proposed arrangements and yet a certain fascination with the vista the words of Pint had opened up. It was Lew Stain who came forward first with a comment.

"I agree that the thing must be carried out on a grand scale. I was as blind as a bat about *that*. But I don't agree we got to deliver ourselves over bag and baggage to Mike and have him slice all the fat profits off the top. What share would you get, Pint?"

"Oh, my dear sir," answered Pint. "I will take good care of myself. I'll do quite well. You may depend on it."

"I'm sure you will," grumbled Stain. "You'll get a damned sight more out of this than I will. And I was the one started it."

"Of course I will."

"What will happen to me?" demanded the actor in a loud and belligerent voice.

"Nothing will happen to you. You'll step down and out. You'll get something each year. It will be like an annuity, an income, Sell. You should be very happy about it but I can see you're not going to be. Well, get this into your head: this will be Mike's show and if you ever blab a single word you'll have him to answer to—and then God help you, Sell."

"I've got to think about this," declared Geist with a pretense at dignity. "After all, I *am* Sir Julian Grace and I've been magnificent in the part, I'll have you know. Why shouldn't I go on with it? Why do you talk about finding someone else?"

"The reasons are many and would be clear to a backward charity child of four. So stow your gab, Sell. I'll get quite impatient with you in a minute and when I'm impatient I'm likely to get unreasonable. I don't suppose, my dear Sell, that you want to turn up someday in the river and *not* in a good state of preservation?

"There are a few more things to be said," went on the little man after a pause. "We must change our initial plan a little. It wouldn't do to deposit all our funds in one bank now that we'll have thirty thousand pounds in our mauleys. We'll divide it three ways, Wantage, Reading, London. We'll draw all of it out as soon as we get to France, the codling and I. None of the rest of you are going. You're staying where you belong and keeping up a good front. They must never have a chance to get suspicious. There's too much at stake now. I think I shall have to insist on most careful rehearsals of our first moves. Every word to be spoken must be understood and memorized. Every step, every movement, must be worked out in advance. We can't have any mistakes, my friends."

"You're taking a pretty high hand about this, Pint," said Lew Stain.

The little man kept his head lowered for a few moments. When he looked up his eyes seemed to have a feral glow in them.

"You have no idea, my dear man, how high a hand I'll take if it becomes necessary," he said. "You have no idea of the lengths I'm prepared to go. If you are wise, you'll not try to find out. And now, scatter, all of you. There's no reason for either of you—I mean you, Stain and Lowfoot—hanging around here like hyenas around a carcass. Get back to the teeming activities of village life. You, Sell, stay in your make-up in readiness for any emergency. You, Mrs. Lowfoot, cook us up a good meal. And now the codling and I will go into a close consultation on what we have to do in the next half dozen days."

## CHAPTER EIGHT

1

Helen Groody's trip to the camp of the Healer had been a success in one respect only. The party enjoyed themselves; it was made up of Mr. Joe Tope himself, Daphne the maid, to look after the comfort of her mistress, and Huruld to drive the horses. They arrived late in the afternoon and were given one of the clump of houses which surrounded the center camp, a place of three small rooms, furnished only with camp cots and washstands, and a few rush-bottomed chairs. They found that everyone went to the central house for the evening meal, some limping along on crutches, some pushed in wheel chairs, all of them very sick people but all extremely optimistic. Those who were allowed regular food were regaled on a great oyster stew (the oysters brought up fresh from the Channel), boiled beef with carrots and cabbage, and a suet pudding positively stuffed with raisins. The rest had whatever invalid food had been prescribed for them.

After supper the pleasurable part began. There was what the Healer called a get-together. The whole company drew into a close circle and sang songs. Individuals favored with numbers of their own. Mr. Joe Tope rendered "Knocked 'Em in the Old Kent Road" and the Duke of Outland's specialty, "Bill Sloggins." Not to be outdone, Daphne stood up and chirped "The Boy I Love Is Up in the Gallery" and "Sweet Kitty Clover." Then the Healer himself, a great giant of a man whose real name was Austin Aloysius Chapman, did some magic tricks which titillated everyone and caused much opening wide of eyes and such exclamations as "Did ye ever now!" and "Well, I siy!" His large hands, which could draw into place recalcitrant bones stubbornly out of place for years, could also move faster than the eye. After he had found a rabbit in Mr. Joe Tope's coat, the evening came to an end and there was a good-night prayer in which all joined.

The next morning the Healer took Helen Groody in hand. He asked innumerable questions and he examined her gnarled fingers and her very painful knee joints, and he listened to her heart. At the finish he gave his black-maned head a rather somber shake.

"You've really got it, haven't you?" he said. "You suffer a great deal, of course."

"A very great deal," she answered. "Last evening, when we were all having such a pleasant time, I was able to forget about my aching bones for a while. But that happens very seldom."

"Well," said the Healer, "I'll see you again this afternoon. In the meantime, talk to some of the others around here. You'll find a few of them quite interesting. You may succeed in forgetting these bones of yours for another welcome spell."

From the windows of the little house they occupied, she could see the place in front of the main camp where the discarded crutches were piled up. There were more than a score of them now and they made a most encouraging spectacle. "He's going to help me," she said to herself. "I'm sure of it because he seems so kind and so capable. Those wonderful hands will do something for me."

But when he came to see her in the afternoon it was evident at once that he was not going to be able to do anything for her. He gave his head a shake as he seated himself facing her.

"My dear lady," he said, "you have had this trouble for a long time."

"Yes, sir. A very long time."

"Do you know that it has reached your heart?"

"Oh yes. I've been told all about it. A specialist from Vienna came to see me not more than a fortnight ago and he told me that there—there would be trouble when the rheumatism really took hold of my heart. I've been reconciled to that."

"My dear lady, it's possible that I could do you some good with my treatments. There is magic in my hands. I can straighten out crooked muscles and I can get displaced bones back into place. If you had come to me when this started—you couldn't have done so, of course, because I wasn't here then—I could have had you as right as a trivet in an hour or two less than nothing. But, my very patient and gentle lady, when it gets to the heart it's a different matter."

The half-believed dream, which had brought her up into the Cotswolds on this pilgrimage, dissolved into nothing. She managed to give him a smile.

"I wasn't at all sure you could help me," she said. "It was just a wild hope."

"It's this way," said the Healer. "When the heart's affected there is sometimes a very sudden ending to things. You know that, so I'm not frightening you by saying it. Now suppose I gave you a treatment and it happened while you were here, or a short time afterward. Do you know what the doctors would do? They would have me arrested and I would be tried for murder. Nothing less, my dear lady. You see, the doctors don't care for this sort of thing. They say I'm a quack and, if they can catch me in anything, they'll send the police right in. And that would mean an end to my efforts to be helpful to my fellow men. You see, dear lady, this is not just a money-making scheme. I have to charge enough to keep the place running but that's all. I know I can help some of the poor sufferers who come to me, and I want to go on doing it."

"I understand, of course," said Helen. "Thank you, Doctor, for being so frank. It has been a pleasure to see what fine results you are getting. I've enjoyed my visit very much."

"Stay over another night," he advised. "Attend another get-together. It will do you good."

2

Mr. Joe Tope was still complaining bitterly as they reached the outskirts of Little Shallow.

"Why did he go and scratch hisself off the list?" he demanded, a reference to the action of the Healer. "Why does he want to turn you over to next door?" It was all a mystery to Mr. Tope. The Healer was there to heal and he should have taken Miss Groody in hand as he had done with all the others.

"It's quite all right, Mr. Tope," asserted Helen. "The Healer has his reasons and I understand them. Anyway the trip has done me some good."

They were to realize quickly how much good the trip had done her. As they reached the main crossroad of the village, Huruld let out a cry from his seat in front. "It's gone! Ma'am, the house! It's burned to the ground."

Helen turned and saw that he was right. The Old Rectory was indeed gone! Where it had stood with its stained chimneys and its pleasant air of mellow old age, there was nothing but a pile of ruins from which a few spirals of smoke still rose in places.

They drove over in furious haste and then halted in front of the property to gaze with sorrowful and still almost incredulous eyes at the sorry trick which circumstances had played them in their brief absence.

"My home!" cried Helen. "Oh, the dear old place! What can have happened?" Then a more detailed realization of what it meant began to take possession of her. "Do you suppose everything has been lost? My books! The portrait of my poor father! My fine, comfortable bed! The Chippendale sideboard!"

A boy had been attracted by the sight of the Groody carriage standing in front of the smoking ruins. As the stables had been burned also, it had been assumed that all the equipment and the horses had been lost and the boy's eyes were round and rather vacant with the shock as he came running over. When he perceived Huruld sitting up in front and Miss Groody herself on the seat below, he let out a curious sound compounded of fear and disbelief.

"Oo ay! It's ghosts, it is! A-come back from graves."

A man heard the boy and turned to look. His jaw dropped open and he seemed ready to join in the flight of the rapidly decamping youngster.

"Cor lumme!" he said. "It's her, damned if it ain't! And it's Huruld sitting up there like real flesh and blood."

In no time at all the whole of the village population had converged on the spot, to become convinced quickly that it was indeed Miss Groody and the members of her household, in real flesh and blood, come back from wherever they had been. Mutual explanations followed and Helen was thus enabled to judge the extent of her good fortune in her choice of a time to visit the camp in the Cotswolds. Mr. Joe Tope had vanished almost as soon as the explanations began. His agile mind, so well trained in the art of scrubbing and chalking, had seen at once that this meant changes in the betting position of Miss Groody as a Tontine contestant. He was frantically getting off a telegram to Herb Biler.

On the heels of the natives came two men whose interest in the return of the party had an official slant. The first to arrive was William Wordsworth Glossop, who had been dispatched promptly to the scene by the Tontine manager when word of Miss Groody's demise had reached London. He had been able to verify the report of the death of the Duchess of Outland and had notified the office that the Tontine had been won by Sir Julian Grace, still alive and in seeming good health at Three Gables. His face was a study as the fact came home to him that there was still competition. He felt, in fact, somewhat aggravated over this inexplicable turn of events. "Why *can't* they make up their minds whether they are dead or alive?" he asked himself.

He came to the side of the carriage to judge for himself. One glance convinced him that this was Miss Groody, sitting there and gazing with mournful eyes at the ruins of her home.

"Good day, Miss Groody," he said. "You remember me, of course. I am William Wordsworth Glossop. From the headquarters of the Waterloo Tontine. I've called on you twice, ma'am."

"Of course, Mr. Glossop. Oh, how sad it is to see what has happened to my beautiful old home! I can't seem to believe it's true."

"But, ma'am, it's splendid to see the owner alive and well," said Glossop. "Particularly as we had every reason to believe she had shared the fate of the house."

"Yes, Mr. Glossop. I suppose I have a great deal to be thankful for. I *am* alive. But it doesn't seem that there will be much pleasure for me in living now that my home is gone."

At this point Mr. Glossop extricated himself from the tight cordon of boggling natives around the carriage, and made off. He also had a report to get in quickly to his superiors in London, having to do with the distribution of the Tontine money on the day following. There would have to be two checks for half the amount instead of one for the full thirty thousand pounds.

His place at the side of the carriage was taken by Guy Chasson Batson. The man from the Home Office had heard the news but did not seem prepared yet to accept it. All the work he had been doing, the endless questioning of people who might know something, the frantic sending off of telegrams, the reports he indited every few hours to the Home Office; all this had been without much purpose if it were true that Helen Groody had not been killed after all. He stared at the delicate little lady in the carriage with almost hostile eyes.

"Ma'am, I am Guy Chasson Batson from London. The Home Office. *Are* you Miss Groody?"

Having no idea who he was or his purpose in being there, she inclined her head. "Yes, I am Helen Groody."

"And may I ask, ma'am, where you have been?"

"Well," she said, still puzzled as to his purpose, "I'm not sure that I should discuss this matter so openly, and with everyone."

"You must discuss it with me, ma'am."

She looked at him more closely. "Your purpose then is official."

"Yes, ma'am. I am in charge of the case."

"I'm sorry I can't invite you in to discuss matters in private. But, as you see, my house is now—well, it doesn't offer any such facilities, does it?"

At this point an acquaintance in the crowd suggested that Miss Groody should put up at the village inn until she could make other arrangements. "Of course," she said. "That is the first thing to do. The unexpectedness of everything has made it difficult for me to think."

"Please, before you go," said a brisk voice from among the spectators. "I'm from the London *Packet*. There are some questions I want to ask, Miss Groody."

Mr. Batson turned angrily in the direction of the voice. "Now see here, Corby. Haven't I told you with all due emphasis and in full clarity that when there's anything to be given out to the press I will do the giving out myself? I see you too, Convery, over there. What I've said to Corby applies to all of you. I won't have you getting in and asking questions first."

"A little sudden authority acts just like schnapps," said the reporter in a disgusted tone of voice. "It goes right up to empty heads and unsettles 'em. Eh, Convery?"

" 'Upon what meat doth this our Caesar feed'!" contributed the tall young man thus addressed, who was on the staff of the London *Times* and felt free to speak his opinion, even of Home Office men.

"I'll have no impudence from you penny-a-liners," asserted Mr. Batson, resorting as usual in disturbed moments to mopping his hands with his scented handkerchief. "Now, Miss Groody, I feel it would be wise for you to go to the inn at once."

In a very short time she was accommodated in a quite pleasant room which had from its windows the best possible view under the circumstances. She could see her shop, which looked very spruce and businesslike in new paint, and she could not see the blank spot where her beloved home had stood for so many years.

"And now, ma'am," said Mr. Batson when he was admitted half an hour later, "I have many questions to ask you. You are aware, of course, that this unexpected development has made necessary a complete change in my activities. Instead of a murder, I have only a case of arson on my hands. With intent, perhaps. I think I shall have little difficulty in proving the intent. But I want you to know first that I shall pursue this lesser breach of the law with as much assiduity as I was displaying before."

A new reason for anxiety took possession of the homeless Helen Groody. "Is it possible," she asked, "that this misunderstanding has not been confined to the people here? Could a false impression have reached as far as London?"

"I'm sure the morning papers all carried long stories of the happenings here," answered Mr. Batson. "These bothersome reporters have been in the village ever since the fire occurred."

"Then," cried Helen, "my niece in London thinks I am dead!" She motioned to her maid, who was arranging their few belongings about the room. "I must get off a telegram, Daphne. To poor Nelly. She will be frantic, I'm afraid."

One of the hotel maids, who was assisting in putting the room to rights, interrupted at this point.

"Please, ma'am," she said, "I heerd as Mr. H'Alfred Carboy was coming in by the morning train."

"Oh, I'm so glad!" cried Helen. "When he gets here I can really begin to plan what I am to do with the ruins of my life. Mr. Batson, can the Home Office wait for a few minutes? I'll let you know when I've sent my telegram off and attended to some other urgent matters."

Guy Chasson Batson bowed rather stiffly. "As there is less urgency about the case," he said, "I suppose there is no reason to disturb you until such time as your mind is free of other matters. But I must demand that you do *not* speak to reporters until you have discussed everything with me. I shall be below when you are ready for me."

When the official had left, Helen's mind began to function with her usual clearness and decision. "Daphne," she said, "find Huruld and tell him to be at the station to meet Mr. Carboy off the first train. Arrange for Mr. Carboy to have lunch with me here. Then go to Mr. Price at the shop and tell him I desire to see him at once. I've decided that we'll have to move back to our old quarters behind the shop until other arrangements can be made. I have no intention of accepting hospitality. I'm always uneasy in other people's houses, particularly since I've become such an invalid. The rooms back of the shop are being used to store stock but Mr. Price will have to move everything out and find other places for it. We won't be very comfortable there, Daphne, but we'll have to put up with it for a while. And I must say there's something almost inspiring in going back to the place where I started so many years ago. I'll find myself with a battle on my hands, you know, and there will be advantages in living where I can keep an eye on everything. Oh dear, if I only had good health! I would be over there already."

CHAPTER NINE

1

The night before the Tontine money was to be distributed, the Rev. Gilbert Tranmer returned from his long holiday in Italy. He came back a new man, refreshed in body and soul, and loaded down with curious things he had picked up on his lone travels. He brought back as well an enthusiasm for bright skies and vivid colorings and hills covered with vineyards, and the sound of melodious voices heard over the shimmering surfaces of blue lakes. His spirits were so very much improved, in fact, that he picked up a notice on his desk about a meeting of the Ladies' Committee for Consideration of New Carpet for the Chancel Steps and said to himself: "The dear ladies! It will be such a pleasure to see them all."

He sang snatches from the operas over his breakfast and talked like a steam en-gine (as Mrs. Culp, the housekeeper, put it) over his boiled egg.

"And how have things been at home?" he asked.

"It's been very quiet, sir," replied Mrs. Culp. "All except for the Tontine. There's been aplenty about that."

"The Tontine? Indeed. Nothing has happened, I trust, to my good friend Sir Julian."

"Just that he's won it," declared the housekeeper. As she had not heard of Helen Groody's emergence from the shades, to quote one of the London newspapers that very day, she gave it out that both ladies were dead, leaving the neighborhood contestant the undisputed winner.

"Well," said the homecomer, heaping marmalade on a piece of toast with a realization that an English breakfast was better than anything he had encountered abroad, "I'm very sorry to hear about Her Grace and Miss Groody. But I must say there's satisfaction in having Sir Julian the winner. I trust there has been no gambling going on, no betting on the results."

"Everybody for miles around had a bit on it. All of it down on Sir Julian, of course."

"Ah, how very reprehensible! You also, Mrs. Culp?"

"Just the ten shillings you left with me, sir. I've got the ticket and we'll divide the winnings as agreed, sir, when the books pays up."

"Quite," said the clergyman. "It will come in most handy, Mrs. Culp, because my journeyings cost me much more than I had anticipated." He paused and took a final sip of tea, saying to himself, "I must pay Sir Julian a call this morning. It will be a chance to kill two birds with one stone."

What he meant was soon apparent. Among the things the good vicar had brought back with him was a coat about which, now that he was home, he had misgivings. It was a very gay affair of cream-colored corduroy with large steel buttons and a twisted belt of the same material in red, white and blue. A handsome thing unquestionably but could it be worn here at home without some loss of dignity? He had no thought other than to don it in the seclusion of his study, particularly in the seasons when the house became chilly, and when he worked in his garden. There was no reason, surely, for him to wear nothing but his clerical clothes and his "dog collar," which he secretly disliked. It had occurred to him that his old friend Sir Julian Grace would give him an honest opinion on this point.

It was around nine o'clock when the Rev. Gilbert Tranmer wheeled out his bicycle from the shed adjoining the stables and threw one leg over the saddle. He was carrying the corduroy coat on his shoulder and he could see the disapproval in Mrs. Culp's eyes as she watched from a kitchen window.

He said something in Italian which was meant to mean, "To blazes with such a stunted view of life!" and he sang "O Sole Mio" as he pedaled off down the road.

It was a beautiful morning. Spring had come. He was feeling in the best of spirits when he reached Three Gables and rested his bicycle against the trunk of one of the tall oaks. But the results of his tap on the door brought a quick change in his mood. It was not the housekeeper of so many years' standing who answered the knock but a woman he recognized at once with surprise and disapproval.

"Oh, Mrs. Lowfoot," he said. "This is a surprise. Where is Mrs. Hiddledy?"

"Gone," said Mary Tindy. "Discharged. I've took her place. Is it Sir Julian you've come to see? Can't be seen, Rev'end."

"And why not? I'm just back from a long holiday in Italy and I'm very anxious to see Sir Julian. He is in good health, I trust."

"No. Bad health. No one is allowed to see him. Not for days yet, Rev'end."

The spirits of the homecomer took an immediate dip. He felt there was something wrong. One did not receive such a gruff reception as this at Three Gables nor was it in accordance with the Grace tradition to employ a woman of the stamp of Mrs. Lowfoot. And where was Noel, his steadiest and best listener in church?

He asked about Noel and got one word as an answer. "Dead."

"Dead! Mrs. Lowfoot, I am indeed sorry! This is very sad. It takes away all of the pleasure I was anticipating from my return. Poor Noel! Still, he was a good man and a sincere believer and it is some consolation to know that he is reaping his full reward." The vicar sighed deeply and then returned to the question of his friend's health. "But, Mrs. Lowfoot, you must tell me more about Sir Julian. I am very much concerned about him."

And then Mary Tindy proceeded to make a great mistake. Instead of repeating that the owner of the house was not strong enough to see anyone, and letting it go at that, she decided on a single little bit of additional information. "His teeth are hurting him something awful, sir."

There was a basis of truth in what she said. The actor who now stood in Sir Julian's stead had developed an ulcerated condition in one of his teeth and was having a very bad time of it. It seemed to the woman that this was a perfectly safe piece of corroborative evidence. It happened, however, that the Rev. Gilbert Tranmer was one of the very few people in existence who knew that two years before Sir Julian Grace had found it advisable to part with his teeth and have a false set made for him.

"Indeed!" said the clergyman, looking at her with immediately sharpened interest. "His teeth are bothering him, you say?"

"Yes, sir. He's just like a bear with the pain of it."

Then the Rev. Gilbert Tranmer made a mistake himself. Instead of going quietly away and spreading the word of what he had discovered, so that steps could be taken in sufficient force, he decided to bluster the situation through himself. A decision which, as will soon be clear, was to prove a costly one for him.

"Nonsense, woman!" he said. "Sir Julian Grace could not have a toothache for the very best of reasons."

"He's suffering, I tell you. Suffering something awful."

"Someone may be. But not your employer. The real Sir Julian has no teeth. And now will you tell me just what is going on here?" He made his way through the door as he spoke.

"I will tell you," said a quiet voice from somewhere inside the house. A small man materialized in front of the indignant clergyman, one who had first been mentioned in this narrative as "an odd and frightening man." He looked up with his strange light eyes and began to speak in the same slow and almost gentle way. "I don't know who you are, sir, but it is clear that you are a person of no discretion whatever. You come into a household where you have no business and you proceed to tell us that you are ready to—shall we say, blow the show? Well, it's very unfortunate for you that you've warned us in advance what you propose to do. Very unfortunate, my dear sir, for we will now find it necessary to be quite violent with you."

The clergyman was not intimidated in the least. "I don't know who you are," he said, "but you're a very questionable character, and you wouldn't be here if something strange hadn't happened. I'm going to get to the bottom of this."

The little man seized the corduroy coat from his arm and threw it on the floor. He then took its owner by the shoulders and shook him back and forth in a fury over this dislocation of their well-laid plans.

"Sell!" called the little man.

The actor, with one side of his jaw badly swollen, came out from his quarters in the Fox wing and took hold of the unwanted visitor by both shoulders. The clergyman was lifted off the floor and held in suspension while Pint produced a handkerchief.

"Let him down," he said. "And now, if you please, we'll have no sound out of you, my good devil-dodger. If you make as much noise as the squeak of a rat in a trap, I'll see to it personally that your throat is neatly cut. From ear to ear."

When the visitor had been securely gagged and his arms bound behind him, Pint sat down and began to ask questions. He looked in sullen fury at Mary Tindy, who was now thoroughly frightened and repentant.

"You!" he said. "What did you tell him?"

"I said he had the toothache," she wailed. "That was all. How was I to know there was anything wrong in saying it?"

Pint raised both hands in the air. "That's the way it goes!" he said. "We have a magnificent plan. We see years of prosperity ahead. And a woman with a head like a cabbage rotting in the frost takes it on herself to tell one little thing she doesn't need to." He turned savagely in the direction of the actor. "Put him away somewhere, Sell. Upstairs in one of those closets.

Make sure he's so well trussed up he can't make a move. Then get down here quick. We've got some things to talk about."

"The cat's out of the bag," said Geist when the clergyman had been attended to and the four of them were sitting together. "And as far as I'm concerned, I don't care. The way this tooth is paining, I just want to get out of this hole and find a dentist."

"That fang has cost us a fortune," said Pint. "Now we can't go on with the grand scheme. All that's left to us is the chance to get this money coming in today. I haven't figured out how it's to be done. But if you'll stop bawling about your jaw and let me do some thinking, I'll find a way. Thirty thousand pounds! We must get our hands on it."

He closed his eyes and leaned his moon-shaped head against the back of the chair. "We can't take the check away with us. They would stop payment at the first hint of doubt and then we wouldn't have a shilling for our pains. There's no bank would cash it for us—not for the whole amount, that is. If we deposit it, as we first planned, and draw out some, that's all we'll ever see. That snooping tusheroon upstairs has done for us. Perhaps, if we're lucky, we'll have as much as three days to work in. Can we manage it in three days?"

Titus was listening to this in a state of horror. The sight of the Rev. Gilbert Tranmer, with the gag in his mouth and his arms bound behind him, being kicked and prodded up the stairs, had thrown him into a fright from which he would not soon recover. "Have I died and gone to hell?" he was wondering. "Are these devils I'm listening to?"

"What are we going to do with the minister?" asked Geist, shaking his head with the swelling in one cheek, and groaning. "We can't keep him locked up long, you know. They'll be searching everywhere for him."

"They won't find him," declared Pint. "Not where we're going to send him. We're going to send him right up to the golden gates he's been preaching about all his life."

"No, I draw the line at murder," said the actor, looking up and forgetting the pain for a moment. "Anything but that. I'm not going to swing for all the money in the world."

"Nor me," said the woman.

Titus was looking at Pint like the bird which cannot move while the snake writhes up to swallow it.

The little man made a gesture with the tip of one finger across his throat. "It's the only way," he said. He began to explain why. They might be able to keep the clergyman hidden for a matter of hours, perhaps for better than a day, but certainly no more. Before they knew it, there would be searching parties around the house, and then it would be all over. A plan was beginning to form in his mind, a way to get all the money out of the country. It would need two days to carry out, perhaps three; so it could not be done with the clergyman alive. As he talked, the woman began to watch him intently as though she were coming over to his side of the question. The actor, shaking his head from side to side, hoping the pain could be eased in that way, was not finding any arguments to put in on the other side.

"But what about the body?" asked the actor finally. "A body can be found as soon as a live man."

"But supposing it isn't found? The good old *corpus delicti*. The law can't do much until they've found the body. It seems to me," added Pint, looking slyly at the still and frightened faces about him, "we are in a fortunate position in that respect. We can reasonably expect our colleague, Mr. Stain, to attend to the little matter of the body."

"Do you suppose," asked the woman timidly, because Pint's angry eyes were still on her, "that he told anyone he was coming here?"

"I've thought of that, of course," said Pint. "There's no way of finding out. He has a stubborn look about him and I don't believe he would tell us the truth, even if we beat him within an inch of his life—what little he has left of it. But I'm hoping he didn't tell. These walkers with the Lord start out to make calls and they're never quite sure where they'll wind up. Kind of hit and miss, do you see?" Suddenly he stopped as a new thought occurred to him. "How did he get here?"

When she did not answer, being too upset, no doubt, for coherent thought, he pounded furiously on the table and repeated the question. "How did he get here, woman? Do you hear me? Did he walk? Did he roll up in a celestial carriage with angels in attendance?"

"No," she answered. "He come on a bicycle."

The little man sprang up with a furious agitation of his short legs and ran to a window. He nodded, turned his head toward her and pointed out the window with a dramatic forefinger.

"There it is," he said. "In clear view. Under a tree. It's saying as plain as day: He's here. Just go inside and you'll find him. He's a prisoner of the thieves and crooks and money-changers inside." He shook his fist at Mary Tindy. "Why did you leave it there? God, woman, why must we be cursed with your help!"

Then he turned to Titus. "Get on this, you! Take that machine and throw it in the river. No, that would be dangerous. Rivers are alive. They're full of eyes. Boats coming silently up and down without any warning. Blabbing little boys fishing everywhere with bent pins. Houses you can't see for the trees, and full of windows with people peering out all the time. No. The river won't do. Take the infernal thing up the road and hide it in the woods. Cover it over with underbrush and leaves. And," taking the corduroy coat and ripping it into two pieces with a furious motion of his arms, "put this with it. Quick, now!"

Titus was reluctant to return after obeying his instructions. Three Gables had become a place of terror. Had Pint followed out his threat and disposed of the Rev. Gilbert Tranmer with as much dispatch as he himself had shown in getting rid of the bicycle? A silence hung over the house which seemed to hint of unspeakable things. "Turn about!" said a resolute voice inside himself. "Go at once and tell what you know. There may still be time to save the old man."

But Titus was less resolute than the voice. He dreaded the consequences of such an action more than what might happen inside the house. It was possible, also, that Pint had already acted to be rid of the unwelcome intruder. If this were the case, it was too late to save himself by giving warning.

The house was in partial darkness when he finally let himself in. He could hear steps in the kitchen where Mary Tindy was working. He assumed that the actor had returned to his uneasy quarters in the Fox wing. But where was the implacable little man who had made himself the master of them all? Titus climbed the back stairs on tiptoe and paused on the upper landing. All of the windows were closed and the blinds drawn. A footstep from below gave notice that Pint was in the front of the house and, with this much assurance, Titus decided he would endeavor to learn what had happened to the clergyman. If the latter had already been killed, there might still be time for him to make his escape and perhaps be free of the consequences.

Before he could move from the landing he became conscious of a very slight sound from somewhere in the darkness. It was a furtive sound and seemed to have been caused by something being dragged on the floor. It was repeated at slow and regular intervals. Titus listened closely and became convinced that it came from his own bedroom on the southwestern angle of the building. The door was partly open but he lacked the courage to venture inside.

"He's alive!" he said to himself. "Somehow he's got free of the cupboard and is trying to reach one of the windows."

Titus was still reluctant to commit himself to the bold and proper course. While he stood in the hall and debated the matter, he could hear the cautious movement repeated at regular intervals. "Pint will kill him out of hand if he finds what he's up to," he thought. This seemed so certain that he considered the advisability of freeing the clergyman of his bonds and blocking the door while they shouted for help from the window. But this called for more courage than he was able to muster.

He had partially retraced his steps down the back stairs when he heard Pint's voice from the front of the house.

"Who came in?" demanded the little man. "I thought I heard steps."

Mary Tindy came to the door of the kitchen. "It's just him—Titus," she said. "I saw him at the back door."

Pint came back and stared up into the semidarkness. "What are you doing there?" he demanded, catching sight of Titus.

It was now too late to act. Titus returned to the lower hall. "I was going up to my room to lie down," he explained.

"Did you get rid of the bicycle?"

"Yes. I did what you said."

Pint has not taken his eyes from the face of the son of the house. It was clear that his suspicions had been aroused. Finally he motioned toward the front room with one thumb. "Get in there, you. I don't like the way you're acting. Are you getting ready to play the nark on us?" His eyes gleamed in the partial darkness. "It's too late. You're in this up to your neck. But I'll feel more comfortable if I have you under my eye."

2

The boy who had discovered the body of Noel lying in the kitchen at Three Gables was a very gentle and unfortunate lad named Wilton, but because of his having a bad leg and needing to use a crutch he was called Three Legs by the other boys in the neighborhood. He could not keep up with them and so he had little part in their games and other activities, which made him very unhappy. His one chance to mingle with them on anything like equal terms had come about when he found the body. They fairly swarmed around him then to get full particulars, saying such things as "Gee, Wilton, what did the body look like?" and "Say, weren't you scared to death?" Wilton had stoutly maintained that he was not frightened but this was no more than a pose. In reality he had been so badly alarmed that he had run away as fast as he could hobble with his crutch.

As a result of his inability to keep up with the other boys, poor little Three Legs was much by himself. He liked to wander along the river, to sit by the weir and watch the play of the fast-darting fish, to follow with rapt eyes the flight of birds. When the season was more advanced he would be a very great deal in the woods, sitting under a tree perhaps, so quietly that sometimes he would see pointed noses come up out of holes and sharp little eyes peer warily out at the world. He was in the habit also of paying many visits to the neighborhood of Three Gables. Some things were going on there which puzzled him. The one he thought about the most was the change in Sir Julian Grace. Several times, after watching the actor strolling in the gardens, he had said to his mother: "Sir Julian must be getting old, Ma. He walks different. Kind of stiff. And sometimes he looks different."

His mother, a widow who depended for their support on a pension her father had been awarded, a very small one, had agreed about the reason. "He's an old 'un, Sir Julian. No wonder he walks different. Pretty soon he won't be doing any walking at all."

"It's strange, Ma," said the observant boy. "He doesn't look as nice as he used to."

Now it happened on this particular day that Three Legs was up in the woods, searching for the first signs of approaching spring and finding reason for jubilation in little shoots of green under the heavy carpet of the leaves, when he saw Titus make his way into the cover of the trees some distance off. The newcomer was carrying a bicycle by the saddle and handlebars and seemed in a great hurry about something. What followed puzzled the small boy very much. Titus placed the machine on the ground behind the

broad trunk of an old oak, placed a kind of coat on top of it and proceeded
to cover it with branches and twigs, packing them down securely. When he
had finished this task he turned and hurried to the road in a manner which
a grownup would have called furtive.

"He's got red hair," said the boy to himself. "He must be Titus Grace.
But why was he hiding the bicycle? Was he playing a trick on someone?"

The boy decided that this was worth looking into and he started off also
in the direction of Three Gables. He did not take the road but hobbled
through the woods by easy routes which he had found for himself, crossing
and recrossing a small stream as many as half a dozen times on the way.
When he arrived opposite the house he ensconced himself behind a tree.
Titus was nowhere in sight. It was clear that the son of the Grace family
had already returned and had gone in. But something else happened almost
immediately which rewarded the boy for his rather tiring trip. A face appeared at an upper window on the side of the house directly opposite him.
The boy gasped with astonishment.

"It's the rector!" said the boy to himself. "It's Mr. Tranmer. But—but
what's wrong with his face?"

Only part of the clergyman's face could be seen, for the lower half was
covered by something in the nature of a white handkerchief. "He's hurt,"
thought the boy, a conclusion which was supported by the fact that Mr.
Tranmer's hair was disheveled and that he had a look in his eyes which
could mean only one thing, that he was consumed with a desperate fear.

As the boy watched, dropping down into the underbrush, the face disappeared from the window with a suddenness which suggested that someone had seized the clergyman from behind and had dragged him away.
The boy showed a degree of discretion unusual for one of his years by
remaining where he was and keeping well down out of sight.

A moment later another face appeared in the window and this time it
was the boy who felt fear. It was a most disturbing kind of face, round in
shape and pasty in color and with eyes which sent a shudder up young
Wilton's spine. The owner of these eyes looked up and down the road with
great care and it was clear to the boy that this very odd man was trying to
find out if anyone had been watching. He remained still and was very
much relieved when the man in the window, having observed no trace of
onlookers, vanished from sight. The shade was pulled down after him.

Three Legs said to himself: "This is very strange, this is. Now why should
they have the rector as a prisoner? Because that's what he is, I think. And
isn't that handkerchief around his face so he can't speak? It's not Sir Julian
Grace that's doing it. It's that bad man with the funny eyes. Sir Julian
is a good man and goes to church regularly. And he and the rector are
friends."

The boy waited a long time, having acquired a wholesome fear of the
bad man with the very light eyes. He was afraid if he made as much as a
single move the bad man would be at the window again, staring down at
him; and a boy with a crutch would not be able to run away very fast.

Finally, however, he got up his courage to leave the screen of the under-brush; for if anything was to be done for the rector it had to be done quickly. He hobbled back into the woods as fast as his legs would carry him.

When he told her what he had seen in the window his mother said to him: "Come now, Wilton, you imagined it." When he persisted she said, "But really, who would want to hurt Mr. Tranmer, who wouldn't hurt a fly himself?" The boy stoutly maintained that the rector was a prisoner in the house and that evil people were acting as his jailers.

"I must get to South Burnley and tell them," he said. "You should have seen Mr. Tranmer's eyes. He was frightened. He needs help."

So the boy started out by himself to walk to the village of South Burnley. The quickest way was by the road which ran down to the river at Three Gables but he knew enough to give that neighborhood a wide berth. Instead he selected a winding road west of the weir, which was rough and hilly and was six whole miles away from South Burnley. He was plodding along very slowly and wondering if he would ever get there when a wagon turned out of a side road and pulled up to wait for him. The boy knew this outfit very well. It belonged to Ramp Poole, who was a higgler and drove all over the countryside, finding things to buy.

"Well, Wilton," said Mr. Poole, "where are you off to? This is pretty rough work for boys with crutches."

Three Legs had started to cry from sheer exhaustion and fear that he would never reach the village. At this he stopped and wiped some of the sweat and dust and tears from his cheeks. "Please, Mr. Poole, I must get to the village. The rector needs help, sir. They'll do him in, sir! His face is bound up in a white rag and I don't think he can breathe well. He's at Three Gables."

"Ham, Shem and Japheth!" said the higgler. "Say that slower. I can't make any sense out of it."

"He's a prisoner, Mr. Poole, sir. At Three Gables. There's an ugly man standing guard over him."

The higgler laughed. "Now, Wilton," he said. "That's a good one. What are you going to be, another Charles Dickens, making up stories like this?"

"No, sir. No, Mr. Poole. It's the truth. I tell you it's the truth."

"Wilton, are you sure you aren't making up a story to equal the time you found the colored man in the kitchen? That's what it sounds like to me. Come now, own up."

"Please," said the boy, "would I be walking all the way to the village up these steep hills just to tell some lies?"

"Ham, Shem and Japheth! Of course not. My boy, I believe you. All right, Wilton, get in. I'll have you there in two shakes of a dead lamb's tail."

Three Legs climbed up to the high seat with some difficulty. With the curiosity of youth he looked at the wagon back of him and saw that the higgler had been having a busy day. There were three crates of chickens, a pair of ducks plucked and ready for the oven, an old bureau with a metal top and six pairs of assorted footmen's clothing, satin stockings and all.

Ramp Poole thumped the reins on the hindquarters of the horse to get it going and then turned into a side road which proved to be a good short cut. In no time at all they had reached South Burnley and had made their way to the inn. By good fortune there was a group of men in the bar: a gamekeeper, two laborers from the fields in stained smocks, several villagers in business clothes and Dr. Sandilands. The doctor had come in to see the ailing wife of the proprietor and was on his way out; but he stopped and waited when he saw the higgler and the dusty cripple.

"Men," said Poole, "and Dr. Sandilands. The boy has something to tell you. It will give you a start just as it did me. But I believe him. I think you'll all believe him too."

He picked Three Legs up and seated him on the bar, crutch and all. The boy looked kind of frightened and held his head down.

"I found him on the Eastbridge road. He was starting out to walk here and plodding along like the game little fellow he is. It would have taken him days to get here but I don't believe he would have quit. All right, Wilton, tell them what you saw."

It must have been apparent to everyone, and very clear indeed to Dr. Sandilands, that the boy would not grow much more and perhaps that he would not live very much longer. That being the case, he was now experiencing what would undoubtedly be the most dramatic moment of his short life. He rose to the occasion. With very few words he made them see the sorry plight of the imprisoned clergyman when he stood at the window silently appealing for help and the terror of the moment when the small man with the terrible eyes took his place. Certainly he made them realize his own fears as he waited to see if the man would catch a glimpse of him and come out to get him.

The story was listened to in silence and at the finish the doctor stepped up closer to the bar. "Wilton," he said, "are you telling us the truth? You saw all this with your own eyes?"

"Yes, Dr. Sandilands."

"You didn't get excited and kind of imagine some of it?"

"No, Doctor. No, sir."

"You say this man at the window was gagged. How could you be sure it was the rector if you could see only part of his face?"

"By the mole on his cheek, sir. It wasn't covered. And by his eyes."

"Well," said the doctor, addressing the company in the bar, "I believe the boy's story. I've had a curious feeling in my bones about that house. As though something queer was going on."

At this point one of the company, who had slipped out in the middle of things to investigate, came back. "It's true!" he said. "Every word of it. I've been over to see Mrs. Culp at the Rectory and she says the rev'end started out on his bicycle early this morning and hasn't come back. He carried with him a coat he brought home from Italy. It's the truth the kincher's telling."

"Ham, Shem and Japheth!" said the higgler. "Do you know what I think? I think Sir Julian is dead and that some crooks are in the house, pretending he's alive to get the Tontine money!"

This was an unpalatable theory to accept, for it meant that the bets on Sir Julian, which they had counted as won and had been spending in their minds, were lost. To the credit of all of them, it can be said that they gave little thought to their losses as soon as they were convinced.

"Men," said the doctor, "we had better get down there right away. We'll send word to the police at Windsor but we can't wait for them. There's a life at stake."

### 3

More than fifty men were recruited in a matter of minutes. They came from the shops and the cider mill and the farms close about, armed with shotguns and revolvers and dueling pistols, and any crude weapons they could get their hands on, including scythes and pruning hooks. There were buggies and fine carriages as well as farm wagons and bicycles to carry them down to the river. The whole village turned out to see them start and cheered them loudly.

Riding in his own buggy with the village grocer as his companion, the doctor said: "That redheaded son must be in it. These are queer times when things like this can happen."

In a very few minutes the doctor noticed something in the vehicle behind him and he raised an arm for the cavalcade to stop. Wilton, riding with Ramp Poole (who had emptied his wagon of goods and filled it with armed volunteers), had turned very white and had slumped back into his seat with closed eyes. The doctor leaped out and ran over to examine him. After feeling the pulse, he gave his head an ominous shake.

"The boy will have to be taken home at once," he announced. "I'm afraid the walk up that steep road has been too much for him. Who will do it? It means missing the show but I won't answer for this brave little fellow's life if he isn't attended to at once. Well, who's for it?"

There was silence for a moment and then the higgler said: "I'll go, Doctor. I hate to miss the fun but I'm fond of this boy. What am I to do?"

"Get him home and have him in bed at once. There's a medicine he'll have to take. His mother will know about that. I'll come over as soon as we have this little unpleasantness started. Thanks, Poole; I consider this very handsome of you."

"Don't mention it," said the higgler. He distributed his passengers among the other vehicles and turned off to the right at the next crossroad. Farewells were shouted to the boy from the whole train but it was doubtful if he realized it.

"I'm afraid of what may come of this," said the doctor, driving on. "He hasn't the strength of a kitten. Imagine him, setting out to walk six miles with a crutch, uphill most of the way! I wonder how many of us would have that much spirit?"

When they reached the last crossroad and had less than half a mile to go, a buggy with two occupants turned in ahead of them. Dr. Sandilands called out a warning. "No one allowed there. Draw in, gentlemen. Who are you, may I ask?"

The buggy came to a stop. The one who was driving leaned out and asked in an aggrieved tone, "What's all this?"

"We have some particular business down there," answered Sandilands, "and we don't want word of our coming carried ahead of us. I am Dr. Sandilands from South Burnley and these are all neighbors of mine. Now will you oblige by telling us who you are?"

"My name is Glossop. I'm the inspector for the Waterloo Tontine. Anything else you want to know?"

"A great deal. You see, sir, it's our opinion that Sir Julian Grace is dead and that they're trying to keep it a secret at Three Gables."

"Nonsense!" said Glossop heatedly. "I saw him not so very long ago. He was very much alive then, I can tell you."

"I wish we could believe you. We are all good friends of his and nothing would please us more than to find you are right."

"There has been enough of this kind of thing!" declared the inspector. "First they're dead and then we're told they are alive; or the other way about. Would you believe it, sir, that we've had to draw fresh checks three times already because of these conflicting reports? Must we do it again? Frankly, gentlemen, I'm getting tired of this."

The other man in the buggy was of rather considerable size and gave the impression of being a retired prize fighter. He had fingers as large a sausages grasping tightly the handle of a dispatch case.

"Am I right in assuming that you are delivering the Tontine money, Mr. Glossop?"

"If I am, it is my own concern, sir. Do you think, sir, I would discuss this matter in the hearing of a multitude of characters who seem to me, I must confess, decidedly suspicious?" Then he relented to the extent of making a partial explanation. "Do you know, Doctor, that Miss Groody turned up this morning in Little Shallow, safe and sound?"

Dr. Sandilands looked quite dumfounded at this information, as did all the members of the cavalcade. "Then we hadn't won anyway," he said. "I agree with you, Mr. Glossop, that things are getting highly complicated."

"I wired to London," declared the inspector, "to tear up the single check and have two made out, dividing the money between Miss Groody and Sir Julian. If what you say is true, we'll have to make still another change, awarding all the money to Miss Groody. But," giving his head a sharp nod, "you still have to prove to me that Sir Julian is dead. And I still believe you are going to find yourselves wrong."

"Come along with us, then, and see for yourself." The doctor looked about him and then called, "Robertson!"

"Yes, Dr. Sandilands," said one of the party in a rear wagon.

"Weren't you in the Crimea? Didn't you see some service later in India?"

"Yes, sir."

"I haven't met you since you moved to South Burnley, Mr. Robertson, but I've heard most favorable reports of you. It's going to be necessary to detach enough of our people to draw a cordon around the house on the east side, all the way from the stables to the river. We don't want any of them ducking out the back way. Will you take charge of this party?"

"Yes, sir. Very much honored, Dr. Sandilands."

"You'll need a dozen men. I think we had better let you have those with the best guns and who know how to use them. If these scoundrels make a break for it and won't stop on command, you'll have to let them have it, Robertson."

"Quite, sir."

"I would suggest you instruct your people to aim at their legs in that event. We don't want them killed. Killing is too good for them."

"Yes, sir."

"You had better use Sepoy Lane, which will take you straight to the cricket grounds. You must have your cordon drawn before we make a start. Will twenty minutes suffice?"

"Plenty, sir."

"Then select your men and get started." The doctor turned to the

Tontine inspector. "While we wait, Mr. Glossop, I'll tell you our reasons for taking these steps."

## 4

While the forces of retribution converged on Three Gables, a bitter controversy was being waged inside the house. The plan hatched in Pint's agile brain amounted to this: instead of depositing the check locally and drawing out as much cash as they dared, they would go at once to London and discount the check for whatever they could get. He insisted that this move was feasible even though it held out small hope of being profitable. It was undoubtedly the safer course, for the city would swallow them up and they would have a much better chance of escaping punishment when the truth came out. He held out no promises that the gimlet-eyed dealers in doubtful property who might conceivably pay them something in the expectation of compounding with the Tontine authorities would be easy to deal with. They might be able to draw out as much as two thousand pounds from a local bank. The most favorable expectations in London would run to half of that.

This was what all their grand plans had dwindled down to, then. No longer a grandiose scheme to set up a permanent impostor on the Continent and draw the full income for as many years as the man lived. No longer even a chance to get their hands on one year's income. They were scrambling now for crumbs, for anything they could get before the arm of the law intervened. They had taken all these risks for nothing. An ill-judged remark to a casual visitor by the female member of the group had made all this difference!

There was the fate of the casual visitor to be settled also. Pint was still determined to put the Rev. Gilbert Tranmer away before they did anything else. Now that they were scrambling for ryers (Pint's own expression, meaning bets for a shilling and six), Geist and the woman were determined not to risk their necks. The actor even contended that they could take the clergyman with them on the London train. The feel of a knife close to his ribs would keep him quiet. Once they had him in London, it would be a simple matter to keep him locked up. If neither the worthy man nor his lifeless body was found, it would be possible to sell the check at a reasonable discount. Geist argued along these lines with a degree of heat which could be attributed in part to the pain from which he was still suffering.

"They're less trouble, dead," said Pint. And then he added in a smoldering fury, "Anyway, what right did he have to come charging in here and upset our plans?"

Titus took no part in the discussion. In the first place, the others neither wanted nor tolerated his opinions. In the second place, he had already made up his mind that they were all risking their lives in a lost cause and he intended to get away before sharing in the consequences of this great folly.

He had the money he had received for his collection of drums and this would have to suffice as the basis for a new start in life.

It will be remembered that when Titus was a small boy he was careful to hoard the money which came his way. To avoid whatever risk there might be in keeping it in one place, he had distributed it in various holes and crannies. Returning to Three Gables, he had resorted to the same plan, even using such of the secret receptacles and croney-holes as he could remember. All that remained for him to do now was to make a tour of the house and the stables and collect his funds before vanishing for good. While the others argued bitterly, paying no attention to him, he was quietly gathering up his capital, ending up in the stables. It was his intention, now that he had his pockets crammed with bank notes, to make a careful exit by way of Sepoy Lane; but before he could put this plan into execution he heard footsteps approaching from that very direction. Peering out cautiously through a cobwebbed window in the haymow, he saw that a party of men had reached the cricket field and had halted there, apparently, for consultation. All of them carried guns or firearms of some description.

The game was up; Titus had no doubts on that score. The people of the neighborhood were taking the law into their own hands. He had little hope now of getting away.

"Get to your posts, men," he heard a cautious voice say. "The rest will be down in a few minutes and then the fun will be starting. Remember, don't fire unless you have to. If they try to break out on this side, challenge 'em. Shoot only if they refuse to stop."

He saw the group break up and the members begin to station themselves behind the line of fir trees which marked the eastern border of the property. Two of them materialized suddenly just below his window. He heard them laugh excitedly and one of them say: "We'd better get inside, Bill. It'll be safer if the barstards start to shoot."

Then he became aware of the sound of many feet on the road. Another party, a large one quite obviously, was approaching the house. This, he judged, would be the main attack. He wondered, without any feeling of concern, if those he had left in the house were aware of what was happening. He hoped not.

The cricket ground was now deserted and he began to entertain some hopes of getting away. To judge by the sounds, the pair below had moved to the front and were watching through the doors of the coach house. Moving with great care, he let himself out of the window and into the branches of a large cherry tree growing close to the wall. In a few moments his feet were on the ground, and he heard no signs of concern from the pair on guard in front. Doubling over to make himself as inconspicuous as possible, he made his way through the thick shrubbery which enclosed the grounds. When he had reached the start of Sepoy Lane, he began to believe that he might escape after all.

From the direction of the house he heard a loud thumping, as of rifle butts being used on a door or at least many impatient knuckles. "They've reached the house," he thought. And then he heard a loud voice raised in command, although he was too far away to catch any of the words.

He began to run at the top of his speed, saying to himself; "Well, they're caught! And I'm glad of it."

It was the hammering of Dr. Sandilands' revolver on the front door at Three Gables which Titus had heard and it was the doughty doctor, moreover, who shouted the words of admonition. What he said was: "Stand back, in there! We're coming in through the door. And take it easy. No shooting, if you place any value on your lives!"

The three inside were taken completely by surprise. The argument among them had been so bitter that they had not heard a sound. The only interruption they had anticipated was the arrival of the mailman or the special messenger who would bring the check from Tontine headquarters. Pint looked at the actor, who was made up to play his part in accepting the money but whose cheeks had gone so white that it was clear he was not prepared for this, and then at Mary Tindy; with loathing for both of them, particularly for the woman whose loose tongue was the cause of everything. He sprang to his feet and drew a revolver from a pocket. Geist *was* prepared for this and, as he had no intention of sharing in any of the fruits of violence, he knocked the gun out of the little man's hand. They both went down on the floor then, each trying to get possession of the firearm, and cursing in rage and frustration. Mary Tindy was on her way to open the door and this brought Pint to his senses. He sat up on the floor, his collar broken open, his hair rumpled, his breathing hard.

"Wait!" he commanded. "Don't be in such a damned hurry. We've lost; but we don't have to run to them, holding out our wrists in eagerness for the handcuffs, do we? Listen to this. I've got one thing to tell you two weaklings who've brought me to this pass. Don't say a word! No matter how many questions they ask, don't give them any answers. Just sit still and keep your mealy mouths shut. We can decide later what we are going to say—when we've seen which way the cat jumps."

"That's sense," conceded Geist. "For once I'll play the part mum. No holding forth, no smothering them with classic abuse. I'll say not a word, no matter how many good lines I think of."

"And you, woman?" asked Pint, looking bitterly at Mary Tindy.

She nodded her head. "I guess you're right about it. Lowfoot allus says, 'Wait, listen, say nothing.'"

"Where's the cub?" asked Pint suddenly. "Do you suppose this is his work? That he's brought this down on us?"

"It wouldn't be a surprise to me," said the actor bitterly.

The woman went to the door then and drew back the bolt. Dr. Sandilands came into the room, followed by a score of others, eager to be about the business of repairing what damage had been done and making the guilty parties pay. The woman, who was no stranger to the doctor, had seated herself on a sofa while the two men occupied chairs, one on each side.

All three wore stubborn and angry looks on their stony features and, when he challenged their presence, they did not answer by a "yes" or a "no" or the more likely "be damned to you."

"Well," said the doctor, "I guess we're not going to get much out of this precious lot. It doesn't matter, of course. This whole horrible and almost unbelievable story is becoming very clear."

The rest of the rescuing party had gone to work at once to ransack the house with the prime object of locating the prisoner. They discovered him quickly, locked into a dark closet and about dead from the lack of air, the merciless tightness of the gag and the pain in his bound limbs. They carried him downstairs very gently and placed him in a chair.

The Rev. Gilbert Tranmer had indeed paid dearly for his rashness in attempting to solve the situation singlehanded. There was a red bar across his face where the gag had constricted the flesh, and his lips were puffed and bleeding. The blood had been kept out of his arms and legs for so long that they hung on his frame as limply as the limbs of a scarecrow in a cherry orchard. In spite of these evidences of the suffering he had endured for many hours, the good rector seemed in cheerful enough spirits.

He managed to articulate: "Well, gentlemen, my thanks, my most hearty and boundless thanks, for arriving in the bare nick of time. I'm inclined to think it wouldn't have done, as the Iron Duke said after Waterloo, if you hadn't come just when you did."

"How do you feel, sir?" asked Sandilands, who had been shocked by the battered appearance of the rector.

The rescued man gave some thought to this question and then said, "I feel very humble. Most completely humble, Dr. Sandilands."

One of the party, who happened to be the clergyman's warden, asked a question. "Humble, sir? But why?"

"Well," said Mr. Tranmer, "I am forced to confess that during the last few hours I did not trust in the Lord as much as I should. I knew, naturally, that He had His own plans as far as I was concerned; when the recall would sound for me, most particularly. I realized also that this young man" —he moved his body with great difficulty in order to look in the direction of Pint, who was staring at him with an immeasurable degree of enmity in his washed-out gray eyes—"this very amiable young man, had decided to rush the Lord, as it were, to force His hand, and finish me off ahead of the appointed time. I should have said to myself, 'The Lord always contrives to get His own way, because it is the only way and the right way. If it is His will that I am to die now and this amiable young man is in reality an instrument of the divine purpose, then I must accept it. But if it isn't His will, then this young man will find himself frustrated and *his* plan knocked into a cocked hat.' In either event, I should have been content to wait. But, gentlemen, I could hardly breathe, and the bonds were cutting into my wrists and ankles, and I was in so much pain and trepidation of spirit that I gave up hope. I fully expected to die before I could be released from that dark hole where they had me.

"But," he concluded, "the Lord *did* contrive to get His own way. He did it by sending you to my rescue. I am very happy that you got here, even though I should never have entertained any doubts whatever. I realize that I have not been equal to the test. And so I am very humble."

"Humility is all very well in its place, Gib," commented the doctor. "But don't carry it too far. It's our combined opinion that you've acted with the utmost courage and resolution."

"I wonder where my own arms and legs are," said the clergyman. "These, clearly, don't belong to me. I have no control over them. It's a curious thing but they have no feeling in them at all."

"You'll soon be very conscious of the fact that they do belong to you," said Sandilands grimly. "Just wait, my friend, until the blood starts to circulate again. Whew! You'll wish they didn't belong to you."

Despite the fact that he was experiencing everything that a scarecrow might feel after being tossed about all night in a wind and sleet storm and losing much of its stuffing, the clergyman managed at this point to achieve a more upright position. He did so in order to study more closely the three silent prisoners.

The head of the police from Windsor, a burly individual of the highly suitable name of Heft, had arrived by this time, having ridden over with four assistants in a smoking and very creditable hurry, and at this moment was engaged in handcuffing the guilty trio together.

"They seem a silent lot," commented the clergyman. "Have they been questioned? And if so, what information have they given you?"

"Not a word," said the doctor. "We tried our hand on them and got nothing for our pains. I'm sure Mr. Heft will now have a go at it, and I wish him more luck than we had."

The police officer said in confident tones: "I'll get 'em chattering, never fear. It's a knack I have. A gift, you might say."

"There's one question of such importance," said the rector, "that I can't leave it until the official query gets under way. It should be asked, and an answer obtained, at once."

"What is it?" asked the officer, turning to look at the victim of Pint's ferocity.

"It's this." The Rev. Gilbert Tranmer sat up very straight at this point and his voice gained in volume. "What did they do with the body of that great good friend of us all, that kind and honorable man, Julian Grace?"

There was a brief moment of silence. Every pair of eyes in the room, numbering well beyond a score, turned in the direction of the silent trio. Mary Tindy swallowed hard, as though she wanted to speak, but the implacable gaze of Pint was on her and she stifled the impulse.

"Well," said Heft finally, "speak up, one of you. What did you worthy characters do with this gentleman's body?"

There was no response. The faces of the trio remained as glum as before. The clergyman suddenly burst out with bitter and passionate words.

"For what they've done to me I'm not asking any redress," he said. "I am even prepared to suggest that they be forgiven for it. Or at any rate that their punishment be fixed without any regard to my pains. But if they have committed any unseemly act of vandalism, if they have been guilty of any indignity to the mortal clay of my dear friend, then I want them treated as the worst of criminals and made to suffer any penalty the law may fix for them!"

"Amen!" said Dr. Sandilands fervently. "We did not ask that question. Do you want it put to them now?"

"If you please. We can't delay in getting at the truth."

"Well, are you listening, you three frozen stumps?" demanded the police officer. "Are you going to give the reverend gentleman the answer he asks?"

There was still no response, not as much as the flicking of an eyelash to give any hint of interest on the part of the prisoners.

"It don't matter," said Heft after a few moments. "I sent on a couple of my men to pick up the other two who's got theirselves mixed up in this pleasant little affair. Mr. Lew Stain and Mr. Casper Lowfoot, to wit. One of them will be got to talk, perhaps both estimable gentlemen. We'll find out from them what was done with the body."

Mary Tindy stared hard at this. Perhaps the certainty that her husband, that silent man with his furtive ways, was going to do some talking, suggested to her that she might be well advised to forestall him. It was clear she was feeling a desire to make face with the authorities for her own single and personal benefit. But a glance from the cold eye of Pint served to curb the desire. She still agreed with him that the least said the soonest mended, if any mending was going to be possible.

"I haven't heard that man Lowfoot say more than a dozen words all the time I've known him," contributed the doctor. "And I've never had what you could call a square look at him. But I think he's the one to try on this."

"I don't care if he looks at me or if he don't," declared the Windsor officer. "He'll be pouring out his life history by the time I get through with him. And," with a hostile glance at the mum prisoners, "the histories of some others I know."

An intensely interested spectator had been sitting in one corner of the room while all this was going on. William Wordsworth Glossop had not said a word but he had heard everything and he had seen everything. At this point he decided he could no longer remain silent.

"Who," he demanded to know, "was the man I talked to?"

Asked to define the nature of his inquiry more explicitly, he explained about the call he had made at Three Gables and the seemingly satisfactory conversation he had carried on with someone who passed for Sir Julian Grace.

"Was it either one of these fine gentlemen?" asked Heft, indicating the two male prisoners.

"Certainly not! It was a tall and handsome old man—charming, erudite, well mannered."

The idea had been growing in Geist's mind that his performance as the Tontine contender had been the top mark in his acting career. He had been watching Mr. Glossop ever since the latter had come into the room with a sense almost of triumph. Now that Glossop had brought the matter up, he could no longer restrain himself.

"You talked to me," he said.

The inspector looked at the prisoner. Geist had made himself up but, seen at close range, the artful devices he had employed had small value. His hair was rumpled, his face swollen.

"Nonsense!" he said. "The man I talked to didn't resemble you in any possible aspect."

The actor grinned. "I am a master of make-up, Mr. Glossop," he said. "How much did the Tontine pay me last year? Come, the exact amount. And what did I say in my report to the Admiralty about the floating dock? Well, I guess that is all the proof you need."

Pint turned on him suddenly and viciously. "Stow your gab! Didn't I tell you not to say anything?"

The actor regarded the little man with a new ease and unconcern. "Pint," he said, "as I've been sitting here, I've been hearing sounds. Clanging sounds, like the swinging to and closing shut of iron gates, and footsteps in long stone corridors, and the clatter of hundreds of dishes in one room. We'll be living in the midst of such sounds for a good many years, Pint, you and me. We're both going to be nothing but numbers. Why should I be afraid of you? So I return the compliment. Stow your own gab, will you?"

5

Titus Grace was seen emerging from Sepoy Lane by old Dad Swayne, a local character, who was engaged in cutting down weeds along the roadside. Dad halted his leisurely scythe to take a look at the tall, redheaded young man. "It's ta son," he said to himself. "And what in t'under makes him sich a wax? Is deyvil atter him?"

Titus was also seen getting on the local coach a half mile down the road and he had fidgeted and turned repeatedly to look back all the way to Windsor. The conductor on the London train collected his ticket and observed that he was in something of a wax still. But he was not on the train when it rolled into Paddington where two officers were on hand to scrutinize the alighting passengers. It was assumed that he had shown sufficient cunning to get off at one of the suburban stops. He was never seen again.

Where did he go? Did he leave the country, and if so how did he manage it? What manner of life did he contrive for himself in the land of his adoption? These questions were rather thoroughly explored and discussed in the newspaper press for some time thereafter, and they never ceased to be topics of conversation in the country adjacent to Three Gables. Occasionally a dispatch would appear in a London daily, reporting that the fugitive had been seen somewhere or other, and there would be much sending of telegrams or cables and much breathless activity on the part of local authorities; but all to no avail.

It may have been that the best clue to his movements was supplied by Mary Tindy. All of the prisoners were sure that Titus had been responsible for bringing the neighbors down on them. His name came up in the course of a police examination and the woman fairly spat in rage.

"That dirty rat!" she exclaimed. "I know where he's off to. He's gone to Bermuda. He'll be trying to cadge something from that woman, you mark my words."

When the police demanded more explicit information, she came forward with the name of Mrs. Beltrade, "as what knew his father, and a nice leddy she is, and fair rolling in oof."

When it developed that a ship had sailed for Bermuda on the day after the arrival of Titus in London, provided that he went there, the clue began to assume substance and probability. But the vessel in question, which had carried the rather vainglorious name of Conqueror, never reached the islands. At first it was believed that the ship had altered its course and had headed straight for the West Indies, and for weeks an officer sat in concealment in the thick underbrush which surrounded the beautiful home of Sue Beltrade, in case the fugitive should slip off one of the many other vessels arriving at the island.

Two months later the silence of the marble-walled Room at Lloyd's of London was disturbed by the ominous sound of the Lutine Bell, which hangs under a metal sounding board and has two functions to perform, to announce the loss of a ship with one stroke and to convey the happy news of a belated arrival with two.

"Clang!" went the Lutine Bell, and everyone in the room turned and waited hopefully for a second strike. But the bell subsided into silence after the first and it took a few seconds only for the information to reach all parts of the Room that the Conqueror had been given up for lost.

None of the crew or passengers had been saved, and so it may have been that this was the true explanation of the complete silence into which Titus Grace had disappeared.

6

Lew Stain and Casper Lowfoot were being held at the Golden Beetle until they could be removed to the county jail. When Lowfoot was brought out the next morning, he did not look at the small group assembled to hear what he had to say: the very much battered rector, Dr. Sandilands, Alfred Carboy, who was present to represent his partner, and police officer Heft from Windsor. The prisoner took the low chair pointed out to him and studied the toes of his dusty boots.

Heft explained what they wanted to know. Lowfoot thought it over, his lips moving with the slow turning of his brain.

"What do I get out of it?" he asked finally.

"Nothing," said Heft emphatically. "Not a day knocked off your sentence.

The only advantage for you in this is that the judge will know what you've done. That may, or it may not, incline him in your favor."

"But them that wants to know badly will pay me something," persisted the prisoner.

"Not a shilling!"

"That's being pretty high and mighty. Supposing then I turns ugly and refuses?"

"Suit yourself," advised the officer. "But be quick about it. If you're going to be ugly we still have your partner and your wife to talk to. Not to mention those two beauties from the city."

There was a long pause, and much tightening and untightening of lips, while the slow eyes worked out the pattern of the dusty boots. Then Lowfoot nodded his head.

"I give in," he said. "Do you want me to show you the place or will you follow directions?"

"Better take him along," advised the police officer. "It will be surer and quicker."

So they started out, in a carriage and a wagon long enough to accomplish the purpose which was taking them from the village. Sitting on the jolting seat of the wagon, his arm drawn through that of the solicitous police officer, Lowfoot paid no attention to the uncomplimentary remarks of the villagers who witnessed the departure. "An actor gets a toothache and I go to jail," he was thinking bitterly. "And I'm badgered and shoved abart and made to take orders. That's luck, that is! If I had a chance to give that woman a piece of my mind!"

They drove direct to the brickyard with its sign which now served as a badge of infamy, "Lew Stain and Casper Lowfoot, Bricks"; and as they drew near they became conscious of a great deal of noise.

"Sounds like a small riot of some kind," remarked the doctor. "Do you suppose the people of the neighborhood are paying their respects to Messrs. Stain and Lowfoot?"

Sure enough, the noise came from the brickyard, where the employees, having learned of the disgrace of the owners, had assembled in considerable numbers and high spirits to display their feelings on such an occasion. A brickyard always presents a rather busy appearance, for it is a tradition of the trade that the barrows are wheeled at a run and never at a walk. They were certainly being wheeled at a run now, being empty and therefore capable of high rates of speed. The idle diggers and wheelers were racing about with them, describing all manner of geometric designs in the dust of the yard and avoiding collisions by the smallest fractions of inches. They were shouting exultantly back and forth.

There was a delighted shout when the two vehicles turned into the yard and the excited employees saw Mr. Lowfoot in the wagon. They gathered around and gave him a noisy welcome.

"Here he is!" shouted one man, dancing up and down furiously and waving his arms. "Here he is, Casper the Grasper! Where's your partner, Lew the Screw?"

"Don't you know, Andy Miller," shouted another of them, "that good old Lew ain't at liberty any more? He wanted to come but the fellow with the keys said, 'No, you belongs here, Mr. Stain.'"

Lowfoot was not looking up but he could be heard muttering to himself. "I'm remembering everything. Everything done and every word said, and who said them. When I get out I'll make 'em pay for it!"

Andy Miller caught what the prisoner was saying and seized upon it with avidity. "He's going to pay us back, boys, when he gets out. Do you hear that? *When he gets out!*"

There was much laughing and doubling up with mirth and slapping of knees at this. "You ain't going to get out, Casper!" "Hark at 'im! Once they gets him they'll take such a fancy to our Casper that they won't never let him go." "Listen, Casper. You and your friend Lew, that stirk, will be swallowing prison slops and squatting on prison privies for the rest of your lives."

Hearing an even greater outburst of laughter, the company in the carriage turned and saw that one of the brickmakers in his soiled clothes was doing a derisive dance behind them. It was a grotesque performance with much tossing of arms and kicking of legs and the air filled with hands in clayish gloves and feet in dusty brodequins. It could be compared only to a giraffe dancing a gavotte.

"Chang Todd!" muttered Lowfoot. "I'll remember you, Mr. Chang Todd. I'll get my own back out of your hide!"

"Now, Lowfoot," said the police officer, impatient to get things over, "where do we go?"

"Over there," muttered the proprietor, pointing a finger with black and broken nails. "That pile of brokes and flaws in the corner. Just behind the pugmill. It's under them."

The rector looked, white-faced and shocked, at the doctor. "About what I feared," he whispered. "This is a pretty grim business, Dr. Sandilands. What do you suppose will happen when these people find out? Will they be ready to tear him limb from limb?"

"I won't raise a finger to protect him if they do!"

The accumulation of many years of broken bricks was cleared away with much difficulty. The employees stood at a distance and watched in a sudden silence, wondering, perhaps knowing, what it was about. Lowfoot had been pressed into service and as he tossed the bricks back of him he volunteered one explanation. "Stain and I come here that night. Just the two of us. It took us hours to move this stuff and pile it back again over the box."

Underneath the bricks, they came finally to a rough pine box, the very roughest and cheapest which could have been obtained. The rector lowered his head and said a prayer while his companions removed their hats and repeated the words after him.

"Let us not feel too badly," the clergyman concluded. "Countless brave men and even gallant knights have been buried in ditches on the battlefields of history. Six feet of unseemly earth do not indicate a man's worth. Julian Grace, had he been left here, would have come out from under these broken bricks on the day of deliverance with a shining face and as ready for fair judgment as if he had emerged from under a marble slab in Westminster Abbey. But, my friends, we may well count it a rare privilege to find him a more suitable bier."

"Sir," said Andy Miller, at the clergyman's shoulder, "we didn't know, none on us. Could we be allowed to help carry the coffin to the wagon, turn and turn about? It would be an honor, sir."

"Yes, Miller, we'll be glad to have you and the rest act as the pallbearers on this very sad occasion."

The rough pine box was carried to the wagon and there covered with a velvet cloak which Allie had brought under his arm. Caps in hand, the employees dropped back.

"Thank you, Andy Miller, and you, Chang Todd, and all the rest," said the Rev. Gilbert Tranmer. "What you have done has been a tribute to the splendid man whose bones have been resting here, unknown to any of you. The services will be at the church tomorrow at two. I trust you will be there. We must see that Sir Julian Grace is buried with all the honor due him."

Alfred looked at the police officer. "Are you attending to things?" he asked.

Heft nodded. "After I gets this worthy gentleman and his distinguished colleague where they belong, behind a row of bars."

"I am acting for my partner, his grandson, who is two thousand miles away. I want to be able to tell him that we did everything possible. You understand, I trust, that no expense is to be spared?"

The rector took the young man's arm as they walked back to the carriage. "I think, Mr. Carboy," he said, "that you will be gratified at the service tomorrow. The schools are being closed all through the countryside. Every man, woman and child will attend to pay their respects. There was nothing but love and admiration for him."

"The actor did a little talking this morning," said Heft. "It seems they had big plans. If they could get a suitable double for Sir Julian, they were going to set him up properly on the Continent and go on collecting the yearly payments. But the fellow got an ulcerated tooth and that upset the whole applecart."

"'God moves in a mysterious way,'" quoted the Rev. Gilbert Tranmer. This suggested another quotation to him. "Mr. Officer, could you drive on well ahead of us and keep Lowfoot with you? 'An honest man, close-buttoned to the chin. But neither broadcloth without nor a warm heart within.' Cowper, I think. The air will be better the farther the distance between us."

## CHAPTER TEN

### 1

Edward Daniel Carboy was a precocious youngster. Here he was, nearly a year and a half old, big for his age, able not only to walk but to run, and talking all the time. One evening when the head of the household returned from his labors at the office, his wife greeted him with a serious air.

"He's had his first fight," she said.

"Who, the Rising Hope of the Carboys?" Allie shook his head. "This is starting early, isn't it? What was it all about?"

"I don't know. I had him in the park, looking so fine in his new clothes and his pink bonnet. There was another child near us. *Much* older and bigger. Before I knew it, they were tugging and shoving at each other in a great rage. They both fell over and they both got hurt. My, the other one's nursemaid was angry!"

"Is he asleep?"

Nell nodded. "Yes, he went right off. I think he was very pleased with himself."

The father tiptoed into the bedroom and came back in a few moments, his eyes beaming with pride. "The little stirk!" he said. "I believe he's going to have a black eye. Isn't it too bad that the first black eye can't be preserved in some way like the first pair of shoes? It would be a memento of childhood which all men would be proud to keep."

Nell nodded in a rather absent-minded way. "Himself used to say, 'Why are boys born into the world except to fight?' Allie, look at this. It's a map of Little Shallow. See, right here. At this corner there's a nice little cottage that can be rented. I think it's the very place."

"The very place for what?" he asked.

"Oh, hadn't I explained?" Nell looked at him with complete gravity. "I'm going to leave you, Mr. Carboy. I'm going to walk right out and take my son with me. For a few weeks or months, as the case may be." Her eyes suddenly filled with tears. "Oh, Allie, we must do it! The poor little thing hasn't much longer to live and she's so lonesome out there. Living behind the shop, seeing so few people, being so very careful about her heart! She just seems to live from visit to visit that we pay her. She worships Edward Daniel Carboy. What I'm trying to tell you, if you'll deign to get that stubborn, un-yielding, unco-operative look off your face, is that we should take the little house and I'll move out there for as—for as long as she lives. Which won't be long, Allie. A few weeks at most, if we can believe half of what the doctors say."

"Wait a minute, you wild Irishwoman!" cried Allie. "Do you mean that I'm to stay in the city, working myself to skin and bone——"

"And gaining weight all the time."

"Never mind that. I take it you have no regard for my comfort or wishes. You'll go to the country so your aunt can see my son every day. What about my side of this? I'm fond of Edward Daniel Carboy myself, you know. I like to see him every day too. And I'm fond of you, although at this exact moment I wonder why."

"Allie, my darling," said Nell, "it will be just as hard for me. You see, I love you very much, even if we have been married over two years and I've taken on two pounds and your hair is getting just a mite thin on top. But here's the way to look at it, my poor, much-abused husband. You're going to live for at least fifty years more. You're going to see Edward Daniel Carboy grow up, go to school, enter the business, get married, have children of his own. Poor Aunt Helen isn't going to live fifty days. Don't you think we ought to be just as generous as we can to her for that small little spell of time?"

Allie sat down and gave the matter some thought. "I'm afraid you're right, my lovely Irish bride," he said grudgingly. "We owe her a great deal, both of us."

"We do indeed, Allie."

"And she's having a very bad time of it. Why in thunderation does she insist on living behind the shop? She can't be short of funds. She got the whole thirty thousand pounds, didn't she?"

"Allie, I'm very much afraid it's all gone. Didn't she send us five thousand pounds? Didn't she send money to your father in South Africa to help him along in his new business? She's afraid Jonathan Bade isn't going to live much longer and she sent him a really big check to help in getting the mission organized so it can be carried on after he's gone. I suspect she took on some obligations as a result of the failure which she's had to pay off. And then there's Huruld and Daphne to be provided for and all her funny old pensioners in the village."

"I had no idea she had stripped herself of everything. Of course, the shop is doing well. She could make herself more comfortable if she wanted to."

"Allie, it goes deeper than that. She thinks it's right and proper to start over again in exactly the same way. I really believe she's happier at the shop than she would be anywhere else. She knows everything that's going on and it helps, I'm sure, to keep her alive. It must be that. All the doctors agree she should have died long ago. Sometimes I can't help thinking it's a pity. She suffers so terribly!"

"I know." Allie gave his head a grave shake. "Well, you've convinced me. It's going to be hard. I've got kind of accustomed to you and Edward Daniel Carboy around the house. You Irish have an insidious way with you, making yourselves indispensable to people! Well, let me have a look at that plan. Where is this house you're talking about? And what absurd and outrageous rental are they asking for it?" He put an arm around her shoulders and gave her a quick and very satisfactory hug. "I'll be down every weekend. And sometimes, perhaps, it could be arranged for my wife and son to pay *me* a visit in London."

2

Immediately following the official announcement that she was the winner of the Waterloo Tontine, Helen Groody had enjoyed a rather strenuous existence. Newspapermen had come to see her, with no Mr. Batson from the Home Office to fend them off, and had asked her innumerable questions. There had been telegrams and, roughly speaking, a barrowful of letters from all over the United Kingdom. She would have enjoyed it very much if it had not been so apparent to her that her heart would not stand much of this sort of thing.

The first Sunday after the check had been placed in her hand, a very much dressed-up Joe Tope had arrived off the early morning train. His raiment seemed to be made of pearl buttons, and even his hat was bedizened with them. He had a companion who was carrying the largest floral horseshoe ever constructed by mortal hands.

"M'em," said Joe Tope, having been granted admittance to her room at the inn, for she had not moved over to the shop at this time, "the compliments of Herb Biler and all the rest on 'em."

"Do you mean to say that they've sent this to me?" she asked, completely taken aback by the sheer size of the horseshoe.

"Yus," answered Joe proudly. "Never been a bigger one built, m'em, not even for Derby winners or furrin soverints. And why not, may I ask? You're the prize skinner on the record books, m'em. Hardly more than a few shillings on you, and you come skating home. Herb Biler made a fortun' out of you, m'em. All on us did well. Why, even Baggsy here," indicating his companion, who had deposited the floral monstrosity in a corner and was standing in an awkward silence, turning his cap in his hands, "even this big hunks was able to afford a new mog for his missus. A catskin tippet, no less. And as for me"—the Tope eye lighted up—"I'm a-moving, you bet. I'm to have my own kit now and someone under me to do the scrubbing and chalking!"

"I'm delighted, Mr. Joe Tope," said Helen, "that all of you have done so well and feel so good about it. I congratulate you on—getting your own kit, was it? And I do hope that Mr. Baggsy's missus enjoys her new—mog? I'm sure it will look very handsome on her. But I can't help feeling sorry for all the poor people who did the losing. They tell me that the whole river country was betting solidly on Sir Julian. And for a time they thought they had won! That must have been a blow for them."

"Never feel sorry for punters, m'em. They're brought into this world to be took. So why shouldn't we be the takers?" asked Joe Tope cheerfully. "And now, m'em, it wur Herb Biler's orders we wur to drink your good health. If you'll excuse us we'll go downstairs and attend to that little chore."

There had been much excitement also about the trials. It took several days to hear all the evidence against the Three Gables Gang, as the public began to call Pint, Selwyn Geist, Mary Tindy, Casper Lowfoot and Lew Stain, and nothing else was talked about anywhere. They were convicted, of course, and they all drew stiff terms, so stiff that Mary Tindy cried out in court that she wouldn't live to see the end of it, and Pint glowered at the judge with his implacable eyes and would have given violent expression to his opinions if he had not been bundled out in a hurry.

It had not been necessary for Helen Groody to appear in court but she was continually disturbed by the aftermath of the events which had led to the death of Her Grace the Duchess of Outland. Alexander Fawkes was not caught. Perhaps the hunt slackened when the charge against him was reduced from murder to arson. The girl Dossie Smith was not found either, and that should not have been a difficult matter at all. Perhaps there was no particular desire to bring either of them into court with the revelations which would inevitably have followed. At any rate Badger Bill remained the sole beneficiary of his own murderous design. He was not called to the stand but the judge made him the recipient of a blistering tirade and he was given a sentence which kept him out of the poaching business for almost the rest of his life.

The day when sentence was passed, and the case was officially closed, His Grace of Outland paid a visit to the shop in Little Shallow behind which Helen Groody had finally established herself.

"You're very snug here," he said, glancing about with an approving eye at the room which had once served as parlor for the whole Groody family. "I find, ma'am, that one appreciates snugness more all the time as one grows older. No one ever called Outland Park a snug place and I hope I never have to go back there. It was not that way with my wife, ma'am. My poor lovely Isabelle was always hoping that something would turn up so we could boot the tenants out and move back ourselves. She really couldn't be content with less than four drawing rooms and at least forty bedrooms, and some bounder with a title or a million in every one of them."

"I intend to finish my days here," said Helen. "It was where I made my start and I find it pleasant to be back. It's easy to believe that my mother is sitting in that armchair under the window and that my father is smoking his pipe in front of the fire. Of course I've had to find other quarters for Huruld. But he's got a place now over the stables at the inn and he's happy about it. You see, our horses are being boarded there and he wouldn't be content if he was too much separated from the old fellows."

"I'm giving up that place where we lived last," said the duke. "I'm going to move into the city and have a small flat. I'll have one man to look after me and I'll have my newspapers. And in the summers I'll be off on my yacht. That's the ticket for me." He paused and lowered his voice. "I'm not a sentimental man, ma'am, but I couldn't bear the house because my poor Isabelle died there."

Things had to quiet down before she could begin to exist as she had planned, the quiet life with no emotional disturbances to play hob with her heart. She had existed for many months in seclusion and quiet when Nell and her son arrived on the scene.

"We've rented the Birdward place, Aunt Helen," announced Mrs. Alfred Carboy, "and we're going to settle down here for a while."

The sick woman looked at them with almost unbelieving eyes. "Nelly, do you mean it?" she managed to gasp finally. "You are really going to be here for some time? You and my little Danny?"

The young wife nodded casually. "Allie and I got to talking about it," she explained, "and we decided it would be the best thing for young Mr. Daddles here. The country air is so much better for him. And he can have a dog here, young Mr. Putty Dunnett can. He's quite mad about dogs but we haven't room for one in that little house in London. And so here we are. Allie will come down every Saturday afternoon and it will be good for him too."

"How wonderful!" said her aunt. "I couldn't ask anything more of life than this. Are you glad, my little Danny, that you're going to live in the country?"

The boy nodded. "Yes, Granty," he said. "Get dog. Big dog. Brown."

"What are you going to call him?"

"Rough," said the boy.

"Rough? Why, is he going to be a big, rough dog?"

The boy, of course, could not explain. All he knew was that when he got his dog he was going to call him Rough. And the very next day they found a big pup with a brown coat which suited the boy perfectly. He became known as Rough immediately.

The Birdward house belonged to a retired army captain who had made it the very model of a house for a retired soldier. It was compact, convenient, neat and full of all manner of timesaving devices. The creation of the house had been a labor of love and, when it became necessary for his wife and himself to spend a year in Italy for their joint health, the captain had decided to rent it, with the greatest reluctance. "Remember, Larkins," he had said, shaking an admonitory forefinger at the agent, "no children and no dogs." The agent argued that Danny was a mere baby and, therefore, could hardly qualify as a child, and succeeded in convincing the tight-lipped little ex-officer that there was a distinction. He forgot to bring up the matter of dogs with the prospective tenants and there was nothing about it in the lease. When he saw Rough on one of his visits to Little Shallow, he drew a long face and said, "Goodness me, this is indeed most unfortunate." It was too late to do anything about it, for by that time Danny and Rough had become inseparable.

It did not seem to matter very much because Nell and her son spent little time in the Birdward house. As soon as the necessary housework had been done—Nell was as quick as a hummingbird over such matters—the two would walk to the shop and spend the rest of the day there. It would not be until the sick woman had been tucked in for the night that mother and son would return, the dog following on their heels.

"Old Rough, nice Rough!" the boy would say. "Rough my dog, Mummy."

Danny was very much interested in the workings of the shop. He soon made the discovery that people called regularly and that their arrival was announced by the jangling of a bell. They were customers, a word which he soon mastered. Whenever the bell rang, he would jump up and run to the door leading to the shop, open it a cautious inch and peep through. He would come back then and say to his great-great-aunt, "Cus'mers, Granty." Sometimes he would open the door a little more and would stand for a longer time, peering through the crack. When he came back his eyes would be shining. "Boy cus'mer," he would say, or even, "Lit' girl cus'mer."

The rest of the time he was content to play with toys on the floor while the old lady watched him from her couch. He had been given an elaborate toy by his father, a really wonderful thing called a Noah's Ark, with barns and haystacks, and all the animals on the face of the earth painted to look like the real thing, and staddles and farm wagons and plows and an almost inexhaustible supply of fences. He played with great concentration, setting out the buildings and making good imitations of a large farm. Gradually, however, his ideas changed. Finding that his supply of fences was almost without limit, he began to branch out, to make larger farms. Before long he was taking in the whole floor, right up to the walls and under the tables and chairs.

One afternoon when the landholdings had been extended to such a degree that nothing was left of the floor for other purposes, and poor Rough had been ordered to a corner with orders not to do as much as give a wag of his tail, the old lady called her niece in from the room beyond.

"Look!" she said. "I never get over the wonder of it, Nell. He's just like his great-grandfather. My Allie. The resemblance is going to be really startling, my dear. But I didn't call you in to say that. Look at the shape of his head. The back particularly. He's got a lot of old Sam Carboy in him. And if you want proof, look at what he's doing. A mere farm is not enough for Edward Daniel Carboy. He must take in everything in sight. He's building right back to the horizon on all sides. He's going to be another of them, a true Carboy, a trade empire-builder."

"I hope not," said the boy's mother. "Don't you think, Aunt Helen, that we've had enough of that in one family?"

"He can't help what he is," said the old lady. "He's a Carboy and he'll be fairly bursting with ambition. I want to see him become a great man, Nell. Have you been keeping your eyes on things? In the world, I mean. Oh, such wonderful changes are under way! Pretty soon we'll be having pictures which move on a big screen—no, don't laugh at me, I read something about it the other day. And carriages which run by power like factories, without any horses. No more coachmen—or coachmen's daughters. And machines which will reproduce the human voice. Oh, Nelly, this world is going to be a wonderful place! I won't see any of these changes but you'll see them all. What a privilege it will be for you! I was born too early. So was old Sam Carboy. But, Nelly, this little son of yours was born at exactly the right time. It's my hope that he'll be having a hand in everything. I think he will; I *know* he will, because you can see it in him already."

That evening the local doctor, whose name was Partridge, came to the Birdward house to talk with Nell. His face reflected the gravity of his errand.

"I think I should warn you, Mrs. Carboy," he said. "Miss Groody is—er—approaching the final stage. I would consider myself negligent and cowardly if I failed to tell you the truth. The whole truth."

Nell had tidied the house and had settled down to make some repairs on a coat of her son's. She looked up over the needle in her busy fingers. "Oh, Doctor, are you sure?" she said, her cheeks becoming pale. "She seemed so well today. I came home feeling quite hopeful. Of course she suffers terribly. I know she's been better since we came to be with her but nothing can relieve her of the pain."

"The rheumatism had been taking control of the heart," said the doctor soberly. "It was attacking the outposts before but now it has made its way into the citadel. When I listened to her heart this evening it was harsh and rough, and very uneven. Her temperature—I hesitate to tell you this because it carries such significance—her temperature, Mrs. Carboy, is one hundred and four."

The fingers of the young wife and mother had continued automatically at their task up to this point. Now they stopped. She looked at the doctor with stricken eyes.

"One hundred and four! That's terribly high, isn't it?"

"It's so high, when considered in the light of her weakened condition, that I've come to give you this warning. She can't last much longer."

"How soon? Be perfectly frank with me, Doctor. I would rather know."

The man of medicine frowned reflectively. "I think many doctors would say that she couldn't last through the night. Of course you can't be sure but I wouldn't be surprised if it occurred at any minute. Certainly, Mrs. Carboy, the extreme limit of possibility is another week."

3

The week that the doctor had set as the limit of possibility for Helen Groody passed. She remained the same. Another week passed. And then a third. The doctor would leave the shop shaking his head and saying to himself: "It beats anything! Where does she find this reserve of strength? What is keeping her alive?" Her temperature would go up to the danger point and then down again. Her pulse was continuously harsh and jerky. On several occasions she seemed to be falling into a coma but each time she opened her eyes on what seemed the very brink of eternity and smiled cheerfully at whoever happened to be in the room.

Once she said to Nell: "That doctor has a strange look about him all the time. As though he's upset. He shakes his head when he listens to my heart and gives a kind of cluck. What's wrong with him?"

"I'm sure," said Nell, "that he's pleased at the way you are doing."

"Or surprised," said the sick lady. "I'm inclined to think that's it."

She never forgot what the bigwig from "Orstrer" had told her. Nothing was allowed to penetrate the sickroom which might lead to emotional disturbance. Sometimes Mr. Price, to whom the world was indigo and who realized that every hand was against him, would go to the door, determined to explain some earth-shaking crisis in the price of commodities. Generally he would recover himself in time and take his hand from the knob. Twice, when the crisis seemed more significant and dire than the perpetual threat of war in the Balkans, Nell had to restrain him by force from entering. The inmate of the room had stopped reading newspapers because the happenings in the world or the tone of the leaders might excite her to thoughts tinged with anger, dismay or apprehension. The magazines and quarterlies, being controversial in the extreme, went unopened. No whisper of gossip ever penetrated into that chamber of peaceful contemplation. "Love is the only emotion which will not affect you adversely," the bigwig had said; and the presence of Nell and her small son did much to maintain the right atmosphere.

Two incidents occurred which proved to be storms in the teacup of these slow days but both of which came close to doing what the bigwig had feared. The first had to do with a clock which Captain Birdward had left in the house against his better judgment. It was a small Queen Anne clock with one hand only and it was extremely valuable. It attracted Danny's attention because it looked so far away on top of the highboy in the master bedroom, almost as though it were up in the clouds. He slipped in often to look at it and one morning his mother heard a loud crash and then a cry of pain and fear, followed by long and steady wailing from the master bedroom. The boy had piled one chair on top of another and they had tumbled, of course, but not until he had his hands on the clock. By some curious chance none of the glass was broken and there did not seem to be a scratch on the mellow walnut body; but inside, the springs had become uncoiled and loose, the arm of the tiny pendulum was bent and three wheels of various sizes had become free of their moorings and were rolling about with every movement of the case.

In response to a frantic telegram from his wife, Alfred Carboy brought a German clockmaker with him the next weekend. The expert, whose name was Albrecht Schotten, worked for two days on it. There was no more than an hour left to train time when he straightened up, wiped his fingers on a piece of cloth and announced in a voice of modulated triumph: "There! It has been put together. That much, at least, I have been able to do."

Allie and Nell ran into the room in a state of great anxiety to learn the result of his long labors. As far as they could see the clock had been restored to its former state.

"Is it fixed?" asked Nell eagerly. "Is it quite all right again?"

Mr. Albrecht Schotten proceeded to wash his hands in a basin beside the bed. "Well, now, my dear young lady, I do not know. It has been put together. But will it run? Ah, that is the question! Have I assembled the works with enough consideration for its great delicacy of balance and interplay of parts? We shall now see."

He produced the key, opened the glass door front and proceeded to wind the clock. Nell and Allie scarcely breathed as they watched. The boy came in and stood behind them, the dog crouched at his heels. There was not a sound in the room save for the slow turning of the key.

When the last revolution had been completed and the key withdrawn, the room was immediately filled with the most welcome of all sounds under the circumstances, the steady and musical *tick-tock, tick-tock* of a clock which knows its business and is going about it as faithfully as when it was first made and set to running, two centuries or more earlier.

But it had been impossible to keep what had happened from the ears of the sick lady. Her niece's worried looks had told her that something was amiss and she had succeeded in getting at the truth. It then became certain that the physician from Orstrer had been right. Before she could be told that the clock had been repaired so well that even Captain Birdward would never know what had happened, she fell into a state of collapse.

"A blister will do no good now," said the doctor when the Carboy family arrived with the news. "The heart still beats but it may stop at any minute."

The brave heart did not stop. She came through the crisis, which a minor worry had created, only to suffer soon after from one of a sharper kind.

One Saturday afternoon, when the snow was falling slowly and damply outside, young Master Carboy grew weary of waiting for his father to arrive. His mother was in the kitchen, preparing something very special for their supper, so Danny conscientiously put on his felt shoes, slipped into his overcoat, wrapped the muffler around his neck, pulled his cap down close to his ears and sallied out.

He had intended to go no farther than the corner where the road from the station came swinging around into the village, but Rough chased an imaginary rabbit in the opposite direction and, of course, his master had to follow to be sure the dog did not become lost. The result was that they were soon in a neighborhood which the boy knew nothing about. The snow was still falling but it was getting colder and it came home to the sole heir of all the Carboys, if the term could still be applied, that small boys were at a disadvantage when they were alone in the outside world. He was completely lost and Rough was of no help to him whatever.

After Alfred Carboy arrived home a frantic search of the neighborhood was made but it was more than an hour before the unhappy pair were found crouching for shelter in a long-abandoned chicken coop. In the meantime Daphne had been injudicious enough to go into the sickroom with tears streaming down her face and a blubbering forecast of total disaster. This was the kind of shock all the doctors had feared. When Alfred and Nell arrived later they found the patient in a sinking condition from anxiety. They sat down beside the bed, their hands clasped together, too heartsick to say a word. A clock on the wall, a very new clock, went on ticking steadily and prosaically, quite unaware of all the trouble and even unaware of what its forerunner of distinguished lineage had caused some time earlier.

"My poor little aunt Helen!" whispered Nell. "I am sure, Allie, she was hoping to live out the year and collect another Tontine check. She spoke many times of what she could do with it."

"It's better not," said Allie. "She's been suffering too much. No one needs the money but she needs the peace she can get only in this way."

After a long half hour of almost unbroken silence, the patient stirred. The doctor had been called away to other responsibilities, so Nell walked on tiptoe to the side of the bed.

"What was his name?" asked the occupant of the couch in a voice so low that it could hardly be heard.

"Come, dear Aunty," said Nell. "Don't try to speak. You haven't the strength."

"But I—I want to know. It keeps running through my head." There was a long pause while the patient summoned the strength for further explanation. "It was a king. A king of England. He said something. What was it he said?"

"But, Aunt Helen, there have been so many kings of England. And they said so many things."

"This one—this one was dying. And he said something. I think—yes, it *was*—it was Charles II. And now I remember. He apologized to the courtiers around him because he was taking so long to die. I guess I kept thinking about it because I'm like the king. I'm taking such a long time to die." Then she went on in her own thoughts. "But I'm different from that king. I mustn't die. I must keep on living for quite a time still. So much still depends on me."

The next morning, when Helen Groody opened her eyes, there was almost a hint of color in her cheeks. This meant little, because she had always had such a high complexion that sickness could not drive it entirely away. It was clear, however, that another crisis, the most severe of them all, had been weathered.

The winter months passed slowly. The patient was not subjected to anything that would create an emotion other than the love she felt so strongly for the little group keeping the vigil with her. Perhaps this was the reason she continued to hold on to life with a heart which fluttered and ebbed and gave no hope of functioning for long. She was too weak to get up but her faculties were still keen enough to make it possible for her to follow everything that went on about her. She watched with a sympathetic eye the bold expansion that Edward Daniel Carboy created with his wooden animals and equipment. Sometimes she whispered suggestions to him. "There's the room behind this one, Danny," she said once. "Why don't you take it in too?" To herself she added, "There are no limits for those with bold hearts."

She talked to Nell quite often about the Tontine. "It would be nice if I could live long enough to collect the money once more," she said several times. "There are so many things to be done with it."

Nell knew all about the demands which were made on her. They came in every mail, from all over the world. "Please, you have so much and our need is so great," was the general tenor of the communications. They had to be read to her each day and she listened always with the greatest concentration. The good judgment which had made her such a remarkable investor in her day rendered it easy for her now to detect the spurious note in most of them. A relative few seemed genuine and these she asked her niece to keep in a basket for later reference. The basket was soon filled.

The letter which interested the sick lady most of all was one signed Mat Blunt. "Who is Mat Blunt?" asked Nell, who was reading the day's mail to her. "He writes a beautifully illiterate letter but he seems confident you'll remember him. And what a life he's had!"

Helen Groody smiled over the memories the name had evoked. "Mat Blunt was one of the Rixby children," she said. "He was the rough little fellow who felt he had to assert himself, even when things were at their worst. When I arrived in Rixby, the first thing I heard was about Mat and the two sisters, Addie and Measy. Addie was lame and when Mat began to make fun of them she hit him with her crutch. Right on the 'snook.' That was the word they used, I seem to remember. Mat was the first to step out on the stage that night and I led him to his place at the head of the line."

"He says," went on Nell, quoting from the letter, "that he has been an enlisted man and fought with Gordon in China. Also he's been with a circus and a professional soccer player with one of the northern teams. Now he's on the gate at the same mill in Rixby where he worked as a child. It seems he has fallen in love with a young woman of such virtue that she won't have anything to do with him unless he turns over a new leaf and takes her out to Canada to raise cattle. He's eager and willing to do everything she wants but there's one little sticker in the way. He hasn't a shilling in his pocket."

"I must get him the money," said Helen Groody eagerly. "I took a great fancy to him and I've often wondered what became of him. He was with a circus, you say? That would be just like him. Was he an acrobat or a clown?"

"Neither," answered Nell, studying the letter. "As far as I can make out, he was feeding the elephants."

"The little girl Addie, the one who hit him with her crutch, has turned into a writer of stories for magazines. I have letters from her every now and then. The sister, Measy, the lazy and sly one, is married and has eight children. I suppose Addie supports them."

The list of those who must be helped, if she lived long enough to receive another Tontine payment, grew every day. And as it grew the winter months

rolled on. Finally spring came. It came with unusual suddenness. One day
a raw March wind was blowing down the streets of Little Shallow, and the
windows were streaked with a heavy rain which turned at intervals to sleet.
It was a dismal day and to Helen Groody, lying so quietly on her couch to
ease the strain on her heart, it seemed fitting that it should be so. "The
last day of waiting," she said to herself. "I'm sure now I'm going to survive
through this night and that will be the end of the struggle. Tomorrow must
be different—warm and bright with all the promise of good we can do with
the money it will bring us."

Tomorrow came, and it was all that she had wished. The wind had blown
itself out and the rain had packed up its pipes and faucets and gone somewhere else. The sun was out and there was a beautifully soft feeling in the
air which could mean only one thing. Spring! She had lived through the
year and the money was hers.

Nell sang as she hurried about the household tasks. "Isn't this the loveliest
day you've ever seen, Mr. John Gilpin?" she said to Danny as she lathered
him and scrubbed him and toweled him strenuously. "There was one better, the day when I married your father, but *you* don't remember that.
Now, get dressed, all by yourself this morning, even to tying your shoes,
and be quick about it, for we must get over there at once."

Edward Daniel Carboy had grown a great deal during that longest of all
winters, so much so, in fact, that now he talked of nothing but ponies.

"Aunt Helen!" called Nell from the door. "Do you know what day this
is?"

"Of course I do. It's the start of the new year. The new Tontine year. I
expect Mr. Glossop will be here with the money. I don't think he'll be very
pleased."

"There are newspapermen at the inn," said Nell, who had been picking
up all the gossip on the way. "Some of them have cameras. And there's an
artist who has come down to make a sketch of you. I'm sure you are going to
see many more mornings like this."

The old lady shook her head. "No, Nelly, this one is the last. I did want
to get through this year for—for so many reasons." The reasons were all contained in the letters piled up in the basket. "But now that the Lord has been
good enough to let me live this long, I'm not going to expect anything
more." To herself she added, "For my own sake, dear Nelly, for my own
sake."

"I hope," said Nell, "that you're going to be sensible about the money and
keep some of it for yourself."

"We'll see. There are so many people I want to help. If there isn't anything left over, it won't matter." She looked then at the boy, who had removed his coat and muffler and hat all by himself and placed them neatly
on a chair. "What do you want me to give you, Danny boy?"

That was a very easy question to answer. "A pony," he said.

"A pony!" The eyes of the sick lady misted over with the memories this
request brought back to her. There was the first Allie Carboy, *her* Allie, who

had been such a fine rider and had not been interested much in anything else. Then there had been Samuel the Younger, who had been bribed to live with her at the Old Rectory by promises of a pony. What had Sammy called it? Turk, that was it; good little Turk, dead for more than forty years and gone to the animal paradise where there was a special place for the beloved ponies of little boys. And now the grandson of Turk's owner was urging the familiar desire. A pony!

"You shall have it, Danny boy," she said. "At first, I'm afraid, it will have to be one to draw you about in a pony cart. But you are growing so fast that very soon you'll have one to ride."

The bell in the shop rang. Danny ran to the door and peered through. He seemed puzzled. "Not cus'mer," he announced.

He was quite right. It was Mr. Glossop, accompanied by the ex-prize fighter.

Helen Groody raised herself to a sitting position, with much effort. Her eyes had a light in them. The struggle had been won; the long months when she had lain still on her couch, afraid to move, afraid to read, even to think, because reading and thinking might create in her mind certain of the emotions which were bad for her tired and resigned heart; the long months of a consuming pain from which there had been no escape and only the most fleeting moments of relief. She had made up her mind that it was necessary to survive, so that this great sum of money would be hers and she would be able to do all the generous acts which were in her mind. She had been determined that no bodily weakness and no shrinking from the continuous, racking pain would be allowed to bring her to an earlier ending.

Mr. Glossop had come and he would see her and know that she was not an impostor, and he would pay over the money. It was no wonder that her eyes had a light in them.

4

On the fifth day after the arrival of William Wordsworth Glossop with that huge and welcome check, all the details in connection with the distribution of the money had been completed. A pile of envelopes, addressed in a neat hand by Nelly, lay on the table in the room back of the shop. The envelopes contained checks and letters which had been most carefully composed to avoid any hint of condescension or what Helen Groody called Lady Bountifulness. As a few of them contained cash, it had been necessary to draw out of the bank a small portion of the total. Of this loose change only six pound notes were left when the last letter had been sealed. The bank account had been completely wiped out.

Helen Groody looked intently at the six pound notes. Then she folded them over and placed them in another envelope. She was holding it in her hand when Daphne and Huruld came in to wrap her up in a fur coat and a multitude of blankets. She had announced her intention of going for a ride that afternoon and the carriage was ready in front of the shop.

Dr. Partridge happened by as the great lady of Little Shallow was carried out to the carriage. He stopped his plodding old nag and his face became almost purple with surprise and indignation.

"Ma'am!" he exploded. "What is the meaning of this? Don't you know you may kill yourself by going out like this?"

Helen looked up at the sky, which was as blue as a great bird's egg, with the sun shining splendidly. "But, Doctor," she said, "it's such a lovely day. I must take advantage of it."

"You might at least have someone with you!" he spluttered. "You are certain to need attention."

"This is a trip I must make all by myself."

"I'm warning you, ma'am! And I'm refusing to take any responsibility for this foolishness!"

"I know this is my last chance to get out," she said to herself. "There couldn't be a better day for it. I almost think it was sent on purpose."

When the wrathful physician had driven on, she said to Huruld, in a voice filled with high anticipation: "And now I want you to drive up to the very top of Purdom Hill. Don't stop until you reach Glocker Spinney."

Huruld obeyed instructions and when they arrived at the spot where the trees of the spinney almost touched from each side of the sandy road, he turned the carriage about. This was a favorite place with people of the vicinity. From here it was possible to see far north into the Vale and to trace for some distance the roads which ran east and west. Four villages were within eyesight, and the spires of three churches. Helen had a particular interest in this vantage point. Far off to the west it was possible on a clear day—and there had never been a clearer day than this—to see a slate gable over the elbow of a hill. This was part of Beaulaw Hall. Soon after the Groodys first came to Little Shallow she had stood on this very spot and had seen a small cloud of dust rising slowly up the crest of the hill, and she had known that it was Allie Carboy riding home at a great rate of speed.

From Purdom Hill they descended to a place north of the village where three roads met, and the view was most exceptional, for it was possible to look a long distance east and west. It was contended by the loyal inhabitants that the grass was greener on this stretch than in any other part of the United Kingdom. Down one of these three roads, moreover, about half a mile, there was a field almost entirely closed in by woods. Helen had the carriage halted here and she sat for several minutes looking at every detail, although her mind clearly was on the past. It was here that the gypsies had made their camp and the Lady Margilda had uttered the prophecies which resulted in the Groody family taking over the shop from Mrs. 'Enry. "How that strange woman changed my life!" thought the old lady. "I suppose that I owe all my happiness to her."

For the better part of an hour the carriage moved amid similar scenes and wherever they stopped there was something which served to lift a corner of the curtain Time had lowered over the past. When this bittersweet experience had come to an end, Helen Groody sighed deeply and said to

Huruld, "And now back to the village, not forgetting to stop at the Crossley cottage."

The Crossley cottage was a small one of whitewashed stone with a fence of white palings around it. When they stopped at the gate she pressed the envelope containing the last six pounds into his hand.

"Now, Huruld, you must do exactly what I say," she instructed. "When you go in, you must give this to poor old Mrs. Crossley but you mustn't let her daughter-in-law see you do it. If she sees, that dreadful creature will have it from the old lady as soon as you're out of the house, and the money in her own pocket."

"She won't catch me at it, mum," promised Huruld. "Ev'buddy knows what that woman is like."

"And then say this to Mrs. Crossley: first that I can't go in to see her for the same reason that she can't come out to see me, we're both too crippled with the rheumatism for that. Then tell her that she's not being left an allowance because that woman would take every shilling of it herself; but arrangements have been made for the doctor to see her once a week, and twice a week things for her comfort will be sent in to her. And now there's this to be said to her; and, Huruld, don't forget one word of it. Tell her that the day when I first came to Little Shallow with my father and mother, on a day very much like this, I saw her standing at this very gate. She had married very young, and she was nice and pretty, with her flaxen pigtails hanging down her back. And she waved to us and we all three said it was the nicest kind of welcome we could have had."

Huruld carried out his instructions with conscientious zeal. It took quite a few minutes and, when he emerged through the gate in the white picket fence, he stared hard at his mistress, bundled up so carefully on the back seat. Then he sprang up and took the reins and drove in a great hurry to the shop. When he arrived there, he did not get down but called in an urgent voice: "Daphne! Daphne, come out! Come out quick!"

When Daphne appeared, wiping damp hands on her apron, he spoke to her in a choking voice:

"Daphne, I'm much feared the good old lady is dead!"